THE GREAT BOOK OF WONDER

THE GREAT BOOK OF WONDER

LORD DUNSANY

WILDSIDE PRESS

CONTENTS

THE GODS OF PEGĀNA (1905)

THE BOOK OF WONDER (1912)

FIFTY-ONE TALES (1915)

THE LAST BOOK OF WONDER (1916)

TALES OF THREE HEMISPHERES (1920)

UNHAPPY FAR-OFF THINGS (1916)

TALES OF WAR (1918)

9 UNCOLLECTED AND RARE STORIES

THE GODS OF PEGĀNA (1905)

PREFACE

In the mists before THE BEGINNING, Fate and Chance cast lots to decide whose the Game should be; and he that won strode through the mists to MANA-YOOD-SUSHAI and said: "Now make gods for Me, for I have won the cast and the Game is to be Mine." Who it was that won the cast, and whether it was Fate or whether Chance that went through the mists before THE BEGINNING to MANA-YOOD-SUSHAI—*none knoweth.*

INTRODUCTION

Before there stood gods upon Olympus, or ever Allah was Allah, had wrought and rested MANA-YOOD-SUSHAI.

There are in Pegana Mung and Sish and Kib, and the maker of all small gods, who is MANA-YOOD-SUSHAI. Moreover, we have a faith in Roon and Slid.

And it has been said of old that all things that have been were wrought by the small gods, excepting only MANA-YOOD-SUSHAI, who made the gods and hath thereafter rested.

And none may pray to MANA-YOOD-SUSHAI but only the gods whom he hath made.

But at the Last will MANA-YOOD-SUSHAI forget to rest, and will make again new gods and other worlds, and will destroy the gods whom he hath made.

And the gods and the worlds shall depart, and there shall be only MANA-YOOD-SUSHAI.

OF SKARL THE DRUMMER

When MANA-YOOD-SUSHAI had made the gods and Skarl, Skarl made a drum, and began to beat upon it that he might drum for ever. Then because he was weary after the making of the gods, and because of the drumming of Skarl, did MANA-YOOD-SUSHAI grow drowsy and fall asleep.

And there fell a hush upon the gods when they saw that MANA rested, and there was silence on Pegana save for the drumming of Skarl. Skarl sitteth upon the mist before the feet of MANA-YOOD-SUSHAI, above the gods of Pegana, and there he beateth his drum. Some say that the Worlds and the Suns are but the echoes of the drumming of Skarl, and others say that they be dreams that arise in the mind of MANA because of the drumming of Skarl, as one may dream whose rest is troubled by sound of song, but none knoweth, for who hath heard the voice of MANA-YOOD-SUSHAI, or who hath seen his drummer?

Whether the season be winter or whether it be summer, whether it be morning among the worlds or whether it be night, Skarl still beateth his drum, for the purposes of the gods are not yet fulfilled. Sometimes the arm of Skarl grows weary; but still he beateth his drum, that the gods may do the work of the gods, and the worlds go on, for if he cease for an instant then MANA-YOOD-SUSHAI will start awake, and there will be worlds nor gods no more.

But, when at the last the arm of Skarl shall cease to beat his drum, silence shall startle Pegana like thunder in a cave, and MANA-YOOD-SUSHAI shall cease to rest.

Then shall Skarl put his drum upon his back and walk forth into the void beyond the worlds, because it is THE END, and the work of Skarl is over.

There may arise some other god whom Skarl may serve, or it may be that he shall perish; but to Skarl it shall matter not, for he shall have done the work of Skarl.

OF THE MAKING OF THE WORLDS

When MANA-YOOD-SUSHAI had made the gods there were only the gods, and They sat in the middle of Time, for there was as much Time before them as behind them, which having no end had neither a beginning.

And Pegana was without heat or light or sound, save for the drumming of Skarl; moreover Pegana was The Middle of All, for there was below Pegana what there was above it, and there lay before it that which lay beyond.

Then said the gods, making the signs of the gods and speaking with Their hands lest the silence of Pegana should blush; then said the gods to one another, speaking with Their hands; "Let Us make worlds to amuse Ourselves while MANA rests. Let Us make worlds and Life and Death, and colours in the sky; only let Us not break the silence upon Pegana."

Then raising Their hands, each god according to his sign, They made the worlds and the suns, and put a light in the houses of the sky.

Then said the gods: "Let Us make one to seek, to seek and never to find out concerning the wherefore of the making of the gods."

And They made by the lifting of Their hands, each god according to his sign, the Bright One with the flaring tail to seek from the end of the Worlds to the end of them again, to return again after a hundred years.

Man, when thou seest the comet, know that another seeketh besides thee nor ever findeth out.

Then said the gods, still speaking with Their hands: "Let there be now a Watcher to regard."

And They made the Moon, with his face wrinkled with many mountains and worn with a thousand valleys, to regard with pale eyes the games of the small gods, and to watch throughout the resting time of MANA-YOOD-SUSHAI; to watch, to regard all things, and be silent.

Then said the gods: "Let Us make one to rest. One not to move among the moving. One not to seek like the comet, nor to go round like the worlds; to rest while MANA rests."

And They made the Star of the Abiding and set it in the North.

Man, when thou seest the Star of the Abiding to the North, know that one resteth as doth MANA-YOOD-SUSHAI, and know that somewhere among the Worlds is rest.

Lastly the gods said: "We have made worlds and suns, and one to seek and another to regard, let Us now make one to wonder."

And They made Earth to wonder, each god by the uplifting of his hand according to his sign.

And Earth was.

OF THE GAME OF THE GODS

A million years passed over the first game of the gods. And MANA-YOOD-SUSHAI still rested, still in the middle of Time, and the gods still played with Worlds. The Moon regarded, and the Bright One sought, and returned again to his seeking.

Then Kib grew weary of the first game of the gods, and raised his hand in Pegana, making the sign of Kib, and Earth became covered with beasts for Kib to play with.

And Kib played with beasts.

But the other gods said one to another, speaking with their hands: "What is it that Kib has done?"

And They said to Kib: "What are these things that move upon The Earth yet move not in circles like the Worlds, that regard like the Moon and yet they do not shine?"

And Kib said: "This is Life."

But the gods said one to another: "If Kib has thus made beasts he will in time make Men, and will endanger the Secret of the gods."

And Mung was jealous of the work of Kib, and sent down Death among the beasts, but could not stamp them out.

A million years passed over the second game of the gods, and still it was the Middle of Time.

And Kib grew weary of the second game, and raised his hand in the Middle of All, making the sign of Kib, and made Men: out of beasts he made them, and Earth was covered with Men.

Then the gods feared greatly for the Secret of the gods, and set a veil between Man and his ignorance that he might not understand. And Mung was busy among Men.

But when the other gods saw Kib playing his new game They came and played it too. And this They will play until MANA arises to rebuke Them, saying: "What do ye playing with Worlds and Suns and Men and Life and Death?" And They shall be ashamed of Their playing in the hour of the laughter of MANA-YOOD-SUSHAI.

It was Kib who first broke the Silence of Pegana, by speaking with his mouth like a man.

And all the other gods were angry with Kib that he had spoken with his mouth.

And there was no longer silence in Pegana or the Worlds.

THE CHAUNT OF THE GODS

There came the voice of the gods singing the chaunt of the gods, singing: "We are the gods; We are the little games of MANA-YOOD-SUSHAI that he hath played and hath forgotten.

"MANA-YOOD-SUSHAI hath made us, and We made the Worlds and the Suns.

"And We play with the Worlds and the Sun and Life and Death until MANA arises to rebuke us, saying: 'What do ye playing with Worlds and Suns?'

"It is a very serious thing that there be Worlds and Suns, and yet most withering is the laughter of MANA-YOOD-SUSHAI.

"And when he arises from resting at the Last, and laughs at us for playing with Worlds and Suns, We will hastily put them behind us, and there shall be Worlds no more."

THE SAYINGS OF KIB

(Sender of Life in all the Worlds)

Kib said: "I am Kib. I am none other than Kib."

Kib is Kib. Kib is he and no other. Believe! Kib said: "When Time was early, when Time was very early indeed—there was only

MANA-YOOD-SUSHAI. MANA-YOOD-SUSHAI was before the beginning of the gods, and shall be after their going."

And Kib said: "After the going of the gods there will be no small worlds nor big."

Kib said: "It will be lonely for MANA-YOOD-SUSHAI."

Because this is written, believe! For is it not written, or are you greater than Kib? Kib is Kib.

CONCERNING SISH

(The Destroyer of Hours)

Time is the hound of Sish.

At Sish's bidding do the hours run before him as he goeth upon his way.

Never hath Sish stepped backward nor ever hath he tarried; never hath he relented to the things that once he knew nor turned to them again.

Before Sish is Kib, and behind him goeth Mung.

Very pleasant are all things before the face of Sish, but behind him they are withered and old.

And Sish goeth ceaselessly upon his way.

Once the gods walked upon Earth as men walk and spake with their mouths like Men. That was in Wornath-Mavai. They walk not now.

And Wornath-Mavai was a garden fairer than all the gardens upon Earth.

Kib was propitious, and Mung raised not his hand against it, neither did Sish assail it with his hours.

Wornath-Mavai lieth in a valley and looketh towards the south, and on the slopes of it Sish rested among the flowers when Sish was young.

Thence Sish went forth into the world to destroy its cities, and to provoke his hours to assail all things, and to batter against them with the rust and with the dust.

And Time, which is the hound of Sish, devoured all things; and Sish sent up the ivy and fostered weeds, and dust fell from the hand of Sish and covered stately things. Only the valley where Sish rested when he and Time were young did Sish not provoke his hours to assail.

There he restrained his old hound Time, and at its borders Mung withheld his footsteps.

Wornath-Mavai still lieth looking towards the south, a garden among gardens, and still the flowers grow about its slopes as they grew when the gods were young; and even the butterflies live in Wornath-Mavai still. For the minds of the gods relent towards their earliest memories, who relent not otherwise at all.

Wornath-Mavai still lieth looking towards the south; but if thou shouldst ever find it thou art then more fortunate than the gods, because they walk not in Wornath-Mavai now.

Once did the prophet think that he discerned it in the distance beyond mountains, a garden exceeding fair with flowers; but Sish arose, and pointed with his hand, and set his hound to pursue him, who hath followed ever since.

Time is the hound of the gods; but it hath been said of old that he will one day turn upon his masters, and seek to slay the gods, excepting only MANA-YOOD-SUSHAI, whose dreams are the gods themselves—dreamed long ago.

THE SAYINGS OF SLID

(Whose Soul is by the Sea)

Slid said: "Let no man pray to MANA-YOOD-SUSHAI, for who shall trouble MANA with mortal woes or irk him with the sorrows of all the houses of Earth?

"Nor let any sacrifice to MANA-YOOD-SUSHAI, for what glory shall he find in sacrifices or altars who hath made the gods themselves?

"Pray to the small gods, who are the gods of Doing; but MANA is the god of Having Done—the god of Having Done and of the Resting.

"Pray to the small gods and hope that they may hear thee. Yet what mercy should the small gods have, who themselves made Death and Pain; or shall they restrain their old hound Time for thee?

"Slid is but a small god. Yet Slid is Slid—it is written and hath been said.

"Pray, thou, therefore, to Slid, and forget not Slid, and it may be that Slid will not forget to send thee Death when most thou needest it."

And the People of Earth said: "There is a melody upon the Earth as though ten thousand streams all sang together for their homes that they had forsaken in the hills."

And Slid said: "I am the Lord of gliding waters and of foaming waters and of still. I am the Lord of all the waters in the world and all that long streams garner in the hills; but the soul of Slid is in the Sea. Thither goes all that glides upon Earth, and the end of all the rivers is the Sea."

And Slid said: "The hand of Slid hath toyed with cataracts, and down the valleys have trod the feet of Slid, and out of the lakes of the plains regard the eyes of Slid; but the soul of Slid is in the sea."

Much homage hath Slid among the cities of men and pleasant are the woodland paths and the paths of the plains, and pleasant the high valleys where he danceth in the hills; but Slid would be fettered neither by banks nor boundaries—so the soul of Slid is in the Sea.

For there may Slid repose beneath the sun and smile at the gods above him with all the smiles of Slid, and be a happier god than Those who sway the Worlds, whose work is Life and Death.

There may he sit and smile, or creep among the ships, or moan and sigh round islands in his great content—the miser lord of wealth in gems and pearls beyond the telling of all fables.

Or there may he, when Slid would fain exult, throw up his great arms, or toss with many a fathom of wandering hair the mighty head of Slid, and cry aloud tumultuous dirges of shipwreck, and feel through all his being the crashing might of Slid, and sway the sea. Then doth the Sea, like venturous legions on the eve of war that exult to acclaim their chief, gather its force together from under all the winds and roar and follow and sing and crash together to vanquish all things—and all at the bidding of Slid, whose soul is in the sea.

There is ease in the soul of Slid and there be calms upon the sea; also, there be storms upon the sea and troubles in the soul of Slid, for the gods have many moods. And Slid is in many places, for he sitteth in high Pegana. Also along the valleys walketh Slid, wherever water moveth or lieth still; but the voice and the cry of Slid are from the sea. And to whoever that cry hath ever come he must needs follow and follow, leaving all stable things; only to be always with Slid in all the moods of Slid, to find no rest until he reaches the sea.

With the cry of Slid before them and the hills of their home behind have gone a hundred thousand to the sea, over whose bones doth Slid lament with the voice of a god lamenting for his people. Even the streams from the inner lands have heard Slid's far-off cry, and all together have forsaken lawns and trees to follow where Slid is gathering up his own, to rejoice where Slid rejoices, singing the chaunt of Slid, even as will at the Last gather all the Lives of the People about the feet of MANA-YOOD-SUSHAI.

THE DEEDS OF MUNG

(Lord of all Deaths between Pegana and the Rim)

Once, as Mung went his way athwart the Earth and up and down its cities and across its plains, Mung came upon a man who was afraid when Mung said: "I am Mung!"

And Mung said: "Were the forty million years before thy coming intolerable to thee?"

And Mung said: "Not less tolerable to thee shall be the forty million years to come!"

Then Mung made against him the sign of Mung and the Life of the Man was fettered no longer with hands and feet.

At the end of the flight of the arrow there is Mung, and in the houses and the cities of Men. Mung walketh in all places at all times. But mostly he loves to walk in the dark and still, along the river mists when the wind hath sank, a little before night meeteth with the morning upon the highway between Pegana and the Worlds.

Sometimes Mung entereth the poor man's cottage; Mung also boweth very low before The King. Then do the Lives of the poor man and of The King go forth among the Worlds.

And Mung said: "Many turnings hath the road that Kib hath given every man to tread upon the earth. Behind one of these turnings sitteth Mung."

One day as a man trod upon the road that Kib had given him to tread he came suddenly upon Mung. And when Mung said: "I am Mung!" the man cried out: "Alas, that I took this road, for had I gone by any other way then had I not met with Mung."

And Mung said: "Had it been possible for thee to go by any other way then had the Scheme of Things been otherwise and the gods had been other gods. When MANA-YOOD-SUSHAI forgets to rest and makes again new gods it may be that They will send thee again into the Worlds; and then thou mayest choose some other way, and not meet with Mung."

Then Mung made the sign of Mung. And the Life of that man went forth with yesterday's regrets and all old sorrows and forgotten things— whither Mung knoweth.

And Mung went onward with his work to sunder Life from flesh, and Mung came upon a man who became stricken with sorrow when he saw the shadow of Mung. But Mung said: "When at the sign of Mung thy Life shall float away there will also disappear thy sorrow at forsaking it." But the man cried out: "O Mung! tarry for a little, and make not the sign of Mung against me now, for I have a family upon the earth with whom sorrow will remain, though mine should disappear because of the sign of Mung."

And Mung said: "With the gods it is always Now. And before Sish hath banished many of the years the sorrows of thy family for thee shall go the way of thine." And the man beheld Mung making the sign of Mung before his eyes, which beheld things no more.

THE CHAUNT OF THE PRIESTS

This is the chaunt of the Priests.
The chaunt of the priests of Mung.
This is the chaunt of the Priests.

All day long to Mung cry out the Priests of Mung, and, yet Mung harkeneth not. What, then, shall avail the prayers of All the People?

Rather bring gifts to the Priests, gifts to the Priests of Mung.

So shall they cry louder unto Mung than ever was their wont.

And it may be that Mung shall hear.

Not any longer than shall fall the Shadow of Mung athwart the hopes of the People.

Not any longer then shall the Tread of Mung darken the dreams of the people.

Not any longer shall the lives of the People be loosened because of Mung.

Bring ye gifts to the Priests, gifts to the Priests of Mung.

This is the chaunt of the Priests.

The chaunt of the Priests of Mung.

This is the chaunt of the Priests.

THE SAYINGS OF LIMPANG-TUNG

(The God of Mirth and of Melodious Minstrels)

And Limpang-Tung said: "The ways of the gods are strange. The flower groweth up and the flower fadeth away. This may be very clever of the gods. Man groweth from his infancy, and in a while he dieth. This may be very clever too.

"But the gods play with a strange scheme.

"I will send jests into the world and a little mirth. And while Death seems to thee as far away as the purple rim of hills; or sorrow as far off as rain in the blue days of summer, then pray to Limpang-Tung. But when thou growest old, or ere thou diest, pray not of Limpang-Tung, for thou becomest part of a scheme that he doth not understand.

"Go out into the starry night, and Limpang-Tung will dance with thee who danced since the gods were young, the god of mirth and of melodious minstrels. Or offer up a jest to Limpang-Tung; only pray not in thy sorrow to Limpang-Tung, for he saith of sorrow: 'It may be very clever of the gods,' but he doth not understand."

And Limpang-Tung said: "I am lesser than the gods; pray, therefore, to the small gods and not to Limpang-Tung.

"Natheless between Pegana and the Earth flutter ten thousand thousand prayers that beat their wings against the face of Death, and never for one of them hath the hand of the Striker been stayed, nor yet have tarried the feet of the Relentless One.

"Utter thy prayer! It may accomplish where failed ten thousand thousand.

"Limpang-Tung is lesser than the gods, and doth not understand."

And Limpang-Tung said: "Lest men grow weary down on the great Worlds through gazing always at a changeless sky, I will paint my pictures in the sky. And I will paint them twice in every day for so long as days shall be. Once as the day ariseth out of the homes of dawn will I paint the Blue, that men may see and rejoice; and ere day falleth under into the night will I paint upon the Blue again, lest men be sad.

"It is a little," said Limpang-Tung, "it is a little even for a god to give some pleasure to men upon the Worlds."

And Limpang-Tung hath sworn that the pictures that he paints shall never be the same for so long as the days shall be, and this he hath sworn by the oath of the gods of Pegana that the gods may never break, laying his hand upon the shoulder of each of the gods and swearing by the light behind Their eyes.

Limpang-Tung hath lured a melody out of the stream and stolen its anthem from the forest; for him the wind hath cried in lonely places and the ocean sung its dirges. There is music for Limpang-Tung in the sounds of the moving of grass and in the voices of the people that lament or in the cry of them that rejoice.

In an inner mountain land where none hath come he hath carved his organ pipes out of the mountains, and there when the winds, his servants, come in from all the world he maketh the melody of Limpang-Tung. But the song, arising at night, goeth forth like a river, winding through all the world, and here and there amid the peoples of earth one heareth, and straightaway all that hath voice to sing crieth aloud in music to his soul.

Or sometimes walking through the dusk with steps unheard by men, in a form unseen by the people, Limpang-Tung goeth abroad, and, standing behind the minstrels in cities of song, waveth his hands above them to and fro, and the minstrels bend to their work, and the voice of the music ariseth; and mirth and melody abound in that city of song, and no one seeth Limpang-Tung as he standeth behind the minstrels.

But through the mists towards morning, in the dark when the minstrels sleep and mirth and melody have sunk to rest, Limpang-Tung goeth back again to his mountain land.

OF YOHARNETH-LAHAI

(The God of Little Dreams and Fancies)

Yaoharneth-Lahai is the god of little dreams and fancies.

All night he sendeth little dreams out of Pegana to please the people of Earth.

He sendeth little dreams to the poor man and to The King.

He is so busy to send his dreams to all before the night be ended that oft he forgetteth which be the poor man and which be The King.

To whom Yoharneth-Lahai cometh not with little dreams and sleep he must endure all night the laughter of the gods, with highest mockery, in Pegana.

All night long Yoharneth-Lahai giveth peace to cities until the dawn hour and the departing of Yoharneth-Lahai, when it is time for the gods to play with men again.

Whether the dreams and the fancies of Yoharneth-Lahai be false and the Things that are done in the Day be real, or the Things that are done in the Day be false and the dreams and the fancies of Yoharneth-Lahai be true, none knoweth saving only MANA-YOOD-SUSHAI, who hath not spoken.

OF ROON, THE GOD OF GOING, AND THE THOUSAND HOME GODS

Roon said: "There be gods of moving and gods of standing still, but I am the god of Going."

It is because of Roon that the worlds are never still, for the moons and the worlds and the comet are stirred by the spirit of Roon, which saith: "Go! Go! Go!"

Roon met the Worlds all in the morning of Things, before there was light upon Pegana, and Roon danced before them in the Void, since when they are never still, Roon sendeth all streams to the Sea, and all the rivers to the soul of Slid.

Roon maketh the sign of Roon before the waters, and lo! they have left the hills; and Roon hath spoken in the ear of the North Wind that he may be still no more.

The footfall of Roon hath been heard at evening outside the houses of men, and thenceforth comfort and abiding know them no more. Before them stretcheth travel over all the lands, long miles, and never resting between their homes and their graves—and all at the bidding of Roon.

The Mountains have set no limit against Roon nor all the seas a boundary.

Whither Roon hath desired there must Roon's people go, and the worlds and their streams and the winds.

I heard the whisper of Roon at evening, saying: "There are islands of spices to the South," and the voice of Roon saying: "Go."

And Roon said: "There are a thousand home gods, the little gods that sit before the hearth and mind the fire—there is one Roon."

Roon saith in a whisper, in a whisper when none heareth, when the sun is low: "What doeth MANA-YOOD-SUSHAI?" Roon is no god that thou mayest worship by thy hearth, nor will he be benignant to thy home.

Offer to Roon thy toiling and thy speed, whose incense is the smoke of the camp fire to the South, whose song is the sound of going, whose temples stand beyond the farthest hills in his lands behind the East.

Yarinareth, Yarinareth, Yarinareth, which signifieth Beyond—these words be carved in letters of gold upon the arch of the great portal of the Temple of Roon that men have builded looking towards the East upon the Sea, where Roon is carved as a giant trumpeter, with his trumpet pointing towards the East beyond the Seas.

Whoso heareth his voice, the voice of Roon at evening, he at once forsaketh the home gods that sit beside the hearth. These be the gods of the hearth: Pitsu, who stroketh the cat; Hobith who calms the dog; and Habaniah, the lord of glowing embers; and little Zumbiboo, the lord of dust; and old Gribaun, who sits in the heart of the fire to turn the wood to ash—all these be home gods, and live not in Pegana and be lesser than Roon.

There is also Kilooloogung, the lord of arising smoke, who taketh the smoke from the hearth and sendeth it to the sky, who is pleased if it reacheth Pegana, so that the gods of Pegana, speaking to the gods, say: "There is Kilooloogung doing the work on earth of Kilooloogung."

All these are gods so small that they be lesser than men, but pleasant gods to have beside the hearth; and often men have prayed to Kilooloogung, saying: "Thou whose smoke ascendeth to Pegana send up with it our prayers, that the gods may hear." And Kilooloogung, who is pleased that men should pray, stretches himself up all grey and lean, with his arms above his head, and sendeth his servant the smoke to seek Pegana, that the gods of Pegana may know that the people pray.

And Jabim is the Lord of broken things, who sitteth behind the house to lament the things that are cast away. And there he sitteth lamenting the broken things until the worlds be ended, or until someone cometh to mend the broken things. Or sometimes he sitteth by the river's edge to lament the forgotten things that drift upon it.

A kindly god is Jabim, whose heart is sore if anything be lost.

There is also Triboogie, the Lord of Dusk, whose children are the shadows, who sitteth in a corner far off from Habaniah and speaketh to none. But after Habaniah hath gone to sleep and old Gribaun hath blinked a hundred times, until he forgetteth which be wood or ash, then doth Triboogie send his children to run about the room and dance upon the walls, but never disturb the silence.

But when there is light again upon the worlds, and dawn comes dancing down the highway from Pegana, then does Triboogie retire into his corner, with his children all around him, as though they had never danced about the room. And the slaves of Habaniah and old Gribaun come and awake them from their sleep upon the hearth, and Pitsu strokes the cat, and Hobith calms the dog, and Kilooloogung stretches aloft his arms towards Pegana, and Triboogie is very still, and his children asleep.

And when it is dark, all in the hour of Triboogie, Hish creepeth from the forest, the Lord of Silence, whose children are the bats, that have broken the command of their father, but in a voice that is ever so low. Hish husheth the mouse and all the whispers in the night; he maketh all noises still. Only the cricket rebelleth. But Hish hath set against him such a spell that after he hath cried a thousand times his voice may be heard no more but becometh part of the silence.

And when he hath slain all sounds Hish boweth low to the ground; then cometh into the house, with never a sound of feet, the god Yoharneth-Lahai.

But away in the forest whence Hish hath come Wohoon, the Lord of Noises in the Night, awaketh in his lair and creepeth round the forest to see whether it be true that Hish hath gone.

Then in some glade Wohoon lifts up his voice and cries aloud, that all the night may hear, that it is he, Wohoon, who is abroad in all the forest. And the wolf and the fox and the owl, and the great beasts and the small, lift up their voices to acclaim Wohoon. And there arise the sounds of voices and the stirring of leaves.

THE REVOLT OF THE HOME GODS

There be three broad rivers of the plain, born before memory or fable, whose mothers are three grey peaks and whose father was the storm. There names be Eimës, Zänës, and Segástrion.

And Eimës is the joy of lowing herds; and Zänës hath bowed his neck to the yoke of man, and carries the timber from the forest far up below the mountain; and Segástrion sings old songs to shepherd boys, singing of his childhood in a lone ravine and of how he once sprang down the mountain sides and far away into the plain to see the world, and of how one day at last he will find the sea. These be the rivers of the plain, wherein the plain rejoices. But old men tell, whose fathers heard it from the ancients, how once the lords of the three rivers of the plain rebelled against the law of the Worlds, and passed beyond their boundaries, and joined together and whelmed cities and slew men, saying: "We now play the game of the gods and slay men for our pleasure, and we be greater than the gods of Pegana."

And all the plain was flooded to the hills.

And Eimës, Zänës, and Segástrion sat upon the mountains, and spread their hands over their rivers that rebelled by their command.

But the prayer of men going upward found Pegana, and cried in the ear of the gods: "There be three home gods who slay us for their pleasure, and say that they be mightier than Pegana's gods, and play Their game with men."

Then were all the gods of Pegana very wroth; but They could not whelm the lords of the three rivers, because being home gods, though small, they were immortal.

And still the home gods spread their hands across their rivers, with their fingers wide apart, and the waters rose and rose, and the voice of their torrent grew louder, crying: "Are we not Eimës, Zänës, and Segástrion?"

Then Mung went down into a waste of Afrik, and came upon the drought Umbool as he sat in the desert upon iron rocks, clawing with miserly grasp at the bones of men and breathing hot.

And Mung stood before him as his dry sides heaved, and ever as they sank his hot breath blasted dry sticks and bones.

Then Mung said: "Friend of Mung! Go, thou and grin before the faces of Eimës, Zänës, and Segástrion till they see whether it be wise to rebel against the gods of Pegana."

And Umbool answered: "I am the beast of Mung."

And Umbool came and crouched upon a hill upon the other side of the waters and grinned across them at the rebellious home gods.

And whenever Eimës, Zänës, and Segástrion stretched out their hands over their rivers they saw before their faces the grinning of Umbool; and because the grinning was like death in a hot and hideous land therefore they turned away and spread their hands no more over their rivers, and the waters sank and sank.

But when Umbool had grinned for thirty days the waters fell back into the river beds and the lords of the rivers slunk away back again to their homes: still Umbool sat and grinned.

Then Eimës sought to hide himself in a great pool beneath a rock, and Zänës crept into the middle of a wood, and Segástrion lay and panted on the sand—still Umbool sat and grinned.

And Eimës grew lean, and was forgotten, so that the men of the plain would say: "Here once was Eimës"; and Zänës scarce had strength to lead his river to the sea; and as Segástrion lay and panted a man stepped over his stream, and Segástrion said: "It is the foot of a man that has passed across my neck, and I have sought to be greater than the gods of Pegana."

Then said the gods of Pegana: "It is enough. We are the gods of Pegana, and none are equal."

Then Mung sent Umbool back to his waste in Afrik to breathe again upon the rocks, and parch the desert, and to sear the memory of Afrik into the brains of all who ever bring their bones away.

And Eimës, Zänës, and Segástrion sang again, and walked once more in their accustomed haunts, and played the game of Life and Death with fishes and frogs, but never essayed to play it any more with men, as do the gods of Pegana.

OF DOROZHAND

(Whose Eyes Regard The End)

Sitting above the lives of the people, and looking, doth Dorozhand see that which is to be.

The god of Destiny is Dorozhand. Upon whom have looked the eyes of Dorozhand he goeth forward to an end that naught may stay; he becometh the arrow from the bow of Dorozhand hurled forward at a mark he may not see—to the goal of Dorozhand. Beyond the thinking of men, beyond the sight of all the other gods, regard the eyes of Dorozhand.

He hath chosen his slaves. And them doth the destiny god drive onward where he will, who, knowing not whither nor even knowing why, feel only his scourge behind them or hear his cry before.

There is something that Dorozhand would fain achieve, and, therefore, hath he set the people striving, with none to cease or rest in all the worlds. But the gods of Pegana, speaking to the gods, say: "What is it that Dorozhand would fain achieve?"

It hath been written and said that not only the destinies of men are the care of Dorozhand but that even the gods of Pegana be not unconcerned by his will.

All the gods of Pegana have felt a fear, for they have seen a look in the eyes of Dorozhand that regardeth beyond the gods.

The reason and purpose of the Worlds is that there should be Life upon the Worlds, and Life is the instrument of Dorozhand wherewith he would achieve his end.

Therefore the Worlds go on, and the rivers run to the sea, and Life ariseth and flieth even in all the Worlds, and the gods of Pegana do the work of the gods—and all for Dorozhand. But when the end of Dorozhand hath been achieved there will be need no longer of Life upon the Worlds, nor any more a game for the small gods to play. Then will Kib tiptoe gently across Pegana to the resting-place in Highest Pegana of MANA-YOOD-SUSHAI, and touching reverently his hand, the hand that wrought the gods, say: "MANA-YOOD-SUSHAI, thou hast rested long."

And MANA-YOOD-SUSHAI shall say: "Not so; for I have rested for but fifty aeons of the gods, each of them scarce more than ten million mortal years of the Worlds that ye have made."

And then shall the gods be afraid when they find that MANA knoweth that they have made Worlds while he rested. And they shall answer: "Nay; but the Worlds came all of themselves."

Then MANA-YOOD-SUSHAI, as one who would have done with an irksome matter, will lightly wave his hand—the hand that wrought the gods—and there shall be gods no more.

When there shall be three moons towards the north above the Star of the Abiding, three moons that neither wax nor wane but regard towards the North.

Or when the comet ceaseth from his seeking and stands still, not any longer moving among the Worlds but tarrying as one who rests after the end of search, then shall arise from resting, because it is THE END, the Greater One, who rested of old time, even MANA-YOOD-SUSHAI.

Then shall the Times that were be Times no more; and it may be that the old, dead days shall return from beyond the Rim, and we who have wept for them shall see those days again, as one who, returning from long travel to his home, comes suddenly on dear, remembered things.

For none shall know of MANA who hath rested for so long, whether he be a harsh or merciful god. It may be that he shall have mercy, and that these things shall be.

THE EYE IN THE WASTE

There lie seven deserts beyond Bodrahan, which is the city of the caravans' end. None goeth beyond. In the first desert lie the tracks of mighty travellers outward from Bodrahan, and some returning. And in the second lie only outward tracks, and none return.

The third is a desert untrodden by the feet of men.

The fourth is the desert of sand, and the fifth is the desert of dust, and the sixth is the desert of stones, and the seventh is the Desert of Deserts.

In the midst of the last of the deserts that lie beyond Bodrahan, in the centre of the Desert of Deserts, standeth the image that hath been hewn of old out of the living hill whose name is Ranorada—the eye in the waste.

About the base of Ranorada is carved in mystic letters that are vaster than the beds of streams these words:

To the god who knows.

Now, beyond the second desert are no tracks, and there is no water in all the seven deserts that lie beyond Bodrahan. Therefore came no man thither to hew that statue from the living hills, and Ranorada was wrought by the hands of gods. Men tell in Bodrahan, where the caravans end and all the drivers of the camels rest, how once the gods hewed Ranorada from the living hill, hammering all night long beyond the deserts. Moreover, they say that Ranorada is carved in the likeness of the god Hoodrazai, who hath found the secret of MANA-YOOD-SUSHAI, and knoweth the wherefore of the making of the gods.

They say that Hoodrazai stands all alone in Pegana and speaks to none because he knows what is hidden from the gods.

Therefore the gods have made his image in a lonely land as one who thinks and is silent—the eye in the waste.

They say that Hoodrazai had heard the murmers of MANA-YOOD-SUSHAI as he muttered to himself, and gleaned the meaning, and knew; and that he was the god of mirth and of abundant joy, but became from the moment of his knowing a mirthless god, even as his image, which regards the deserts beyond the track of man.

But the camel drivers, as they sit and listen to the tales of the old men in the market-place of Bodrahan, at evening, while the camels rest, say:

"If Hoodrazai is so very wise and yet is sad, let us drink wine, and banish wisdom to the wastes that lie beyond Bodrahan." Therefore is there feasting and laughter all night long in the city where the caravans end.

All this the camel drivers tell when the caravans come in from Bodrahan; but who shall credit tales that camel drivers have heard from aged men in so remote a city?

OF THE THING THAT IS NEITHER GOD NOR BEAST

Seeing that wisdom is not in cities nor happiness in wisdom, and because Yadin the prophet was doomed by the gods ere he was born to go in search of wisdom, he followed the caravans to Bodrahan. There in the evening, where the camels rest, when the wind of the day ebbs out into the desert sighing amid the palms its last farewells and leaving the caravans still, he sent his prayer with the wind to drift into the desert calling to Hoodrazai.

And down the wind his prayer went calling: "Why do the gods endure, and play their game with men? Why doth not Skarl forsake his drumming, and MANA cease to rest?" and the echo of seven deserts answered: "Who knows? Who knows?"

But out in the waste, beyond the seven deserts where Ranorada looms enormous in the dusk, at evening his prayer was heard; and from the rim of the waste whither had gone his prayer, came three flamingoes flying, and their voices said: "Going South, Going South" at every stroke of their wings.

But as they passed by the prophet they seemed so cool and free and the desert so blinding and hot that he stretched up his arms towards them. Then it seemed happy to fly and pleasant to follow behind great white wings, and he was with the three flamingoes up in the cool above the desert, and their voices cried before him: "Going South, Going South," and the desert below him mumbled: "Who knows? Who knows?"

Sometimes the earth stretched up towards them with peaks of mountains, sometimes it fell away in steep ravines, blue rivers sang to them as they passed above them, or very faintly came the song of breezes in lone orchards, and far away the sea sang mighty dirges of old forsaken isles. But it seemed that in all the world there was nothing only to be going South.

It seemed that somewhere the South was calling to her own, and that they were going South.

But when the prophet saw that they had passed above the edge of Earth, and that far away to the North of them lay the Moon, he perceived that he was following no mortal birds but some strange messengers of Hoodrazai whose nest had lain in one of Pegana's vales below the mountains whereon sit the gods.

Still they went South, passing by all the Worlds and leaving them to the North, till only Araxes, Zadres, and Hyraglion lay still to the South of them, where great Ingazi seemed only a point of light, and Yo and Mindo could be seen no more.

Still they went South till they passed below the South and came to the Rim of the Worlds.

There there is neither South nor East nor West, but only North and Beyond; there is only North of it where lie the Worlds, and Beyond it where lies the Silence, and the Rim is a mass of rocks that were never used by the gods when They made the Worlds, and on it sat Trogool. Trogool is the Thing that is neither god nor beast, who neither howls nor breathes, only *It* turns over the leaves of a great book, black and white, black and white for ever until THE END.

And all that is to be is written in the book is also all that was.

When *It* turneth a black page it is night, and when *It* turneth a white page it is day.

Because it is written that there are gods—there are the gods.

Also there is writing about thee and me until the page where our names no more are written.

Then as the prophet watched *It*, Trogool turned a page—a black one, and night was over, and day shone on the Worlds.

Trogool is the Thing that men in many countries have called by many names, *It* is the Thing that sits behind the gods, whose book is the Scheme of Things.

But when Yadin saw that old remembered days were hidden away with the part that *It* had turned, and knew that upon one whose name is writ no more the last page had turned for ever a thousand pages back. Then did he utter his prayer in the fact of Trogool who only turns the pages and never answers prayer. He prayed in the face of Trogool: "Only turn back thy pages to the name of one which is writ no more, and far away upon a place named Earth shall rise the prayers of a little people that acclaim the name of Trogool, for there is indeed far off a place called Earth where men shall pray to Trogool."

Then spake Trogool who turns the pages and never answers prayer, and his voice was like the murmurs of the waste at night when echoes have been lost: "Though the whirlwind of the South should tug with his claws at a page that hath been turned yet shall he not be able to ever turn it back."

Then because of words in the book that said that it should be so, Yadin found himself lying in the desert where one gave him water, and afterwards carried him on a camel into Bodrahan.

There some said that he had but dreamed when thirst seized him while he wandered among the rocks in the desert. But certain aged men of Bodrahan say that indeed there sitteth somewhere a Thing that is called Trogool, that is neither god nor beast, that turneth the leaves of a book, black and white, black and white, until he come to the words: *Mai Doon Izahn*, which means The End For Ever, and book and gods and worlds shall be no more.

YONATH THE PROPHET

Yonath was the first among prophets who uttered unto men.

These are the words of Yonath, the first among all prophets:

There be gods upon Pegana.

Upon a night I slept. And in my sleep Pegana came very near. And Pegana was full of gods.

I saw the gods beside me as one might see wonted things.

Only I saw not MANA-YOOD-SUSHAI.

And in that hour, in the hour of my sleep, I knew.

And the end and the beginning of my knowing, and all of my knowing that there was, was this—that Man Knoweth Not.

Seek thou to find at night the utter edge of the darkness, or seek to find the birthplace of the rainbow where he leapeth upward from the hills, only seek not concerning the wherefore of the making of the gods.

The gods have set a brightness upon the farther side of the Things to Come that they may appear more felititous to men than the Things that Are.

To the gods the Things to Come are but as the Things that Are, and nothing altereth in Pegana.

The gods, although not merciful, are not ferocious gods. They are the destroyers of the Days that Were, but they set a glory about the Days to Be.

Man must endure the Days that Are, but the gods have left him his ignorance as a solace.

Seek not to know. Thy seeking will weary thee, and thou wilt return much worn, to rest at last about the place from whence thou settest out upon thy seeking.

Seek not to know. Even I, Yonath, the oldest prophet, burdened with the wisdom of great years, and worn with seeking, know only that man knoweth not.

Once I set out seeking to know all things. Now I know one thing only, and soon the Years will carry me away.

The path of my seeking, that leadeth to seeking again, must be trodden by very many more, when Yonath is no longer even Yonath.

Set not thy foot upon that path.

Seek not to know.

These be the Words of Yonath.

YUG THE PROPHET

When the Years had carries away Yonath, and Yonath was dead, there was no longer a prophet among men.

And still men sought to know.

Therefore they said unto Yug: "Be thou our prophet, and know all things, and tell us concerning the wherefore of It All."

And Yug said: "I know all things." And men were pleased.

And Yug said of the Beginning that it was in Yug's own garden, and of the End that it was in the sight of Yug.

And men forgot Yug.

One day Yug saw Mung behind the hills making the sign of Mung. And Yug was Yug no more.

ALHIRETH-HOTEP THE PROPHET

When Yug was Yug no more men said unto Alhireth-Hotep: "Be thou our prophet, and be as wise as Yug."

And Alhireth-Hotep said: "I am as wise as Yug." And men were very glad.

And Alhireth-Hotep said of Life and Death: "These be the affairs of Alhireth-Hotep." And men brought gifts to him.

One day Alhireth-Hotep wrote in a book: "Alhireth-Hotep knoweth All Things, for he hath spoken with Mung."

And Mung stepped from behind him, making the sign of Mung, saying: "Knowest thou All Things, then, Alhireth-Hotep?" And Alhireth-Hotep became among the Things that Were.

KABOK THE PROPHET

When Alhireth-Hotep was among the Things that Were, and still men sought to know, they said unto Kabok: "Be thou as wise as was Alhireth-Hotep."

And Kabok grew wise in his own sight and in the sight of men.

And Kabok said: "Mung maketh his signs against men or withholdeth it by the advice of Kabok."

And he said unto one: "Thou hast sinned against Kabok, therefore will Mung make the sign of Mung against thee." And to another: "Thou has brought Kabok gifts, therefore shall Mung forbear to make against thee the sign of Mung."

One night as Kabok fattened upon the gifts that men had brought him he heard the tread of Mung treading in the garden of Kabok about his house at night.

And because the night was very still it seemed most evil to Kabok that Mung should be treading in his garden, without the advice of Kabok, about his house at night.

And Kabok, who knew All Things, grew afraid, for the treading was very loud and the night still, and he knew not what lay behind the back of Mung, which none had ever seen.

But when the morning grew to brightness, and there was light upon the Worlds, and Mung trod no longer in the garden, Kabok forgot his fears, and said: "Perhaps it was but a herd of cattle that stampeded in the garden of Kabok."

And Kabok went about his business, which was that of knowing All Things, and telling All Things unto men, and making light of Mung.

But that night Mung trod again in the garden of Kabok, about his house at night, and stood before the window of the house like a shadow standing erect, so that Kabok knew indeed that it was Mung.

And a great fear fell upon the throat of Kabok, so that his speech was hoarse; and he cried out: "Thou art Mung!"

And Mung slightly inclined his head, and went on to tread in the garden of Kabok, about his house at night.

And Kabok lay and listened with horror at his heart.

But when the second morning grew to brightness, and there was light upon the Worlds, Mung went from treading in the garden of Kabok; and for a little while Kabok hoped, but looked with great dread for the coming of the third night.

And when the third night was come, and the bat had gone to his home, and the wind had sank, the night was very still.

And Kabok lay and listened, to whom the wings of the night flew very slow.

But, ere night met the morning upon the highway between Pegana and the Worlds, there came the tread of Mung in the garden of Kabok towards Kabok's door.

And Kabok fled out of his house as flees a hunted beast and flung himself before Mung.

And Mung made the sign of Mung, pointing towards THE END.

And the fears of Kabok had rest from troubling Kabok any more, for they and he were among accomplished things.

OF THE CALAMITY THAT BEFELL YUN-ILARA BY THE SEA, AND OF THE BUILDING OF THE TOWER OF THE ENDING OF DAYS

When Kabok and his fears had rest the people sought a prophet who should have no fear of Mung, whose hand was against the prophets.

And at last they found Yun-Ilara, who tended sheep and had no fear of Mung, and the people brought him to the town that he might be their prophet.

And Yun-Ilara built a tower towards the sea that looked upon the setting of the Sun. And he called it the Tower of the Ending of Days.

And about the ending of the day would Yun-Ilara go up to his tower's top and look towards the setting of the Sun to cry his curses against Mung, crying: "O Mung! whose hand is against the Sun, whom men abhor but worship because they fear thee, here stands and speaks a man who fears thee not. Assassin lord of murder and dark things, abhorrent, merciless, make thou the sign of Mung against me when thou wilt, but until silence settles upon my lips, because of the sign of Mung, I will curse Mung to his face." And the people in the street below would gaze up with wonder towards Yun-Ilara, who had no fear of Mung, and brought him gifts; only in their homes after the falling of the night would they pray again with reverence to Mung. But Mung said: "Shall a man curse a god?"

And still Mung came not nigh to Yun-Ilara as he cried his curses against Mung from his tower towards the sea.

And Sish throughout the Worlds hurled Time away, and slew the Hours that had served him well, and called up more out of the timeless waste that lieth beyond the Worlds, and drave them forth to assail all things. And Sish cast a whiteness over the hairs of Yun-Ilara, and ivy about his tower, and weariness over his limbs, for Mung passed by him still.

And when Sish became a god less durable to Yun-Ilara than ever Mung hath been he ceased at last to cry from his tower's top his curses against Mung whenever the sun went down, till there came the day when weariness of the gift of Kib fell heavily upon Yun-Ilara.

Then from the tower of the Ending of Days did Yun-Ilara cry out thus to Mung, crying: "O Mung! O loveliest of the gods! O Mung, most dearly to be desired! thy gift of Death is the heritage of Man, with ease and rest and silence and returning to the Earth. Kib giveth but toil and trouble; and Sish, he sendeth regrets with each of his hours wherewith he assails the World. Yoharneth-Lahai cometh nigh no more. I can no longer be glad with Limpang-Tung. When the other gods forsake him a man hath only Mung."

But Mung said: "Shall a man curse a god?"

And every day and all night long did Yun-Ilara cry aloud: "Ah, now for the hour of the mourning of many, and the pleasant garlands of flowers and the tears, and the moist, dark earth. Ah, for repose down underneath the grass, where the firm feet of the trees grip hold upon the world, where never shall come the wind that now blows through my bones, and the rain shall come warm and trickling, not driven by storm, where is the easeful falling asunder of bone from bone in the dark." Thus prayed Yun-Ilara, who had cursed in his folly and youth, while never heeded Mung.

Still from a heap of bones that are Yun-Ilara still, lying about the ruined base of the tower that once he builded, goes up a shrill voice with the wind crying out for the mercy of Mung, if any such there be.

OF HOW THE GODS WHELMED SIDITH

There was dole in the valley of Sidith. For three years there had been pestilence, and in the last of the three a famine; moreover, there was imminence of war.

Throughout all Sidith men died night and day, and night and day within the Temple of All the gods save One (for none may pray to MANA-YOOD-SUSHAI) did the priests of the gods pray hard.

For they said: "For a long while a man may hear the droning of little insects and yet not be aware that he hath heard them, so may the gods not hear our prayers at first until they have been very oft repeated. But when your praying has troubled the silence long it may be that some god as he strolls in Pegana's glades may come on one of our lost prayers, that flutters like a butterfly tossed in storm when all its wings are broken; then if the gods be merciful they may ease our fears in Sidith, or else they may crush us, being petulant gods, and so we shall see trouble in Sidith no longer, with its pestilence and dearth and fears of war."

But in the fourth year of the pestilence and in the second year of the famine, and while still there was imminence of war, came all the people of Sidith to the door of the Temple of All the gods save One, where none may enter but the priests—but only leave gifts and go.

And there the people cried out: "O High Prophet of All the gods save One, Priest of Kib, Priest of Sish, and Priest of Mung, Teller of the mysteries of Dorozhand, Receiver of the gifts of the People, and Lord of Prayer, what doest thou within the Temple of All the gods save One?"

And Arb-Rin-Hadith, who was the High Prophet, answered: "I pray for all the People."

But the people answered: "O High Prophet of All the gods save One, Priest of Kib, Priest of Sish, and Priest of Mung, Teller of the mysteries of Dorozhand, Receiver of the gifts of the People, and Lord of Prayer, for four long years hast thou prayed with the priests of all thine order, while we brought ye gifts and died. Now, therefore, since They have not heard thee in four grim years, thou must go and carry to Their faces the prayer of the people of Sidith when They go to drive the thunder to his pasture upon the mountain Aghrinaun, or else there shall no longer be gifts upon thy temple door, whenever falls the dew, that thou and thine order may fatten.

"Then thou shalt say before Their faces: 'O All the gods save One, Lords of the Worlds, whose child is the eclipse, take back thy pestilence from Sidith, for ye have played the game of the gods too long with the people of Sidith, who would fain have done with the gods'."

Then in great fear answered the High Prophet, saying: "What if the gods be angry and whelm Sidith?" And the people answered: "Then are we sooner done with pestilence and famine and the imminence of war."

That night the thunder howled upon Aghrinaun, which stood a peak above all others in the land of Sidith. And the people took Arb-Rin-Hadith from his Temple and drave him to Aghrinaun, for they said: "There walk to-night upon the mountain All the gods save One."

And Arb-Rin-Hadith went trembling to the gods.

Next morning, white and frightened from Aghrinaun, came Arb-Rin-Hadith back into the valley, and there spake to the people, saying: "The faces of the gods are iron and their mouths set hard. There is no hope from the gods."

Then said the people: "Thou shalt go to MANA-YOOD-SUSHAI, to whom no man may pray: seek him upon Aghrinaun where it lifts clear into the stillness before morning, and on its summit, where all things seem to rest surely there rests also MANA-YOOD-SUSHAI. Go to him, and say: 'Thou hast made evil gods, and They smite Sidith.' Perchance he hath forgotten all his gods, or hath not heard of Sidith. Thou hast escaped the thunder of the gods, surely thou shalt also escape the stillness of MANA-YOOD-SUSHAI."

Upon a morning when the sky and lakes were clear and the world still, and Aghrinaun was stiller than the world, Arb-Rin-Hadith crept in fear towards the slopes of Aghrinaun because the people were urgent.

All that day men saw him climbing. At night he rested near the top. But ere the morning of the day that followed, such as rose early saw him in the silence, a speck against the blue, stretch up his arms upon the summit to MANA-YOOD-SUSHAI. Then instantly they saw him not, nor was he ever seen of men again who had dared to trouble the stillness of MANA-YOOD-SUSHAI.

Such as now speak of Sidith tell of a fierce and potent tribe that smote away a people in a valley enfeebled by pestilence, where stood a temple to "All the gods save One" in which was no high priest.

OF HOW IMBAUN BECAME HIGH PROPHET
IN ARADEC OF ALL THE GODS SAVE ONE

Imbaun was to be made High Prophet in Aradec, of All the Gods save One.

From Ardra, Rhoodra, and the lands beyond came all High Prophets of the Earth to the Temple in Aradec of All the gods save One.

And then they told Imbaun how The Secret of Things was upon the summit of the dome of the Hall of Night, but faintly writ, and in an unknown tongue.

Midway in the night, between the setting and the rising sun, they led Imbaun into the Hall of Night, and said to him, chaunting altogether: "Imbaun, Imbaun, Imbaun, look up to the roof, where is writ The Secret of Things, but faintly, and in an unknown tongue."

And Imbaun looked up, but darkness was so deep within the Hall of Night that Imbaun was not even the High Prophets who came from Ardra, Rhoodra, and the lands beyond, nor saw he aught in the Hall of Night at all.

Then called the High Prophets: "What seest thou, Imbaun?"

And Imbaun said: "I see naught."

Then called the High Prophets: "What knowest thou Imbaun?"

And Imbaun said: "I know naught."

Then spake the High Prophet of Eld of All the gods save One, who is first on Earth of prophets: "O Imbaun! we have all looked upwards in the Hall of Night towards the secret of Things, and ever it was dark, and the Secret faint and in an unknown tongue. And now thou knowest what all High Prophets know."

And Imbaun answered: "I know."

So Imbaun became High Prophet in Aradec of All the gods save One, and prayed for all the people, who knew not that there was darkness in the Hall of Night or that the secret was writ faint and in an unknown tongue.

These are the words of Imbaun that he wrote in a book that all the people might know:

"In the twentieth night of the nine hundredth moon, as night came up the valley, I performed the mystic rites of each of the gods in the temple as is my wont, lest any of the gods should grow angry in the night and whelm us while we slept.

"And as I uttered the last of certain secret words I fell asleep in the temple, for I was weary, with my head against the altar of Dorozhand. Then in the stillness, as I slept, there entered Dorozhand by the temple door in the guise of a man, and touched me on the shoulder, and I awoke.

"But when I saw that his eyes shone blue and lit the whole of the temple I knew that he was a god though he came in mortal guise. And Dorozhand said: 'Prophet of Dorozhand, behold that the people may know.' And he showed me the paths of Sish stretching far down into the future time. Then he bade me arise and follow whither he pointed, speaking no words but commanding with his eyes.

"Therefore upon the twentieth night of the nine hundredth moon I walked with Dorozhand adown the paths of Sish into the future time.

"And ever beside the way did men slay men. And the sum of their slaying was greater than the slaying of the pestilence of any of the evils of the gods.

"And cities arose and shed their houses in dust, and ever the desert returned again to its own, and covered over and hid the last of all that had troubled its repose.

"And still men slew men.

"And I came at last to a time when men set their yoke no longer upon beasts but made them beasts of iron.

"And after that did men slay men with mists.

"Then, because the slaying exceeded their desire, there came peace upon the world that was brought by the hand of the slayer, and men slew men no more.

"And cities multiplied, and overthrew the desert and conquered its repose.

"And suddenly I beheld that THE END was near, for there was a stirring above Pegana as of One who grows weary of resting, and I saw the hound Time crouch to spring, with his eyes upon the throats of the gods, shifting from throat to throat, and the drumming of Skarl grew faint.

"And if a god may fear, it seemed that there was fear upon the face of Dorozhand, and he seized me by the hand and led me back along the paths of Time that I might not see THE END.

"Then I saw cities rise out of the dust again and fall back into the desert whence they had arisen; and again I slept in the Temple of All the gods save One, with my head against the altar of Dorozhand.

"Then again the Temple was alight, but not with light from the eyes of Dorozhand; only dawn came all blue out of the East and shone through the arches of the Temple. Then I awoke and performed the morning rites and mysteries of All the gods save One, lest any of the gods be angry in the day and take away the Sun.

"And I knew that because I who had been so near to it had not beheld THE END that a man should never behold it or know the doom of the gods. This They have hidden."

OF HOW IMBAUN MET ZODRAK

The prophet of the gods lay resting by the river to watch the stream run by.

And as he lay he pondered on the Scheme of Things and the works of all the gods. And it seemed to the prophet of the gods as he watched the stream run by that the Scheme was a right scheme and the gods benignant gods; yet there was sorrow in the Worlds. It seemed that Kib was bountiful, that Mung calmed all who suffer, that Sish dealt not too harshly with the hours, and that all the gods were good; yet there was sorrow in the Worlds.

Then said the prophet of the gods as he watched the stream run by: "There is some other god of whom naught is writ." And suddenly the prophet was aware of an old man who bemoaned beside the river, crying: "Alas! alas!"

His face was marked by the sign and the seal of exceeding many years, and there was yet vigour in his frame. These be the words of the prophet that he wrote in his book: "I said: 'Who art thou that bemoans beside the river?' And he answered: 'I am the fool.' I said: 'Upon thy brow are the marks of wisdom such as is stored in books.' He said: 'I am Zodrak. Thousands of years ago I tended sheep upon a hill that sloped towards the sea. The gods have many moods. Thousands of years ago They were in a mirthful mood. They said: 'Let Us call up a man before Us that We may laugh in Pegana.'"

"'And Their eyes that looked on me saw not me alone but also saw THE BEGINNING and THE END and all the Worlds besides. Then said the gods, speaking as speak the gods: "Go, back to thy sheep."

"'But I, who am the fool, had heard it said on earth that whoso seeth the gods upon Pegana becometh as the gods, if so he demand to Their faces, who may not slay him who hath looked them in the eyes.

"'And I, the fool, said: "I have looked in the eyes of the gods, and I demand what a man may demand of the gods when he hath seen Them in Pegana." And the gods inclined Their heads and Hoodrazai said: "It is the law of the gods."

"'And I, who was only a shepherd, how could I know?

"'I said: "I will make men rich." And the gods said: "What is rich?"

"'And I said: "I will send them love." And the gods said: "What is love?" And I sent gold into the Worlds, and, alas! I sent with it poverty and strife. And I sent love into the Worlds, and with it grief.

"'And now I have mixed gold and love most woefully together, and I can never remedy what I have done, for the deeds of the gods are done, and nothing may undo them.

"'Then I said: "I will give men wisdom that they may be glad." And those who got my wisdom found that they knew nothing, and from having been happy became glad no more.

"'And I, who would make men happy, have made them sad, and I have spoiled the beautiful scheme of the gods.

"'And now my hand is for ever on the handle of Their plough. I was only a shepherd, and how should I have known?

"'Now I come to thee as thou restest by the river to ask of thee thy forgiveness, for I would fain have the forgiveness of a man.'

"And I answered: 'O Lord of seven skies, whose children are the storms, shall a man forgive a god?'

"He answered: 'Men have sinned not against the gods as the gods have sinned against men since I came into Their councils.'

"And I, the prophet, answered: 'O Lord of seven skies, whose plaything is the thunder, thou art amongst the gods, what need hast thou for words from any man?'

"He said: 'Indeed I am amongst the gods, who speak to me as they speak to other gods, yet is there always a smile about Their mouths, and a look in Their eyes that saith: "Thou wert a man."'

"I said: 'O Lord of seven skies, about whose feet the Worlds are as drifted sand, because thou biddest me, I, a man, forgive thee.'

"And he answered: 'I was but a shepherd, and I could not know.' Then he was gone."

PEGANA

The prophet of the gods cried out to the gods: "O! All the gods save One" for none may pray to MANA-YOOD-SUSHAI, "where shall the life of a man abide when Mung hath made against his body the sign of Mung?—for the people with whom ye play have sought to know."

But the gods answered, speaking through the mist:

"Though thou shouldst tell thy secrets to the beasts, even that the beasts should understand, yet will not the gods divulge the secret of the gods to thee, that gods and beasts and men shall be all the same, all knowing the same things."

That night Yoharneth-Lahai same to Aradec, and said unto Imbaun: "Wherefore wouldst thou know the secret of the gods that not the gods may tell thee?

"When the wind blows not, where, then, is the wind?

"Or when thou art not living, where art thou?

"What should the wind care for the hours of calm or thou for death?

"Thy life is long, Eternity is short.

"So short that, shouldst thou die and Eternity should pass, and after the passing of Eternity thou shouldst live again, thou wouldst say: 'I closed mine eyes but for an instant.'

"There is an eternity behind thee as well as one before. Hast thou bewailed the aeons that passed without thee, who art so much afraid of the aeons that shall pass?"

Then said the prophet: "How shall I tell the people that the gods have not spoken and their prophet doth not know? For then should I be prophet no longer, and another would take the people's gifts instead of me."

Then said Imbaun to the people: "The gods have spoken, saying: 'O Imbaun, Our prophet, it is as the people believe whose wisdom hath discovered the secret of the gods, and the people when they die shall come to Pegāna, and there live with the gods, and there have pleasure without toil. And Pegāna is a place all white with the peaks of mountains, on each of them a god, and the people shall lie upon the slopes of the mountains each under the god that he hath worshipped most when his lot was in the Worlds. And there shall music beyond thy dreaming come drifting through the scent of all the orchards in the Worlds, with somewhere someone singing an old song that shall be as a half-remembered thing. And there shall be gardens that have always sunlight, and streams that are lost in no sea beneath skies for ever blue. And there shall be no rain nor no regrets. Only the roses that in highest Pegāna have achieved their prime shall shed their petals in showers at thy feet, and only far away on the forgotten earth shall voices drift up to thee that cheered thee in thy childhood about the gardens of thy youth. And if thou sighest for any memory of earth because thou hearest unforgotten voices, then will the gods send messengers on wings to soothe thee in Pegāna, saying to them: "There one sigheth who hath remembered Earth." And they shall make Pegāna more seductive for thee still, and they shall take thee by the hand and whisper in thine ear till the old voices are forgot.

"'And besides the flowers of Pegāna there shall have climbed by then until it hath reached to Pegāna the rose that clambered about the house where thou wast born. Thither shall also come the wandering echoes of all such music as charmed thee long ago.

"'Moreover, as thou sittest on the orchard lawns that clothe Pegāna's mountains, and as thou hearkenest to melody that sways the souls of the gods, there shall stretch away far down beneath thee the great unhappy Earth, till gazing from rapture upon sorrows thou shalt be glad that thou wert dead.

"'And from the three great mountains that stand aloof and over all the others—Grimbol, Zeebol, and Trehagobol—shall blow the wind of the morning and the wind of all the day, borne upon the wings of all the butterflies that have died upon the Worlds, to cool the gods and Pegāna.

"'Far through Pegāna a silvery fountain, lured upward by the gods from the Central Sea, shall fling its waters aloft, and over the highest of Pegāna's peaks, above Trehagobol, shall burst into gleaming mists, to cover Highest Pegāna, and make a curtain about the resting-place of MANA-YOOD-SUSHAI.

"'Alone, still and remote below the base of one of the inner mountains, lieth a great blue pool.

"'Whoever looketh down into its waters may behold all his life that was upon the Worlds and all the deeds that he hath done.

"'None walk by the pool and none regard its depths, for all in Pegāna have suffered and all have sinned some sin, and it lieth in the pool.

"'And there is no darkness in Pegāna, for when night hath conquered the sun and stilled the Worlds and turned the white peaks of Pegāna into grey then shine the blue eyes of the gods like sunlight on the sea, where each god sits upon his mountain.

"'And at the Last, upon some afternoon, perhaps in summer, shall the gods say, speaking to the gods: "What is the likeness of MANA-YOOD-SUSHAI and what THE END?"

"'And then shall MANA-YOOD-SUSHAI draw back with his hand the mists that cover his resting, saying: "This is the Face of MANA-YOOD-SUSHAI and this THE END."'"

Then said the people to the prophet: "Shall not black hills draw round in some forsaken land, to make a vale-wide cauldron wherein the molten rock shall seethe and roar, and where the crags of mountains shall be hurled upward to the surface and bubble and go down again, that there our enemies may boil for ever?"

And the prophet answered: "It is writ large about the bases of Pegāna's mountains, upon which sit the gods: 'Thine Enemies Are Forgiven.'"

THE SAYINGS OF IMBAUN

The Prophet of the gods said: "Yonder beside the road there sitteth a false prophet; and to all who seek to know the hidden days he saith: 'Upon the morrow the King shall speak to thee as his chariot goeth by.'"

Moreover, all the people bring him gifts, and the false prophet hath more to listen to his words than hath the Prophet of the gods.

Then said Imbaun: "What knoweth the Prophet of the gods? I know only that I and men know naught concerning the gods or aught concerning men. Shall I, who am their prophet, tell the people this?

"For wherefore have the people chosen prophets but that they should speak the hopes of the people, and tell the people that their hopes be true?"

The false prophet saith: "Upon the morrow the king shall speak to thee."

Shall not I say: "Upon The Morrow the gods shall speak with thee as thou restest upon Pegāna?"

So shall the people be happy, and know that their hopes be true who have believed the words that they have chosen a prophet to say.

But what shall know the Prophet of the gods, to whom none may come to say: "Thy hopes are true," for whom none may make strange signs before his eyes to quench his fear of death, for whom alone the chaunt of his priests availeth naught?

The Prophet of the gods hath sold his happiness for wisdom, and hath given his hopes for the people.

Said also Imbaun: "When thou art angry at night observe how calm be the stars; and shall small ones rail when there is such a calm among the great ones? Or when thou art angry by day regard the distant hills, and see the calm that doth adorn their faces. Shalt thou be angry while they stand so serene?

"Be not angry with men, for they are driven as thou art by Dorozhand. Do bullocks goad one another on whom the same yoke rests?

"And be not angry with Dorozhand, for then thou beatest thy bare fingers against iron cliffs.

"All that is is so because it was to be. Rail not, therefore, against what is, for it was all to be."

And Imbaun said: "The Sun ariseth and maketh a glory about all the things that he seeth, and drop by drop he turneth the common dew to every kind of gem. And he maketh a splendour in the hills.

"And also man is born. And there rests a glory about the gardens of his youth. Both travel afar to do what Dorozhand would have them do.

"Soon now the sun will set, and very softly come twinkling in the stillness all the stars.

"Also man dieth. And quietly about his grave will all the mourners weep.

"Will not his life arise again somewhere in all the worlds? Shall he not again behold the gardens of his youth? Or does he set to end?"

OF HOW IMBAUN SPAKE OF DEATH TO THE KING

There trod such pestilence in Aradec that, the King as he looked abroad out of his palace saw men die. And when the King saw Death he feared that one day even the King should die. Therefore he commanded guards to bring before him the wisest prophet that should be found in Aradec.

Then heralds came to the temple of All the gods save One, and cried aloud, having first commanded silence, crying: "Rhazahan, King over Aradec, Prince by right of Ildun and Ildaun, and Prince by conquest of Pathia, Ezek, and Azhan, Lord of the Hills, to the High Prophet of All the gods save One sends salutations."

Then they bore him before the King.

The King said unto the prophet: "O Prophet of All the gods save One, shall I indeed die?"

And the prophet answered: "O King! thy people may not rejoice for ever, and some day the King will die."

And the King answered: "This may be so, but certainly thou shalt die. It may be that one day I shall die, but till then the lives of the people are in my hands."

Then guards led the prophet away.

And there arose prophets in Aradec who spake not of death to Kings.

OF OOD

Men say that if thou comest to Sundari, beyond all the plains, and shalt climb to his summit before thou art seized by the avalanche which sitteth always on his slopes, that then there lie before thee many peaks. And if thou shalt climb these and cross their valleys (of which there be seven and also seven peaks) thou shalt come at last to the land of forgotten hills, where amid many valleys and white snow there standeth the "Great Temple of One god Only."

Therein is a dreaming prophet who doeth naught, and a drowsy priesthood about him.

These be the priests of MANA-YOOD-SUSHAI.

Within the temple it is forbidden to work, also it is forbidden to pray. Night differeth not from day within its doors. They rest as MANA rests. And the name of their prophet is Ood.

Ood is a greater prophet than any of all the prophets of Earth, and it hath been said by some that were Ood and his priests to pray chaunting all together and calling upon MANA-YOOD-SUSHAI that MANA-YOOD-SUSHAI would then awake, for surely he would hear the prayers of his own prophet—then would there be Worlds no more.

There is also another way to the land of forgotten hills, which is a smooth road and a straight, that lies through the heart of the mountains. But for certain hidden reasons it were better for thee to go by the peaks and snow, even though thou shouldst perish by the way, that thou shouldst seek to come to the house of Ood by the smooth, straight road.

THE RIVER

There arises a river in Pegana that is neither a river of water nor yet a river of fire, and it flows through the skies and the Worlds to the Rim of the Worlds, a river of silence. Through all the Worlds are sounds, the noises of moving, and the echoes of voices and song; but upon the River is no sound ever heard, for there all echoes die.

The River arises out of the drumming of Skarl, and flows for ever between banks of thunder, until it comes to the waste beyond the Worlds, behind the farthest star, down to the Sea of Silence.

I lay in the desert beyond all cities and sounds, and above me flowed the River of Silence through the sky; and on the desert's edge night fought against the Sun, and suddenly conquered.

Then on the River I saw the dream-built ship of the god Yoharneth-Lahai, whose great prow lifted grey into the air above the River of Silence.

Her timbers were olden dreams dreamed long ago, and poets' fancies made her tall, straight masts, and her rigging was wrought out of the people's hopes.

Upon her deck were rowers with dream-made oars, and the rowers were the people of men's fancies, and princes of old story and people who had died, and people who had never been.

These swung forward and swung back to row Yoharneth-Lahai through the Worlds with never a sound of rowing. For ever on every wind float up to Pegana the hopes and the fancies of the people which have no home in the Worlds, and there Yoharneth-Lahai weaves them into dreams, to take them to the people again.

And every night in his dream-built ship Yoharneth-Lahai setteth forth, with all his dreams on board, to take again their old hopes back to the people and all forgotten fancies.

But ere the day comes back to her own again, and all the conquering armies of the dawn hurl their red lances in the face of the night, Yoharneth-Lahai leaves the sleeping Worlds, and rows back up the River of Silence, that flows from Pegana into the Sea of Silence that lies beyond the Worlds.

And the name of the River is Imrana the River of Silence. All they that be weary of the sound of cities and very tired of clamour creep down in the night-time to Yoharneth-Lahai's ship, and going aboard it, among the dreams and the fancies of old times, lie down upon the deck, and pass from sleeping to the River, while Mung, behind them, makes the sign of Mung because they would have it so. And, lying there upon the deck among their own remembered fancies, and songs that were never sung, and they drift up Imrana ere the dawn, where the sound of the cities comes not, nor the voice of the thunder is heard, nor the midnight howl of Pain as he gnaws at the bodies of men, and far away and forgotten bleat the small sorrows that trouble all the Worlds.

But where the River flows through Pegana's gates, between the great twin constellations Yum and Gothum, where Yum stands sentinel upon the left and Gothum upon the right, there sits Sirami, the lord of All Forgetting. And, when the ship draws near, Sirami looketh with his sapphire eyes into the faces and beyond them of those that were weary of cities, and as he gazes, as one that looketh before him remembering naught, he gently waves his hands. And amid the waving of Sirami's hands there fall from all that behold him all their memories, save certain things that may not be forgotten even beyond the Worlds.

It hath been said that when Skarl ceases to drum, and MANA-YOOD-SUSHAI awakes, and the gods of Pegana know that it is THE END, that then the gods will enter galleons of gold, and with dream-born rowers glide down Imrana (who knows whither or why?) till they come where the River enters the Silent Sea, and shall there be gods of nothing, where nothing is, and never a sound shall come. And far away upon the River's banks shall bay their old hound Time, that shall seek to rend his masters; while MANA-YOOD-SUSHAI shall think some other plan concerning gods and worlds.

THE BIRD OF DOOM AND THE END

For at the last shall the thunder, fleeing to escape from the doom of the gods, roar horribly among the Worlds; and Time, the hound of the gods, shall bay hungrily at his masters because he is lean with age.

And from the innermost of Pegana's vales shall the bird of doom, Mosahn, whose voice is like the trumpet, soar upward with boisterous beatings of his wings above Pegana's mountains and the gods, and there with his trumpet voice acclaim THE END.

Then in the tumult and amid the fury of their hound the gods shall make for the last time in Pegana the sign of all the gods, and go with dignity and quiet down to Their galleons of gold, and sail away down the River of Silence, not ever to return.

Then shall the River overflow its banks, and a tide come setting in from the Silent Sea, till all the Worlds and the Skies are drowned in silence; while MANA-YOOD-SUSHAI in the Middle of All sits deep in thought. And the hound Time, when all the Worlds and cities are swept away whereon he used to raven, having no more to devour, shall suddenly die.

But there are some that hold—and this is the heresy of the Saigoths—that when the gods go down at the last into their galleons of gold Mung shall turn alone, and, setting his back against Trehagobol and wielding the Sword of Severing which is called Death, shall fight out his last fight with the hound Time, his empty scabbard Sleep clattering loose beside him.

There under Trehagobol they shall fight alone when all the gods are gone.

And the Saigoths say that for two days and nights the hound shall leer and snarl before the face of Mung-days and nights that shall be lit by neither sun nor moons, for these shall go dipping down the sky with all the Worlds as the galleons glide away, because the gods that made them are gods no more.

And then shall the hound, springing, tear out the throat of Mung, who, making for the last time the sign of Mung, shall bring down Death crashing through the shoulders of the hound, and in the blood of Time that Sword shall rust away.

Then shall MANA-YOOD-SUSHAI be all alone, with neither Death nor Time, and never the hours singing in his ears, nor the swish of the passing lives.

But far away from Pegana shall go the galleons of gold that bear the gods away, upon whose faces shall be utter calm, because They are the gods knowing that it is THE END.

TIME AND THE GODS (1906)

PREFACE

These tales are of the things that befell gods and men in Yarnith, Averon, and Zarkandhu, and in the other countries of my dreams.

TIME AND THE GODS

Once when the gods were young and only Their swarthy servant Time was without age, the gods lay sleeping by a broad river upon earth. There in a valley that from all the earth the gods had set apart for Their repose the gods dreamed marble dreams. And with domes and pinnacles the dreams arose and stood up proudly between the river and the sky, all shimmering white to the morning. In the city's midst the gleaming marble of a thousand steps climbed to the citadel where arose four pinnacles beckoning to heaven, and midmost between the pinnacles there stood the dome, vast, as the gods had dreamed it. All around, terrace by terrace, there went marble lawns well guarded by onyx lions and carved with effigies of all the gods striding amid the symbols of the worlds. With a sound like tinkling bells, far off in a land of shepherds hidden by some hill, the waters of many fountains turned again home. Then the gods awoke and there stood Sardathrion. Not to common men have the gods given to walk Sardathrion's streets, and not to common eyes to see her fountains. Only to those to whom in lonely passes in the night the gods have spoken, leaning through the stars, to those that have heard the voices of the gods above the morning or seen Their faces bending above the sea, only to those hath it been given to see Sardathrion, to stand where her pinnacles gathered together in the night fresh from the dreams of gods. For round the valley a great desert lies through which no common traveller may come, but those whom the gods have chosen feel suddenly a great longing at heart, and crossing the mountains that divide the desert from the world, set out across it driven by the gods, till hidden in the desert's midst they find the valley at last and look with eyes upon Sardathrion.

In the desert beyond the valley grow a myriad thorns, and all pointing towards Sardathrion. So may many that the gods have loved come to the marble city, but none can return, for other cities are no fitting home for men whose feet have touched Sardathrion's marble streets, where even the gods have not been ashamed to come in the guise of men with Their cloaks wrapped about their faces. Therefore no city shall ever hear the songs that are sung in the marble citadel by those in whose ears have rung the voices of the gods. No report shall ever come to other lands of the music of the fall of Sardathrion's fountains, when the waters which went heavenward return again into the lake where the gods cool Their brows sometimes in the guise of men. None may ever hear the speech of the poets of that city, to whom the gods have spoken.

It stands a city aloof. There hath been no rumour of it—I alone have dreamed of it, and I may not be sure that my dreams are true.

* * * *

Above the Twilight the gods were seated in the after years, ruling the worlds. No longer now They walked at evening in the Marble City hearing the fountains splash, or listening to the singing of the men they loved, because it was in the after years and the work of the gods was to be done.

But often as they rested a moment from doing the work of the gods, from hearing the prayers of men or sending here the Pestilence or there Mercy, They would speak awhile with one another of the olden years saying, "Rememberest thou not Sardathrion?" and another would answer "Ah! Sardathrion, and all Sardathrion's mist-draped marble lawns whereon we walk not now."

Then the gods turned to do the work of the gods, answering the prayers of men or smiting them, and ever They sent Their swarthy servant Time to heal or overwhelm. And Time went forth into the worlds to obey the commands of the gods, yet he cast furtive glances at his masters, and the gods distrusted Time because he had known the worlds or ever the gods became.

One day when furtive Time had gone into the worlds to nimbly smite some city whereof the gods were weary, the gods above the twilight speaking to one another said:

"Surely we are the lords of Time and gods of the worlds besides. See how our city Sardathrion lifts over other cities. Others arise and perish but Sardathrion standeth yet, the first and the last of cities. Rivers are lost in the sea and streams forsake the hills, but ever Sardathrion's fountains arise in our dream city. As was Sardathrion when the gods were young, so are her streets to-day as a sign that we are the gods."

Suddenly the swart figure of Time stood up before the gods, with both hands dripping with blood and a red sword dangling idly from his fingers, and said:

"Sardathrion is gone! I have overthrown it!"

And the gods said:

"Sardathrion? Sardathrion, the marble city? Thou, thou hast over-thrown it? Thou, the slave of the gods?"

And the oldest of the gods said:

"Sardathrion, Sardathrion, and is Sardathrion gone?"

And furtively Time looked him in the face and edged towards him fingering with his dripping fingers the hilt of his nimble sword.

Then the gods feared with a new fear that he that had overthrown Their city would one day slay the gods. And a new cry went wailing through the Twilight, the lament of the gods for Their dream city, crying:

"Tears may not bring again Sardathrion.

"But this the gods may do who have seen, and seen with unrelenting eyes, the sorrows of ten thousand worlds—thy gods may weep for thee.

"Tears may not bring again Sardathrion.

"Believe it not, Sardathrion, that ever thy gods sent this doom to thee; he that hath overthrown thee shall overthrow thy gods.

"How oft when Night came suddenly on Morning playing in the fields of Twilight did we watch thy pinnacles emerging from the darkness, Sardathrion, Sardathrion, dream city of the gods, and thine onyx lions looming limb by limb from the dusk.

"How often have we sent our child the Dawn to play with thy fountain tops; how often hath Evening, loveliest of our goddesses, strayed long upon thy balconies.

"Let one fragment of thy marbles stand up above the dust for thine old gods to caress, as a man when all else is lost treasures one lock of the hair of his beloved.

"Sardathrion, the gods must kiss once more the place where thy streets were once.

"There were wonderful marbles in thy streets, Sardathrion."

"Sardathrion, Sardathrion, the gods weep for thee."

THE COMING OF THE SEA

Once there was no sea, and the gods went walking over the green plains of earth.

Upon an evening of the forgotten years the gods were seated on the hills, and all the little rivers of the world lay coiled at Their feet asleep, when Slid, the new god, striding through the stars, came suddenly upon earth lying in a corner of space. And behind Slid there marched a million waves, all following Slid and tramping up the twilight; and Slid touched Earth in one of her great green valleys that divide the south, and here he encamped for the night with all his waves about him. But to the gods as They sat upon Their hilltops a new cry came crying over the green spaces that lay below the hills, and the gods said:

"This is neither the cry of life nor yet the whisper of death. What is this new cry that the gods have never commanded, yet which comes to the ears of the gods?"

And the gods together shouting made the cry of the south, calling the south wind to them. And again the gods shouted all together making the cry of the north, calling the north wind to Them; and thus They gathered to Them all Their winds and sent these four down into the low plains to find what thing it was that called with the new cry, and to drive it away from the gods.

Then all the winds harnessed up their clouds and drave forth till they came to the great green valley that divides the south in twain, and there found Slid with all his waves about him. Then for a space Slid and the four winds struggled with one another till the strength of the winds was gone, and they limped back to the gods, their masters, and said:

"We have met this new thing that has come upon the earth and have striven against its armies, but could not drive them forth; and the new thing is beautiful but very angry, and is creeping towards the gods."

But Slid advanced and led his armies up the valley, and inch by inch and mile by mile he conquered the lands of the gods. Then from Their hills the gods sent down a great array of cliffs against hard, red rocks, and bade them march against Slid. And the cliffs marched down till they came and stood before Slid and leaned their heads forward and frowned and stood staunch to guard the lands of the gods against the might of the sea, shutting Slid off from the world. Then Slid sent some of his smaller waves to search out what stood against him, and the cliffs shattered them. But Slid went back and gathered together a hoard of his greatest waves and hurled them against the cliffs, and the cliffs shattered them. And again Slid called up out of his deep a mighty array of waves and sent them roaring against the guardians of the gods, and the red rocks frowned and smote them. And once again Slid gathered his greater waves and hurled them against the cliffs; and when the waves were scattered like those before them the feet of the cliffs were no longer standing firm, and their faces were scarred and battered. Then into every cleft that stood in the rocks Slid sent his hugest wave and others followed behind it, and Slid himself seized hold of huge rocks with his claws and tore them down and stamped them under his feet. And when the tumult was over the sea had won, and over the broken remnants of those red cliffs the armies of Slid marched on and up the long green valley.

Then the gods heard Slid exulting far away and singing songs of triumph over Their battered cliffs, and ever the tramp of his armies sounded nearer and nearer in the listening ears of the gods.

Then the gods called to Their downlands to save Their world from Slid, and the downlands gathered themselves and marched away, a great white line of gleaming cliffs, and halted before Slid. Then Slid advanced no more and lulled his legions, and while his waves were low he softly crooned a song such as once long ago had troubled the stars and brought down tears out of the twilight.

Sternly the white cliffs stood on guard to save the world of the gods, but the song that once had troubled the stars went moaning on awaking pent desires, till full at the feet of the gods the melody fell. Then the blue rivers that lay curled asleep opened their gleaming eyes, uncurled themselves and shook their rushes, and, making a stir among the hills, crept down to find the sea. And passing across the world they came at last to where the white cliffs stood, and, coming behind them, split them here and there and went through their broken ranks to Slid at last. And the gods were angry with Their traitorous streams.

Then Slid ceased from singing the song that lures the world, and gathered up his legions, and the rivers lifted up their heads with the waves, and all went marching on to assail the cliffs of the gods. And wherever the rivers had broken the ranks of the cliffs, Slid's armies went surging in and broke them up into islands and shattered the islands away. And the gods on Their hill-tops heard once more the voice of Slid exulting over Their cliffs.

Already more than half the world lay subject to Slid, and still his armies advanced; and the people of Slid, the fishes and the long eels, went in and out of arbours that once were dear to the gods. Then the gods feared for Their dominion, and to the innermost sacred recesses of the mountains, to the very heart of the hills, the gods trooped off together and there found Tintaggon, a mountain of black marble, staring far over the earth, and spake thus to him with the voices of the gods:

"O eldest born of our mountains, when first we devised the earth we made thee, and thereafter fashioned fields and hollows, valleys and other hills, to lie about thy feet. And now, Tintaggon, thine ancient lords, the gods, are facing a new thing which overthrows the old. Go therefore, thou, Tintaggon, and stand up against Slid, that the gods be still the gods and the earth still green."

And hearing the voices of his sires, the elder gods, Tintaggon strode down through the evening, leaving a wake of twilight broad behind him as he strode: and going across the green earth came down to Ambrady at the valley's edge, and there met the foremost of Slid's fierce armies conquering the world.

And against him Slid hurled the force of a whole bay, which lashed itself high over Tintaggon's knees and streamed around his flanks and then fell and was lost. Tintaggon still stood firm for the honour and dominion of his lords, the elder gods. Then Slid went to Tintaggon and said: "Let us now make a truce. Stand thou back from Ambrady and let me pass through thy ranks that mine armies may now pass up the valley which opens on the world, that the green earth that dreams around the feet of older gods shall know the new god Slid. Then shall mine armies strive with thee no more, and thou and I shall be the equal lords of the whole earth when all the world is singing the chaunt of Slid, and thy head alone shall be lifted above mine armies when rival hills are dead. And I will deck thee with all the robes of the sea, and all the plunder that I have taken in rare cities shall be piled before thy feet. Tintaggon, I have conquered all the stars, my song swells through all the space besides, I come victorious from Mahn and Khanagat on the furthest edge of the worlds, and thou and I are to be equal lords when the old gods are gone and the green earth knoweth Slid. Behold me gleaming azure and fair with a thousand smiles, and swayed by a thousand moods." And Tintaggon answered: "I am staunch and black and have one mood, and this—to defend my masters and their green earth."

Then Slid went backward growling and summoned together the waves of a whole sea and sent them singing full in Tintaggon's face. Then from Tintaggon's marble front the sea fell backwards crying on to a broken shore, and ripple by ripple straggled back to Slid saying: "Tintaggon stands."

Far out beyond the battered shore that lay at Tintaggon's feet Slid rested long and sent the nautilus to drift up and down before Tintaggon's eyes, and he and his armies sat singing idle songs of dreamy islands far away to the south, and of the still stars whence they had stolen forth, of twilight evenings and of long ago. Still Tintaggon stood with his feet planted fair upon the valley's edge defending the gods and Their green earth against the sea.

And all the while that Slid sang his songs and played with the nautilus that sailed up and down he gathered his oceans together. One morning as Slid sang of old outrageous wars and of most enchanting peace and of dreamy islands and the south wind and the sun, he suddenly launched five oceans out of the deep all to attack Tintaggon. And the five oceans sprang upon Tintaggon and passed above his head. One by one the grip of the oceans loosened, one by one they fell back into the deep and still Tintaggon stood, and on that morning the might of all five oceans lay dead at Tintaggon's feet. That which Slid had conquered he still held, and there is now no longer a great green valley in the south, but all that Tintaggon had guarded against Slid he gave back to the gods. Very calm the sea lies now about Tintaggon's feet, where he stands all black amid crumbled cliffs of white, with red rocks piled about his feet. And often the sea retreats far out along the shore, and often wave by wave comes marching in with the sound of the tramping of armies, that all may still remember the great fight that surged about Tintaggon once, when he guarded the gods and the green earth against Slid.

Sometimes in their dreams the war-scarred warriors of Slid still lift their heads and cry their battle cry; then do dark clouds gather about Tintaggon's swarthy brow and he stands out menacing, seen afar by ships, where once he conquered Slid. And the gods know well that while Tintaggon stands They and Their world are safe; and whether Slid shall one day smite Tintaggon is hidden among the secrets of the sea.

A LEGEND OF THE DAWN

When the worlds and All began the gods were stern and old and They saw the Beginning from under eyebrows hoar with years, all but Inzana, Their child, who played with the golden ball. Inzana was the child of all the gods. And the law before the Beginning and thereafter was that all should obey the gods, yet hither and thither went all Pegana's gods to obey the Dawnchild because she loved to be obeyed.

It was dark all over the world and even in Pegana, where dwell the gods, it was dark when the child Inzana, the Dawn, first found her golden ball. Then running down the stairway of the gods with tripping feet, chalcedony, onyx, chalcedony, onyx, step by step, she cast her golden ball across the sky. The golden ball went bounding up the sky, and the Dawnchild with her flaring hair stood laughing upon the stairway of the gods, and it was day. So gleaming fields below saw the first of all the days that the gods have destined. But towards evening certain mountains, afar and aloof, conspired together to stand between the world and the golden ball and to wrap their crags about it and to shut it from the world, and all the world was darkened with their plot. And the Dawnchild up in Pegana cried for her golden ball. Then all the gods came down the stairway right to Pegana's gate to see what ailed the Dawnchild and to ask her why she cried. Then Inzana said that her golden ball had been taken away and hidden by mountains black and ugly, far away from Pegana, all in a world of rocks under the rim of the sky, and she wanted her golden ball and could not love the dark.

Thereat Umborodom, whose hound was the thunder, took his hound in leash, and strode away across the sky after the golden ball until he came to the mountains afar and aloof. There did the thunder put his nose to the rocks and bay along the valleys, and fast at his heels followed Umborodom. And the nearer the hound, the thunder, came to the golden ball the louder did he bay, but haughty and silent stood the mountains whose plot had darkened the world. All in the dark among the crags in a mighty cavern, guarded by two twin peaks, at last they found the golden ball for which the Dawnchild wept. Then under the world went Umborodom with his thunder panting behind him, and came in the dark before the morning from underneath the world and gave the Dawnchild back her golden ball. And Inzana laughed and took it in her hands, and Umborodom went back into Pegana, and at its threshold the thunder went to sleep.

Again the Dawnchild tossed the golden ball far up into the blue across the sky, and the second morning shone upon the world, on lakes and oceans, and on drops of dew. But as the ball went bounding on its way, the prowling mists and the rain conspired together and took it and wrapped it in their tattered cloaks and carried it away. And through the rents in their garments gleamed the golden ball, but they held it fast and carried it right away and underneath the world. Then on an onyx step Inzana sat down and wept, who could no more be happy without her golden ball. And again the gods were sorry, and the South Wind came to tell her tales of most enchanted islands, to whom she listened not, nor yet to the tales of temples in lone lands that the East Wind told her, who had stood beside her when she flung her golden ball. But from far away the West Wind came with news of three grey travellers wrapt round with battered cloaks that carried away between them a golden ball.

Then up leapt the North Wind, he who guards the pole, and drew his sword of ice out of his scabbard of snow and sped away along the road that leads across the blue. And in the darkness underneath the world he met the three grey travellers and rushed upon them and drove them far before him, smiting them with his sword till their grey cloaks streamed with blood. And out of the midst of them, as they fled with flapping cloaks all red and grey and tattered, he leapt up with the golden ball and gave it to the Dawnchild.

Again Inzana tossed the ball into the sky, making the third day, and up and up it went and fell towards the fields, and as Inzana stooped to pick it up she suddenly heard the singing of all the birds that were. All the birds in the world were singing all together and also all the streams, and Inzana sat and listened and thought of no golden ball, nor ever of chalcedony and onyx, nor of all her fathers the gods, but only of all the birds. Then in the woods and meadows where they had all suddenly sung, they suddenly ceased. And Inzana, looking up, found that her ball was lost, and all alone in the stillness one owl laughed. When the gods heard Inzana crying for her ball They clustered together on the threshold and peered into the dark, but saw no golden ball. And leaning forward They cried out to the bat as he passed up and down: "Bat that seest all things, where is the golden ball?"

And though the bat answered none heard. And none of the winds had seen it nor any of the birds, and there were only the eyes of the gods in the darkness peering for the golden ball. Then said the gods: "Thou hast lost thy golden ball," and They made her a moon of silver to roll about the sky. And the child cried and threw it upon the stairway and chipped and broke its edges and asked for the golden ball. And Limpang Tung, the Lord of Music, who was least of all the gods, because the child cried still for her golden ball, stole out of Pegana and crept across the sky, and found the birds of all the world sitting in trees and ivy, and whispering in the dark. He asked them one by one for news of the golden ball. Some had last seen it on a neighbouring hill and others in trees, though none knew where it was. A heron had seen it lying in a pond, but a wild duck in some reeds had seen it last as she came home across the hills, and then it was rolling very far away.

At last the cock cried out that he had seen it lying beneath the world. There Limpang Tung sought it and the cock called to him through the darkness as he went, until at last he found the golden ball. Then Limpang Tung went up into Pegāna and gave it to the Dawnchild, who played with the moon no more. And the cock and all his tribe cried out: "We found it. We found the golden ball."

Again Inzana tossed the ball afar, laughing with joy to see it, her hands stretched upwards, her golden hair afloat, and carefully she watched it as it fell. But alas! it fell with a splash into the great sea and gleamed and shimmered as it fell till the waters became dark above it and could be seen no more. And men on the world said: "How the dew has fallen, and how the mists set in with breezes from the streams."

But the dew was the tears of the Dawnchild, and the mists were her sighs when she said: "There will no more come a time when I play with my ball again, for now it is lost for ever."

And the gods tried to comfort Inzana as she played with her silver moon, but she would not hear Them, and went in tears to Slid, where he played with gleaming sails, and in his mighty treasury turned over gems and pearls and lorded it over the sea. And she said: "O Slid, whose soul is in the sea, bring back my golden ball."

And Slid stood up, swarthy, and clad in seaweed, and mightily dived from the last chalcedony step out of Pegāna's threshold straight into ocean. There on the sand, among the battered navies of the nautilus and broken weapons of the swordfish, hidden by dark water, he found the golden ball. And coming up in the night, all green and dripping, he carried it gleaming to the stairway of the gods and brought it back to Inzana from the sea; and out of the hands of Slid she took it and tossed it far and wide over his sails and sea, and far away it shone on lands that knew not Slid, till it came to its zenith and dropped towards the world.

But ere it fell the Eclipse dashed out from his hiding, and rushed at the golden ball and seized it in his jaws. When Inzana saw the Eclipse bearing her plaything away she cried aloud to the thunder, who burst from Pegāna and fell howling upon the throat of the Eclipse, who dropped the golden ball and let it fall towards earth. But the black mountains disguised themselves with snow, and as the golden ball fell down towards them they turned their peaks to ruby crimson and their lakes to sapphires gleaming amongst silver, and Inzana saw a jewelled casket into which her plaything fell. But when she stooped to pick it up again she found no jewelled casket with rubies, silver or sapphires, but only wicked mountains disguised in snow that had trapped her golden ball. And then she cried because there was none to find it, for the thunder was far away chasing the Eclipse, and all the gods lamented when They saw her sorrow. And Limpang Tung, who was least of all the gods, was yet the saddest at the Dawnchild's grief, and when the gods said: "Play with your silver moon," he stepped lightly from the rest, and coming down the stairway of the gods, playing an instrument of music, went out towards the world to find the golden ball because Inzana wept.

And into the world he went till he came to the nether cliffs that stand by the inner mountains in the soul and heart of the earth where the Earthquake dwelleth alone, asleep but astir as he sleeps, breathing and moving his legs, and grunting aloud in the dark. Then in the ear of the Earthquake Limpang Tung said a word that only the gods may say, and the Earthquake started to his feet and flung the cave away, the cave wherein he slept between the cliffs, and shook himself and went galloping abroad and overturned the mountains that hid the golden ball, and bit the earth beneath them and hurled their crags about and covered himself with rocks and fallen hills, and went back ravening and growling into the soul of the earth, and there lay down and slept again for a hundred years. And the golden ball rolled free, passing under the shattered earth, and so rolled back to Pegana; and Limpang Tung came home to the onyx step and took the Dawnchild by the hand and told not what he had done but said it was the Earthquake, and went away to sit at the feet of the gods. But Inzana went and patted the Earthquake on the head, for she said it was dark and lonely in the soul of the earth. Thereafter, returning step by step, chalcedony, onyx, chalcedony, onyx, up the stairway of the gods, she cast again her golden ball from the Threshold afar into the blue to gladden the world and the sky, and laughed to see it go.

And far away Trogool upon the utter Rim turned a page that was numbered six in a cipher that none might read. And as the golden ball went through the sky to gleam on lands and cities, there came the Fog towards it, stooping as he walked with his dark brown cloak about him, and behind him slunk the Night. And as the golden ball rolled past the Fog suddenly Night snarled and sprang upon it and carried it away. Hastily Inzana gathered the gods and said: "The Night hath seized my golden ball and no god alone can find it now, for none can say how far the Night may roam, who prowls all round us and out beyond the worlds."

At the entreaty of Their Dawnchild all the gods made Themselves stars for torches, and far away through all the sky followed the tracks of Night as far as he prowled abroad. And at one time Slid, with the Pleiades in his hand, came nigh to the golden ball, and at another Yoharneth-Lahai, holding Orion for a torch, but lastly Limpang Tung, bearing the morning star, found the golden ball far away under the world near to the lair of Night.

And all the gods together seized the ball, and Night turning smote out the torches of the gods and thereafter slunk away; and all the gods in triumph marched up the gleaming stairway of the gods, all praising little Limpang Tung, who through the chase had followed Night so close in search of the golden ball. Then far below on the world a human child cried out to the Dawnchild for the golden ball, and Inzana ceased from her play that illumined world and sky, and cast the ball from the Threshold of the gods to the little human child that played in the fields below, and would one day die. And the child played all day long with the golden ball down in the little fields where the humans lived, and went to bed at evening and put it beneath his pillow, and went to sleep, and no one worked in all the world because the child was playing. And the light of the golden ball streamed up from under the pillow and out through the half shut door and shone in the western sky, and Yoharneth-Lahai in the night time tip-toed into the room, and took the ball gently (for he was a god) away from under the pillow and brought it back to the Dawnchild to gleam on an onyx step.

But some day Night shall seize the golden ball and carry it right away and drag it down to his lair, and Slid shall dive from the Threshold into the sea to see if it be there, and coming up when the fishermen draw their nets shall find it not, nor yet discover it among the sails. Limpang Tung shall seek among the birds and shall not find it when the cock is mute, and up the valleys shall go Umborodom to seek among the crags. And the hound, the thunder, shall chase the Eclipse and all the gods go seeking with Their stars, but never find the ball. And men, no longer having light of the golden ball, shall pray to the gods no more, who, having no worship, shall be no more the gods.

These things be hidden even from the gods.

THE VENGEANCE OF MEN

Ere the Beginning the gods divided earth into waste and pasture. Pleasant pastures They made to be green over the face of earth, orchards They made in valleys and heather upon hills, but Harza They doomed, predestined and foreordained to be a waste for ever.

When the world prayed at evening to the gods and the gods answered-prayers They forgot the prayers of all the Tribes of Arim. Therefore the men of Arim were assailed with wars and driven from land to land and yet would not be crushed. And the men of Arim made them gods for themselves, appointing men as gods until the gods of Pegana should remember them again. And their leaders, Yoth and Haneth, played the part of gods and led their people on though every tribe assailed them. At last they came to Harza, where no tribes were, and at last had rest from war, and Yoth and Haneth said: "The work is done, and surely now Pegana's gods will remember." And they built a city in Harza and tilled the soil, and the green came over the waste as the wind comes over the sea, and there were fruit and cattle in Harza and the sounds of a million sheep. There they rested from their flight from all the tribes, and builded fables out of all their sorrows till all men smiled in Harza and children laughed.

Then said the gods, "Earth is no place for laughter." Thereat They strode to Pegana's outer gate, to where the Pestilence lay curled asleep, and waking him up They pointed toward Harza, and the Pestilence leapt forward howling across the sky.

That night he came to the fields near Harza, and stalking through the grass sat down and glared at the lights, and licked his paws and glared at the lights again.

But the next night, unseen, through laughing crowds, the Pestilence crept into the city, and stealing into the houses one by one, peered into the people's eyes, looking even through their eyelids, so that when morning came men stared before them crying out that they saw the Pestilence whom others saw not, and thereafter died, because the green eyes of the Pestilence had looked into their souls. Chill and damp was he, yet there came heat from his eyes that parched the souls of men. Then came the physicians and the men learned in magic, and made the sign of the physicians and the sign of the men of magic and cast blue water upon herbs and chanted spells; but still the Pestilence crept from house to house and still he looked into the souls of men. And the lives of the people streamed away from Harza, and whither they went is set in many books. But the Pestilence fed on the light that shines in the eyes of men, which never appeased his hunger; chiller and damper he grew, and the heat from his eyes increased when night by night he galloped through the city, going by stealth no more.

Then did men pray in Harza to the gods, saying:

"High gods! Show clemency to Harza."

And the gods listened to their prayers, but as They listened They pointed with their fingers and cheered the Pestilence on. And the Pestilence grew bolder at his masters' voices and thrust his face close up before the eyes of men.

He could be seen by none saving those he smote. At first he slept by day, lying in misty hollows, but as his hunger increased he sprang up even in sunlight and clung to the chests of men and looked down through their eyes into their souls that shrivelled, until almost he could be dimly seen even by those he smote not.

Adro, the physician, sat in his chamber with one light burning, making a mixing in a bowl that should drive the Pestilence away, when through his door there blew a draught that set the light a-flickering.

Then because the draught was cold the physician shivered and went and closed the door, but as he turned again he saw the Pestilence lapping at his mixing, who sprang and set one paw upon Adro's shoulder and another upon his cloak, while with two he clung to his waist, and looked him in the eyes.

Two men were walking in the street; one said to the other: "Upon the morrow I will sup with thee."

And the Pestilence grinned a grin that none beheld, baring his dripping teeth, and crept away to see whether upon the morrow those men should sup together.

A traveller coming in said: "This is Harza. Here will I rest."

But his life went further than Harza upon that day's journey.

All feared the Pestilence, and those that he smote beheld him, but none saw the great shapes of the gods by starlight as They urged Their Pestilence on.

Then all men fled from Harza, and the Pestilence chased dogs and rats and sprang upward at the bats as they sailed above him, who died and lay in the streets. But soon he returned and pursued the men of Harza where they fled, and sat by rivers where they came to drink, away below the city. Then back to Harza went the people of Harza pursued by the Pestilence still, and gathered in the Temple of All the gods save One, and said to the High Prophet: "What may now be done?" who answered:

"All the gods have mocked at prayer. This sin must now be punished by the vengeance of men."

And the people stood in awe.

The High Prophet went up to the Tower beneath the sky whereupon beat the eyes of all the gods by starlight. There in the sight of the gods he spake in the ear of the gods, saying: "High gods! Ye have made mock of men. Know therefore that it is writ in ancient lore and found by prophecy that there is an *End* that waiteth for the gods, who shall go down from Pegana in galleons of gold all down the Silent River and into the Silent Sea, and there Their galleons shall go up in mist and They shall be gods no more. And men shall gain harbour from the mocking of the gods at last in the warm moist earth, but to the gods shall no ceasing ever come from being the Things that were the gods. When Time and worlds and death are gone away nought shall then remain but worn regrets and Things that were once gods.

"In the sight of the gods.

"In the ear of the gods."

Then the gods shouted all together and pointed with Their hands at the High Prophet's throat, and the Pestilence sprang.

Long since the High Prophet is dead and his words are forgotten by men, but the gods know not yet whether it be true that *The End* is waiting for the gods, and him who might have told Them They have slain. And the gods of Pegana are fearing the fear that hath fallen upon the gods because of the vengeance of men, for They know not when *The End* shall be, or whether it shall come.

WHEN THE GODS SLEPT

All the gods were sitting in Pegana, and Their slave, Time, lay idle at Pegana's gate with nothing to destroy, when They thought of worlds, worlds large and round and gleaming, and little silver moons. Then (who knoweth when?), as the gods raised Their hands making the sign of the gods, the thoughts of the gods became worlds and silver moons. And the worlds swam by Pegana's gate to take their places in the sky, to ride at anchor for ever, each where the gods had bidden. And because they were round and big and gleamed all over the sky, the gods laughed and shouted and all clapped Their hands. Then upon earth the gods played out the game of the gods, the game of life and death, and on the other worlds They did a secret thing, playing a game that is hidden.

At last They mocked no more at life and laughed at death no more, and cried aloud in Pegana: "Will no new thing be? Must those four march for ever round the world till our eyes are wearied with the treading of the feet of the Seasons that will not cease, while Night and Day and Life and Death drearily rise and fall?"

And as a child stares at the bare walls of a narrow hut, so the gods looked all listlessly upon the worlds, saying:

"Will no new thing be?"

And in Their weariness the gods said: "Ah! to be young again. Ah! to be fresh once more from the brain of *Mana-Yood-Sushai*."

And They turned away Their eyes in weariness from all the gleaming worlds and laid Them down upon Pegana's floor, for They said:

"It may be that the worlds shall pass and we would fain forget them."

Then the gods slept. Then did the comet break loose from his moorings and the eclipse roamed about the sky, and down on the earth did Death's three children—Famine, Pestilence, and Drought—come out to feed. The eyes of the Famine were green, and the eyes of the Drought were red, but the Pestilence was blind and smote about all round him with his claws among the cities.

But as the gods slept, there came from beyond the Rim, out of the dark and unknown, three Yozis, spirits of ill, that sailed up the river of Silence in galleons with silver sails. Far away they had seen Yum and Gothum, the stars that stand sentinel over Pegana's gate, blinking and falling asleep, and as they neared Pegana they found a hush wherein the gods slept heavily. Ya, Ha, and Snyrg were these three Yozis, the lords of evil, madness, and of spite. When they crept from their galleons and stole over Pegana's silent threshold it boded ill for the gods. There in Pegana lay the gods asleep, and in a corner lay the Power of the gods alone upon the floor, a thing wrought of black rock and four words graven upon it, whereof I might not give thee any clue, if even I should find it—four words of which none knoweth. Some say they tell of the opening of a flower towards dawn, and others say they concern earthquakes among hills, and others that they tell of the death of fishes, and others that the words be these: Power, Knowledge, Forgetting, and another word that not the gods themselves may ever guess. These words the Yozis read, and sped away in dread lest the gods should wake, and going aboard their galleons, bade the rowers haste. Thus the Yozis became gods, having the power of gods, and they sailed away to the earth, and came to a mountainous island in the sea. There they sat upon the rocks, sitting as the gods sit, with their right hands uplifted, and having the power of gods, only none came to worship. Thither came no ships nigh them, nor ever at evening came the prayers of men, nor smell of incense, nor screams from the sacrifice. Then said the Yozis:

"Of what avails it that we be gods if no one worship us nor give us sacrifice?"

And Ya, Ha, and Snyrg set sail in their silver galleons, and went looming down the sea to come to the shores of men. And first they came to an island where were fisher folk; and the folk of the island, running down to the shore cried out to them:

"Who be ye?"

And the Yozis answered:

"We be three gods, and we would have your worship."

But the fisher folk answered:

"Here we worship Rahm, the Thunder, and have no worship nor sacrifice for other gods."

Then the Yozis snarled with anger and sailed away, and sailed till they came to another shore, sandy and low and forsaken. And at last they found an old man upon the shore, and they cried out to him:

"Old man upon the shore! We be three gods that it were well to worship, gods of great power and apt in the granting of prayer."

The old man answered:

"We worship Pegāna's gods, who have a fondness for our incense and the sound of our sacrifice when it squeals upon the altar."

Then answered Snyrg:

"Asleep are Pegāna's gods, nor will They wake for the humming of thy prayers which lie in the dust upon Pegāna's floor, and over Them Sniracte, the spider of the worlds, hath woven a web of mist. And the squealing of the sacrifice maketh no music in ears that are closed in sleep."

The old man answered, standing upon the shore:

"Though all the gods of old shall answer our prayers no longer, yet still to the gods of old shall all men pray here in Syrinais."

But the Yozis turned their ships about and angrily sailed away, all cursing Syrinais and Syrinais's gods, but most especially the old man that stood upon the shore.

Still the three Yozis lusted for the worship of men, and came, on the third night of their sailing, to a city's lights; and nearing the shore they found it a city of song wherein all folks rejoiced. Then sat each Yozi on his galleon's prow, and leered with his eyes upon the city, so that the music stopped and the dancing ceased, and all looked out to sea at the strange shapes of the Yozis beneath their silver sails. Then Snyrg demanded their worship, promising increase of joys, and swearing by the light of his eyes that he would send little flames to leap over the grass, to pursue the enemies of that city and to chase them about the world.

But the people answered that in that city men worshipped Agrodaun, the mountain standing alone, and might not worship other gods even though they came in galleons with silver sails, sailing from over the sea. But Snyrg answered:

"Certainly Agrodaun is only a mountain, and in no manner a god."

But the priests of Agrodaun sang answer from the shore:

"If the sacrifice of men make not Agrodaun a god, nor blood still young on his rocks, nor the little fluttering prayers of ten thousand hearts, nor two thousands years of worship and all the hopes of the people and the whole strength of our race, then are there no gods and ye be common sailors, sailing from over the sea."

Then said the Yozis:

"Hath Agrodaun answered prayer?" And the people heard the words that the Yozis said.

Then went the priests of Agrodaun away from the shore and up the steep streets of the city, the people following, and over the moor beyond it to the foot of Agrodaun, and then said:

"Agrodaun, if thou art not our god, go back and herd with yonder common hills, and put a cap of snow upon thy head and crouch far off as they do beneath the sky; but if we have given thee divinity in two thousand years, if our hopes are all about thee like a cloak, then stand and look upon thy worshippers from over our city for ever." And the smoke that ascended from his feet stood still and there fell a hush over great Agrodaun; and the priests went back to the sea and said to the three Yozis:

"New gods shall have our worship when Agrodaun grows weary of being our god, or when in some night-time he shall stride away, leaving us nought to gaze at that is higher than our city."

And the Yozis sailed away and cursed towards Agrodaun, but could not hurt him, for he was but a mountain.

And the Yozis sailed along the coast till they came to a river running to the sea, and they sailed up the river till they came to a people at work, who furrowed the soil and sowed, and strove against the forest. Then the Yozis called to the people as they worked in the fields:

"Give us your worship and ye shall have many joys."

But the people answered:

"We may not worship you."

Then answered Snyrg:

"Ye also, have ye a god?"

And the people answered:

"We worship the years to come, and we set the world in order for their coming, as one layeth raiment on the road before the advent of a King. And when those years shall come, they shall accept the worship of a race they knew not, and their people shall make their sacrifice to the years that follow them, who, in their turn, shall minister to the End."

Then answered Snyrg:

"Gods that shall recompense you not. Rather give us your prayers and have our pleasures, the pleasures that we shall give you, and when your gods shall come, let them be wroth—they cannot punish you."

But the people continued to sacrifice their labour to their gods, the years to come, making the world a place for gods to dwell in, and the Yozis cursed those gods and sailed away. And Ya, the Lord of malice, swore that when those years should come, they should see whether it were well for them to have snatched away the worship from three Yozis.

And still the Yozis sailed, for they said:

"It were better to be birds and have no air to fly in, than to be gods having neither prayers nor worship."

But where sky met with ocean, the Yozis saw land again, and thither sailed; and there the Yozis saw men in strange old garments performing ancient rites in a land of many temples. And the Yozis called to the men as they performed their ancient rites and said:

"We be three gods well versed in the needs of men, to worship whom were to obtain instant joy."

But the men said:

"We have already gods."

And Snyrg replied:

"Ye, too?"

The men answered:

"For we worship the things that have been and all the years that were. Divinely have they helped us, therefore we give them worship that is their due."

And the Yozis answered the people:

"We be gods of the present and return good things for worship."

But the people answered, saying from the shore:

"Our gods have given us already the good things, and we return Them the worship that is Their due."

And the Yozis set their faces to landward, and cursed all things that had been and all the years that were, and sailed in their galleons away.

A rocky shore in an inhuman land stood up against the sea. Thither the Yozis came and found no man, but out of the dark from inland towards evening came a herd of great baboons and chattered greatly when they saw the ships.

Then spake Snyrg to them:

"Have ye, too, a god?"

And the baboons spat.

Then said the Yozis:

"We be seductive gods, having a particular remembrance for little prayers."

But the baboons leered fiercely at the Yozis and would have none of them for gods.

One said that prayers hindered the eating of nuts. But Snyrg leaned forward and whispered, and the baboons went down upon their knees and clasped their hands as men clasp, and chattered prayer and said to one another that these were the gods of old, and gave the Yozis their worship—for Snyrg had whispered in their ears that, if they would worship the Yozis, he would make them men. And the baboons arose from worshipping, smoother about the face and a little shorter in the arms, and went away and hid their bodies in clothing, and afterwards galloped away from the rocky shore and went and herded with men. And men could not discern what they were, for their bodies were bodies of men, though their souls were still the souls of beasts and their worship went to the Yozis, spirits of ill.

And the lords of malice, hatred and madness sailed back to their island in the sea and sat upon the shore as gods sit, with right hand uplifted; and at evening foul prayers from the baboons gathered about them and infested the rocks.

But in Pegana the gods awoke with a start.

THE KING THAT WAS NOT

The land of Runazar hath no King nor ever had one; and this is the law of the land of Runazar that, seeing that it hath never had a King, it shall not have one for ever. Therefore in Runazar the priests hold sway, who tell people that never in Runazar hath there been a King.

Althazar, King of Runazar, and lord of all lands near by, commanded for the closer knowledge of the gods that Their images should be carven in Runazar, and in all lands near by. And when Althazar's command, wafted abroad by trumpets, came tinkling in the ear of all the gods, right glad were They at the sound of it. Therefore men quarried marble from the earth, and sculptors busied themselves in Runazar to obey the edict of the King. But the gods stood by starlight on the hills where the sculptors might see Them, and draped the clouds about Them, and put upon Them Their divinest air, that sculptors might do justice to Pegana's gods. Then the gods strode back into Pegana and the sculptors hammered and wrought, and there came a day when the Master of Sculptors took audience of the King, saying:

"Althazar, King of Runazar, High Lord moreover of all the lands near by, to whom be the gods benignant, humbly have we completed the images of all such gods as were in thine edict named."

Then the King commanded a great space to be cleared among the houses in his city, and there the images of all the gods were borne and set before the King, and there were assembled the Master of Sculptors and all his men; and before each stood a soldier bearing a pile of gold upon a jewelled tray, and behind each stood a soldier with a drawn sword pointing against their necks, and the King looked upon the images. And lo! they stood as gods with the clouds all draped about them, making the sign of the gods, but their bodies were those of men, and lo! their faces were very like the King's, and their beards were as the King's beard. And the King said:

"These be indeed Pegana's gods."

And the soldiers that stood before the sculptors were caused to present to them the piles of gold, and the soldiers that stood behind the sculptors were caused to sheath their swords. And the people shouted:

"These be indeed Pegana's gods, whose faces we are permitted to see by the will of Althazar the King, to whom be the gods benignant." And heralds were sent abroad through the cities of Runazar and of all the lands near by, proclaiming of the images:

"These be Pegana's gods."

But up in Pegana the gods howled with wrath and Mung leant forward to make the sign of Mung against Althazar the King. But the gods laid Their hands upon his shoulder saying:

"Slay him not, for it is not enough that Althazar shall die, who hath made the faces of the gods to be like the faces of men, but he must not even have ever been."

Then said the gods:

"Spake we of Althazar, a King?"

And the gods said:

"Nay, we spake not." And the gods said:

"Dreamed we of one Althazar?" And the gods said:

"Nay, we dreamed not."

But in the royal palace of Runazar, Althazar, passing suddenly out of the remembrance of the gods, became no longer a thing that was or had ever been.

And by the throne of Althazar lay a robe, and near it lay a crown, and the priests of the gods entered his palace and made it a temple of the gods. And the people coming to worship said:

"Whose was this robe and to what purpose is this crown?"

And the priests answered:

"The gods have cast away the fragment of a garment and lo! from the fingers of the gods hath slipped one little ring."

And the people said to the priests:

"Seeing that Runazar hath never had a King, therefore be ye our rulers, and make ye our laws in the sight of Pegana's gods."

THE CAVE OF KAI

The pomp of crowning was ended, the rejoicings had died away, and Khanazar, the new King, sat in the seat of the Kings of Averon to do his work upon the destinies of men. His uncle, Khanazar the Lone, had died, and he had come from a far castle to the south, with a great procession, to Ilaun, the citadel of Averon; and there they had crowned him King of Averon and of the mountains, and Lord, if there be aught beyond those mountains, of all such lands as are. But now the pomp of the crowning was gone away and Khanazar sat afar off from his home, a very mighty King.

Then the King grew weary of the destinies of Averon and weary of the making of commands. So Khanazar sent heralds through all cities saying:

"Hear! The will of the King! Hear! The will of the King of Averon and of the mountains and Lord, if there be aught beyond those mountains, of all such lands as are. Let there come together to Ilaun all such as have an art in secret matters. Hear!"

And there gathered together to Ilaun the wise men of all the degrees of magic, even to the seventh, who had made spells before Khanazar the Lone; and they came before the new King in his palace placing their hands upon his feet. Then said the King to the magicians:

"I have a need."

And they answered:

"The earth touches the feet of the King in token of submission."

But the King answered:

"My need is not of the earth; but I would find certain of the hours that have been, and sundry days that were."

And all the wise folks were silent, till there spake out mournfully the wisest of them all, who made spells in the seventh degree, saying:

"The days that were, and the hours, have winged their way to Mount Agdora's summit, and there, dipping, have passed away from sight, not ever to return, for haply they have not heard the King's command."

Of these wise folks are many things chronicled. Moreover, it is set in writing of the scribes how they had audience of King Khanazar and of the words they spake, but of their further deeds there is no legend. But it is told how the King sent men to run and pass through all the cities till they should find one that was wiser even than the magicians that had made spells before Khanazar the Lone. Far up the mountains that limit Averon they found Syrahn, the prophet, among the goats, who was of none of the degrees of magic, and who had cast no spells before the former King. Him they brought to Khanazar, and the King said unto him:

"I have a need."

And Syrahn answered:

"Thou art a man."

And the King said:

"Where lie the days that were and certain hours?"

And Syrahn answered:

"These things lie in a cave afar from here, and over the cave stands sentinel one Kai, and this cave Kai hath guarded from the gods and men since ever the Beginning was made. It may be that he shall let Khanazar pass by."

Then the King gathered elephants and camels that carried burdens of gold, and trusty servants that carried precious gems, and gathered an army to go before him and an army to follow behind, and sent out horsemen to warn the dwellers of the plains that the King of Averon was afoot.

And he bade Syrahn to lead to that place where the days of old lie hid and all forgotten hours.

Across the plain and up Mount Agdora, and dipping beyond its summit went Khanazar the King, and his two armies who followed Syrahn. Eight times the purple tent with golden border had been pitched for the King of Averon, and eight times it had been struck ere the King and the King's armies came to a dark cave in a valley dark, where Kai stood guard over the days that were. And the face of Kai was as a warrior that vanquisheth cities and burdeneth himself not with captives, and his form was as the forms of gods, but his eyes were the eyes of beasts; before whom came the King of Averon with elephants and camels bearing burdens of gold, and trusty servants carrying precious gems.

Then said the King:

"Yonder behold my gifts. Give back to me my yesterday with its waving banners, my yesterday with its music and blue sky and all its cheering crowds that made me King, the yesterday that sailed with gleaming wings over my Averon."

And Kai answered, pointing to his cave:

"Thither, dishonoured and forgot, thy yesterday slunk away. And who amid the dusty heap of the forgotten days shall grovel to find thy yesterday?"

Then answered the King of Averon and of the mountains and Lord, if there be aught beyond them, of all such lands as are:

"I will go down on my knees in yon dark cave and search with my hands amid the dust, if so I may find my yesterday again and certain hours that are gone."

And the King pointed to his piles of gold that stood where elephants were met together, and beyond them to the scornful camels. And Kai answered:

"The gods have offered me the gleaming worlds and all as far as the Rim, and whatever lies beyond it as far as the gods may see—and thou comest to me with elephants and camels."

Then said the King:

"Across the orchards of my home there hath passed one hour whereof thou knowest well, and I pray to thee, who wilt take no gifts borne upon elephants or camels, to give me of thy mercy one second back, one grain of dust that clings to that hour in the heap that lies within thy cave."

And, at the word mercy, Kai laughed. And the King turned his armies to the east. Therefore the armies returned to Averon and the heralds before them cried:

"Here cometh Khanazar, King of Averon and of the mountains and Lord, if there be aught beyond those mountains, of all such lands as are."

And the King said to them:

"Say rather that here comes one greatly wearied who, having accomplished nought, returneth from a quest forlorn."

So the King came again to Averon.

But it is told how there came into Ilaun one evening as the sun was setting a harper with a golden harp desiring audience of the King.

And it is told how men led him to Khanazar, who sat frowning alone upon his throne, to whom said the harper:

"I have a golden harp; and to its strings have clung like dust some seconds out of the forgotten hours and little happenings of the days that were."

And Khanazar looked up and the harper touched the strings, and the old forgotten things were stirring again, and there arose a sound of songs that had passed away and long since voices. Then when the harper saw that Khanazar looked not angrily upon him his fingers tramped over the chords as the gods tramp down the sky, and out of the golden harp arose a haze of memories; and the King leaning forward and staring before him saw in the haze no more his palace walls, but saw a valley with a stream that wandered through it, and woods upon either hill, and an old castle standing lonely to the south. And the harper, seeing a strange look upon the face of Khanazar, said:

"Is the King pleased who lords it over Averon and the mountains, and, if there be aught beyond them, over all such lands as are?"

And the King said:—

"Seeing that I am a child again in a valley to the south, how may I say what may be the will of the great King?"

When the stars shone high over Ilaun and still the King sat staring straight before him, all the courtiers drew away from the great palace, save one that stayed and kept one taper burning, and with them went the harper.

And when the dawn came up through silent archways into the marble palace, making the taper pale, the King still stared before him, and still he sat there when the stars shone again clearly and high above Ilaun.

But on the second morning the King arose and sent for the harper and said to him:—

"I am King again, and thou that hast a skill to stay the hours and mayest may bring again to men their forgotten days, thou shalt stand sentinel over my great to-morrow; and when I go forth to conquer Ziman-ho and make my armies mighty thou shalt stand between that morrow and the cave of Kai, and haply some deed of mine and the battling of my armies shall cling to thy golden harp and not go down dishonoured into the cave. For my to-morrow, who with such resounding stride goes trampling through my dreams, is far too kingly to herd with forgotten days in the dust of things that were. But on some future day, when Kings are dead and all their deeds forgotten, some harper of that time shall come and from those golden strings awake those deeds that echo in my dreams, till my to-morrow shall stride forth among the lesser days and tell the years that Khanazar was a King."

And answered the harper:

"I will stand sentinel over thy great to-morrow, and when thou goest forth to conquer Ziman-ho and make thine armies mighty I will stand between thy morrow and the cave of Kai, till thy deeds and the battling of thine armies shall cling to my golden harp and not go down dishonoured into the cave. So that when Kings are dead and all their deeds forgotten the harpers of the future time shall awake from these golden chords those deeds of thine. This will I do."

Men of these days, that be skilled upon the harp, tell still of Khanazar, how that he was King of Averon and of the mountains, and claimed lordship of certain lands beyond, and how he went with armies against Ziman-ho and fought great battles, and in the last gained victory and was slain. But Kai, as he waited with his claws to gather in the last days of Khanazar that they might loom enormous in his cave, still found them not, and only gathered in some meaner deeds and the days and hours of lesser men, and was vexed by the shadow of a harper that stood between him and the world.

THE SORROW OF SEARCH

It is told also of King Khanazar how he bowed very low unto the gods of Old. None bowed so low unto the gods of Old as did King Khanazar.

One day the King returning from the worship of the gods of Old and from bowing before them in the temple of the gods commanded their prophets to appear before him, saying:

"I would know somewhat concerning the gods."

Then came the prophets before King Khanazar, burdened with many books, to whom the King said:

"It is not in books."

Thereat the prophets departed, bearing away with them a thousand methods well devised in books whereby men may gain wisdom of the gods. One alone remained, a master prophet, who had forgotten books, to whom the King said:

"The gods of Old are mighty."

And answered the master prophet:

"Very mighty are the gods of Old."

Then said the King:

"There are no gods but the gods of Old."

And answered the prophet:

"There are none other."

And they two being alone within the palace the King said:

"Tell me aught concerning gods or men if aught of the truth be known."

Then said the master prophet:

"Far and white and straight lieth the road to Knowing, and down it in the heat and dust go all wise people of the earth, but in the fields before they come to it the very wise lie down or pluck the flowers. By the side of the road to Knowing—O King, it is hard and hot—stand many temples, and in the doorway of every temple stand many priests, and they cry to the travellers that weary of the road, crying to them:

"This is the End."

And in the temples are the sounds of music, and from each roof arises the savour of pleasant burning; and all that look at a cool temple, whichever temple they look at, or hear the hidden music, turn in to see whether it be indeed the End. And such as find that their temple is not indeed the End set forth again upon the dusty road, stopping at each temple as they pass for fear they miss the End, or striving onwards on the road, and see nothing in the dust, till they can walk no longer and are taken worn and weary of their journey into some other temple by a kindly priest who shall tell them that this also is the End. Neither on that road may a man gain any guiding from his fellows, for only one thing that they say is surely true, when they say:

"Friend, we can see nothing for the dust."

And of the dust that hides the way much has been there since ever that road began, and some is stirred up by the feet of all that travel upon it, and more arises from the temple doors.

And, O King, it were better for thee, travelling upon that road, to rest when thou hearest one calling: "This is the End," with the sounds of music behind him. And if in the dust and darkness thou pass by Lo and Mush and the pleasant temple of Kynash, or Sheenath with his opal smile, or Sho with his eyes of agate, yet Shilo and Mynarthitep, Gazo and Amurund and Slig are still before thee and the priests of their temples will not forget to call thee.

And, O King, it is told that only one discerned the end and passed by three thousand temples, and the priests of the last were like the priests of the first, and all said that their temple was at the end of the road, and the dark of the dust lay over them all, and all were very pleasant and only the road was weary. And in some were many gods, and in a few only one, and in some the shrine was empty, and all had many priests, and in all the travellers were happy as they rested. And into some his fellow travellers tried to force him, and when he said:

"I will travel further," many said:

"This man lies, for the road ends here."

And he that travelled to the End hath told that when the thunder was heard upon the road there arose the sound of the voices of all the priests as far as he could hear, crying:

"Hearken to Shilo"—"Hear Mush"—"Lo! Kynash"—"The voice of Sho"—"Mynarthitep is angry"—"Hear the word of Slig!"

And far away along the road one cried to the traveller that Sheenath stirred in his sleep.

O King this is very doleful. It is told that that traveller came at last to the utter End and there was a mighty gulf, and in the darkness at the bottom of the gulf one small god crept, no bigger than a hare, whose voice came crying in the cold:

"I know not."

And beyond the gulf was nought, only the small god crying.

And he that travelled to the End fled backwards for a great distance till he came to temples again, and entering one where a priest cried:

"This is the End," lay down and rested on a couch. There Yush sat silent, carved with an emerald tongue and two great eyes of sapphire, and there many rested and were happy. And an old priest, coming from comforting a child, came over to that traveller who had seen the End and said to him:

"This is Yush and this is the End of wisdom."

And the traveller answered:

"Yush is very peaceful and this indeed the End."

"O King, wouldst thou hear more?"

And the King said:

"I would hear all."

And the master prophet answered:

"There was also another prophet and his name was Shaun, who had such reverence for the gods of Old that he became able to discern their forms by starlight as they strode, unseen by others, among men. Each night did Shaun discern the forms of the gods and every day he taught concerning them, till men in Averon knew how the gods appeared all grey against the mountains, and how Rhoog was higher than Mount Scagadon, and how Skun was smaller, and how Asgool leaned forward as he strode, and how Trodath peered about him with small eyes. But one night as Shaun watched the gods of Old by starlight, he faintly discerned some other gods that sat far up the slopes of the mountains in the stillness behind the gods of Old. And the next day he hurled his robe away that he wore as Averon's prophet and said to his people:

"There be gods greater than the gods of Old, three gods seen faintly on the hills by starlight looking on Averon."

And Shaun set out and travelled many days and many people followed him. And every night he saw more clearly the shapes of the three new gods who sat silent when the gods of Old were striding among men. On the higher slopes of the mountain Shaun stopped with all his people, and there they built a city and worshipped the gods, whom only Shaun could see, seated above them on the mountain. And Shaun taught how the gods were like grey streaks of light seen before dawn, and how the god on the right pointed upward toward the sky, and how the god on the left pointed downward toward the ground, but the god in the middle slept.

And in the city Shaun's followers built three temples. The one on the right was a temple for the young, and the one on the left a temple for the old, and the third was a temple for the old, and the third was a temple with doors closed and barred—therein none ever entered. One night as Shaun watched before the three gods sitting like pale light against the mountain, he saw on the mountain's summit two gods that spake together and pointed, mocking the gods of the hill, only he heard no sound. The next day Shaun set out and a few followed him to climb to the mountain's summit in the cold, to find the gods who were so great that they mocked at the silent three. And near the two gods they halted and built for themselves huts. Also they built a temple wherein the Two were carved by the hand of Shaun with their heads turned towards each other, with mockery on Their faces and Their fingers pointing, and beneath Them were carved the three gods of the hill as actors making sport. None remembered now Asgool, Trodath, Skun, and Rhoog, the gods of Old.

For many years Shaun and his few followers lived in their huts upon the mountain's summit worshipping gods that mocked, and every night Shaun saw the two gods by starlight as they laughed to one another in the silence. And Shaun grew old.

One night as his eyes were turned towards the Two, he saw across the mountains in the distance a great god seated in the plain and looming enormous to the sky, who looked with angry eyes towards the Two as they sat and mocked. Then said Shaun to his people, the few that had followed him thither:

"Alas that we may not rest, but beyond us in the plain sitteth the one true god and he is wroth with mocking. Let us therefore leave these two that sit and mock and let us find the truth in the worship of that greater god, who even though he kill shall yet not mock us."

But the people answered:

"Thou hast taken from us many gods and taught us now to worship gods that mock, and if there is laughter on their faces as we die, lo! thou alone canst see it, and we would rest."

But three men who had grown old with following followed still.

And down the steep mountain on the further side Shaun led them, saying:

"Now we shall surely know."

And the three old men answered:

"We shall know indeed, O last of all the prophets."

That night the two gods mocking at their worshippers mocked not at Shaun nor his three followers, who coming to the plain still travelled on till they came at last to a place where the eyes of Shaun at night could closely see the vast form of their god. And beyond them as far as the sky there lay a marsh. There they rested, building such shelters as they could, and said to one another:

"This is the End, for Shaun discerneth that there are no more gods, and before us lieth the marsh and old age hath come upon us."

And since they could not labour to build a temple, Shaun carved upon a rock all that he saw by starlight of the great god of the plain; so that if ever others forsook the gods of Old because they saw beyond them the Greater Three, and should thence come to knowledge of the Twain that mocked, and should yet persevere in wisdom till they saw by starlight him whom Shaun named the Ultimate god, they should still find there upon the rock what one had written concerning the end of search. For three years Shaun carved upon the rock, and rising one night from carving, saying:

"Now is my labour done," saw in the distance four greater gods beyond the Ultimate god. Proudly in the distance beyond the marsh these gods were tramping together, taking no heed of the god upon the plain. Then said Shaun to his three followers:

"Alas that we know not yet, for there be gods beyond the marsh."

None would follow Shaun, for they said that old age must end all quests, and that they would rather wait there in the plain for Death than that he should pursue them across the marsh.

Then Shaun said farewell to his followers, saying:

"You have followed me well since ever we forsook the gods of Old to worship greater gods. Farewell. It may be that your prayers at evening shall avail when you pray to the god of the plain, but I must go onward, for there be gods beyond."

So Shaun went down into the marsh, and for three days struggled through it, and on the third night saw the four gods not very far away, yet could not discern Their faces. All the next day Shaun toiled on to see Their faces by starlight, but ere the night came up or one star shone, at set of sun, Shaun fell down before the feet of his four gods. The stars came out, and the faces of the four shone bright and clear, but Shaun saw them not, for the labour of toiling and seeing was over for Shaun; and lo! They were Asgool, Trodath, Skun, and Rhoog—The gods of Old.

Then said the King:

"It is well that the sorrow of search cometh only to the wise, for the wise are very few."

Also the King said:

"Tell me this thing, O prophet. Who are the true gods?"

The master prophet answered:

"Let the King command."

THE MEN OF YARNITH

The men of Yarnith hold that nothing began until Yarni Zai uplifted his hand. Yarni Zai, they say, has the form of a man but is greater and is a thing of rock. When he uplifted his hand all the rocks that wandered beneath the Dome, by which name they call the sky, gathered together around Yarni Zai.

Of the other worlds they say nought, but hold that the stars are the eyes of all the other gods that look on Yarni Zai and laugh, for they are all greater than he, though they have gathered no worlds around them.

Yet though they be greater than Yarni Zai, and though they laugh at him when they speak together beneath the Dome, they all speak of Yarni Zai.

Unheard is the speaking of the gods to all except the gods, but the men of Yarnith tell of how their prophet Iraun lying in the sand desert, Azrakhan, heard once their speaking and knew thereby how Yarni Zai departed from all the other gods to clothe himself with rocks and make a world.

Certain it is that every legend tells that at the end of the valley of Yodeth, where it becomes lost among black cliffs, there sits a figure colossal, against a mountain, whose form is the form of a man with the right hand uplifted, but vaster than the hills. And in the Book of Secret Things which the prophets keep in the Temple that stands in Yarnith is writ the story of the gathering of the world as Iraun heard it when the gods spake together, up in the stillness above Azrakhan.

And all that read this may learn how Yarni Zai drew the mountains about him like a cloak, and piled the world below him. It is not set in writing for how many years Yarni Zai sat clothed with rocks at the end of the Valley of Yodeth, while there was nought in all the world save rocks and Yarni Zai.

But one day there came another god running over the rocks across the world, and he ran as the clouds run upon days of storm, and as he sped towards Yodeth, Yarni Zai, sitting against his mountain with right hand uplifted, cried out:

"What dost thou, running across my world, and whither art thou going?"

And the new god answered never a word, but sped onwards, and as he went to left of him and to right of him there sprang up green things all over the rocks of the world of Yarni Zai.

So the new god ran round the world and made it green, saying in the valley where Yarni Zai sat monstrous against his mountain and certain lands wherein Cradoa, the drought, browsed horribly at night.

Further, the writing in the book tells of how there came yet another god running speedily out of the east, as swiftly as the first, with his face set westward, and nought to stay his running; and how he stretched both arms outward beside him, and to left of him and to right of him as he ran the whole world whitened.

And Yarni Zai called out:

"What dost thou, running across my world?"

And the new god answered:

"I bring the snow for all the world—whiteness and resting and stillness."

And he stilled the running of streams and laid his hand even upon the head of Yarni Zai and muffled the noises of the world, till there was no sound in all lands, but the running of the new god that brought the snow as he sped across the plains.

But the two new gods chased each other for ever round the world, and every year they passed again, running down the valleys and up the hills and away across the plains before Yarni Zai, whose hand uplifted had gathered the world about him.

And, furthermore, the very devout may read how all the animals came up the valley of Yodeth to the mountain whereon rested Yarni Zai, saying:

"Give us leave to live, to be lions, rhinoceroses and rabbits, and to go about the world."

And Yarni Zai gave leave to the animals to be lions, rhinoceroses and rabbits, and all the other kinds of beasts, and to go about the world. But when they all had gone he gave leave to the bird to be a bird and to go about the sky.

And further there came a man into that valley who said:

"Yarni Zai, thou hast made animals into thy world. O Yarni Zai, ordain that there be men."

So Yarni Zai made men.

Then was there in the world Yarni Zai, and two strange gods that brought the greenness and the growing and the whiteness and the stillness, and animals and men.

And the god of the greenness pursued the god of the whiteness, and the god of the whiteness pursued the god of the greenness, and men pursued animals, and animals pursued men. But Yarni Zai sat still against his mountain with his right hand uplifted. But the men of Yarnith say that when the arm of Yarni Zai shall cease to be uplifted the world shall be flung behind him, as a man's cloak is flung away. And Yarni Zai, no longer clad with the world, shall go back into the emptiness beneath the Dome among the stars, as a diver seeking pearls goes down from the islands.

It is writ in Yarnith's histories by scribes of old that there passed a year over the valley of Yarnith that bore not with it any rain; and the Famine from the wastes beyond, finding that it was dry and pleasant in Yarnith, crept over the mountains and down their slopes and sunned himself at the edge of Yarnith's fields.

And men of Yarnith, labouring in the fields, found the Famine as he nibbled at the corn and chased the cattle, and hastily they drew water from deep wells and cast it over the Famine's dry grey fur and drove him back to the mountains. But the next day when his fur was dry again the Famine returned and nibbled more of the corn and chased the cattle further, and again men drove him back. But again the Famine returned, and there came a time when there was no more water in the wells to frighten the Famine with, and he nibbled the corn till all of it was gone and the cattle that he chased grew very lean. And the Famine drew nearer, even to the houses of men and trampled on their gardens at night and ever came creeping nearer to their doors. At last the cattle were able to run no more, and one by one the Famine took them by their throats and dragged them down, and at night he scratched in the ground, killing even the roots of things, and came and peered in at the doorways and started back and peered in at the door again a little further, but yet was not bold enough to enter altogether, for fear that men should have water to throw over his dry grey fur.

Then did the men of Yarnith pray to Yarni Zai as he sat far off beyond the valley, praying to him night and day to call his Famine back, but the Famine sat and purred and slew all the cattle and dared at last to take men for his food.

And the histories tell how he slew children first and afterwards grew bolder and tore down women, till at last he even sprang at the throats of men as they laboured in the fields.

Then said the men of Yarnith:

"There must go one to take our prayers to the feet of Yarni Zai; for the world at evening utters many prayers, and it may be that Yarni Zai, as he hears all earth lamenting when the prayers at evening flutter to his feet, may have missed among so many the prayers of the men of Yarnith. But if one go and say to Yarni Zai: 'There is a little crease in the outer skirts of thy cloak that men call the valley of Yarnith, where the Famine is a greater lord than Yarni Zai,' it may be that he shall remember for an instant and call his Famine back."

Yet all men feared to go, seeing that they were but men and Yarni Zai was Lord of the whole earth, and the journey was far and rocky. But that night Hothrun Dath heard the Famine whining outside his house and paw-ing at his door; therefore, it seemed to him more meet to wither before the glance of Yarni Zai than that the whining of that Famine should ever again fall upon his ears.

So about the dawn, Hothrun Dath crept away, fearing still to hear behind him the breathing of the Famine, and set out upon his journey whither pointed the graves of men. For men in Yarnith are buried with their feet and faces turned toward Yarni Zai, lest he might beckon to them in their night and call them to him.

So all day long did Hothrun Dath follow the way of the graves. It is told that he even journeyed for three days and nights with nought but the graves to guide him, as they pointed towards Yarni Zai where all the world slopes upwards towards Yodeth, and the great black rocks that are nearest to Yarni Zai lie gathered together by clans, till he came to the two great black pillars of asdarinth and saw the rocks beyond them piled in a dark valley, narrow and aloof, and knew that this was Yodeth. Then did he haste no more, but walked quietly up the valley, daring not to disturb the stillness, for he said:

"Surely this is the stillness of Yarni Zai, which lay about him before he clothed himself with rocks."

Here among the rocks which first had gathered to the call of Yarni Zai, Hothrun Dath felt a mighty fear, but yet went onwards because of all his people and because he knew that thrice in every hour in some dark chamber Death and Famine met to speak two words together, "The End."

But as dawn turned the darkness into grey, he came to the valley's end, and even touched the foot of Yarni Zai, but saw him not, for he was all hidden in the mist. Then Hothrun Dath feared that he might not behold him to look him in the eyes when he sent up his prayer. But laying his forehead against the foot of Yarni Zai he prayed for the men of Yarnith, saying:

"O Lord of Famine and Father of Death, there is a spot in the world that thou hast cast about thee which men call Yarnith, and there men die before the time thou hast apportioned, passing out of Yarnith. Perchance the Famine hath rebelled against thee, or Death exceeds his powers. O Master of the World, drive out the Famine as a moth out of thy cloak, lest the gods beyond that regard thee with their eyes say—there is Yarni Zai, and lo! his cloak is tattered."

And in the mist no sign made Yarni Zai. Then did Hothrun Dath pray to Yarni Zai to make some sign with his uplifted hand that he might know he heard him. In the awe and silence he waited, until nigh the dawn the mist that hid the figure rolled upwards. Serene above the mountains he brooded over the world, silent, with right hand uplifted.

What Hothrun Dath saw there upon the face of Yarni Zai no history telleth, or how he came again alive to Yarnith, but this is writ that he fled, and none hath since beheld the face of Yarni Zai. Some say that he saw a look on the face of the image that set a horror tingling through his soul, but it is held in Yarnith that he found the marks of instruments of carving about the figure's feet, and discerning thereby that Yarni Zai was wrought by the hands of men, he fled down the valley screaming:

"There are no gods, and all the world is lost." And hope departed from him and all the purposes of life. Motionless behind him, lit by the rising sun, sat the colossal figure with right hand uplifted that man had made in his own image.

But the men of Yarnith tell how Hothrun Dath came back again panting to his own city, and told the people that there were no gods and that Yarnith had no hope from Yarni Zai. Then the men of Yarnith when they knew that the Famine came not from the gods, arose and strove against him. They dug deep for wells, and slew goats for food high up on Yarnith's mountains and went afar and gathered blades of grass, where yet it grew, that their cattle might live. Thus they fought the Famine, for they said: "If Yarni Zai be not a god, then is there nothing mightier in Yarnith than men, and who is the Famine that he should bare his teeth against the lords of Yarnith?"

And they said: "If no help cometh from Yarni Zai then is there no help but from our own strength and might, and we be Yarnith's gods with the saving of Yarnith burning within us or its doom according to our desire."

And some more the Famine slew, but others raised their hands saying: "These be the hands of gods," and drave the Famine back till he went from the houses of men and out among the cattle, and still the men of Yarnith pursued him, till above the heat of the fight came the million whispers of rain heard faintly far off towards evening. Then the Famine fled away howling back to the mountains and over the mountains' crests, and became no more than a thing that is told in Yarnith's legends.

A thousand years have passed across the graves of those that fell in Yarnith by the Famine. But the men of Yarnith still pray to Yarni Zai, carved by men's hands in the likeness of a man, for they say—"It may be that the prayers we offer to Yarni Zai may roll upwards from his image as do the mists at dawn, and somewhere find at last the other gods or that God who sits behind the others of whom our prophets know not."

FOR THE HONOUR OF THE GODS

Of the great wars of the Three Islands are many histories writ and of how the heroes of the olden time one by one were slain, but nought is told of the days before the olden time, or ever the people of the isles went forth to war, when each in his own land tended cattle or sheep, and listless peace obscured those isles in the days before the olden time. For then the people of the Islands played like children about the feet of Chance and had no gods and went not forth to war. But sailors, cast by strange winds upon those shores which they named the Prosperous Isles, and finding a happy people which had no gods, told how they should be happier still and know the gods and fight for the honour of the gods and leave their names writ large in histories and at the last die proclaiming the names of the gods. And the people of the islands met and said:

"The beasts we know, but lo! these sailors tell of things beyond that know us as we know the beasts and use us for their pleasure as we use the beasts, but yet are apt to answer idle prayer flung up at evening near the hearth, when a man returneth from the ploughing of the fields. Shall we now seek these gods?" And some said:

"We are lords of the Three Islands and have none to trouble us, and while we live we find prosperity, and when we die our bones have ease in the quiet. Let us not therefore seek those who may loom greater than we do in the Islands Three or haply harry our bones when we be dead."

But others said:

"The prayers that a man mutters, when the drought hath come and all the cattle die, go up unheeded to the heedless clouds, and if somewhere there be those that garner prayer let us send men to seek them and to say: 'There be men in the Isles called Three, or sometimes named by sailors the Prosperous Isles (and they be in the Central Sea), who ofttimes pray, and it hath been told us that ye love the worship of men, and for it answer prayer, and we be travellers from the Islands Three.'"

And the people of the Islands were greatly allured by the thought of strange things neither men nor beasts who at evening answered prayer.

Therefore they sent men down in ships with sails to sail across the sea, and in safety over the sea to a far shore Chance brought the ships. Then over hill and valley three men set forth seeking to find the gods, and their comrades beached the ships and waited on the shore. And they that sought the gods followed for thirty nights the lightnings in the sky over five mountains, and as they came to the summit of the last, they saw a valley beneath them, and lo! the gods. For there the gods sat, each on a marble hill, each sitting with an elbow on his knee, and his chin upon his hand, and all the gods were smiling about Their lips. And below them there were armies of little men, and about the feet of the gods they fought against each other and slew one another for the honour of the gods, and for the glory of the name of the gods. And round them in the valley their cities that they had builded with the toil of their hands, they burned for the honour of the gods, where they died for the honour of the gods, and the gods looked down and smiled. And up from the valley fluttered the prayers of men and here and there the gods did answer a prayer, but oftentimes They mocked them, and all the while men died.

And they that had sought the gods from the Islands Three, having seen what they had seen, lay down on the mountain summit lest the gods should see them. Then they crept backward a little space, still lying down, and whispered together and then stooped low and ran, and travelled across the mountains in twenty days and came again to their comrades by the shore.

But their comrades asked them if their quest had failed and the three men only answered:

"We have seen the gods."

And setting sail the ships hove back across the Central Sea and came again to the Islands Three, where rest the feet of Chance, and said to the people:

"We have seen the gods."

But to the rulers of the Islands they told how the gods drove men in herds; and went back and tended their flocks again all in the Prosperous Isles, and were kinder to their cattle after they had seen how that the gods used men.

But the gods walking large about Their valley, and peering over the great mountain's rim, saw one morning the tracks of the three men. Then the gods bent their faces low over the tracks and leaning forward ran, and came before the evening of the day to the shore where the men had set sail in ships, and saw the tracks of ships upon the sand, and waded far out into the sea, and yet saw nought. Still it had been well for the Islands Three had not certain men that had heard the travellers' tale sought also to see the gods themselves. These in the night-time slipped away from the Isles in ships, and ere the gods had retreated to the hills, They saw where ocean meets with sky the full white sails of those that sought the gods upon an evil day. Then for a while the people of those gods had rest while the gods lurked behind the mountain, waiting for the travellers from the Prosperous Isles. But the travellers came to shore and beached their ships, and sent six of their number to the mountain whereof they had been told. But they after many days returned, having not seen the gods but only the smoke that went upward from burned cities, and vultures that stood in the sky instead of answered prayer. And they all ran down their ships again into the sea, and set sail again and came to the Prosperous Isles. But in the distance crouching behind the ships the gods came wading through the sea that They might have the worship of the isles. And to every isle of the three the gods showed themselves in different garb and guise, and to all they said:

"Leave your flocks. Go forth and fight for the honour of the gods."

And from one of the isles all the folk came forth in ships to battle for gods that strode through the isle like kings. And from another they came to fight for gods that walked like humble men upon the earth in beggars' rags; and the people of the other isle fought for the honour of gods that were clothed in hair like beasts; and had many gleaming eyes and claws upon their foreheads. But of how these people fought till the isles grew desolate but very glorious, and all for the fame of the gods, are many histories writ.

NIGHT AND MORNING

Once in an arbour of the gods above the fields of twilight Night wandering alone came suddenly on Morning. Then Night drew from his face his cloak of dark grey mists and said: "See, I am Night," and they two sitting in that arbour of the gods, Night told wondrous stories of old mysterious happenings in the dark. And Morning sat and wondered, gazing into the face of Night and at his wreath of stars. And Morning told how the rains of Snamarthis smoked in the plain, but Night told how Snamarthis held riot in the dark, with revelry and drinking and tales told by kings, till all the hosts of Meenath crept against it and the lights went out and there arose the din of arms or ever Morning came. And Night told how Sindana the beggar had dreamed that he was a King, and Morning told how she had seen Sindana find suddenly an army in the plain, and how he had gone to it thinking he was King and the army had believed him, and Sindana now ruled over Marthis and Targadrides, Dynath, Zahn, and Tumeida. And most Night loved to tell of Assarnees, whose ruins are scant memories on the desert's edge, but Morning told of the twin cities of Nardis and Timaut that lorded over the plain. And Night told terribly of what Mynandes found when he walked through his own city in the dark. And ever at the elbow of regal Night whispers arose saying: "Tell Morning *this*."

And ever Night told and ever Morning wondered. And Night spake on, and told what the dead had done when they came in the darkness on the King that had led them into battle once. And Night knew who slew Darnex and how it was done. Moreover, he told why the seven Kings tortured Sydatheris and what Sydatheris said just at the last, and how the Kings went forth and took their lives.

And Night told whose blood had stained the marble steps that lead to the temple in Ozahn, and why the skull within it wears a golden crown, and whose soul is in the wolf that howls in the dark against the city. And Night knew whither the tigers go out of the Irasian desert and the place where they meet together, and who speaks to them and what she says and why. And he told why human teeth had bitten the iron hinge in the great gate that swings in the walls of Mondas, and who came up out of the marsh alone in the darktime and demanded audience of the King and told the King a lie, and how the King, believing it, went down into the vaults of his palace and found only toads and snakes, who slew the King. And he told of ventures in palace towers in the quiet, and knew the spell whereby a man might send the light of the moon right into the soul of his foe. And Night spoke of the forest and the stirring of shadows and soft feet pattering and peering eyes, and of the fear that sits behind the trees taking to itself the shape of something crouched to spring.

But far under that arbour of the gods down on the earth the mountain peak Mondana looked Morning in the eyes and forsook his allegiance to

Night, and one by one the lesser hills about Mondana's knees greeted the Morning. And all the while in the plains the shapes of cities came looming out of the dusk. And Kongros stood forth with all her pinnacles, and the winged figure of Poesy carved upon the eastern portal of her gate, and the squat figure of Avarice carved facing it upon the west; and the bat began to tire of going up and down her streets, and already the owl was home. And the dark lions went up out of the plain back to their caves again. Not as yet shone any dew upon the spider's snare nor came the sound of any insects stirring or bird of the day, and full allegiance all the valleys owned still to their Lord the Night. Yet earth was preparing for another ruler, and kingdom by kingdom she stole away from Night, and there marched through the dreams of men a million heralds that cried with the voice of the cock: "Lo! Morning come behind us." But in that arbour of the gods above the fields of twilight the star wreath was paling about the head of Night, and ever more wonderful on Morning's brow appeared the mark of power. And at the moment when the camp fires pale and the smoke goes grey to the sky, and camels sniff the dawn, suddenly Morning forgot Night. And out of that arbour of the gods, and away to the haunts of the dark, Night with his swart cloak slunk away; and Morning placed her hand upon the mists and drew them upward and revealed the earth, and drove the shadows before her, and they followed Night. And suddenly the mystery quitted haunting shapes, and an old glamour was gone, and far and wide over the fields of earth a new splendour arose.

USURY

The men of Zonu hold that Yahn is God, who sits as a usurer behind a heap of little lustrous gems and ever clutches at them with both his arms. Scarce larger than a drop of water are the gleaming jewels that lie under the grasping talons of Yahn, and every jewel is a life. Men tell in Zonu that the earth was empty when Yahn devised his plan, and on it no life stirred. Then Yahn lured to him shadows whose home was beyond the Rim, who knew little of joys and nought of any sorrow, whose place was beyond the Rim before the birth of Time. These Yahn lured to him and showed them his heap of gems; and in the jewels there was light, and green fields glistened in them, and there were glimpses of blue sky and little streams, and very faintly little gardens showed that flowered in orchard lands. And some showed winds in the heaven, and some showed the arch of the sky with a waste plain drawn across it, with grasses bent in the wind and never aught but the plain. But the gems that changed the most had in their centre the ever changing sea. Then the shadows gazed into the Lives and saw the green fields and the sea and earth and the gardens of earth. And Yahn said: "I will loan you each a Life, and you may do your work with it upon the Scheme of Things, and have each a shadow for his servant in green fields and in gardens, only for these things you shall polish these Lives with experience and cut their edges with your griefs, and in the end shall return them again to me."

And thereto the shadows consented, that they might have gleaming Lives and have shadows for their servants, and this thing became the Law. But the shadows, each with his Life, departed and came to Zonu and to other lands, and there with experience they polished the Lives of Yahn, and cut them with human griefs until they gleamed anew. And ever they found new scenes to gleam within these Lives, and cities and sails and men shone in them where there had been before only green fields and sea, and ever Yahn the usurer cried out to remind them of their bargain. When men added to their Lives scenes that were pleasant to Yahn, then was Yahn silent, but when they added scenes that pleased not the eyes of Yahn, then did he take a toll of sorrow from them because it was the Law.

But men forgot the usurer, and there arose some claiming to be wise in the Law, who said that after their labour, which they wrought upon their Lives, was done, those Lives should be theirs to possess; so men took comfort from their toil and labour and the grinding and cutting of their griefs. But as their Lives began to shine with experience of many things, the thumb and forefinger of Yahn would suddenly close upon a Life, and the man became a shadow. But away beyond the Rim the shadows say:

"We have greatly laboured for Yahn, and have gathered griefs in the world, and caused his Lives to shine, and Yahn doeth nought for us. Far better had we stayed where no cares are, floating beyond the Rim."

And there the shadows fear lest ever again they be lured by specious promises to suffer usury at the hands of Yahn, who is overskilled in Law. Only Yahn sits and smiles, watching his hoard increase in preciousness, and hath no pity for the poor shadows whom he hath lured from their quiet to toil in the form of men.

And ever Yahn lures more shadows and sends them to brighten his Lives, sending the old Lives out again to make them brighter still; and sometimes he gives to a shadow a Life that was once a king's and sendeth him with it down to the earth to play the part of a beggar, or sometimes he sendeth a beggar's Life to play the part of a king. What careth Yahn?

The men of Zonu have been promised by those that claim to be wise in the Law that their Lives which they have toiled at shall be theirs to possess for ever, yet the men of Zonu fear that Yahn is greater and overskilled in the Law. Moreover it hath been said that Time will bring the hour when the wealth of Yahn shall be such as his dreams have lusted for. Then shall Yahn leave the earth at rest and trouble the shadows no more, but sit and gloat with his unseemly face over his hoard of Lives, for his soul is a usurer's soul. But others say, and they swear that this is true, that there are gods of Old, who be far greater than Yahn, who made the Law wherein Yahn is overskilled, and who will one day drive a bargain with him that shall be too hard for Yahn. Then Yahn shall wander away, a mean forgotten god, and perchance in some forsaken land shall haggle with the rain for a drop of water to drink, for his soul is a usurer's soul. And the Lives—who knoweth the gods of Old or what Their will shall be?

MLIDEEN

Upon an evening of the forgotten years the gods were seated upon Mowrah Nawut above Mlideen holding the avalanche in leash.

All in the Middle City stood the Temples of the city's priests, and hither came all the people of Mlideen to bring them gifts, and there it was the wont of the City's priests to carve them gods for Mlideen. For in a room apart in the Temple of Eld in the midst of the temples that stood in the Middle City of Mlideen there lay a book called the Book of Beautiful Devices, writ in a language that no man may read and writ long ago, telling how a man may make for himself gods that shall neither rage nor seek revenge against a little people. And ever the priests came forth from reading in the Book of Beautiful Devices and ever they sought to make benignant gods, and all the gods that they made were different from each other, only their eyes turned all upon Mlideen.

But upon Mowrah Nawut for all of the forgotten years the gods had waited and forborne until the people of Mlideen should have carven one hundred gods. Never came lightnings from Mowrah Nawut crashing upon Mlideen, nor blight on harvests nor pestilence in the city, only upon Mowrah Nawut the gods sat and smiled. The people of Mlideen had said: "Yoma is god." And the gods sat and smiled. And after the forgetting of Yoma and the passing of years the people had said: "Zungari is god." And the gods sat and smiled.

Then on the altar of Zungari a priest had set a figure squat, carven in purple agate, saying: "Yazun is god." Still the gods sat and smiled.

About the feet of Yonu, Bazun, Nidish and Sundrao had gone the worship of the people of Mlideen, and still the gods sat holding the avalanche in leash above the city.

There set a great calm towards sunset over the heights, and Mowrah Nawut stood up still with gleaming snow, and into the hot city cool breezes blew from his benignant slopes as Tarsi Zalo, high prophet of Mlideen, carved out of a great sapphire the city's hundredth god, and then upon Mowrah Nawut the gods turned away saying: "One hundred infamies have now been wrought." And they looked no longer upon Mlideen and held the avalanche no more in leash, and he leapt forward howling.

Over the Middle City of Mlideen now lies a mass of rocks, and on the rocks a new city is builded wherein people dwell who know not old Mlideen, and the gods are seated on Mowrah Nawut still. And in the new city men worship carven gods, and the number of the gods that they have carven is ninety and nine, and I, the prophet, have found a curious stone and go to carve it into the likeness of a god for all Mlideen to worship.

THE SECRET OF THE GODS

Zyni Moe, the small snake, saw the cool river gleaming before him afar off and set out over the burning sand to reach it.

Uldoon, the prophet, came out of the desert and followed up the bank of the river towards his old home. Thirty years since Uldoon had left the city, where he was born, to live his life in a silent place where he might search for the secret of the gods. The name of his home was the City by the River, and in that city many prophets taught concerning many gods, and men made many secrets for themselves, but all the while none knew the Secret of the gods. Nor might any seek to find it, for if any sought men said of him:

"This man sins, for he giveth no worship to the gods that speak to our prophets by starlight when none heareth."

And Uldoon perceived that the mind of a man is as a garden, and that his thoughts are as the flowers, and the prophets of a man's city are as many gardeners who weed and trim, and who have made in the garden paths both smooth and straight, and only along these paths is a man's soul permitted to go lest the gardeners say, "This soul transgresseth." And from the paths the gardeners weed out every flower that grows, and in the garden they cut off all flowers that grow tall, saying:

"It is customary," and "it is written," and "this hath ever been," or "that hath not been before."

Therefore Uldoon saw that not in that city might he discover the Secret of the gods. And Uldoon said to the people:

"When the worlds began, the Secret of the gods lay written clear over the whole earth, but the feet of many prophets have trampled it out. Your prophets are all true men, but I go into the desert to find a truth which is truer than your prophets." Therefore Uldoon went into the desert and in storm and still he sought for many years. When the thunder roared over the mountains that limited the desert he sought the Secret in the thunder, but the gods spake not by the thunder. When the voices of the beasts disturbed the stillness under the stars he sought the secret there, but the gods spake not by the beasts.

Uldoon grew old and all the voices of the desert had spoken to Uldoon, but not the gods, when one night he heard Them whispering beyond the hills. And the gods whispered one to another, and turning Their faces earthward They all wept. And Uldoon though he saw not the gods yet saw Their shadows turn as They went back to a great hollow in the hills; and there, all standing in the valley's mouth, They said:

"Oh, Morning Zai, oh, oldest of the gods, the faith of thee is gone, and yesterday for the last time thy name was spoken upon earth." And turning earthward they all wept again. And the gods tore white clouds out of the sky and draped them about the body of Morning Zai and bore him forth from his valley behind the hills, and muffled the mountain peaks with snow, and beat upon their summits with drum sticks carved of ebony, playing the dirge of the gods. And the echoes rolled about the passes and the winds howled, because the faith of the olden days was gone, and with it had sped the soul of Morning Zai. So through the mountain passes the gods came at night bearing Their dead father. And Uldoon followed. And the gods came to a great sepulchre of onyx that stood upon four fluted pillars of white marble, each carved out of four mountains, and therein the gods laid Morning Zai because the old faith was fallen. And there at the tomb of Their father the gods spake and Uldoon heard the Secret of the gods, and it became to him a simple thing such as a man might well guess—yet hath not. Then the soul of the desert arose and cast over the tomb its wreath of forgetfulness devised of drifting sand, and the gods strode home across the mountains to Their hollow land. But Uldoon left the desert and travelled many days, and so came to the river where it passes beyond the city to seek the sea, and following its bank came near to his old home. And the people of the City by the River, seeing him far off, cried out:

"Hast thou found the Secret of the gods?"

And he answered:

"I have found it, and the Secret of the gods is this"—:

Zyni Moe, the small snake, seeing the figure and the shadow of a man between him and the cool river, raised his head and struck once. And the gods are pleased with Zyni Moe, and have called him the protector of the Secret of the gods.

THE SOUTH WIND

Two players sat down to play a game together to while eternity away, and they chose the gods as pieces wherewith to play their game, and for their board of playing they chose the sky from rim to rim, whereon lay a little dust; and every speck of dust was a world upon the board of playing. And the players were robed and their faces veiled, and the robes and veils were alike, and their names were Fate and Chance. And as they played their game and moved the gods hither and thither about the board, the dust arose, and shone in the light from the players' eyes that gleamed behind the veils. Then said the gods: "See how We stir the dust."

It chanced, or was ordained (who knoweth which?) that Ord, a prophet, one night saw the gods as They strode knee deep among the stars. But as he gave Them worship, he saw the hand of a player, enormous over Their heads, stretched out to make his move. Then Ord, the prophet, knew. Had he been silent it might have still been well with Ord, but Ord went about the world crying out to all men, "There is a power over the gods."

This the gods heard. Then said They, "Ord hath seen."

Terrible is the vengeance of the gods, and fierce were Their eyes when They looked on the head of Ord and snatched out of his mind all knowledge of Themselves. And that man's soul went wandering afield to find for itself gods, for ever finding them not. Then out of Ord's Dream of Life the gods plucked the moon and the stars, and in the night-time he only saw black sky and saw the lights no more. Next the gods took from him, for Their vengeance resteth not, the birds and butterflies, flowers and leaves and insects and all small things, and the prophet looked on the world that was strangely altered, yet knew not of the anger of the gods. Then the gods sent away his familiar hills, to be seen no more by him, and all the pleasant woodlands on their summits and the further fields; and in a narrower world Ord walked round and round, now seeing little, and his soul still wandered searching for some gods and finding none.

Lastly, the gods took away the fields and stream and left to the prophet only his house and the larger things that were in it. Day by day They crept about him drawing films of mist between him and familiar things, till at last he beheld nought at all and was quite blind and unaware of the anger of the gods. Then Ord's world became only a world of sound, and only by hearing he kept his hold upon Things. All the profit that he had out of his days was here some song from the hills or there the voice of the birds, and sound of the stream, or the drip of the falling rain. But the anger of the gods ceases not with the closing of flowers, nor is it assuaged by all the winter's snows, nor doth it rest in the full glare of summer, and They snatched away from Ord one night his world of sound and he awoke deaf. But as a man may smite away the hive of the bee, and the bee with all his fellows builds again, knowing not what hath smitten his hive or that it shall smite again, so Ord built for himself a world out of old memories and set it in the past. There he builded himself cities out of former joys, and therein built palaces of mighty things achieved, and with his memory as a key he opened golden locks and had still a world to live in, though the gods had taken from him the world of sound and all the world of sight. But the gods tire not from pursuing, and They seized his world of former things and took his memory away and covered up the paths that led into the past, and left him blind and deaf and forgetful among men, and caused all men to know that this was he who once had said that the gods were little things.

And lastly the gods took his soul, and out of it They fashioned the South Wind to roam the seas for ever and not have rest; and well the South Wind knows that he hath once understood somewhere and long ago, and so he moans to the islands and cries along southern shores, "I have known," and "I have known."

But all things sleep when the South Wind speaks to them and none heed his cry that he hath known, but are rather content to sleep. But still the South Wind, knowing that there is something that he hath forgot, goes on crying, "I have known," seeking to urge men to arise and to discover it. But none heed the sorrows of the South Wind even when he driveth his tears out of the South, so that though the South Wind cries on and on and never findeth rest none heed that there is aught that may be known, and the Secret of the gods is safe. But the business of the South Wind is with the North, and it is said that the time will one day come when he shall overcome the bergs and sink the seas of ice and come where the Secret of the gods is graven upon the pole. And the game of Fate and Chance shall suddenly cease and He that loses shall cease to be or ever to have been, and from the board of playing Fate or Chance (who knoweth which shall win?) shall sweep the gods away.

IN THE LAND OF TIME

Thus Karnith, King of Alatta, spake to his eldest son: "I bequeath to thee my city of Zoon, with its golden eaves, whereunder hum the bees. And I bequeath to thee also the land of Alatta, and all such other lands as thou art worthy to possess, for my three strong armies which I leave thee may well take Zindara and over-run Istahn, and drive back Onin from his frontier, and leaguer the walls of Yan, and beyond that spread conquest over the lesser lands of Hebith, Ebnon, and Karida. Only lead not thine armies against Zeenar, nor ever cross the Eidis."

Thereat in the city of Zoon in the land of Alatta, under his golden eaves, died King Karnith, and his soul went whither had gone the souls of his sires the elder Kings, and the souls of their slaves.

Then Karnith Zo, the new King, took the iron crown of Alatta and afterwards went down to the plains that encircle Zoon and found his three strong armies clamouring to be led against Zeenar, over the river Eidis.

But the new King came back from his armies, and all one night in the great palace alone with his iron crown, pondered long upon war; and a little before dawn he saw dimly through his palace window, facing east over the city of Zoon and across the fields of Alatta, to far off where a valley opened on Istahn. There, as he pondered, he saw the smoke arising tall and straight over small houses in the plain and the fields where the sheep fed. Later the sun rose shining over Alatta as it shone over Istahn, and there arose a stir about the houses both in Alatta and Istahn, and cocks crowded in the city and men went out into the fields among the bleating sheep; and the King wondered if men did otherwise in Istahn. And men and women met as they went out to work and the sound of laughter arose from streets and fields; the King's eyes gazed into the distance toward Istahn and still the smoke went upward tall and straight from the small houses. And the sun rose higher that shone upon Alatta and Istahn, causing the flowers to open wide in each, and the birds to sing and the voices of men and women to arise. And in the market place of Zoon caravans were astir that set out to carry merchandise to Istahn, and afterwards passed camels coming to Alatta with many tinkling bells. All this the King saw as he pondered much, who had not pondered before. Westward the Agnid mountains frowned in the distance guarding the river Eidis; behind them the fierce people of Zeenar lived in a bleak land.

Later the King, going abroad through his new kingdom, came on the Temple of the gods of Old. There he found the roof shattered and the marble columns broken and tall weeds met together in the inner shrine, and the gods of Old, bereft of worship or sacrifice, neglected and forgotten. And the King asked of his councillors who it was that had overturned this temple of the gods or caused the gods Themselves to be thus forsaken. And they answered him:

"Time has done this."

Next the King came upon a man bent and crippled, whose face was furrowed and worn, and the King having seen no such sight within the court of his father said to the man:

"Who hath done this thing to you?"

And the old man answered:

"Time hath ruthlessly done it."

But the King and his councillors went on, and next they came upon a body of men carrying among them a hearse. And the King asked his councillors closely concerning death, for these things had not before been expounded to the King. And the oldest of the councillors answered:

"Death, O King, is a gift sent by the gods by the hand of their servant Time, and some receive it gladly, and some are forced reluctantly to take it, and before others it is suddenly flung in the middle of the day. And with this gift that Time hath brought him from the gods a man must go forth into the dark to possess no other thing for so long as the gods are willing."

But the King went back to his palace and gathered the greatest of his prophets and his councillors and asked them more particularly concerning Time. And they told the King how that Time was a great figure standing like a tall shadow in the dusk or striding, unseen, across the world, and how that he was the slave of the gods and did Their bidding, but ever chose new masters, and how all the former masters of Time were dead and Their shrines forgotten. And one said:

"I have seen him once when I went down to play again in the garden of my childhood because of certain memories. And it was towards evening and the light was pale, and I saw Time standing over the little gate, pale like the light, and he stood between me and that garden and had stolen my memories because he was mightier than I."

And another said:

"I, too, have seen the Enemy of my House. For I saw him when he strode over the fields that I knew well and led a stranger by the hand to place him in my home to sit where my forefathers sat. And I saw him afterwards walk thrice round the house and stoop and gather up the glamour from the lawns and brush aside the tall poppies in the garden and spread weeds in his pathway where he strode through the remembered nooks."

And another said:

"He went one day into the desert and brought up life out of the waste places, and made it cry bitterly and covered it with the desert again."

And another said:

"I too saw him once seated in the garden of a child tearing the flowers, and afterwards he went away through many woodlands and stooped down as he went, and picked the leaves one by one from the trees."

And another said:

"I saw him once by moonlight standing tall and black amidst the ruins of a shrine in the old kingdom of Amarna, doing a deed by night. And he wore a look on his face such as murderers wear as he busied himself to cover over something with weeds and dust. Thereafter in Amarna the people of that old Kingdom missed their god, in whose shrine I saw Time crouching in the night, and they have not since beheld him."

And all the while from the distance at the city's edge rose a hum from the three armies of the King clamouring to be led against Zeenar. Thereat the King went down to his three armies and speaking to their chiefs said:

"I will not go down clad with murder to be King over other lands. I have seen the same morning arising on Istahn that also gladdened Alatta, and have heard Peace lowing among the flowers. I will not desolate homes to rule over an orphaned land and a land widowed. But I will lead you against the pledged enemy of Alatta who shall crumble the towers of Zoon and hath gone far to overthrow our gods. He is the foe of Zindara and Istahn and many-citadeled Yan, Hebith and Ebnon may not overcome him nor Karida be safe against him among her bleakest mountains. He is a foe mightier than Zeenar with frontiers stronger than Eidis; he leers at all the peoples of the earth and mocks their gods and covets their builded cities. Therefore we will go forth and conquer Time and save the gods of Alatta from his clutch, and coming back victorious shall find that Death is gone and age and illness departed, and here we shall live for ever by the golden eaves of Zoon, while the bees hum among unrusted gables and never crumbling towers. There shall be neither fading nor forgetting, nor ever dying nor sorrow, when we shall have freed the people and pleasant fields of the earth from inexorable Time."

And the armies swore that they would follow the King to save the world and the gods.

So the next day the King set forth with his three armies and crossed many rivers and marched through many lands, and wherever they went they asked for news of Time.

And the first day they met a woman with her face furrowed and lined, who told them that she had been beautiful and that Time had smitten her in the face with his five claws.

Many an old man they met as they marched in search of Time. All had seen him but none could tell them more, except that some said he went that way and pointed to a ruined tower or to an old and broken tree.

And day after day and month by month the King pushed on with his armies, hoping to come at last on Time. Sometimes they encamped at night near palaces of beautiful design or beside gardens of flowers, hoping to find their enemy when he came to desecrate in the dark. Sometimes they came on cobwebs, sometimes on rusted chains and houses with broken roofs or crumbling walls. Then the armies would push on apace thinking that they were closer upon the track of Time.

As the weeks passed by and weeks grew to months, and always they heard reports and rumours of Time, but never found him, the armies grew weary of the great march, but the King pushed on and would let none turn back, saying always that the enemy was near at hand.

Month in, month out, the King led on his now unwilling armies, till at last they had marched for close upon a year and came to the village of Astarma very far to the north. There many of the King's weary soldiers deserted from his armies and settled down in Astarma and married Astarmian girls. By these soldiers we have the march of the armies clearly chronicled to the time when they came to Astarma, having been nigh a year upon the march. And the army left that village and the children cheered them as they went up the street, and five miles distant they passed over a ridge of hills and out of sight. Beyond this less is known, but the rest of this chronicle is gathered from the tales that the veterans of the King's armies used to tell in the evenings about the fires in Zoon and remembered afterwards by the men of Zeenar.

It is mostly credited in these days that such of the King's armies as went on past Astarma came at last (it is not known after how long a time) over a crest of a slope where the whole earth slanted green to the north. Below it lay green fields and beyond them moaned the sea with never shore nor island so far as the eye could reach. Among the green fields lay a village, and on this village the eyes of the King and his armies were turned as they came down the slope. It lay beneath them, grave with seared antiquity, with old-world gables stained and bent by the lapse of frequent years, with all its chimneys awry. Its roofs were tiled with antique stones covered over deep with moss, each little window looked with a myriad strange cut panes on the gardens shaped with quaint devices and overrun with weeds. On rusted hinges the doors sung to and fro and were fashioned of planks of immemorial oak with black knots gaping from their sockets. Against it all there beat the thistle-down, about it clambered the ivy or swayed the weeds; tall and straight out of the twisted chimneys arose blue columns of smoke, and blades of grass peeped upward between the huge cobbles of the unmolested street. Between the gardens and the cobbled streets stood hedges higher than a horseman might look, of stalwart thorn, and upward through it clambered the convolvulus to peer into the garden from the top. Before each house there was cut a gap in the hedge, and in it swung a wicket gate of timber soft with the rain and years, and green like the moss. Over all ôf it there brooded age and the full hush of things bygone and forgotten. Upon this derelict that the years had cast up out of antiquity the King and his armies gazed long. Then on the hill slope the King made his armies halt, and went down alone with one of his chiefs into the village.

Presently there was a stir in one of the houses, and a bat flew out of the door into the daylight, and three mice came running out of the doorway down the step, an old stone cracked in two and held together by moss; and there followed an old man bending on a stick with a white beard coming to the ground, wearing clothes that were glossed with use, and presently there came others out of the other houses, all of them as old, and all hobbling on sticks. These were the oldest people that the King had ever beheld, and he asked them the name of the village and who they were; and one of them answered, "This is the City of the Aged in the Territory of Time."

And the King said, "Is Time then here?"

And one of the old men pointed to a great castle standing on a steep hill and said: "Therein dwells Time, and we are his people;" and they all looked curiously at King Karnith Zo, and the eldest of the villagers spoke again and said: "Whence do you come, you that are so young?" and Karnith Zo told him how he had come to conquer Time to save the world and the gods, and asked them whence they came.

And the villagers said:

"We are older than always, and know not whence we came, but we are the people of Time, and here from the Edge of Everything he sends out his hours to assail the world, and you may never conquer Time." But the King went back to his armies, and pointed towards the castle on the hill and told them that at last they had found the Enemy of the Earth; and they that were older than always went back slowly into their houses with the creaking of olden doors. And there they went across the fields and passed the village. From one of his towers Time eyed them all the while, and in battle order they closed in on the steep hill as Time sat still in his great tower and watched.

But as the feet of the foremost touched the edge of the hill Time hurled five years against them, and the years passed over their heads and the army still came on, an army of older men. But the slope seemed steeper to the King and to every man in his army, and they breathed more heavily. And

Time summoned up more years, and one by one he hurled them at Karnith Zo and at all his men. And the knees of the army stiffened, and their beards grew and turned grey, and the hours and days and the months went singing over their heads, and their hair turned whiter and whiter, and the conquering hours bore down, and the years rushed on and swept the youth of that army clear away till they came face to face under the walls of the castle of Time with a mass of howling years, and found the top of the slope too steep for aged men. Slowly and painfully, harassed with agues and chills, the King rallied his aged army that tottered down the slope.

Slowly the King led back his warriors over whose heads had shrieked the triumphant years. Year in, year out, they straggled southwards, always towards Zoon; they came, with rust upon their spears and long beards flowing, again into Astarma, and none knew them there. They passed again by towns and villages where once they had inquired curiously concerning Time, and none knew them there either. They came again to the palaces and gardens where they had waited for Time in the night, and found that Time had been there. And all the while they set a hope before them that they should come on Zoon again and see its golden eaves. And no one knew that unperceived behind them there lurked and followed the gaunt figure of Time cutting off stragglers one by one and overwhelming them with his hours, only men were missed from the army every day, and fewer and fewer grew the veterans of Karnith Zo.

But at last after many a month, one night as they marched in the dusk before the morning, dawn suddenly ascending shone on the eaves of Zoon, and a great cry ran through the army:

"Alatta, Alatta!"

But drawing nearer they found that the gates were rusted and weeds grew tall along the outer walls, many a roof had fallen, gables were blackened and bent, and the golden eaves shone not as heretofore. And the soldiers entering the city expecting to find their sisters and sweethearts of a few years ago saw only old women wrinkled with great age and knew not who they were.

Suddenly someone said:

"He has been here too."

And then they knew that while they searched for Time, Time had gone forth against their city and leaguered it with the years, and had taken it while they were far away and enslaved their women and children with the yoke of age. So all that remained of the three armies of Karnith Zo settled in the conquered city. And presently the men of Zeenar crossed over the river Eidis and easily conquering an army of aged men took all Alatta for themselves, and their kings reigned thereafter in the city of Zoon. And sometimes the men of Zeenar listened to the strange tales that the old Alattans told of the years when they made battle against Time. Such of these tales as the men of Zeenar remembered they afterwards set forth, and this is all that may be told of those adventurous armies that went to war with Time to save the world and the gods, and were overwhelmed by the hours and the years.

THE RELENTING OF SARNIDAC

The lame boy Sarnidac tended sheep on a hill to the southward of the city. Sarnidac was a dwarf and greatly derided in the city. For the women said:

"It is very funny that Sarnidac is a dwarf," and they would point their fingers at him saying:—"This is Sarnidac, he is a dwarf; also he is very lame."

Once the doors of all the temples in the world swung open to the morning, and Sarnidac with his sheep upon the hill saw strange figures going down the white road, always southwards. All the morning he saw the dust rising above the strange figures and always they went southwards right as far as the rim of the Nydoon hills where the white road could be seen no more. And the figures stooped and seemed to be larger than men, but all men seemed very large to Sarnidac, and he could not see clearly through the dust. And Sarnidac shouted to them, as he hailed all people that passed down the long white road, and none of the figures looked to left or right and none of them turned to answer Sarnidac. But then few people ever answered him because he was lame, and a small dwarf.

Still the figures went striding swiftly, stooping forward through the dust, till at last Sarnidac came running down his hill to watch them closer. As he came to the white road the last of the figures passed him, and Sarnidac ran limping behind him down the road.

For Sarnidac was weary of the city wherein all derided him, and when he saw these figures all hurrying away he thought that they went perhaps to some other city beyond the hills over which the sun shone brighter, or where there was more food, for he was poor, even perhaps where people had not the custom of laughing at Sarnidac. So this procession of figures that stooped and seemed larger than men went southward down the road and a lame dwarf hobbled behind them.

Khamazan, now called the City of the Last of Temples, lies southward of the Nydoon hills. This is the story of Pompeides, now chief prophet of the only temple in the world, and greatest of all the prophets that have been:

On the slopes of Nydoon I was seated once above Khamazan. There I saw figures in the morning striding through much dust along the road that leads across the world. Striding up the hill they came towards me, not with the gait of men, and soon the first one came to the crest of the hill where the road dips to find the plains again, where lies Khamazan. And now I swear by all the gods that are gone that this thing happened as I shall say it, and was surely so. When those that came striding up the hill came to its summit they took not the road that goes down into the plains nor trod the dust any longer, but went straight on and upwards, striding as they strode before, as though the hill had not ended nor the road dipped. And they strode as though they trod no yielding substance, yet they stepped upwards through the air.

This the gods did, for They were not born men who strode that day so strangely away from earth.

But I, when I saw this thing, when already three had passed me, leaving earth, cried out before the fourth:

'Gods of my childhood, guardians of little homes, whither are ye going, leaving the round earth to swim alone and forgotten in so great a waste of sky?'

And one answered:

'Heresy apace shoots her fierce glare over the world and men's faith grows dim and the gods go. Men shall make iron gods and gods of steel when the wind and the ivy meet within the shrines of the temples of the gods of old.'

And I left that place as a man leaves fire by night, and going plainwards down the white road that the gods spurned cried out to all that I passed to follow me, and so crying came to the city's gates. And there I shouted to all near the gates:

'From yonder hilltop the gods are leaving earth.'

Then I gathered many, and we all hastened to the hill to pray the gods to tarry, and there we cried out to the last of the departing gods:

'Gods of old prophecy and of men's hopes, leave not the earth, and all our worship shall hum about Your ears as never it hath before, and oft the sacrifice shall squeal upon Your altars.'

And I said:—

'Gods of still evenings and quiet nights, go not from earth and leave not Your carven shrines, and all men shall worship You still. For between us and yonder still blue spaces oft roam the thunder and the storms, there in his hiding lurks the dark eclipse, and there are stored all snows and hails and lightnings that shall vex the earth for a million years. Gods of our hopes, how shall men's prayers crying from empty shrines pass through such terrible spaces; how shall they ever fare above the thunder and many storms to whatever place the gods may go in that blue waste beyond?'

But the gods bent straight forward, and trampled through the sky and looked not to the right nor left nor downwards, nor ever heeded my prayer.

And one cried out hoping yet to stay the gods, though nearly all were gone, saying:—

'O gods, rob not the earth of the dim hush that hangs round all Your temples, bereave not all the world of old romance, take not the glamour from the moonlight nor tear the wonder out of the white mists in every land; for, O ye gods of the childhood of the world, when You have left the earth you shall have taken the mystery from the sea and all its glory from antiquity, and You shall have wrenched out hope from the dim future. There shall be no strange cries at night time half understood, nor songs in the twilight, and the whole of the wonder shall have died with last year's flowers in little gardens or hill-slopes leaning south; for with the gods must go the enchantment of the plains and all the magic of dark woods, and something shall be lacking from the quiet of early dawn. For it would scarce befit the gods to leave the earth and not take with Them that which They had given it. Out beyond the still blue spaces Ye will need the holiness of sunset for Yourselves and little sacred memories and the thrill that is in stories told by firesides long ago. One strain of music, one song, one line of poetry and one kiss, and a memory of one pool with rushes, and each one the best, shall the gods take to whom the best belongs, when the gods go.

'Sing a lamentation, people of Khamazan, sing a lamentation for all the children of earth at the feet of the departing gods. Sing a lamentation for the children of earth who now must carry their prayers to empty shrines and around empty shrines must rest at last.'

Then when our prayers were ended and our tears shed, we beheld the last and smallest of the gods halted upon the hilltop. Twice he called to Them with a cry somewhat like the cry wherewith our shepherds hail their brethren, and long gazed after Them, and then deigned to look no longer and to tarry upon earth and turn his eyes on men. Then a great shout went up when we saw that our hopes were saved and that there was still on earth a haven for our prayers. Smaller than men now seemed the figures that had loomed so big, as one behind the other far over our heads They still strode upwards. But the small god that had pitied the world came with us down the hill, still deigning to tread the road, though strangely, not as men tread, and into Khamazan. There we housed him in the palace of the King, for that was before the building of the temple of gold, and the King made sacrifice before him with his own hands, and he that had pitied the world did eat the flesh of the sacrifice.

And the Book of the Knowledge of the gods in Khamazan tells how the small god that pitied the world told his prophets that his name was Sarnidac and that he herded sheep, and that therefore he is called the shepherd god, and sheep are sacrificed upon his altars thrice a day, and the North, East, West and the South are the four hurdles of Sarnidac and the white clouds are his sheep. And the Book of the Knowledge of the gods tells further how the day on which Pompeides found the gods shall be kept for ever as a fast until the evening and called the Fast of the Departing, but in the evening shall a feast be held which is named the Feast of the Relenting, for on that evening Sarnidac pitied the whole world and tarried.

And the people of Khamazan all prayed to Sarnidac, and dreamed their dreams and hoped their hopes because their temple was not empty.

Whether the gods that are departed be greater than Sarnidac none know in Khamazan, but some believe that in their azure windows They have set lights that lost prayers swarming upwards may come to them like moths and at last find haven and light far up above the evening and the stillness where sit the gods.

But Sarnidac wondered at the strange figures, at the people of Khamazan, and at the palace of the King and the customs of the prophets, but wondered not more greatly at aught in Khamazan than he had wondered at the city which he had left. For Sarnidac, who had not known why men were unkind to him, thought that he had found at last the land for which the gods had let him hope, where men should have the custom of being kind to Sarnidac.

THE JEST OF THE GODS

Once the Older gods had need of laughter. Therefore They made the soul of a king, and set in it ambitions greater than kings should have, and lust for territories beyond the lust of other kings, and in this soul They set strength beyond the strength of others and fierce desire for power and a strong pride. Then the gods pointed earthward and sent that soul into the fields of men to live in the body of a slave. And the slave grew, and the pride and lust for power began to arise in his heart, and he wore shackles on his arms. Then in the Fields of Twilight the gods prepared to laugh.

But the slave went down to the shore of the great sea, and cast his body away and the shackles that were upon it, and strode back to the Fields of Twilight and stood up before the gods and looked Them in Their faces. This thing the gods, when They had prepared to laugh, had not foreseen. Lust for power burned strong in that King's soul, and there was all the strength and pride in it that the gods had placed therein, and he was too strong for the Older gods. He whose body had borne the lashes of men could brook no longer the dominion of the gods, and standing before Them he bade the gods to go. Up to Their lips leapt all the anger of the Older gods, being for the first time commanded, but the King's soul faced Them still, and Their anger died away and They averted Their eyes. Then Their thrones became empty, and the Fields of Twilight bare as the gods slunk far away. But the soul chose new companions.

THE DREAMS OF THE PROPHET

I

When the gods drave me forth to toil and assailed me with thirst and beat me down with hunger, then I prayed to the gods. When the gods smote the cities wherein I dwelt, and when Their anger scorched me and Their eyes burned, then did I praise the gods and offer sacrifice. But when I came again to my green land and found that all was gone, and the old mysterious haunts wherein I prayed as a child were gone, and when the gods tore up the dust and even the spider's web from the last remembered nook, then did I curse the gods, speaking it to Their faces, saying:—

"Gods of my prayers! Gods of my sacrifice! because Ye have forgotten the sacred places of my childhood, and they have therefore ceased to be, yet may I not forget. Because Ye have done this thing, Ye shall see cold altars and shall lack both my fear and praise. I shall not wince at Your lightnings, nor be awed when Ye go by."

Then looking seawards I stood and cursed the gods, and at this moment there came to me one in the garb of a poet, who said:—

"Curse not the gods."

And I said to him:

"Wherefore should I not curse Those that have stolen my sacred places in the night, and trodden down the gardens of my childhood?"

And he said "Come, and I will show thee." And I followed him to where two camels stood with their faces towards the desert. And we set out and I travelled with him for a great space, he speaking never a word, and so we came at last to a waste valley hid in the desert's midst. And herein, like fallen moons, I saw vast ribs that stood up white out of the sand, higher than the hills of the desert. And here and there lay the enormous shapes of skulls like the white marble domes of palaces built for tyrannous kings a long while since by armies of driven slaves. Also there lay in the desert other bones, the bones of vast legs and arms, against which the desert, like a besieging sea, ever advanced and already had half drowned. And as I gazed in wonder at these colossal things the poet said to me:

"The gods are dead."

And I gazed long in silence, and I said:

"These fingers, that are now so dead and so very white and still, tore once the flowers in gardens of my youth."

But my companion said to me:

"I have brought thee here to ask of thee thy forgiveness of the gods, for I, being a poet, knew the gods, and would fain drive off the curses that hover above Their bones and bring Them men's forgiveness as an offering at the last, that the weeds and the ivy may cover Their bones from the sun."

And I said:

"They made Remorse with his fur grey like a rainy evening in the autumn, with many rending claws, and Pain with his hot hands and lingering feet, and Fear like a rat with two cold teeth carved each out of the ice of either pole, and Anger with the swift flight of the dragonfly in summer having burning eyes. I will not forgive these gods."

But the poet said:

"Canst thou be angry with these beautiful white bones?" And I looked long at those curved and beautiful bones that were no longer able to hurt the smallest creature in all the worlds that they had made. And I thought long of the evil that they had done, and also of the good. But when I thought of Their great hands coming red and wet from battles to make a primrose for a child to pick, then I forgave the gods.

And a gentle rain came falling out of heaven and stilled the restless sand, and a soft green moss grew suddenly and covered the bones till they looked like strange green hills, and I heard a cry and awoke and found that I had dreamed, and looking out of my house into the street I found that a flash of lightning had killed a child. Then I knew that the gods still lived.

II

I lay asleep in the poppy fields of the gods in the valley of Alderon, where the gods come by night to meet together in council when the moon is low. And I dreamed that this was the Secret.

Fate and Chance had played their game and ended, and all was over, all the hopes and tears, regrets, desires and sorrows, things that men wept for and unremembered things, and kingdoms and little gardens and the sea, and the worlds and the moons and the suns; and what remained was nothing, having neither colour nor sound.

Then said Fate to Chance: "Let us play our old game again." And they played it again together, using the gods as pieces, as they had played it oft before. So that those things which have been shall all be again, and under the same bank in the same land a sudden glare of singlight on the same spring day shall bring the same daffodil to bloom once more and the same child shall pick it, and not regretted shall be the billion years that fell between. And the same old faces shall be seen again, yet not bereaved of their familiar haunts. And you and I shall in a garden meet again upon an afternoon in summer when the sun stands midway between his zenith and the sea, where we met oft before. For Fate and Chance play but one game together with every move the same, and they play it oft to while eternity away.

THE JOURNEY OF THE KING

I

One day the King turned to the women that danced and said to them: "Dance no more," and those that bore the wine in jewelled cups he sent away. The palace of King Ebalon was emptied of sound of song and there rose the voices of heralds crying in the streets to find the prophets of the land.

Then went the dancers, the cupbearer and the singers down into the hard streets among the houses, Pattering Leaves, Silvern Fountain and Summer Lightning, the dancers whose feet the gods had not devised for stony ways, which had only danced for princes. And with them went the singer, Soul of the South, and the sweet singer, Dream of the Sea, whose voices the gods had attuned to the ears of kings, and old Istahn the cupbearer left his life's work in the palace to tread the common ways, he that had stood at the elbows of three kings of Zarkandhu and had watched his ancient vintage feeding their valour and mirth as the waters of Tondaris feed the green plains to the south. Ever he had stood grave among their jests, but his heart warmed itself solely by the fire of the mirth of Kings. He too, with the singers and dancers, went out into the dark.

And throughout the land the heralds sought out the prophets thereof. Then one evening as King Ebalon sat alone within his palace there were brought before him all who had repute for wisdom and who wrote the histories of the times to be. Then the King spake, saying: "The King goeth upon a journey with many horses, yet riding upon none, when the pomp of travelling shall be heard in the streets and the sound of the lute and the drum and the name of the King. And I would know what princes and what people shall greet me on the other shore in the land to which I travel."

Then fell a hush upon the prophets for they murmured: "All knowledge is with the King."

Then said the King: "Thou first, Samahn, High Prophet of the Temple of gold in Azinorn, answer or thou shalt write no more the history of the times to be, but shalt toil with thy hand to make record of the little happenings of the days that were, as do the common men."

Then said Samahn: "All knowledge is with the King," and when the pomp of travelling shall be heard in the streets and the slow horses whereon the King rideth not go behind lute and drum, then, as the King well knoweth, thou shalt go down to the great white house of Kings and, entering the portals where none are worthy to follow, shalt make obeisance alone to all the elder Kings of Zarkandhu, whose bones are seated upon golden thrones grasping their sceptres still. Therein thou shalt go with robes and sceptre through the marble porch, but thou shalt leave behind thee thy gleaming crown that others may wear it, and as the times go by come in to swell the number of the thirty Kings that sit in the great white house on golden thrones. There is one doorway in the great white house, and it stands wide with marble portals yawning for kings, but when it shall receive thee, and thine obeisance hath been made because of thine obligation to the thirty Kings, thou shalt find at the back of the house an unknown door through which the soul of a King may just pass, and leaving thy bones upon a golden throne thou shalt go unseen out of the great white house to tread the velvet spaces that lie among the worlds. Then, O King, it were well to travel fast and not to tarry about the houses of men as do the souls of some who still bewail the sudden murder that sent them upon the journey before their time, and who, being yet both to go, linger in dark chambers all the night. These, setting forth to travel in the dawn and travelling all the day, see earth behind them gleaming when an evening falls, and again are loth to leave its pleasant haunts, and come back again through dark woods and up into some old loved chamber, and ever tarry between home and flight and find no rest.

Thou wilt set forth at once because the journey is far and lasts for many hours; but the hours on the velvet spaces are the hours of the gods, and we may not say what time such an hour may be if reckoned in mortal years.

At last thou shalt come to a grey place filled with mist, with grey shapes standing before it which are altars, and on the altars rise small red flames from dying fires that scarce illumine the mist. And in the mist it is dark and cold because the fires are low. These are the altars of the people's faiths, and the flames are the worship of men, and through the mist the gods of Old go groping in the dark and in the cold. There thou shalt hear a voice cry feebly: "Inyani, Inyani, lord of the thunder, where art thou, for I cannot see?" And a voice shall answer faintly in the cold: "O maker of many worlds, I am here." And in that place the gods of Old are nearly deaf for the prayers of men grow few, they are nigh blind because the fires burn low upon the altars of men's faiths and they are very cold. And all about the place of mist there lies a moaning sea which is called the Sea of Souls. And behind the place of mist are the dim shapes of mountains, and on the peak of one there glows a silvern light that shines in the moaning sea; and ever as the flames on the altars die before the gods of Old the light on the mountain increases, and the light shines over the mist and never through it as the gods of Old grow blind. It is said that the light on the mountain shall one day become a new god who is not of the gods of Old.

There, O King, thou shalt enter the Sea of Souls by the shore where the altars stand which are covered in mist. In that sea are the souls of all that ever lived on the worlds and all that ever shall live, all freed from earth and flesh. And all the souls in that sea are aware of one another but more than with hearing or sight or by taste or touch or smell, and they all speak to each other yet not with lips, with voices which need no sound. And over the sea lies music as winds o'er an ocean on earth, and there unfettered by language great thoughts set outward through the souls as on earth the currents go.

Once did I dream that in a mist-built ship I sailed upon that sea and heard the music that is not of instruments, and voices not from lips, and woke and found that I was upon the earth and that the gods had lied to me in the night. Into this sea from fields of battle and cities come down the rivers of lives, and ever the gods have taken onyx cups and far and wide into the worlds again have flung the souls out of the sea, that each soul may find a prison in the body of a man with five small windows closely barred, and each one shackled with forgetfulness.

But all the while the light on the mountain grows, and none may say what work the god that shall be born of the silvern light shall work on the Sea of Souls, when the gods of Old are dead and the Sea is living still.

And answer made the King:

"Thou that art a prophet of the gods of Old, go back and see that those red flames burn more brightly on the altars in the mist, for the gods of Old are easy and pleasant gods, and thou canst not say what toil shall vex our souls when the god of the light on the mountain shall stride along the shore where bleach the huge bones of the gods of Old."

And Samahn answered: "All knowledge is with the King."

II

Then the King called to Ynath bidding him speak concerning the journey of the King. Ynath was the prophet that sat at the Eastern gate of the Temple of Gorandhu. There Ynath prayed his prayers to all the passers by lest ever the gods should go abroad, and one should pass him dressed in mortal guise. And men are pleased as they walk by that Eastern gate that Ynath should pray to them for fear that they be gods, so men bring gifts to Ynath in the Eastern gate.

And Ynath said: "All knowledge is with the King. When a strange ship comes to anchor in the air outside thy chamber window, thou shalt leave thy well-kept garden and it shall become a prey to the nights and days and be covered again with grass. But going aboard thou shalt set sail over the Sea of Time and well shall the ship steer through the many worlds and still sail on. If other ships shall pass thee on the way and hail thee saying: 'From what port' thou shalt answer them: 'From Earth.' And if they ask thee 'whither bound?' then thou shalt answer: 'The End.' Or thou shalt hail them saying: 'From what port?' And they shall answer: 'From The End called also The Beginning, and bound to Earth.' And thou shalt sail away till like an old sorrow dimly felt by happy men the worlds shall gleam in the distance like one star, and as the star pales thou shalt come to the shore of space where aeons rolling shorewards from Time's sea shall lash up centuries to foam away in years. There lies the Centre Garden of the gods, facing full seawards. All around lie songs that on earth were never sung, fair thoughts not heard among the worlds, dream pictures never seen that drifted over Time without a home till at last the aeons swept them on to the shore of space. And in the Centre Garden of the gods bloom many fancies. Therein once some souls were playing where the gods walked up and down and to and fro. And a dream came in more beauteous than the rest on the crest of a wave of Time, and one soul going downward to the shore clutched at the dream and caught it. Then over the dreams and stories and old songs that lay on the shore of space the hours came sweeping back, and the centuries caught that soul and swirled him with his dream far out to the Sea of Time, and the aeons swept him earthwards and cast him into a palace with all the might of the sea and left him there with his dream. The child grew to a King and still clutched at his dream till the people wondered and laughed. Then, O King, Thou didst cast thy dream back into the Sea, and Time drowned it and men laughed no more, but thou didst forget that a certain sea beat on a distant shore and that there was a garden and therein souls. But at the end of the journey that thou shalt take, when thou comest to the shore of space again thou shalt go up the beach, and coming to a garden gate that stands in a garden wall shalt remember these things again, for it stands where the hours assail not above the beating of Time, far up the shore, and nothing altereth there. So thou shalt go through the garden gate and hear again the whispering of the souls when they talk low where sing the voices of the gods. There with kindred souls thou shalt speak as thou didst of yore and tell them what befell thee beyond the tides of time and how they took thee and made of thee a King so that thy soul found no rest. There in the Centre Garden thou shalt sit at ease and watch the gods all rainbow-clad go up and down and to and fro on the paths of dreams and songs, and shalt not venture down to the cheerless sea. For that which a man loves most is not on this side of Time, and all which drifts on its aeons is a lure.

"All knowledge is with the King."

Then said the King: "Ay, there was a dream once but Time hath swept it away."

III

Then spake Monith, Prophet of the Temple of Azure that stands on the snow-peak of Ahmoon and said: "All knowledge is with the King. Once thou didst set out upon a one day's journey riding thy horse and before thee had gone a beggar down the road, and his name was Yeb. Him thou didst overtake and when he heeded not thy coming thou didst ride over him.

"Upon the journey that thou shalt one day take riding upon no horse, this beggar has set out before thee and is labouring up the crystal steps towards the moon as a man goeth up the steps of a high tower in the dark. On the moon's edge beneath the shadow of Mount Angises he shall rest awhile and then shall climb the crystal steps again. Then a great journey lies before him before he may rest again till he come to that star that is called the left eye of Gundo. Then a journey of many crystal steps lieth before him again with nought to guide him but the light of Omrazu. On the edge of Omrazu shall Yeb tarry long, for the most dreadful part of his journey lieth before him. Up the crystal steps that lie beyond Omrazu he must go, and any that follow, though the howling of all the meteors that ride the sky; for in that part of the crystal space go many meteors up and down all squealing in the dark, which greatly perplex all travellers. And, if he may see though the gleaming of the meteors and in spite of their uproar come safely through, he shall come to the star Omrund at the edge of the Track of Stars. And from star to star along the Track of Stars the soul of a man may travel with more ease, and there the journey lies no more straight forward, but curves to the right."

Then said King Ebalon:

"Of this beggar whom my horse smote down thou hast spoken much, but I sought to know by what road a King should go when he taketh his last royal journey, and what princes and what people should meet him upon another shore."

Then answered Monith:

"All knowledge is with the King. It hath been doomed by the gods, who speak not in jest, that thou shalt follow the soul that thou didst send alone upon its journey, that that soul go not unattended up the crystal steps.

"Moreover, as this beggar went upon his lonely journey he dared to curse the King, and his curses lie like a red mist along the valleys and hollows wherever he uttered them. By these red mists, O King, thou shalt track him as a man follows a river by night until thou shalt fare at last to the land wherein he hath blessed thee (repenting of anger at last), and thou shalt see his blessing lie over the land like a blaze of golden sunshine illumining fields and gardens."

Then said the King:

"The gods have spoken hard above the snowy peak of this mountain Ahmoon."

And Monith said:

"How a man may come to the shore of space beyond the tides of time I know not, but it is doomed that thou shalt certainly first follow the beggar past the moon, Omrund and Omrazu till thou comest to the Track of Stars, and up the Track of Stars coming towards the right along the edge of it till thou comest to Ingazi. There the soul of the beggar Yeb sat long, then, breathing deep, set off on his great journey earthward adown the crystal steps. Straight through the spaces where no stars are found to rest at, following the dull gleam of earth and her fields till he come at last where journeys end and start."

Then said King Ebalon:

"If this hard tale be true, how shall I find the beggar that I must follow when I come again to the earth?"

And the Prophet answered:

"Thou shalt know him by his name and find him in this place, for that beggar shall be called King Ebalon and he shall be sitting upon the throne of the Kings of Zarkandhu."

And the King answered:

"If one sit upon this throne whom men call King Ebalon, who then shall I be?"

And the Prophet answered:

"Thou shalt be a beggar and thy name shall be Yeb, and thou shalt ever tread the road before the palace waiting for alms from the King whom men shall call Ebalon."

Then said the King:

"Hard gods indeed are those that tramp the snows of Ahmoon about the temple of Azure, for if I sinned against this beggar called Yeb, they too have sinned against him when they doomed him to travel on this weary journey though he hath not offended."

And Monith said:

"He too hath offended, for he was angry as thy horse struck him, and the gods smite anger. And his anger and his curses doom him to journey without rest as also they doom thee."

Then said the King:

"Thou that sittest upon Ahmoon in the Temple of Azure, dreaming thy dreams and making prophecies, foresee the ending of this weary quest and tell me where it shall be?"

And Monith answered:

"As a man looks across great lakes I have gazed into the days to be, and as the great flies come upon four wings of gauze to skim over blue waters, so have my dreams come sailing two by two out of the days to be. And I dreamed that King Ebalon, whose soul was not thy soul, stood in his palace in a time far hence, and beggars thronged the street outside, and among them was Yeb, a beggar, having thy soul. And it was on the morning of a festival and the King came robed in white, with all his prophets and his seers and magicians, all down the marble steps to bless the land and all that stood therein as far as the purple hills, because it was the morning of festival. And as the King raised up his hand over the beggars' heads to bless the fields and rivers and all that stood therein, I dreamed that the quest was ended.

"All knowledge is with the King."

IV

Evening darkened and above the palace domes gleamed out the stars whereon haply others missed the secret too.

And outside the palace in the dark they that had borne the wine in jewelled cups mocked in low voices at the King and at the wisdom of his prophets.

Then spake Ynar, called the prophet of the Crystal Peak; for there rises Amanath above all that land, a mountain whose peak is crystal, and Ynar beneath its summit hath his Temple, and when day shines no longer on the world Amanath takes the sunlight and gleams afar as a beacon in a bleak land lit at night. And at the hour when all faces are turned on Amanath, Ynar comes forth beneath the Crystal peak to weave strange spells and to make signs that people say are surely for the gods. Therefore it is said in all those lands that Ynar speaks at evening to the gods when all the world is still.

And Ynar said:

"All knowledge is with the King, and without doubt it hath come to the King's ears how certain speech is held at evening on the Peak of Amanath.

"They that speak to me at evening on the Peak are They that live in a city through whose streets Death walketh not, and I have heard it from Their Elders that the King shall take no journey; only from thee the hills shall slip away, the dark woods, the sky and all the gleaming worlds that fill the night, and the green fields shall go on untrodden by thy feet and the blue sky ungazed at by thine eyes, and still the rivers shall all run seaward but making no music in thine ears. And all the old laments shall still be spoken, troubling thee not, and to the earth shall fall the tears of the children of earth and never grieving thee. Pestilence, heat and cold, ignorance, famine and anger, these things shall grip their claws upon all men as heretofore in fields and roads and cities but shall not hold thee. But from thy soul, sitting in the old worn track of the worlds when all is gone away, shall fall off the shackles of circumstance and thou shalt dream thy dreams alone.

"And thou shalt find that dreams are real where there is nought as far as the Rim but only thy dreams and thee.

"With them thou shalt build palaces and cities resting upon nothing and having no place in time, not to be assailed by the hours or harmed by ivy or rust, not to be taken by conquerors, but destroyed by thy fancy if thou dost wish it so or by thy fancy rebuilded. And nought shall ever disturb these dreams of thine which here are troubled and lost by all the happenings of earth, as the dreams of one who sleeps in a tumultuous city. For these thy dreams shall sweep outward like a strong river over a great waste plain wherein are neither rocks nor hills to turn it, only in that place there shall be no boundaries nor sea, neither hindrance nor end. And it were well for thee that thou shouldst take few regrets into thy waste dominions from the world wherein thou livest, for such regrets or any memory of deeds ill done must sit beside thy soul forever in that waste, singing one song always of forlorn remorse; and they too shall be only dreams but very real.

"There nought shall hinder thee among thy dreams, for even the gods may harass thee no more when flesh and earth and events with which They bound thee shall have slipped away."

Then said the King:

"I like not this grey doom, for dreams are empty. I would see action roaring through the world, and men and deeds."

Then answered the Prophet:

"Victory, jewels and dancing but please thy fancy. What is the sparkle of the gem to thee without thy fancy which it allures, and thy fancy is all a dream. Action and deeds and men are nought without dreams and do but fetter them, and only dreams are real, and where thou stayest when the worlds shall drift away there shall be only dreams."

And the King answered:

"A mad prophet."

And Ynar said:

"A mad prophet, but believing that his soul possesseth all things of which his soul may become aware and that he is master of that soul, and thou a high-minded King believing only that thy soul possesseth such few countries as are leaguered by thine armies and the sea, and that thy soul is possessed by certain strange gods of whom thou knowest not, who shall deal with it in a way whereof thou knowest not. Until a knowledge come to us that either is wrong I have wider realms, I King, than thee and hold them beneath no overlords."

Then said the King:

"Thou hast said no overlords! To whom then dost thou speak by strange signs at evening above the world?"

And Ynar went forward and whispered to the King. And the King shouted:

"Seize ye this prophet for he is a hypocrite and speaks to no gods at evening above the world, but has deceived us with his signs."

And Ynar said:

"Come not near me or I shall point towards you when I speak at evening upon the mountain with Those that ye know of."

Then Ynar went away and the guards touched him not.

V

Then spake the prophet Thun, who was clad in seaweed and had no Temple, but lived apart from men. All his life he had lived on a lonely beach and had heard for ever the wailing of the sea and the crying of the wind in hollows among the cliffs. Some said that having lived so long by the full beating of the sea, and where always the wind cries loudest, he could not feel the joys of other men, but only felt the sorrow of the sea crying in his soul for ever.

"Long ago on the path of stars, midmost between the worlds, there strode the gods of Old. In the bleak middle of the worlds They sat and the worlds went round and round, like dead leaves in the wind at Autumn's end, with never a life on one, while the gods went sighing for the things that might not be. And the centuries went over the gods to go where the centuries go, toward the End of Things, and with Them went the sighs of all the gods as They longed for what might not be.

"One by one in the midst of the worlds, fell dead the gods of Old, still sighing for the things that might not be, all slain by Their own regrets. Only Shimono Kani, the youngest of the gods, made him a harp out of the heart strings of all the elder gods, and, sitting upon the Path of Stars in the Middle of Things, played upon the harp a dirge for the gods of Old. And the song told of all vain regrets and of unhappy loves of the gods in the olden time, and of Their great deeds that were to adorn the future years. But into the dirge of Shimono Kani came voices crying out of the heart strings of the gods, all sighing still for the things that might not be. And the dirge and the voices crying, go drifting away from the Path of Stars, away from the Midst of Things, till they come twittering among the Worlds, like a great host of birds that are lost by night. And every note is a life, and many notes become caught up among the worlds to be entangled with flesh for a little while before they pass again on their journey to the great Anthem that roars at the End of Time. Shimono Kani hath given a voice to the wind and added a sorrow to the sea. But when in lighted chambers after feasting there arises the voice of the singer to please the King, then is the soul of that singer crying aloud to his fellows from where he stands chained to earth. And when at the sound of the singing the heart of the King grows sad and his princes lament then they remember, though knowing not that, they remember it, the sad face of Shimono Kani sitting by his dead brethren, the elder gods, playing on the harp of crying heart strings whereby he sent their souls among the worlds.

"And when the music of one lute is lonely on the hills at night, then one soul calleth to his brother souls—the notes of Shimono Kani's dirge which have not been caught among the worlds—and he knoweth not to whom he calls or why, but knoweth only that minstrelsy is his only cry and sendeth it out into the dark.

"But although in the prison houses of earth all memories must die, yet as there sometimes clings to a prisoner's feet some dust of the fields wherein he was captured, so sometimes fragments of remembrance cling to a man's soul after it hath been taken to earth. Then a great minstrel arises, and, weaving together the shreds of his memories, maketh some melody such as the hand of Shimono Kani smites out of his harp; and they that pass by say: 'Hath there not been some such melody before?' and pass on sad at heart for memories which are not.

"Therefore, O King, one day the great gates of thy palace shall lie open for a procession wherein the King comes down to pass through a people, lamenting with lute and drum; and on the same day a prison door shall be opened by relenting hands, and one more lost note of Shimono Kani's dirge shall go back to swell his melody again.

"The dirge of Shimono Kani shall roll on till one day it shall come with all its notes complete to overwhelm the Silence that sits at the End of Things. Then shall Shimono Kani say to his brethren's bones: The things that might not be have at last become.'

"But very quiet shall be the bones of the gods of Old, and only Their voices shall live which cried from the harp of heart strings, for the things which might not be."

VI

When the caravans, saying farewell to Zandara, set out across the waste northwards towards Einandhu, they follow the desert track for seven days before they come to water where Shubah Onath rises black out of the waste, with a well at its foot and herbage on its summit. On this rock a prophet hath his Temple and is called the Prophet of Journeys, and hath carven in a southern window smiling along the camel track all gods that are benignant to caravans.

There a traveller may learn by prophecy whether he shall accomplish the ten days' journey thence across the desert and so come to the white city of Einandhu, or whether his bones shall lie with the bones of old along the desert track.

No name hath the Prophet of Journeys, for none is needed in that desert where no man calls nor ever a man answers.

Thus spake the Prophet of Journeys standing before the King:

"The journey of the King shall be an old journey pushed on apace.

"Many a year before the making of the moon thou camest down with dream camels from the City without a name that stands beyond all the stars. And then began thy journey over the Waste of Nought, and thy dream camel bore thee well when those of certain of thy fellow travellers fell down in the Waste and were covered over by the silence and were turned again to nought; and those travellers when their dream camels fell, having nothing to carry them further over the Waste, were lost beyond and never found the earth. These are those men that might have been but were not. And all about thee fluttered the myriad hours travelling in great swarms across the Waste of Nought.

"How many centuries passed across the cities while thou wast making thy journey none may reckon, for there is no time in the Waste of Nought, but only the hours fluttering earthwards from beyond to do the work of Time. At last the dream-borne travellers saw far off a green place gleaming and made haste towards it and so came to Earth. And there, O King, ye rest for a little while, thou and those that came with thee, making an encampment upon earth before journeying on. There the swarming hours alight, settling on every blade of grass and tree, and spreading over your tents and devouring all things, and at last bending your very tent poles with their weight and wearying you.

"Behind the encampment in the shadow of the tents lurks a dark figure with a nimble sword, having the name of Time. This is he that hath called the hours from beyond and he it is that is their master, and it is his work that the hours do as they devour all green things upon the earth and tatter the tents and weary all the travellers. As each of the hours does the work of Time, Time smites him with his nimble sword as soon as his work is done, and the hour falls severed to the dust with his bright wings scattered, as a locust cut asunder by the scimitar of a skillful swordsman.

"One by one, O King, with a stir in the camp, and the folding up of the tents one by one, the travellers shall push on again on the journey begun so long before out of the City without a name to the place where dream camels go, striding free through the Waste. So into the Waste, O King, thou shalt set forth ere long, perhaps to renew friendships begun during thy short encampment upon earth.

"Other green places thou shalt meet in the Waste and thereon shalt encamp again until driven thence by the hours. What prophet shall relate how many journeys thou shalt make or how many encampments? But at last thou shalt come to the place of The Resting of Camels, and there shall gleaming cliffs that are named The Ending of Journeys lift up out of the Waste of Nought, Nought at their feet, Nought laying wide before them, with only the glint of worlds far off to illumine the Waste. One by one, on tired dream camels, the travellers shall come in, and going up the pathway through the cliff in that land of The Resting of Camels shall come on The City of Ceasing. There, the dream-wrought pinnacles and the spires that are builded of men's hopes shall rise up real before thee, seen only hitherto as a mirage in the Waste.

"So far the swarming hours may not come, and far away among the tents shall stand the dark figure with the nimble sword. But in the scintillant streets, under the song-built abodes of the last of cities, thy journey, O King, shall end."

VII

In the valley beyond Sidono there lies a garden of poppies, and where the poppies' heads are all a-swing with summer breezes that go up the valley there lies a path well strewn with ocean shells. Over Sidono's summit the birds come streaming to the lake that lies in the valley of the garden, and behind them rises the sun sending Sidono's shadow as far as the edge of the lake. And down the path of many ocean shells when they begin to gleam in the sun, every morning walks an aged man clad in a silken robe with strange devices woven. A little temple where the old man lives stands at the edge of the path. None worship there, for Zornadhu, the old prophet, hath forsaken men to walk among his poppies.

For Zornadhu hath failed to understand the purport of Kings and cities and the moving up and down of many people to the tune of the clinking of gold. Therefore hath Zornadhu gone far away from the sound of cities and from those that are ensnared thereby, and beyond Sidono's mountain hath come to rest where there are neither kings nor armies nor bartering for gold, but only the heads of the poppies that sway in the wind together and the birds that fly from Sidono to the lake, and then the sunrise over Sidono's summit; and afterwards the flight of birds out of the lake and over Sidono again, and sunset behind the valley, and high over lake and garden the stars that know not cities. There Zornadhu lives in his garden of poppies with Sidono standing between him and the whole world of men; and when the wind blowing athwart the valley sways the heads of the tall poppies against the Temple wall, the old prophet says: "The flowers are all praying, and lo! they be nearer to the gods than men."

But the heralds of the King coming after many days of travel to Sidono perceived the garden valley. By the lake they saw the poppy garden gleaming round and small like a sunrise over water on a misty morning seen by some shepherd from the hills. And descending the bare mountain for three days they came to the gaunt pines, and ever between the tall trunks came the glare of the poppies that shone from the garden valley. For a whole day they travelled through the pines. That night a cold wind came up the garden valley crying against the poppies. Low in his Temple, with a song of exceeding grief, Zornadhu in the morning made a dirge for the passing of poppies, because in the night time there had fallen petals that might not return or ever come again into the garden valley. Outside the Temple on the path of ocean shells the heralds halted, and read the names and honours of the King; and from the Temple came the voice of Zornadhu still singing his lament. But they took him from his garden because of the King's command, and down his gleaming path of ocean shells and away up Sidono, and left the Temple empty with none to lament when silken poppies died. And the will of the wind of the autumn was wrought upon the poppies, and the heads of the poppies that rose from the earth went down to the earth again, as the plume of a warrior smitten in a heathen fight far away, where there are none to lament him. Thus out of his land of flowers went Zornadhu and came perforce into the lands of men, and saw cities, and in the city's midst stood up before the King.

And the King said:

"Zornadhu, what of the journey of the King and of the princes and the people that shall meet me?"

Zornadhu answered:

"I know nought of Kings, but in the night time the poppy made his journey a little before dawn. Thereafter the wildfowl came as is their wont over Sidono's summit, and the sun rising behind them gleamed upon Sidono, and all the flowers of the lake awoke. And the bee passing up and down the garden went droning to other poppies, and the flowers of the lake, they that had known the poppy, knew him no more. And the sun's rays slanting from Sidono's crest lit still a garden valley where one poppy waved his petals to the dawn no more. And I, O King, that down a path of gleaming ocean shells walk in the morning, found not, nor have since found, that poppy again, that hath gone on the journey whence there is not returning, out of my garden valley. And I, O King, made a dirge to cry beyond that valley and the poppies bowed their heads; but there is no cry nor no lament that may adjure the life to return again to a flower that grew in a garden once and hereafter is not.

"Unto what place the lives of poppies have gone no man shall truly say. Sure it is that to that place are only outward tracks. Only it may be that when a man dreams at evening in a garden where heavily the scent of poppies hangs in the air, when the winds have sunk, and far away the sound of a lute is heard on lonely hills, as he dreams of silken-scarlet poppies that once were a-swing together in the gardens of his youth, the lives of those old lost poppies shall return, living again in his dream. *So there may dream the gods.* And through the dreams of some divinity reclining in tinted fields above the morning we may haply pass again, although our bodies have long swirled up and down the world with other dust. In these strange dreams our lives may be again, all in the centre of our hopes, rejoicings and laments, until above the morning the gods wake to go about their work, haply to remember still Their idle dreams, haply to dream them all again in the stillness when shines the starlight of the gods."

VIII

Then said the King: "I like not these strange journeys nor this faint wandering through the dreams of gods like the shadow of a weary camel that may not rest when the sun is low. The gods that have made me to love the earth's cool woods and dancing streams do ill to send me into the starry spaces that I love not, with my soul still peering earthward through the eternal years, as a beggar who once was noble staring from the street at lighted halls. For wherever the gods may send me I shall be as the gods have made me, a creature loving the green fields of earth.

"Now if there stand one prophet here that hath the ear of those too splendid gods that stride above the glories of the orient sky, tell them that there is on earth one King in the land called Zarkandhu to the south of the opal mountains, who would fain tarry among the many gardens of earth, and would leave to other men the splendours that the gods shall give the dead above the twilight that surrounds the stars."

Then spake Yamen, prophet of the Temple of Obin that stands on the shores of a great lake, facing east. Yamen said: "I pray oft to the gods who sit above the twilight behind the east. When the clouds are heavy and red at sunset, or when there is boding of thunder or eclipse, then I pray not, lest my prayers be scattered and beaten earthward. But when the sun sets in a tranquil sky, pale green or azure, and the light of his farewells stays long upon lonely hills, then I send forth my prayers to flutter upward to gods that are surely smiling, and the gods hear my prayers. But, O King, boons sought out of due time from the gods are never wholly to be desired, and, if They should grant to thee to tarry on the earth, old age would trouble thee with burdens more and more till thou wouldst become the driven slave of the hours in fetters that none may break."

The King said: "They that have devised this burden of age may surely stay it, pray therefore on the calmest evening of the year to the gods above the twilight that I may tarry always on the earth and always young, while over my head the scourges of the gods pass and alight not."

Then answered Yamen: "The King hath commanded, yet among the blessings of the gods there always cries a curse. The great princes that make merry with the King, who tell of the great deeds that the King wrought in the former time, shall one by one grow old. And thou, O King, seated at the feast crying, 'make merry' and extolling the former time shall find about thee white heads nodding in sleep, and men that are forgetting the former time. Then one by one the names of those that sported with thee once called by the gods, one by one the names of the singers that sing the songs thou lovest called by the gods, lastly of those that chased the grey boar by night and took him in Orghoom river—only the King. Then a new people that have not known the old deeds of the King nor fought and chased with him, who dare not make merry with the King as did his long dead princes. And all the while those princes that are dead growing dearer and greater in thy memory, and all the while the men that served thee then growing more small to thee. And all the old things fading and new things arising which are not as the old things were, the world changing yearly before thine eyes and the gardens of thy childhood overgrown. Because thy childhood was in the olden years thou shalt love the olden years, but ever the new years shall overthrow them and their customs, and not the will of a King may stay the changes that the gods have planned for all the customs of old. Ever thou shalt say 'This was not so,' and ever the new custom shall prevail even against a King. When thou hast made merry a thousand times thou shalt grow tired of making merry. At last thou shalt become weary of the chase, and still old age shall not come near to thee to stifle desires that have been too oft fulfilled; then, O King, thou shalt be a hunter yearning for the chase but with nought to pursue that hath not been oft overcome. Old age shall come not to bury thine ambitions in a time when there is nought for thee to aspire to any more. Experience of many centuries shall make thee wise but hard and very sad, and thou shalt be a mind apart from thy fellows and curse them all for fools, and they shall not perceive thy wisdom because thy thoughts are not their thoughts and the gods that they have made are not the gods of the olden time. No solace shall thy wisdom bring thee but only an increasing knowledge that thou knowest nought, and thou shalt feel as a wise man in a world of fools, or else as a fool in a world of wise men, when all men feel so sure and ever thy doubts increase. When all that spake with thee of thine old deeds are dead, those that saw them not shall speak of them again to thee; till one speaking to thee of thy deeds of valour add more than even a man should when speaking to a King, and thou shalt suddenly doubt whether these great deeds were; and there shall be none to tell thee, only the echoes of the voices of the gods still singing in thine ears when long ago They called the princes that were thy friends. And thou shalt hear the knowledge of the olden time most wrongly told and afterwards forgotten. Then many prophets shall arise claiming discovery of that old knowledge. Then thou shalt find that seeking knowledge is vain, as the chase is vain, as making merry is vain, as all things are vain. One day thou shalt find that it is vain to be a King. Greatly then will the acclamations of the people weary thee, till the time when people grow aweary of Kings. Then thou shalt know that thou hast been uprooted from thine olden time and set to live in uncongenial years, and jests all new to royal ears shall smite thee on the head like hailstones, when thou hast lost thy crown, when those to whose grandsires thou hadst granted to bring them as children to kiss the feet of the King shall mock at thee because thou hast not learnt to barter with gold.

"Not all the marvels of the future time shall atone to thee for those old memories that glow warmer and brighter every year as they recede into the ages that the gods have gathered. And always dreaming of thy long dead princes and of the great Kings of other kingdoms in the olden time thou shalt fail to see the grandeur to which a hurrying jesting people shall attain in that kingless age. Lastly, O King, thou shalt perceive men changing in a way that thou shalt not comprehend, knowing what thou canst not know, till thou shalt discover that these are men no more and a new race holds dominion over the earth whose forefathers were men. These shall speak to thee no more as they hurry upon a quest that thou shalt never understand, and thou shalt know that thou canst no longer take thy part in shaping destinies, but in a world of cities only pine for air and the waving grass again and the sound of a wind in trees. Then even this shall end with the shapes of the gods in the darkness gathering all lives but thine, when the hills shall fling up earth's long stored heat back to the heavens again, when earth shall be old and cold, with nothing alive upon it but one King."

Then said the King: "Pray to those hard gods still, for those that have loved the earth with all its gardens and woods and singing streams will love earth still when it is old and cold and with all its gardens gone and all the purport of its being failed and nought but memories."

IX

Then spake Paharn, a prophet of the land of Hurn.

And Paharn said:

"There was one man that knew, but he stands not here."

And the King said:

"Is he further than my heralds might travel in the night if they went upon fleet horses?"

And the prophet answered:

"He is no further than thy heralds may well travel in the night, but further than they may return from in all the years. Out of this city there goes a valley wandering through all the world and opens out at last on the green land of Hurn. On the one side in the distance gleams the sea, and on the other side a forest, black and ancient, darkens the fields of Hurn; beyond the forest and the sea there is no more, saving the twilight and beyond that the gods. In the mouth of the valley sleeps the village of Rhistaun.

"Here I was born, and heard the murmur of the flocks and herds, and saw the tall smoke standing between the sky and the still roofs of Rhistaun, and learned that men might not go into the dark forest, and that beyond the forest and the sea was nought saving the twilight, and beyond that the gods. Often there came travellers from the world all down the winding valley, and spake with strange speech in Rhistaun and returned again up the valley going back to the world. Sometimes with bells and camels and men running on foot, Kings came down the valley from the world, but always the travellers returned by the valley again and none went further than the land of Hurn.

"And Kithneb also was born in the land of Hurn and tended the flocks with me, but Kithneb would not care to listen to the murmur of the flocks and herds and see the tall smoke standing between the roofs and the sky, but needed to know how far from Hurn it was that the world met the twilight, and how far across the twilight sat the gods.

"And often Kithneb dreamed as he tended the flocks and herds, and when others slept he would wander near to the edge of the forest wherein men might not go. And the elders of the land of Hurn reproved Kithneb when he dreamed; yet Kithneb was still as other men and mingled with his fellows until the day of which I will tell thee, O King. For Kithneb was aged about a score of years, and he and I were sitting near the flocks, and he gazed long at the point where the dark forest met the sea at the end of the land of Hurn. But when night drove the twilight down under the forest we brought the flocks together to Rhistaun, and I went up the street between the houses to see four princes that had come down the valley from the world, and they were clad in blue and scarlet and wore plumes upon their heads, and they gave us in exchange for our sheep some gleaming stones which they told us were of great value on the word of princes. And I sold them three sheep, and Darniag sold them eight.

"But Kithneb came not with the others to the market place where the four princes stood, but went alone across the fields to the edge of the forest.

"And it was upon the next morning that the strange thing befell Kithneb; for I saw him in the morning coming from the fields, and I hailed him with the shepherd's cry wherewith we shepherds call to one another, and he answered not. Then I stopped and spake to him, and Kithneb said not a word till I became angry and left him.

"Then we spake together concerning Kithneb, and others had hailed him, and he had not answered them, but to one he had said that he had heard the voices of the gods speaking beyond the forest and so would never listen more to the voices of men.

"Then we said: 'Kithneb is mad,' and none hindered him.

"Another took his place among the flocks, and Kithneb sat in the evenings by the edge of the forest on the plain, alone.

"So Kithneb spake to none for many days, but when any forced him to speak he said that every evening he heard the gods when they came to sit in the forest from over the twilight and sea, and that he would speak no more with men.

"But as the months went by, men in Rhistaun came to look on Kithneb as a prophet, and we were wont to point to him when strangers came down the valley from the world, saying:

"'Here in the land of Hurn we have a prophet such as you have not among your cities, for he speaks at evening with the gods.'

"A year had passed over the silence of Kithneb when he came to me and spake. And I bowed before him because we believed that he spake among the gods. And Kithneb said:

"'I will speak to thee before the end because I am most lonely. For how may I speak again with men and women in the little streets of Rhistaun among the houses, when I have heard the voices of the gods singing above the twilight? But I am more lonely than ever Rhistaun wonts of, for this I tell thee, *when I hear the gods I know not what They say*. Well indeed I know the voice of each, for ever calling me away from contentment; well I know Their voices as they call to my soul and trouble it; I know by Their tone when They rejoice, and I know when They are sad, for even the gods feel sadness. I know when over fallen cities of the past, and the curved white bones of heroes They sing the dirges of the gods' lament. But alas! Their words I know not, and the wonderful strains of the melody of Their speech beat on my soul and pass away unknown.

"'Therefore I travelled from the land of Hurn till I came to the house of the prophet Arnin-Yo, and told him that I sought to find the meaning of the gods; and Arnin-Yo told me to ask the shepherds concerning all the gods, for what the shepherds knew it was meet for a man to know, and, beyond that, knowledge turned into trouble.

"'But I told Arnin-Yo that I had heard myself the voices of the gods and knew that They were there beyond the twilight and so could never more bow down to the gods that the shepherds made from the red clay which they scooped with their hands out of the hillside.

"'Then said Arnin-Yo to me:

"'"Natheless forget that thou hast heard the gods and bow down again to the gods of the red clay that the shepherds make, and find thereby the ease that the shepherds find, and at last die, remembering devoutly the gods of the red clay that the shepherds scooped with their hands out of the hill. For the gifts of the gods that sit beyond the twilight and smile at the gods of clay, are neither ease nor contentment."

"'And I said:

"'"The god that my mother made out of the red clay that she had got from the hill, fashioning it with many arms and eyes as she sang me songs of its power, and told me stories of its mystic birth, this god is lost and broken; and ever in my ears is ringing the melody of the gods."

"'And Arnin-Yo said:

"'"If thou wouldst still seek knowledge know that only those that come behind the gods may clearly know their meaning. And this thou canst only do by taking ship and putting out to sea from the land of Hurn and sailing up the coast towards the forest. There the sea cliffs turn to the left or southward, and full upon them beats the twilight from over the sea, and there thou mayest come round behind the forest. Here where the world's edge mingles with the twilight the gods come in the evening, and if thou canst come behind Them thou shalt hear Their voices clear, beating full seaward and filling all the twilight with sound of song, and thou shalt know the meaning of the gods. But where the cliffs turn southward there sits behind the gods Brimdono, the oldest whirlpool in the sea, roaring to guard his masters. Him the gods have chained for ever to the floor of the twilit sea to guard the door of the forest that lieth above the cliffs. Here, then, if thou canst hear the voices of the gods as thou hast said, thou wilt know their meaning clear, but this will profit thee little when Brimdono drags thee down and all thy ship.'"

"Thus spake Kithneb to me.

"But I said:

"'O Kithneb, forget those whirlpool-guarded gods beyond the forest, and if thy small god be lost thou shalt worship with me the small god that my mother made. Thousands of years ago he conquered cities but is not any longer an angry god. Pray to him, Kithneb, and he shall bring thee comfort and increase to thy flocks and a mild spring, and at the last a quiet ending for thy days.'

"But Kithneb heeded not, and only bade me find a fisher ship and men to row it. So on the next day we put forth from the land of Hurn in a boat that the fisher folk use. And with us came four of the fisher folk who rowed the boat while I held the rudder, but Kithneb sat and spake not in the prow. And we rowed westward up the coast till we came at evening where the cliffs turned southward and the twilight gleamed upon them and the sea.

"There we turned southwards and saw at once Brimdono. And as a man tears the purple cloak of a king slain in battle to divide it with other warriors,—Brimdono tore the sea. And ever around and around him with a gnarled hand Brimdono whirled the sail of some adventurous ship, the trophy of some calamity wrought in his greed for shipwreck long ago where he sat to guard his masters from all who fare on the sea. And ever one far-reaching empty hand swung up and down so that we durst go no nearer.

"Only Kithneb neither saw Brimdono nor heard his roar, and when we would go no further bade us lower a small boat with oars out of the ship. Into this boat Kithneb descended, not heeding words from us, and onward rowed alone. A cry of triumph over ships and men Brimdono uttered before him, but Kithneb's eyes were turned toward the forest as he came behind the gods. Upon his face the twilight beat full from the haunts of evening to illumine the smiles that grew about his eyes as he came behind the gods. Him that had found the gods above Their twilit cliffs, him that had heard Their voices close at last and knew Their meaning clear, him, from the cheerless world with its doubtings and prophets that lie, from all hidden meanings, where truth rang clear at last, Brimdono took."

But when Paharn ceased to speak, in the King's ears the roar of Brimdono exulting over ancient triumphs and the whelming of ships seemed still to ring.

X

Then Mohontis spake, the hermit prophet, who lived in the deep untravelled woods that seclude Lake Ilana.

"I dreamed that to the west of all the seas I saw by vision the mouth of Munra-O, guarded by golden gates, and through the bars of the gates that guard the mysterious river of Munra-O I saw the flashes of golden barques, wherein the gods went up and down, and to and fro through the evening dusk. And I saw that Munra-O was a river of dreams such as came through remembered gardens in the night, to charm our infancy as we slept beneath the sloping gables of the houses of long ago. And Munra-O rolled down her dreams from the unknown inner land and slid them under the golden gates and out into the waste, unheeding sea, till they beat far off upon low-lying shores and murmured songs of long ago to the islands of the south, or shouted tumultuous paeans to the Northern crags; or cried forlornly against rocks where no one came, dreams that might not be dreamed.

"Many gods there be, that through the dusk of an evening in the summer go up and down this river. There I saw, in a high barque all of gold, gods the of the pomp of cities; there I saw gods of splendour, in boats bejewelled to the keels; gods of magnificence and gods of power. I saw the dark ships and the glint of steel of the gods whose trade was war, and I heard the melody of the bells of silver arow in the rigging of harpstrings as the gods of melody went sailing through the dusk on the river of Munra—O. Wonderful river of Munra—O! I saw a grey ship with sails of the spider's web all lit with dewdrop lanterns, and on its prow was a scarlet cock with its wings spread far and wide when the gods of the dawn sailed also on Munra-O.

"Down this river it is the wont of the gods to carry the souls of men eastward to where the world in the distance faces on Munra-O. Then I knew that when the gods of the Pride of Power and gods of the Pomp of Cities went down the river in their tall gold ships to take earthward other souls, swiftly adown the river and between the ships had gone in this boat of birch bark the god Tarn, the hunter, bearing my soul to the world. And I know now that he came down the stream in the dusk keeping well to the middle, and that he moved silently and swiftly among the ships, wielding a twin-bladed oar. I remember, now, the yellow gleaming of the great boats of the gods of the Pomp of Cities, and the huge prow above me of the gods of the Pride of Power, when Tarn, dipping his right blade into the river, lifted his left blade high, and the drops gleamed and fell. Thus Tarn the hunter took me to the world that faces across the sea of the west on the gate of Munra-O. And so it was that there grew upon me the glamour of the hunt, though I had forgotten Tarn, and took me into mossy places and into dark woods, and I became the cousin of the wolf and looked into the lynx's eyes and knew the bear; and the birds called to me with half-remembered notes, and there grew in me a deep love of great rivers and of all western seas, and a distrust of cities, and all the while I had forgotten Tarn.

"I know not what high galleon shall come for thee, O King, nor what rowers, clad with purple, shall row at the bidding of gods when thou goest back with pomp to the river of Munra-O. But for me Tarn waits where the Seas of the West break over the edge of the world, and, as the years pass over me and the love of the chase sinks low, and as the glamour of the dark woods and mossy places dies down in my soul, ever louder and louder lap the ripples against the canoe of birch bark where, holding his twin-bladed oar, Tarn waits.

"But when my soul hath no more knowledge of the woods nor kindred any longer with the creatures of the dark, and when all that Tarn hath given it shall be lost, then Tarn shall take me back over the western seas, where all the remembered years lie floating idly aswing with the ebb and flow, to bring me again to the river of Munra-O. Far up that river we shall haply chase those creatures whose eyes are peering in the night as they prowl around the world, for Tarn was ever a hunter."

XI

Then Ulf spake, the prophet who in Sistrameides lives in a temple anciently dedicated to the gods. Rumour hath guessed that there the gods walked once some time towards evening. But Time whose hand is against the temples of the gods hath dealt harshly with it and overturned its pillars and set upon its ruins his sign and seal: now Ulf dwells there alone. And Ulf said, "There sets, O King, a river outward from earth which meets with a mighty sea whose waters roll through space and fling their billows on the shores of every star. These are the river and the sea of the Tears of Men."

And the King said:

"Men have not written of this sea."

And the prophet answered:

"Have not tears enough burst in the night time out of sleeping cities? Have not the sorrows of 10,000 homes sent streams into this river when twilight fell and it was still and there was none to hear? Have there not been hopes, and were they all fulfilled? Have there not been conquests and bitter defeats? And have not flowers when spring was over died in the gardens of many children? Tears enough, O King, tears enough have gone down out of earth to make such a sea; and deep it is and wide and the gods know it and it flings its spray on the shores of all the stars. Down this river and across this sea thou shalt fare in a ship of sighs and all around thee over the sea shall fly the prayers of men which rise on white wings higher than their sorrows. Sometimes perched in the rigging, sometimes crying around thee, shall go the prayers that availed not to stay thee in Zarkandhu. Far over the waters, and on the wings of the prayers beats the light of an inaccessible star. No hand hath touched it, none hath journeyed to it, it hath no substance, it is only a light, it is the star of Hope, and it shines far over the sea and brightens the world. It is nought but a light, but the gods gave it.

"Led only by the light of this star the myriad prayers that thou shalt see all around thee fly to the Hall of the gods.

"Sighs shall waft thy ship of sighs over the sea of Tears. Thou shalt pass by islands of laughter and lands of song lying low in the sea, and all of them drenched with tears flung over their rocks by the waves of the sea all driven by the sighs.

"But at last thou shalt come with the prayers of men to the great Hall of the gods where the chairs of the gods are carved of onyx grouped round the golden throne of the eldest of the gods. And there, O King, hope not to find the gods, but reclining upon the golden throne wearing a cloak of his master's thou shalt see the figure of Time with blood upon his hands, and loosely dangling from his fingers a dripping sword, and spattered with blood but empty shall stand the onyx chairs.

"There he sits on his master's throne dangling idly his sword, or with it flicking cruelly at the prayers of men that lie in a great heap bleeding at his feet.

"For a while, O King, the gods had sought to solve the riddles of Time, for a while They made him Their slave, and Time smiled and obeyed his masters, for a while, O King, for a while. He that hath spared nothing hath not spared the gods, nor yet shall he spare thee."

Then the King spake dolefully in the Hall of Kings, and said:

"May I not find at last the gods, and must it be that I may not look in Their faces at the last to see whether They be kindly? They that have sent me on my earthward journey I would greet on my returning, if not as a King coming again to his own city, yet as one who having been ordered had obeyed, and obeying had merited something of those for whom he toiled. I would look Them in Their faces, O prophet, and ask Them concerning many things and would know the wherefore of much. I had hoped, O prophet, that those gods that had smiled upon my childhood, Whose voices stirred at evening in gardens when I was young, would hold dominion still when at last I came to seek Them. O prophet, if this is not to be, make you a great dirge for my childhood's gods and fashion silver bells and, setting them mostly a-swing amidst such trees as grew in the garden of my childhood, sing you this dirge in the dusk: and sing it when the low moth flies up and down and the bat first comes peering from her home, sing it when white mists come rising from the river, when smoke is pale and grey, while flowers are yet closing, ere voices are yet hushed, sing it while all things yet lament the day, or ever the great lights of heaven come blazing forth and night with her splendours takes the place of day. For, if the old gods die, let us lament Them or ever new knowledge comes, while all the world still shudders at Their loss.

"For at the last, O prophet, what is left? Only the gods of my childhood dead, and only Time striding large and lonely through the spaces, chilling the moon and paling the light of stars and scattering earthward out of both his hands the dust of forgetfulness over the fields of heroes and smitten Temples of the older gods."

But when the other prophets heard with what doleful words the King spake in the Hall they all cried out:

"It is not as Ulf has said but as I have said—and I."

Then the King pondered long, not speaking. But down in the city in a street between the houses stood grouped together they that were wont to dance before the King, and they that had borne his wine in jewelled cups. Long they had tarried in the city hoping that the King might relent, and once again regard them with kindly faces calling for wine and song. The next morning they were all to set out in search of some new Kingdom, and they were peering between the houses and up the long grey street to see for the last time the palace of King Ebalon; and Pattering Leaves, the dancer, cried:

"Not any more, not any more at all shall we drift up the carven hall to dance before the King. He that now watches the magic of his prophets will behold no more the wonder of the dance, and among ancient parchments, strange and wise, he shall forget the swirl of drapery when we swing together through the Dance of the Myriad Steps."

And with her were Silvern Fountain and Summer Lightning and Dream of the Sea, each lamenting that they should dance no more to please the eyes of the King.

And Intahn who had carried at the banquet for fifty years the goblet of the King set with its four sapphires each as large as an eye, said as he spread his hands towards the palace making the sign of farewell:

"Not all the magic of prophecy nor yet foreseeing nor perceiving may equal the power of wine. Through the small door in the King's Hall one goes by one hundred steps and many sloping corridors into the cool of the earth where lies a cavern vaster than the Hall. Therein, curtained by the spider, repose the casks of wine that are wont to gladden the hearts of the Kings of Zarkandhu. In islands far to the eastward the vine, from whose heart this wine was long since wrung, hath climbed aloft with many a clutching finger and beheld the sea and ships of the olden time and men since dead, and gone down into the earth again and been covered over with weeds. And green with the damp of years there lie three casks that a city gave not up until all her defenders were slain and her houses fired; and ever to the soul of that wine is added a more ardent fire as ever the years go by. Thither it was my pride to go before a banquet in the olden years, and coming up to bear in the sapphire goblet the fire of the elder Kings and to watch the King's eye flash and his face grow nobler and more like his sires as he drank the gleaming wine.

"And now the King seeks wisdom from his prophets while all the glory of the past and all the clattering splendour of today grows old, far down, forgotten beneath his feet."

And when he ceased the cupbearers and the women that danced looked long in silence at the palace. Then one by one all made the farewell sign before they turned to go, and as they did this a herald unseen in the dark was speeding towards them.

After a long silence the King spake:

"Prophets of my Kingdom," he said, "you have not prophesied alike, and the words of each prophet condemn his fellows' words so that wisdom may not be discovered among prophets. But I command that none in my Kingdom shall doubt that the earliest King of Zarkandhu stored wine beneath this palace before the building of the city or ever the palace arose, and I shall cause commands to be uttered for the making of a banquet at once within this Hall, so that ye shall perceive that the power of my wine is greater than all your spells, and dancing more wondrous than prophecy."

The dancers and the winebearers were summoned back, and as the night wore on a banquet was spread and all the prophets bidden to be seated, Samahn, Ynath, Monith, Ynar Thun, the prophet of Journeys, Zornadhu, Yamen, Paharn, Ilana, Ulf, and one that had not spoken nor yet revealed his name, and who wore his prophet's cloak across his face.

And the prophets feasted as they were commanded and spake as other men spake, save he whose face was hidden, who neither ate nor spake. Once he put out his hand from under his cloak and touched a blossom among the flowers upon the table and the blossom fell.

And Pattering Leaves came in and danced again, and the King smiled, and Pattering Leaves was happy though she had not the wisdom of the prophets. And in and out, in and out, in and out among the columns of the Hall went Summer Lightning in the maze of the dance. And Silvern Fountain bowed before the King and danced and danced and bowed again, and old Intahn went to and fro from the cavern to the King gravely through the midst of the dancers but with kindly eyes, and when the King had often drunk of the old wine of the elder Kings he called for Dream of the Sea and bade her sing. And Dream of the Sea came through the arches and sang of an island builded by magic out of pearls, that lay set in a ruby sea, and how it lay far off and under the south, guarded by jagged reefs whereon the sorrows of the world were wrecked and never came to the island. And how a low sunset always reddened the sea and lit the magic isle and never turned to night, and how someone sang always and endlessly to lure the soul of a King who might by enchantment pass the guarding reefs to find rest on the pearl island and not be troubled more, but only see sorrows on the outer reef battered and broken. Then Soul of the South rose up and sang a song of a fountain that ever sought to reach the sky and was ever doomed to fall to the earth again until at last....

Then whether it was the art of Pattering Leaves or the song of Dream of the Sea, or whether it was the fire of the wine of the elder Kings, Ebalon bade farewell kindly to the prophets when morning paled the stars. Then along the torchlit corridors the King went to his chamber, and having shut the door in the empty room, beheld suddenly a figure wearing the cloak of a prophet; and the King perceived that it was he whose face was hidden at the banquet, who had not revealed his name.

And the King said:

"Art thou, too, a prophet?"

And the figure answered:

"I am a prophet."

And the King said: "Knowest *thou* aught concerning the journey of the King?" And the figure answered: "I know, but have never said."

And the King said: "Who art thou that knowest so much and has not told it?"

And he answered:

"I am *The End*."

Then the cloaked figure strode away from the palace; and the King, unseen by the guards, followed upon his journey.

THE SWORD OF WELLERAN (1908)

DEDICATED

with deep gratitude to those few, known to me or unknown, who have cared for either of my former books, *The Gods of Pegana, Time and the Gods*.

THE SWORD OF WELLERAN

Where the great plain of Tarphet runs up, as the sea in estuaries, among the Cyresian mountains, there stood long since the city of Merimna well-nigh among the shadows of the crags. I have never seen a city in the world so beautiful as Merimna seemed to me when first I dreamed of it. It was a marvel of spires and figures of bronze, and marble fountains, and trophies of fabulous wars, and broad streets given over wholly to the Beautiful. Right through the centre of the city there went an avenue fifty strides in width, and along each side of it stood likenesses in bronze of the Kings of all the countries that the people of Merimna had ever known. At the end of that avenue was a colossal chariot with three bronze horses driven by the winged figure of Fame, and behind her in the chariot the huge form of Welleran, Merimna's ancient hero, standing with extended sword. So urgent was the mien and attitude of Fame, and so swift the pose of the horses, that you had sworn that the chariot was instantly upon you, and that its dust already veiled the faces of the Kings. And in the city was a mighty hall wherein were stored the trophies of Merimna's heroes. Sculptured it was and domed, the glory of the art of masons a long while dead, and on the summit of the dome the image of Rollory sat gazing across the Cyresian mountains towards the wide lands beyond, the lands that knew his sword. And beside Rollory, like an old nurse, the figure of Victory sat, hammering into a golden wreath of laurels for his head the crowns of fallen Kings.

Such was Merimna, a city of sculptured Victories and warriors of bronze. Yet in the time of which I write the art of war had been forgotten in Merimna, and the people almost slept. To and fro and up and down they would walk through the marble streets, gazing at memorials of the things achieved by their country's swords in the hands of those that long ago had loved Merimna well. Almost they slept, and dreamed of Welleran, Soore-nard, Mommolek, Rollory, Akanax, and young Iraine. Of the lands beyond the mountains that lay all round about them they knew nothing, save that they were the theatre of the terrible deeds of Welleran, that he had done with his sword. Long since these lands had fallen back into the possession of the nations that had been scourged by Merimna's armies. Nothing now remained to Merimna's men save their inviolate city and the glory of the remembrance of their ancient fame. At night they would place sentinels far out in the desert, but these always slept at their posts dreaming of Rollory, and three times every night a guard would march around the city clad in purple, bearing lights and singing songs of Welleran. Always the guard went unarmed, but as the sound of their song went echoing across the plain towards the looming mountains, the desert robbers would hear the name of Welleran and steal away to their haunts. Often dawn would come across the plain, shimmering marvellously upon Merimna's spires, abashing all the stars, and find the guard still singing songs of Welleran, and would change the colour of their purple robes and pale the lights they bore. But the guard would go back leaving the ramparts safe, and one by one the sentinels in the plain would awake from dreaming of Rollory and shuffle back into the city quite cold. Then something of the menace would pass away from the faces of the Cyresian mountains, that from the north and the west and the south lowered upon Merimna, and clear in the morning the statues and the pillars would arise in the old inviolate city. You would wonder that an unarmed guard and sentinels that slept could defend a city that was stored with all the glories of art, that was rich in gold and bronze, a haughty city that had erst oppressed its neighbours, whose people had forgotten the art of war. Now this is the reason that, though all her other lands had long been taken from her, Merimna's city was safe. A strange thing was believed or feared by the fierce tribes beyond the mountains, and it was credited among them that at certain stations round Merimna's ramparts there still rode Welleran, Soorenard, Mommolek, Rollory, Akanax, and young Iraine. Yet it was close on a hundred years since Iraine, the youngest of Merimna's heroes, fought his last battle with the tribes.

Sometimes indeed there arose among the tribes young men who doubt-ed and said: 'How may a man for ever escape death?'

But graver men answered them: 'Hear us, ye whose wisdom has dis-cerned so much, and discern for us how a man may escape death when two score horsemen assail him with their swords, all of them sworn to kill him, and all of them sworn upon their country's gods; as often Welleran hath. Or discern for us how two men alone may enter a walled city by night, and bring away from it that city's king, as did Soorenard and Mommolek. Surely men that have escaped so many swords and so many sleety arrows shall escape the years and Time.'

And the young men were humbled and became silent. Still, the suspicion grew. And often when the sun set on the Cyresian mountains, men in Merimna discerned the forms of savage tribesmen black against the light, peering towards the city.

All knew in Merimna that the figures round the ramparts were only statues of stone, yet even there a hope lingered among a few that some day their old heroes would come again, for certainly none had ever seen them die. Now it had been the wont of these six warriors of old, as each received his last wound and knew it to be mortal, to ride away to a certain deep ravine and cast his body in, as somewhere I have read great elephants do, hiding their bones away from lesser beasts. It was a ravine steep and narrow even at the ends, a great cleft into which no man could come by any path. There rode Welleran alone, panting hard; and there later rode Soorenard and Mommolek, Mommolek with a mortal wound upon him not to return, but Soorenard was unwounded and rode back alone from leaving his dear friend resting among the mighty bones of Welleran. And there rode Soorenard, when his day was come, with Rollory and Akanax, and Rollory rode in the middle and Soorenard and Akanax on either side. And the long ride was a hard and weary thing for Soorenard and Akanax, for they both had mortal wounds; but the long ride was easy for Rollory, for he was dead. So the bones of these five heroes whitened in an enemy's land, and very still they were, though they had troubled cities, and none knew where they lay saving only Iraine, the young captain, who was but twenty-five when Mommolek, Rollory, and Akanax rode away. And among them were strewn their saddles and their bridles, and all the accoutrements of their horses, lest any man should ever find them afterwards and say in some foreign city: 'Lo! the bridles or the saddles of Merimna's captains, taken in war,' but their beloved trusty horses they turned free.

Forty years afterwards, in the hour of a great victory, his last wound came upon Iraine, and the wound was terrible and would not close. And Iraine was the last of the captains, and rode away alone. It was a long way to the dark ravine, and Iraine feared that he would never come to the resting-place of the old heroes, and he urged his horse on swiftly, and clung to the saddle with his hands. And often as he rode he fell asleep, and dreamed of earlier days, and of the times when he first rode forth to the great wars of Welleran, and of the time when Welleran first spake to him, and of the faces of Welleran's comrades when they led charges in the battle. And ever as he awoke a great longing arose in his soul as it hovered on his body's brink, a longing to lie among the bones of the old heroes. At last when he saw the dark ravine making a scar across the plain, the soul of Iraine slipped out through his great wound and spread its wings, and pain departed from the poor hacked body, and, still urging his horse forward, Iraine died. But the old true horse cantered on till suddenly he saw before him the dark ravine and put his forefeet out on the very edge of it and stopped. Then the body of Iraine came toppling forward over the right shoulder of the horse, and his bones mingle and rest as the years go by with the bones of Merimna's heroes.

Now there was a little boy in Merimna named Rold. I saw him first, I, the dreamer, that sit before my fire asleep, I saw him first as his mother led him through the great hall where stand the trophies of Merimna's heroes. He was five years old, and they stood before the great glass casket wherein lay the sword of Welleran, and his mother said: 'The sword of Welleran.' And Rold said: 'What should a man do with the sword of Welleran?' And his mother answered: 'Men look at the sword and remember Welleran.' And they went on and stood before the great red cloak of Welleran, and the child said: 'Why did Welleran wear this great red cloak?' And his mother answered: 'It was the way of Welleran.'

When Rold was a little older he stole out of his mother's house quite in the middle of the night when all the world was still, and Merimna asleep dreaming of Welleran, Soorenard, Mommolek, Rollory, Akanax, and young Iraine. And he went down to the ramparts to hear the purple guard go by singing of Welleran. And the purple guard came by with lights, all singing in the stillness, and dark shapes out in the desert turned and fled. And Rold went back again to his mother's house with a great yearning towards the name of Welleran, such as men feel for very holy things.

And in time Rold grew to know the pathway all round the ramparts, and the six equestrian statues that were there guarding Merimna still. These statues were not like other statues, they were so cunningly wrought of many-coloured marbles that none might be quite sure until very close that they were not living men. There was a horse of dappled marble, the horse of Akanax. The horse of Rollory was of alabaster, pure white, his armour was wrought out of a stone that shone, and his horseman's cloak was made of a blue stone, very precious. He looked northwards.

But the marble horse of Welleran was pure black, and there sat Welleran upon him looking solemnly westwards. His horse it was whose cold neck Rold most loved to stroke, and it was Welleran whom the watchers at sunset on the mountains the most clearly saw as they peered towards the city. And Rold loved the red nostrils of the great black horse and his rider's jasper cloak.

Now beyond the Cyresians the suspicion grew that Merimna's heroes were dead, and a plan was devised that a man should go by night and come close to the figures upon the ramparts and see whether they were Welleran, Soorenard, Mommolek, Rollory, Akanax, and young Iraine. And all were agreed upon the plan, and many names were mentioned of those who should go, and the plan matured for many years. It was during these years that watchers clustered often at sunset upon the mountains but came no nearer. Finally, a better plan was made, and it was decided that two men who had been by chance condemned to death should be given a pardon if they went down into the plain by night and discovered whether or not Merimna's heroes lived. At first the two prisoners dared not go, but after a while one of them, Seejar, said to his companion, Sajar-Ho: 'See now, when the King's axeman smites a man upon the neck that man dies.'

And the other said that this was so. Then said Seejar: 'And even though Welleran smite a man with his sword no more befalleth him than death.'

Then Sajar-Ho thought for a while. Presently he said: 'Yet the eye of the King's axeman might err at the moment of his stroke or his arm fail him, and the eye of Welleran hath never erred nor his arm failed. It were better to bide here.'

Then said Seejar: 'Maybe that Welleran is dead and that some other holds his place upon the ramparts, or even a statue of stone.'

But Sajar-Ho made answer: 'How can Welleran be dead when he even escaped from two score horsemen with swords that were sworn to slay him, and all sworn upon our country's gods?'

And Seejar said: 'This story his father told my grandfather concerning Welleran. On the day that the fight was lost on the plains of Kurlistan he saw a dying horse near to the river, and the horse looked piteously towards the water but could not reach it. And the father of my grandfather saw Welleran go down to the river's brink and bring water from it with his own hand and give it to the horse. Now we are in as sore a plight as was that horse, and as near to death; it may be that Welleran will pity us, while the King's axeman cannot because of the commands of the King.'

Then said Sajar-Ho: 'Thou wast ever a cunning arguer. Thou broughtest us into this trouble with thy cunning and thy devices, we will see if thou canst bring us out of it. We will go.'

So news was brought to the King that the two prisoners would go down to Merimna.

That evening the watchers led them to the mountain's edge, and Seejar and Sajar-Ho went down towards the plain by the way of a deep ravine, and the watchers watched them go. Presently their figures were wholly hid in the dusk. Then night came up, huge and holy, out of waste marshes to the eastwards and low lands and the sea; and the angels that watched over all men through the day closed their great eyes and slept, and the angels that watched over all men through the night awoke and ruffled their deep blue feathers and stood up and watched. But the plain became a thing of mystery filled with fears. So the two spies went down the deep ravine, and coming to the plain sped stealthily across it. Soon they came to the line of sentinels asleep upon the sand, and one stirred in his sleep calling on Rollory, and a great dread seized upon the spies and they whispered 'Rollory lives,' but they remembered the King's axeman and went on. And next they came to the great bronze statue of Fear, carved by some sculptor of the old glorious years in the attitude of flight towards the mountains, calling to her children as she fled. And the children of Fear were carved in the likeness of the armies of all the trans-Cyresian tribes with their backs towards Merimna, flocking after Fear. And from where he sat on his horse behind the ramparts the sword of Welleran was stretched out over their heads as ever it was wont. And the two spies kneeled down in the sand and kissed the huge bronze foot of the statue of Fear, saying: 'O Fear, Fear.' And as they knelt they saw lights far off along the ramparts coming nearer and nearer, and heard men singing of Welleran. And the purple guard came nearer and went by with their lights, and passed on into the distance round the ramparts still singing of Welleran. And all the while the two spies clung to the foot of the statue, muttering: 'O Fear, Fear.' But when they could hear the name of Welleran no more they arose and came to the ramparts and climbed over them and came at once upon the figure of Welleran, and they bowed low to the ground, and Seejar said: 'O Welleran, we came to see whether thou didst yet live.' And for a long while they waited with their faces to the earth. At last Seejar looked up towards Welleran's terrible sword, and it was still stretched out pointing to the carved armies that followed after Fear. And Seejar bowed to the ground again and touched the horse's hoof, and it seemed cold to him. And he moved his hand higher and touched the leg of the horse, and it seemed quite cold. At last he touched Welleran's foot, and the armour on it seemed hard and stiff. Then as Welleran moved not and spake not, Seejar climbed up at last and touched his hand, the terrible hand of Welleran, and it was marble. Then Seejar laughed aloud, and he and Sajar-Ho sped down the empty pathway and found Rollory, and he was marble too. Then they climbed down over the ramparts and went back across the plain, walking contemptuously past the figure of Fear, and heard the guard returning round the ramparts for the third time, singing of Welleran; and Seejar said: 'Ay, you may sing of Welleran, but Welleran is dead and a doom is on your city.'

And they passed on and found the sentinel still restless in the night and calling on Rollory. And Sajar-Ho muttered: 'Ay, you may call on Rollory, but Rollory is dead and naught can save your city.'

And the two spies went back alive to their mountains again, and as they reached them the first ray of the sun came up red over the desert behind Merimna and lit Merimna's spires. It was the hour when the purple guard were wont to go back into the city with their tapers pale and their robes a brighter colour, when the cold sentinels came shuffling in from dreaming in the desert; it was the hour when the desert robbers hid themselves away, going back to their mountain caves; it was the hour when gauze-winged insects are born that only live for a day; it was the hour when men die that are condemned to death; and in this hour a great peril, new and terrible, arose for Merimna and Merimna knew it not.

Then Seejar turning said: 'See how red the dawn is and how red the spires of Merimna. They are angry with Merimna in Paradise and they bode its doom.'

So the two spies went back and brought the news to their King, and for a few days the Kings of those countries were gathering their armies together; and one evening the armies of four Kings were massed together at the top of the deep ravine, all crouching below the summit waiting for the sun to set. All wore resolute and fearless faces, yet inwardly every man was praying to his gods, unto each one in turn.

Then the sun set, and it was the hour when the bats and the dark creatures are abroad and the lions come down from their lairs, and the desert robbers go into the plains again, and fevers rise up winged and hot out of chill marshes, and it was the hour when safety leaves the thrones of Kings, the hour when dynasties change. But in the desert the purple guard came swinging out of Merimna with their lights to sing of Welleran, and the sentinels lay down to sleep.

Now into Paradise no sorrow may ever come, but may only beat like rain against its crystal walls, yet the souls of Merimna's heroes were half aware of some sorrow far away as some sleeper feels that some one is chilled and cold yet knows not in his sleep that it is he. And they fretted a little in their starry home. Then unseen there drifted earthward across the setting sun the souls of Welleran, Soorenard, Mommolek, Rollory, Akanax, and young Iraine. Already when they reached Merimna's ramparts it was just dark, already the armies of the four Kings had begun to move, jingling, down the deep ravine. But when the six warriors saw their city again, so little changed after so many years, they looked towards her with a longing that was nearer to tears than any that their souls had known before, crying to her:

'O Merimna, our city: Merimna, our walled city.

'How beautiful thou art with all thy spires, Merimna. For thee we left the earth, its kingdoms and little flowers, for thee we have come away for awhile from Paradise.

'It is very difficult to draw away from the face of God—it is like a warm fire, it is like dear sleep, it is like a great anthem, yet there is a stillness all about it, a stillness full of lights.

'We have left Paradise for awhile for thee, Merimna.

'Many women have we loved, Merimna, but only one city.

'Behold now all the people dream, all our loved people. How beautiful are dreams! In dreams the dead may live, even the long dead and the very silent. Thy lights are all sunk low, they have all gone out, no sound is in thy streets. Hush! Thou art like a maiden that shutteth up her eyes and is asleep, that draweth her breath softly and is quite still, being at ease and untroubled.

'Behold now the battlements, the old battlements. Do men defend them still as we defended them? They are worn a little, the battlements,' and drifting nearer they peered anxiously. 'It is not by the hand of man that they are worn, our battlements. Only the years have done it and indomitable

Time. Thy battlements are like the girdle of a maiden, a girdle that is round about her. See now the dew upon them, they are like a jewelled girdle.

'Thou art in great danger, Merimna, because thou art so beautiful. Must thou perish tonight because we no more defend thee, because we cry out and none hear us, as the bruised lilies cry out and none have known their voices?'

Thus spake those strong-voiced, battle-ordering captains, calling to their dear city, and their voices came no louder than the whispers of little bats that drift across the twilight in the evening. Then the purple guard came near, going round the ramparts for the first time in the night, and the old warriors called to them, 'Merimna is in danger! Already her enemies gather in the darkness.' But their voices were never heard because they were only wandering ghosts. And the guard went by and passed unheeding away, still singing of Welleran.

Then said Welleran to his comrades: 'Our hands can hold swords no more, our voices cannot be heard, we are stalwart men no longer. We are but dreams, let us go among dreams. Go all of you, and thou too, young Iraine, and trouble the dreams of all the men that sleep, and urge them to take the old swords of their grandsires that hang upon the walls, and to gather at the mouth of the ravine; and I will find a leader and make him take my sword.'

Then they passed up over the ramparts and into their dear city. And the wind blew about, this way and that, as he went, the soul of Welleran who had upon his day withstood the charges of tempestuous armies. And the souls of his comrades, and with them young Iraine, passed up into the city and troubled the dreams of every man who slept, and to every man the souls said in their dreams: 'It is hot and still in the city. Go out now into the desert, into the coolunder the mountains, but take with thee the old sword that hangs upon the wall for fear of the desert robbers.'

And the god of that city sent up a fever over it, and the fever brooded over it and the streets were hot; and all that slept awoke from dreaming that it would be cool and pleasant where the breezes came down the ravine out of the mountains; and they took the old swords that their grandsires had, according to their dreams, for fear of the desert robbers. And in and out of dreams passed the souls of Welleran's comrades, and with them young Iraine, in great haste as the night wore on; and one by one they troubled the dreams of all Merimna's men and caused them to arise and go out armed, all save the purple guard who, heedless of danger, sang of Welleran still, for waking men cannot hear the souls of the dead.

But Welleran drifted over the roofs of the city till he came to the form of Rold lying fast asleep. Now Rold was grown strong and was eighteen years of age, and he was fair of hair and tall like Welleran, and the soul of Welleran hovered over him and went into his dreams as a butterfly flits through trellis-work into a garden of flowers, and the soul of Welleran said to Rold in his dreams: 'Thou wouldst go and see again the sword of Welleran, the great curved sword of Welleran. Thou wouldst go and look at it in the night with the moonlight shining upon it.'

And the longing of Rold in his dreams to see the sword caused him to walk still sleeping from his mother's house to the hall wherein were the trophies of the heroes. And the soul of Welleran urging the dreams of Rold caused him to pause before the great red cloak, and there the soul said among the dreams: 'Thou art cold in the night; fling now a cloak around thee.'

And Rold drew round about him the huge red cloak of Welleran. Then Rold's dreams took him to the sword, and the soul said to the dreams: 'Thou hast a longing to hold the sword of Welleran: take up the sword in thy hand.'

But Rold said: 'What should a man do with the sword of Welleran?'

And the soul of the old captain said to the dreams: 'It is a good sword to hold: take up the sword of Welleran.'

And Rold, still sleeping and speaking aloud, said: 'It is not lawful; none may touch the sword.'

And Rold turned to go. Then a great and terrible cry arose in the soul of Welleran, all the more bitter for that he could not utter it, and it went round and round his soul finding no utterance, like a cry evoked long since by some murderous deed in some old haunted chamber that whispers through the ages heard by none.

And the soul of Welleran cried out to the dreams of Rold: 'Thy knees are tied! Thou art fallen in a marsh! Thou canst not move.'

And the dreams of Rold said to him: 'Thy knees are tied, thou art fallen in a marsh,' and Rold stood still before the sword. Then the soul of the warrior wailed among Rold's dreams, as Rold stood before the sword.

'Welleran is crying for his sword, his wonderful curved sword. Poor Welleran, that once fought for Merimna, is crying for his sword in the night. Thou wouldst not keep Welleran without his beautiful sword when he is dead and cannot come for it, poor Welleran who fought for Merimna.'

And Rold broke the glass casket with his hand and took the sword, the great curved sword of Welleran; and the soul of the warrior said among Rold's dreams: 'Welleran is waiting in the deep ravine that runs into the mountains, crying for his sword.'

And Rold went down through the city and climbed over the ramparts, and walked with his eyes wide open but still sleeping over the desert to the mountains.

Already a great multitude of Merimna's citizens were gathered in the desert before the deep ravine with old swords in their hands, and Rold passed through them as he slept holding the sword of Welleran, and the people cried in amaze to one another as he passed: 'Rold hath the sword of Welleran!'

And Rold came to the mouth of the ravine, and there the voices of the people woke him. And Rold knew nothing that he had done in his sleep, and looked in amazement at the sword in his hand and said: 'What art thou, thou beautiful thing? Lights shimmer in thee, thou art restless. It is the sword of Welleran, the curved sword of Welleran!'

And Rold kissed the hilt of it, and it was salt upon his lips with the battle-sweat of Welleran. And Rold said: 'What should a man do with the sword of Welleran?'

And all the people wondered at Rold as he sat there with the sword in his hand muttering, 'What should a man do with the sword of Welleran?'

Presently there came to the ears of Rold the noise of a jingling up in the ravine, and all the people, the people that knew naught of war, heard the jingling coming nearer in the night; for the four armies were moving on Merimna and not yet expecting an enemy. And Rold gripped upon the hilt of the great curved sword, and the sword seemed to lift a little. And a new thought came into the hearts of Merimna's people as they gripped their grandsires' swords. Nearer and nearer came the heedless armies of the four Kings, and old ancestral memories began to arise in the minds of Merimna's people in the desert with their swords in their hands sitting behind Rold. And all the sentinels were awake holding their spears, for Rollory had put their dreams to flight, Rollory that once could put to flight armies and now was but a dream struggling with other dreams.

And now the armies had come very near. Suddenly Rold leaped up, crying: 'Welleran! And the sword of Welleran!' And the savage, lusting sword that had thirsted for a hundred years went up with the hand of Rold and swept through a tribesman's ribs. And with the warm blood all about it there came a joy into the curved soul of that mighty sword, like to the joy of a swimmer coming up dripping out of warm seas after living for long in a dry land. When they saw the red cloak and that terrible sword a cry ran through the tribal armies, 'Welleran lives!' And there arose the sounds of the exulting of victorious men, and the panting of those that fled, and the sword singing softly to itself as it whirled dripping through the air. And the last that I saw of the battle as it poured into the depth and darkness of the ravine was the sword of Welleran sweeping up and falling, gleaming blue in the moonlight whenever it arose and afterwards gleaming red, and so disappearing into the darkness.

But in the dawn Merimna's men came back, and the sun arising to give new life to the world, shone instead upon the hideous things that the sword of Welleran had done. And Rold said: 'O sword, sword! How horrible thou art! Thou art a terrible thing to have come among men. How many eyes shall look upon gardens no more because of thee? How many fields must go empty that might have been fair with cottages, white cottages with children all about them? How many valleys must go desolate that might have nursed warm hamlets, because thou hast slain long since the men that might have built them? I hear the wind crying against thee, thou sword! It comes from the empty valleys. It comes over the bare fields. There are children's voices in it. They were never born. Death brings an end to crying for those that had life once, but these must cry for ever. O sword! sword! why did the gods send thee among men?' And the tears of Rold fell down upon the proud sword but could not wash it clean.

And now that the ardour of battle had passed away, the spirits of Merimna's people began to gloom a little, like their leader's, with their fatigue and with the cold of the morning; and they looked at the sword of Welleran in Rold's hand and said: 'Not any more, not any more for ever will Welleran now return, for his sword is in the hand of another. Now we know indeed that he is dead. O Welleran, thou wast our sun and moon and all our stars. Now is the sun fallen down and the moon broken, and all the stars are scattered as the diamonds of a necklace that is snapped off one who is slain by violence.'

Thus wept the people of Merimna in the hour of their great victory, for men have strange moods, while beside them their old inviolate city slumbered safe. But back from the ramparts and beyond the mountains and over the lands that they had conquered of old, beyond the world and back again to Paradise, went the souls of Welleran, Soorenard, Mommolek, Rollory, Akanax, and young Iraine.

The Fall of Babbulkund

I said: 'I will arise now and see Babbulkund, City of Marvel. She is of one age with the earth; the stars are her sisters. Pharaohs of the old time coming conquering from Araby first saw her, a solitary mountain in the desert, and cut the mountain into towers and terraces. They destroyed one of the hills of God, but they made Babbulkund. She is carven, not built; her palaces are one with her terraces, there is neither join nor cleft. Hers is the beauty of the youth of the world. She deemeth herself to be the middle of Earth, and hath four gates facing outward to the Nations. There sits outside her eastern gate a colossal god of stone. His face flushes with the lights of dawn. When the morning sunlight warms his lips they part a little, and he giveth utterance to the words "Oon Oom," and the language is long since dead in which he speaks, and all his worshippers are gathered to their tombs, so that none knoweth what the words portend that he uttereth at dawn. Some say that he greets the sun as one god greets another in the language thereof, and others say that he proclaims the day, and others that he uttereth warning. And at every gate is a marvel not credible until beholden.'

And I gathered three friends and said to them: 'We are what we have seen and known. Let us journey now and behold Babbulkund, that our minds may be beautified with it and our spirits made holier.'

So we took ship and travelled over the lifting sea, and remembered not things done in the towns we knew, but laid away the thoughts of them like soiled linen and put them by, and dreamed of Babbulkund.

But when we came to the land of which Babbulkund is the abiding glory, we hired a caravan of camels and Arab guides, and passed southwards in the afternoon on the three days' journey through the desert that should bring us to the white walls of Babbulkund. And the heat of the sun shone upon us out of the bright grey sky, and the heat of the desert beat up at us from below.

About sunset we halted and tethered our horses, while the Arabs unloaded the provisions from the camels and prepared a fire out of the dry scrub, for at sunset the heat of the desert departs from it suddenly, like a bird. Then we saw a traveller approaching us on a camel coming from the south. When he was come near we said to him:

'Come and encamp among us, for in the desert all men are brothers, and we will give thee meat to eat and wine, or, if thou art bound by thy faith, we will give thee some other drink that is not accursed by the prophet.'

The traveller seated himself beside us on the sand, and crossed his legs and answered:

'Hearken, and I will tell you of Babbulkund, City of Marvel. Babbulkund stands just below the meeting of the rivers, where Oonrana, River of Myth, flows into the Waters of Fable, even the old stream Plegáthanees. These, together, enter her northern gate rejoicing. Of old they flowed in the dark through the Hill that Nehemoth, the first of Pharaohs, carved into the City of Marvel. Sterile and desolate they float far through the desert, each in the appointed cleft, with life upon neither bank, but give birth in Babbulkund to the sacred purple garden whereof all nations sing. Thither all the bees come on a pilgrimage at evening by a secret way of the air. Once, from his twilit kingdom, which he rules equally with the sun, the moon saw and loved Babbulkund, clad with her purple garden; and the moon wooed Babbulkund, and she sent him weeping away, for she is more beautiful than all her sisters the stars. Her sisters come to her at night into her maiden chamber. Even the gods speak sometimes of Babbulkund, clad with her purple garden. Listen, for I perceive by your eyes that ye have not seen Babbulkund; there is a restlessness in them and an unappeased wonder. Listen. In the garden whereof I spoke there is a lake that hath no twin or fellow in the world; there is no companion for it among all the lakes. The shores of it are of glass, and the bottom of it. In it are great fish having golden and scarlet scales, and they swim to and fro. Here it is the wont of the eighty-second Nehemoth (who rules in the city today) to come, after the dusk has fallen, and sit by the lake alone, and at this hour eight hundred slaves go down by steps through caverns into vaults beneath the lake. Four hundred of them carrying purple lights march one behind the other, from east to west, and four hundred carrying green lights march one behind the other, from west to east. The two lines cross and re-cross each other in and out as the slaves go round and round, and the fearful fish flash up and down and to and fro.'

But upon that traveller speaking night descended, solemn and cold, and we wrapped ourselves in our blankets and lay down upon the sand in the sight of the astral sisters of Babbulkund. And all that night the desert said many things, softly and in a whisper, but I knew not what he said. Only the sand knew and arose and was troubled and lay down again, and the wind knew. Then, as the hours of the night went by, these two discovered the foot-tracks wherewith we had disturbed the holy desert, and they troubled over them and covered them up; and then the wind lay down and the sand rested. Then the wind arose again and the sand danced. This they did many times. And all the while the desert whispered what I shall not know.

Then I slept awhile and awoke just before sunrise, very cold. Suddenly the sun leapt up and flamed upon our faces; we all threw off our blankets and stood up. Then we took food, and afterwards started southwards, and in the heat of the day rested, and afterwards pushed on again. And all the while the desert remained the same, like a dream that will not cease to trouble a tired sleeper.

And often travellers passed us in the desert, coming from the City of Marvel, and there was a light and a glory in their eyes from having seen Babbulkund.

That evening, at sunset, another traveller neared us, and we hailed him, saying:

'Wilt thou eat and drink with us, seeing that all men are brothers in the desert?'

And he descended from his camel and sat by us and said:

'When morning shines on the colossus Neb and Neb speaks, at once the musicians of King Nehemoth in Babbulkund awake.

'At first their fingers wander over their golden harps, or they stroke idly their violins. Clearer and clearer the note of each instrument ascends like larks arising from the dew, till suddenly they all blend together and a new melody is born. Thus, every morning, the musicians of King Nehemoth make a new marvel in the City of Marvel; for these are no common musicians, but masters of melody, raided by conquest long since, and carried away in ships from the Isles of Song. And, at the sound of the music, Nehemoth awakes in the eastern chamber of his palace, which is carved in the form of a great crescent, four miles long, on the northern side of the city. Full in the windows of its eastern chamber the sun rises, and full in the windows of its western chamber the sun sets.

'When Nehemoth awakes he summons slaves who bring a palanquin with bells, which the King enters, having lightly robed. Then the slaves run and bear him to the onyx Chamber of the Bath, with the sound of small bells ringing as they run. And when Nehemoth emerges thence, bathed and anointed, the slaves run on with their ringing palanquin and bear him to the Orient Chamber of Banquets, where the King takes the first meal of the day. Thence, through the great white corridor whose windows all face sunwards, Nehemoth, in his palanquin, passes on to the Audience Chamber of Embassies from the North, which is all decked with Northern wares.

'All about it are ornaments of amber from the North and carven chalices of the dark brown Northern crystal, and on its floors lie furs from Baltic shores.

'In adjoining chambers are stored the wonted food of the hardy Northern men, and the strong wine of the North, pale but terrible. Therein the King receives barbarian princes from the frigid lands. Thence the slaves bear him swiftly to the Audience Chamber of Embassies from the East, where the walls are of turquoise, studded with the rubies of Ceylon, where the gods are the gods of the East, where all the hangings have been devised in the gorgeous heart of Ind, and where all the carvings have been wrought with the cunning of the isles. Here, if a caravan hath chanced to have come in from Ind or from Cathay, it is the King's wont to converse awhile with Moguls or Mandarins, for from the East come the arts and knowledge of the world, and the converse of their people is polite. Thus Nehemoth passes on through the other Audience Chambers and receives, perhaps, some Sheikhs of the Arab folk who have crossed the great desert from the West, or receives an embassy sent to do him homage from the shy jungle people to the South. And all the while the slaves with the ringing palanquin run westwards, following the sun, and ever the sun shines straight into the chamber where Nehemoth sits, and all the while the music from one or other of his bands of musicians comes tinkling to his ears. But when the middle of the day draws near, the slaves run to the cool groves that lie along the verandahs on the northern side of the palace, forsaking the sun, and as the heat overcomes the genius of the musicians, one by one their hands fall from their instruments, till at last all melody ceases. At this moment Nehemoth falls asleep, and the slaves put the palanquin down and lie down beside it. At this hour the city becomes quite still, and the palace of Nehemoth and the tombs of the Pharaohs of old face to the sunlight, all alike in silence. Even the jewellers in the market-place, selling gems to princes, cease from their bargaining and cease to sing; for in Babbulkund the vendor of rubies sings the song of the ruby, and the vendor of sapphires sings the song of the sapphire, and each stone hath its song, so that a man, by his song, proclaims and makes known his wares.

'But all these sounds cease at the meridian hour, the jewellers in the market-place lie down in what shadow they can find, and the princes go back to the cool places in their palaces, and a great hush in the gleaming air hangs over Babbulkund. But in the cool of the late afternoon, one of the King's musicians will awake from dreaming of his home and will pass his fingers, perhaps, over the strings of his harp and, with the music, some memory may arise of the wind in the glens of the mountains that stand in the Isles of Song. Then the musician will wrench great cries out of the soul of his harp for the sake of the old memory, and his fellows will awake and all make a song of home, woven of sayings told in the harbour when the ships came in, and of tales in the cottages about the people of old time. One by one the other bands of musicians will take up the song, and Babbulkund, City of Marvel, will throb with this marvel anew. Just now Nehemoth awakes, the slaves leap to their feet and bear the palanquin to the outer side of the great crescent palace between the south and the west, to behold the sun again. The palanquin, with its ringing bells, goes round once more; the voices of the jewellers sing again, in the market-place, the song of the emerald, the song of the sapphire; men talk on the housetops, beggars wail in the streets, the musicians bend to their work, all the sounds blend together into one murmur, the voice of Babbulkund speaking at evening. Lower and lower sinks the sun, till Nehemoth, following it, comes with his panting slaves to the great purple garden of which surely thine own country has its songs, from wherever thou art come.

'There he alights from his palanquin and goes up to a throne of ivory set in the garden's midst, facing full westwards, and sits there alone, long regarding the sunlight until it is quite gone. At this hour trouble comes into the face of Nehemoth. Men have heard him muttering at the time of sunset: "Even I too, even I too." Thus do King Nehemoth and the sun make their glorious ambits about Babbulkund.

'A little later, when the stars come out to envy the beauty of the City of Marvel, the King walks to another part of the garden and sits in an alcove of opal all alone by the marge of the sacred lake. This is the lake whose shores and floors are of glass, which is lit from beneath by slaves with purple lights and with green lights intermingling, and is one of the seven wonders of Babbulkund. Three of the wonders are in the city's midst and four are at her gates. There is the lake, of which I tell thee, and the purple garden of which I have told thee and which is a wonder even to the stars, and there is Ong Zwarba, of which I shall tell thee also. And the wonders at the gates are these. At the eastern gate Neb. And at the northern gate the wonder of the river and the arches, for the River of Myth, which becomes one with the Waters of Fable in the desert outside the city, floats under a gate of pure gold, rejoicing, and under many arches fantastically carven that are one with either bank. The marvel at the western gate is the marvel of Annolith and the dog Voth. Annolith sits outside the western gate facing towards the city. He is higher than any of the towers or palaces, for his head was carved from the summit of the old hill; he hath two eyes of sapphire wherewith he regards Babbulkund, and the wonder of the eyes is that they are today in the same sockets wherein they glowed when first the world began, only the marble that covered them has been carven away and the light of day let in and the sight of the envious stars. Larger than a lion is the dog Voth beside him; every hair is carven upon the back of Voth, his war hackles are erected and his teeth are bared. All the Nehemoths have worshipped the god Annolith, but all their people pray to the dog Voth, for the law of the land is that none but a Nehemoth may worship the god Annolith. The marvel at the southern gate is the marvel of the jungle, for he comes with all his wild untravelled sea of darkness and trees and tigers and sunward-aspiring orchids right through a marble gate in the city wall and enters the city, and there widens and holds a space in its midst of many miles across. Moreover, he is older than the City of Marvel, for he dwelt long since in one of the valleys of the mountain which Nehemoth, first of Pharaohs, carved into Babbulkund.

'Now the opal alcove in which the King sits at evening by the lake stands at the edge of the jungle, and the climbing orchids of the jungle have long since crept from their homes through clefts of the opal alcove, lured by the lights of the lake, and now bloom there exultingly. Near to this alcove are the hareems of Nehemoth.

'The King hath four hareems—one for the stalwart women from the mountains to the north, one for the dark and furtive jungle women, one for the desert women that have wandering souls and pine in Babbulkund, and one for the princesses of his own kith, whose brown cheeks blush with the blood of ancient Pharaohs and who exult with Babbulkund in her surpassing beauty, and who know nought of the desert or the jungle or the bleak hills to the north. Quite unadorned and clad in simple garments go all the kith of Nehemoth, for they know well that he grows weary of pomp. Unadorned all save one, the Princess Linderith, who weareth Ong Zwarba and the three lesser gems of the sea. Such a stone is Ong Zwarba that there are none like it even in the turban of Nehemoth nor in all the sanctuaries of the sea. The same god that made Linderith made long ago Ong Zwarba; she and Ong Zwarba shine together with one light, and beside this marvellous stone gleam the three lesser ones of the sea.

'Now when the King sitteth in his opal alcove by the sacred lake with the orchids blooming around him all sounds are become still. The sound of the tramping of the weary slaves as they go round and round never comes to the surface. Long since the musicians sleep, and their hands have fallen dumb upon their instruments, and the voices in the city have died away. Perhaps a sigh of one of the desert women has become half a song, or on a hot night in summer one of the women of the hills sings softly a song of snow; all night long in the midst of the purple garden sings one nightingale; all else is still; the stars that look on Babbulkund arise and set, the cold unhappy moon drifts lonely through them, the night wears on; at last the dark figure of Nehemoth, eighty-second of his line, rises and moves stealthily away.'

The traveller ceased to speak. For a long time the clear stars, sisters of Babbulkund, had shone upon him speaking, the desert wind had arisen and whispered to the sand, and the sand had long gone secretly to and fro; none of us had moved, none of us had fallen asleep, not so much from wonder at his tale as from the thought that we ourselves in two days' time should see that wondrous city. Then we wrapped our blankets around us and lay down with our feet towards the embers of our fire and instantly were asleep, and in our dreams we multiplied the fame of the City of Marvel.

The sun arose and flamed upon our faces, and all the desert glinted with its light. Then we stood up and prepared the morning meal, and, when we had eaten, the traveller departed. And we commended his soul to the god of the land whereto he went, of the land of his home to the northward, and he commended our souls to the God of the people of the land wherefrom we had come. Then a traveller overtook us going on foot; he wore a brown cloak that was all in rags and he seemed to have been walking all night, and he walked hurriedly but appeared weary, so we offered him food and drink, of which he partook thankfully. When we asked him where he was going, he answered 'Babbulkund.' Then we offered him a camel upon which to ride, for we said, 'We also go to Babbulkund.' But he answered strangely:

'Nay, pass on before me, for it is a sore thing never to have seen Babbulkund, having lived while yet she stood. Pass on before me and behold her, and then flee away at once, returning northwards.'

Then, though we understood him not, we left him, for he was insistent, and passed on our journey southwards through the desert, and we came before the middle of the day to an oasis of palm trees standing by a well and there we gave water to the haughty camels and replenished our water-bottles and soothed our eyes with the sight of green things and tarried for many hours in the shade. Some of the men slept, but of those that remained awake each man sang softly the songs of his own country, telling of Babbulkund. When the afternoon was far spent we travelled a little way southwards, and went on through the cool evening until the sun fell low and we encamped, and as we sat in our encampment the man in rags overtook us, having travelled all the day, and we gave him food and drink again, and in the twilight he spoke, saying:

'I am the servant of the Lord the God of my people, and I go to do his work on Babbulkund. She is the most beautiful city in the world; there hath been none like her, even the stars of God go envious of her beauty. She is all white, yet with streaks of pink that pass through her streets and houses like flames in the white mind of a sculptor, like desire in Paradise. She hath been carved of old out of a holy hill, no slaves wrought the City of Marvel, but artists toiling at the work they loved. They took no pattern from the houses of men, but each man wrought what his inner eye had seen and carved in marble the visions of his dream. All over the roof of one of the palace chambers winged lions flit like bats, the size of every one is the size of the lions of God, and the wings are larger than any wing created; they are one above the other more than a man can number, they are all carven out of one block of marble, the chamber itself is hollowed from it, and it is borne aloft upon the carven branches of a grove of clustered tree-ferns wrought by the hand of some jungle mason that loved the tall fern well. Over the River of Myth, which is one with the Waters of Fable, go bridges, fashioned like the wisteria tree and like the drooping laburnum, and a hundred others of wonderful devices, the desire of the souls of masons a long while dead. Oh! very beautiful is white Babbulkund, very beautiful she is, but proud; and the Lord the God of my people hath seen her in her pride, and looking towards her hath seen the prayers of Nehemoth going up to the abomination Annolith and all the people following after Voth. She is very beautiful, Babbulkund; alas that I may not bless her. I could live always on one of her inner terraces looking on the mysterious jungle in her midst and the heavenward faces of the orchids that, clambering from the darkness, behold the sun. I could love Babbulkund with a great love, yet am I the servant of the Lord the God of my people, and the King hath sinned unto the abomination Annolith, and the people lust exceedingly for Voth. Alas for thee, Babbulkund, alas that I may not even now turn back, for tomorrow I must prophesy against thee and cry out against thee, Babbulkund. But ye travellers that have entreated me hospitably, rise and pass on with your camels, for I can tarry no longer, and I go to do the work on Babbulkund of the Lord the God of my people. Go now and see the beauty of Babbulkund before I cry out against her, and then flee swiftly northwards.'

A smouldering fragment fell in upon our camp fire and sent a strange light into the eyes of the man in rags. He rose at once, and his tattered cloak swirled up with him like a great wing; he said no more, but turned round from us instantly southwards, and strode away into the darkness towards Babbulkund. Then a hush fell upon our encampment, and the smell of the tobacco of those lands arose. When the last flame died down in our camp fire I fell asleep, but my rest was troubled by shifting dreams of doom.

Morning came, and our guides told us that we should come to the city ere nightfall. Again we passed southwards through the changeless desert; sometimes we met travellers coming from Babbulkund, with the beauty of its marvels still fresh in their eyes.

When we encamped near the middle of the day we saw a great number of people on foot coming towards us running, from the southwards. These we hailed when they were come near, saying, 'What of Babbulkund?'

They answered: 'We are not of the race of the people of Babbulkund, but were captured in youth and taken away from the hills that are to the northward. Now we have all seen in visions of the stillness the Lord the God of our people calling to us from His hills, and therefore we all flee northwards. But in Babbulkund King Nehemoth hath been troubled in the nights by unkingly dreams of doom, and none may interpret what the dreams portend. Now this is the dream that King Nehemoth dreamed on the first night of his dreaming. He saw move through the stillness a bird all black, and beneath the beatings of his wings Babbulkund gloomed and darkened; and after him flew a bird all white, beneath the beatings of whose wings Babbulkund gleamed and shone; and there flew by four more birds alternately black and white. And, as the black ones passed Babbulkund darkened, and when the white ones appeared her streets and houses shone. But after the sixth bird there came no more, and Babbulkund vanished from her place, and there was only the empty desert where she had stood, and the rivers Oonrana and Plegáthanees mourning alone. Next morning all the prophets of the King gathered before their abominations and questioned them of the dream, and the abominations spake not. But when the second night stepped down from the halls of God, dowered with many stars, King Nehemoth dreamed again; and in this dream King Nehemoth saw four birds only, black and white alternately as before. And Babbulkund darkened again as the black ones passed, and shone when the white came by; only after the four birds came no more, and Babbulkund vanished from her place, leaving only the forgetful desert and the mourning rivers.

'Still the abominations spake not, and none could interpret the dream. And when the third night came forth from the divine halls of her home dowered like her sisters, again King Nehemoth dreamed. And he saw a bird all black go by again, beneath whom Babbulkund darkened, and then a white bird and Babbulkund shone; and after them came no more, and Babbulkund passed away. And the golden day appeared, dispelling dreams, and still the abominations were silent, and the King's prophets answered not to portend the omen of the dream. One prophet only spake before the King, saying: "The sable birds, O King, are the nights, and the white birds are the days…" This thing the King had feared, and he arose and smote the prophet with his sword, whose soul went crying away and had to do no more with nights and days.

'It was last night that the King dreamed his third dream, and this morning we fled away from Babbulkund. A great heat lies over it, and the orchids of the jungle droop their heads. All night long the women in the hareem of the North have wailed horribly for their hills. A fear hath fallen upon the city, and a boding. Twice hath Nehemoth gone to worship Annolith, and all the people have prostrated themselves before Voth. Thrice the horologers have looked into the great crystal globe wherein are foretold all happenings to be, and thrice the globe was blank. Yea, though they went a fourth time yet was no vision revealed; and the people's voice is hushed in Babbulkund.'

Soon the travellers arose and pushed on northwards again, leaving us wondering. Through the heat of the day we rested as well as we might, but the air was motionless and sultry and the camels ill at ease. The Arabs said that it boded a desert storm, and that a great wind would arise full of sand. So we arose in the afternoon, and travelled swiftly, hoping to come to shelter before the storm. And the air burned in the stillness between the baked desert and the glaring sky.

Suddenly a wind arose out of the South, blowing from Babbulkund, and the sand lifted and went by in great shapes, all whispering. And the wind blew violently, and wailed as it blew, and hundreds of sandy shapes went towering by, and there were little cries among them and the sounds of a passing away. Soon the wind sank quite suddenly, and its cries died, and the panic ceased among the driven sands. And when the storm departed the air was cool, and the terrible sultriness and the boding were passed away, and the camels had ease among them. And the Arabs said that the storm which was to be had been, as was willed of old by God.

The sun set and the gloaming came, and we neared the junction of Oonrana and Plegáthanees, but in the darkness discerned not Babbulkund. We pushed on hurriedly to reach the city ere nightfall, and came to the junction of the River of Myth where he meets with the Waters of Fable, and still saw not Babbulkund. All round us lay the sand and rocks of the unchanging desert, save to the southwards where the jungle stood with its orchids facing skywards. Then we perceived that we had arrived too late, and that her doom had come to Babbulkund; and by the river in the empty desert on the sand the man in rags was seated, with his face hidden in his hands, weeping bitterly.

* * * *

Thus passed away in the hour of her iniquities before Annolith, in the two thousand and thirty-second year of her being, in the six thousand and fiftieth year of the building of the World, Babbulkund, City of Marvel, sometime called by those that hated her City of the Dog, but hourly mourned in Araby and Ind and wide through jungle and desert; leaving no memorial in stone to show that she had been, but remembered with an abiding love, in spite of the anger of God, by all that knew her beauty, whereof still they sing.

THE KITH OF THE ELF FOLK

CHAPTER I

The north wind was blowing, and red and golden the last days of Autumn were streaming hence. Solemn and cold over the marshes arose the evening.

It became very still.

Then the last pigeon went home to the trees on the dry land in the distance, whose shapes already had taken upon themselves a mystery in the haze.

Then all was still again.

As the light faded and the haze deepened, mystery crept nearer from every side.

Then the green plover came in crying, and all alighted.

And again it became still, save when one of the plover arose and flew a little way uttering the cry of the waste. And hushed and silent became the earth, expecting the first star. Then the duck came in, and the widgeon, company by company: and all the light of day faded out of the sky saving one red band of light. Across the light appeared, black and huge, the wings of a flock of geese beating up wind to the marshes. These, too, went down among the rushes.

Then the stars appeared and shone in the stillness, and there was silence in the great spaces of the night.

Suddenly the bells of the cathedral in the marshes broke out, calling to evensong.

Eight centuries ago on the edge of the marsh men had built the huge cathedral, or it may have been seven centuries ago, or perhaps nine—it was all one to the Wild Things.

So evensong was held, and candles lighted, and the lights through the windows shone red and green in the water, and the sound of the organ went roaring over the marshes. But from the deep and perilous places, edged with bright mosses, the Wild Things came leaping up to dance on the reflection of the stars, and over their heads as they danced the marsh-lights rose and fell.

The Wild Things are somewhat human in appearance, only all brown of skin and barely two feet high. Their ears are pointed like the squirrel's, only far larger, and they leap to prodigious heights. They live all day under deep pools in the loneliest marshes, but at night they come up and dance. Each Wild Thing has over its head a marsh-light, which moves as the Wild Thing moves; they have no souls, and cannot die, and are of the kith of the Elf-folk.

All night they dance over the marshes, treading upon the reflection of the stars (for the bare surface of the water will not hold them by itself); but when the stars begin to pale, they sink down one by one into the pools of their home. Or if they tarry longer, sitting upon the rushes, their bodies fade from view as the marsh-fires pale in the light, and by daylight none may see the Wild Things of the kith of the Elf-folk. Neither may any see them even at night unless they were born, as I was, in the hour of dusk, just at the moment when the first star appears.

Now, on the night that I tell of, a little Wild Thing had gone drifting over the waste, till it came right up to the walls of the cathedral and danced upon the images of the coloured saints as they lay in the water among the reflection of the stars. And as it leaped in its fantastic dance, it saw through the painted windows to where the people prayed, and heard the organ roaring over the marshes. The sound of the organ roared over the marshes, but the song and prayers of the people streamed up from the cathedral's highest tower like thin gold chains, and reached to Paradise, and up and down them went the angels from Paradise to the people, and from the people to Paradise again.

Then something akin to discontent troubled the Wild Thing for the first time since the making of the marshes; and the soft grey ooze and the chill of the deep water seemed to be not enough, nor the first arrival from northwards of the tumultuous geese, nor the wild rejoicing of the wings of the wildfowl when every feather sings, nor the wonder of the calm ice that comes when the snipe depart and beards the rushes with frost and clothes the hushed waste with a mysterious haze where the sun goes red and low, nor even the dance of the Wild Things in the marvellous night; and the little Wild Thing longed to have a soul, and to go and worship God.

And when evensong was over and the lights were out, it went back crying to its kith.

But on the next night, as soon as the images of the stars appeared in the water, it went leaping away from star to star to the farthest edge of the marshlands, where a great wood grew where dwelt the Oldest of the Wild Things.

And it found the Oldest of Wild Things sitting under a tree, sheltering itself from the moon.

And the little Wild Thing said: 'I want to have a soul to worship God, and to know the meaning of music, and to see the inner beauty of the marshlands and to imagine Paradise.'

And the Oldest of the Wild Things said to it: 'What have we to do with God? We are only Wild Things, and of the kith of the Elf-folk.'

But it only answered, 'I want to have a soul.'

Then the Oldest of the Wild Things said: 'I have no soul to give you; but if you got a soul, one day you would have to die, and if you knew the meaning of music you would learn the meaning of sorrow, and it is better to be a Wild Thing and not to die.'

So it went weeping away.

But they that were kin to the Elf-folk were sorry for the little Wild Thing; and though the Wild Things cannot sorrow long, having no souls to sorrow with, yet they felt for awhile a soreness where their souls should be, when they saw the grief of their comrade.

So the kith of the Elf-folk went abroad by night to make a soul for the little Wild Thing. And they went over the marshes till they came to the high fields among the flowers and grasses. And there they gathered a large piece of gossamer that the spider had laid by twilight; and the dew was on it.

Into this dew had shone all the lights of the long banks of the ribbed sky, as all the colours changed in the restful spaces of evening. And over it the marvellous night had gleamed with all its stars.

Then the Wild Things went with their dew-bespangled gossamer down to the edge of their home. And there they gathered a piece of the grey mist that lies by night over the marshlands. And into it they put the melody of the waste that is borne up and down the marshes in the evening on the wings of the golden plover. And they put into it, too, the mournful song that the reeds are compelled to sing before the presence of the arrogant North Wind. Then each of the Wild Things gave some treasured memory of the old marshes, 'For we can spare it,' they said. And to all this they added a few images of the stars that they gathered out of the water. Still the soul that the kith of the Elf-folk were making had no life.

Then they put into it the low voices of two lovers that went walking in the night, wandering late alone. And after that they waited for the dawn. And the queenly dawn appeared, and the marsh-lights of the Wild Things paled in the glare, and their bodies faded from view; and still they waited by the marsh's edge. And to them waiting came over field and marsh, from the ground and out of the sky, the myriad song of the birds.

This, too, the Wild Things put into the piece of haze that they had gathered in the marshlands, and wrapped it all up in their dew-bespangled gossamer. Then the soul lived.

And there it lay in the hands of the Wild Things no larger than a hedge-hog; and wonderful lights were in it, green and blue; and they changed ceaselessly, going round and round, and in the grey midst of it was a purple flare.

And the next night they came to the little Wild Thing and showed her the gleaming soul. And they said to her: 'If you must have a soul and go and worship God, and become a mortal and die, place this to your left breast a little above the heart, and it will enter and you will become a human. But if you take it you can never be rid of it to become immortal again unless you pluck it out and give it to another; and we will not take it, and most of the humans have a soul already. And if you cannot find a human without a soul you will one day die, and your soul cannot go to Paradise, because it was only made in the marshes.'

Far away the little Wild Thing saw the cathedral windows alight for evensong, and the song of the people mounting up to Paradise, and all the angels going up and down. So it bid farewell with tears and thanks to the Wild Things of the kith of Elf-folk, and went leaping away towards the green dry land, holding the soul in its hands.

And the Wild Things were sorry that it had gone, but could not be sorry long, because they had no souls.

At the marsh's edge the little Wild Thing gazed for some moments over the water to where the marsh-fires were leaping up and down, and then pressed the soul against its left breast a little above the heart.

Instantly it became a young and beautiful woman, who was cold and frightened. She clad herself somehow with bundles of reeds, and went towards the lights of a house that stood close by. And she pushed open the door and entered, and found a farmer and a farmer's wife sitting over their supper.

And the farmer's wife took the little Wild Thing with the soul of the marshes up to her room, and clothed her and braided her hair, and brought her down again, and gave her the first food that she had ever eaten. Then the farmer's wife asked many questions.

'Where have you come from?' she said.

'Over the marshes.'

'From what direction?' said the farmer's wife.

'South,' said the little Wild Thing with the new soul.

'But none can come over the marshes from the south,' said the farmer's wife.

'No, they can't do that,' said the farmer.

'I lived in the marshes.'

'Who are you?' asked the farmer's wife.

'I am a Wild Thing, and have found a soul in the marshes, and we are kin to the Elf-folk.'

Talking it over afterwards, the farmer and his wife agreed that she must be a gipsy who had been lost, and that she was queer with hunger and exposure.

So that night the little Wild Thing slept in the farmer's house, but her new soul stayed awake the whole night long dreaming of the beauty of the marshes.

As soon as dawn came over the waste and shone on the farmer's house, she looked from the window towards the glittering waters, and saw the inner beauty of the marsh. For the Wild Things only love the marsh and know its haunts, but now she perceived the mystery of its distances and the glamour of its perilous pools, with their fair and deadly mosses, and felt the marvel of the North Wind who comes dominant out of unknown icy lands, and the wonder of that ebb and flow of life when the wildfowl whirl in at evening to the marshlands and at dawn pass out to sea. And she knew that over her head above the farmer's house stretched wide Paradise, where perhaps God was now imagining a sunrise while angels played low on lutes, and the sun came rising up on the world below to gladden fields and marsh.

And all that heaven thought, the marsh thought too; for the blue of the marsh was as the blue of heaven, and the great cloud shapes in heaven became the shapes in the marsh, and through each ran momentary rivers of purple, errant between banks of gold. And the stalwart army of reeds appeared out of the gloom with all their pennons waving as far as the eye could see. And from another window she saw the vast cathedral gathering its ponderous strength together, and lifting it up in towers out of the marshlands.

She said, 'I will never, never leave the marsh.'

An hour later she dressed with great difficulty and went down to eat the second meal of her life. The farmer and his wife were kindly folk, and taught her how to eat.

'I suppose the gipsies don't have knives and forks,' one said to the other afterwards.

After breakfast the farmer went and saw the Dean, who lived near his cathedral, and presently returned and brought back to the Dean's house the little Wild Thing with the new soul.

'This is the lady,' said the farmer. 'This is Dean Murnith.' Then he went away.

'Ah,' said the Dean, 'I understand you were lost the other night in the marshes. It was a terrible night to be lost in the marshes.'

'I love the marshes,' said the little Wild Thing with the new soul.

'Indeed! How old are you?' said the Dean.

'I don't know,' she answered.

'You must know about how old you are,' he said.

'Oh, about ninety,' she said, 'or more.'

'Ninety years!' exclaimed the Dean.

'No, ninety centuries,' she said; 'I am as old as the marshes.'

Then she told her story—how she had longed to be a human and go and worship God, and have a soul and see the beauty of the world, and how all the Wild Things had made her a soul of gossamer and mist and music and strange memories.

'But if this is true,' said Dean Murnith, 'this is very wrong. God cannot have intended you to have a soul.

'What is your name?'

'I have no name,' she answered.

'We must find a Christian name and a surname for you. What would you like to be called?'

'Song of the Rushes,' she said.

'That won't do at all,' said the Dean.

'Then I would like to be called Terrible North Wind, or Star in the Waters,' she said.

'No, no, no,' said Dean Murnith; 'that is quite impossible. We could call you Miss Rush if you like. How would Mary Rush do? Perhaps you had better have another name—say Mary Jane Rush.'

So the little Wild Thing with the soul of the marshes took the names that were offered her, and became Mary Jane Rush.

'And we must find something for you to do,' said Dean Murnith. 'Meanwhile we can give you a room here.'

'I don't want to do anything,' replied Mary Jane; 'I want to worship God in the cathedral and live beside the marshes.'

Then Mrs. Murnith came in, and for the rest of that day Mary Jane stayed at the house of the Dean.

And there with her new soul she perceived the beauty of the world; for it came grey and level out of misty distances, and widened into grassy fields and ploughlands right up to the edge of an old gabled town; and solitary in the fields far off an ancient windmill stood, and his honest hand-made sails went round and round in the free East Anglian winds. Close by, the gabled houses leaned out over the streets, planted fair upon sturdy timbers that grew in the olden time, all glorying among themselves upon their beauty. And out of them, buttress by buttress, growing and going upwards, aspiring tower by tower, rose the cathedral.

And she saw the people moving in the streets all leisurely and slow, and unseen among them, whispering to each other, unheard by living men and concerned only with bygone things, drifted the ghosts of very long ago. And wherever the streets ran eastwards, wherever were gaps in the houses, always there broke into view the sight of the great marshes, like to some bar of music weird and strange that haunts a melody, arising again and again, played on the violin by one musician only, who plays no other bar, and he is swart and lank about the hair and bearded about the lips, and his moustache droops long and low, and no one knows the land from which he comes.

All these were good things for a new soul to see.

Then the sun set over green fields and ploughland and the night came up. One by one the merry lights of cheery lamp-lit windows took their stations in the solemn night.

Then the bells rang, far up in a cathedral tower, and their melody fell on the roofs of the old houses and poured over their eaves until the streets were full, and then flooded away over green fields and plough, till it came to the sturdy mill and brought the miller trudging to evensong, and far away eastwards and seawards the sound rang out over the remoter marshes. And it was all as yesterday to the old ghosts in the streets.

Then the Dean's wife took Mary Jane to evening service, and she saw three hundred candles filling all the aisle with light. But sturdy pillars stood there in unlit vastnesses; great colonnades going away into the gloom, where evening and morning, year in year out, they did their work in the dark, holding the cathedral roof aloft. And it was stiller than the marshes are still when the ice has come and the wind that brought it has fallen.

Suddenly into this stillness rushed the sound of the organ, roaring, and presently the people prayed and sang.

No longer could Mary Jane see their prayers ascending like thin gold chains, for that was but an elfin fancy, but she imagined clear in her new soul the seraphs passing in the ways of Paradise, and the angels changing guard to watch the World by night.

When the Dean had finished service, a young curate, Mr. Millings, went up into the pulpit.

He spoke of Abana and Pharpar, rivers of Damascus: and Mary Jane was glad that there were rivers having such names, and heard with wonder of Nineveh, that great city, and many things strange and new.

And the light of the candles shone on the curate's fair hair, and his voice went ringing down the aisle, and Mary Jane rejoiced that he was there.

But when his voice stopped she felt a sudden loneliness, such as she had not felt since the making of the marshes; for the Wild Things never are lonely and never unhappy, but dance all night on the reflection of the stars, and having no souls, desire nothing more.

After the collection was made, before anyone moved to go, Mary Jane walked up the aisle to Mr. Millings.

'I love you,' she said.

CHAPTER II

Nobody sympathised with Mary Jane.

'So unfortunate for Mr. Millings,' every one said; 'such a promising young man.'

Mary Jane was sent away to a great manufacturing city of the Midlands, where work had been found for her in a cloth factory. And there was nothing in that town that was good for a soul to see. For it did not know that beauty was to be desired; so it made many things by machinery, and became hurried in all its ways, and boasted its superiority over other cities and became richer and richer, and there was none to pity it.

In this city Mary Jane had had lodgings found for her near the factory.

At six o'clock on those November mornings, about the time that, far away from the city, the wildfowl rose up out of the calm marshes and passed to the troubled spaces of the sea, at six o'clock the factory uttered a prolonged howl and gathered the workers together, and there they worked, saving two hours for food, the whole of the daylit hours and into the dark till the bells tolled six again.

There Mary Jane worked with other girls in a long dreary room, where giants sat pounding wool into a long thread-like strip with iron, rasping hands. And all day long they roared as they sat at their soulless work. But the work of Mary Jane was not with these, only their roar was ever in her ears as their clattering iron limbs went to and fro.

Her work was to tend a creature smaller, but infinitely more cunning.

It took the strip of wool that the giants had threshed, and whirled it round and round until it had twisted it into hard thin thread. Then it would make a clutch with fingers of steel at the thread that it had gathered, and waddle away about five yards and come back with more.

It had mastered all the subtlety of skilled workers, and had gradually displaced them; one thing only it could not do, it was unable to pick up the ends if a piece of the thread broke, in order to tie them together again. For this a human soul was required, and it was Mary Jane's business to pick up broken ends; and the moment she placed them together the busy soulless creature tied them for itself.

All here was ugly; even the green wool as it whirled round and round was neither the green of the grass nor yet the green of the rushes, but a sorry muddy green that befitted a sullen city under a murky sky.

When she looked out over the roofs of the town, there too was ugliness; and well the houses knew it, for with hideous stucco they aped in grotesque mimicry the pillars and temples of old Greece, pretending to one another to be that which they were not. And emerging from these houses and going in, and seeing the pretence of paint and stucco year after year until it all peeled away, the souls of the poor owners of those houses sought to be other souls until they grew weary of it.

At evening Mary Jane went back to her lodgings. Only then, after the dark had fallen, could the soul of Mary Jane perceive any beauty in that city, when the lamps were lit and here and there a star shone through the smoke. Then she would have gone abroad and beheld the night, but this the old woman to whom she was confided would not let her do. And the days multiplied themselves by seven and became weeks, and the weeks passed by, and all days were the same. And all the while the soul of Mary Jane was crying for beautiful things, and found not one, saving on Sundays, when she went to church, and left it to find the city greyer than before.

One day she decided that it was better to be a wild thing in the lovely marshes, than to have a soul that cried for beautiful things and found not one. From that day she determined to be rid of her soul, so she told her story to one of the factory girls, and said to her:

'The other girls are poorly clad and they do soulless work; surely some of them have no souls and would take mine.'

But the factory girl said to her: 'All the poor have souls. It is all they have.'

Then Mary Jane watched the rich whenever she saw them, and vainly sought for some one without a soul.

One day at the hour when the machines rested and the human beings that tended them rested too, the wind being at that time from the direction of the marshlands, the soul of Mary Jane lamented bitterly. Then, as she stood outside the factory gates, the soul irresistibly compelled her to sing, and a wild song came from her lips, hymning the marshlands. And into her song came crying her yearning for home, and for the sound of the shout of the North Wind, masterful and proud, with his lovely lady the Snow; and she sang of tales that the rushes murmured to one another, tales that the teal knew and the watchful heron. And over the crowded streets her song went crying away, the song of waste places and of wild free lands, full of wonder and magic, for she had in her elf-made soul the song of the birds and the roar of the organ in the marshes.

At this moment Signor Thompsoni, the well-known English tenor, happened to go by with a friend. They stopped and listened; everyone stopped and listened.

'There has been nothing like this in Europe in my time,' said Signor Thompsoni.

So a change came into the life of Mary Jane.

People were written to, and finally it was arranged that she should take a leading part in the Covent Garden Opera in a few weeks.

So she went to London to learn.

London and singing lessons were better than the City of the Midlands and those terrible machines. Yet still Mary Jane was not free to go and live as she liked by the edge of the marshlands, and she was still determined to be rid of her soul, but could find no one that had not a soul of their own.

One day she was told that the English people would not listen to her as Miss Rush, and was asked what more suitable name she would like to be called by.

'I would like to be called Terrible North Wind,' said Mary Jane, 'or Song of the Rushes.'

When she was told that this was impossible and Signorina Maria Russiano was suggested, she acquiesced at once, as she had acquiesced when they took her away from her curate; she knew nothing of the ways of humans.

At last the day of the Opera came round, and it was a cold day of the winter.

And Signorina Russiano appeared on the stage before a crowded house.

And Signorina Russiano sang.

And into the song went all the longing of her soul, the soul that could not go to Paradise, but could only worship God and know the meaning of music, and the longing pervaded that Italian song as the infinite mystery of the hills is borne along the sound of distant sheep-bells. Then in the souls that were in that crowded house arose little memories of a great while since that were quite quite dead, and lived awhile again during that marvellous song.

And a strange chill went into the blood of all that listened, as though they stood on the border of bleak marshes and the North Wind blew.

And some it moved to sorrow and some to regret, and some to an unearthly joy,—then suddenly the song went wailing away like the winds of the winter from the marshlands when Spring appears from the South.

So it ended. And a great silence fell fog-like over all that house, breaking in upon the end of a chatty conversation that Cecilia, Countess of Birmingham, was enjoying with a friend.

In the dead hush Signorina Russiano rushed from the stage; she appeared again running among the audience, and dashed up to Lady Birmingham.

'Take my soul,' she said; 'it is a beautiful soul. It can worship God, and knows the meaning of music and can imagine Paradise. And if you go to the marshlands with it you will see beautiful things; there is an old town there built of lovely timbers, with ghosts in its streets.'

Lady Birmingham stared. Everyone was standing up. 'See,' said Signorina Russiano, 'it is a beautiful soul.'

And she clutched at her left breast a little above the heart, and there was the soul shining in her hand, with the green and blue lights going round and round and the purple flare in the midst.

'Take it,' she said, 'and you will love all that is beautiful, and know the four winds, each one by his name, and the songs of the birds at dawn. I do not want it, because I am not free. Put it to your left breast a little above the heart.'

Still everybody was standing up, and Lady Birmingham felt uncomfortable.

'Please offer it to some one else,' she said.

'But they all have souls already,' said Signorina Russiano.

And everybody went on standing up. And Lady Birmingham took the soul in her hand.

'Perhaps it is lucky,' she said.

She felt that she wanted to pray.

She half-closed her eyes, and said '*Unberufen*'. Then she put the soul to her left breast a little above the heart, and hoped that the people would sit down and the singer go away.

Instantly a heap of clothes collapsed before her. For a moment, in the shadow among the seats, those who were born in the dusk hour might have seen a little brown thing leaping free from the clothes, then it sprang into the bright light of the hall, and became invisible to any human eye.

It dashed about for a little, then found the door, and presently was in the lamplit streets.

To those that were born in the dusk hour it might have been seen leaping rapidly wherever the streets ran northwards and eastwards, disappearing from human sight as it passed under the lamps and appearing again beyond them with a marsh-light over its head.

Once a dog perceived it and gave chase, and was left far behind.

The cats of London, who are all born in the dusk hour, howled fearfully as it went by.

Presently it came to the meaner streets, where the houses are smaller. Then it went due north-eastwards, leaping from roof to roof. And so in a few minutes it came to more open spaces, and then to the desolate lands, where market gardens grow, which are neither town nor country. Till at last the good black trees came into view, with their demoniac shapes in the night, and the grass was cold and wet, and the night-mist floated over it. And a great white owl came by, going up and down in the dark. And at all these things the little Wild Thing rejoiced elvishly.

And it left London far behind it, reddening the sky, and could distinguish no longer its unlovely roar, but heard again the noises of the night.

And now it would come through a hamlet glowing and comfortable in the night; and now to the dark, wet, open fields again; and many an owl it overtook as they drifted through the night, a people friendly to the Elf-folk. Sometimes it crossed wide rivers, leaping from star to star; and, choosing its way as it went, to avoid the hard rough roads, came before midnight to the East Anglian lands.

And it heard there the shout of the North Wind, who was dominant and angry, as he drove southwards his adventurous geese; while the rushes bent before him chaunting plaintively and low, like enslaved rowers of some fabulous trireme, bending and swinging under blows of the lash, and singing all the while a doleful song.

And it felt the good dank air that clothes by night the broad East Anglian lands, and came again to some old perilous pool where the soft green mosses grew, and there plunged downward and downward into the dear dark water till it felt the homely ooze once more coming up between its toes. Thence, out of the lovely chill that is in the heart of the ooze, it arose renewed and rejoicing to dance upon the image of the stars.

I chanced to stand that night by the marsh's edge, forgetting in my mind the affairs of men; and I saw the marsh-fires come leaping up from all the perilous places. And they came up by flocks the whole night long to the number of a great multitude, and danced away together over the marshes.

And I believe that there was a great rejoicing all that night among the kith of the Elf-folk.

THE HIGHWAYMEN

Tom o' the Roads had ridden his last ride, and was now alone in the night. From where he was, a man might see the white recumbent sheep and the black outline of the lonely downs, and the grey line of the farther and lonelier downs beyond them; or in hollows far below him, out of the pitiless wind, he might see the grey smoke of hamlets arising from black valleys. But all alike was black to the eyes of Tom, and all the sounds were silence in his ears; only his soul struggled to slip from the iron chains and to pass southwards into Paradise. And the wind blew and blew.

For Tom tonight had nought but the wind to ride; they had taken his true black horse on the day when they took from him the green fields and the sky, men's voices and the laughter of women, and had left him alone with chains about his neck to swing in the wind for ever. And the wind blew and blew.

But the soul of Tom o' the Roads was nipped by the cruel chains, and whenever it struggled to escape it was beaten backwards into the iron collar by the wind that blows from Paradise from the south. And swinging there by the neck, there fell away old sneers from off his lips, and scoffs that he had long since scoffed at God fell from his tongue, and there rotted old bad lusts out of his heart, and from his fingers the stains of deeds that were evil; and they all fell to the ground and grew there in pallid rings and clusters. And when these ill things had all fallen away, Tom's soul was clean again, as his early love had found it, a long while since in spring; and it swung up there in the wind with the bones of Tom, and with his old torn coat and rusty chains.

And the wind blew and blew.

And ever and anon the souls of the sepultured, coming from consecrated acres, would go by beating up wind to Paradise past the Gallows Tree and past the soul of Tom, that might not go free.

Night after night Tom watched the sheep upon the downs with empty hollow sockets, till his dead hair grew and covered his poor dead face, and hid the shame of it from the sheep. And the wind blew and blew.

Sometimes on gusts of the wind came someone's tears, and beat and beat against the iron chains, but could not rust them through. And the wind blew and blew.

And every evening all the thoughts that Tom had ever uttered came flocking in from doing their work in the world, the work that may not cease, and sat along the gallows branches and chirruped to the soul of Tom, the soul that might not go free. All the thoughts that he had ever uttered! And the evil thoughts rebuked the soul that bore them because they might not die. And all those that he had uttered the most furtively, chirruped the loudest and the shrillest in the branches all the night.

And all the thoughts that Tom had ever thought about himself now pointed at the wet bones and mocked at the old torn coat. But the thoughts that he had had of others were the only companions that his soul had to soothe it in the night as it swung to and fro. And they twittered to the soul and cheered the poor dumb thing that could have dreams no more, till there came a murderous thought and drove them all away.

And the wind blew and blew.

Paul, Archbishop of Alois and Vayence, lay in his white sepulchre of marble, facing full to the southwards towards Paradise. And over his tomb was sculptured the Cross of Christ, that his soul might have repose. No wind howled here as it howled in lonely tree-tops up upon the downs, but came with gentle breezes, orchard scented, over the low lands from Paradise from the southwards, and played about forget-me-nots and grasses in the consecrated land where lay the Reposeful round the sepulchre of Paul,

Archbishop of Alois and Vayence. Easy it was for a man's soul to pass from such a sepulchre, and, flitting low over remembered fields, to come upon the garden lands of Paradise and find eternal ease.

And the wind blew and blew.

In a tavern of foul repute three men were lapping gin. Their names were Joe and Will and the gypsy Puglioni; none other names had they, for of whom their fathers were they had no knowledge, but only dark suspicions.

Sin had caressed and stroked their faces often with its paws, but the face of Puglioni Sin had kissed all over the mouth and chin. Their food was robbery and their pastime murder. All of them had incurred the sorrow of God and the enmity of man. They sat at a table with a pack of cards before them, all greasy with the marks of cheating thumbs. And they whispered to one another over their gin, but so low that the landlord of the tavern at the other end of the room could hear only muffled oaths, and knew not by Whom they swore or what they said.

These three were the staunchest friends that ever God had given unto a man. And he to whom their friendship had been given had nothing else besides, saving some bones that swung in the wind and rain, and an old torn coat and iron chains, and a soul that might not go free.

But as the night wore on the three friends left their gin and stole away, and crept down to that graveyard where rested in his sepulchre Paul, Archbishop of Alois and Vayence. At the edge of the graveyard, but outside the consecrated ground, they dug a hasty grave, two digging while one watched in the wind and rain. And the worms that crept in the unhallowed ground wondered and waited.

And the terrible hour of midnight came upon them with its fears, and found them still beside the place of tombs. And the three friends trembled at the horror of such an hour in such a place, and shivered in the wind and drenching rain, but still worked on. And the wind blew and blew.

Soon they had finished. And at once they left the hungry grave with all its worms unfed, and went away over the wet fields stealthily but in haste, leaving the place of tombs behind them in the midnight. And as they went they shivered, and each man as he shivered cursed the rain aloud. And so they came to the spot where they had hidden a ladder and a lantern. There they held long debate whether they should light the lantern, or whether they should go without it for fear of the King's men. But in the end it seemed to them better that they should have the light of their lantern, and risk being taken by the King's men and hanged, than that they should come suddenly face to face in the darkness with whatever one might come face to face with a little after midnight about the Gallows Tree.

On three roads in England whereon it was not the wont of folk to go their ways in safety, travellers tonight went unmolested. But the three friends, walking several paces wide of the King's highway, approached the Gallows Tree, and Will carried the lantern and Joe the ladder, but Puglioni carried a great sword wherewith to do the work which must be done. When they came close, they saw how bad was the case with Tom, for little remained of that fine figure of a man and nothing at all of his great resolute spirit, only as they came they thought they heard a whimpering cry like the sound of a thing that was caged and unfree.

To and fro, to and fro in the winds swung the bones and the soul of Tom, for the sins that he had sinned on the King's highway against the laws of the King; and with shadows and a lantern through the darkness, at the peril of their lives, came the three friends that his soul had won before it swung in chains. Thus the seeds of Tom's own soul that he had sown all his life had grown into a Gallows Tree that bore in season iron chains in clusters; while the careless seeds that he had strewn here and there, a kindly jest and a few merry words, had grown into the triple friendship that would not desert his bones.

Then the three set the ladder against the tree, and Puglioni went up with his sword in his right hand, and at the top of it he reached up and began to hack at the neck below the iron collar. Presently, the bones and the old coat and the soul of Tom fell down with a rattle, and a moment afterwards his head that had watched so long alone swung clear from the swinging chain. These things Will and Joe gathered up, and Puglioni came running down his ladder, and they heaped upon its rungs the terrible remains of their friend, and hastened away wet through with the rain, with the fear of phantoms in their hearts and horror lying before them on the ladder. By two o'clock they were down again in the valley out of the bitter wind, but they went on past the open grave into the graveyard all among the tombs, with their lantern and their ladder and the terrible thing upon it, which kept their friendship still. Then these three, that had robbed the Law of its due and proper victim, still sinned on for what was still their friend, and levered out the marble slabs from the sacred sepulchre of Paul, Archbishop of Alois and Vayence. And from it they took the very bones of the Archbishop himself, and carried them away to the eager grave that they had left, and put them in and shovelled back the earth. But all that lay on the ladder they placed, with a few tears, within the great white sepulchre under the Cross of Christ, and put back the marble slabs.

Thence the soul of Tom, arising hallowed out of sacred ground, went at dawn down the valley, and, lingering a little about his mother's cottage and old haunts of childhood, passed on and came to the wide lands beyond the clustered homesteads. There, there met with it all the kindly thoughts that the soul of Tom had ever had, and they flew and sang beside it all the way southwards, until at last, with singing all about it, it came to Paradise.

But Will and Joe and the gypsy Puglioni went back to their gin, and robbed and cheated again in the tavern of foul repute, and knew not that in their sinful lives they had sinned one sin at which the Angels smiled.

IN THE TWILIGHT

The lock was quite crowded with boats when we capsized. I went down backwards for some few feet before I started to swim, then I came spluttering upwards towards the light; but, instead of reaching the surface, I hit my head against the keel of a boat and went down again. I struck out almost at once and came up, but before I reached the surface my head crashed against a boat for the second time, and I went right to the bottom. I was confused and thoroughly frightened. I was desperately in need of air, and knew that if I hit a boat for the third time I should never see the surface again. Drowning is a horrible death, notwithstanding all that has been said to the contrary. My past life never occurred to my mind, but I thought of many trivial things that I might not do or see again if I were drowned. I swam up in a slanting direction, hoping to avoid the boat that I had struck. Suddenly I saw all the boats in the lock quite clearly just above me, and every one of their curved varnished planks and the scratches and chips upon their keels. I saw several gaps among the boats where I might have swam up to the surface, but it did not seem worthwhile to try and get there, and I had forgotten why I wanted to. Then all the people leaned over the sides of their boats: I saw the light flannel suits of the men and the coloured flowers in the women's hats, and I noticed details of their dresses quite distinctly. Everybody in the boats was looking down at me; then they all said to one another, 'We must leave him now,' and they and the boats went away; and there was nothing above me but the river and the sky, and on either side of me were the green weeds that grew in the mud, for I had somehow sunk back to the bottom again. The river as it flowed by murmured not unpleasantly in my ears, and the rushes seemed to be whispering quite softly among themselves. Presently the murmuring of the river took the form of words, and I heard it say, 'We must go on to the sea; we must leave him now.'

Then the river went away, and both its banks; and the rushes whispered, 'Yes, we must leave him now.' And they too departed, and I was left in a great emptiness staring up at the blue sky. Then the great sky bent over me, and spoke quite softly like a kindly nurse soothing some little foolish child, and the sky said, 'Goodbye. All will be well. Goodbye.' And I was sorry to lose the blue sky, but the sky went away. Then I was alone, with nothing round about me; I could see no light, but it was not dark—there was just absolutely nothing, above me and below me and on every side. I thought that perhaps I was dead, and that this might be eternity; when suddenly some great southern hills rose up all round about me, and I was lying on the warm, grassy slope of a valley in England. It was a valley that I had known well when I was young, but I had not seen it now for many years. Beside me stood the tall flower of the mint; I saw the sweet-smelling thyme flower and one or two wild strawberries. There came up to me from fields below me the beautiful smell of hay, and there was a break in the voice of the cuckoo. There was a feeling of summer and of evening and of lateness and of Sabbath in the air; the sky was calm and full of a strange colour, and the sun was low; the bells in the church in the village were all a-ring, and the chimes went wandering with echoes up the valley towards the sun, and whenever the echoes died a new chime was born. And all the people of the village walked up a stone-paved path under a black oak porch and went into the church, and the chimes stopped and the people of the village began to sing, and the level sunlight shone on the white tombstones that stood all round the church. Then there was a stillness in the village, and shouts and laughter came up from the valley no more, only the occasional sound of the organ and of song. And the blue butterflies, those that love the chalk, came and perched themselves on the tall grasses, five or six sometimes on a single piece of grass, and they closed their wings and slept, and the grass bent a little beneath them. And from the woods along the tops of the hills the rabbits came hopping out and nibbled the grass, and hopped a little further and nibbled again, and the large daisies closed their petals up and the birds began to sing.

Then the hills spoke, all the great chalk hills that I loved, and with a deep and solemn voice they said, 'We have come to you to say Goodbye.'

Then they all went away, and there was nothing again all round about me upon every side. I looked everywhere for something on which to rest the eye. Nothing. Suddenly a low grey sky swept over me and a moist air met my face; a great plain rushed up to me from the edge of the clouds; on two sides it touched the sky, and on two sides between it and the clouds a line of low hills lay. One line of hills brooded grey in the distance, the other stood a patchwork of little square green fields, with a few white cottages about it. The plain was an archipelago of a million islands each about a yard square or less, and everyone of them was red with heather. I was back on the Bog of Allen again after many years, and it was just the same as ever, though I had heard that they were draining it. I was with an old friend whom I was glad to see again, for they had told me that he died some years ago. He seemed strangely young, but what surprised me most was that he stood upon a piece of bright green moss which I had always learned to think would never bear. I was glad, too, to see the old bog again, and all the lovely things that grew there—the scarlet mosses and the green mosses and the firm and friendly heather, and the deep silent water. I saw a little stream that wandered vaguely through the bog, and little white shells down in the clear depths of it; I saw, a little way off, one of the great pools where no islands are, with rushes round its borders, where the duck love to come. I looked long at that untroubled world of heather, and then I looked at the white cottages on the hill, and saw the grey smoke curling from their chimneys and knew that they burned turf there, and longed for the smell of burning turf again. And far away there arose and came nearer the weird cry of wild and happy voices, and a flock of geese appeared that was coming from the northward. Then their cries blended into one great voice of exultation, the voice of freedom, the voice of Ireland, the voice of the Waste; and the voice said 'Goodbye to you. Goodbye!' and passed away into the distance; and as it passed, the tame geese on the farms cried out to their brothers up above them that they were free. Then the hills went away, and the bog and the sky went with them, and I was alone again, as lost souls are alone.

Then there grew up beside me the red brick buildings of my first school and the chapel that adjoined it. The fields a little way off were full of boys in white flannels playing cricket. On the asphalt playing ground, just by the schoolroom windows, stood Agamemnon, Achilles, and Odysseus, with their Argives armed behind them; but Hector stepped down out of a ground-floor window, and in the schoolroom were all Priam's sons and the Achæans and fair Helen; and a little farther away the Ten Thousand drifted across the playground, going up into the heart of Persia to place Cyrus on his brother's throne. And the boys that I knew called to me from the fields, and said 'Goodbye,' and they and the fields went away; and the Ten Thousand said 'Goodbye,' each file as they passed me marching swiftly, and they too disappeared. And Hector and Agamemnon said 'Goodbye,' and the host of the Argives and of the Achæans; and they all went away and the old school with them, and I was alone again.

The next scene that filled the emptiness was rather dim: I was being led by my nurse along a little footpath over a common in Surrey. She was quite young. Close by a band of gypsies had lit their fire, near them their romantic caravan stood unhorsed, and the horse cropped grass beside it. It was evening, and the gypsies muttered round their fire in a tongue unknown and strange. Then they all said in English, 'Goodbye'. And the evening and the common and the campfire went away. And instead of this a white highway with darkness and stars below it that led into darkness and stars, but at the near end of the road were common fields and gardens, and there I stood close to a large number of people, men and women. And I saw a man walking alone down the road away from me towards the darkness and the stars, and all the people called him by his name, and the man would not hear them, but walked on down the road, and the people went on calling him by his name. But I became irritated with the man because he would not stop or turn round when so many people called him by his name, and it was a very strange name. And I became weary of hearing the strange name so very often repeated, so that I made a great effort to call him, that he might listen and that the people might stop repeating this strange name. And with the effort I opened my eyes wide, and the name that the people called was my own name, and I lay on the river's bank with men and women bending over me, and my hair was wet.

THE GHOSTS

The argument that I had with my brother in his great lonely house will scarcely interest my readers. Not those, at least, whom I hope may be attracted by the experiment that I undertook, and by the strange things that befell me in that hazardous region into which so lightly and so ignorantly I allowed my fancy to enter. It was at Oneleigh that I had visited him.

Now Oneleigh stands in a wide isolation, in the midst of a dark gathering of old whispering cedars. They nod their heads together when the North Wind comes, and nod again and agree, and furtively grow still again, and say no more awhile. The North Wind is to them like a nice problem among wise old men; they nod their heads over it, and mutter about it all together. They know much, those cedars, they have been there so long. Their grandsires knew Lebanon, and the grandsires of these were the servants of the King of Tyre and came to Solomon's court. And amidst these black-haired children of grey-headed Time stood the old house of Oneleigh. I know not how many centuries had lashed against it their evanescent foam of years; but it was still unshattered, and all about it were the things of long ago, as cling strange growths to some sea-defying rock. Here, like the shells of long-dead limpets, was armour that men encased themselves in long ago; here, too, were tapestries of many colours, beautiful as seaweed; no modern flotsam ever drifted hither, no early Victorian furniture, no electric light. The great trade routes that littered the years with empty meat tins and cheap novels were far from here. Well, well, the centuries will shatter it and drive its fragments on to distant shores. Meanwhile, while it yet stood, I went on a visit there to my brother, and we argued about ghosts. My brother's intelligence on this subject seemed to me to be in need of correction. He mistook things imagined for things having an actual existence; he argued that second-hand evidence of persons having seen ghosts proved ghosts to exist. I said that even if they had seen ghosts, this was no proof at all; nobody believes that there are red rats, though there is plenty of first-hand evidence of men having seen them in delirium. Finally, I said I would see ghosts myself, and continue to argue against their actual existence. So I collected a handful of cigars and drank several cups of very strong tea, and went without my dinner, and retired into a room where there was dark oak and all the chairs were covered with tapestry; and my brother went to bed bored with our argument, and trying hard to dissuade me from making myself uncomfortable. All the way up the old stairs as I stood at the bottom of them, and as his candle went winding up and up, I heard him still trying to persuade me to have supper and go to bed.

It was a windy winter, and outside the cedars were muttering I know not what about; but I think that they were Tories of a school long dead, and were troubled about something new. Within, a great damp log upon the fireplace began to squeak and sing, and struck up a whining tune, and a tall flame stood up over it and beat time, and all the shadows crowded round and began to dance. In distant corners old masses of darkness sat still like chaperones and never moved. Over there, in the darkest part of the room, stood a door that was always locked. It led into the hall, but no one ever used it; near that door something had happened once of which the family are not proud. We do not speak of it. There in the firelight stood the venerable forms of the old chairs; the hands that had made their tapestries lay far beneath the soil, the needles with which they wrought were many separate flakes of rust. No one wove now in that old room—no one but the assiduous ancient spiders who, watching by the deathbed of the things of yore, worked shrouds to hold their dust. In shrouds about the cornices already lay the heart of the oak wainscot that the worm had eaten out.

Surely at such an hour, in such a room, a fancy already excited by hunger and strong tea might see the ghosts of former occupants. I expected nothing less. The fire flickered and the shadows danced, memories of strange historic things rose vividly in my mind; but midnight chimed solemnly from a seven-foot clock, and nothing happened. My imagination would not be hurried, and the chill that is with the small hours had come upon me, and I had nearly abandoned myself to sleep, when in the hall adjoining there arose the rustling of silk dresses that I had waited for and expected. Then there entered two by two the high-born ladies and their gallants of Jacobean times. They were little more than shadows—very dignified shadows, and almost indistinct; but you have all read ghost stories before, you have all seen in museums the dresses of those times—there is little need to describe them; they entered, several of them, and sat down on the old chairs, perhaps a little carelessly considering the value of the tapestries. Then the rustling of their dresses ceased.

Well—I had seen ghosts, and was neither frightened nor convinced that ghosts existed. I was about to get up out of my chair and go to bed, when there came a sound of pattering in the hall, a sound of bare feet coming over the polished floor, and every now and then a foot would slip and I heard claws scratching along the wood as some four-footed thing lost and regained its balance. I was not frightened, but uneasy. The pattering came straight towards the room that I was in, then I heard the sniffing of expectant nostrils; perhaps 'uneasy' was not the most suitable word to describe my feelings then. Suddenly a herd of black creatures larger than bloodhounds came galloping in; they had large pendulous ears, their noses were to the ground sniffing, they went up to the lords and ladies of long ago and fawned about them disgustingly. Their eyes were horribly bright, and ran down to great depths. When I looked into them I knew suddenly what these creatures were, and I was afraid. They were the sins, the filthy, immortal sins of those courtly men and women.

How demure she was, the lady that sat near me on an old-world chair—how demure she was, and how fair, to have beside her with its jowl upon her lap a sin with such cavernous red eyes, a clear case of murder. And you, yonder lady with the golden hair, surely not you—and yet that fearful beast with the yellow eyes slinks from you to yonder courtier there, and whenever one drives it away it slinks back to the other. Over there a lady tries to smile as she strokes the loathsome furry head of another's sin, but one of her own is jealous and intrudes itself under her hand. Here sits an old nobleman with his grandson on his knee, and one of the great black sins of the grandfather is licking the child's face and has made the child its own. Sometimes a ghost would move and seek another chair, but always his pack of sins would move behind him. Poor ghosts, poor ghosts! how many flights they must have attempted for two hundred years from their hated sins, how many excuses they must have given for their presence, and the sins were with them still—and still unexplained. Suddenly one of them seemed to scent my living blood, and bayed horribly, and all the others left their ghosts at once and dashed up to the sin that had given tongue. The brute had picked up my scent near the door by which I had entered, and they moved slowly nearer to me sniffing along the floor, and uttering every now and then their fearful cry. I saw that the whole thing had gone too far. But now they had seen me, now they were all about me, they sprang up trying to reach my throat; and whenever their claws touched me, horrible thoughts came into my mind and unutterable desires dominated my heart. I planned bestial things as these creatures leaped around me, and planned them with a masterly cunning. A great red-eyed murder was among the foremost of those furry things from whom I feebly strove to defend my throat. Suddenly it seemed to me good that I should kill my brother. It seemed important to me that I should not risk being punished. I knew where a revolver was kept; after I had shot him, I would dress the body up and put flour on the face like a man that had been acting as a ghost. It would be very simple. I would say that he had frightened me—and the servants had heard us talking about ghosts. There were one or two trivialities that would have to be arranged, but nothing escaped my mind. Yes, it seemed to me very good that I should kill my brother as I looked into the red depths of this creature's eyes. But one last effort as they dragged me down—'If two straight lines cut one another,' I said, 'the opposite angles are equal. Let AB, CD, cut one another at E, then the angles CEA, CEB equal two right angles (prop. xiii.). Also CEA, AED equal two right angles.'

I moved towards the door to get the revolver; a hideous exultation arose among the beasts. 'But the angle CEA is common, therefore AED equals CEB. In the same way CEA equals DEB. *QED*.' It was proved. Logic and reason re-established themselves in my mind, there were no dark hounds of sin, the tapestried chairs were empty. It seemed to me an inconceivable thought that a man should murder his brother.

THE WHIRLPOOL

Once going down to the shore of the great sea I came upon the Whirlpool lying prone upon the sand and stretching his huge limbs in the sun.

I said to him: 'Who art thou?'

And he said:

'I am named Nooz Wana, the Whelmer of Ships, and from the Straits of Pondar Obed I am come, wherein it is my wont to vex the seas. There I chased Leviathan with my hands when he was young and strong; often he slipped through my fingers, and away into the weed forests that grow below the storms in the dusk on the floor of the sea; but at last I caught and tamed him. For there I lurk upon the ocean's floor, midway between the knees of either cliff, to guard the passage of the Straits from all the ships that seek the Further Seas; and whenever the white sails of the tall ships come swelling round the corner of the crag out of the sunlit spaces of the Known Sea and into the dark of the Straits, then standing firm upon the ocean's floor, with my knees a little bent, I take the waters of the Straits in both my hands and whirl them round my head. But the ship comes gliding on with the sound of the sailors singing on her decks, all singing songs of the islands and carrying the rumour of their cities to the lonely seas, till they see me suddenly astride athwart their course, and are caught in the waters as I whirl them round my head. Then I draw in the waters of the Straits towards me and downwards, nearer and nearer to my terrible feet, and hear in my ears above the roar of my waters the ultimate cry of the ship; for just before I drag them to the floor of ocean and stamp them asunder with my wrecking feet, ships utter their ultimate cry, and with it go the lives of all the sailors and passes the soul of the ship. And in the ultimate cry of ships are the songs the sailors sing, and their hopes and all their loves, and the song of the wind among the masts and timbers when they stood in the forest long ago, and the whisper of the rain that made them grow, and the soul of the tall pine-tree or the oak. All this a ship gives up in one cry which she makes at the last. And at that moment I would pity the tall ship if I might; but a man may feel pity who sits in comfort by his fireside telling tales in the winter—no pity are they permitted ever to feel who do the work of the gods; and so when I have brought her circling from round my shoulders to my waist and thence, with her masts all sloping inwards, to my knees, and lower still and downwards till her topmast pennants flutter against my ankles, then I, Nooz Wana, Whelmer of Ships, lift up my feet and trample her beams asunder, and there go up again to the surface of the Straits only a few broken timbers and the memories of the sailors and of their early loves to drift for ever down the empty seas.

'Once in every hundred years, for one day only, I go to rest myself along the shore and to sun my limbs on the sand, that the tall ships may go through the unguarded Straits and find the Happy Isles. And the Happy

Isles stand midmost among the smiles of the sunny Further Seas, and there the sailors may come upon content and long for nothing; or if they long for aught, they shall possess it.

'There comes not Time with his devouring hours; nor any of the evils of the gods or men. These are the islands whereto the souls of the sailors every night put in from all the world to rest from going up and down the seas, to behold again the vision of far-off intimate hills that lift their orchards high above the fields facing the sunlight, and for a while again to speak with the souls of old. But about the dawn dreams twitter and arise, and circling thrice around the Happy Isles set out again to find the world of men, then follow the souls of the sailors, as, at evening, with slow stroke of stately wings the heron follows behind the flight of multitudinous rooks; but the souls returning find awakening bodies and endure the toil of the day. Such are the Happy Isles, whereunto few have come, save but as roaming shadows in the night, and for only a little while.

'But longer than is needed to make me strong and fierce again I may not stay, and at set of sun, when my arms are strong again, and when I feel in my legs that I can plant them fair and bent upon the floor of ocean, then I go back to take a new grip upon the waters of the Straits, and to guard the Further Seas again for a hundred years. Because the gods are jealous, lest too many men shall pass to the Happy Isles and find content. *For the gods have not content.*'

THE HURRICANE

One night I sat alone on the great down, looking over the edge of it at a murky, sullen city. All day long with its smoke it had troubled the holy sky, and now it sat there roaring in the distance and glared at me with its furnaces and lighted factory windows. Suddenly I became aware that I was not the only enemy of that city, for I perceived the colossal form of the Hurricane walking over the down towards me, playing idly with the flowers as he passed, and near me he stopped and spake to the Earthquake, who had come up mole-like but vast out of a cleft in the earth.

'Old friend,' said the Hurricane, 'rememberest when we wrecked the nations and drave the herds of the sea into new pasturage?'

'Yes,' said the Earthquake, drowsily; 'Yes, yes.'

'Old friend,' said the Hurricane, 'there are cities everywhere. Over thy head while thou didst sleep they have built them constantly. My four children the Winds suffocate with the fumes of them, the valleys are desolate of flowers, and the lovely forests are cut down since last we went abroad together.'

The Earthquake lay there, with his snout towards the city, blinking at the lights, while the tall Hurricane stood beside him pointing fiercely at it.

'Come,' said the Hurricane, 'let us fare forth again and destroy them, that all the lovely forests may come back and the furry creeping things. Thou shalt whelm these cities utterly and drive the people forth, and I will smite them in the shelterless places and sweep their desecrations from the sea. Wilt thou come forth with me and do this thing for the glory of it? Wilt thou wreck the world again as we did, thou and I, or ever Man had come? Wilt thou come forth to this place at this hour tomorrow night?'

'Yes,' said the Earthquake, 'Yes,' and he crept to his cleft again, and head foremost waddled down into the abysses.

When the Hurricane strode away, I got up quietly and departed, but at that hour of the next night I came up cautiously to the same spot. There I found the huge grey form of the Hurricane alone, with his head bowed in his hands, weeping; for the Earthquake sleeps long and heavily in the abysses, and he would not wake.

THE FORTRESS UNVANQUISHABLE, SAVE FOR SACNOTH

In a wood older than record, a foster brother of the hills, stood the village of Allathurion; and there was peace between the people of that village and all the folk who walked in the dark ways of the wood, whether they were human or of the tribes of the beasts or of the race of the fairies and the elves and the little sacred spirits of trees and streams. Moreover, the village people had peace among themselves and between them and their lord, Lorendiac. In front of the village was a wide and grassy space, and beyond this the great wood again, but at the back the trees came right up to the houses, which, with their great beams and wooden framework and thatched roofs, green with moss, seemed almost to be a part of the forest.

Now in the time I tell of, there was trouble in Allathurion, for of an evening fell dreams were wont to come slipping through the tree trunks and into the peaceful village; and they assumed dominion of men's minds and led them in watches of the night through the cindery plains of Hell. Then the magician of that village made spells against those fell dreams; yet still the dreams came flitting through the trees as soon as the dark had fallen, and led men's minds by night into terrible places and caused them to praise Satan openly with their lips.

And men grew afraid of sleep in Allathurion. And they grew worn and pale, some through the want of rest, and others from fear of the things they saw on the cindery plains of Hell.

Then the magician of the village went up into the tower of his house, and all night long those whom fear kept awake could see his window high up in the night glowing softly alone. The next day, when the twilight was far gone and night was gathering fast, the magician went away to the forest's edge, and uttered there the spell that he had made. And the spell was a compulsive, terrible thing, having a power over evil dreams and over spirits of ill; for it was a verse of forty lines in many languages, both living and dead, and had in it the word wherewith the people of the plains are wont to curse their camels, and the shout wherewith the whalers of the north lure the whales shoreward to be killed, and a word that causes elephants to trumpet; and every one of the forty lines closed with a rhyme for 'wasp'.

And still the dreams came flitting through the forest, and led men's souls into the plains of Hell. Then the magician knew that the dreams were from Gaznak. Therefore he gathered the people of the village, and told them that he had uttered his mightiest spell—a spell having power over all that were human or of the tribes of the beasts; and that since it had not availed the dreams must come from Gaznak, the greatest magician among the spaces of the stars. And he read to the people out of the Book of Magicians, which tells the comings of the comet and foretells his coming again. And he told them how Gaznak rides upon the comet, and how he visits Earth once in every two hundred and thirty years, and makes for himself a vast, invincible fortress and sends out dreams to feed on the minds of men, and may never be vanquished but by the sword Sacnoth.

And a cold fear fell on the hearts of the villagers when they found that their magician had failed them.

Then spake Leothric, son of the Lord Lorendiac, and twenty years old was he: 'Good Master, what of the sword Sacnoth?'

And the village magician answered: 'Fair Lord, no such sword as yet is wrought, for it lies as yet in the hide of Tharagavverug, protecting his spine.'

Then said Leothric: 'Who is Tharagavverug, and where may he be encountered?'

And the magician of Allathurion answered: 'He is the dragon-crocodile who haunts the Northern marshes and ravages the homesteads by their marge. And the hide of his back is of steel, and his under parts are of iron; but along the midst of his back, over his spine, there lies a narrow strip of unearthly steel. This strip of steel is Sacnoth, and it may be neither cleft nor molten, and there is nothing in the world that may avail to break it, nor even leave a scratch upon its surface. It is of the length of a good sword, and of the breadth thereof. Shouldst thou prevail against Tharagavverug, his hide may be melted away from Sacnoth in a furnace; but there is only one thing that may sharpen Sacnoth's edge, and this is one of Tharagavverug's own steel eyes; and the other eye thou must fasten to Sacnoth's hilt, and it will watch for thee. But it is a hard task to vanquish Tharagavverug, for no sword can pierce his hide; his back cannot be broken, and he can neither burn nor drown. In one way only can Tharagavverug die, and that is by starving.'

Then sorrow fell upon Leothric, but the magician spoke on:

'If a man drive Tharagavverug away from his food with a stick for three days, he will starve on the third day at sunset. And though he is not vulnerable, yet in one spot he may take hurt, for his nose is only of lead. A sword would merely lay bare the uncleavable bronze beneath, but if his nose be smitten constantly with a stick he will always recoil from the pain, and thus may Tharagavverug, to left and right, be driven away from his food.'

Then Leothric said: 'What is Tharagavverug's food?'

And the magician of Allathurion said: 'His food is men.'

But Leothric went straightway thence, and cut a great staff from a hazel tree, and slept early that evening. But the next morning, awaking from troubled dreams, he arose before the dawn, and, taking with him provisions for five days, set out through the forest northwards towards the marshes. For some hours he moved through the gloom of the forest, and when he emerged from it the sun was above the horizon shining on pools of water in the waste land. Presently he saw the claw-marks of Tharagavverug deep in the soil, and the track of his tail between them like a furrow in a field. Then Leothric followed the tracks till he heard the bronze heart of Tharagavverug before him, booming like a bell.

And Tharagavverug, it being the hour when he took the first meal of the day, was moving towards a village with his heart tolling. And all the people of the village were come out to meet him, as it was their wont to do; for they abode not the suspense of awaiting Tharagavverug and of hearing him sniffing brazenly as he went from door to door, pondering slowly in his metal mind what habitant he should choose. And none dared to flee, for in the days when the villagers fled from Tharagavverug, he, having chosen his victim, would track him tirelessly, like a doom. Nothing availed them against Tharagavverug. Once they climbed the trees when he came, but Tharagavverug went up to one, arching his back and leaning over slightly, and rasped against the trunk until it fell. And when Leothric came near, Tharagavverug saw him out of one of his small steel eyes and came towards him leisurely, and the echoes of his heart swirled up through his open mouth. And Leothric stepped sideways from his onset, and came between him and the village and smote him on the nose, and the blow of the stick made a dint in the soft lead. And Tharagavverug swung clumsily away, uttering one fearful cry like the sound of a great church bell that had become possessed of a soul that fluttered upward from the tombs at night—an evil soul, giving the bell a voice. Then he attacked Leothric, snarling, and again Leothric leapt aside, and smote him on the nose with his stick. Tharagavverug uttered like a bell howling. And whenever the dragon-crocodile attacked him, or turned towards the village, Leothric smote him again.

So all day long Leothric drove the monster with a stick, and he drove him farther and farther from his prey, with his heart tolling angrily and his voice crying out for pain.

Towards evening Tharagavverug ceased to snap at Leothric, but ran before him to avoid the stick, for his nose was sore and shining; and in the gloaming the villagers came out and danced to cymbal and psaltery. When Tharagavverug heard the cymbal and psaltery, hunger and anger came upon him, and he felt as some lord might feel who was held by force from the banquet in his own castle and heard the creaking spit go round and round and the good meat crackling on it. And all that night he attacked Leothric fiercely, and oft-times nearly caught him in the darkness; for his gleaming eyes of steel could see as well by night as by day. And Leothric gave ground slowly till the dawn, and when the light came they were near the village again; yet not so near to it as they had been when they encountered, for Leothric drove Tharagavverug farther in the day than Tharagavverug had forced him back in the night. Then Leothric drove him again with his stick till the hour came when it was the custom of the dragon-crocodile to find his man. One third of his man he would eat at the time he found him, and the rest at noon and evening. But when the hour came for finding his man a great fierceness came on Tharagavverug, and he grabbed rapidly at Leothric, but could not seize him, and for a long while neither of them would retire. But at last the pain of the stick on his leaden nose overcame the hunger of the dragon-crocodile, and he turned from it howling. From that moment Tharagavverug weakened. All that day Leothric drove him with his stick, and at night both held their ground; and when the dawn of the third day was come the heart of Tharagavverug beat slower and fainter. It was as though a tired man was ringing a bell. Once Tharagavverug nearly seized a frog, but Leothric snatched it away just in time. Towards noon the dragon-crocodile lay still for a long while, and Leothric stood near him and leaned on his trusty stick. He was very tired and sleepless, but had more leisure now for eating his provisions. With Tharagavverug the end was coming fast, and in the afternoon his breath came hoarsely, rasping in his throat. It was as the sound of many huntsmen blowing blasts on horns, and towards evening his breath came faster but fainter, like the sound of a hunt going furious to the distance and dying away, and he made desperate rushes towards the village; but Leothric still leapt about him, battering his leaden nose. Scarce audible now at all was the sound of his heart: it was like a church bell tolling beyond hills for the death of some one unknown and far away. Then the sun set and flamed in the village windows, and a chill went over the world, and in some small garden a woman sang; and Tharagavverug lifted up his head and starved, and his life went from his invulnerable body, and Leothric lay down beside him and slept. And later in the starlight the villagers came out and carried Leothric, sleeping, to the village, all praising him in whispers as they went. They laid him down upon a couch in a house, and danced outside in silence, without psaltery or cymbal. And the next day, rejoicing, to Allathurion they hauled the dragon-crocodile. And Leothric went with them, holding his battered staff; and a tall, broad man, who was smith of Allathurion, made a great furnace, and melted Tharagavverug away till only Sacnoth was left, gleaming among the ashes. Then he took one of the small eyes that had been chiselled out, and filed an edge on Sacnoth, and gradually the steel eye wore away facet by facet, but ere it was quite gone it had sharpened redoubtably Sacnoth. But the other eye they set in the butt of the hilt, and it gleamed there bluely.

And that night Leothric arose in the dark and took the sword, and went westwards to find Gaznak; and he went through the dark forest till the dawn, and all the morning and till the afternoon. But in the afternoon he came into the open and saw in the midst of The Land Where No Man Goeth the fortress of Gaznak, mountainous before him, little more than a mile away.

And Leothric saw that the land was marsh and desolate. And the fortress went up all white out of it, with many buttresses, and was broad below but narrowed higher up, and was full of gleaming windows with the light upon them. And near the top of it a few white clouds were floating, but above them some of its pinnacles reappeared. Then Leothric advanced into the marshes, and the eye of Tharagavverug looked out warily from the hilt of Sacnoth; for Tharagavverug had known the marshes well, and the sword nudged Leothric to the right or pulled him to the left away from the dangerous places, and so brought him safely to the fortress walls.

And in the wall stood doors like precipices of steel, all studded with boulders of iron, and above every window were terrible gargoyles of stone; and the name of the fortress shone on the wall, writ large in letters of brass: 'The Fortress Unvanquishable, Save For Sacnoth.'

Then Leothric drew and revealed Sacnoth, and all the gargoyles grinned, and the grin went flickering from face to face right up into the cloud-abiding gables.

And when Sacnoth was revealed and all the gargoyles grinned, it was like the moonlight emerging from a cloud to look for the first time upon a field of blood, and passing swiftly over the wet faces of the slain that lie together in the horrible night. Then Leothric advanced towards a door, and it was mightier than the marble quarry, Sacremona, from which of old men cut enormous slabs to build the Abbey of the Holy Tears. Day after day they wrenched out the very ribs of the hill until the Abbey was builded, and it was more beautiful than anything in stone. Then the priests blessed Sacremona, and it had rest, and no more stone was ever taken from it to build the houses of men. And the hill stood looking southwards lonely in the sunlight, defaced by that mighty scar. So vast was the door of steel. And the name of the door was The Porte Resonant, the Way of Egress for War.

Then Leothric smote upon the Porte Resonant with Sacnoth, and the echo of Sacnoth went ringing through the halls, and all the dragons in the fortress barked. And when the baying of the remotest dragon had faintly joined in the tumult, a window opened far up among the clouds below the twilit gables, and a woman screamed, and far away in Hell her father heard her and knew that her doom was come.

And Leothric went on smiting terribly with Sacnoth, and the grey steel of the Porte Resonant, the Way of Egress for War, that was tempered to resist the swords of the world, came away in ringing slices.

Then Leothric, holding Sacnoth in his hand, went in through the hole that he had hewn in the door, and came into the unlit, cavernous hall.

An elephant fled trumpeting. And Leothric stood still, holding Sacnoth. When the sound of the feet of the elephant had died away in the remoter corridors, nothing more stirred, and the cavernous hall was still.

Presently the darkness of the distant halls became musical with the sound of bells, all coming nearer and nearer.

Still Leothric waited in the dark, and the bells rang louder and louder, echoing through the halls, and there appeared a procession of men on camels riding two by two from the interior of the fortress, and they were armed with scimitars of Assyrian make and were all clad with mail, and chainmail hung from their helmets about their faces, and flapped as the camels moved. And they all halted before Leothric in the cavernous hall, and the camel bells clanged and stopped. And the leader said to Leothric:

'The Lord Gaznak has desired to see you die before him. Be pleased to come with us, and we can discourse by the way of the manner in which the Lord Gaznak has desired to see you die.'

And as he said this he unwound a chain of iron that was coiled upon his saddle, and Leothric answered:

'I would fain go with you, for I am come to slay Gaznak.'

Then all the camel-guard of Gaznak laughed hideously, disturbing the vampires that were asleep in the measureless vault of the roof. And the leader said:

'The Lord Gaznak is immortal, save for Sacnoth, and weareth armour that is proof even against Sacnoth himself, and hath a sword the second most terrible in the world.'

Then Leothric said: 'I am the Lord of the sword Sacnoth.'

And he advanced towards the camel-guard of Gaznak, and Sacnoth lifted up and down in his hand as though stirred by an exultant pulse. Then the camel-guard of Gaznak fled, and the riders leaned forward and smote their camels with whips, and they went away with a great clamour of bells through colonnades and corridors and vaulted halls, and scattered into the inner darknesses of the fortress. When the last sound of them had died away, Leothric was in doubt which way to go, for the camel-guard was dispersed in many directions, so he went straight on till he came to a great stairway in the midst of the hall. Then Leothric set his foot in the middle of a wide step, and climbed steadily up the stairway for five minutes. Little light was there in the great hall through which Leothric ascended, for it only entered through arrow slits here and there, and in the world outside evening was waning fast. The stairway led up to two folding doors, and they stood a little ajar, and through the crack Leothric entered and tried to continue straight on, but could get no farther, for the whole room seemed to be full of festoons of ropes which swung from wall to wall and were looped and draped from the ceiling. The whole chamber was thick and black with them. They were soft and light to the touch, like fine silk, but Leothric was unable to break any one of them, and though they swung away from him as he pressed forward, yet by the time he had gone three yards they were all about him like a heavy cloak. Then Leothric stepped back and drew Sacnoth, and Sacnoth divided the ropes without a sound, and without a sound the severed pieces fell to the floor. Leothric went forward slowly, moving Sacnoth in front of him up and down as he went. When he was come into the middle of the chamber, suddenly, as he parted with Sacnoth a great hammock of strands, he saw a spider before him that was larger than a ram, and the spider looked at him with eyes that were little, but in which there was much sin, and said:

'Who are you that spoil the labour of years all done to the honour of Satan?'

And Leothric answered: 'I am Leothric, son of Lorendiac.'

And the spider said: 'I will make a rope at once to hang you with.'

Then Leothric parted another bunch of strands, and came nearer to the spider as he sat making his rope, and the spider, looking up from his work, said: 'What is that sword which is able to sever my ropes?'

And Leothric said: 'It is Sacnoth.'

Thereat the black hair that hung over the face of the spider parted to left and right, and the spider frowned; then the hair fell back into its place, and hid everything except the sin of the little eyes which went on gleaming lustfully in the dark. But before Leothric could reach him, he climbed away with his hands, going up by one of his ropes to a lofty rafter, and there sat, growling. But clearing his way with Sacnoth, Leothric passed through the chamber, and came to the farther door; and the door being shut, and the handle far up out of his reach, he hewed his way through it with Sacnoth in the same way as he had through the Porte Resonant, the Way of Egress for War. And so Leothric came into a well-lit chamber, where Queens and Princes were banqueting together, all at a great table; and thousands of candles were glowing all about, and their light shone in the wine that the Princes drank and on the huge gold candelabra, and the royal faces were irradiant with the glow, and the white table-cloth and the silver plates and the jewels in the hair of the Queens, each jewel having a historian all to itself, who wrote no other chronicles all his days. Between the table and the door there stood two hundred footmen in two rows of one hundred facing one another. Nobody looked at Leothric as he entered through the hole in the door, but one of the Princes asked a question of a footman, and the question was passed from mouth to mouth by all the hundred footmen till it came to the last one nearest Leothric; and he said to Leothric, without looking at him:

'What do you seek here?'

And Leothric answered: 'I seek to slay Gaznak.'

And footman to footman repeated all the way to the table: 'He seeks to slay Gaznak.'

And another question came down the line of footmen: 'What is your name?'

And the line that stood opposite took his answer back.

Then one of the Princes said: 'Take him away where we shall not hear his screams.'

And footman repeated it to footman till it came to the last two, and they advanced to seize Leothric.

Then Leothric showed to them his sword, saying, 'This is Sacnoth,' and both of them said to the man nearest: 'It is Sacnoth;' then screamed and fled away.

And two by two, all up the double line, footman to footman repeated, 'It is Sacnoth,' then screamed and fled, till the last two gave the message to the table, and all the rest had gone. Hurriedly then arose the Queens and Princes, and fled out of the chamber. And the goodly table, when they were all gone, looked small and disorderly and awry. And to Leothric, pondering in the desolate chamber by what door he should pass onwards, there came from far away the sounds of music, and he knew that it was the magical musicians playing to Gaznak while he slept.

Then Leothric, walking towards the distant music, passed out by the door opposite to the one through which he had cloven his entrance, and so passed into a chamber vast as the other, in which were many women, weirdly beautiful. And they all asked him of his quest, and when they heard that it was to slay Gaznak, they all besought him to tarry among them, saying that Gaznak was immortal, save for Sacnoth, and also that they had need of a knight to protect them from the wolves that rushed round and round the wainscot all the night and sometimes broke in upon them through the mouldering oak. Perhaps Leothric had been tempted to tarry had they been human women, for theirs was a strange beauty, but he perceived that instead of eyes they had little flames that flickered in their sockets, and knew them to be the fevered dreams of Gaznak. Therefore he said:

'I have a business with Gaznak and with Sacnoth,' and passed on through the chamber.

And at the name of Sacnoth those women screamed, and the flames of their eyes sank low and dwindled to sparks.

And Leothric left them, and, hewing with Sacnoth, passed through the farther door.

Outside he felt the night air on his face, and found that he stood upon a narrow way between two abysses. To left and right of him, as far as he could see, the walls of the fortress ended in a profound precipice, though the roof still stretched above him; and before him lay the two abysses full of stars, for they cut their way through the whole Earth and revealed the under sky; and threading its course between them went the way, and it sloped upward and its sides were sheer. And beyond the abysses, where the way led up to the farther chambers of the fortress, Leothric heard the musicians playing their magical tune. So he stepped on to the way, which was scarcely a stride in width, and moved along it holding Sacnoth naked. And to and fro beneath him in each abyss whirred the wings of vampires passing up and down, all giving praise to Satan as they flew. Presently he perceived the dragon Thok lying upon the way, pretending to sleep, and his tail hung down into one of the abysses.

And Leothric went towards him, and when he was quite close Thok rushed at Leothric.

And he smote deep with Sacnoth, and Thok tumbled into the abyss, screaming, and his limbs made a whirring in the darkness as he fell, and he fell till his scream sounded no louder than a whistle and then could be heard no more. Once or twice Leothric saw a star blink for an instant and reappear again, and this momentary eclipse of a few stars was all that remained in the world of the body of Thok. And Lunk, the brother of Thok, who had lain a little behind him, saw that this must be Sacnoth and fled lumbering away. And all the while that he walked between the abysses, the mighty vault of the roof of the fortress still stretched over Leothric's head, all filled with gloom. Now, when the further side of the abyss came into view, Leothric saw a chamber that opened with innumerable arches upon the twin abysses, and the pillars of the arches went away into the distance and vanished in the gloom to left and right.

Far down the dim precipice on which the pillars stood he could see windows small and closely barred, and between the bars there showed at moments, and disappeared again, things that I shall not speak of.

There was no light here except for the great Southern stars that shone below the abysses, and here and there in the chamber through the arches lights that moved furtively without the sound of footfall.

Then Leothric stepped from the way, and entered the great chamber.

Even to himself he seemed but a tiny dwarf as he walked under one of those colossal arches.

The last faint light of evening flickered through a window painted in sombre colours commemorating the achievements of Satan upon Earth. High up in the wall the window stood, and the streaming lights of candles lower down moved stealthily away.

Other light there was none, save for a faint blue glow from the steel eye of Tharagavverug that peered restlessly about it from the hilt of Sacnoth. Heavily in the chamber hung the clammy odour of a large and deadly beast.

Leothric moved forward slowly with the blade of Sacnoth in front of him feeling for a foe, and the eye in the hilt of it looking out behind.

Nothing stirred.

If anything lurked behind the pillars of the colonnade that held aloft the roof, it neither breathed nor moved.

The music of the magical musicians sounded from very near.

Suddenly the great doors on the far side of the chamber opened to left and right. For some moments Leothric saw nothing move, and waited clutching Sacnoth. Then Wong Bongerok came towards him, breathing.

This was the last and faithfullest guard of Gaznak, and came from slobbering just now his master's hand.

More as a child than a dragon was Gaznak wont to treat him, giving him often in his fingers tender pieces of man all smoking from his table.

Long and low was Wong Bongerok, and subtle about the eyes, and he came breathing malice against Leothric out of his faithful breast, and behind him roared the armoury of his tail, as when sailors drag the cable of the anchor all rattling down the deck.

And well Wong Bongerok knew that he now faced Sacnoth, for it had been his wont to prophesy quietly to himself for many years as he lay curled at the feet of Gaznak.

And Leothric stepped forward into the blast of his breath, and lifted Sacnoth to strike.

But when Sacnoth was lifted up, the eye of Tharagavverug in the butt of the hilt beheld the dragon and perceived his subtlety.

For he opened his mouth wide, and revealed to Leothric the ranks of his sabre teeth, and his leather gums flapped upwards. But while Leothric made to smite at his head, he shot forward scorpion-wise over his head the length of his armoured tail. All this the eye perceived in the hilt of Sacnoth, who smote suddenly sideways. Not with the edge smote Sacnoth, for, had he done so, the severed end of the tail had still come hurtling on, as some pine tree that the avalanche has hurled point foremost from the cliff right through the broad breast of some mountaineer. So had Leothric been transfixed; but Sacnoth smote sideways with the flat of his blade, and sent the tail whizzing over Leothric's left shoulder; and it rasped upon his armour as it went, and left a groove upon it. Sideways then at Leothric smote the foiled tail of Wong Bongerok, and Sacnoth parried, and the tail went shrieking up the blade and over Leothric's head. Then Leothric and Wong Bongerok fought sword to tooth, and the sword smote as only Sacnoth can, and the evil faithful life of Wong Bongerok the dragon went out through the wide wound.

Then Leothric walked on past that dead monster, and the armoured body still quivered a little. And for a while it was like all the ploughshares in a county working together in one field behind tired and struggling horses; then the quivering ceased, and Wong Bongerok lay still to rust.

And Leothric went on to the open gates, and Sacnoth dripped quietly along the floor.

By the open gates through which Wong Bongerok had entered, Leothric came into a corridor echoing with music. This was the first place from which Leothric could see anything above his head, for hitherto the roof had ascended to mountainous heights and had stretched indistinct in the gloom. But along the narrow corridor hung huge bells low and near to his head, and the width of each brazen bell was from wall to wall, and they were one behind the other. And as he passed under each the bell uttered, and its voice was mournful and deep, like to the voice of a bell speaking to a man for the last time when he is newly dead. Each bell uttered once as Leothric came under it, and their voices sounded solemnly and wide apart at ceremonious intervals. For if he walked slow, these bells came closer together, and when he walked swiftly they moved farther apart. And the echoes of each bell tolling above his head went on before him whispering to the others. Once when he stopped they all jangled angrily till he went on again.

Between these slow and boding notes came the sound of the magical musicians. They were playing a dirge now very mournfully.

And at last Leothric came to the end of the Corridor of the Bells, and beheld there a small black door. And all the corridor behind him was full of the echoes of the tolling, and they all muttered to one another about the ceremony; and the dirge of the musicians came floating slowly through them like a procession of foreign elaborate guests, and all of them boded ill to Leothric.

The black door opened at once to the hand of Leothric, and he found himself in the open air in a wide court paved with marble. High over it shone the moon, summoned there by the hand of Gaznak.

There Gaznak slept, and around him sat his magical musicians, all playing upon strings. And, even sleeping, Gaznak was clad in armour, and only his wrists and face and neck were bare.

But the marvel of that place was the dreams of Gaznak; for beyond the wide court slept a dark abyss, and into the abyss there poured a white cascade of marble stairways, and widened out below into terraces and balconies with fair white statues on them, and descended again in a wide stairway, and came to lower terraces in the dark, where swart uncertain shapes went to and fro. All these were the dreams of Gaznak, and issued from his mind, and, becoming gleaming marble, passed over the edge of the abyss as the musicians played. And all the while out of the mind of Gaznak, lulled by that strange music, went spires and pinnacles beautiful and slender, ever ascending skywards. And the marble dreams moved slow in time to the music. When the bells tolled and the musicians played their dirge, ugly gargoyles came out suddenly all over the spires and pinnacles, and great shadows passed swiftly down the steps and terraces, and there was hurried whispering in the abyss.

When Leothric stepped from the black door, Gaznak opened his eyes. He looked neither to left nor right, but stood up at once facing Leothric.

Then the magicians played a deathspell on their strings, and there arose a humming along the blade of Sacnoth as he turned the spell aside. When Leothric dropped not down, and they heard the humming of Sacnoth, the magicians arose and fled, all wailing, as they went, upon their strings.

Then Gaznak drew out screaming from its sheath the sword that was the mightiest in the world except for Sacnoth, and slowly walked towards Leothric; and he smiled as he walked, although his own dreams had foretold his doom. And when Leothric and Gaznak came together, each looked at each, and neither spoke a word; but they smote both at once, and their swords met, and each sword knew the other and from whence he came. And whenever the sword of Gaznak smote on the blade of Sacnoth it rebounded gleaming, as hail from off slated roofs; but whenever it fell upon the armour of Leothric, it stripped it off in sheets. And upon Gaznak's armour Sacnoth fell oft and furiously, but ever he came back snarling, leaving no mark behind, and as Gaznak fought he held his left hand hovering close over his head. Presently Leothric smote fair and fiercely at his enemy's neck, but Gaznak, clutching his own head by the hair, lifted it high aloft, and Sacnoth went cleaving through an empty space. Then Gaznak replaced his head upon his neck, and all the while fought nimbly with his sword; and again and again Leothric swept with Sacnoth at Gaznak's bearded neck, and ever the left hand of Gaznak was quicker than the stroke, and the head went up and the sword rushed vainly under it.

And the ringing fight went on till Leothric's armour lay all round him on the floor and the marble was splashed with his blood, and the sword of Gaznak was notched like a saw from meeting the blade of Sacnoth. Still Gaznak stood unwounded and smiling still.

At last Leothric looked at the throat of Gaznak and aimed with Sacnoth, and again Gaznak lifted his head by the hair; but not at his throat flew Sacnoth, for Leothric struck instead at the lifted hand, and through the wrist of it went Sacnoth whirring, as a scythe goes through the stem of a single flower.

And bleeding, the severed hand fell to the floor; and at once blood spurted from the shoulders of Gaznak and dripped from the fallen head, and the tall pinnacles went down into the earth, and the wide fair terraces all rolled away, and the court was gone like the dew, and a wind came and the colonnades drifted thence, and all the colossal halls of Gaznak fell. And the abysses closed up suddenly as the mouth of a man who, having told a tale, will for ever speak no more.

Then Leothric looked around him in the marshes where the night mist was passing away, and there was no fortress nor sound of dragon or mortal, only beside him lay an old man, wizened and evil and dead, whose head and hand were severed from his body.

And gradually over the wide lands the dawn was coming up, and ever growing in beauty as it came, like to the peal of an organ played by a master's hand, growing louder and lovelier as the soul of the master warms, and at last giving praise with all its mighty voice.

Then the birds sang, and Leothric went homeward, and left the marshes and came to the dark wood, and the light of the dawn ascending lit him upon his way. And into Allathurion he came ere noon, and with him brought the evil wizened head, and the people rejoiced, and their nights of trouble ceased.

* * * *

This is the tale of the vanquishing of The Fortress Unvanquishable, Save For Sacnoth, and of its passing away, as it is told and believed by those who love the mystic days of old.

Others have said, and vainly claim to prove, that a fever came to Allathurion, and went away; and that this same fever drove Leothric into the marshes by night, and made him dream there and act violently with a sword.

And others again say that there hath been no town of Allathurion, and that Leothric never lived.

Peace to them. The gardener hath gathered up this autumn's leaves. Who shall see them again, or who wot of them? And who shall say what hath befallen in the days of long ago?

THE LORD OF CITIES

I came one day upon a road that wandered so aimlessly that it was suited to my mood, so I followed it, and it led me presently among deep woods. Somewhere in the midst of them Autumn held his court, sitting wreathed with gorgeous garlands; and it was the day before his annual festival of the Dance of Leaves, the courtly festival upon which hungry Winter rushes mob-like, and there arise the furious cries of the North Wind triumphing, and all the splendour and grace of the woods is gone, and Autumn flees away, discrowned and forgotten, and never again returns. Other Autumns arise, other Autumns, and fall before other Winters. A road led away to the left, but my road went straight on. The road to the left had a trodden appearance; there were wheel tracks on it, and it seemed the correct way to take. It looked as if no one could have any business with the road that led straight on and up the hill. Therefore I went straight on and up the hill; and here and there on the road grew blades of grass undisturbed in the repose and hush that the road had earned from going up and down the world; for you can go by this road, as you can go by all roads, to London, to Lincoln, to the North of Scotland, to the West of Wales, and to Wrellisford where roads end. Presently the woods ended, and I came to the open fields and at the same moment to the top of the hill, and saw the high places of Somerset and the downs of Wilts spread out along the horizon. Suddenly I saw underneath me the village of Wrellisford, with no sound in its street but the voice of the Wrellis roaring as he tumbled over a weir above the village. So I followed my road down over the crest of the hill, and the road became more languid as I descended, and less and less concerned with the cares of a highway. Here a spring broke out in the middle of it, and here another. The road never heeded. A stream ran right across it, still it straggled on. Suddenly it gave up the minimum property that a road should possess, and, renouncing its connection with High Streets, its lineage of Piccadilly, shrank to one side and became an unpretentious footpath. Then it led me to the old bridge over the stream, and thus I came to Wrellisford, and found after travelling in many lands a village with no wheel tracks in its street. On the other side of the bridge, my friend the road struggled a few yards up a grassy slope, and there ceased. Over all the village hung a great stillness, with the roar of the Wrellis cutting right across it, and there came occasionally the bark of a dog that kept watch over the broken stillness and over the sanctity of that untravelled road. That terrible and wasting fever that, unlike so many plagues, comes not from the East but from the West, the fever of hurry, had not come here—only the Wrellis hurried on his eternal quest, but it was a calm and placid hurry that gave one time for song. It was in the early afternoon, and nobody was about. Either they worked beyond the mysterious valley that nursed Wrellisford and hid it from the world, or else they secluded themselves within their old-time houses that were roofed with tiles of stone. I sat down upon the old stone bridge and watched the Wrellis, who seemed to me to be the only traveller that came from far away into this village where roads end, and passed on beyond it. And yet the Wrellis comes singing out of eternity, and tarries for a very little while in the village where roads end, and passes on into eternity again; and so surely do all that dwell in Wrellisford. I wondered as I leaned upon the bridge in what place the Wrellis would first find the sea, whether as he wound idly through meadows on his long quest he would suddenly behold him, and, leaping down over some rocky cliff, take to him at once the message of the hills. Or whether, widening slowly into some grand and tidal estuary, he would take his waste of waters to the sea and the might of the river should meet with the might of the waves, like to two Emperors clad in gleaming mail meeting midway between two hosts of war; and the little Wrellis would become a haven for returning ships and a setting-out place for adventurous men.

A little beyond the bridge there stood an old mill with a ruined roof, and a small branch of the Wrellis rushed through its emptiness shouting, like a boy playing alone in a corridor of some desolate house. The mill-wheel was gone, but there lay there still great bars and wheels and cogs, the bones of some dead industry. I know not what industry was once lord in that house, I know not what retinue of workers mourns him now; I only know who is lord there today in all those empty chambers. For as soon as I entered, I saw a whole wall draped with his marvellous black tapestry, without price because inimitable and too delicate to pass from hand to hand amongmerchants. I looked at the wonderful complexity of its infinite threads, my finger sank into it for more than an inch without feeling the touch; so black it was and so carefully wrought, sombrely covering the whole of the wall, that it might have been worked to commemorate the deaths of all that ever lived there, as indeed it was. I looked through a hole in the wall into an inner chamber where a worn-out driving band went among many wheels, and there this priceless inimitable stuff not merely clothed the walls but hung from bars and ceiling in beautiful draperies, in marvellous festoons. Nothing was ugly in this desolate house, for the busy artist's soul of its present lord had beautified everything in its desolation. It was the unmistakable work of the spider, in whose house I was, and the house was utterly desolate but for him, and silent but for the roar of the Wrellis and the shout of the little stream. Then I turned homewards; and as I went up and over the hill and lost the sight of the village, I saw the road whiten and harden and gradually broaden out till the tracks of wheels appeared; and it went afar to take the young men of Wrellisford into the wide ways of the earth—to the new West and the mysterious East, and into the troubled South.

And that night, when the house was still and sleep was far off, hushing hamlets and giving ease to cities, my fancy wandered up that aimless road and came suddenly to Wrellisford. And it seemed to me that the travelling of so many people for so many years between Wrellisford and John o' Groat's, talking to one another as they went or muttering alone, had given the road a voice. And it seemed to me that night that the road spoke to the river by Wrellisford bridge, speaking with the voice of many pilgrims. And the road said to the river: 'I rest here. How is it with you?'

And the river, who is always speaking, said: 'I rest nowhere from do-ing the Work of the World. I carry the murmur of inner lands to the sea, and to the abysses voices of the hills.'

'It is I,' said the road, 'that do the Work of the World, and take from city to city the rumour of each. There is nothing higher than Man and the making of cities. What do you do for Man?'

And the river said: 'Beauty and song are higher than Man. I carry the news seaward of the first song of the thrush after the furious retreat of win-ter northward, and the first timid anemone learns from me that she is safe and that spring has truly come. Oh but the song of all the birds in spring is more beautiful than Man, and the first coming of the hyacinth more delectable than his face! When spring is fallen upon the days of summer, I carry away with mournful joy at night petal by petal the rhododendron's bloom. No lit procession of purple kings is nigh so fair as that. No beautiful death of well-beloved men hath such a glory of forlornness. And I bear far away the pink and white petals of the apple-blossom's youth when the laborious time comes for his work in the world and for the bearing of apples. And I am robed each day and every night anew with the beauty of heaven, and I make lovely visions of the trees. But Man! What is Man? In the ancient parliament of the elder hills, when the grey ones speak together, they say nought of Man, but concern themselves only with their brethren the stars. Or when they wrap themselves in purple cloaks at evening, they lament some old irreparable wrong, or, uttering some mountain hymn, all mourn the set of sun.'

'Your beauty,' said the road, 'and the beauty of the sky, and of the rhododendron blossom and of spring, live only in the mind of Man, and except in the mind of Man the mountains have no voices. Nothing is beautiful that has not been seen by Man's eye. Or if your rhododendron blossom was beautiful for a moment, it soon withered and was drowned, and spring soon passes away; beauty can only live on in the mind of Man. I bring thought into the mind of Man swiftly from distant places every day. I know the Telegraph—I know him well; he and I have walked for hundreds of miles together. There is no work in the world except for Man and the making of his cities. I take wares to and fro from city to city.'

'My little stream in the field there,' said the river, 'used to make wares in that house for awhile once.'

'Ah,' said the road, 'I remember, but I brought cheaper ones from distant cities. Nothing is of any importance but making cities for Man.'

'I know so little about him,' said the river, 'but I have a great deal of work to do—I have all this water to send down to the sea; and then tomorrow or next day all the leaves of Autumn will be coming this way. It will be very beautiful. The sea is a very, very wonderful place. I know all about it; I have heard shepherd boys singing of it, and sometimes before a storm the gulls come up. It is a place all blue and shining and full of pearls, and has in it coral islands and isles of spice, and storms and galleons and the bones of Drake. The sea is much greater than Man. When I come to the sea, he will know that I have worked well for him. But I must hurry, for I have much to do. This bridge delays me a little; some day I will carry it away.'

'Oh, you must not do that,' said the road.

'Oh, not for a long time,' said the river. 'Some centuries perhaps—and I have much to do besides. There is my song to sing, for instance, and that alone is more beautiful than any noise that Man makes.'

'All work is for Man,' said the road, 'and for the building of cities. There is no beauty or romance or mystery in the sea except for the men that sail abroad upon it, and for those that stay at home and dream of them. As for your song, it rings night and morning, year in, year out, in the ears of men that are born in Wrellisford; at night it is part of their dreams, at morning it is the voice of day, and so it becomes part of their souls. But the song is not beautiful in itself. I take these men with your song in their souls up over the edge of the valley and a long way off beyond, and I am a strong and dusty road up there, and they go with your song in their souls and turn it into music and gladden cities. But nothing is the Work of the World except work for Man.'

'I wish I was quite sure about the Work of the World,' said the stream; 'I wish I knew for certain for whom we work. I feel almost sure that it is for the sea. He is very great and beautiful. I think that there can be no greater master than the sea. I think that some day he may be so full of romance and mystery and sound of sheep bells and murmur of mist-hidden hills, which we streams shall have brought him, that there will be no more music or beauty left in the world, and all the world will end; and perhaps the streams shall gather at the last, we all together, to the sea. Or perhaps the sea will give us at the last unto each one his own again, giving back all that he has garnered in the years—the little petals of the apple-blossom and the mourned ones of the rhododendron, and our old visions of the trees and sky; so many memories have left the hills. But who may say? For who knows the tides of the sea?'

'Be sure that it is all for Man,' said the road. 'For Man and the making of cities.'

Something had come near on utterly silent feet.

'Peace, peace!' it said. 'You disturb the queenly night, who, having come into this valley, is a guest in my dark halls. Let us have an end to this discussion.'

It was the spider who spoke.

'The Work of the World is the making of cities and palaces. But it is not for Man. What is Man? He only prepares my cities for me, and mellows them. All his works are ugly, his richest tapestries are coarse and clumsy. He is a noisy idler. He only protects me from mine enemy the wind; and the beautiful work in my cities, the curving outlines and the delicate weavings, is all mine. Ten years to a hundred it takes to build a city, for five or six hundred more it mellows, and is prepared for me; then I inhabit it, and hide away all that is ugly, and draw beautiful lines about it to and fro. There is nothing so beautiful as cities and palaces; they are the loveliest places in the world, because they are the stillest, and so most like the stars. They are noisy at first, for a little, before I come to them; they have ugly corners not yet rounded off, and coarse tapestries, and then they become ready for me and my exquisite work, and are quite silent and beautiful. And there I entertain the regal nights when they come there jewelled with stars, and all their train of silence, and regale them with costly dust. Already nods, in a city that I wot of, a lonely sentinel whose lords are dead, who grows too old and sleepy to drive away the gathering silence that infests the streets; tomorrow I go to see if he be still at his post. For me Babylon was built, and rocky Tyre; and still men build my cities! All the Work of the World is the making of cities, and all of them I inherit.'

THE DOOM OF LA TRAVIATA

Evening stole up out of mysterious lands and came down on the streets of Paris, and the things of the day withdrew themselves and hid away, and the beautiful city was strangely altered, and with it the hearts of men. And with lights and music, and in silence and in the dark, the other life arose, the life that knows the night, and dark cats crept from the houses and moved to silent places, and dim streets became haunted with dusk shapes. At this hour in a mean house, near to the Moulin Rouge, La Traviata died; and her death was brought to her by her own sins, and not by the years of God. But the soul of La Traviata drifted blindly about the streets where she had sinned till it struck against the wall of Notre Dame de Paris. Thence it rushed upwards, as the sea mist when it beats against a cliff, and streamed away to Paradise, and was there judged. And it seemed to me, as I watched from my place of dreaming, when La Traviata came and stood before the seat of judgment, that clouds came rushing up from the far Paradisal hills and gathered together over the head of God, and became one black cloud; and the clouds moved swiftly as shadows of the night when a lantern is swung in the hand, and more and more clouds rushed up, and ever more and more, and, as they gathered, the cloud a little above the head of God became no larger, but only grew blacker and blacker. And the halos of the saints settled lower upon their heads and narrowed and became pale, and the singing of the choirs of the seraphim faltered and sunk low, and the converse of the blessed suddenly ceased. Then a stern look came into the face of God, so that the seraphim turned away and left Him, and the saints. Then God commanded, and seven great angels rose up slowly through the clouds that carpet Paradise, and there was pity on their faces, and their eyes were closed. Then God pronounced judgment, and the lights of Paradise went out, and the azure crystal windows that look towards the world, and the windows rouge and verd, became dark and colourless, and I saw no more. Presently the seven great angels came out by one of Heaven's gates and set their faces Hellwards, and four of them carried the young soul of La Traviata, and one of them went on before and one of them followed behind. These six trod with mighty strides the long and dusty road that is named the Way of the Damned. But the seventh flew above them all the way, and the light of the fires of Hell that was hidden from the six by the dust of that dreadful road flared on the feathers of his breast.

Presently the seven angels, as they swept Hellwards, uttered speech.

'She is very young,' they said; and 'She is very beautiful,' they said; and they looked long at the soul of La Traviata, looking not at the stains of sin, but at that portion of her soul wherewith she had loved her sister a long while dead, who flitted now about an orchard on one of Heaven's hills with a low sunlight ever on her face, who communed daily with the saints when they passed that way going to bless the dead from Heaven's utmost edge. And as they looked long at the beauty of all that remained beautiful in her soul they said: 'It is but a young soul;' and they would have taken her to one of Heaven's hills, and would there have given her a cymbal and a dulcimer, but they knew that the Paradisal gates were clamped and barred against La Traviata. And they would have taken her to a valley in the world where there were a great many flowers and a loud sound of streams, where birds were singing always and church bells rang on Sabbaths, only this they durst not do. So they swept onwards nearer and nearer Hell. But when they were come quite close and the glare was on their faces, and they saw the gates already divide and prepare to open outwards, they said: 'Hell is a terrible city, and she is tired of cities;' then suddenly they dropped her by the side of the road, and wheeled and flew away. But into a great pink flower that was horrible and lovely grew the soul of La Traviata; and it had in it two eyes but no eyelids, and it stared constantly into the faces of all the passers-by that went along the dusty road to Hell; and the flower grew in the glare of the lights of Hell, and withered but could not die; only, one petal turned back towards the heavenly hills as an ivy leaf turns outwards to the day, and in the soft and silvery light of Paradise it withered not nor faded, but heard at times the commune of the saints coming murmuring from the distance, and sometimes caught the scent of orchards wafted from the heavenly hills, and felt a faint breeze cool it every evening at the hour when the saints to Heaven's edge went forth to bless the dead.

But the Lord arose with His sword, and scattered His disobedient angels as a thresher scatters chaff.

ON THE DRY LAND

Over the marshes hung the gorgeous night with all his wandering bands of nomad stars, and his whole host of still ones blinked and watched.

Over the safe dry land to eastward, grey and cold, the first clear pallor of dawn was coming up above the heads of the immortal gods.

Then, as they neared at last the safety of the dry land, Love looked at the man whom he had led for so long through the marshes, and saw that his hair was white, for it was shining in the pallor of the dawn.

Then they stepped together on to the land, and the old man sat down weary on the grass, for they had wandered in the marshes for many years; and the light of the grey dawn widened above the heads of the gods.

And Love said to the old man, 'I will leave you now.'

And the old man made no answer, but wept softly.

Then Love was grieved in his little careless heart, and he said: 'You must not be sorry that I go, nor yet regret me, nor care for me at all.

'I am a very foolish child, and was never kind to you, nor friendly. I never cared for your great thoughts, or for what was good in you, but perplexed you by leading you up and down the perilous marshes. And I was so heartless that, had you perished where I led you, it would have been nought to me, and I only stayed with you because you were good to play with.

'And I am cruel and altogether worthless and not such a one as any should be sorry for when I go, or one to be regretted, or even cared for at all.'

And still the old man spoke not, but wept softly; and Love grieved bitterly in his kindly heart.

And Love said: 'Because I am so small my strength has been concealed from you, and the evil that I have done. But my strength is great, and I have used it unjustly. Often I pushed you from the causeway through the marshes, and cared not if you drowned. Often I mocked you, and caused others to mock you. And often I led you among those that hated me, and laughed when they revenged themselves upon you.

'So weep not, for there is no kindness in my heart, but only murder and foolishness, and I am no companion for one so wise as you, but am so frivolous and silly that I laughed at your noble dreams and hindered all your deeds. See now, you have found me out, and now you will send me away, and here you will live at ease, and, undisturbed, have noble dreams of the immortal gods.

'See now, here is dawn and safety, and *there* is darkness and peril.'

Still the old man wept softly.

Then Love said: 'Is it thus with you?' and his voice was grave now and quiet. 'Are you so troubled? Old friend of so many years, there is grief in my heart for you. Old friend of perilous ventures, I must leave you now. But I will send my brother soon to you—my little brother Death. And he will come up out of the marshes to you, and will not forsake you, but will be true to you as I have not been true.'

And dawn grew brighter over the immortal gods, and the old man smiled through his tears, which glistened wondrously in the increasing light. But Love went down to the night and to the marshes, looking backward over his shoulder as he went, and smiling beautifully about his eyes. And in the marshes whereunto he went, in the midst of the gorgeous night, and under the wandering bands of nomad stars, rose shouts of laughter and the sounds of the dance.

And after a while, with his face towards the morning, Death out of the marshes came up tall and beautiful, and with a faint smile shadowy on his lips, and lifted in his arms the lonely man, being gentle with him, and, murmuring with his low deep voice an ancient song, carried him to the morning to the gods.

A DREAMER'S TALES (1910)

PREFACE

I hope for this book that it may come into the hands of those that were kind to my others and that it may not disappoint them.

—Lord Dunsany

POLTARNEES, BEHOLDER OF OCEAN

Toldees, Mondath, Arizim, these are the Inner Lands, the lands whose sentinels upon their borders do not behold the sea. Beyond them to the east there lies a desert, for ever untroubled by man: all yellow it is, and spotted with shadows of stones, and Death is in it, like a leopard lying in the sun. To the south they are bounded by magic, to the west by a mountain, and to the north by the voice and anger of the Polar wind. Like a great wall is the mountain to the west. It comes up out of the distance and goes down into the distance again, and it is named Poltarnees, Beholder of Ocean. To the northward red rocks, smooth and bare of soil, and without any speck of moss or herbage, slope up to the very lips of the Polar wind, and there is nothing else there by the noise of his anger. Very peaceful are the Inner Lands, and very fair are their cities, and there is no war among them, but quiet and ease. And they have no enemy but age, for thirst and fever lie sunning themselves out in the mid-desert, and never prowl into the Inner Lands. And the ghouls and ghosts, whose highway is the night, are kept in the south by the boundary of magic. And very small are all their pleasant cities, and all men are known to one another therein, and bless one another by name as they meet in the streets. And they have a broad, green way in every city that comes in out of some vale or wood or downland, and wanders in and out about the city between the houses and across the streets, and the people walk along it never at all, but every year at her appointed time Spring walks along it from the flowery lands, causing the anemone to bloom on the green way and all the early joys of hidden woods, or deep, secluded vales, or triumphant downlands, whose heads lift up so proudly, far up aloof from cities.

Sometimes waggoners or shepherds walk along this way, they that have come into the city from over cloudy ridges, and the townsmen hinder them not, for there is a tread that troubleth the grass and a tread that troubleth it not, and each man in his own heart knoweth which tread he hath. And in the sunlit spaces of the weald and in the wold's dark places, afar from the music of cities and from the dance of the cities afar, they make there the music of the country places and dance the country dance. Amiable, near and friendly appears to these men the sun, and as he is genial to them and tends their younger vines, so they are kind to the little woodland things and any rumour of the fairies or old legend. And when the light of some little distant city makes a slight flush upon the edge of the sky, and the happy golden windows of the homesteads stare gleaming into the dark, then the old and holy figure of Romance, cloaked even to the face, comes down out of hilly woodlands and bids dark shadows to rise and dance, and sends the forest creatures forth to prowl, and lights in a moment in her bower of grass the little glowworm's lamp, and brings a hush down over the grey lands, and out of it rises faintly on far-off hills the voice of a lute. There are not in the world lands more prosperous and happy than Toldees, Mondath, Arizim.

From these three little kingdoms that are named the Inner Lands the young men stole constantly away. One by one they went, and no one knew why they went save that they had a longing to behold the Sea. Of this longing they spoke little, but a young man would become silent for a few days, and then, one morning very early, he would slip away and slowly climb Poltarnee's difficult slope, and having attained the top pass over and never return. A few stayed behind in the Inner Lands and became the old men, but none that had ever climbed Poltarnees from the very earliest times had ever come back again. Many had gone up Poltarnees sworn to return. Once a king sent all his courtiers, one by one, to report the mystery to him, and then went himself; none ever returned.

Now, it was the wont of the folk of the Inner Lands to worship rumours and legends of the Sea, and all that their prophets discovered of the Sea was writ in a sacred book, and with deep devotion on days of festival or mourning read in the temples by the priests. Now, all their temples lay open to the west, resting upon pillars, that the breeze from the Sea might enter them, and they lay open on pillars to the east that the breezes of the Sea might not be hindered by pass onward wherever the Sea list. And this is the legend that they had of the Sea, whom none in the Inner Lands had ever beholden. They say that the Sea is a river heading towards Hercules, and they say that he touches against the edge of the world, and that Poltarnees looks upon him. They say that all the worlds of heaven go bobbing on this river and are swept down with the stream, and that Infinity is thick and furry with forests through which the river in his course sweeps on with all the worlds of heaven. Among the colossal trunks of those dark trees, the smallest fronds of whose branches are man nights, there walk the gods. And whenever its thirst, glowing in space like a great sun, comes upon the beast, the tiger of the gods creeps down to the river to drink. And the tiger of the gods drinks his fill loudly, whelming worlds the while, and the level of the river sinks between its banks ere the beast's thirst is quenched and ceases to glow like a sun. And many worlds thereby are heaped up dry and stranded, and the gods walk not among them evermore, because they are hard to their feet. These are the worlds that have no destiny, whose people know no god. And the river sweeps onwards ever. And the name of the River is Oriathon, but men call it Ocean. This is the Lower Faith of the Inner Lands. And there is a Higher Faith which is not told to all. Oriathon sweeps on through the forests of Infinity and all at once falls roaring over an Edge, whence Time has long ago recalled his hours to fight in his war with the gods; and falls unlit by the flash of nights and days, with his flood unmeasured by miles, into the deeps of nothing.

Now as the centuries went by and the one way by which a man could climb Poltarnees became worn with feet, more and more men surmounted it, not to return. And still they knew not in the Inner Lands upon what mystery Poltarnees looked. For on a still day and windless, while men walked happily about their beautiful streets or tended flocks in the country, suddenly the west wind would bestir himself and come in from the Sea. And he would come cloaked and grey and mournful and carry to someone the hungry cry of the Sea calling out for bones of men. And he that heard it would move restlessly for some hours, and at last would rise suddenly, irresistibly up, setting his face to Poltarnees, and would say, as is the custom of those lands when men part briefly, "Till a man's heart remembereth," which means "Farewell for a while"; but those that loved him, seeing his eyes on Poltarnees, would answer sadly, "Till the gods forget," which means "Farewell."

Now the king of Arizim had a daughter who played with the wild wood flowers, and with the fountains in her father's court, and with the little blue heaven-birds that came to her doorway in the winter to shelter from the snow. And she was more beautiful than the wild wood flowers, or than all the fountains in her father's court, or than the blue heaven-birds in their full winter plumage when they shelter from the snow. The old wise kings of Mondath and of Toldees saw her once as she went lightly down the little paths of her garden, and turning their gaze into the mists of thought, pondered the destiny of their Inner Lands. And they watched her closely by the stately flowers, and standing alone in the sunlight, and passing and repassing the strutting purple birds that the king's fowlers had brought from Asagéhon. When she was of the age of fifteen years the King of Mondath called a council of kings. And there met with him the kings of Toldees and Arizim. And the King of Mondath in his Council said:

"The call of the unappeased and hungry Sea (and at the word 'Sea' the three kings bowed their heads) lures every year out of our happy kingdoms more and more of our men, and still we know not the mystery of the Sea, and no devised oath has brought one man back. Now thy daughter, Arizim, is lovelier than the sunlight, and lovelier than those stately flowers of thine that stand so tall in her garden, and hath more grace and beauty than those strange birds that the venturous fowlers bring in creaking wagons out of Asagéhon, whose feathers are alternate purple and white. Now, he that shall love thy daughter, Hilnaric, whoever he shall be, is the man to climb Poltarnees and return, as none hath ever before, and tell us upon what Poltarnees looks; for it may be that they daughter is more beautiful than the Sea."

Then from his Seat of Council arose the King of Arizim. He said: "I fear that thou hast spoken blasphemy against the Sea, and I have a dread that ill will come of it. Indeed I had not thought she was so fair. It is such a short while ago that she was quite a small child with her hair still unkempt and not yet attired in the manner of princesses, and she would go up into the wild woods unattended and come back with her robes unseemly and all torn, and would not take reproof with a humble spirit, but made grimaces even in my marble court all set about with fountains."

Then said the King of Toldees:

"Let us watch more closely and let us see the Princess Hilnaric in the season of the orchard-bloom when the great birds go by that know the Sea, to rest in our inland places; and if she be more beautiful than the sunrise over our folded kingdoms when all the orchards bloom, it may be that she is more beautiful than the Sea."

And the King of Arizim said:

"I fear this is terrible blasphemy, yet will I do as you have decided in council."

And the season of the orchard-bloom appeared. One night the King of Arizim called his daughter forth on his outer balcony of marble. And the moon was rising huge and round and holy over dark woods, and all the fountains were singing to the night. And the moon touched the marble palace gables, and they glowed in the land. And the moon touched the heads of all the fountains, and the grey columns broke into fairy lights. And the moon left the dark ways of the forest and lit the whole white palace and its fountains and shone on the forehead of the Princess, and the palace of Arizim glowed afar, and the fountains became columns of gleaming jewels and song. And the moon made a music at its rising, but it fell a little short of mortal ears. And Hilnaric stood there wondering, clad in white, with the moonlight shining on her forehead; and watching her from the shadows on the terrace stood the kings of Mondath and Toldees. They said.

"She is more beautiful than the moonrise." And the season of the orchard-bloom appeared. One night the King of Arizim called his daughter forth on his outer balcony of marble. And the moon was rising huge and round and holy over dark woods, and all the fountains were singing to the night. And the moon touched the marble palace gables, and they glowed in the land. And the moon touched the heads of all the fountains, and the grey columns broke into fairy lights. And the moon left the dark ways of the forest and lit the whole white palace and its fountains and shone on the forehead of the Princess, and the palace of Arizim glowed afar, and the fountains became columns of gleaming jewels and song. And the moon made a music at its rising, but it fell a little short of mortal ears. And Hilnaric stood there wondering, clad in white, with the moonlight shining on her forehead; and watching her from the shadows on the terrace stood the kings of Mondath and Toldees. They said:

"She is more beautiful than the moonrise." And on another day the King of Arizim bade his daughter forth at dawn, and they stood again upon the balcony. And the sun came up over a world of orchards, and the sea-mists went back over Poltarnees to the Sea; little wild voices arose in all the thickets, the voices of the fountains began to die, and the song arose, in all the marble temples, of the birds that are sacred to the Sea. And Hilnaric stood there, still glowing with dreams of heaven.

"She is more beautiful," said the kings, "than morning."

Yet one more trial they made of Hilnaric's beauty, for they watched her on the terraces at sunset ere yet the petals of the orchards had fallen, and all along the edge of neighbouring woods the rhododendron was blooming with the azalea. And the sun went down under craggy Poltarnees, and the sea-mist poured over his summit inland. And the marble temples stood up clear in the evening, but films of twilight were drawn between the mountain and the city. Then from the Temple ledges and eaves of palaces the bats fell headlong downwards, then spread their wings and floated up and down through darkening ways; lights came blinking out in golden windows, men cloaked themselves against the grey sea-mist, the sound of small songs arose, and the face of Hilnaric became a resting-place for mysteries and dreams.

"Than all these things," said the kings, "she is more lovely: but who can say whether she is lovelier than the Sea?"

Prone in a rhododendron thicket at the edge of the palace lawns a hunter had waited since the sun went down. Near to him was a deep pool where the hyacinths grew and strange flowers floated upon it with broad leaves; and there the great bull gariachs came down to drink by starlight; and, waiting there for the gariachs to come, he saw the white form of the Princess leaning on her balcony. Before the stars shone out or the bulls came down to drink he left his lurking-place and moved closer to the palace to see more nearly the Princess. The palace lawns were full of untrodden dew, and everything was still when he came across them, holding his great spear. In the farthest corner of the terraces the three old kings were discussing the beauty of Hilnaric and the destiny of the Inner Lands. Moving lightly, with a hunter's tread, the watcher by the pool came very near, even in the still evening, before the Princess saw him. When he saw her closely he exclaimed suddenly:

"She must be more beautiful than the Sea."

When the Princess turned and saw his garb and his great spear she knew that he was a hunter of gariachs.

When the three kings heard the young man exclaim they said softly to one another:

"This must be the man."

Then they revealed themselves to him, and spoke to him to try him. They said:

"Sir, you have spoken blasphemy against the Sea."

And the young man muttered:

"She is more beautiful than the Sea."

And the kings said:

"We are older than you and wiser, and know that nothing is more beautiful than the Sea."

And the young man took off the gear of his head, and became downcast, and he knew that he spake with kings, yet he answered:

"By this spear, she is more beautiful than the Sea."

And all the while the Princess stared at him, knowing him to be a hunter of gariachs.

Then the king of Arizim said to the watcher by the pool:

"If thou wilt go up Poltarnees and come back, as none have come, and report to us what lure or magic is in the Sea, we will pardon thy blasphemy, and thou shalt have the Princess to wife and sit among the Council of Kings."

And gladly thereunto the young man consented. And the Princess spoke to him, and asked him his name. And he told her that his name was Athelvok, and great joy arose in him at the sound of her voice. And to the three kings he promised to set out on the third day to scale the slope of Poltarnees and to return again, and this was the oath by which they bound him to return:

"I swear by the Sea that bears the worlds away, by the river of Oriathon, which men call Ocean, and by the gods and their tiger, and by the doom of the worlds, that I will return again to the Inner Lands, having beheld the Sea."

And that oath he swore with solemnity that very night in one of the temples of the Sea, but the three kings trusted more to the beauty of Hilnaric even than to the power of the oath.

The next day Athelvok came to the palace of Arizim with the morning, over the fields to the East and out of the country of Toldees, and Hilnaric came out along her balcony and met him on the terraces. And she asked him if he had ever slain a gariach, and he said that he had slain three, and then he told her how he had killed his first down by the pool in the wood. For he had taken his father's spear and gone down to the edge of the pool, and had lain under the azaleas there waiting for the stars to shine, by whose first light the gariachs go to the pools to drink; and he had gone too early and had had long to wait, and the passing hours seemed longer than they were. And all the birds came in that home at night, and the bat was abroad, and the hour of the duck went by, and still no gariach came down to the pool; and Athelvok felt sure that none would come. And just as this grew to a certainty in his mind the thicket parted noiselessly and a huge bull gariach stood facing him on the edge of the water, and his great horns swept out sideways from his head, and at the ends curved upwards, and were four strides in width from tip to tip. And he had not seen Athelvok, for the great bull was on the far side of the little pool, and Athelvok could not creep round to him for fear of meeting the wind (for the gariachs, who can see little in the dark forests, rely on hearing and smell). But he devised swiftly in his mind while the bull stood there with head erect just twenty strides from him across the water. And the bull sniffed the wind cautiously and listened, then lowered his great head down to the pool and drank. At that instant Athelvok leapt into the water and shot forward through its weedy depths among the stems of the strange flowers that floated upon broad leaves on the surface. And Athelvok kept his spear out straight before him, and the fingers of his left hand he held rigid and straight, not pointing upwards, and so did not come to the surface, but was carried onward by the strength of his spring and passed unentangled through the stems of the flowers. When Athelvok jumped into the water the bull must have thrown his head up, startled at the splash, then he would have listened and have sniffed the air, and neither hearing nor scenting any danger he must have remained rigid for some moments, for it was in that attitude that Athelvok found him as he emerged breathless at his feet. And, striking at once, Athelvok drove the spear into his throat before the head and the terrible horns came down. But Athelvok had clung to one of the great horns, and had been carried at terrible speed through the rhododendron bushes until the gariach fell, but rose at once again, and died standing up, still struggling, drowned in its own blood.

But to Hilnaric listening it was as though one of the heroes of old time had come back again in the full glory of his legendary youth.

And long time they went up and down the terraces, saying those things which were said before and since, and which lips shall yet be made to say again. And above them stood Poltarnees beholding the Sea.

And the day came when Athelvok should go. And Hilnaric said to him:

"Will you not indeed most surely come back again, having just looked over the summit of Poltarnees?"

Athelvok answered: "I will indeed come back, for thy voice is more beautiful than the hymn of the priests when they chant and praise the Sea, and though many tributary seas ran down into Oriathon and he and all the others poured their beauty into one pool below me, yet would I return swearing that thou were fairer than they."

And Hilnaric answered:

"The wisdom of my heart tells me, or old knowledge or prophecy, or some strange lore, that I shall never hear thy voice again. And for this I give thee my forgiveness."

But he, repeating the oath that he had sworn, set out, looking often backwards until the slope became to step and his face was set to the rock. It was in the morning that he started, and he climbed all the day with little rest, where every foot-hole was smooth with many feet. Before he reached the top the sun disappeared from him, and darker and darker grew the Inner Lands. Then he pushed on so as to see before dark whatever thing Poltarnees had to show. The dusk was deep over the Inner Lands, and the lights of cities twinkled through the sea-mist when he came to Poltarnees's summit, and the sun before him was not yet gone from the sky.

And there below him was the old wrinkled Sea, smiling and murmuring song. And he nursed little ships with gleaming sails, and in his hands were old regretted wrecks, and mast all studded over with golden nails that he had rent in anger out of beautiful galleons. And the glory of the sun was among the surges as they brought driftwood out of isles of spice, tossing their golden heads. And the grey currents crept away to the south like companionless serpents that love something afar with a restless, deadly love. And the whole plain of water glittering with late sunlight, and the surges and the currents and the white sails of ships were all together like the face of a strange new god that has looked at a man for the first time in the eyes at the moment of his death; and Athelvok, looking on the wonderful Sea, knew why it was that the dead never return, for there is something that the dead feel and know, and the living would never understand even though the dead should come and speak to them about it. And there was the Sea smiling at him, glad with the glory of the sun. And there was a haven there for homing ships, and a sunlit city stood upon its marge, and people walked about the streets of it clad in the unimagined merchandise of far sea-bordering lands.

An easy slope of loose rock went from the top of Poltarnees to the shore of the Sea.

For a long while Athelvok stood there regretfully, knowing that there had come something into his soul that no one in the Inner Lands could understand, where the thoughts of their minds had gone no farther than the three little kingdoms. Then, looking long upon the wandering ships, and the marvelous merchandise from alien lands, and the unknown colour that wreathed the brows of the Sea, he turned his face to the darkness and the Inner Lands.

At that moment the Sea sang a dirge at sunset for all the harm that he had done in anger and all the ruin wrought on adventurous ships; and there were tears in the voice of the tyrannous Sea, for he had loved the galleons that he had overwhelmed, and he called all men to him and all living things that he might make amends, because he had loved the bones that he had strewn afar. And Athelvok turned and set one foot upon the crumbled slope, and then another, and walked a little way to be nearer to the Sea, and then a dream came upon him and he felt that men had wronged the lovely Sea because he had been angry a little, because he had been sometimes cruel; he felt that there was trouble among the tides of the Sea because he had loved the galleons who were dead. Still he walked on and the crumbled stones rolled with him, and just as the twilight faded and a star appeared he came to the golden shore, and walked on till the surges were about his knees, and he heard the prayer-like blessings of the Sea. Long he stood thus, while the stars came out above him and shone again in the surges; more stars came wheeling in their courses up from the Sea, lights twinkled out through all the haven city, lanterns were slung from the ships, the purple night burned on; and Earth, to the eyes of the gods as they sat afar, glowed as with one flame. Then Athelvok went into the haven city; there he met many who had left the Inner Lands before him; none of them wished to return to the people who had not seen the Sea; many of them had forgotten the three little kingdoms, and it was rumoured that one man, who had once tried to return, had found the shifting, crumbled slope impossible to climb.

Hilnaric never married. But her dowry was set aside to build a temple wherein men curse the ocean.

Once every year, with solemn rite and ceremony, they curse the tides of the Sea; and the moon looks in and hates them.

BLAGDAROSS

On a waste place strewn with bricks in the outskirts of a town twilight was falling. A star or two appeared over the smoke, and distant windows lit mysterious lights. The stillness deepened and the loneliness. Then all the outcast things that are silent by day found voices.

An old cork spoke first. He said: "I grew in Andalusian woods, but never listened to the idle songs of Spain. I only grew strong in the sunlight waiting for my destiny. One day the merchants came and took us all away and carried us all along the shore of the sea, piled high on the backs of donkeys, and in a town by the sea they made me into the shape that I am now. One day they sent me northward to Provence, and there I fulfilled my destiny. For they set me as a guard over the bubbling wine, and I faithfully stood sentinel for twenty years. For the first few years in the bottle that I guarded the wine slept, dreaming of Provence; but as the years went on he grew stronger and stronger, until at last whenever a man went by the wind would put out all his might against me, saying, 'Let me go free; let me go free!' And every year his strength increased, and he grew more clamourous when men went by, but never availed to hurl me from my post. But when I had powerfully held him for twenty years they brought him to the banquet and took me from my post, and the wine arose rejoicing and leapt through the veins of men and exalted their souls within them till they stood up in their places and sang Provençal songs. But me they cast away—me that had been sentinel for twenty years, and was still as strong and staunch as when first I went on guard. Now I am an outcast in a cold northern city, who once have known the Andalusian skies and guarded long ago Provençal suns that swam in the heart of the rejoicing wine."

An unstruck match that somebody had dropped spoke next. "I am a child of the sun," he said, "and an enemy of cities; there is more in my heart than you know of. I am a brother of Etna and Stromboli; I have fires lurking in me that will one day rise up beautiful and strong. We will not go into servitude on any hearth nor work machines for our food, but we will take out own food where we find it on that day when we are strong. There are wonderful children in my heart whose faces shall be more lively than the rainbow; they shall make a compact with the North wind, and he shall lead them forth; all shall be black behind them and black above them, and there shall be nothing beautiful in the world but them; they shall seize upon the earth and it shall be theirs, and nothing shall stop them but our old enemy the sea."

Then an old broken kettle spoke, and said: "I am the friend of cities. I sit among the slaves upon the hearth, the little flames that have been fed with coal. When the slaves dance behind the iron bars I sit in the middle of the dance and sing and make our masters glad. And I make songs about the comfort of the cat, and about the malice that is towards her in the heart of the dog, and about the crawling of the baby, and about the ease that is in the lord of the house when we brew the good brown tea; and sometimes when the house is very warm and slaves and masters are glad, I rebuke the hostile winds that prowl about the world."

And then there spoke the piece of an old cord. "I was made in a place of doom, and doomed men made my fibres, working without hope. Therefore there came a grimness into my heart, so that I never let anything go free when once I was set to bind it. Many a thing have I bound relentlessly for months and years; for I used to come coiling into warehouses where the great boxes lay all open to the air, and one of them would be suddenly closed up, and my fearful strength would be set on him like accurse, and if his timbers groaned when first I seized them, or if they creaked aloud in the lonely night, thinking of woodlands out of which they came, then I only gripped them tighter still, for the poor useless hate is in my soul of those that made me in the place of doom. Yet, for all the things that my prison-clutch has held, the last work that I did was to set something free. I lay idle one night in the gloom on the warehouse floor. Nothing stirred there, and even the spider slept. Towards midnight a great flock of echoes suddenly leapt up from the wooden planks and circled round the roof. A man was coming towards me all alone. And as he came his soul was reproaching him, and I saw that there was a great trouble between the man and his soul, for his soul would not let him be, but went on reproaching him.

"Then the man saw me and said, 'This at least will not fail me.' When I heard him say this about me, I determined that whatever he might require of me it should be done to the uttermost. And as I made this determination in my unfaltering heart, he picked me up and stood on an empty box that I should have bound on the morrow, and tied one end of me to a dark rafter; and the knot was carelessly tied, because his soul was reproaching him all the while continually and giving him no ease. Then he made the other end of me into a noose, but when the man's soul saw this it stopped reproaching the man, and cried out to him hurriedly, and besought him to be at peace with it and to do nothing sudden; but the man went on with his work, and put the noose down over his face and underneath his chin, and the soul screamed horribly.

"Then the man kicked the box away with his foot, and the moment he did this I knew that my strength was not great enough to hold him; but I remembered that he had said I would not fail him, and I put all my grim vigour into my fibres and held by sheer will. Then the soul shouted to me to give way, but I said:

"'No; you vexed the man.'

"Then it screamed for me to leave go of the rafter, and already I was slipping, for I only held on to it by a careless knot, but I gripped with my prison grip and said:

"'You vexed the man.'

"And very swiftly it said other things to me, but I answered not; and at last the soul that vexed the man that had trusted me flew away and left him at peace. I was never able to bind things any more, for every one of my fibres was worn and wrenched, and even my relentless heart was weakened by the struggle. Very soon afterwards I was thrown out here. I have done my work."

So they spoke among themselves, but all the while there loomed above them the form of an old rocking-horse complaining bitterly. He said: "I am Blagdaross. Woe is me that I should lie now an outcast among these worthy but little people. Alas! for the days that are gathered, and alas for the Great One that was a master and a soul to me, whose spirit is now shrunken and can never know me again, and no more ride abroad on knightly quests. I was Bucephalus when he was Alexander, and carried him victorious as far as Ind. I encountered dragons with him when he was St. George, I was the horse of Roland fighting for Christendom, and was often Rosinante. I fought in tournays and went errant upon quests, and met Ulysses and the heroes and the fairies. Or late in the evening, just before the lamps in the nursery were put out, he would suddenly mount me, and we would gallop through Africa. There we would pass by night through tropic forests, and come upon dark rivers sweeping by, all gleaming with the eyes of crocodiles, where the hippopotamus floated down with the stream, and mysterious craft loomed suddenly out of the dark and furtively passed away. And when we had passed through the forest lit by the fireflies we would come to the open plains, and gallop onwards with scarlet flamingoes flying along beside us through the lands of dusky kings, with golden crowns upon their heads and scepters in their hands, who came running out of their palaces to see us pass. Then I would wheel suddenly, and the dust flew up from my four hooves as I turned and we galloped home again, and my master was put to bed. And again he would ride abroad on another day till we came to magical fortresses guarded by wizardry and overthrew the dragons at the gate, and ever came back with a princess fairer than the sea.

"But my master began to grow larger in his body and smaller in his soul, and then he rode more seldom upon quests. At last he saw gold and never came again, and I was cast out here among these little people."

But while the rocking-horse was speaking two boys stole away, unnoticed by their parents, from a house on the edge of the waste place, and were coming across it looking for adventures. One of them carried a broom, and when he saw the rocking-horse he said nothing, but broke off the handle from the broom and thrust it between his braces and his shirt on the left side. Then he mounted the rocking-horse, and drawing forth the broomstick, which was sharp and spiky at the end, said, "Saladin is in this desert with all his paynims, and I am Coeur de Lion." After a while the other boy said: "Now let me kill Saladin too." But Blagdaross in his wooden heart, that exulted with thoughts of battle, said: "I am Blagdaross yet!"

THE MADNESS OF ANDELSPRUTZ

I first saw the city of Andelsprutz on an afternoon in spring. The day was full of sunshine as I came by the way of the fields, and all that morning I had said, "There will be sunlight on it when I see for the first time the beautiful conquered city whose fame has so often made for me lovely dreams." Suddenly I saw its fortifications lifting out of the fields, and behind them stood its belfries. I went in by a gate and saw its houses and streets, and a great disappointment came upon me. For there is an air about a city, and it has a way with it, whereby a man may recognized one from another at once. There are cities full of happiness and cities full of pleasure, and cities full of gloom. There are cities with their faces to heaven, and some with their faces to earth; some have a way of looking at the past and others look at the future; some notice you if you come among them, others glance at you, others let you go by. Some love the cities that are their neighbours, others are dear to the plains and to the heath; some cities are bare to the wind, others have purple cloaks and others brown cloaks, and some are clad in white. Some tell the old tale of their infancy, with others it is secret; some cities sing and some mutter, some are angry, and some have broken hearts, and each city has her way of greeting Time.

I had said: "I will see Andelsprutz arrogant with her beauty," and I had said: "I will see her weeping over her conquest."

I had said: "She will sing songs to me," and "she will be reticent," "she will be all robed," and "she will be bare but splendid."

But the windows of Andelsprutz in her houses looked vacantly over the plains like the eyes of a dead madman. At the hour her chimes sounded unlovely and discordant, some of them were out of tune, and the bells of some were cracked, her roofs were bald and without moss. At evening no pleasant rumour arose in her streets. When the lamps were lit in the houses no mystical flood of light stole out into the dusk, you merely saw that there were lighted lamps; Andelsprutz had no way with her and no air about her. When the night fell and the blinds were all drawn down, then I perceived what I had not thought in the daylight. I knew then that Andelsprutz was dead.

I saw a fair-haired man who drank beer in a café, and I said to him:

"Why is the city of Andelsprutz quite dead, and her soul gone hence?"

He answered: "Cities do not have souls and there is never any life in bricks."

And I said to him: "Sir, you have spoken truly."

And I asked the same question of another man, and he gave me the same answer, and I thanked him for his courtesy. And I saw a man of a more slender build, who had black hair, and channels in his cheeks for tears to run in, and I said to him:

"Why is Andelsprutz quite dead, and when did her soul go hence?"

And he answered: "Andelsprutz hoped too much. For thirty years would she stretch out her arms toward the land of Akla every night, to Mother Akla from whom she had been stolen. Every night she would be hoping and sighing, and stretching out her arms to Mother Akla. At midnight, once a year, on the anniversary of the terrible day, Akla would send spies to lay a wreath against the walls of Andelsprutz. She could do no more. And on this night, once in every year, I used to weep, for weeping was the mood of the city that nursed me. Every night while other cities slept did Andelsprutz sit brooding here and hoping, till thirty wreaths lay mouldering by her walls, and still the armies of Akla could not come.

"But after she had hoped so long, and on the night that faithful spies had brought her thirtieth wreath, Andelsprutz went suddenly mad. All the bells clanged hideously in the belfries, horses bolted in the streets, the dogs all howled, the stolid conquerors awoke and turned in their beds and slept again; and I saw the grey shadowy form of Andelsprutz rise up, decking her hair with the phantasms of cathedrals, and stride away from her city. And the great shadowy form that was the soul of Andelsprutz went away muttering to the mountains, and there I followed her—for had she not been my nurse? Yes, I went away alone into the mountains, and for three days, wrapped in a cloak, I slept in their misty solitudes. I had no food to eat, and to drink I had only the water of the mountain streams. By day noliving thing was near to me, and I heard nothing but the noise of the wind, and the mountain streams roaring. But for three nights I heard all round me on the mountain the sounds of a great city: I saw the lights of tall cathedral windows flash momentarily on the peaks, and at times the glimmering lantern of some fortress patrol. And I saw the huge misty outline of the soul of Andelsprutz sitting decked with her ghostly cathedrals, speaking to herself, with her eyes fixed before her in a mad stare, telling of ancient wars. And her confused speech for all those nights upon the mountain was sometimes the voice of traffic, and then of church bells, and then of bugles, but oftenest it was the voice of red war; and it was all incoherent, and she was quite mad.

"The third night it rained heavily all night long, but I stayed up there to watch the soul of my native city. And she still sat staring straight before her, raving; but here voice was gentler now, there were more chimes in it, and occasional song. Midnight passed, and the rain still swept down on me, and still the solitudes of the mountain were full of the mutterings of the poor mad city. And the hours after midnight came, the cold hours wherein sick men die.

"Suddenly I was aware of great shapes moving in the rain, and heard the sound of voices that were not of my city nor yet of any that I ever knew. And presently I discerned, though faintly, the souls of a great concourse of cities, all bending over Andelsprutz and comforting her, and the ravines of the mountains roared that night with the voices of cities that had lain still for centuries. For there came the soul of Camelot that had so long ago forsaken Usk; and there was Ilion, all girt with towers, still cursing the sweet face of ruinous Helen; I saw there Babylon and Persepolis, and the bearded face of bull-like Nineveh, and Athens mourning her immortal gods.

"All these souls if cities that were dead spoke that night on the mountain to my city and soothed her, until at last she muttered of war no longer, and her eyes stared wildly no more, but she hid her face in her hands and for some while wept softly. At last she arose, and walking slowly and with bended head, and leaning upon Ilion and Carthage, went mournfully eastwards; and the dust of her highways swirled behind her as she went, a ghostly dust that never turned to mud in all that drenching rain. And so the souls of the cities led her away, and gradually they disappeared from the mountain, and the ancient voices died away in the distance.

"Now since then have I seen my city alive; but once I met with a traveler who said that somewhere in the midst of a great desert are gathered together the souls of all dead cities. He said that he was lost once in a place where there was no water, and he heard their voices speaking all the night."

But I said: "I was once without water in a desert and heard a city speaking to me, but knew not whether it really spoke to me or not, for on that day I heard so many terrible things, and only some of them were true."

And the man with the black hair said: "I believe it to be true, though whither she went I know not. I only know that a shepherd found me in the morning faint with hunger and cold, and carried me down here; and when I came to Andelsprutz it was, as you have perceived it, dead."

WHERE THE TIDES EBB AND FLOW

I dreamt that I had done a horrible thing, so that burial was to be denied me either in soil or sea, neither could there be any hell for me.

I waited for some hours, knowing this. Then my friends came for me, and slew me secretly and with ancient rite, and lit great tapers, and carried me away.

It was all in London that the thing was done, and they went furtively at dead of night along grey streets and among mean houses until they came to the river. And the river and the tide of the sea were grappling with one another between the mud-banks, and both of them were black and full of lights. A sudden wonder came in to the eyes of each, as my friends came near to them with their glaring tapers. All these things I saw as they carried me dead and stiffening, for my soul was still among my bones, because there was no hell for it, and because Christian burial was denied me.

They took me down a stairway that was green with slimy things, and so came slowly to the terrible mud. There, in the territory of forsaken things, they dug a shallow grave. When they had finished they laid me in the grave, and suddenly they cast their tapers to the river. And when the water had quenched the flaring lights the tapers looked pale and small as they bobbed upon the tide, and at once the glamour of the calamity was gone, and I noticed then the approach of the huge dawn; and my friends cast their cloaks over their faces, and the solemn procession was turned into many fugitives that furtively stole away.

Then the mud came back wearily and covered all but my face. There I lay alone with quite forgotten things, with drifting things that the tides will take no farther, with useless things and lost things, and with the horrible unnatural bricks that are neither stone nor soil. I was rid of feeling, because I had been killed, but perception and thought were in my unhappy soul. The dawn widened, and I saw the desolate houses that crowded the marge of the river, and their dead windows peered into my dead eyes, windows with bales behind them instead of human souls. I grew so weary looking at these forlorn things that I wanted to cry out, but could not, because I was dead. Then I knew, as I had never known before, that for all the years that herd of desolate houses had wanted to cry out too, but, being dead, were dumb. And I knew then that it had yet been well with the forgotten drifting things if they had wept, but they were eyeless and without life. And I, too, tried to weep, but there were no tears in my dead eyes. And I knew then that the river might have cared for us, might have caressed us, might have sung to us, but he swept broadly onwards, thinking of nothing but the princely ships.

At last the tide did what the river would not, and came and covered me over, and my soul had rest in the green water, and rejoiced and believed that it had the Burial of the Sea. But with the ebb the water fell again, and left me alone again with the callous mud among the forgotten things that drift no more, and with the sight of all those desolate houses, and with the knowledge among all of us that each was dead.

In the mournful wall behind me, hung with green weeds, forsaken of the sea, dark tunnels appeared, and secret narrow passages that were clamped and barred. From these at last the stealthy rats came down to nibble me away, and my soul rejoiced thereat and believed that he would be free perforce from the accursed bones to which burial was refused. Very soon the rats ran away a little space and whispered among themselves. They never came any more. When I found that I was accursed even among the rats I tried to weep again.

Then the tide came swinging back and covered the dreadful mud, and hid the desolate houses, and soothed the forgotten things, and my soul had ease for a while in the sepulture of the sea. And then the tide forsook me again.

To and fro it came about me for many years. Then the County Council found me, and gave me decent burial. It was the first grave that I had ever slept in. That very night my friends came for me. They dug me up and put me back again in the shallow hold in the mud.

Again and again through the years my bones found burial, but always behind the funeral lurked one of those terrible men who, as soon as night fell, came and dug them up and carried them back again to the hole in the mud.

And then one day the last of those men died who once had done to me this terrible thing. I heard his soul go over the river at sunset.

And again I hoped.

A few weeks afterwards I was found once more, and once more taken out of that restless place and given deep burial in sacred ground, where my soul hoped that it should rest.

Almost at once men came with cloaks and tapers to give me back to the mud, for the thing had become a tradition and a rite. And all the forsaken things mocked me in their dumb hearts when they saw me carried back, for they were jealous of me because I had left the mud. It must be remembered that I could not weep.

And the years went by seawards where the black barges go, and the great derelict centuries became lost at sea, and still I lay there without any cause to hope, and daring not to hope without a cause, because of the terrible envy and the anger of the things that could drift no more.

Once a great storm rode up, even as far as London, out of the sea from the South; and he came curving into the river with the fierce East wind. And he was mightier than the dreary tides, and went with great leaps over the listless mud. And all the sad forgotten things rejoiced, and mingled with things that were haughtier than they, and rode once more amongst the lordly shipping that was driven up and down. And out of their hideous home he took my bones, never again, I hoped, to be vexed with the ebb and flow. And with the fall of the tide he went riding down the river and turned to the southwards, and so went to his home. And my bones he scattered among many isles and along the shores of happy alien mainlands. And for a moment, while they were far asunder, my soul was almost free.

Then there arose, at the will of the moon, the assiduous flow of the tide, and it undid at once the work of the ebb, and gathered my bones from the marge of sunny isles, and gleaned them all along the mainland's shores, and went rocking northwards till it came to the mouth of the Thames, and there turned westwards its relentless face, and so went up the river and came to the hole in the mud, and into it dropped my bones; and partly the mud covered them, and partly it left them white, for the mud cares not for its forsaken things.

Then the ebb came, and I saw the dead eyes of the houses and the jealousy of the other forgotten things that the storm had not carried thence.

And some more centuries passed over the ebb and flow and over the loneliness of things for gotten. And I lay there all the while in the careless grip of the mud, never wholly covered, yet never able to go free, and I longed for the great caress of the warm Earth or the comfortable lap of the Sea.

Sometimes men found my bones and buried them, but the tradition never died, and my friends' successors always brought them back. At last the barges went no more, and there were fewer lights; shaped timbers no longer floated down the fairway, and there came instead old wind-uprooted trees in all their natural simplicity.

At last I was aware that somewhere near me a blade of grass was growing, and the moss began to appear all over the dead houses. One day some thistledown went drifting over the river.

For some years I watched these signs attentively, until I became certain that London was passing away. Then I hoped once more, and all along both banks of the river there was anger among the lost things that anything should dare to hope upon the forsaken mud. Gradually the horrible houses crumbled, until the poor dead things that never had had life got decent burial among the weeds and moss. At last the may appeared and the convolvulus. Finally, the wild rose stood up over mounds that had been wharves and warehouses. Then I knew that the cause of Nature had triumphed, and London had passed away.

The last man in London came to the wall by the river, in an ancient cloak that was one of those that once my friends had worn, and peered over the edge to see that I still was there. Then he went, and I never saw men again: they had passed away with London.

A few days after the last man had gone the birds came into London, all the birds that sing. When they first saws me they all looked sideways at me, then they went away a little and spoke among themselves.

"He only sinned against Man," they said; "it is not our quarrel."

"Let us be kind to him," they said.

Then they hopped nearer me and began to sing. It was the time of the rising of the dawn, and from both banks of the river, and from the sky, and from the thickets that were once the streets, hundreds of birds were singing. As the light increased the birds sang more and more; they grew thicker and thicker in the air above my head, till there were thousands of them singing there, and then millions, and at last I could see nothing but a host of flickering wings with the sunlight on them, and little gaps of sky. Then when there was nothing to be heard in London but the myriad notes of that exultant song, my soul rose up from the bones in the hole in the mud and began to climb heavenwards. And it seemed that a lane-way opened amongst the wings of the birds, and it went up and up, and one of the smaller gates of Paradise stood ajar at the end of it. And then I knew by a sign that the mud should receive me no more, for suddenly I found that I could weep.

At this moment I opened my eyes in bed in a house in London, and outside some sparrows were twittering in a tree in the light of the radiant morning; and there were tears still wet upon my face, for one's restraint is feeble while one sleeps. But I arose and opened the window wide, and stretching my hands out over the little garden, I blessed the birds whose song had woken me up from the troubled and terrible centuries of my dream.

BETHMOORA

There is a faint freshness in the London night as though some strayed reveler of a breeze had left his comrades in the Kentish uplands and had entered the town by stealth. The pavements are a little damp and shiny. Upon one's ears that at this late hour have become very acute there hits the tap of a remote footfall. Louder and louder grow the taps, filling the whole night. And a black cloaked figure passes by, and goes tapping into the dark. One who has danced goes homewards. Somewhere a ball has closed its doors and ended. Its yellow lights are out, its musicians are silent, its dancers have all gone into the night air, and Time has said of it, "Let it be past and over, and among the things that I have put away."

Shadows begin to detach themselves from their great gathering places. No less silently than those shadows that are thin and dead move homewards the stealthy cats. Thus have we even in London our faint forebodings of the dawn's approach, which the birds and the beasts and the stars are crying aloud to the untrammeled fields.

At what moment I know not I perceive that the night itself is irrevocably overthrown. It is suddenly revealed to me by the weary pallor of the street lamps that the streets are silent and nocturnal still, not because there is any strength in night, but because men have not yet arisen from sleep to defy him. So have I seen dejected and untidy guards still bearing antique muskets in palatial gateways, although the realms of the monarch that they guard have shrunk to a single province which no enemy yet has troubled to overrun.

And it is now manifest from the aspect of the street lamps, those abashed dependants of night, that already English mountain peaks have seen the dawn, that the cliffs of Dover are standing white to the morning, that the sea-mist has lifted and is pouring inland.

And now men with a hose have come and are sluicing out the streets.

Behold now night is dead.

What memories, what fancies throng one's mind! A night but just now gathered out of London by the horrific hand of Time. A million common artificial things all cloaked for a while in mystery, like beggars robed in purple, and seated on dread thrones. Four million people asleep, dreaming perhaps. What worlds have they gone into? Whom have they met? But my thoughts are far off with Bethmoora in her loneliness, whose gates swing to and fro. To and fro they swing, and creak and creak in the wind, but no one hears them. They are of green copper, very lovely, but no one sees them now. The desert wind pours sand into their hinges, no watchman comes to ease them. No guard goes round Bethmoora's battlements, no enemy assails them. There are no lights in her houses, no footfall on her streets, she stands there dead and lonely beyond the Hills of Hap, and I would see Bethmoora once again, but dare not.

It is many a year, they tell me, since Bethmoora became desolate.

Her desolation is spoken of in taverns where sailors meet, and certain travellers have told me of it.

I had hoped to see Bethmoora once again. It is many a year ago, they say, when the vintage was last gathered in from the vineyards that I knew, where it is all desert now. It was a radiant day, and the people of the city were dancing by the vineyards, while here and there one played upon the kalipac. The purple flowering shrubs were all in bloom, and the snow shone upon the Hills of Hap.

Outside the copper gates they crushed the grapes in vats to make the syrabub. It had been a goodly vintage.

In the little gardens at the desert's edge men beat the tambang and the tittibuk, and blew melodiously the zootibar.

All there was mirth and song and dance, because the vintage had been gathered in, and there would be ample syrabub for the winter months, and much left over to exchange for turquoises and emeralds with the merchants who come down from Oxuhahn. Thus they rejoiced all day over their vintage on the narrow strip of cultivated ground that lay between Bethmoora and the desert which meets the sky to the South. And when the heat of the day began to abate, and the sun drew near to the snows on the Hills of Hap, the note of the zootibar still rose clear from the gardens, and the brilliant dresses of the dancers still wound among the flowers. All that day three men on mules had been noticed crossing the face of the Hills of Hap. Backwards and forwards they moved as the track wound lower and lower, three little specks of black against the snow. They were seen first in the very early morning up near the shoulder of Peol Jagganoth, and seemed to be coming out of Utnar Véhi. All day they came. And in the evening, just before the lights come out and colours change, they appeared before Bethmoora's copper gates. They carried staves, such as messengers bear in those lands, and seemed sombrely clad when the dancers all came round them with their green and lilac dresses. Those Europeans who were present and heard the message given were ignorant of the language, and only caught the name of Utnar Véhi. But it was brief, and passed rapidly from mouth to mouth, and almost at once the people burnt their vineyards and began to flee away from Bethmoora, going for the most part northwards, though some went to the East. They ran down out of their fair white houses, and streamed through the copper gate; the throbbing of the tambang and the tittibuk suddenly ceased with the note of the Zootibar, and the clinking kalipac stopped a moment after. The three strange travellers went back the way they came the instant their message was given. It was the hour when a light would have appeared in some high tower, and window after window would have poured into the dusk its lion-frightening light, and the cooper gates would have been fastened up. But no lights came out in windows there that night and have not ever since, and those copper gates were left wide and have never shut, and the sound arose of the red fire crackling in the vineyards, and the pattering of feet fleeing softly. There were no cries, no other sounds at all, only the rapid and determined flight. They fled as swiftly and quietly as a herd of wild cattle flee when they suddenly see a man. It was as though something had befallen which had been feared for generations, which could only be escaped by instant flight, which left no time for indecision.

Then fear took the Europeans also, and they too fled. And what the message was I have never heard.

Many believe that it was a message from Thuba Mleen, the mysterious emperor of those lands, who is never seen by man, advising that Bethmoora should be left desolate. Others say that the message was one of warning from the gods, whether from friendly gods or from adverse ones they know not.

And others hold that the Plague was ravaging a line of cities over in Utnar Véhi, following the South-west wind which for many weeks had been blowing across them towards Bethmoora.

Some say that the terrible gnousar sickness was upon the three travellers, and that their very mules were dripping with it, and suppose that they were driven to the city by hunger, but suggest no better reason for so terrible a crime.

But most believe that it was a message from the desert himself, who owns all the Earth to the southwards, spoken with his peculiar cry to those three who knew his voice—men who had been out on the sand-wastes without tents by night, who had been by day without water, men who had been out there where the desert mutters, and had grown to know his needs and his malevolence. They say that the desert had a need for Bethmoora, that he wished to come into her lovely streets, and to send into her temples and her houses his storm-winds draped with sand. For he hates the sound and the sight of men in his old evil heart, and he would have Bethmoora silent and undisturbed, save for the weird love he whispers to her gates.

If I knew what that message was that the three men brought on mules, and told in the copper gate, I think that I should go and see Bethmoora once again. For a great longing comes on me here in London to see once more that white and beautiful city, and yet I dare not, for I know not the danger I should have to face, whether I should risk the fury of unknown dreadful gods, or some disease unspeakable and slow, or the desert's curse or torture in some little private room of the Emperor Thuba Mleen, or something that the travelers have not told—perhaps more fearful still.

IDLE DAYS ON THE YANN

So I came down through the wood on the bank of Yann and found, as had been prophesied, the ship *Bird of the River* about to loose her cable.

The captain sat cross-legged upon the white deck with his scimitar lying beside him in its jeweled scabbard, and the sailors toiled to spread the nimble sails to bring the ship into the central stream of Yann, and all the while sang ancient soothing songs. And the wind of the evening descending cool from the snowfields of some mountainous abode of distant gods came suddenly, like glad tidings to an anxious city, into the wing-like sails.

And so we came into the central stream, whereat the sailors lowered the greater sails. But I had gone to bow before the captain, and to inquire concerning the miracles, and appearances among men, of the most holy gods of whatever land he had come from. And the captain answered that he came from fair Belzoond, and worshipped gods that were the least and humblest, who seldom sent the famine or the thunder, and were easily appeased with little battles. And I told how I came from Ireland, which is of Europe, whereat the captain and all the sailors laughed, for they said, "There are no such places in all the land of dreams." When they had ceased to mock me, I explained that my fancy mostly dwelt in the desert of Cuppar-Nombo, about a beautiful blue city called Golthoth the Damned, which was sentinelled all round by wolves and their shadows, and had been utterly desolate for years and years, because of a curse which the gods once spoke in anger and could never since recall. And sometimes my dreams took me as far as Pungar Vees, the red walled city where the fountains are, which trades with the Isles and Thul. When I said this they complimented me upon the abode of my fancy, saying that, though they had never seen these cities, such places might well be imagined. For the rest of that evening I bargained with the captain over the sum that I should pay him for any fare if God and the tide of Yann should bring us safely as far as the cliffs by the sea, which are named Bar-Wul-Yann, the Gate of Yann.

And now the sun had set, and all the colours of the world and heaven had held a festival with him, and slipped one by one away before the imminent approach of night. The parrots had all flown home to the jungle on either bank, the monkeys in rows in safety on high branches of the trees were silent and asleep, the fireflies in the deeps of the forest were going up and down, and the great stars came gleaming out to look on the face of Yann. Then the sailors lighted lanterns and hung them round the ship, and the light flashed out on a sudden and dazzled Yann, and the ducks that fed along his marshy banks all suddenly arose, and made wide circles in the upper air, and saw the distant reaches of the Yann and the white mist that softly cloaked the jungle, before they returned again to their marshes.

And then the sailors knelt on the decks and prayed, not all together, but five or six at a time. Side by side there kneeled down together five or six, for there only prayed at the same time men of different faiths, so that no god should hear two men praying to him at once. As soon as any one had finished his prayer, another of the same faith would take his place. Thus knelt the row of five or six with bended heads under the fluttering sail, while the central stream of the River Yann took them on towards the sea, and their prayers rose up from among the lanterns and went towards the stars. And behind them in the after end of the ship the helmsman prayed aloud the helmsman's prayer, which is prayed by all who follow his trade upon the River Yann, of whatever faith they be. And the captain prayed to his little lesser gods, to the gods that bless Belzoond.

And I too felt that I would pray. Yet I liked not to pray to a jealous God there where the frail affectionate gods whom the heathen love were being humbly invoked; so I bethought me, instead, of Sheol Nugganoth, whom the men of the jungle have long since deserted, who is now unworshipped and alone; and to him I prayed.

And upon us praying the night came suddenly down, as it comes upon all men who pray at evening and upon all men who do not; yet our prayers comforted our own souls when we thought of the Great Night to come.

And so Yann bore us magnificently onwards, for he was elate with molten snow that the Poltiades had brought him from the Hills of Hap, and the Marn and Migris were swollen with floods; and he bore us in his full might past Kyph and Pir, and we saw the lights of Goolunza.

Soon we all slept except the helmsman, who kept the ship in the mid-stream of Yann.

When the sun rose the helmsman ceased to sing, for by song he cheered himself in the lonely night. When the song ceased we suddenly all awoke, and another took the helm, and the helmsman slept.

We knew that soon we should come to Mandaroon. We made a meal, and Mandaroon appeared. Then the captain commanded, and the sailors loosed again the greater sails, and the ship turned and left the stream of Yann and came into a harbour beneath the ruddy walls of Mandaroon. Then while the sailors went and gathered fruits I came alone to the gate of Mandaroon. A few huts were outside it, in which lived the guard. A sentinel with a long white beard was standing in the gate, armed with a rusty pike. He wore large spectacles, which were covered with dust. Through the gate I saw the city. A deathly stillness was over all of it. The ways seemed untrodden, and moss was thick on doorsteps; in the market-place huddled figures lay asleep. A scent of incense came wafted through the gateway, of incense and burned poppies, and there was a hum of the echoes of distant bells. I said to the sentinel in the tongue of the region of Yann, "Why are they all asleep in this still city?"

He answered: "None may ask questions in this gate for fear they will wake the people of the city. For when the people of this city wake the gods will die. And when the gods die men may dream no more." And I began to ask him what gods that city worshipped, but he lifted his pike because none might ask questions there. So I left him and went back to the *Bird of the River*.

Certainly Mandaroon was beautiful with her white pinnacles peering over her ruddy walls and the green of her copper roofs.

When I came back again to the *Bird of the River*, I found the sailors were returned to the ship. Soon we weighed anchor, and sailed out again, and so came once more to the middle of the river. And now the sun was moving toward his heights, and there had reached us on the River Yann the song of those countless myriads of choirs that attend him in his progress round the world. For the little creatures that have many legs had spread their gauze wings easily on the air, as a man rests his elbows on a balcony and gave jubilant, ceremonial praises to the sun, or else they moved together on the air in wavering dances intricate and swift, or turned aside to avoid the onrush of some drop of water that a breeze had shaken from a jungle orchid, chilling the air and driving it before it, as it fell whirring in its rush to the earth; but all the while they sang triumphantly. "For the day is for us," they said, "whether our great and sacred father the Sun shall bring up more life like us from the marshes, or whether all the world shall end tonight." And there sang all those whose notes are known to human ears, as well as those whose far more numerous notes have been never heard by man.

To these a rainy day had been as an era of war that should desolate continents during all the lifetime of a man.

And there came out also from the dark and steaming jungle to behold and rejoice in the Sun the huge and lazy butterflies. And they danced, but danced idly, on the ways of the air, as some haughty queen of distant conquered lands might in her poverty and exile dance, in some encampment of the gipsies, for the mere bread to live by, but beyond that would never abate her pride to dance for a fragment more.

And the butterflies sung of strange and painted things, of purple orchids and of lost pink cities and the monstrous colours of the jungle's decay. And they, too, were among those whose voices are not discernible by human ears. And as they floated above the river, going from forest to forest, their splendour was matched by the inimical beauty of the birds who darted out to pursue them. Or sometimes they settled on the white and wax-like blooms of the plant that creeps and clambers about the trees of the forest; and their purple wings flashed out on the great blossoms as, when the caravans go from Nurl to Thace, the gleaming silks flash out upon the snow, where the crafty merchants spread them one by one to astonish the mountaineers of the Hills of Noor.

But upon men and beasts the sun sent drowsiness. The river monsters along the river's marge lay dormant in the slime. The sailors pitched a pavilion, with golden tassels, for the captain upon the deck, and then went, all but the helmsman, under a sail that they had hung as an awning between two masts. Then they told tales to one another, each of his own city or of the miracles of his god, until all were fallen asleep. The captain offered me the shade of his pavillion with the gold tassels, and there we talked for a while, he telling me that he was taking merchandise to Perdóndaris, and that he would take back to fair Belzoond things appertaining to the affairs of the sea. Then, as I watched through the pavilion's opening the brilliant birds and butterflies that crossed and recrossed over the river, I fell asleep, and dreamed that I was a monarch entering his capital underneath arches of flags, and all the musicians of the world were there, playing melodiously their instruments; but no one cheered.

In the afternoon, as the day grew cooler again, I awoke and found the captain buckling on his scimitar, which he had taken off him while he rested.

And now we were approaching the wide court of Astahahn, which opens upon the river. Strange boats of antique design were chained there to the steps. As we neared it we saw the open marble court, on three sides of which stood the city fronting on colonnades. And in the court and along the colonnades the people of that city walked with solemnity and care according to the rites of ancient ceremony. All in that city was of ancient device; the carving on the houses, which, when age had broken it, remained unrepaired, was of the remotest times, and everywhere were represented in stone beasts that have long since passed away from Earth—the dragon, the griffin, the hippogriffin, and the different species of gargoyle. Nothing was to be found, whether material or custom, that was new in Astahahn. Now they took no notice at all of us as we went by, but continued their processions and ceremonies in the ancient city, and the sailors, knowing their custom, took no notice of them. But I called, as we came near, to one who stood beside the water's edge, asking him what men did in Astahahn and what their merchandise was, and with whom they traded. He said, "Here we have fettered and manacled Time, who would otherwise slay the gods."

I asked him what gods they worshipped in that city, and he said, "All those gods whom Time has not yet slain." Then he turned from me and would say no more, but busied himself in behaving in accordance with ancient custom. And so, according to the will of Yann, we drifted onwards and left Astahahn. The river widened below Astahahn, and we found in greater quantities such birds as prey on fishes. And they were very wonderful in their plumage, and they came not out of the jungle, but flew, with their long necks stretched out before them, and their legs lying on the wind behind, straight up the river over the mid-stream.

And now the evening began to gather in. A thick white mist had appeared over the river, and was softly rising higher. It clutched at the trees with long impalpable arms, it rose higher and higher, chilling the air; and white shapes moved away into the jungle as though the ghosts of shipwrecked mariners were searching stealthily in the darkness for the spirits of evil that long ago had wrecked them on the Yann.

As the sun sank behind the field of orchids that grew on the matted summit of the jungle, the river monsters came wallowing out of the slime in which they had reclined during the heat of the day, and the great beasts of the jungle came down to drink. The butterflies a while since were gone to rest. In little narrow tributaries that we passed night seemed already to have fallen, though the sun which had disappeared from us had not yet set.

And now the birds of the jungle came flying home far over us, with the sunlight glistening pink upon their breasts, and lowered their pinions as soon as they saw the Yann, and dropped into the trees. And the widgeon began to go up the river in great companies, all whistling, and then would suddenly wheel and all go down again. And there shot by us the small and arrow-like teal; and we heard the manifold cries of flocks of geese, which the sailors told me had recently come in from crossing over the Lispasian ranges; every year they come by the same way, close by the peak of Mluna, leaving it to the left, and the mountain eagles know the way they come and—men say—the very hour, and every year they expect them by the same way as soon as the snows have fallen upon the Northern Plains. But soon it grew so dark that we heard those birds no more, and only heard the whirring of their wings, and of countless others besides, until they all settled down along the banks of the river, and it was the hour when the birds of the night went forth. Then the sailors lit the lanterns for the night, and huge moths appeared, flapping about the ship, and at moments their gorgeous colours would be revealed by the lanterns, then they would pass into the night again, where all was black. And again the sailors prayed, and thereafter we supped and slept, and the helmsman took our lives into his care.

When I awoke I found that we had indeed come to Perdóndaris, that famous city. For there it stood upon the left of us, a city fair and notable, and all the more pleasant for our eyes to see after the jungle that was so long with us. And we were anchored by the market-place, and the captain's merchandise was all displayed, and a merchant of Perdóndaris stood looking at it. And the captain had his scimitar in his hand, and was beating with it in anger upon the deck, and the splinters were flying up from the white planks; for the merchant had offered him a price for his merchandise that the captain declared to be an insult to himself and his country's gods, whom he now said to be great and terrible gods, whose curses were to be dreaded. But the merchant waved his hands, which were of great fatness, showing the pink palms, and swore that of himself he thought not at all, but only of the poor folk in the huts beyond the city to whom he wished to sell the merchandise for as low a price as possible, leaving no remuneration for himself. For the merchandise was mostly the thick toomarund carpets that in the winter keep the wind from the floor, and tollub which the people smoke in pipes. Therefore the merchant said if he offered a piffek more the poor folk must go without their toomarunds when the winter came, and without their tollub in the evenings, or else he and his aged father must starve together. Thereat the captain lifted his scimitar to his own throat, saying that he was now a ruined man, and that nothing remained to him but death. And while he was carefully lifting his beard with his left hand, the merchant eyed the merchandise again, and said that rather than see so worthy a captain die, a man for whom he had conceived an especial love when first he saw the manner in which he handled his ship, he and his aged father should starve together and therefore he offered fifteen piffeks more.

When he said this the captain prostrated himself and prayed to his gods that they might yet sweeten this merchant's bitter heart—to his little lesser gods, to the gods that bless Belzoond.

At last the merchant offered yet five piffeks more. Then the captain wept, for he said that he was deserted of his gods; and the merchant also wept, for he said that he was thinking of his aged father, and of how he soon would starve, and he hid his weeping face with both his hands, and eyed the tollub again between his fingers. And so the bargain was concluded, and the merchant took the toomarund and tollub, paying for them out of a great clinking purse. And these were packed up into bales again, and three of the merchant's slaves carried them upon their heads into the city. And all the while the sailors had sat silent, cross-legged in a crescent upon the deck, eagerly watching the bargain, and now a murmur of satisfaction arose among them, and they began to compare it among themselves with other bargains that they had known. And I found out from them that there are seven merchants in Perdóndaris, and that they had all come to the captain one by one before the bargaining began, and each had warned him privately against the others. And to all the merchants the captain had offered the wine of his own country, that they make in fair Belzoond, but could in no wise persuade them to it. But now that the bargain was over, and the sailors were seated at the first meal of the day, the captain appeared among them with a cask of that wine, and we broached it with care and all made merry together. And the captain was glad in his heart because he knew that he had much honour in the eyes of his men because of the bargain that he had made. So the sailors drank the wine of their native land, and soon their thoughts were back in fair Belzoond and the little neighbouring cities of Durl and Duz.

But for me the captain poured into a little jar some heavy yellow wine from a small jar which he kept apart among his sacred things. Thick and sweet it was, even like honey, yet there was in its heart a mighty, ardent fire which had authority over souls of men. It was made, the captain told me, with great subtlety by the secret craft of a family of six who lived in a hut on the mountains of Hian Min. Once in these mountains, he said, he followed the spoor of a bear, and he came suddenly on a man of that family who had hunted the same bear, and he was at the end of a narrow way with precipice all about him, and his spear was sticking in the bear, and the wound was not fatal, and he had no other weapon. And the bear was walking towards the man, very slowly because his wound irked him—yet he was now very close. And what he captain did he would not say, but every year as soon as the snows are hard, and travelling is easy on the Hian Min, that man comes down to the market in the plains, and always leaves for the captain in the gate of fair Belzoond a vessel of that priceless secret wine.

And as I sipped the wine and the captain talked, I remembered me of stalwart noble things that I had long since resolutely planned, and my soul seemed to grow mightier within me and to dominate the whole tide of the Yann. It may be that I then slept. Or, if I did not, I do not now minutely recollect every detail of that morning's occupations. Towards evening, I awoke and wishing to see Perdóndaris before we left in the morning, and being unable to wake the captain, I went ashore alone. Certainly Perdóndaris was a powerful city; it was encompassed by a wall of great strength and altitude, having in it hollow ways for troops to walk in, and battlements along it all the way, and fifteen strong towers on it in every mile, and copper plaques low down where men could read them, telling in all the languages of those parts of the earth—one language on each plaque—the tale of how an army once attacked Perdóndaris and what befell that army. Then I entered Perdóndaris and found all the people dancing, clad in brilliant silks, and playing on the tambang as they danced. For a fearful thunderstorm had terrified them while I slept, and the fires of death, they said, had danced over Perdóndaris, and now the thunder had gone leaping away large and black and hideous, they said, over the distant hills, and had turned round snarling at them, shoving his gleaming teeth, and had stamped, as he went, upon the hilltops until they rang as though they had been bronze. And often and again they stopped in their merry dances and prayed to the God they knew not, saying, "O, God that we know not, we thank Thee for sending the thunder back to his hills." And I went on and came to the market-place, and lying there upon the marble pavement I saw the merchant fast asleep and breathing heavily, with his face and the palms of his hands towards the sky, and slaves were fanning him to keep away the flies. And from the market-place I came to a silver temple and then to a palace of onyx, and there were many wonders in Perdóndaris, and I would have stayed and seen them all, but as I came to the outer wall of the city I suddenly saw in it a huge ivory gate. For a while I paused and admired it, then I came nearer and perceived the dreadful truth. The gate was carved out of one solid piece!

I fled at once through the gateway and down to the ship, and even as I ran I thought that I heard far off on the hills behind me the tramp of the fearful beast by whom that mass of ivory was shed, who was perhaps even then looking for his other tusk. When I was on the ship again I felt safer, and I said nothing to the sailors of what I had seen.

And now the captain was gradually awakening. Now night was rolling up from the East and North, and only the pinnacles of the towers of Perdóndaris still took the fallen sunlight. Then I went to the captain and told him quietly of the thing I had seen. And he questioned me at once about the gate, in a low voice, that the sailors might not know; and I told him how the weight of the thing was such that it could not have been brought from afar, and the captain knew that it had not been there a year ago. We agreed that such a beast could never have been killed by any assault of man, and that the gate must have been a fallen tusk, and one fallen near and recently. Therefore he decided that it were better to flee at once; so he commanded, and the sailors went to the sails, and others raised the anchor to the deck, and just as the highest pinnacle of marble lost the last rays of the sun we left Perdóndaris, that famous city. And night came down and cloaked Perdóndaris and hid it from our eyes, which as things have happened will never see it again; for I have heard since that something swift and wonderful has suddenly wrecked Perdóndaris in a day—towers, walls and people.

And the night deepened over the River Yann, a night all white with stars. And with the night there rose the helmsman's song. As soon as he had prayed he began to sing to cheer himself all through the lonely night. But first he prayed, praying the helmsman's prayer. And this is what I remember of it, rendered into English with a very feeble equivalent of the rhythm that seemed so resonant in those tropic nights.

To whatever god may hear.

Wherever there be sailors whether of river or sea: whether their way be dark or whether through storm: whether their peril be of beast or of rock: or from enemy lurking on land or pursuing on sea: wherever the tiller is cold or the helmsman stiff: wherever sailors sleep or helmsmen watch: guard, guide and return us to the old land, that has known us: to the far homes that we know.

To all the gods that are.

To whatever god may hear.

So he prayed, and there was silence. And the sailors laid them down to rest for the night. The silence deepened, and was only broken by the ripples of Yann that lightly touched our prow. Sometimes some monster of the river coughed.

Silence and ripples, ripples and silence again.

And then his loneliness came upon the helmsman, and he began to sing. And he sang the market songs of Durl and Duz, and the old dragon-legends of Belzoond.

Many a song he sang, telling to spacious and exotic Yann the little tales and trifles of his city of Durl. And the songs welled up over the black jungle and came into the clear cold air above, and the great bands of stars that look on Yann began to know the affairs of Durl and Duz, and of the shepherds that dwelt in the fields between, and the flocks that they had, and the loves that they had loved, and all the little things that they had hoped to do. And as I lay wrapped up in skins and blankets, listening to those songs, and watching the fantastic shapes of the great trees like to black giants stalking through the night, I suddenly fell asleep.

When I awoke great mists were trailing away from the Yann. And the flow of the river was tumbling now tumultuously, and little waves appeared; for Yann had scented from afar the ancient crags of Glorm, and knew that their ravines lay cool before him wherein he should meet the merry wild Irillion rejoicing from fields of snow. So he shook off from him the torpid sleep that had come upon him in the hot and scented jungle, and forgot its orchids and its butterflies, and swept on turbulent, expectant, strong; and soon the snowy peaks of the Hills of Glorm came glittering into view. And now the sailors were waking up from sleep. Soon we all ate, and then the helmsman laid him down to sleep while a comrade took his place, and they all spread over him their choicest furs.

And in a while we heard the sound that the Irillion made as she came down dancing from the fields of snow.

And then we saw the ravine in the Hills of Glorm lying precipitous and smooth before us, into which we were carried by the leaps of Yann. And now we left the steamy jungle and breathed the mountain air; the sailors stood up and took deep breaths of it, and thought of their own far off Acroctian hills on which were Durl and Duz—below them in the plains stands fair Belzoond.

A great shadow brooded between the cliffs of Glorm, but the crags were shining above us like gnarled moons, and almost lit the gloom. Louder and louder came the Irillion's song, and the sound of her dancing down from the fields of snow. And soon we saw her white and full of mists, and wreathed with rainbows delicate and small that she had plucked up near the mountain's summit from some celestial garden of the Sun. Then she went away seawards with the huge grey Yann and the ravine widened, and opened upon the world, and our rocking ship came through to the light of the day.

And all that morning and all the afternoon we passed through the marshes of Pondoovery; and Yann widened there, and flowed solemnly and slowly, and the captain bade the sailors beat on bells to overcome the dreariness of the marshes.

At last the Irusian mountains came in sight, nursing the villages of Pen-Kai and Blut, and the wandering streets of Mlo, where priests propitiate the avalanche with wine and maize. Then night came down over the plains of Tlun, and we saw the lights of Cappadarnia. We heard the Pathnites beating upon drums as we passed Imaut and Golzunda, then all but the helmsman slept. And villages scattered along the banks of the Yann heard all that night in the helmsman's unknown tongue the little songs of cities that they knew not.

I awoke before dawn with a feeling that I was unhappy before I remembered why. Then I recalled that by the evening of the approaching day, according to all foreseen probabilities, we should come to Bar-Wul-Yann, and I should part from the captain and his sailors. And I had liked the man because he had given me of his yellow wine that was set apart among his sacred things, and many a story he had told me about his fair Belzoond between the Acroctian hills and the Hian Min. And I had liked the ways that his sailors had, and the prayers that they prayed at evening side by side, grudging not one another their alien gods. And I had a liking too for the tender way in which they often spoke of Durl and Duz, for it is good that men should love their native cities and the little hills that hold those cities up.

And I had come to know who would meet them when they returned to their homes, and where they thought the meetings would take place, some in a valley of the Acroctian hills where the road comes up from Yann, others in the gateway of one or another of the three cities, and others by the fireside in the home. And I thought of the danger that had menaced us all alike outside Perdóndaris, a danger that, as things have happened, was very real.

And I thought too of the helmsman's cheery song in the cold and lonely night, and how he had held our lives in his careful hands. And as I thought of this the helmsman ceased to sing, and I looked up and saw a pale light had appeared in the sky, and the lonely night had passed; and the dawn widened, and the sailors awoke.

And soon we saw the tide of the Sea himself advancing resolute between Yann's borders, and Yann sprang lithely at him and they struggled awhile; then Yann and all that was his were pushed back northward, so that the sailors had to hoist the sails and, the wind being favorable, we still held onwards.

And we passed Gondara and Narl and Haz. And we saw memorable, holy Golnuz, and heard the pilgrims praying.

When we awoke after the midday rest we were coming near to Nen, the last of the cities on the River Yann. And the jungle was all about us once again, and about Nen; but the great Mloon ranges stood up over all things, and watched the city from beyond the jungle.

Here we anchored, and the captain and I went up into the city and found that the Wanderers had come into Nen.

And the Wanderers were a weird, dark, tribe, that once in every seven years came down from the peaks of Mloon, having crossed by a pass that is known to them from some fantastic land that lies beyond. And the people of Nen were all outside their houses, and all stood wondering at their own streets. For the men and women of the Wanderers had crowded all the ways, and every one was doing some strange thing. Some danced astounding dances that they had learned from the desert wind, rapidly curving and swirling till the eye could follow no longer. Others played upon instruments beautiful wailing tunes that were full of horror, which souls had taught them lost by night in the desert, that strange far desert from which the Wanderers came.

None of their instruments were such as were known in Nen nor in any part of the region of the Yann; even the horns out of which some were made were of beasts that none had seen along the river, for they were barbed at the tips. And they sang, in the language of none, songs that seemed to be akin to the mysteries of night and to the unreasoned fear that haunts dark places.

Bitterly all the dogs of Nen distrusted them. And the Wanderers told one another fearful tales, for though no one in Nen knew ought of their language yet they could see the fear on the listeners' faces, and as the tale wound on the whites of their eyes showed vividly in terror as the eyes of some little beast whom the hawk has seized. Then the teller of the tale would smile and stop, and another would tell his story, and the teller of the first tale's lips would chatter with fear. And if some deadly snake chanced to appear the Wanderers would greet him as a brother, and the snake would seem to give his greetings to them before he passed on again. Once that most fierce and lethal of tropic snakes, the giant lythra, came out of the jungle and all down the street, the central street of Nen, and none of the Wanderers moved away from him, but they all played sonorously on drums, as though he had been a person of much honour; and the snake moved through the midst of them and smote none.

Even the Wanderers' children could do strange things, for if any one of them met with a child of Nen the two would stare at each other in silence with large grave eyes; then the Wanderers' child would slowly draw from his turban a live fish or snake. And the children of Nen could do nothing of that kind at all.

Much I should have wished to stay and hear the hymn with which they greet the night, that is answered by the wolves on the heights of Mloon, but it was now time to raise the anchor again that the captain might return from Bar-Wul-Yann upon the landward tide. So we went on board and continued down the Yann. And the captain and I spoke little, for we were thinking of our parting, which should be for long, and we watched instead the splendour of the westering sun. For the sun was a ruddy gold, but a faint mist cloaked the jungle, lying low, and into it poured the smoke of the little jungle cities, and the smoke of them met together in the mist and joined into one haze, which became purple, and was lit by the sun, as the thoughts of men become hallowed by some great and sacred thing. Some times one column from a lonely house would rise up higher than the cities' smoke, and gleam by itself in the sun.

And now as the sun's last rays were nearly level, we saw the sight that I had come to see, for from two mountains that stood on either shore two cliffs of pink marble came out into the river, all glowing in the light of the low sun, and they were quite smooth and of mountainous altitude, and they nearly met, and Yann went tumbling between them and found the sea.

And this was Bar-Wul-Yann, the Gate of Yann, and in the distance through that barrier's gap I saw the azure indescribable sea, where little fishing-boats went gleaming by.

And the sun set, and the brief twilight came, and the exultation of the glory of Bar-Wul-Yann was gone, yet still the pink cliffs glowed, the fairest marvel that the eye beheld—and this in a land of wonders. And soon the twilight gave place to the coming out of stars, and the colours of Bar-Wul-Yann went dwindling away. And the sight of those cliffs was to me as some chord of music that a master's hand had launched from the violin, and which carries to Heaven or Faëry the tremulous spirits of men.

And now by the shore they anchored and went no further, for they were sailors of the river and not of the sea, and knew the Yann but not the tides beyond.

And the time was come when the captain and I must part, he to go back to his fair Belzoond in sight of the distant peaks of the Hian Min, and I to find my way by strange means back to those hazy fields that all poets know, wherein stand small mysterious cottages through whose windows, looking westwards, you may see the fields of men, and looking eastwards see glittering elfin mountains, tipped with snow, going range on range into the region of Myth, and beyond it into the kingdom of Fantasy, which pertain to the Lands of Dream. Long we regarded one another, knowing that we should meet no more, for my fancy is weakening as the years slip by, and I go ever more seldom into the Lands of Dream. Then we clasped hands, uncouthly on his part, for it is not the method of greeting in his country, and he commended my soul to the care of his own gods, to his little lesser gods, the humble ones, to the gods that bless Belzoond.

THE SWORD AND THE IDOL

It was a cold winter's evening late in the Stone Age; the sun had gone down blazing over the plains of Thold; there were no clouds, only the chill blue sky and the imminence of stars; and the surface of the sleeping Earth began to harden against the cold of the night. Presently from their lairs arose, and shook themselves and went stealthily forth, those of Earth's children to whom it is the law to prowl abroad as soon as the dusk has fallen. And they went pattering softly over the plain, and their eyes shone in the dark, and crossed and recrossed one another in their courses. Suddenly there became manifest in the midst of the plain that fearful portent of the presence of Man—a little flickering fire. And the children of

Earth who prowl abroad by night looked sideways at it and snarled and edged away; all but the wolves, who came a little nearer, for it was winter and the wolves were hungry, and they had come in thousands from the mountains, and they said in their hearts, "We are strong." Around the fire a little tribe was encamped. They, too, had come from the mountains, and from lands beyond them, but it was in the mountains that the wolves first winded them; they picked up bones at first that the tribe had dropped, but they were closer now and on all sides. It was Loz who had lit the fire. He had killed a small furry beast, hurling his stone axe at it, and had gathered a quantity of reddish-brown stones, and had laid them in a long row, and placed bits of the small beast all along it; then he lit a fire on each side, and the stones heated, and the bits began to cook. It was at this time that the tribe noticed that the wolves who had followed them so far were no longer content with the scraps of deserted encampments. A line of yellow eyes surrounded them, and when it moved it was to come nearer. So the men of the tribe hastily tore up brushwood, and felled a small tree with their flint axes, and heaped it all over the fire that Loz had made, and for a while the great heap hid the flame, and the wolves came trotting in and sat down again on their haunches much closer than before; and the fierce and valiant dogs that belonged to the tribe believed that their end was about to come while fighting, as they had long since prophesied it would. Then the flame caught the lofty stack of brushwood, and rushed out of it, and ran up the side of it, and stood up haughtily far over the top, and the wolves seeing this terrible ally of Man reveling there in his strength, and knowing nothing of this frequent treachery to his masters, went slowly away as though they had other purposes. And for the rest of that night the dogs of the encampment cried out to them and besought them to come back. But the tribe lay down all round the fire under thick furs and slept. And a great wind arose and blew into the roaring heart of the fire till it was red no longer, but all pallid with heat. With the dawn the tribe awoke.

Loz might have known that after such a mighty conflagration nothing could remain of his small furry beast, but there was hunger in him and little reason as he searched among the ashes. What he found there amazed him beyond measure; there was no meat, there was not even his row of reddish-brown stones, but something longer than a man's leg and narrower than his hand, was lying there like a great flattened snake. When Loz looked at its thin edges and saw that it ran to a point, he picked up stones to chip it and make it sharp. It was the instinct of Loz to sharpen things. When he found that it could not be chipped his wonderment increased. It was many hours before he discovered that he could sharpen the edges by rubbing them with a stone; but at last the point was sharp, and all one side of it except near the end, where Loz held it in his hand. And Loz lifted it and brandished it, and the Stone Age was over. That afternoon in the little encampment, just as the tribe moved on, the Stone Age passed away, which, for perhaps thirty or forty thousand years, had slowly lifted Man from among the beasts and left him with his supremacy beyond all hope of reconquest.

It was not for many days that any other man tried to make for himself an iron sword by cooking the same kind of small furry beast that Loz had tried to cook. It was not for many years that any thought to lay the meat along stones as Loz had done; and when they did, being no longer on the plains of Thold, they used flints or chalk. It was not for many generations that another piece of iron ore was melted and the secret slowly guessed. Nevertheless one of Earth's many veils was torn aside by Loz to give us ultimately the steel sword and the plough, machinery and factories; let us not blame Loz if we think that he did wrong, for he did all in ignorance. The tribe moved on until it came to water, and there it settled down under a hill, and they built their huts there. Very soon they had to fight with another tribe, a tribe that was stronger than they; but the sword of Loz was terrible and his tribe slew their foes. You might make one blow at Loz, but then would come one thrust from that iron sword, and there was no way of surviving it. No one could fight with Loz. And he became ruler of the tribe in the place of Iz, who hitherto had ruled it with his sharp axe, as his father had before him.

Now Loz begat Lo, and in his old age gave his sword to him, and Lo ruled the tribe with it. And Lo called the name of the sword Death, because it was so swift and terrible.

And Iz begat Ird, who was of no account. And Ird hated Lo because he was of no account by reason of the iron sword of Lo.

One night Ird stole down to the hut of Lo, carrying his sharp axe, and he went very softly, but Lo's dog, Warner, heard him coming, and he growled softly by his master's door. When Ird came to the hut he heard Lo talking gently to his sword. And Lo was saying, "Lie still, Death. Rest, rest, old sword," and then, "What, again, Death? Be still. Be still."

And then again: "What, art thou hungry, Death? Or thirsty, poor old sword? Soon, Death, soon. Be still only a little."

But Ird fled, for he did not like the gentle tone of Lo as he spoke to his sword.

And Lo begat Lod. And when Lo died Lod took the iron sword and ruled the tribe.

And Ird begat Ith, who was of no account, like his father.

Now when Lod had smitten a man or killed a terrible beast, Ith would go away for a while into the forest rather than hear the praises that would be given to Lod.

And once, as Ith sat in the forest waiting for the day to pass, he suddenly thought he saw a tree trunk looking at him as with a face. And Ith was afraid, for trees should not look at men. But soon Ith saw that it was only a tree and not a man, though it was like a man. Ith used to speak to this tree, and tell it about Lod, for he dared not speak to any oneelse about him. And Ith found comfort in speaking about Lod.

One day Ith went with his stone axe into the forest, and stayed there many days.

He came back by night, and the next morning when the tribe awoke they saw something that was like a man and yet was not a man. And it sat on the hill with its elbows pointing outwards and was quite still. And Ith was crouching before it, and hurriedly placing before it fruits and flesh, and then leaping away from it and looking frightened. Presently all the tribe came out to see, but dared not come quite close because of the fear that they saw on the face of Ith. And Ith went to his hut, and came back again with a hunting spear-head and valuable small stone knives, and reached out and laid them before the thing that was like a man, and then sprang away from it.

And some of the tribe questioned Ith about the still thing that was like a man, and Ith said, "This is Ged." Then they asked, "Who is Ged?" and Ith said, "Ged sends the crops and the rain; and the sun and the moon are Ged's."

Then the tribe went back to their huts, but later in the day some came again, and they said to Ith, "Ged is only as we are, having hands and feet." And Ith pointed to the right hand of Ged, which was not as his left, but was shaped like the paw of a beast, and Ith said, "By this ye may know that he is not as any man."

Then they said, "He is indeed Ged." But Lod said, "He speaketh not, nor doth he eat," and Ith answered, "The thunder is his voice and the famine is his eating."

After this the tribe copied Ith, and brought little gifts of meat to Ged; and Ith cooked them before him that Ged might smell the cooking.

One day a great thunderstorm came trampling up from the distance and raged among the hills, and the tribe all hid away from it in their huts. And Ith appeared among the huts looking unafraid. And Ith said little, but the tribe thought that he had expected the terrible storm because the meat that they had laid before Ged had been tough meat, and not the best parts of the beasts they slew.

And Ged grew to have more honour among the tribe than Lod. And Lod was vexed.

One night Lod arose when all were asleep, and quieted his dog, and took his iron sword and went away to the hill. And he came on Ged in the starlight, sitting still, with his elbows pointing outwards, and his beast's paw, and the mark of the fire on the ground where his food had been cooked.

And Lod stood there for a while in great fear, trying to keep to his purpose. Suddenly he stepped up close to Ged and lifted his iron sword, and Ged neither hit nor shrank. Then the thought came into Lod's mind, "Ged does not hit. What will Ged do instead?"

And Lod lowered his sword and struck not, and his imagination began to work on that "What will Ged do instead?"

And the more Lod thought, the worse was his fear of Ged.

And Lod ran away and left him.

Lod still ruled the tribe in battle or in the hunt, but the chiefest spoils of battle were given to Ged, and the beasts that they slew were Ged's; and all questions that concerned war or peace, and questions of law and disputes, were always brought to him, and Ith gave the answers after speaking to Ged by night.

At last Ith said, the day after an eclipse, that the gifts which they brought to Ged were not enough, that some far greater sacrifice was needed, that Ged was very angry even now, and not to be appeased by any ordinary sacrifice.

And Ith said that to save the tribe from the anger of Ged he would speak to Ged that night, and ask him what new sacrifice he needed.

Deep in his heart Lod shuddered, for his instinct told him that Ged wanted Lod's only son, who should hold the iron sword when Lod was gone.

No one would dare touch Lod because of the iron sword, but his instinct said in his slow mind again and again, "Ged loves Ith. Ith has said so. Ith hates the sword-holders."

"Ith hates the sword-holders. Ged loves Ith."

Evening fell and the night came when Ith should speak with Ged, and Lod became ever surer of the doom of his race.

He lay down but could not sleep.

Midnight had barely come when Lod arose and went with his iron sword again to the hill.

And there sat Ged. Had Ith been to him yet? Ith whom Ged loved, who hated the sword-holders.

And Lod looked long at the old sword of iron that had come to his grandfather on the plains of Thold.

Good-bye, old sword! And Lod laid it on the knees of Ged, then went away.

And when Ith came, a little before dawn, the sacrifice was found acceptable unto Ged.

THE IDLE CITY

There was once a city which was an idle city, wherein men told vain tales.

And it was that city's custom to tax all men that would enter in, with the toll of some idle story in the gate.

So all men paid to the watchers in the gate the toll of an idle story, and passed into the city unhindered and unhurt. And in a certain hour of the night when the king of that city arose and went pacing swiftly up and down the chamber of his sleeping, and called upon the name of the dead queen, then would the watchers fasten up the gate and go into that chamber to the king, and, sitting on the floor, would tell him all the tales that they had gathered. And listening to them some calmer mood would come upon the king, and listening still he would lie down again and at last fall asleep, and all the watchers silently would arise and steal away from the chamber.

A while ago wandering, I came to the gate of that city. And even as I came a man stood up to pay his toll to the watchers. They were seated cross-legged on the ground between him and the gate, and each one held a spear. Near him two other travellers sat on the warm sand waiting. And the man said:

"Now the city of Nombros forsook the worship of the gods and turned towards God. So the gods threw their cloaks over their faces and strode away from the city, and going into the haze among the hills passed through the trunks of the olive groves into the sunset. But when they had already left the Earth, they turned and looked through the gleaming folds of the twilight for the last time at their city; and they looked half in anger and half in regret, then turned and went away for ever. But they sent back a Death, who bore a scythe, saying to it: 'Slay half in the city that forsook us, but half of them spare alive that they may yet remember their old forsaken gods.'

"But God sent a destroying angel to show that He was God, saying unto him: 'Go into that city and slay half of the dwellers therein, yet spare a half of them that they may know that I am God.'

"And at once the destroying angel put his hand to his sword, and the sword came out of the scabbard with a deep breath, like to the breath that a broad woodman takes before his first blow at some giant oak. Thereat the angel pointed his arms downwards, and bending his head between them, fell forward from Heaven's edge, and the spring of his ankles shot him downwards with his wings furled behind him. So he went slanting earthward through the evening with his sword stretched out before him, and he was like a javelin that some hunter hath hurled that returneth again to the earth: but just before he touched it he lifted his head and spread his wings with the under feathers forward, and alighted by the bank of the broad Flavro that divides the city of Nombros. And down the bank of the Flavro he fluttered low, like to a hawk over a new-cut cornfield when the little creatures of the corn are shelterless, and at the same time down the other bank the Death from the gods went mowing.

"At once they saw each other, and the angel glared at the Death, and the Death leered back at him, and the flames in the eyes of the angel illumined with a red glare the mist that lay in the hollows of the sockets of the Death. Suddenly they fell on one another, sword to scythe. And the angel captured the temples of the gods, and set up over them the sign of God, and the Death captured the temples of God, and led into them the ceremonies and sacrifices of the gods; and all the while the centuries slipped quietly by, going down the Flavro seawards.

"And now some worship God in the temple of the gods, and others worship the gods in the temple of God, and still the angel hath not returned again to the rejoicing choirs, and still the Death hath not gone back to die with the dead gods; but all through Nombros they fight up and down, and still on each side of the Flavro the city lives."

And the watchers in the gate said, "Enter in."

Then another traveler rose up, and said:

"Solemnly between Huhenwazy and Nitcrana the huge grey clouds came floating. And those great mountains, heavenly Huhenwazi and Nitcrana, the king of peaks, greeted them, calling them brothers. And the clouds were glad of their greeting, for they meet with companions seldom in the lonely heights of the sky.

"But the vapours of evening said unto the earth-mist, 'What are those shapes that dare to move above us and to go where Nitcrana is and Huhenwazi?'

"And the earth-mist said in answer unto the vapours of evening, 'It is only an earth-mist that has become mad and has left the warm and comfortable earth, and has in his madness thought that his place is with Huhenwazi and Nitcrana.'

"'Once,' said the vapours of evening, 'there were clouds, but this was many and many a day ago, as our forefathers have said. Perhaps the mad one thinks he is the clouds.'

"Then spake the earth-worms from the warm deeps of the mud, saying 'O earth-mist, thou art indeed the clouds, and there are no clouds but thou. And as for Huhenwazi and Nitcrana, I cannot see them, and therefore they are not high, and there are no mountains in the world but those that I cast up every morning out of the deeps of the mud.'

"And the earth-mist and the vapours of evening were glad at the voice of the earth-worms, and looking earthward believed what they had said.

"And indeed it is better to be as the earth-mist, and to keep close to the warm mud at night, and to hear the earth-worm's comfortable speech, and not to be a wanderer in the cheerless heights, but to leave the mountains alone with their desolate snow, to draw what comfort they can from their vast aspect over all the cities of men, and from the whispers that they hear at evening of unknown distant gods."

And the watchers in the gate said, "Enter in."

Then a man stood up who came out of the west, and told a western tale. He said:

"There is a road in Rome that runs through an ancient temple that once the gods had loved; it runs along the top of a great wall, and the floor of the temple lies far down beneath it, of marble, pink and white.

"Upon the temple floor I counted to the number of thirteen hungry cats.

"'Sometimes,' they said among themselves, 'it was the gods that lived here, sometimes it was men, and now it's cats. So let us enjoy the sun on the hot marble before another people comes.'

"For it was at that hour of a warm afternoon when my fancy is able to hear silent voices.

"And the awful leanness of all those thirteen cats moved me to go into a neighbouring fish shop, and there to buy a quantity of fishes. Then I returned and threw them all over the railing at the top of the great wall, and they fell for thirty feet, and hit the sacred marble with a smack.

"Now, in any other town but Rome, or in the minds of any other cats, the sight of fishes falling out of heaven had surely excited wonder. They rose slowly, and all stretched themselves, then they came leisurely towards the fishes. 'It is only a miracle,' they said in their hearts."

And the watchers in the gate said, "Enter in."

Proudly and slowly, as they spoke, drew up to them a camel, whose rider sought entrance to the city. His face shone with the sunset by which for long he had steered for the city's gate. Of him they demanded toll. Whereat he spoke to his camel, and the camel roared and kneeled, and the man descended from him. And the man unwrapped from many silks a box of divers metals wrought by the Japanese, and on the lid of it were figures of men who gazed from some shore at an isle of the Inland Sea. This he showed to the watchers, and when they had seen it, said, "It has seemed to me that these speak to each other thus:

"'Behold now Oojni, the dear one of the sea, the little mother sea that hath no storms. She goeth out from Oojni singing a song, and she returneth singing over her sands. Little is Oojni in the lap of the sea, and scarce to be perceived by wondering ships. White sails have never wafted her legends afar, they are told not by bearded wanderers of the sea. Her fireside tales are known not to the North, the dragons of China have not heard of them, nor those that ride on elephants through Ind.

"'Men tell the tales and the smoke ariseth upwards; the smoke departeth and the tales are told.

"'Oojni is not a name among the nations, she is not know of where the merchants meet, she is not spoken of by alien lips.

"'Indeed, but Oojni is a little among the isles, yet is she loved by those that know her coasts and her inland places hidden from the sea.

"Without glory, without fame, and without wealth, Oojni is greatly loved by a little people, and by a few; yet not by few, for all her dead still love her, and oft by night come whispering through her woods. Who could forget Oojni even among the dead?

"For here in Oojni, wot you, are homes of men, and gardens, and golden temples of the gods, and sacred places inshore from the sea, and many murmurous woods. And there is a path that winds over the hills to go into mysterious holy lands where dance by night the spirits of the woods, or sing unseen in the sunlight; and no one goes into these holy lands, for who that love Oojni could rob her of her mysteries, and the curious aliens come not. Indeed, but we love Oojni though she is so little; she is the little mother of our race, and the kindly nurse of all seafaring birds.

"And behold, even now caressing her, the gentle fingers of the mother sea, whose dreams are far with that old wanderer Ocean.

"And yet let us forget not Fuzi-Yama, for he stands manifest over clouds and sea, misty below, and vague and indistinct, but clear above for all the isles to watch. The ships make all their journeys in his sight, the nights and the days go by him like a wind, the summers and winters under him flicker and fade, the lives of men pass quietly here and hence, and Fuzi-Yama watches there—and knows."

And the watchers in the gate said, "Enter in."

And I, too, would have told them a tale, very wonderful and very true; one that I had told in many cities, which as yet had no believers. But now the sun had set, and the brief twilight gone, and ghostly silences were rising from far and darkening hills. A stillness hung over that city's gate. And the great silence of the solemn night was more acceptable to the watchers in the gate than any sound of man. Therefore they beckoned to us, and motioned with their hands that we should pass untaxed into the city. And softly we went up over the sand, and between the high rock pillars of the gate, and a deep stillness settled among the watchers, and the stars over them twinkled undisturbed.

For how short a while man speaks, and withal how vainly. And for how long he is silent. Only the other day I met a king in Thebes, who had been silent already for four thousand years.

THE HASHISH MAN

I was at a dinner in London the other day. The ladies had gone upstairs, and no one sat on my right; on my left there was a man I did not know, but he knew my name somehow apparently, for he turned to me after a while, and said, "I read a story of yours about Bethmoora in a review."

Of course I remembered the tale. It was about a beautiful Oriental city that was suddenly deserted in a day—nobody quite knew why. I said, "Oh, yes," and slowly searched in my mind for some more fitting acknowledgment of the compliment that his memory had paid me.

I was greatly astonished when he said, "You were wrong about the gnousar sickness; it was not that at all."

I said, "Why! Have you been there?"

And he said, "Yes; I do it with hashish. I know Bethmoora well." And he took out of his pocket a small box full of some black stuff that looked like tar, but had a stranger smell. He warned me not to touch it with my finger, as the stain remained for days. "I got it from a gipsy," he said. "He had a lot of it, as it had killed his father." But I interrupted him, for I wanted to know for certain what it was that had made desolate that beautiful city, Bethmoora, and why they fled from it swiftly in a day. "Was it because of the Desert's curse?" I asked. And he said, "Partly it was the fury of the Desert and partly the advice of the Emperor Thuba Mleen, for that fearful beast is in some way connected with the Desert on his mother's side." And he told me this strange story: "You remember the sailor with the black scar, who was there on the day that you described when the messengers came on mules to the gate of Bethmoora, and all the people fled. I met this man in a tavern, drinking rum, and he told me all about the flight from Bethmoora, but knew no more than you did what the message was, or who had sent it. However, he said he would see Bethmoora once more whenever he touched again at an eastern port, even if he had to face the Devil. He often said that he would face the Devil to find out the mystery of that message that emptied Bethmoora in a day. And in the end he had to face Thuba Mleen, whose weak ferocity he had not imagined. For one day the sailor told me he had found a ship, and I met him no more after that in the tavern drinking rum. It was about that time that I got the hashish from the gipsy, who had a quantity that he did not want. It takes one literally out of oneself. It is like wings. You swoop over distant countries and into other worlds. Once I found out the secret of the universe. I have forgotten what it was, but I know that the Creator does not take Creation seriously, for I remember that He sat in Space with all His work in front of Him and laughed. I have seen incredible things in fearful worlds. As it is your imagination that takes you there, so it is only by your imagination that you can get back. Once out in aether I met a battered, prowling spirit, that had belonged to a man whom drugs had killed a hundred years ago; and he led me to regions that I had never imagined; and we parted in anger beyond the Pleiades, and I could not imagine my way back. And I met a huge grey shape that was the Spirit of some great people, perhaps of a whole star, and I besought It to show me my way home, and It halted beside me like a sudden wind and pointed, and, speaking quite softly, asked me if I discerned a certain tiny light, and I saw a far star faintly, and then It said to me, 'That is the Solar System,' and strode tremendously on. And somehow I imagined my way back, and only just in time, for my body was already stiffening in a chair in my room; and the fire had gone out and everything was cold, and I had to move each finger one by one, and there were pins and needles in them, and dreadful pains in the nails, which began to thaw; and at last I could move one arm, and reached a bell, and for a long time no one came, because every one was in bed. But at last a man appeared, and they got a doctor; and HE said that it was hashish poisoning, but it would have been all right if I hadn't met that battered, prowling spirit.

"I could tell you astounding things that I have seen, but you want to know who sent that message to Bethmoora. Well, it was Thuba Mleen. And this is how I know. I often went to the city after that day you wrote of (I used to take hashish of an evening in my flat), and I always found it uninhabited. Sand had poured into it from the desert, and the streets were yellow and smooth, and through open, swinging doors the sand had drifted.

"One evening I had put the guard in front of the fire, and settled into a chair and eaten my hashish, and the first thing that I saw when I came to Bethmoora was the sailor with the black scar, strolling down the street, and making footprints in the yellow sand. And now I knew that I should see what secret power it was that kept Bethmoora uninhabited.

"I saw that there was anger in the Desert, for there were storm clouds heaving along the skyline, and I heard a muttering amongst the sand.

"The sailor strolled on down the street, looking into the empty houses as he went; sometimes he shouted and sometimes he sang, and sometimes he wrote his name on a marble wall. Then he sat down on a step and ate his dinner. After a while he grew tired of the city, and came back up the street. As he reached the gate of green copper three men on camels appeared.

"I could do nothing. I was only a consciousness, invisible, wandering: my body was in Europe. The sailor fought well with his fists, but he was over-powered and bound with ropes, and led away through the Desert.

"I followed for as long as I could stay, and found that they were going by the way of the Desert round the Hills of Hap towards Utnar Véhi, and then I knew that the camel men belonged to Thuba Mleen.

"I work in an insurance office all day, and I hope you won't forget me if ever you want to insure—life, fire, or motor—but that's no part of my story. I was desperately anxious to get back to my flat, though it is not good to take hashish two days running; but I wanted to see what they would do to the poor fellow, for I had heard bad rumours about Thuba Mleen. When at last I got away I had a letter to write; then I rang for my servant, and told him that I must not be disturbed, though I left my door unlocked in case of accidents. After that I made up a good fire, and sat down and partook of the pot of dreams. I was going to the palace of Thuba Mleen.

"I was kept back longer than usual by noises in the street, but suddenly I was up above the town; the European countries rushed by beneath me, and there appeared the thin white palace spires of horrible Thuba Mleen. I found him presently at the end of a little narrow room. A curtain of red leather hung behind him, on which all the names of God, written in Yannish, were worked with a golden thread. Three windows were small and high. The Emperor seemed no more than about twenty, and looked small and weak. No smiles came on his nasty yellow face, though he tittered continually. As I looked from his low forehead to his quivering under lip, I became aware that there was some horror about him, though I was not able to perceive what it was. And then I saw it—the man never blinked; and though later on I watched those eyes for a blink, it never happened once.

"And then I followed the Emperor's rapt glance, and I saw the sailor lying on the floor, alive but hideously rent, and the royal torturers were at work all round him. They had torn long strips from him, but had not detached them, and they were torturing the ends of them far away from the sailor." The man that I met at dinner told me many things which I must omit. "The sailor was groaning softly, and every time he groaned Thuba Mleen tittered. I had no sense of smell, but I could hear and see, and I do not know which was the most revolting—the terrible condition of the sailor or the happy unblinking face of horrible Thuba Mleen.

"I wanted to go away, but the time was not yet come, and I had to stay where I was.

"Suddenly the Emperor's face began to twitch violently and his under lip quivered faster, and he whimpered with anger, and cried with a shrill voice, in Yannish, to the captain of his torturers that there was a spirit in the room. I feared not, for living men cannot lay hands on a spirit, but all the torturers were appalled at his anger, and stopped their work, for their hands trembled in fear. Then two men of the spear-guard slipped from the room, and each of them brought back presently a golden bowl, with knobs on it, full of hashish; and the bowls were large enough for heads to have floated in had they been filled with blood. And the two men fell to rapidly, each eating with two great spoons—there was enough in each spoonful to have given dreams to a hundred men. And there came upon them soon the hashish state, and their spirits hovered, preparing to go free, while I feared horribly, but ever and anon they fell back again to their bodies, recalled by some noise in the room. Still the men ate, but lazily now, and without ferocity. At last the great spoons dropped out of their hands, and their spirits rose and left them. I could not flee. And the spirits were more horrible than the men, because they were young men, and not yet wholly moulded to fit their fearful souls. Still the sailor groaned softly, evoking little titters from the Emperor Thuba Mleen. Then the two spirits rushed at me, and swept me thence as gusts of wind sweep butterflies, and away we went from that small, pale, heinous man. There was no escaping from these spirits' fierce insistence. The energy in my minute lump of the drug was overwhelmed by the huge spoonsful that these men had eaten with both hands. I was whirled over Arvle Woondery, and brought to the lands of Snith, and swept on still until I came to Kragua, and beyond this to those bleak lands that are nearly unknown to fancy. And we came at last to those ivory hills that are named the Mountains of Madness, and I tried to struggle against the spirits of that frightful Emperor's men, for I heard on the other side of the ivory hills the pittering of those beasts that prey on the mad, as they prowled up and down. It was no fault of mine that my little lump of hashish could not fight with their horrible spoonsful...."

Some one was tugging at the hall-door bell. Presently a servant came and told our host that a policeman in the hall wished to speak to him at once. He apologised to us, and went outside, and we heard a man in heavy boots, who spoke in a low voice to him. My friend got up and walked over to the window, and opened it, and looked outside. "I should think it will be a fine night," he said. Then he jumped out. When we put our astonished heads out of the window to look for him, he was already out of sight.

POOR OLD BILL

On an antique haunt of sailors, a tavern of the sea, the light of day was fading. For several evenings I had frequented this place, in the hope of hearing something from the sailors, as they sat over strange wines, about a rumour that had reached my ears of a certain fleet of galleons of old Spain still said to be afloat in the South Seas in some uncharted region.

In this I was again to be disappointed. Talk was low and seldom, and I was about to leave, when a sailor, wearing ear-rings of pure gold, lifted up his head from his wine, and looking straight before him at the wall, told his tale loudly:

(When later on a storm of rain arose and thundered on the tavern's leaded panes, he raised his voice without effort and spoke on still. The darker it got the clearer his wild eyes shone.)

"A ship with sails of the olden time was nearing fantastic isles. We had never seen such isles.

"We all hated the captain, and he hated us. He hated us all alike, there was no favouritism about him. And he never would talk a word with any of us, except sometimes in the evening when it was getting dark he would stop and look up and talk a bit to the men he had hanged at the yard-arm.

"We were a mutinous crew. But Captain was the only man that had pistols. He slept with one under his pillow and kept one close beside him. There was a nasty look about the isles. They were small and flat as though they had come up only recently from the sea, and they had no sand or rocks like honest isles, but green grass down to the water. And there were little cottages there whose looks we did not like. Their thatches came almost down to the ground, and were strangely turned up at the corners, and under the low eaves were queer dark windows whose little leaded panes were too thick to see through. And no one, man or beast, was walking about, so that you could not know what kind of people lived there. But Captain knew. And he went ashore and into one of the cottages, and someone lit lights inside, and the little windows wore an evil look.

"It was quite dark when he came aboard again, and he bade a cheery good-night to the men that swung from the yard-arm and he eyed us in a way that frightened poor old Bill.

"Next night we found that he had learned to curse, for he came on a lot of us asleep in our bunks, and among them poor old Bill, and he pointed at us with a finger, and made a curse that our souls should stay all night at the top of the masts. And suddenly there was the soul of poor old Bill sitting like a monkey at the top of the mast, and looking at the stars, and freezing through and through.

"We got up a little mutiny after that, but Captain comes up and points with his finger again, and this time poor old Bill and all the rest are swimming behind the ship through the cold green water, though their bodies remain on deck.

"It was the cabin-boy who found out that Captain couldn't curse when he was drunk, though he could shoot as well at one time as another.

"After that it was only a matter of waiting, and of losing two men when the time came. Some of us were murderous fellows, and wanted to kill Captain, but poor old Bill was for finding a bit of an island, out of the track of ships, and leaving him there with his share of our year's provisions. And everybody listened to poor old Bill, and we decided to maroon Captain as soon as we caught him when he couldn't curse.

"It was three whole days before Captain got drunk again, and poor old Bill and all had a dreadful time, for Captain invented new curses every day, and wherever he pointed his finger our souls had to go; and the fishes got to know us, and so did the stars, and none of them pitied us when we froze on the masts or were hurried through forests of seaweed and lost our way—both stars and fishes went about their businesses with cold, unastonished eyes. Once when the sun had set and it was twilight, and the moon was showing clearer and clearer in the sky, and we stopped our work for a moment because Captain seemed to be looking away from us at the colours in the sky, he suddenly turned and sent our souls to the Moon. And it was colder there than ice at night; and there were horrible mountains making shadows; and it was all as silent as miles of tombs; and Earth was shining up in the sky as big as the blade of a scythe, and we all got homesick for it, but could not speak nor cry. It was quite dark when we got back, and we were very respectful to Captain all the next day, but he cursed several of us again very soon. What we all feared most was that he would curse our souls to Hell, and none of us mentioned Hell above a whisper for fear that it should remind him. But on the third evening the cabin-boy came and told us that Captain was drunk. And we all went to his cabin, and we found him lying there across his bunk, and he shot as he had never shot before; but he had no more than the two pistols, and he would only have killed two men if he hadn't caught Joe over the head with the end of one of his pistols. And then we tied him up. And poor old Bill put the rum between the Captain's teeth, and kept him drunk for two days, so that he could not curse, till we found a convenient rock. And before sunset of the second day we found a nice bare island for Captain, out of the track of ships, about a hundred yards long and about eighty wide; and we rowed him along to it in a little boat, and gave him provisions for a year, the same as we had ourselves, because poor old Bill wanted to be fair. And we left him sitting comfortable with his back to a rock singing a sailor's song.

"When we could no longer hear Captain singing we all grew very cheerful and made a banquet out of our year's provisions, as we all hoped to be home again in under three weeks. We had three great banquets every day for a week—every man had more than he could eat, and what was left over we threw on the floor like gentlemen. And then one day, as we saw San Huëgédos, and wanted to sail in to spend our money, the wind changed round from behind us and beat us out to sea. There was no tacking against it, and no getting into the harbour, though other ships sailed by us and anchored there. Sometimes a dead calm would fall on us, while fishing boats all around us flew before half a gale, and sometimes the wind would beat us out to sea when nothing else was moving. All day we tried, and at night we laid to and tried again the next day. And all the sailors of the other ships were spending their money in San Huëgédos and we could not come nigh it. Then we spoke horrible things against the wind and against San Huëgédos, and sailed away.

"It was just the same at Norenna.

"We kept close together now and talked in low voices. Suddenly poor old Bill grew frightened. As we went all along the Siractic coast-line, we tried again and again, and the wind was waiting for us in every harbour and sent us out to sea. Even the little islands would not have us. And then we knew that there was no landing yet for poor old Bill, and every one upbraided his kind heart that had made them maroon Captain on a rock, so as not to have his blood upon their heads. There was nothing to do but to drift about the seas. There were no banquets now, because we feared that Captain might live his year and keep us out to sea.

"At first we used to hail all passing ships, and used to try to board them in the boats; but there was no towing against Captain's curse, and we had to give that up. So we played cards for a year in Captain's cabin, night and day, storm and fine, and every one promised to pay poor old Bill when we got ashore.

"It was horrible to us to think what a frugal man Captain really was, he that used to get drunk every other day whenever he was at sea, and here he was still alive, and sober too, for his curse still kept us out of every port, and our provisions were gone.

"Well, it came to drawing lots, and Jim was the unlucky one. Jim only kept us about three days, and then we drew lots again, and this time it was the nigger. The nigger didn't keep us any longer, and we drew again, and this time it was Charlie, and still Captain was alive.

"As we got fewer one of us kept us longer. Longer and longer a mate used to last us, and we all wondered how ever Captain did it. It was five weeks over the year when we drew Mike, and he kept us for a week, and Captain was still alive. We wondered he didn't get tired of the same old curse; but we supposed things looked different when one is alone on an island.

"When there was only Jakes and poor old Bill and the cabin-boy and Dick, we didn't draw any longer. We said that the cabin-boy had had all the luck, and he mustn't expect any more. Then poor old Bill was alone with Jakes and Dick, and Captain was still alive. When there was no more boy, and the Captain still alive, Dick, who was a huge strong man like poor old Bill, said that it was Jakes' turn, and he was very lucky to have lived as long as he had. But poor old Bill talked it all over with Jakes, and they thought it better than Dick should take his turn.

"Then there was Jakes and poor old Bill; and Captain would not die.

"And these two used to watch one another night and day, when Dick was gone and no one else was left to them. And at last poor old Bill fell down in a faint and lay there for an hour. Then Jakes came up to him slowly with his knife, and makes a stab at poor old Bill as he lies there on the deck. And poor old Bill caught hold of him by the wrist, and put his knife into him twice to make quite sure, although it spoiled the best part of the meat. Then poor old Bill was all alone at sea.

"And the very next week, before the food gave out, Captain must have died on his bit of an island; for poor old Bill heard the Captain's soul going cursing over the sea, and the day after that the ship was cast on a rocky coast.

"And Captain's been dead now for over a hundred years, and poor old Bill is safe ashore again. But it looks as if Captain hadn't done with him yet, for poor old Bill doesn't ever get any older, and somehow or other he doesn't seem to die. Poor old Bill!"

When this was over the man's fascination suddenly snapped, and we all jumped up and left him.

It was not only his revolting story, but it was the fearful look in the eyes of the man who told it, and the terrible ease with which his voice surpassed the roar of the rain, that decided me never again to enter that haunt of sailors—the tavern of the sea.

THE BEGGARS

I was walking down Piccadilly not long ago, thinking of nursery rhymes and regretting old romance.

As I saw the shopkeepers walk by in their black frock-coats and their black hats, I thought of the old line in nursery annals: "The merchants of London, they wear scarlet."

The streets were all so unromantic, dreary. Nothing could be done for them, I thought—nothing. And then my thoughts were interrupted by barking dogs. Every dog in the street seemed to be barking—every kind of dog, not only the little ones but the big ones too. They were all facing East towards the way I was coming by. Then I turned round to look and had this vision, in Piccadilly, on the opposite side to the houses just after you pass the cab-rank.

Tall bent men were coming down the street arrayed in marvelous cloaks. All were sallow of skin and swarthy of hair, and most of them wore strange beards. They were coming slowly, and they walked with staves, and their hands were out for alms.

All the beggars had come to town.

I would have given them a gold doubloon engraven with the towers of Castile, but I had no such coin. They did not seem the people to who it were fitting to offer the same coin as one tendered for the use of a taxicab (O marvelous, ill-made word, surely the pass-word somewhere of some evil order). Some of them wore purple cloaks with wide green borders, and the border of green was a narrow strip with some, and some wore cloaks of old and faded red, and some wore violet cloaks, and none wore black. And they begged gracefully, as gods might beg for souls.

I stood by a lamp-post, and they came up to it, and one addressed it, calling the lamp-post brother, and said, "O lamp-post, our brother of the dark, are there many wrecks by thee in the tides of night? Sleep not, brother, sleep not. There were many wrecks an it were not for thee."

It was strange: I had not thought of the majesty of the street lamp and his long watching over drifting men. But he was not beneath the notice of these cloaked strangers.

And then one murmured to the street: "Art thou weary, street? Yet a little longer they shall go up and down, and keep thee clad with tar and wooden bricks. Be patient, street. In a while the earthquake cometh."

"Who are you?" people said. "And where do you come from?"

"Who may tell what we are," they answered, "or whence we come?"

And one turned towards the smoke-stained houses, saying, "Blessed be the houses, because men dream therein."

Then I perceived, what I had never thought, that all these staring houses were not alike, but different one from another, because they held different dreams.

And another turned to a tree that stood by the Green Park railings, saying, "Take comfort, tree, for the fields shall come again."

And all the while the ugly smoke went upwards, the smoke that has stifled Romance and blackened the birds. This, I thought, they can neither praise nor bless. And when they saw it they raised their hands towards it, towards the thousand chimneys, saying, "Behold the smoke. The old coal-forests that have lain so long in the dark, and so long still, are dancing now and going back to the sun. Forget not Earth, O our brother, and we wish thee joy of the sun."

It had rained, and a cheerless stream dropped down a dirty gutter. It had come from heaps of refuse, foul and forgotten; it had gathered upon its way things that were derelict, and went to somber drains unknown to man or the sun. It was this sullen stream as much as all other causes that had made me say in my heart that the town was vile, that Beauty was dead in it, and Romance fled.

Even this thing they blessed. And one that wore a purple cloak with broad green border, said, "Brother, be hopeful yet, for thou shalt surely come at last to the delectable Sea, and meet the heaving, huge, and travelled ships, and rejoice by isles that know the golden sun." Even thus they blessed the gutter, and I felt no whim to mock.

And the people that went by, in their black unseemly coats and their misshapen, monstrous, shiny hats, the beggars also blessed. And one of them said to one of these dark citizens: "O twin of Night himself, with thy specks of white at wrist and neck like to Night's scattered stars. How fearfully thou dost veil with black thy hid, unguessed desires. They are deep thoughts in thee that they will not frolic with colour, that they say 'No' to purple, and to lovely green 'Begone.' Thou hast wild fancies that they must needs be tamed with black, and terrible imaginings that they must be hidden thus. Has thy soul dreams of the angels, and of the walls of faëry that thou hast guarded it so utterly, lest it dazzle astonished eyes? Even so God hid the diamond deep down in miles of clay.

"The wonder of thee is not marred by mirth.

"Behold thou art very secret.

"Be wonderful. Be full of mystery."

Silently the man in the black frock-coat passed on. And I came to understand when the purple beggar had spoken, that the dark citizen had trafficked perhaps with Ind, that in his heart were strange and dumb ambitions; that his dumbness was founded by solemn rite on the roots of ancient tradition; that it might be overcome one day by a cheer in the street or by some one singing a song, and that when this shopman spoke there might come clefts in the world and people peering over at the abyss.

Then turning towards Green Park, where as yet Spring was not, the beggars stretched out their hands, and looking at the frozen grass and the yet unbudding trees they, chanting all together, prophesied daffodils.

A motor omnibus came down the street, nearly running over some of the dogs that were barking ferociously still. It was sounding its horn noisily.

And the vision went then.

In a letter from a friend whom I have never seen, one of those that read my books, this line was quoted—"But he, he never came to Carcassonne." I do not know the origin of the line, but I made this tale about it.

CARCASSONNE

When Camorak reigned at Arn, and the world was fairer, he gave a festival to all the weald to commemorate the splendour of his youth.

They say that his house at Arn was huge and high, and its ceiling painted blue; and when evening fell men would climb up by ladders and light the scores of candles hanging from slender chains. And they say, too, that sometimes a cloud would come, and pour in through the top of one of the oriel windows, and it would come over the edge of the stonework as the sea-mist comes over a sheer cliffs shaven lip where an old wind has blown for ever and ever (he has swept away thousands of leaves and thousands of centuries, they are all one to him, he owes no allegiance to Time). And the cloud would re-shape itself in the hall's lofty vault and drift on through it slowly, and out to the sky again through another window. And from its shape the knights in Camorak's hall would prophesy the battles and sieges of the next season of war. They say of the hall of Camorak at Arn that there hath been none like it in any land, and foretell that there will be never.

Hither had come in the folk of the Weald from sheepfold and from forest, revolving slow thoughts of food, and shelter, and love, and they sat down wondering in that famous hall; and therein also were seated the men of Arn, the town that clustered round the King's high house, and all was roofed with red, maternal earth.

If old songs may be trusted, it was a marvelous hall.

Many who sat there could only have seen it distantly before, a clear shape in the landscape, but smaller than a hill. Now they beheld along the wall the weapons of Camorak's men, of which already the lute-players made songs, and tales were told at evening in the byres. There they described the shield of Camorak that had gone to and fro across so many battles, and the sharp but dinted edges of his sword; there were the weapons of Gadriol the Leal, and Norn, and Athoric of the Sleety Sword, Heriel the Wild, Yarold, and Thanga of Esk, their arms hung evenly all round the hall, low where a man could reach them; and in the place of honour in the midst, between the arms of Camorak and of Gadriol the Leal, hung the harp of Arleon. And of all the weapons hanging on those walls none were more calamitous to Camorak's foes than was the harp of Arleon. For to a man that goes up against a strong place on foot, pleasant indeed is the twang and jolt of some fearful engine of war that his fellow-warriors are working behind him, from which huge rocks go sighing over his head and plunge among his foes; and pleasant to a warrior in the wavering light are the swift commands of his King, and a joy to him are his comrades' instant cheers exulting suddenly at a turn of the war. All this and more was the harp to Camorak's men; for not only would it cheer his warriors on, but many a time would Arleon of the Harp strike wild amazement into opposing hosts by some rapturous prophecy suddenly shouted out while his hand swept over the roaring strings. Moreover, no war was ever declared till Camorak and his men had listened long to the harp, and were elate with the music and mad against peace. Once Arleon, for the sake of a rhyme, had made war upon Estabonn; and an evil king was overthrown, and honour and glory won; from such queer motives does good sometimes accrue.

Above the shields and the harps all round the hall were the painted figures of heroes of fabulous famous songs. Too trivial, because too easily surpassed by Camorak's men, seemed all the victories that the earth had known; neither was any trophy displayed of Camorak's seventy battles, for these were as nothing to his warriors or him compared with those things that their youth had dreamed and which they mightily purposed yet to do.

Above the painted pictures there was darkness, for evening was closing in, and the candles swinging on their slender chain were not yet lit in the roof; it was as though a piece of the night had been builded into the edifice like a huge natural rock that juts into a house. And there sat all the warriors of Arn and the Weald-folk wondering at them; and none were more than thirty, and all were skilled in war. And Camorak sat at the head of all, exulting in his youth.

We must wrestle with Time for some seven decades, and he is a weak and puny antagonist in the first three bouts.

Now there was present at this feast a diviner, one who knew the schemes of Fate, and he sat among the people of the Weald and had no place of honour, for Camorak and his men had no fear of Fate. And when the meat was eaten and the bones cast aside, the king rose up from his chair, and having drunken wine, and being in the glory of his youth and with all his knights about him, called to the diviner, saying, "Prophesy."

And the diviner rose up, stroking his grey beard, and spake guardedly—"There are certain events," he said, "upon the ways of Fate that are veiled even from a diviner's eyes, and many more are clear to us that were better veiled from all; much I know that is better unforetold, and some things that I may not foretell on pain of centuries of punishment. But this I know and foretell—that you will never come to Carcassonne."

Instantly there was a buzz of talk telling of Carcassonne—some had heard of it in speech or song, some had read of it, and some had dreamed of it. And the king sent Arleon of the Harp down from his right hand to mingle with the Weald-folk to hear aught that any told of Carcassonne. But the warriors told of the places they had won to—many a hard-held fortress, many a far-off land, and swore that they would come to Carcassonne.

And in a while came Arleon back to the king's right hand, and raised his harp and chanted and told of Carcassonne. Far away it was, and far and far away, a city of gleaming ramparts rising one over other, and marble terraces behind the ramparts, and fountains shimmering on the terraces. To Carcassonne the elf-kings with their fairies had first retreated from men, and had built it on an evening late in May by blowing their elfin horns. Carcassonne! Carcassonne!

Travellers had seen it sometimes like a clear dream, with the sun glittering on its citadel upon a far-off hilltop, and then the clouds had come or a sudden mist; no one had seen it long or come quite close to it; though once there were some men that came very near, and the smoke from the houses blew into their faces, a sudden gust—no more, and these declared that some one was burning cedarwood there. Men had dreamed that there is a witch there, walking alone through the cold courts and corridors of marmorean palaces, fearfully beautiful and still for all her fourscore centuries, singing the second oldest song, which was taught her by the sea, shedding tears for loneliness from eyes that would madden armies, yet will she not call her dragons home—Carcassonne is terribly guarded. Sometimes she swims in a marble bath through whose deeps a river tumbles, or lies all morning on the edge of it to dry slowly in the sun, and watches the heaving river trouble the deeps of the bath. It flows through the caverns of earth for further than she knows, and coming to light in the witch's bath goes down through the earth again to its own peculiar sea.

In autumn sometimes it comes down black with snow that spring has molten in unimagined mountains, or withered blooms of mountain shrubs go beautifully by.

When there is blood in the bath she knows there is war in the mountains; and yet she knows not where those mountains are.

When she sings the fountains dance up from the dark earth, when she combs her hair they say there are storms at sea, when she is angry the wolves grow brave and all come down to the byres, when she is sad the sea is sad, and both are sad for ever. Carcassonne! Carcassonne!

This city is the fairest of the wonders of Morning; the sun shouts when he beholdeth it; for Carcassonne Evening weepeth when Evening passeth away.

And Arleon told how many goodly perils were round about the city, and how the way was unknown, and it was a knightly venture. Then all the warriors stood up and sang of the splendour of the venture. And Camorak swore by the gods that had builded Arn, and by the honour of his warriors that, alive or dead, he would come to Carcassonne.

But the diviner rose and passed out of the hall, brushing the crumbs from him with his hands and smoothing his robe as he went.

Then Camorak said, "There are many things to be planned, and counsels to be taken, and provender to be gathered. Upon what day shall we start?" And all the warriors answering shouted, "Now." And Camorak smiled thereat, for he had but tried them. Down then from the walls they took their weapons, Sikorix, Kelleron, Aslof, Wole of the Axe; Huhenoth, Peace-breaker; Wolwuf, Father of War; Tarion, Lurth of the Warcry and many another. Little then dreamed the spiders that sat in that ringing hall of the unmolested leisure they were soon to enjoy.

When they were armed they all formed up and marched out of the hall, and Arleon strode before them singing of Carcassonne.

But the talk of the Weald arose and went back well fed to byres. They had no need of wars or of rare perils. They were ever at war with hunger. A long drought or hard winter were to them pitched battles; if the wolves entered a sheep-fold it was like the loss of a fortress, a thunder-storm on the harvest was like an ambuscade. Well-fed, they went back slowly to their byres, being at truce with hunger; and the night filled with stars.

And black against the starry sky appeared the round helms of the warriors as they passed the tops of the ridges, but in the valleys they sparkled now and then as the starlight flashed on steel.

They followed behind Arleon going south, whence rumours had always come of Carcassonne: so they marched in the starlight, and he before them singing.

When they had marched so far that they heard no sound from Arn, and even inaudible were her swinging bells, when candles burning late far up in towers no longer sent them their disconsolate welcome; in the midst of the pleasant night that lulls the rural spaces, weariness came upon Arleon and his inspiration failed. It failed slowly. Gradually he grew less sure of the way to Carcassonne. Awhile he stopped to think, and remembered the way again; but his clear certainty was gone, and in its place were efforts in his mind to recall old prophecies and shepherd's songs that told of the marvelous city. Then as he said over carefully to himself a song that a wanderer had learnt from a goatherd's boy far up the lower slope of ultimate southern mountains, fatigue came down upon his toiling mind like snow on the winding ways of a city noisy by night, stilling all.

He stood, and the warriors closed up to him. For long they had passed by great oaks standing solitary here and there, like giants taking huge breaths of the night air before doing some furious deed; now they had come to the verge of a black forest; the tree-trunks stood like those great columns in an Egyptian hall whence God in an older mood received the praise of men; the top of it sloped the way of an ancient wind. Here they all halted and lighted a fire of branches, striking sparks from flint into a heap of bracken. They eased them of their armour, and sat round the fire, and Camorak stood up there and addressed them, and Camorak said: "We go to war with Fate, who has doomed that I shall not come to Carcassonne. And if we turn aside but one of the dooms of Fate, then the whole future of the world is ours, and the future that Fate has ordered is like the dry course of an averted river. But if such men as we, such resolute conquerors, cannot prevent one doom that Fate has planned, then is the race of man enslaved for ever to do its petty and allotted task."

Then they all drew their swords, and waved them high in the firelight, and declared war on Fate.

Nothing in the somber forest stirred or made any sound.

Tired men do not dream of war. When morning came over the gleaming fields a company that had set out from Arn discovered the discovered the camping-place of the warriors, and brought pavilions and provender. And the warriors feasted, and the birds in the forest sang, and the inspiration of Arleon awoke.

Then they rose, and following Arleon, entered the forest, and marched away to the South. And many a woman of Arn sent her thoughts with them as they played alone some old monotonous tune, but their own thoughts were far before them, skimming over the bath through whose deeps the river tumbles in marble Carcassonne.

When butterflies were dancing on the air, and the sun neared the zenith, pavilions were pitched, and all the warriors rested; and then they feasted again, and then played knightly games, and late in the afternoon marched on once more, singing of Carcassonne.

And night came down with its mystery on the forest, and gave their demoniac look again to the trees, and rolled up out of misty hollows a huge and yellow moon.

And the men of Arn lit fires, and sudden shadows arose and leaped fantastically away. And the night-wind blew, arising like a ghost, and passed between the tree trunks, and slipped down shimmering glades, and waked the prowling beasts still dreaming of day, and drifted nocturnal birds afield to menace timorous things, and beat the roses of the befriending night, and wafted to the ears of wandering men the sound of a maiden's song, and gave a glamour to the lutanist's tune played in his loneliness on distant hills; and the deep eyes of moths glowed like a galleon's lamps, and they spread their wings and sailed their familiar sea. Upon this night-wind also the dreams of Camorak's men floated to Carcassonne.

All the next morning they marched, and all the evening, and knew they were nearing now the deeps of the forest. And the citizens of Arn kept close together and close behind the warriors. For the deeps of the forest were all unknown to travellers, but not unknown to those tales of fear that men tell at evening to their friends, in the comfort and the safety of their hearths. Then night appeared, and an enormous moon. And the men of Camorak slept. Sometimes they woke, and went to sleep again; and those that stayed awake for long and listened heard heavy two-footed creatures pad through the night on paws.

As soon as it was light the unarmed men of Arn began to slip away, and went back by bands through the forest. When darkness came they did not stop to sleep, but continued their flight straight on until they came to Arn, and added there by the tales they told to the terror of the forest.

But the warriors feasted, and afterwards Arleon rose, and played his harp, and led them on again; and a few faithful servants stayed with them still. And they marched all day through a gloom that was as old as night, but Arleon's inspiration burned in his mind like a star. And he led them till the birds began to drop into the treetops, and it was evening and they all encamped. They had only one pavilion left to them now, and near it they lit a fire, and Camorak posted a sentry with drawn sword just beyond the glow of the firelight. Some of the warriors slept in the pavilion and others round about it.

When dawn came something terrible had killed and eaten the sentry. But the splendour of the rumours of Carcassonne and Fate's decree that they should never come there, and the inspiration of Arleon and his harp, all urged the warriors on; and they marched deeper and deeper all day into the forest.

Once they saw a dragon that had caught a bear and was playing with it, letting it run a little way and overtaking it with a paw.

They came at last to a clear space in the forest just before nightfall. An odour of flowers arose from it like a mist, and every drop of dew interpreted heaven unto itself.

It was the hour when twilight kisses Earth.

It was the hour when a meaning comes into senseless things, and trees out-majesty the pomp of monarchs, and the timid creatures steal abroad to feed, and as yet the beasts of prey harmlessly dream, and Earth utters a sigh, and it is night.

In the midst of the wide clearing Camorak's warriors camped, and rejoiced to see stars again appearing one by one.

That night they ate the last of their provisions, and slept unmolested by the prowling things that haunt the gloom of the forest.

On the next day some of the warriors hunted stags, and others lay in rushes by a neighbouring lake and shot arrows at water-fowl. One stag was killed, and some geese, and several teal.

Here the adventurers stayed, breathing the pure wild air that cities know not; by day they hunted, and lit fires by night, and sang and feasted, and forgot Carcassonne. The terrible denizens of the gloom never molested them, venison was plentiful, and all manner of water-fowl: they loved the chase by day, and by night their favourite songs. Thus day after day went by, thus week after week. Time flung over this encampment a handful of moons, the gold and silver moons that waste the year away; Autumn and Winter passed, and Spring appeared; and still the warriors hunted and feasted there.

One night of the springtide they were feasting about a fire and telling tales of the chase, and the soft moths came out of the dark and flaunted their colours in the firelight, and went out grey into the dark again; and the night wind was cool upon the warriors' necks, and the camp-fire was warm in their faces, and a silence had settled among them after some song, and Arleon all at once rose suddenly up, remembering Carcassonne. And his hand swept over the strings of his harp, awaking the deeper chords, like the sound of a nimble people dancing their steps on bronze, and the music rolled away into the night's own silence, and the voice of Arleon rose:

"When there is blood in the bath she knows there is war in the mountains and longs for the battle-shout of kingly men."

And suddenly all shouted, "Carcassonne!" And at that word their idleness was gone as a dream is gone from a dreamer waked with a shout. And soon the great march began that faltered no more nor wavered. Unchecked by battles, undaunted in lonesome spaces, ever unwearied by the vulturous years, the warriors of Camorak held on; and Arleon's inspiration led them still. They cleft with the music of Arleon's harp the gloom of ancient silences; they went singing into battles with terrible wild men, and came out singing, but with fewer voices; they came to villages in valleys full of the music of bells, or saw the lights at dusk of cottages sheltering others.

They became a proverb for wandering, and a legend arose of strange, disconsolate men. Folks spoke of them at nightfall when the fire was warm and rain slipped down the eaves; and when the wind was high small children feared the Men Who Would Not Rest were going clattering past. Strange tales were told of men in old grey armour moving at twilight along the tops of the hills and never asking shelter; and mothers told their boys who grew impatient of home that the grey wanderers were once so impatient and were now hopeless of rest, and were driven along with the rain whenever the wind was angry.

But the wanderers were cheered in their wandering by the hope of coming to Carcassonne, and later on by anger against Fate, and at last they marched on still because it seemed better to march on than to think.

For many years they had wandered and had fought with many tribes; often they gathered legends in villages and listened to idle singers singing songs; and all the rumours of Carcassonne still came from the South.

And then one day they came to a hilly land with a legend in it that only three valleys away a man might see, on clear days, Carcassonne. Tired though they were and few, and worn with the years which had all brought them wars, they pushed on instantly, led still by Arleon's inspiration which dwindled in his age, though he made music with his old harp still.

All day they climbed down into the first valley and for two days ascended, and came to the Town That May Not Be Taken In War below the top of the mountain, and its gates were shut against them, and there was no way round. To left and right steep precipices stood for as far as eye could see or legend tell of, and the pass lay through the city. Therefore Camorak drew up his remaining warriors in line of battle to wage their last war, and they stepped forward over the crisp bones of old, unburied armies.

No sentinel defied them in the gate, no arrow flew from any tower of war. One citizen climbed alone to the mountain's top, and the rest hid themselves in sheltered places.

Now, in the top of the mountain was a deep, bowl-like cavern in the rock, in which fires bubbled softly. But if any cast a boulder into the fires, as it was the custom for one of those citizens to do when enemies approached them, the mountain hurled up intermittent rocks for three days, and the rocks fell flaming all over the town and all round about it. And just as Camorak's men began to batter the gate they heard a crash on the mountain, and a great rock fell beyond them and rolled into the valley. The next two fell in front of them on the iron roofs of the town. Just as they entered the town a rock found them crowded in a narrow street, and shattered two of them. The mountain smoked and panted; with every pant a rock plunged into the streets or bounced along the heavy iron roof, and the smoke went slowly up, and up, and up.

When they had come through the long town's empty streets to the locked gate at the end, only fifteen were left. When they had broken down the gate there were only ten alive. Three more were killed as they went up the slope, and two as they passed near the terrible cavern. Fate let the rest go some way down the mountain upon the other side, and then took three of them. Camorak and Arleon alone were left alive. And night came down on the valley to which they had come, and was lit by flashes from the fatal mountain; and the two mourned for their comrades all night long.

But when the morning came they remembered their war with Fate, and their old resolve to come to Carcassonne, and the voice of Arleon rose in a quavering song, and snatches of music from his old harp, and he stood up and marched with his face southwards as he had done for years, and behind him Camorak went. And when at last they climbed from the third valley, and stood on the hill's summit in the golden sunlight of evening, their aged eyes saw only miles of forest and the birds going to roost.

Their beards were white, and they had travelled very far and hard; it was the time with them when a man rests from labours and dreams in light sleep of the years that were and not of the years to come.

Long they looked southwards; and the sun set over remoter forests, and glow-worms lit their lamps, and the inspiration of Arleon rose and flew away for ever, to gladden, perhaps, the dreams of younger men.

And Arleon said: "My King, I know no longer the way to Carcassonne."

And Camorak smiled, as the aged smile, with little cause for mirth, and said: "The years are going by us like huge birds, whom Doom and Destiny and the schemes of God have frightened up out of some old grey marsh. And it may well be that against these no warrior may avail, and that Fate has conquered us, and that our quest has failed."

And after this they were silent.

Then they drew their swords, and side by side went down into the forest, still seeking Carcassonne.

I think they got not far; for there were deadly marshes in that forest, and gloom that outlasted the nights, and fearful beasts accustomed to its ways. Neither is there any legend, either in verse or among the songs of the people of the fields, of any having come to Carcassonne.

IN ZACCARATH

"Come," said the King in sacred Zaccarath, "and let our prophets prophesy before us."

A far-seen jewel of light was the holy palace, a wonder to the nomads on the plains.

There was the King with all his underlords, and the lesser kings that did him vassalage, and there were all his queens with all their jewels upon them.

Who shall tell of the splendour in which they sat; of the thousand lights and the answering emeralds; of the dangerous beauty of that hoard of queens, or the flash of their laden necks?

There was a necklace there of rose-pink pearls beyond the art of the dreamer to imagine. Who shall tell of the amethyst chandeliers, where torches, soaked in rare Bhyrinian oils, burned and gave off a scent of blethany?

(This herb marvellous, which, growing near the summit of Mount Zaumnos, scents all the Zaumnian range, and is smelt far out on the Kepuscran plains, and even, when the wind is from the mountains, in the streets of the city of Ognoth. At night it closes its petals and is heard to breathe, and its breath is a swift poison. This it does even by day if the snows are disturbed about it. No plant of this has ever been captured alive by a hunter.)

Enough to say that when the dawn came up it appeared by contrast pallid and unlovely and stripped bare of all its glory, so that it hid itself with rolling clouds.

"Come," said the King, "let our prophets prophesy."

Then the heralds stepped through the ranks of the King's silk-clad warriors who lay oiled and scented upon velvet cloaks, with a pleasant breeze among them caused by the fans of slaves; even their casting-spears were set with jewels; through their ranks the heralds went with mincing steps, and came to the prophets, clad in brown and black, and one of them they brought and set him before the King. And the King looked at him and said, "Prophesy unto us."

And the prophet lifted his head, so that his beard came clear from his brown cloak, and the fans of the slaves that fanned the warriors wafted the tip of it a little awry. And he spake to the King, and spake thus:

"Woe unto thee, King, and woe unto Zaccarath. Woe unto thee, and woe unto thy women, for your fall shall be sore and soon. Already in Heaven the gods shun thy god: they know his doom and what is written of him: he sees oblivion before him like a mist. Thou hast aroused the hate of the mountaineers. They hate thee all along the crags of Droom. The evilness of thy days shall bring down the Zeedians on thee as the suns of springtide bring the avalanche down. They shall do unto Zaccarath as the avalanche doth unto the hamlets of the valley." When the queens chattered or tittered among themselves, he merely raised his voice and still spake on: "Woe to these walls and the carven things upon them. The hunter shall know the camping-places of the nomads by the marks of the camp-fires on the plain, but he shall not know the place of Zaccarath."

A few of the recumbent warriors turned their heads to glance at the prophet when he ceased. Far overhead the echoes of his voice hummed on awhile among the cedarn rafters.

"Is he not splendid?" said the King. And many of that assembly beat with their palms upon the polished floor in token of applause. Then the prophet was conducted back to his place at the far end of that mighty hall, and for a while musicians played on marvellous curved horns, while drums throbbed behind them hidden in a recess. The musicians were sitting crosslegged on the floor, all blowing their huge horns in the brilliant torchlight, but as the drums throbbed louder in the dark they arose and moved slowly nearer to the King. Louder and louder drummed the drums in the dark, and nearer and nearer moved the men with the horns, so that their music should not be drowned by the drums before it reached the King.

A marvellous scene it was when the tempestuous horns were halted before the King, and the drums in the dark were like the thunder of God; and the queens were nodding their heads in time to the music, with their diadems flashing like heavens of falling stars; and the warriors lifted their heads and shook, as they lifted them, the plumes of those golden birds which hunters wait for by the Liddian lakes, in a whole lifetime killing scarcely six, to make the crests that the warriors wore when they feasted in Zaccarath. Then the King shouted and the warriors sang—almost they remembered then old battle-chants. And, as they sang, the sound of the drums dwindled, and the musicians walked away backwards, and the drumming became fainter and fainter as they walked, and altogether ceased, and they blew no more on their fantastic horns. Then the assemblage beat on the floor with their palms. And afterwards the queens besought the King to send for another prophet. And the heralds brought a singer, and placed him before the King; and the singer was a young man with a harp. And he swept the strings of it, and when there was silence he sang of the iniquity of the King. And he foretold the onrush of the Zeedians, and the fall and the forgetting of Zaccarath, and the coming again of the desert to its own, and the playing about of little lion cubs where the courts of the palace had stood.

"Of what is he singing?" said a queen to a queen.

"He is singing of everlasting Zaccarath."

As the singer ceased the assemblage beat listlessly on the floor, and the King nodded to him, and he departed.

When all the prophets had prophesied to them and all the singers sung, that royal company arose and went to other chambers, leaving the hall of festival to the pale and lonely dawn. And alone were left the lion-headed gods that were carven out of the walls; silent they stood, and their rocky arms were folded. And shadows over their faces moved like curious thoughts as the torches flickered and the dull dawn crossed the fields. And the colours began to change in the chandeliers.

When the last lutanist fell asleep the birds began to sing.

Never was greater splendour or a more famous hall. When the queens went away through the curtained door with all their diadems, it was as though the stars should arise in their stations and troop together to the West at sunrise.

And only the other day I found a stone that had undoubtedly been a part of Zaccarath, it was three inches long and an inch broad; I saw the edge of it uncovered by the sand. I believe that only three other pieces have been found like it.

THE FIELD

When one has seen Spring's blossom fall in London, and Summer appear and ripen and decay, as it does early in cities, and one is in London still, then, at some moment or another, the country places lift their flowery heads and call to one with an urgent, masterful clearness, upland behind upland in the twilight like to some heavenly choir arising rank on rank to call a drunkard from his gambling-hell. No volume of traffic can drown the sound of it, no lure of London can weaken its appeal. Having heard it one's fancy is gone, and evermore departed, to some coloured pebble agleam in a rural brook, and all that London can offer is swept from one's mind like some suddenly smitten metropolitan Goliath.

The call is from afar both in leagues and years, for the hills that call one are the hills that were, and their voices are the voices of long ago, when the elf-kings still had horns.

I see them now, those hills of my infancy (for it is they that call), with their faces upturned to the purple twilight, and the faint diaphanous figures of the fairies peering out from under the bracken to see if evening is come. I do not see upon their regal summits those desirable mansions, and highly desirable residences, which have lately been built for gentlemen who would exchange customers for tenants.

When the hills called I used to go to them by road, riding a bicycle. If you go by train you miss the gradual approach, you do not cast off London like an old forgiven sin, nor pass by little villages on the way that must have some rumour of the hills; nor, wondering if they are still the same, come at last upon the edge of their far-spread robes, and so on to their feet, and see far off their holy, welcoming faces. In the train you see them suddenly round a curve, and there they all are sitting in the sun.

I imagine that as one penetrated out from some enormous forest of the tropics, the wild beasts would become fewer, the gloom would lighten, and the horror of the place would slowly lift. Yet as one emerges nearer to the edge of London, and nearer to the beautiful influence of the hills, the houses become uglier, the streets viler, the gloom deepens, the errors of civilisation stand bare to the scorn of the fields.

Where ugliness reaches the height of its luxuriance, in the dense misery of the place, where one imagines the builder saying, "Here I culminate. Let us give thanks to Satan," there is a bridge of yellow brick, and through it, as through some gate of filigree silver opening on fairyland, one passes into the country.

To left and right, as far as one can see, stretches that monstrous city; before one are the fields like an old, old song.

There is a field there that is full of king-cups. A stream runs through it, and along the stream is a little wood of osiers. There I used often to rest at the streams edge before my long journey to the hills.

There I used to forget London, street by street. Sometimes I picked a bunch of king-cups to show them to the hills.

I often came there. At first I noticed nothing about the field except its beauty and its peacefulness.

But the second time that I came I thought there was something ominous about the field.

Down there among the king-cups by the little shallow stream I felt that something terrible might happen in just such a place.

I did not stay long there, because I thought that too much time spent in London had brought on these morbid fancies and I went on to the hills as fast as I could.

I stayed for some days in the country air, and when I came back I went to the field again to enjoy that peaceful spot before entering London. But there was still something ominous among the osiers.

A year elapsed before I went there again. I emerged from the shadow of London into the gleaming sun; the bright green grass and the king-cups were flaming in the light, and the little stream was singing a happy song. But the moment I stepped into the field my old uneasiness returned, and worse than before. It was as though the shadow was brooding there of some dreadful future thing and a year had brought it nearer.

I reasoned that the exertion of bicycling might be bad for one, and that the moment one rested this uneasiness might result.

A little later I came back past the field by night, and the song of the stream in the hush attracted me down to it. And there the fancy came to me that it would be a terribly cold place to be in the starlight, if for some reason one was hurt and could not get away.

I knew a man who was minutely acquainted with the past history of that locality, and him I asked if anything historical had ever happened in that field. When he pressed me for my reason in asking him this, I said that the field had seemed to me such a good place to hold a pageant in. But he said that nothing of any interest had ever occurred there, nothing at all.

So it was from the future that the field's terrible trouble came.

For three years off and on I made visits to the field, and every time more clearly it boded evil things, and my uneasiness grew more acute every time that I was lured to go and rest among the cool green grass under the beautiful osiers. Once to distract my thoughts I tried to gauge how fast the stream was trickling, but I found myself wondering if it flowed faster than blood.

I felt that it would be a terrible place to go mad in, one would hear voices.

At last I went to a poet whom I knew, and woke him from huge dreams, and put before him the whole case of the field. He had not been out of London all that year, and he promised to come with me and look at the field, and tell me what was going to happen there. It was late in July when we went. The pavement, the air, the houses and the dirt had been all baked dry by the summer, the weary traffic dragged on, and on, and on, and Sleep spreading her wings soared up and floated from London and went to walk beautifully in rural places.

When the poet saw the field he was delighted, the flowers were out in masses all along the stream, he went down to the little wood rejoicing. By the side of the stream he stood and seemed very sad. Once or twice he looked up and down it mournfully, then he bent and looked at the king-cups, first one and then another, very closely, and shaking his head.

For a long while he stood in silence, and all my old uneasiness returned, and my bodings for the future.

And then I said, "What manner of field is it?"

And he shook his head sorrowfully.

"It is a battlefield," he said.

THE DAY OF THE POLL

In the town by the sea it was the day of the poll, and the poet regarded it sadly when he woke and saw the light of it coming in at his window between two small curtains of gauze. And the day of the poll was beautifully bright; stray bird-songs came to the poet at the window; the air was crisp and wintry, but it was the blaze of sunlight that had deceived the birds.

He heard the sound of the sea that the moon led up the shore, dragging the months away over the pebbles and shingles and piling them up with the years where the worn-out centuries lay; he saw the majestic downs stand facing mightily south-wards; saw the smoke of the town float up to their heavenly faces—column after column rose calmly into the morning as house by house was waked by peering shafts of the sunlight and lit its fires for the day; column by column went up toward the serene downs' faces, and failed before they came there and hung all white over houses; and every one in the town was raving mad.

It was a strange thing that the poet did, for he hired the largest motor in the town and covered it with all the flags he could find, and set out to save an intelligence. And he presently found a man whose face was hot, who shouted that the time was not far distant when a candidate, whom he named, would be returned at the head of the poll by a thumping majority. And by him the poet stopped and offered him a seat in the motor that was covered with flags. When the man saw the flags that were on the motor, and that it was the largest in the town, he got in. He said that his vote should be given for that fiscal system that had made us what we are, in order that the poor man's food should not be taxed to make the rich man richer. Or else it was that he would give his vote for that system of tariff reform which should unite us closer to our colonies with ties that should long endure, and give employment to all. But it was not to the polling-booth that the motor went, it passed it and left the town and came by a small white winding road to the very top of the downs. There the poet dismissed the car and let that wondering voter on to the grass and seated himself on a rug. And for long the voter talked of those imperial traditions that our forefathers had made for us and which he should uphold with his vote, or else it was of a people oppressed by a feudal system that was out of date and effete, and that should be ended or mended. But the poet pointed out to him small, distant, wandering ships on the sunlit strip of sea, and the birds far down below them, and the houses below the birds, with the little columns of smoke that could not find the downs.

And at first the voter cried for his polling-booth like a child; but after a while he grew calmer, save when faint bursts of cheering came twittering up to the downs, when the voter would cry out bitterly against the misgovernment of the Radical party, or else it was—I forget what the poet told me—he extolled its splendid record.

"See," said the poet, "these ancient beautiful things, the downs and the old-time houses and the morning, and the grey sea in the sunlight going mumbling round the world. And this is the place they have chosen to go man in!"

And standing there with all broad England behind him, rolling north-ward, down after down, and before him the glittering sea too far for the sound of the roar of it, there seemed to the voter to grow less important the questions that troubled the town. Yet he was still angry.

"Why did you bring me here?" he said again.

"Because I grew lonely," said the poet, "when all the town went mad."

Then he pointed out to the voter some old bent thorns, and showed him the way that a wind had blown for a million years, coming up at dawn from the sea; and he told him of the storms that visit the ships, and their names and whence they come, and the currents they drive afield, and the way that the swallows go. And he spoke of the down where they sat, when the summer came, and the flowers that were not yet, and the different butterflies, and about the bats and the swifts, and the thoughts in the heart of man. He spoke of the aged windmill that stood on the down, and of how to children it seemed a strange old man who was only dead by day. And as he spoke, and as the sea-wind blew on that high and lonely place, there began to slip away from the voter's mind meaningless phrases that had crowded it long—thumping majority—victory in the fight—terminological inexactitudes—and the smell of paraffin lamps dangling in heated schoolrooms, and quotations taken from ancient speeches because the words were long. They fell away, though slowly, and slowly the voter saw a wider world and the wonder of the sea. And the afternoon wore on, and the winter evening came, and the night fell, and all black grew the sea, and about the time that the stars come blinking out to look upon our littleness, the polling-booth closed in the town.

When they got back the turmoil was on the wane in the streets; night hid the glare of the posters; and the tide, finding the noise abated and being at the flow, told an old tale that he had learned in his youth about the deeps of the sea, the same which he had told to coastwise ships that brought it to Babylon by the way of Euphrates before the doom of Troy.

I blame my friend the poet, however lonely he was, for preventing this man from registering his vote (the duty of every citizen); but perhaps it matters less, as it was a foregone conclusion, because the losing candidate, either through poverty or sheer madness, had neglected to subscribe to a single football club.

THE UNHAPPY BODY

"Why do you not dance with us and rejoice with us?" they said to a certain body. And then that body made the confession of its trouble. It said: "I am united with a fierce and violent soul, that is altogether tyrannous and will not let me rest, and he drags me away from the dances of my kin to make me toil at his detestable work; and he will not let me do the little things, that would give pleasure to the folk I love, but only cares to please posterity when he has done with me and left me to the worms; and all the while he makes absurd demands of affection from those that are near to me, and is too proud even to notice any less than he demands, so that those that should be kind to me all hate me." And the unhappy body burst into tears.

And they said: "No sensible body cares for its soul. A soul is a little thing, and should not rule a body. You should drink and smoke more till he ceases to trouble you." But the body only wept, and said, "Mine is a fearful soul. I have driven him away for a little while with drink. But he will soon come back. Oh, he will soon come back!"

And the body went to bed hoping to rest, for it was drowsy with drink. But just as sleep was near it, it looked up, and there was its soul sitting on the windowsill, a misty blaze of light, and looking into the river.

"Come," said the tyrannous soul, "and look into the street."

"I have need of sleep," said the body.

"But the street is a beautiful thing," the soul said vehemently; "a hundred of the people are dreaming there."

"I am ill through want of rest," the body said.

"That does not matter," the soul said to it. "There are millions like you in the earth, and millions more to go there. The people's dreams are wandering afield; they pass the seas and mountains of faëry, threading the intricate passes led by their souls; they come to golden temples a-ring with a thousand bells; they pass up steep streets lit by paper lanterns, where the doors are green and small; they know their way to witches' chambers and castles of enchantment; they know the spell that brings them to the causeway along the ivory mountains—on one side looking downward they behold the fields of their youth and on the other lie the radiant plains of the future. Arise and write down what the people dream."

"What reward is there for me," said the body, "if I write down what you bid me?"

"There is no reward," said the soul.

"Then I shall sleep," said the body.

And the soul began to hum an idle song sung by a young man in a fabulous land as he passed a golden city (where fiery sentinels stood), and knew that his wife was within it, though as yet but a little child, and knew by prophecy that furious wars, not yet arisen in far and unknown mountains, should roll above him with their dust and thirst before he ever came to that city again—the young man sang it as he passed the gate, and was now dead with his wife a thousand years.

"I cannot sleep for that abominable song," the body cried to the soul.

"Then do as you are commanded," the soul replied. And wearily the body took a pen again. Then the soul spoke merrily as he looked through the window. "There is a mountain lifting sheer above London, part crystal and part myst. Thither the dreamers go when the sound of the traffic has fallen. At first they scarcely dream because of the roar of it, but before midnight it stops, and turns, and ebbs with all its wrecks. Then the dreamers arise and scale the shimmering mountain, and at its summit find the galleons of dream. Thence some sail East, some West, some into the Past and some into the Future, for the galleons sail over the years as well as over the spaces, but mostly they head for the Past and the olden harbours, for thither the sighs of men are mostly turned, and the dream-ships go before them, as the merchantmen before the continual trade-winds go down the African coast. I see the galleons even now raise anchor after anchor; the stars flash by them; they slip out of the night; their prows go gleaming into the twilight of memory, and night soon lies far off, a black cloud hanging low, and faintly spangled with stars, like the harbour and shore of some low-lying land seen afar with its harbour lights."

Dream after dream that soul related as he sat there by the window. He told of tropical forests seen by unhappy men who could not escape from London, and never would—forests made suddenly wondrous by the song of some passing bird flying to unknown eyries and singing an unknown song. He saw the old men lightly dancing to the tune of elfin pipes—beautiful dances with fantastic maidens—all night on moonlit imaginary mountains; he heard far off the music of glittering Springs; he saw the fairness of blossoms of apple and may thirty years fallen; he heard old voices—old tears came glistening back; Romance sat cloaked and crowned upon southern hills, and the soul knew him.

One by one he told the dreams of all that slept in that street. Sometimes he stopped to revile the body because it worked badly and slowly. Its chill fingers wrote as fast as they could, but the soul cared not for that. And so the night wore on till the soul heard tinkling in Oriental skies far footfalls of the morning.

"See now," said the soul, "the dawn that the dreamers dread. The sails of light are paling on those unwreckable galleons; the mariners that steer them slip back into fable and myth; that other sea the traffic is turning now at its ebb, and is about to hide its pallid wrecks, and to come swinging back, with its tumult, at the flow. Already the sunlight flashes in the gulfs behind the east of the world; the gods have seen it from their palace of twilight that the built above the sunrise; they warm their hands at its glow as it streams through their gleaming arches, before it reaches the world; all the gods are there that have ever been, and all the gods that shall be; they sit there in the morning, chanting and praising Man."

"I am numb and very cold for want of sleep," said the body.

"You shall have centuries of sleep," said the soul, "but you must not sleep now, for I have seen deep meadows with purple flowers flaming tall and strange above the brilliant grass, and herds of pure white unicorns that gambol there for joy, and a river running by with a glittering galleon on it, all of gold, that goes from an unknown inland to an unknown isle of the sea to take a song from the King of Over-the-Hills to the Queen of Far-Away.

"I will sing that song to you, and you shall write it down."

"I have toiled for you for years," the body said. "Give me now but one night's rest, for I am exceeding weary."

"Oh, go and rest. I am tired of you. I am off," said the soul.

And he arose and went, we know not whither. But the body they laid in the earth. And the next night at midnight the wraiths of the dead came drifting from their tombs to felicitate that body.

"You are free here, you know," they said to their new companion.

"Now I can rest," said the body.

THE BOOK OF WONDER (1912)

THE BRIDE OF THE MAN-HORSE

In the morning of his two hundred and fiftieth year Shepperalk the centaur went to the golden coffer, wherein the treasure of the centaurs was, and taking from it the hoarded amulet that his father, Jyshak, in the years of his prime, had hammered from mountain gold and set with opals bartered from the gnomes, he put it upon his wrist, and said no word, but walked from his mother's cavern. And he took with him too that clarion of the centaurs, that famous silver horn, that in its time had summoned to surrender seventeen cities of Man, and for twenty years had brayed at star-girt walls in the Siege of Tholdenblarna, the citadel of the gods, what time the centaurs waged their fabulous war and were not broken by any force of arms, but retreated slowly in a cloud of dust before the final miracle of the gods that They brought in Their desperate need from Their ultimate armoury. He took it and strode away, and his mother only sighed and let him go.

She knew that today he would not drink at the stream coming down from the terraces of Varpa Niger, the inner land of the mountains, that today he would not wonder awhile at the sunset and afterwards trot back to the cavern again to sleep on rushes pulled by rivers that know not Man. She knew that it was with him as it had been of old with his father, and with Goom the father of Jyshak, and long ago with the gods. Therefore she only sighed and let him go.

But he, coming out from the cavern that was his home, went for the first time over the little stream, and going round the corner of the crags saw glittering beneath him the mundane plain. And the wind of the autumn that was gilding the world, rushing up the slopes of the mountain, beat cold on his naked flanks. He raised his head and snorted.

"I am a man-horse now!" he shouted aloud; and leaping from crag to crag he galloped by valley and chasm, by torrent-bed and scar of avalanche, until he came to the wandering leagues of the plain, and left behind him for ever the Athraminaurian mountains.

His goal was Zretazoola, the city of Sombelenë. What legend of Sombelenë's inhuman beauty or of the wonder of her mystery had ever floated over the mundane plain to the fabulous cradle of the centaurs' race, the

Athraminaurian mountains, I do not know. Yet in the blood of man there is a tide, an old sea-current rather, that is somehow akin to the twilight, which brings him rumours of beauty from however far away, as driftwood is found at sea from islands not yet discovered: and this spring-tide of current that visits the blood of man comes from the fabulous quarter of his lineage, from the legendary, the old; it takes him out to the woodlands, out to the hills; he listens to ancient song. So it may be that Shepperalk's fabulous blood stirred in those lonely mountains away at the edge of the world to rumours that only the airy twilight knew and only confided secretly to the bat, for Shepperalk was more legendary even than man. Certain it was that he headed from the first for the city of Zretazoola, where Sombelenë in her temple dwelt; though all the mundane plain, its rivers and mountains, lay between Shepperalk's home and the city he sought.

When first the feet of the centaur touched the grass of that soft alluvial earth he blew for joy upon the silver horn, he pranced and caracoled, he gambolled over the leagues; pace came to him like a maiden with a lamp, a new and beautiful wonder; the wind laughed as it passed him. He put his head down low to the scent of the flowers, he lifted it up to be nearer the unseen stars, he revelled through kingdoms, took rivers in his stride; how shall I tell you, ye that dwell in cities, how shall I tell you what he felt as he galloped? He felt for strength like the towers of Bel-Narana; for lightness like those gossamer palaces that the fairy-spider builds 'twixt heaven and sea along the coasts of Zith; for swiftness like some bird racing up from the morning to sing in some city's spires before daylight comes. He was the sworn companion of the wind. For joy he was as a song; the lightnings of his legendary sires, the earlier gods, began to mix with his blood; his hooves thundered. He came to the cities of men, and all men trembled, for they remembered the ancient mythical wars, and now they dreaded new battles and feared for the race of man. Not by Clio are these wars recorded; history does not know them, but what of that? Not all of us have sat at historians' feet, but all have learned fable and myth at their mothers' knees. And there were none that did not fear strange wars when they saw Shepperalk swerve and leap along the public ways. So he passed from city to city.

By night he lay down unpanting in the reeds of some marsh or a forest; before dawn he rose triumphant, and hugely drank of some river in the dark, and splashing out of it would trot to some high place to find the sunrise, and to send echoing eastwards the exultant greetings of his jubilant horn. And lo! the sunrise coming up from the echoes, and the plains new-lit by the day, and the leagues spinning by like water flung from a top, and that gay companion, the loudly laughing wind, and men and the fears of men and their little cities; and, after that, great rivers and waste spaces and huge new hills, and then new lands beyond them, and more cities of men, and always the old companion, the glorious wind. Kingdom by kingdom slipt by, and still his breath was even. "It is a golden thing to gallop on good turf in one's youth," said the young man-horse, the centaur. "Ha, ha," said the wind of the hills, and the winds of the plain answered.

Bells pealed in frantic towers, wise men consulted parchments, astrologers sought of the portent from the stars, the aged made subtle prophecies. "Is he not swift?" said the young. "How glad he is," said children.

Night after night brought him sleep, and day after day lit his gallop, till he came to the lands of the Athalonian men who live by the edges of the mundane plain, and from them he came to the lands of legend again such as those in which he was cradled on the other side of the world, and which fringe the marge of the world and mix with the twilight. And there a mighty thought came into his untired heart, for he knew that he neared Zretazoola now, the city of Sombelenë.

It was late in the day when he neared it, and clouds coloured with evening rolled low on the plain before him; he galloped on into their golden mist, and when it hid from his eyes the sight of things, the dreams in his heart awoke and romantically he pondered all those rumours that used to come to him from Sombelenë, because of the fellowship of fabulous things. She dwelt (said evening secretly to the bat) in a little temple by a lone lakeshore. A grove of cypresses screened her from the city, from Zretazoola of the climbing ways. And opposite her temple stood her tomb, her sad lake-sepulchre with open door, lest her amazing beauty and the centuries of her youth should ever give rise to the heresy among men that lovely Sombelenë was immortal: for only her beauty and her lineage were divine.

Her father had been half centaur and half god; her mother was the child of a desert lion and that sphinx that watches the pyramids;—she was more mystical than Woman.

Her beauty was as a dream, was as a song; the one dream of a lifetime dreamed on enchanted dews, the one song sung to some city by a deathless bird blown far from his native coasts by storm in Paradise. Dawn after dawn on mountains of romance or twilight after twilight could never equal her beauty; all the glow-worms had not the secret among them nor all the stars of night; poets had never sung it nor evening guessed its meaning; the morning envied it, it was hidden from lovers.

She was unwed, unwooed.

The lions came not to woo her because they feared her strength, and the gods dared not love her because they knew she must die.

This was what evening had whispered to the bat, this was the dream in the heart of Shepperalk as he cantered blind through the mist. And suddenly there at his hooves in the dark of the plain appeared the cleft in the legendary lands, and Zretazoola sheltering in the cleft, and sunning herself in the evening.

Swiftly and craftily he bounded down by the upper end of the cleft, and entering Zretazoola by the outer gate which looks out sheer on the stars, he galloped suddenly down the narrow streets. Many that rushed out on to balconies as he went clattering by, many that put their heads from glittering windows, are told of in olden song. Shepperalk did not tarry to give greetings or to answer challenges from martial towers, he was down through the earthward gateway like the thunderbolt of his sires, and, like Leviathan who has leapt at an eagle, he surged into the water between temple and tomb.

He galloped with half-shut eyes up the temple-steps, and, only seeing dimly through his lashes, seized Sombelenë by the hair, undazzled as yet by her beauty, and so haled her away; and, leaping with her over the floorless chasm where the waters of the lake fall unremembered away into a hole in the world, took her we know not where, to be her slave for all centuries that are allowed to his race.

Three blasts he gave as he went upon that silver horn that is the world-old treasure of the centaurs. These were his wedding bells.

DISTRESSING TALE OF THANGOBRIND THE JEWELLER

When Thangobrind the jeweller heard the ominous cough, he turned at once upon that narrow way. A thief was he, of very high repute, being patronized by the lofty and elect, for he stole nothing smaller than the Moomoo's egg, and in all his life stole only four kinds of stone—the ruby, the diamond, the emerald, and the sapphire; and, as jewellers go, his honesty was great. Now there was a Merchant Prince who had come to Thangobrind and had offered his daughter's soul for the diamond that is larger than the human head and was to be found on the lap of the spider-idol, Hlo-hlo, in his temple of Moung-ga-ling; for he had heard that Thangobrind was a thief to be trusted.

Thangobrind oiled his body and slipped out of his shop, and went secretly through byways, and got as far as Snarp, before anybody knew that he was out on business again or missed his sword from its place under the counter. Thence he moved only by night, hiding by day and rubbing the edges of his sword, which he called Mouse because it was swift and nimble. The jeweller had subtle methods of travelling; nobody saw him cross the plains of Zid; nobody saw him come to Mursk or Tlun. O, but he loved shadows! Once the moon peeping out unexpectedly from a tempest had betrayed an ordinary jeweller; not so did it undo Thangobrind: the watchman only saw a crouching shape that snarled and laughed: "'Tis but a hyena," they said. Once in the city of Ag one of the guardians seized him, but Thangobrind was oiled and slipped from his hand; you scarcely heard his bare feet patter away. He knew that the Merchant Prince awaited his return, his little eyes open all night and glittering with greed; he knew how his daughter lay chained up and screaming night and day. Ah, Thangobrind knew. And had he not been out on business he had almost allowed himself one or two little laughs. But business was business, and the diamond that he sought still lay on the lap of Hlo-hlo, where it had been for the last two million years since Hlo-hlo created the world and gave unto it all things except that precious stone called Dead Man's Diamond. The jewel was often stolen, but it had a knack of coming back again to the lap of Hlo-hlo. Thangobrind knew this, but he was no common jeweller and hoped to outwit Hlo-hlo, perceiving not the trend of ambition and lust and that they are vanity.

How nimbly he threaded his way through he pits of Snood!—now like a botanist, scrutinising the ground; now like a dancer, leaping from crumbling edges. It was quite dark when he went by the towers of Tor, where archers shoot ivory arrows at strangers lest any foreigner should alter their laws, which are bad, but not to be altered by mere aliens. At night they shoot by the sound of the strangers' feet. O, Thangobrind, Thangobrind, was ever a jeweller like you! He dragged two stones behind him by long cords, and at these the archers shot. Tempting indeed was the snare that they set in Woth, the emeralds loose-set in the city's gate; but Thangobrind discerned the golden cord that climbed the wall from each and the weights that would topple upon him if he touched one, and so he left them, though he left them weeping, and at last came to Theth. There all men worship Hlo-hlo; though they are willing to believe in other gods, as missionaries attest, but only as creatures of the chase for the hunting of Hlo-hlo, who wears Their halos, so these people say, on golden hooks along his hunting-belt. And from Theth he came to the city of Moung and the temple of Moung-ga-ling, and entered and saw the spider-idol, Hlo-hlo, sitting there with Dead Man's Diamond glittering on his lap, and looking for all the world like a full moon, but a full moon seen by a lunatic who had slept too long in its rays, for there was in Dead Man's Diamond a certain sinister look and a boding of things to happen that are better not mentioned here. The face of the spider-idol was lit by that fatal gem; there was no other light. In spite of his shocking limbs and that demoniac body, his face was serene and apparently unconscious.

A little fear came into the mind of Thangobrind the jeweller, a passing tremor—no more; business was business and he hoped for the best. Thangobrind offered honey to Hlo-hlo and prostrated himself before him. Oh, he was cunning! When the priests stole out of the darkness to lap up the honey they were stretched senseless on the temple floor, for there was a drug in the honey that was offered to Hlo-hlo. And Thangobrind the jeweller picked Dead Man's Diamond up and put it on his shoulder and trudged away from the shrine; and Hlo-hlo the spider-idol said nothing at all, but he laughed softly as the jeweller shut the door. When the priests awoke out of the grip of the drug that was offered with the honey to Hlo-hlo, they rushed to a little secret room with an outlet on the stars and cast a horoscope of the thief. Something that they saw in the horoscope seemed to satisfy the priests.

It was not like Thangobrind to go back by the road by which he had come. No, he went by another road, even though it led to the narrow way, night-house and spider-forest.

The city of Moung went towering by behind him, balcony above balcony, eclipsing half the stars, as he trudged away with his diamond. Though when a soft pittering as of velvet feet arose behind him he refused to acknowledge that it might be what he feared, yet the instincts of his trade told him that it is not well when any noise whatever follows a diamond by night, and this was one of the largest that had ever come to him in the way of business. When he came to the narrow way that leads to spider-forest, Dead Man's Diamond feeling cold and heavy, and the velvety footfall seeming fearfully close, the jeweller stopped and almost hesitated. He looked behind him; there was nothing there. He listened attentively; there was no sound now. Then he thought of the screams of the Merchant Prince's daughter, whose soul was the diamond's price, and smiled and went stoutly on. There watched him, apathetically, over the narrow way, that grim and dubious woman whose house is the Night. Thangobrind, hearing no longer the sound of suspicious feet, felt easier now. He was all but come to the end of the narrow way, when the woman listlessly uttered that ominous cough.

The cough was too full of meaning to be disregarded. Thangobrind turned round and saw at once what he feared. The spider-idol had not stayed at home. The jeweller put his diamond gently upon the ground and drew his sword called Mouse. And then began that famous fight upon the narrow way in which the grim old woman whose house was Night seemed to take so little interest. To the spider-idol you saw at once it was all a horrible joke. To the jeweller it was grim earnest. He fought and panted and was pushed back slowly along the narrow way, but he wounded Hlo-hlo all the while with terrible long gashes all over his deep, soft body till Mouse was slimy with blood. But at last the persistent laughter of Hlo-hlo was too much for the jeweller's nerves, and, once more wounding his demoniac foe, he sank aghast and exhausted by the door of the house called Night at the feet of the grim old woman, who having uttered once that ominous cough interfered no further with the course of events. And there carried Thangobrind the jeweller away those whose duty it was, to the house where the two men hang, and taking down from his hook the left-hand one of the two, they put that venturous jeweller in his place; so that there fell on him the doom that he feared, as all men know though it is so long since, and there abated somewhat the ire of the envious gods.

And the only daughter of the Merchant Prince felt so little gratitude for this great deliverance that she took to respectability of a militant kind, and became aggressively dull, and called her home the English Riviera, and had platitudes worked in worsted upon her tea-cosy, and in the end never died, but passed away at her residence.

THE HOUSE OF THE SPHINX

When I came to the House of the Sphinx it was already dark. They made me eagerly welcome. And I, in spite of the deed, was glad of any shelter from that ominous wood. I saw at once that there had been a deed, although a cloak did all that a cloak may do to conceal it. The mere uneasiness of the welcome made me suspect that cloak.

The Sphinx was moody and silent. I had not come to pry into the secrets of Eternity nor to investigate the Sphinx's private life, and so had little to say and few questions to ask; but to whatever I did say she remained morosely indifferent. It was clear that either she suspected me of being in search of the secrets of one of her gods, or of being boldly inquisitive about her traffic with Time, or else she was darkly absorbed with brooding upon the deed.

I saw soon enough that there was another than me to welcome; I saw it from the hurried way that they glanced from the door to the deed and back to the door again. And it was clear that the welcome was to be a bolted door. But such bolts, and such a door! Rust and decay and fungus had been there far too long, and it was not a barrier any longer that would keep out even a determined wolf. And it seemed to be something worse than a wolf that they feared.

A little later on I gathered from what they said that some imperious and ghastly thing was looking for the Sphinx, and that something that had happened had made its arrival certain. It appeared that they had slapped the Sphinx to vex her out of her apathy in order that she should pray to one of her gods, whom she had littered in the house of Time; but her moody silence was invincible, and her apathy Oriental, ever since the deed had happened. And when they found that they could not make her pray, there was nothing for them to do but to pay little useless attentions to the rusty lock of the door, and to look at the deed and wonder, and even pretend to hope, and to say that after all it might not bring that destined thing from the forest, which no one named.

It may be said I had chosen a gruesome house, but not if I had described the forest from which I came, and I was in need of any spot wherein I could rest my mind from the thought of it.

I wondered very much what thing would come from the forest on account of the deed; and having seen that forest—as you, gentle reader, have not—I had the advantage of knowing that anything might come. It was useless to ask the Sphinx—she seldom reveals things, like her paramour Time (the gods take after her), and while this mood was on her, rebuff was certain. So I quietly began to oil the lock of the door. And as soon as they saw this simple act I won their confidence. It was not that my work was of any use—it should have been done long before; but they saw that my interest was given for the moment to the thing that they thought vital. They clustered round me then. They asked me what I thought of the door, and whether I had seen better, and whether I had seen worse; and I told them about all the doors I knew, and said that the doors of the baptistry in Florence were better doors, and the doors made by a certain firm of builders in London were worse. And then I asked them what it was that was coming after the Sphinx because of the deed. And at first they would not say, and I stopped oiling the door; and then they said that it was the arch-inquisitor of the forest, who is investigator and avenger of all silverstrian things; and from all that they said about him it seemed to me that this person was quite white, and was a kind of madness that would settle down quite blankly upon a place, a kind of mist in which reason could not live; and it was the fear of this that made them fumble nervously at the lock of that rotten door; but with the Sphinx it was not so much fear as sheer prophecy.

The hope that they tried to hope was well enough in its way, but I did not share it; it was clear that the thing that they feared was the corollary of the deed—one saw that more by the resignation upon the face of the Sphinx than by their sorry anxiety for the door.

The wind soughed, and the great tapers flared, and their obvious fear and the silence of the Sphinx grew more than ever a part of the atmosphere, and bats went restlessly through the gloom of the wind that beat the tapers low.

Then a few things screamed far off, then a little nearer, and something was coming towards us, laughing hideously. I hastily gave a prod to the door that they guarded; my finger sank right into the mouldering wood—there was not a chance of holding it. I had not leisure to observe their fright; I thought of the back-door, for the forest was better than this; only the Sphinx was absolutely calm, her prophecy was made and she seemed to have seen her doom, so that no new thing could perturb her.

But by mouldering rungs of ladders as old as Man, by slippery edges of the dreaded abyss, with an ominous dizziness about my heart and a feeling of horror in the soles of my feet, I clambered from tower to tower till I found the door that I sought; and it opened on to one of the upper branches of a huge and sombre pine, down which I climbed on to the floor of the forest. And I was glad to be back again in the forest from which I had fled.

And the Sphinx in her menaced house—I know not how she fared—whether she gazes for ever, disconsolate, at the deed, remembering only in her smitten mind, at which the little boys now leer, that she once knew well those things at which man stands aghast; or whether in the end she crept away, and clambering horribly from abyss to abyss, came at last to higher things, and is wise and eternal still. For who knows of madness whether it is divine or whether it be of the pit?

PROBABLE ADVENTURE OF THE THREE LITERARY MEN

When the nomads came to El Lola they had no more songs, and the question of stealing the golden box arose in all its magnitude. On the one hand, many had sought the golden box, the receptacle (as the Aethiopians know) of poems of fabulous value; and their doom is still the common talk of Arabia. On the other hand, it was lonely to sit around the camp-fire by night with no new songs.

It was the tribe of Heth that discussed these things one evening upon the plains below the peak of Mluna. Their native land was the track across the world of immemorial wanderers; and there was trouble among the elders of the nomads because there were no new songs; while, untouched by human trouble, untouched as yet by the night that was hiding the plains away, the peak of Mluna, calm in the after-glow, looked on the Dubious Land. And it was there on the plain upon the known side of Mluna, just as the evening star came mouse-like into view and the flames of the camp-fire lifted their lonely plumes uncheered by any song, that that rash scheme was hastily planned by the nomads which the world has named The Quest of the Golden Box.

No measure of wiser precaution could the elders of the nomads have taken than to choose for their thief that very Slith, that identical thief that (even as I write) in how many school-rooms governesses teach stole a march on the King of Westalia. Yet the weight of the box was such that others had to accompany him, and Sippy and Slorg were no more agile thieves than may be found today among vendors of the antique.

So over the shoulder of Mluna these three climbed next day and slept as well as they might among its snows rather than risk a night in the woods of the Dubious Land. And the morning came up radiant and the birds were full of song, but the forest underneath and the waste beyond it and the bare and ominous crags all wore the appearance of an unuttered threat.

Though Slith had an experience of twenty years of theft, yet he said little; only if one of the others made a stone roll with his foot, or, later on in the forest, if one of them stepped on a twig, he whispered sharply to them always the same words: "That is not business." He knew that he could not make them better thieves during a two days' journey, and whatever doubts he had he interfered no further.

From the shoulder of Mluna they dropped into the clouds, and from the clouds to the forest, to whose native beasts, as well the three thieves knew, all flesh was meat, whether it were the flesh of fish or man. There the thieves drew idolatrously from their pockets each one a separate god and prayed for protection in the unfortunate wood, and hoped therefrom for a threefold chance of escape, since if anything should eat one of them it were certain to eat them all, and they confided that the corollary might be true and all should escape if one did. Whether one of these gods was propitious and awake, or whether all of the three, or whether it was chance that brought them through the forest unmouthed by detestable beasts, none knoweth; but certainly neither the emissaries of the god that most they feared, nor the wrath of the topical god of that ominous place, brought their doom to the three adventurers there or then. And so it was that they came to Rumbly Heath, in the heart of the Dubious Land, whose stormy hillocks were the ground-swell and the after-wash of the earthquake lulled for a while. Something so huge that it seemed unfair to man that it should move so softly stalked splendidly by them, and only so barely did they escape its notice that one word rang and echoed through their three imaginations—"If—if—if." And when this danger was at last gone by they moved cautiously on again and presently saw the little harmless mipt, half fairy and half gnome, giving shrill, contented squeaks on the edge of the world. And they edged away unseen, for they said that the inquisitiveness of the mipt had become fabulous, and that, harmless as he was, he had a bad way with secrets; yet they probably loathed the way that he nuzzles dead white bones, and would not admit their loathing; for it does not become adventurers to care who eats their bones. Be this as it may, they edged away from the mipt, and came almost at once to the wizened tree, the goal-post of their adventure, and knew that beside them was the crack in the world and the bridge from Bad to Worse, and that underneath them stood the rocky house of Owner of the Box.

This was their simple plan: to slip into the corridor in the upper cliff; to run softly down it (of course with naked feet) under the warning to travellers that is graven upon stone, which interpreters take to be "It Is Better Not"; not to touch the berries that are there for a purpose, on the right side going down; and so to come to the guardian on his pedestal who had slept for a thousand years and should be sleeping still; and go in through the open window. One man was to wait outside by the crack in the World until the others came out with the golden box, and, should they cry for help, he was to threaten at once to unfasten the iron clamp that kept the crack together. When the box was secured they were to travel all night and all the following day, until the cloud-banks that wrapped the slopes of Mluna were well between them and Owner of the Box.

The door in the cliff was open. They passed without a murmur down the cold steps, Slith leading them all the way. A glance of longing, no more, each gave to the beautiful berries. The guardian upon his pedestal was still asleep. Slorg climbed by a ladder, that Slith knew where to find, to the iron clamp across the crack in the World, and waited beside it with a chisel in his hand, listening closely for anything untoward, while his friends slipped into the house; and no sound came. And presently Slith and Sippy found the golden box: everything seemed happening as they had planned, it only remained to see if it was the right one and to escape with it from that dreadful place. Under the shelter of the pedestal, so near to the guardian that they could feel his warmth, which paradoxically had the effect of chilling the blood of the boldest of them, they smashed the emerald hasp and opened the golden box; and there they read by the light of ingenious sparks which Slith knew how to contrive, and even this poor light they hid with their bodies. What was their joy, even at that perilous moment, as they lurked between the guardian and the abyss, to find that the box contained fifteen peerless odes in the alcaic form, five sonnets that were by far the most beautiful in the world, nine ballads in the manner of Provence that had no equal in the treasuries of man, a poem addressed to a moth in twenty-eight perfect stanzas, a piece of blank verse of over a hundred lines on a level not yet known to have been attained by man, as well as fifteen lyrics on which no merchant would dare to set a price. They would have read them again, for they gave happy tears to a man and memories of dear things done in infancy, and brought sweet voices from far sepulchres; but Slith pointed imperiously to the way by which they had come, and extinguished the light; and Slorg and Sippy sighed, then took the box.

The guardian still slept the sleep that survived a thousand years.

As they came away they saw that indulgent chair close by the edge of the World in which Owner of the Box had lately sat reading selfishly and alone the most beautiful songs and verses that poet ever dreamed.

They came in silence to the foot of the stairs; and then it befell that as they drew near safely, in the night's most secret hour, some hand in an upper chamber lit a shocking light, lit it and made no sound.

For a moment it might have been an ordinary light, fatal as even that could very well be at such a moment as this; but when it began to follow them like an eye and to grow redder and redder as it watched them, then even optimism despaired.

And Sippy very unwisely attempted flight, and Slorg even as unwisely tried to hide; but Slith, knowing well why that light was lit in that secret upper chamber and *who* it was that lit it, leaped over the edge of the World and is falling from us still through the unreverberate blackness of the abyss.

THE INJUDICIOUS PRAYERS OF
POMBO THE IDOLATER

Pombo the idolater had prayed to Ammuz a simple prayer, a necessary prayer, such as even an idol of ivory could very easily grant, and Ammuz had not immediately granted it. Pombo had therefore prayed to Tharma for the overthrow of Ammuz, an idol friendly to Tharma, and in doing this offended against the etiquette of the gods. Tharma refused to grant the little prayer. Pombo prayed frantically to all the gods of idolatry, for though it was a simple matter, yet it was very necessary to a man. And gods that were older than Ammuz rejected the prayers of Pombo, and even gods that were younger and therefore of greater repute. He prayed to them one by one, and they all refused to hear him; nor at first did he think at all of that subtle, divine etiquette against which he had offended. It occurred to him all at once as he prayed to his fiftieth idol, a little green-jade god whom the Chinese know, that all the idols were in league against him. When Pombo discovered this he resented his birth bitterly, and made lamentation and alleged that he was lost. He might have been seen then in any part of London haunting curiosity-shops and places where they sold idols of ivory or of stone, for he dwelt in London with others of his race though he was born in Burmah among those who hold Ganges holy. On drizzly evenings of November's worst his haggard face could be seen in the glow of some shop pressed close against the glass, where he would supplicate some calm, cross-legged idol till policemen moved him on. And after closing hours back he would go to his dingy room, in that part of our capital where English is seldom spoken, to supplicate little idols of his own. And when Pombo's simple, necessary prayer was equally refused by the idols of museums, auction-rooms, shops, then he took counsel with himself and purchased incense and burned it in a brazier before his own cheap little idols, and played the while upon an instrument such as that wherewith men charm snakes. And still the idols clung to their etiquette.

Whether Pombo knew about this etiquette and considered it frivolous in the face of his need, or whether his need, now grown desperate, unhinged his mind, I know not, but Pombo the idolater took a stick and suddenly turned iconoclast.

Pombo the iconoclast immediately left his house, leaving his idols to be swept away with the dust and so to mingle with Man, and went to an arch-idolater of repute who carved idols out of rare stones, and put his case before him. The arch-idolater who made idols of his own rebuked Pombo in the name of Man for having broken his idols—"for hath not Man made them?" the arch-idolater said; and concerning the idols themselves he spoke long and learnedly, explaining divine etiquette, and how Pombo had offended, and how no idol in the world would listen to Pombo's prayer. When Pombo heard this he wept and made bitter outcry, and cursed the gods of ivory and the gods of jade, and the hand of Man that made them, but most of all he cursed their etiquette that had undone, as he said, an innocent man; so that at last that arch-idolater, who made idols of his own, stopped in his work upon an idol of jasper for a king that was weary of Wosh, and took compassion on Pombo, and told him that though no idol in the world would listen to his prayer, yet only a little way over the edge of it a certain disreputable idol sat who knew nothing of etiquette, and granted prayers that no respectable god would ever consent to hear. When Pombo heard this he took two handfuls of the arch-idolater's beard and kissed them joyfully, and dried his tears and became his old impertinent self again. And he that carved from jasper the usurper of Wosh explained how in the village of World's End, at the furthest end of Last Street, there is a hole that you take to be a well, close by the garden wall, but that if you lower yourself by your hands over the edge of the hole, and feel about with your feet till they find a ledge, that is the top step of a flight of stairs that takes you down over the edge of the World. "For all that men know, those stairs may have a purpose and even a bottom step," said the arch-idolater, "but discussion about the lower flights is idle." Then the teeth of Pombo chattered, for he feared the darkness, but he that made idols of his own explained that those stairs were always lit by the faint blue gloaming in which the World spins. "Then," he said, "you will go by Lonely House and under the bridge that leads from the House to Nowhere, and whose purpose is not guessed; thence past Maharrion, the god of flowers, and his high-priest, who is neither bird nor cat; and so you will come to the little idol Duth, the disreputable god that will grant your prayer." And he went on carving again at his idol of jasper for the king who was weary of Wosh; and Pombo thanked him and went singing away, for in his vernacular mind he thought that "he *had* the gods."

It is a long journey from London to World's End, and Pombo had no money left, yet within five weeks he was strolling along Last Street; but how he contrived to get there I will not say, for it was not entirely honest. And Pombo found the well at the end of the garden beyond the end house of Last Street, and many thoughts ran through his mind as he hung by his hands from the edge, but chiefest of all those thoughts was one that said the gods were laughing at him through the mouth of the arch-idolater, their prophet, and the thought beat in his head till it ached like his wrists ...and then he found the step.

And Pombo walked downstairs. There, sure enough, was the gloaming in which the world spins, and stars shone far off in it faintly; there was nothing before him as he went downstairs but that strange blue waste of gloaming, with its multitudes of stars, and comets plunging through it on outward journeys and comets returning home. And then he saw the lights of the bridge to Nowhere, and all of a sudden he was in the glare of the shimmering parlour-window of Lonely House; and he heard voices there pronouncing words, and the voices were nowise human, and but for his bitter need he had screamed and fled. Halfway between the voices and Maharrion, whom he now saw standing out from the world, covered in rainbow halos, he perceived the weird grey beast that is neither cat nor bird. As Pombo hesitated, chilly with fear, he heard those voices grow louder in Lonely House, and at that he stealthily moved a few steps lower, and then rushed past the beast. The beast intently watched Maharrion hurling up bubbles that are every one a season of spring in unknown constellations, calling the swallows home to unimagined fields, watched him without even turning to look at Pombo, and saw him drop into the Linlunlarna, the river that rises at the edge of the World, the golden pollen that sweetens the tide of the river and is carried away from the World to be a joy to the Stars. And there before Pombo was the little disreputable god who cares nothing for etiquette and will answer prayers that are refused by all the respectable idols. And whether the view of him, at last, excited Pombo's eagerness, or whether his need was greater than he could bear that it drove him so swiftly downstairs, or whether, as is most likely, he ran too fast past the beast, I do not know, and it does not matter to Pombo; but at any rate he could not stop, as he had designed, in attitude of prayer at the feet of Duth, but ran on past him down the narrowing steps, clutching at smooth, bare rocks till he fell from the World as, when our hearts miss a beat, we fall in dreams and wake up with a dreadful jolt; but there was no waking up for Pombo, who still fell on towards the incurious stars, and his fate is even one with the fate of Slith.

THE LOOT OF BOMBASHARNA

Things had grown too hot for Shard, captain of pirates, on all the seas that he knew. The ports of Spain were closed to him; they knew him in San Domingo; men winked in Syracuse when he went by; the two Kings of the Sicilies never smiled within an hour of speaking of him; there were huge rewards for his head in every capital city, with pictures of it for identification—*and all the pictures were unflattering*. Therefore Captain Shard decided that the time had come to tell his men the secret.

Riding off Teneriffe one night, he called them all together. He generously admitted that there were things in the past that might require explanation: the crowns that the Princes of Aragon had sent to their nephews the Kings of the two Americas had certainly never reached their Most Sacred Majesties. Where, men might ask, were the eyes of Captain Stobbud? Who had been burning towns on the Patagonian seaboard? Why should such a ship as theirs choose pearls for cargo? Why so much blood on the decks and so many guns? And where was the *Nancy*, the *Lark*, or the *Margaret Belle*? Such questions as these, he urged, might be asked by the inquisitive, and if counsel for the defence should happen to be a fool, and unacquainted with the ways of the sea, they might become involved in troublesome legal formulae. And Bloody Bill, as they rudely called Mr. Gagg, a member of the crew, looked up at the sky, and said that it was a windy night and looked like hanging. And some of those present thoughtfully stroked their necks while Captain Shard unfolded to them his plan. He said the time was come to quit the *Desperate Lark*, for she was too well known to the navies of four kingdoms, and a fifth was getting to know her, and others had suspicions. (More cutters than even Captain Shard suspected were already looking for her jolly black flag with its neat skull-and-crossbones in yellow.) There was a little archipelago that he knew of on the wrong side of the Sargasso Sea; there were about thirty islands there, bare, ordinary islands, but one of them floated. He had noticed it years ago, and had gone ashore and never told a soul, but had quietly anchored it with the anchor of his ship to the bottom of the sea, which just there was profoundly deep, and had made the thing the secret of his life, determining to marry and settle down there if it ever became impossible to earn his livelihood in the usual way at sea. When first he saw it, it was drifting slowly, with the wind in the tops of the trees; but if the cable had not rusted away, it should be still where he left it, and they would make a rudder and hollow out cabins below, and at night they would hoist sails to the trunks of the trees and sail wherever they liked.

And all the pirates cheered, for they wanted to set their feet on land again somewhere where the hangman would not come and jerk them off it at once; and bold men though they were, it was a strain seeing so many lights coming their way at night. Even then…! But it swerved away again and was lost in the mist.

And Captain Shard said that they would need to get provisions first, and he, for one, intended to marry before he settled down; and so they should have one more fight before they left the ship, and sack the sea-coast city of Bombasharna and take from it provisions for several years, while he himself would marry the Queen of the South. And again the pirates cheered, for often they had seen seacoast Bombasharna, and had always envied its opulence from the sea.

So they set all sail, and often altered their course, and dodged and fled from strange lights till dawn appeared, and all day long fled southwards. And by evening they saw the silver spires of slender Bombasharna, a city that was the glory of the coast. And in the midst of it, far away though they were, they saw the palace of the Queen of the South; and it was so full of windows all looking toward the sea, and they were so full of light, both from the sunset that was fading upon the water and from candles that maids were lighting one by one, that it looked far off like a pearl, shimmering still in its haliotis shell, still wet from the sea.

So Captain Shard and his pirates saw it, at evening over the water, and thought of rumours that said that Bombasharna was the loveliest city of the coasts of the world, and that its palace was lovelier even than Bombasharna; but for the Queen of the South rumour had no comparison. Then night came down and hid the silver spires, and Shard slipped on through the gathering darkness until by midnight the piratic ship lay under the seaward battlements.

And at the hour when sick men mostly die, and sentries on lonely ramparts stand to arms, exactly half-an-hour before dawn, Shard, with two rowing boats and half his crew, with craftily muffled oars, landed below the battlements. They were through the gateway of the palace itself before the alarm was sounded, and as soon as they heard the alarm Shard's gunners at sea opened upon the town, and before the sleepy soldiery of Bombasharna knew whether the danger was from the land or the sea, Shard had successfully captured the Queen of the South. They would have looted all day that silver sea-coast city, but there appeared with dawn suspicious topsails just along the horizon. Therefore the captain with his Queen went down to the shore at once and hastily re-embarked and sailed away with what loot they had hurriedly got, and with fewer men, for they had to fight a good deal to get back to the boat. They cursed all day the interference of those ominous ships which steadily grew nearer. There were six ships at first, and that night they slipped away from all but two; but all the next day those two were still in sight, and each of them had more guns than the *Desperate Lark*. All the next night Shard dodged about the sea, but the two ships separated and one kept him in sight, and the next morning it was alone with Shard on the sea, and his archipelago was just in sight, the secret of his life.

And Shard saw he must fight, and a bad fight it was, and yet it suited Shard's purpose, for he had more merry men when the fight began than he needed for his island. And they got it over before any other ship came up; and Shard put all adverse evidence out of the way, and came that night to the islands near the Sargasso Sea.

Long before it was light the survivors of the crew were peering at the sea, and when dawn came there was the island, no bigger than two ships, straining hard at its anchor, with the wind in the tops of the trees.

And then they landed and dug cabins below and raised the anchor out of the deep sea, and soon they made the island what they called shipshape. But the *Desperate Lark* they sent away empty under full sail to sea, where more nations than Shard suspected were watching for her, and where she was presently captured by an admiral of Spain, who, when he found none of that famous crew on board to hang by the neck from the yard-arm, grew ill through disappointment.

And Shard on his island offered the Queen of the South the choicest of the old wines of Provence, and for adornment gave her Indian jewels looted from galleons with treasure for Madrid, and spread a table where she dined in the sun, while in some cabin below he bade the least coarse of his mariners sing; yet always she was morose and moody towards him, and often at evening he was heard to say that he wished he knew more about the ways of Queens. So they lived for years, the pirates mostly gambling and drinking below, Captain Shard trying to please the Queen of the South, and she never wholly forgetting Bombasharna. When they needed new provisions they hoisted sails on the trees, and as long as no ship came in sight they scudded before the wind, with the water rippling over the beach of the island; but as soon as they sighted a ship the sails came down, and they became an ordinary uncharted rock.

They mostly moved by night; sometimes they hovered off sea-coast towns as of old, sometimes they boldly entered river-mouths, and even attached themselves for a while to the mainland, whence they would plunder the neighbourhood and escape again to sea. And if a ship was wrecked on their island of a night they said it was all to the good. They grew very crafty in seamanship, and cunning in what they did, for they knew that any news of the *Desperate Lark*'s old crew would bring hangmen from the interior running down to every port.

And no one is known to have found them out or to have annexed their island; but a rumour arose and passed from port to port and every place where sailors meet together, and even survives to this day, of a dangerous uncharted rock anywhere between Plymouth and the Horn, which would suddenly rise in the safest track of ships, and upon which vessels were supposed to have been wrecked, leaving, strangely enough, no evidence of their doom. There was a little speculation about it at first, till it was silenced by the chance remark of a man old with wandering: "It is one of the mysteries that haunt the sea."

And almost Captain Shard and the Queen of the South lived happily ever after, though still at evening those on watch in the trees would see their captain sit with a puzzled air or hear him muttering now and again in a discontented way: "I wish I knew more about the ways of Queens."

MISS CUBBIDGE AND THE
DRAGON OF ROMANCE

This tale is told in the balconies of Belgrave Square and among the towers of Pont Street; men sing it at evening in the Brompton Road.

Little upon her eighteenth birthday thought Miss Cubbidge, of Number 12A Prince of Wales' Square, that before another year had gone its way she would lose the sight of that unshapely oblong that was so long her home. And, had you told her further that within that year all trace of that so-called square, and of the day when her father was elected by a thumping majority to share in the guidance of the destinies of the empire, should utterly fade from her memory, she would merely have said in that affected voice of hers, "Go to!"

There was nothing about it in the daily Press, the policy of her father's party had no provision for it, there was no hint of it in conversation at evening parties to which Miss Cubbidge went: there was nothing to warn her at all that a loathsome dragon with golden scales that rattled as he went should have come up clean out of the prime of romance and gone by night (so far as we know) through Hammersmith, and come to Ardle Mansions, and then had turned to his left, which of course brought him to Miss Cubbidge's father's house.

There sat Miss Cubbidge at evening on her balcony quite alone, waiting for her father to be made a baronet. She was wearing walking-boots and a hat and a low-necked evening dress; for a painter was but just now painting her portrait and neither she nor the painter saw anything odd in the strange combination. She did not notice the roar of the dragon's golden scales, nor distinguish above the manifold lights of London the small, red glare of his eyes. He suddenly lifted his head, a blaze of gold, over the balcony; he did not appear a yellow dragon then, for his glistening scales reflected the beauty that London puts upon her only at evening and night. She screamed, but to no knight, nor knew what knight to call on, nor guessed where were the dragons' overthrowers of far, romantic days, nor what mightier game they chased, or what wars they waged; perchance they were busy even then arming for Armageddon.

Out of the balcony of her father's house in Prince of Wales' Square, the painted dark-green balcony that grew blacker every year, the dragon lifted Miss Cubbidge and spread his rattling wings, and London fell away like an old fashion. And England fell away, and the smoke of its factories, and the round material world that goes humming round the sun vexed and pursued by time, until there appeared the eternal and ancient lands of Romance lying low by mystical seas.

You had not pictured Miss Cubbidge stroking the golden head of one of the dragons of song with one hand idly, while with the other she sometimes played with pearls brought up from lonely places of the sea. They filled huge haliotis shells with pearls and laid them there beside her, they brought her emeralds which she set to flash among the tresses of her long black hair, they brought her threaded sapphires for her cloak: all this the princes of fable did and the elves and the gnomes of myth. And partly she still lived, and partly she was one with long-ago and with those sacred tales that nurses tell, when all their children are good, and evening has come, and the fire is burning well, and the soft pat-pat of the snowflakes on the pane is like the furtive tread of fearful things in old, enchanted woods. If at first she missed those dainty novelties among which she was reared, the old, sufficient song of the mystical sea singing of faery lore at first soothed and at last consoled her. Even, she forgot those advertisements of pills that are so dear to England; even, she forgot political cant and the things that one discusses and the things that one does not, and had perforce to content herself with seeing sailing by huge golden-laden galleons with treasure for Madrid, and the merry skull-and-cross-bones of the pirateers, and the tiny nautilus setting out to sea, and ships of heroes trafficking in romance or of princes seeking for enchanted isles.

It was not by chains that the dragon kept her there, but by one of the spells of old. To one to whom the facilities of the daily Press had for so long been accorded spells would have palled—you would have said—and galleons after a time and all things out-of-date. After a time. But whether the centuries passed her or whether the years or whether no time at all, she did not know. If anything indicated the passing of time it was the rhythm of elfin horns blowing upon the heights. If the centuries went by her the spell that bound her gave her also perennial youth, and kept alight for ever the lantern by her side, and saved from decay the marble palace facing the mystical sea. And if no time went by her there at all, her single moment on those marvellous coasts was turned as it were to a crystal reflecting a thousand scenes. If it was all a dream, it was a dream that knew no morning and no fading away. The tide roamed on and whispered of mastery and of myth, while near that captive lady, asleep in his marble tank the golden dragon dreamed: and a little way out from the coast all that the dragon dreamed showed faintly in the mist that lay over the sea. He never dreamed of any rescuing knight. So long as he dreamed, it was twilight; but when he came up nimbly out of his tank night fell and starlight glistened on the dripping, golden scales.

There he and his captive either defeated Time or never encountered him at all; while, in the world we know, raged Roncesvalles or battles yet to be—I know not to what part of the shore of Romance he bore her. Perhaps she became one of those princesses of whom fable loves to tell, but let it suffice that there she lived by the sea: and kings ruled, and Demons ruled, and kings came again, and many cities returned to their native dust, and still she abided there, and still her marble palace passed not away nor the power that there was in the dragon's spell.

And only once did there ever come to her a message from the world that of old she knew. It came in a pearly ship across the mystical sea; it was from an old school-friend that she had had in Putney, merely a note, no more, in a little, neat, round hand: it said, "It is not Proper for you to be there alone."

THE QUEST OF THE QUEEN'S TEARS

Sylvia, Queen of the Woods, in her woodland palace, held court, and made a mockery of her suitors. She would sing to them, she said, she would give them banquets, she would tell them tales of legendary days, her jugglers should caper before them, her armies salute them, her fools crack jests with them and make whimsical quips, only she could not love them.

This was not the way, they said, to treat princes in their splendour and mysterious troubadours concealing kingly names; it was not in accordance with fable; myth had no precedent for it. She should have thrown her glove, they said, into some lion's den, she should have asked for a score of venomous heads of the serpents of Licantara, or demanded the death of any notable dragon, or sent them all upon some deadly quest, but that she could not love them—! It was unheard of—it had no parallel in the annals of romance.

And then she said that if they must needs have a quest she would offer her hand to him who first should move her to tears: and the quest should be called, for reference in histories or song, the Quest of the Queen's Tears, and he that achieved them she would wed, be he only a petty duke of lands unknown to romance.

And many were moved to anger, for they hoped for some bloody quest; but the old lords chamberlain said, as they muttered among themselves in a far, dark end of the chamber, that the quest was hard and wise, for that if she could ever weep she might also love. They had known her all her childhood; she had never sighed. Many men had she seen, suitors and courtiers, and had never turned her head after one went by. Her beauty was as still sunsets of bitter evenings when all the world is frore, a wonder and a chill. She was as a sun-stricken mountain uplifted alone, all beautiful with ice, a desolate and lonely radiance late at evening far up beyond the comfortable world, not quite to be companioned by the stars, the doom of the mountaineer.

If she could weep, they said, she could love, they said.

And she smiled pleasantly on those ardent princes, and troubadours concealing kingly names.

Then one by one they told, each suitor prince the story of his love, with outstretched hands and kneeling on the knee; and very sorry and pitiful were the tales, so that often up in the galleries some maid of the palace wept. And very graciously she nodded her head like a listless magnolia in the deeps of the night moving idly to all the breezes its glorious bloom.

And when the princes had told their desperate loves and had departed away with no other spoil than of their own tears only, even then there came the unknown troubadours and told their tales in song, concealing their gracious names.

And there was one, Ackronnion, clothed with rags, on which was the dust of roads, and underneath the rags was war-scarred armour whereon were the dints of blows; and when he stroked his harp and sang his song, in the gallery above maidens wept, and even old lords chamberlain whimpered among themselves and thereafter laughed through their tears and said: "It is easy to make old people weep and to bring idle tears from lazy girls; but he will not set a-weeping the Queen of the Woods."

And graciously she nodded, and he was the last. And disconsolate went away those dukes and princes, and troubadours in disguise. Yet Ackronnion pondered as he went away.

King he was of Afarmah, Lool and Haf, over-lord of Zeroora and hilly Chang, and duke of the dukedoms of Molong and Mlash, none of them unfamiliar with romance or unknown or overlooked in the making of myth. He pondered as he went in his thin disguise.

Now by those that do not remember their childhood, having other things to do, be it understood that underneath fairyland, which is, as all men know, at the edge of the world, there dwelleth the Gladsome Beast. A synonym he for joy.

It is known how the lark in its zenith, children at play out-of-doors, good witches and jolly old parents have all been compared—how aptly!—with this very same Gladsome Beast. Only one "crab" he has (if I may use slang for a moment to make myself perfectly clear), only one drawback, and that is that in the gladness of his heart he spoils the cabbages of the Old Man Who Looks After Fairyland,—and of course he eats men.

It must further be understood that whoever may obtain the tears of the Gladsome Beast in a bowl, and become drunken upon them, may move all persons to shed tears of joy so long as he remains inspired by the potion to sing or to make music.

Now Ackronnion pondered in this wise: that if he could obtain the tears of the Gladsome Beast by means of his art, withholding him from violence by the spell of music, and if a friend should slay the Gladsome Beast before his weeping ceased—for an end must come to weeping even with men—that so he might get safe away with the tears, and drink them before the Queen of the Woods and move her to tears of joy. He sought out therefore a humble knightly man who cared not for the beauty of Sylvia, Queen of the Woods, but had found a woodland maiden of his own once long ago in summer. And the man's name was Arrath, a subject of Ackronnion, a knight-at-arms of the spear-guard: and together they set out through the fields of fable until they came to Fairyland, a kingdom sunning itself (as all men know) for leagues along the edges of the world. And by a strange old pathway they came to the land they sought, through a wind blowing up the pathway sheer from space with a kind of metallic taste from the roving stars. Even so they came to the windy house of thatch where dwells the Old Man Who Looks After Fairyland sitting by parlour windows that look away from the world. He made them welcome in his star-ward parlour, telling them tales of Space, and when they named to him their perilous quest he said it would be a charity to kill the Gladsome Beast; for he was clearly one of those that liked not its happy ways. And then he took them out through his back door, for the front door had no pathway nor even a step—from it the old man used to empty his slops sheer on to the Southern Cross—and so they came to the garden wherein his cabbages were, and those flowers that only blow in Fairyland, turning their faces always towards the comet, and he pointed them out the way to the place he called Underneath, where the Gladsome Beast had his lair. Then they manoeuvred. Ackronnion was to go by the way of the steps with his harp and an agate bowl, while Arrath went round by a crag on the other side. Then the Old Man Who Looks After Fairyland went back to his windy house, muttering angrily as he passed his cabbages, for he did not love the ways of the Gladsome Beast; and the two friends parted on their separate ways.

Nothing perceived them but that ominous crow glutted overlong already upon the flesh of man.

The wind blew bleak from the stars.

At first there was dangerous climbing, and then Ackronnion gained the smooth, broad steps that led from the edge to the lair, and at that moment heard at the top of the steps the continuous chuckles of the Gladsome Beast.

He feared then that its mirth might be insuperable, not to be saddened by the most grievous song; nevertheless he did not turn back then, but softly climbed the stairs and, placing the agate bowl upon a step, struck up the chaunt called Dolorous. It told of desolate, regretted things befallen happy cities long since in the prime of the world. It told of how the gods and beasts and men had long ago loved beautiful companions, and long ago in vain. It told of the golden host of happy hopes, but not of their achieving. It told how Love scorned Death, but told of Death's laughter. The contented chuckles of the Gladsome Beast suddenly ceased in his lair. He rose and shook himself. He was still unhappy. Ackronnion still sang on the chaunt called Dolorous. The Gladsome Beast came mournfully up to him. Ackronnion ceased not for the sake of his panic, but still sang on. He sang of the malignity of time. Two tears welled large in the eyes of the Gladsome Beast. Ackronnion moved the agate bowl to a suitable spot with his foot. He sang of autumn and of passing away. Then the beast wept as the frore hills weep in the thaw, and the tears splashed big into the agate bowl. Ackronnion desperately chaunted on; he told of the glad unnoticed things men see and do not see again, of sunlight beheld unheeded on faces now withered away. The bowl was full. Ackronnion was desperate: the Beast was so close. Once he thought that its mouth was watering!—but it was only the tears that had run on the lips of the Beast. He felt as a morsel! The Beast was ceasing to weep! He sang of worlds that had disappointed the gods. And all of a sudden, crash! and the staunch spear of Arrath went home behind the shoulder, and the tears and the joyful ways of the Gladsome Beast were ended and over for ever.

And carefully they carried the bowl of tears away, leaving the body of the Gladsome Beast as a change of diet for the ominous crow; and going by the windy house of thatch they said farewell to the Old Man Who Looks After Fairyland, who when he heard of the deed rubbed his hands together and mumbled again and again, "And a very good thing, too. My cabbages! My cabbages!"

And not long after Ackronnion sang again in the sylvan palace of the Queen of the Woods, having first drunk all the tears in his agate bowl. And it was a gala night, and all the court were there and ambassadors from the lands of legend and myth, and even some from Terra Cognita.

And Ackronnion sang as he never sang before, and will not sing again. O, but dolorous, dolorous, are all the ways of man, few and fierce are his days, and the end trouble, and vain, vain his endeavour: and woman—who shall tell of it?—her doom is written with man's by listless, careless gods with their faces to other spheres.

Somewhat thus he began, and then inspiration seized him, and all the trouble in the beauty of his song may not be set down by me: there was much of gladness in it, and all mingled with grief: it was like the way of man: it was like our destiny.

Sobs arose at his song, sighs came back along echoes: seneschals, soldiers, sobbed, and a clear cry made the maidens; like rain the tears came down from gallery to gallery.

All round the Queen of the Woods was a storm of sobbing and sorrow.

But no, she would not weep.

THE HOARD OF THE GIBBELINS

The Gibbelins eat, as is well known, nothing less good than man. Their evil tower is joined to Terra Cognita, to the lands we know, by a bridge. Their hoard is beyond reason; avarice has no use for it; they have a separate cellar for emeralds and a separate cellar for sapphires; they have filled a hole with gold and dig it up when they need it. And the only use that is known for their ridiculous wealth is to attract to their larder a continual supply of food. In times of famine they have even been known to scatter rubies abroad, a little trail of them to some city of Man, and sure enough their larders would soon be full again.

Their tower stands on the other side of that river known to Homer—*ho rhoos okeanoio*, as he called it—which surrounds the world. And where the river is narrow and fordable the tower was built by the Gibbelins' gluttonous sires, for they liked to see burglars rowing easily to their steps. Some nourishment that common soil has not the huge trees drained there with their colossal roots from both banks of the river.

There the Gibbelins lived and discreditably fed.

Alderic, Knight of the Order of the City and the Assault, hereditary Guardian of the King's Peace of Mind, a man not unremembered among makers of myth, pondered so long upon the Gibbelins' hoard that by now he deemed it his. Alas that I should say of so perilous a venture, undertaken at dead of night by a valorous man, that its motive was sheer avarice! Yet upon avarice only the Gibbelins relied to keep their larders full, and once in every hundred years sent spies into the cities of men to see how avarice did, and always the spies returned again to the tower saying that all was well.

It may be thought that, as the years went on and men came by fearful ends on that tower's wall, fewer and fewer would come to the Gibbelins' table: but the Gibbelins found otherwise.

Not in the folly and frivolity of his youth did Alderic come to the tower, but he studied carefully for several years the manner in which burglars met their doom when they went in search of the treasure that he considered his. *In every case they had entered by the door.*

He consulted those who gave advice on this quest; he noted every detail and cheerfully paid their fees, and determined to do nothing that they advised, for what were their clients now? No more than examples of the savoury art, and mere half-forgotten memories of a meal; and many, perhaps, no longer even that.

These were the requisites for the quest that these men used to advise: a horse, a boat, mail armour, and at least three men-at-arms. Some said, "Blow the horn at the tower door"; others said, "Do not touch it."

Alderic thus decided: he would take no horse down to the river's edge, he would not row along it in a boat, and he would go alone and by way of the Forest Unpassable.

How pass, you may say, the unpassable? This was his plan: there was a dragon he knew of who if peasants' prayers are heeded deserved to die, not alone because of the number of maidens he cruelly slew, but because he was bad for the crops; he ravaged the very land and was the bane of a dukedom.

Now Alderic determined to go up against him. So he took horse and spear and pricked till he met the dragon, and the dragon came out against him breathing bitter smoke. And to him Alderic shouted, "Hath foul dragon ever slain true knight?" And well the dragon knew that this had never been, and he hung his head and was silent, for he was glutted with blood. "Then," said the knight, "if thou would'st ever taste maiden's blood again thou shalt be my trusty steed, and if not, by this spear there shall befall thee all that the troubadours tell of the dooms of thy breed."

And the dragon did not open his ravening mouth, nor rush upon the knight, breathing out fire; for well he knew the fate of those that did these things, but he consented to the terms imposed, and swore to the knight to become his trusty steed.

It was on a saddle upon this dragon's back that Alderic afterwards sailed above the unpassable forest, even above the tops of those measure-less trees, children of wonder. But first he pondered that subtle plan of his which was more profound than merely to avoid all that had been done before; and he commanded a blacksmith, and the blacksmith made him a pickaxe.

Now there was great rejoicing at the rumour of Alderic's quest, for all folk knew that he was a cautious man, and they deemed that he would succeed and enrich the world, and they rubbed their hands in the cities at the thought of largesse; and there was joy among all men in Alderic's country, except perchance among the lenders of money, who feared they would soon be paid. And there was rejoicing also because men hoped that when the Gibbelins were robbed of their hoard, they would shatter their high-built bridge and break the golden chains that bound them to the world, and drift back, they and their tower, to the moon, from which they had come and to which they rightly belonged. There was little love for the Gibbelins, though all men envied their hoard.

So they all cheered, that day when he mounted his dragon, as though he was already a conqueror, and what pleased them more than the good that they hoped he would do to the world was that he scattered gold as he rode away; for he would not need it, he said, if he found the Gibbelins' hoard, and he would not need it more if he smoked on the Gibbelins' table.

When they heard that he had rejected the advice of those that gave it, some said that the knight was mad, and others said he was greater than those what gave the advice, but none appreciated the worth of his plan.

He reasoned thus: for centuries men had been well advised and had gone by the cleverest way, while the Gibbelins came to expect them to come by boat and to look for them at the door whenever their larder was empty, even as a man looketh for a snipe in a marsh; but how, said Alderic, if a snipe should sit in the top of a tree, and would men find him there? Assuredly never! So Alderic decided to swim the river and not to go by the door, but to pick his way into the tower through the stone. Moreover, it was in his mind to work below the level of the ocean, the river (as Homer knew) that girdles the world, so that as soon as he made a hole in the wall the water should pour in, confounding the Gibbelins, and flooding the cellars, rumoured to be twenty feet in depth, and therein he would dive for emeralds as a diver dives for pearls.

And on the day that I tell of he galloped away from his home scattering largesse of gold, as I have said, and passed through many kingdoms, the dragon snapping at maidens as he went, but being unable to eat them because of the bit in his mouth, and earning no gentler reward than a spur-thrust where he was softest. And so they came to the swart arboreal precipice of the unpassable forest. The dragon rose at it with a rattle of wings. Many a farmer near the edge of the world saw him up there where yet the twilight lingered, a faint, black, wavering line; and mistaking him for a row of geese going inland from the ocean, went into their houses cheerily rubbing their hands and saying that winter was coming, and that we should soon have snow. Soon even there the twilight faded away, and when they descended at the edge of the world it was night and the moon was shining. Ocean, the ancient river, narrow and shallow there, flowed by and made no murmur. Whether the Gibbelins banqueted or whether they watched by the door, they also made no murmur. And Alderic dismounted and took his armour off, and saying one prayer to his lady, swam with his pickaxe. He did not part from his sword, for fear that he meet with a Gibbelin. Landed the other side, he began to work at once, and all went well with him. Nothing put out its head from any window, and all were lighted so that nothing within could see him in the dark. The blows of his pickaxe were dulled in the deep walls. All night he worked, no sound came to molest him, and at dawn the last rock swerved and tumbled inwards, and the river poured in after. Then Alderic took a stone, and went to the bottom step, and hurled the stone at the door; he heard the echoes roll into the tower, then he ran back and dived through the hole in the wall.

He was in the emerald-cellar. There was no light in the lofty vault above him, but, diving through twenty feet of water, he felt the floor all rough with emeralds, and open coffers full of them. By a faint ray of the moon he saw that the water was green with them, and, easily filling a satchel, he rose again to the surface; and there were the Gibbelins waist-deep in the water, with torches in their hands! And, without saying a word, *or even smiling*, they neatly hanged him on the outer wall—and the tale is one of those that have not a happy ending.

HOW NUTH WOULD HAVE PRACTISED HIS ART UPON THE GNOLES

Despite the advertisements of rival firms, it is probable that every tradesman knows that nobody in business at the present time has a position equal to that of Mr. Nuth. To those outside the magic circle of business, his name is scarcely known; he does not need to advertise, he is consummate. He is superior even to modern competition, and, whatever claims they boast, his rivals know it. His terms are moderate, so much cash down when the goods are delivered, so much in blackmail afterwards. He consults your convenience. His skill may be counted upon; I have seen a shadow on a windy night move more noisily than Nuth, for Nuth is a burglar by trade. Men have been known to stay in country houses and to send a dealer afterwards to bargain for a piece of tapestry that they saw there—some article of furniture, some picture. This is bad taste: but those whose culture is more elegant invariably send Nuth a night or two after their visit. He has a way with tapestry; you would scarcely notice that the edges had been cut. And often when I see some huge, new house full of old furniture and portraits from other ages, I say to myself, "These mouldering chairs, these full-length ancestors and carved mahogany are the produce of the incomparable Nuth."

It may be urged against my use of the word incomparable that in the burglary business the name of Slith stands paramount and alone; and of this I am not ignorant; but Slith is a classic, and lived long ago, and knew nothing at all of modern competition; besides which the surprising nature of his doom has possibly cast a glamour upon Slith that exaggerates in our eyes his undoubted merits.

It must not be thought that I am a friend of Nuth's; on the contrary such politics as I have are on the side of Property; and he needs no words from me, for his position is almost unique in trade, being among the very few that do not need to advertise.

At the time that my story begins Nuth lived in a roomy house in Belgrave Square: in his inimitable way he had made friends with the caretaker. The place suited Nuth, and, whenever anyone came to inspect it before purchase, the caretaker used to praise the house in the words that Nuth had suggested. "If it wasn't for the drains," she would say, "it's the finest house in London," and when they pounced on this remark and asked questions about the drains, she would answer them that the drains also were good, but not so good as the house. They did not see Nuth when they went over the rooms, but Nuth was there.

Here in a neat black dress on one spring morning came an old woman whose bonnet was lined with red, asking for Mr. Nuth; and with her came her large and awkward son. Mrs. Eggins, the caretaker, glanced up the street, and then she let them in, and left them to wait in the drawing-room amongst furniture all mysterious with sheets. For a long while they waited, and then there was a smell of pipe-tobacco, and there was Nuth standing quite close to them.

"Lord," said the old woman whose bonnet was lined with red, "you did make me start." And then she saw by his eyes that that was not the way to speak to Mr. Nuth.

And at last Nuth spoke, and very nervously the old woman explained that her son was a likely lad, and had been in business already but wanted to better himself, and she wanted Mr. Nuth to teach him a livelihood.

First of all Nuth wanted to see a business reference, and when he was shown one from a jeweller with whom he happened to be hand-in-glove the upshot of it was that he agreed to take young Tonker (for this was the surname of the likely lad) and to make him his apprentice. And the old woman whose bonnet was lined with red went back to her little cottage in the country, and every evening said to her old man, "Tonker, we must fasten the shutters of a night-time, for Tommy's a burglar now."

The details of the likely lad's apprenticeship I do not propose to give; for those that are in the business know those details already, and those that are in other businesses care only for their own, while men of leisure who have no trade at all would fail to appreciate the gradual degrees by which Tommy Tonker came first to cross bare boards, covered with little obstacles in the dark, without making any sound, and then to go silently up creaky stairs, and then to open doors, and lastly to climb.

Let it suffice that the business prospered greatly, while glowing reports of Tommy Tonker's progress were sent from time to time to the old woman whose bonnet was lined with red in the labourious handwriting of Nuth. Nuth had given up lessons in writing very early, for he seemed to have some prejudice against forgery, and therefore considered writing a waste of time. And then there came the transaction with Lord Castlenorman at his Surrey residence. Nuth selected a Saturday night, for it chanced that Saturday was observed as Sabbath in the family of Lord Castlenorman, and by eleven o'clock the whole house was quiet. Five minutes before midnight Tommy Tonker, instructed by Mr. Nuth, who waited outside, came away with one pocketful of rings and shirt-studs. It was quite a light pocketful, but the jewellers in Paris could not match it without sending specially to Africa, so that Lord Castlenorman had to borrow bone shirt-studs.

Not even rumour whispered the name of Nuth. Were I to say that this turned his head, there are those to whom the assertion would give pain, for his associates hold that his astute judgment was unaffected by circumstance. I will say, therefore, that it spurred his genius to plan what no burglar had ever planned before. It was nothing less than to burgle the house of the gnoles. And this that abstemious man unfolded to Tonker over a cup of tea. Had Tonker not been nearly insane with pride over their recent transaction, and had he not been blinded by a veneration for Nuth, he would have—but I cry over spilt milk. He expostulated respectfully; he said he would rather not go; he said it was not fair; he allowed himself to argue; and in the end, one windy October morning with a menace in the air found him and Nuth drawing near to the dreadful wood.

Nuth, by weighing little emeralds against pieces of common rock, had ascertained the probable weight of those house-ornaments that the gnoles are believed to possess in the narrow, lofty house wherein they have dwelt from of old. They decided to steal two emeralds and to carry them between them on a cloak; but if they should be too heavy one must be dropped at once. Nuth warned young Tonker against greed, and explained that the emeralds were worth less than cheese until they were safe away from the dreadful wood.

Everything had been planned, and they walked now in silence.

No track led up to the sinister gloom of the trees, either of men or cattle; not even a poacher had been there snaring elves for over a hundred years. You did not trespass twice in the dells of the gnoles. And, apart from the things that were done there, the trees themselves were a warning, and did not wear the wholesome look of those that we plant ourselves.

The nearest village was some miles away with the backs of all its houses turned to the wood, and without one window at all facing in that direction. They did not speak of it there, and elsewhere it is unheard of.

Into this wood stepped Nuth and Tommy Tonker. They had no fire-arms. Tonker had asked for a pistol, but Nuth replied that the sound of a shot "would bring everything down on us," and no more was said about it.

Into the wood they went all day, deeper and deeper. They saw the skeleton of some early Georgian poacher nailed to a door in an oak tree; sometimes they saw a fairy scuttle away from them; once Tonker stepped heavily on a hard, dry stick, after which they both lay still for twenty minutes. And the sunset flared full of omens through the tree trunks, and night fell, and they came by fitful starlight, as Nuth had foreseen, to that lean, high house where the gnoles so secretly dwelt.

All was so silent by that unvalued house that the faded courage of Tonker flickered up, but to Nuth's experienced sense it seemed too silent; and all the while there was that look in the sky that was worse than a spoken doom, so that Nuth, as is often the case when men are in doubt, had leisure to fear the worst. Nevertheless he did not abandon the business, but sent the likely lad with the instruments of his trade by means of the ladder to the old green casement. And the moment that Tonker touched the withered boards, the silence that, though ominous, was earthly, became unearthly like the touch of a ghoul. And Tonker heard his breath offending against that silence, and his heart was like mad drums in a night attack, and a string of one of his sandals went tap on a rung of a ladder, and the leaves of the forest were mute, and the breeze of the night was still; and Tonker prayed that a mouse or a mole might make any noise at all, but not a creature stirred, even Nuth was still. And then and there, while yet he was undiscovered, the likely lad made up his mind, as he should have done long before, to leave those colossal emeralds where they were and have nothing further to do with the lean, high house of the gnoles, but to quit this sinister wood in the nick of time and retire from business at once and buy a place in the country. Then he descended softly and beckoned to Nuth. But the gnoles had watched him through knavish holes that they bore in trunks of the trees, and the unearthly silence gave way, as it were with a grace, to the rapid screams of Tonker as they picked him up from behind—screams that came faster and faster until they were incoherent. And where they took him it is not good to ask, and what they did with him I shall not say.

Nuth looked on for a while from the corner of the house with a mild surprise on his face as he rubbed his chin, for the trick of the holes in the trees was new to him; then he stole nimbly away through the dreadful wood.

"And did they catch Nuth?" you ask me, gentle reader.

"Oh, no, my child" (for such a question is childish). "Nobody ever catches Nuth."

HOW ONE CAME, AS WAS FORETOLD, TO THE CITY OF NEVER

The child that played about the terraces and gardens in sight of the Surrey hills never knew that it was he that should come to the Ultimate City, never knew that he should see the Under Pits, the barbicans and the holy minarets of the mightiest city known. I think of him now as a child with a little red watering-can going about the gardens on a summer's day that lit the warm south country, his imagination delighted with all tales of quite little adventures, and all the while there was reserved for him that feat at which men wonder.

Looking in other directions, away from the Surrey hills, through all his infancy he saw that precipice that, wall above wall and mountain above mountain, stands at the edge of the World, and in perpetual twilight alone with the Moon and the Sun holds up the inconceivable City of Never. To tread its streets he was destined; prophecy knew it. He had the magic halter, and a worn old rope it was; an old wayfaring woman had given it to him: it had the power to hold any animal whose race had never known captivity, such as the unicorn, the hippogriff Pegasus, dragons and wyverns; but with a lion, giraffe, camel or horse it was useless.

How often we have seen that City of Never, that marvel of the Nations! Not when it is night in the World, and we can see no further than the stars; not when the sun is shining where we dwell, dazzling our eyes; but when the sun has set on some stormy days, all at once repentant at evening, and those glittering cliffs reveal themselves which we almost take to be clouds, and it is twilight with us as it is for ever with them, then on their gleaming summits we see those golden domes that overpeer the edges of the World and seem to dance with dignity and calm in that gentle light of evening that is Wonder's native haunt. Then does the City of Never, unvisited and afar, look long at her sister the World.

It had been prophecied that he should come there. They knew it when the pebbles were being made and before the isles of coral were given unto the sea. And thus the prophecy came unto fulfilment and passed into history, and so at length to Oblivion, out of which I drag it as it goes floating by, into which I shall one day tumble. The hippogriffs dance before dawn in the upper air; long before sunrise flashes upon our lawns they go to glitter in light that has not yet come to the World, and as the dawn works up from the ragged hills and the stars feel it they go slanting earthwards, till sunlight touches the tops of the tallest trees, and the hippogriffs alight with a rattle of quills and fold their wings and gallop and gambol away till they come to some prosperous, wealthy, detestable town, and they leap at once from the fields and soar away from the sight of it, pursued by the horrible smoke of it until they come again to the pure blue air.

He whom prophecy had named from of old to come to the City of Never, went down one midnight with his magic halter to a lake-side where the hippogriffs alighted at dawn, for the turf was soft there and they could gallop far before they came to a town, and there he waited hidden near their hoofmarks. And the stars paled a little and grew indistinct; but there was no other sign as yet of the dawn, when there appeared far up in the deeps of the night two little saffron specks, then four and five: it was the hippogriffs dancing and twirling around in the sun. Another flock joined them, there were twelve of them now; they danced there, flashing their colours back to the sun, they descended in wide curves slowly; trees down on earth revealed against the sky, jet-black each delicate twig; a star disappeared from a cluster, now another; and dawn came on like music, like a new song. Ducks shot by to the lake from still dark fields of corn, far voicesuttered, a colour grew upon water, and still the hippogriffs gloried in the light, revelling up in the sky; but when pigeons stirred on the branches and the first small bird was abroad, and little coots from the rushes ventured to peer about, then there came down on a sudden with a thunder of feathers the hippogriffs, and, as they landed from their celestial heights all bathed with the day's first sunlight, the man whose destiny it was as from of old to come to the City of Never, sprang up and caught the last with the magic halter. It plunged, but could not escape it, for the hippogriffs are of the uncaptured races, and magic has power over the magical, so the man mounted it, and it soared again for the heights whence it had come, as a wounded beast goes home. But when they came to the heights that venturous rider saw huge and fair to the left of him the destined City of Never, and he beheld the towers of Lel and Lek, Neerib and Akathooma, and the cliffs of Toldenarba a-glistening in the twilight like an alabaster statue of the Evening. Towards them he wrenched the halter, towards Toldenarba and the Under Pits; the wings of the hippogriff roared as the halter turned him. Of the Under Pits who shall tell? Their mystery is secret. It is held by some that they are the sources of night, and that darkness pours from them at evening upon the world; while others hint that knowledge of these might undo our civilization.

There watched him ceaselessly from the Under Pits those eyes whose duty it is; from further within and deeper, the bats that dwell there arose when they saw the surprise in the eyes; the sentinels on the bulwarks beheld that stream of bats and lifted up their spears as it were for war. Nevertheless when they perceived that that war for which they watched was not now come upon them, they lowered their spears and suffered him to enter, and he passed whirring through the earthward gateway. Even so he came, as foretold, to the City of Never perched upon Toldenarba, and saw late twilight on those pinnacles that know no other light. All the domes were of copper, but the spires on their summits were gold. Little steps of onyx ran all this way and that. With cobbled agates were its streets a glory.

Through small square panes of rose-quartz the citizens looked from their houses. To them as they looked abroad the World far-off seemed happy. Clad though that city was in one robe always, in twilight, yet was its beauty worthy of even so lovely a wonder: city and twilight were both peerless but for each other. Built of a stone unknown in the world we tread were its bastions, quarried we know not where, but called by the gnomes *abyx*, it so flashed back to the twilight its glories, colour for colour, that none can say of them where their boundary is, and which the eternal twilight, and which the City of Never; they are the twin-born children, the fairest daughters of Wonder. Time had been there, but not to work destruction; he had turned to a fair, pale green the domes that were made of copper, the rest he had left untouched, even he, the destroyer of cities, by what bribe I know not averted. Nevertheless they often wept in Never for change and passing away, mourning catastrophes in other worlds, and they built temples sometimes to ruined stars that had fallen flaming down from the Milky Way, giving them worship still when by us long since forgotten. Other temples they have—who knows to what divinities?

And he that was destined alone of men to come to the City of Never was well content to behold it as he trotted down its agate street, with the wings of his hippogriff furled, seeing at either side of him marvel on marvel of which even China is ignorant. Then as he neared the city's further rampart by which no inhabitant stirred, and looked in a direction to which no houses faced with any rose-pink windows, he suddenly saw far-off, dwarfing the mountains, an even greater city. Whether that city was built upon the twilight or whether it rose from the coasts of some other world he did not know. He saw it dominate the City of Never, and strove to reach it; but at this unmeasured home of unknown colossi the hippogriff shied frantically, and neither the magic halter nor anything that he did could make the monster face it. At last, from the City of Never's lonely outskirts where no inhabitants walked, the rider turned slowly earthward. He knew now why all the windows faced this way—the denizens of the twilight gazed at the world and not at a greater than them. Then from the last step of the earthward stairway, like lead past the Under Pits and down the glittering face of Toldenarba, down from the overshadowed glories of the gold-tipped City of Never and out of perpetual twilight, swooped the man on his winged monster: the wind that slept at the time leaped up like a dog at their onrush, it uttered a cry and ran past them. Down on the World it was morning; night was roaming away with his cloak trailed behind him, white mists turned over and over as he went, the orb was grey but it glittered, lights blinked surprisingly in early windows, forth over wet, dim fields went cows from their houses: even in this hour touched the fields again the feet of the hippogriff. And the moment that the man dismounted and took off his magic halter the hippogriff flew slanting away with a whirr, going back to some airy dancing-place of his people.

And he that surmounted glittering Toldenarba and came alone of men to the City of Never has his name and his fame among nations; but he and the people of that twilit city well know two things unguessed by other men, they that there is another city fairer than theirs, and he—a deed unaccomplished.

THE CORONATION OF MR. THOMAS SHAP

It was the occupation of Mr. Thomas Shap to persuade customers that the goods were genuine and of an excellent quality, and that as regards the price their unspoken will was consulted. And in order to carry on this occupation he went by train very early every morning some few miles nearer to the City from the suburb in which he slept. This was the use to which he put his life.

From the moment when he first perceived (not as one reads a thing in a book, but as truths are revealed to one's instinct) the very beastliness of his occupation, and of the house that he slept in, its shape, make and pretensions, and even of the clothes that he wore; from that moment he withdrew his dreams from it, his fancies, his ambitions, everything in fact except that ponderable Mr. Shap that dressed in a frock-coat, bought tickets and handled money and could in turn be handled by the statistician. The priest's share in Mr. Shap, the share of the poet, never caught the early train to the City at all.

He used to take little flights of fancy at first, dwelt all day in his dreamy way on fields and rivers lying in the sunlight where it strikes the world more brilliantly further South. And then he began to imagine butterflies there; after that, silken people and the temples they built to their gods.

They noticed that he was silent, and even absent at times, but they found no fault with his behaviour with customers, to whom he remained as plausible as of old. So he dreamed for a year, and his fancy gained strength as he dreamed. He still read halfpenny papers in the train, still discussed the passing day's ephemeral topic, still voted at elections, though he no longer did these things with the whole Shap—his soul was no longer in them.

He had had a pleasant year, his imagination was all new to him still, and it had often discovered beautiful things away where it went, southeast at the edge of the twilight. And he had a matter-of-fact and logical mind, so that he often said, "Why should I pay my twopence at the electric theatre when I can see all sorts of things quite easily without?" Whatever he did was logical before anything else, and those that knew him always spoke of Shap as "a sound, sane, level-headed man."

On far the most important day of his life he went as usual to town by the early train to sell plausible articles to customers, while the spiritual Shap roamed off to fanciful lands. As he walked from the station, dreamy but wide awake, it suddenly struck him that the real Shap was not the one walking to Business in black and ugly clothes, but he who roamed along a jungle's edge near the ramparts of an old and Eastern city that rose up sheer from the sand, and against which the desert lapped with one eternal wave. He used to fancy the name of that city was Larkar. "After all, the fancy is as real as the body," he said with perfect logic. It was a dangerous theory.

For that other life that he led he realized, as in Business, the importance and value of method. He did not let his fancy roam too far until it perfectly knew its first surroundings. Particularly he avoided the jungle—he was not afraid to meet a tiger there (after all it was not real), but stranger things might crouch there. Slowly he built up Larkar: rampart by rampart, towers for archers, gateway of brass, and all. And then one day he argued, and quite rightly, that all the silk-clad people in its streets, their camels, their wares that came from Inkustahn, the city itself, were all the things of his will—and then he made himself King. He smiled after that when people did not raise their hats to him in the street, as he walked from the station to Business; but he was sufficiently practical to recognize that it was better not to talk of this to those that only knew him as Mr. Shap.

Now that he was King in the city of Larkar and in all the desert that lay to the East and North he sent his fancy to wander further afield. He took the regiments of his camel-guards and went jingling out of Larkar, with little silver bells under the camels' chins, and came to other cities far-off on the yellow sand, with clear white walls and towers, uplifting themselves in the sun. Through their gates he passed with his three silken regiments, the light-blue regiment of the camel-guards being upon his right and the green regiment riding at his left, the lilac regiment going on before. When he had gone through the streets of any city and observed the ways of its people, and had seen the way that the sunlight struck its towers, he would proclaim himself King there, and then ride on in fancy. So he passed from city to city and from land to land. Clear-sighted though Mr. Shap was, I think he overlooked the lust of aggrandizement to which kings have so often been victims; and so it was that when the first few cities had opened their gleaming gates and he saw peoples prostrate before his camel, and spearmen cheering along countless balconies, and priests come out to do him reverence, he that had never had even the lowliest authority in the familiar world became unwisely insatiate. He let his fancy ride at inordinate speed, he forsook method, scarce was he king of a land but he yearned to extend his borders; so he journeyed deeper and deeper into the wholly unknown. The concentration that he gave to this inordinate progress through countries of which history is ignorant and cities so fantastic in their bulwarks that, though their inhabitants were human, yet the foe that they feared seemed something less or more; the amazement with which he beheld gates and towers unknown even to art, and furtive people thronging intricate ways to acclaim him as their sovereign—all these things began to affect his capacity for Business. He knew as well as any that his fancy could not rule these beautiful lands unless that other Shap, however unimportant, were well sheltered and fed: and shelter and food meant money, and money, Business. His was more like the mistake of some gambler with cunning schemes who overlooks human greed. One day his fancy, riding in the morning, came to a city gorgeous as the sunrise, in whose opalescent wall were gates of gold, so huge that a river poured between the bars, floating in, when the gates were opened, large galleons under sail. Thence there came dancing out a company with instruments, and made a melody all around the wall; that morning Mr. Shap, the bodily Shap in London, forgot the train to town.

Until a year ago he had never imagined at all; it is not to be wondered at that all these things now newly seen by his fancy should play tricks at first with the memory of even so sane a man. He gave up reading the papers altogether, he lost all interest in politics, he cared less and less for things that were going on around him. This unfortunate missing of the morning train even occurred again, and the firm spoke to him severely about it. But he had his consolation. Were not Arathrion and Argun Zeerith and all the level coasts of Oora his? And even as the firm found fault with him his fancy watched the yaks on weary journeys, slow specks against the snow-fields, bringing tribute; and saw the green eyes of the mountain men who had looked at him strangely in the city of Nith when he had entered it by the desert door. Yet his logic did not forsake him; he knew well that his strange subjects did not exist, but he was prouder of having created them with his brain, than merely of ruling them only; thus in his pride he felt himself something more great than a king, he did not dare to think what! He went into the temple of the city of Zorra and stood some time there alone: all the priests kneeled to him when he came away.

He cared less and less for the things we care about, for the affairs of Shap, the business-man in London. He began to despise the man with a royal contempt.

One day when he sat in Sowla, the city of the Thuls, throned on one amethyst, he decided, and it was proclaimed on the moment by silver trumpets all along the land, that he would be crowned as king over all the lands of Wonder.

By that old temple where the Thuls were worshipped, year in, year out, for over a thousand years, they pitched pavilions in the open air. The trees that blew there threw out radiant scents unknown in any countries that know the map; the stars blazed fiercely for that famous occasion. A fountain hurled up, clattering, ceaselessly into the air armfuls on armfuls of diamonds. A deep hush waited for the golden trumpets, the holy coronation night was come. At the top of those old, worn steps, going down we know not whither, stood the king in the emerald-and-amethyst cloak, the ancient garb of the Thuls; beside him lay that Sphinx that for the last few weeks had advised him in his affairs.

Slowly, with music when the trumpets sounded, came up towards him from we know not where, one-hundred-and-twenty archbishops, twenty angels and two archangels, with that terrific crown, the diadem of the Thuls. They knew as they came up to him that promotion awaited them all because of this night's work. Silent, majestic, the king awaited them.

The doctors downstairs were sitting over their supper, the warders softly slipped from room to room, and when in that cosy dormitory of Hanwell they saw the king still standing erect and royal, his face resolute, they came up to him and addressed him:

"Go to bed," they said—"pretty bed." So he lay down and soon was fast asleep: the great day was over.

CHU-BU AND SHEEMISH

It was the custom on Tuesdays in the temple of Chu-bu for the priests to enter at evening and chant, "There is none but Chu-bu."

And all the people rejoiced and cried out, "There is none but Chu-bu." And honey was offered to Chu-bu, and maize and fat. Thus was he magnified.

Chu-bu was an idol of some antiquity, as may be seen from the colour of the wood. He had been carved out of mahogany, and after he was carved he had been polished. Then they had set him up on the diorite pedestal with the brazier in front of it for burning spices and the flat gold plates for fat. Thus they worshipped Chu-bu.

He must have been there for over a hundred years when one day the priests came in with another idol into the temple of Chu-bu, and set it up on a pedestal near Chu-bu's and sang, "There is also Sheemish."

And all the people rejoiced and cried out, "There is also Sheemish."

Sheemish was palpably a modern idol, and although the wood was stained with a dark-red dye, you could see that he had only just been carved. And honey was offered to Sheemish as well as Chu-bu, and also maize and fat.

The fury of Chu-bu knew no time-limit: he was furious all that night, and next day he was furious still. The situation called for immediate miracles. To devastate the city with a pestilence and kill all his priests was scarcely within his power, therefore he wisely concentrated such divine powers as he had in commanding a little earthquake. "Thus," thought Chu-bu, "will I reassert myself as the only god, and men shall spit upon Sheemish."

Chu-bu willed it and willed it and still no earthquake came, when suddenly he was aware that the hated Sheemish was daring to attempt a miracle too. He ceased to busy himself about the earthquake and listened, or shall I say felt, for what Sheemish was thinking; for gods are aware of what passes in the mind by a sense that is other than any of our five. Sheemish was trying to make an earthquake too.

The new god's motive was probably to assert himself. I doubt if Chu-bu understood or cared for his motive; it was sufficient for an idol already aflame with jealousy that his detestable rival was on the verge of a miracle. All the power of Chu-bu veered round at once and set dead against an earthquake, even a little one. It was thus in the temple of Chu-bu for some time, and then no earthquake came.

To be a god and to fail to achieve a miracle is a despairing sensation; it is as though among men one should determine upon a hearty sneeze and as though no sneeze should come; it is as though one should try to swim in heavy boots or remember a name that is utterly forgotten: all these pains were Sheemish's.

And upon Tuesday the priests came in, and the people, and they did worship Chu-bu and offered fat to him, saying, "O Chu-bu who made everything," and then the priests sang, "There is also Sheemish"; and Chu-bu was put to shame and spake not for three days.

Now there were holy birds in the temple of Chu-bu, and when the third day was come and the night thereof, it was as it were revealed to the mind of Chu-bu, that there was dirt upon the head of Sheemish.

And Chu-bu spake unto Sheemish as speak the gods, moving no lips nor yet disturbing the silence, saying, "There is dirt upon thy head, O Sheemish." All night long he muttered again and again, "there is dirt upon Sheemish's head." And when it was dawn and voices were heard far off, Chu-bu became exultant with Earth's awakening things, and cried out till the sun was high, "Dirt, dirt, dirt, upon the head of Sheemish," and at noon he said, "So Sheemish would be a god." Thus was Sheemish confounded.

And with Tuesday one came and washed his head with rose-water, and he was worshipped again when they sang "There is also Sheemish." And yet was Chu-bu content, for he said, "The head of Sheemish has been defiled," and again, "His head was defiled, it is enough." And one evening lo! there was dirt on the head of Chu-bu also, and the thing was perceived of Sheemish.

It is not with the gods as it is with men. We are angry one with another and turn from our anger again, but the wrath of the gods is enduring. Chu-bu remembered and Sheemish did not forget. They spake as we do not speak, in silence yet heard of each other, nor were their thoughts as our thoughts. We should not judge them merely by human standards. All night long they spake and all night said these words only: "Dirty Chu-bu," "Dirty Sheemish." "Dirty Chu-bu," "Dirty Sheemish," all night long. Their wrath had not tired at dawn, and neither had wearied of his accusation. And gradually Chu-bu came to realize that he was nothing more than the equal of Sheemish. All gods are jealous, but this equality with the upstart

Sheemish, a thing of painted wood a hundred years newer than Chu-bu, and this worship given to Sheemish in Chu-bu's own temple, were particularly bitter. Chu-bu was jealous even for a god; and when Tuesday came again, the third day of Sheemish's worship, Chu-bu could bear it no longer. He felt that his anger must be revealed at all costs, and he returned with all the vehemence of his will to achieving a little earthquake. The worshippers had just gone from his temple when Chu-bu settled his will to attain this miracle. Now and then his meditations were disturbed by that now familiar dictum, "Dirty Chu-bu," but Chu-bu willed ferociously, not even stopping to say what he longed to say and had already said nine hundred times, and presently even these interruptions ceased.

They ceased because Sheemish had returned to a project that he had never definitely abandoned, the desire to assert himself and exalt himself over Chu-bu by performing a miracle, and the district being volcanic he had chosen a little earthquake as the miracle most easily accomplished by a small god.

Now an earthquake that is commanded by two gods has double the chance of fulfilment than when it is willed by one, and an incalculably greater chance than when two gods are pulling different ways; as, to take the case of older and greater gods, when the sun and the moon pull in the same direction we have the biggest tides.

Chu-bu knew nothing of the theory of tides, and was too much occupied with his miracle to notice what Sheemish was doing. And suddenly the miracle was an accomplished thing.

It was a very local earthquake, for there are other gods than Chu-bu or even Sheemish, and it was only a little one as the gods had willed, but it loosened some monoliths in a colonnade that supported one side of the temple and the whole of one wall fell in, and the low huts of the people of that city were shaken a little and some of their doors were jammed so that they would not open; it was enough, and for a moment it seemed that it was all; neither Chu-bu nor Sheemish commanded there should be more, but they had set in motion an old law older than Chu-bu, the law of gravity that that colonnade had held back for a hundred years, and the temple of Chu-bu quivered and then stood still, swayed once and was overthrown, on the heads of Chu-bu and Sheemish.

No one rebuilt it, for nobody dared to near such terrible gods. Some said that Chu-bu wrought the miracle, but some said Sheemish, and thereof schism was born. The weakly amiable, alarmed by the bitterness of rival sects, sought compromise and said that both had wrought it, but no one guessed the truth that the thing was done in rivalry.

And a saying arose, and both sects held this belief in common, that whoso toucheth Chu-bu shall die or whoso looketh upon Sheemish.

That is how Chu-bu came into my possession when I travelled once beyond the hills of Ting. I found him in the fallen temple of Chu-bu with his hands and toes sticking up out of the rubbish, lying upon his back, and in that attitude just as I found him I keep him to this day on my mantle-piece, as he is less liable to be upset that way. Sheemish was broken, so I left him where he was.

And there is something so helpless about Chu-bu with his fat hands stuck up in the air that sometimes I am moved out of compassion to bow down to him and pray, saying, "O Chu-bu, thou that made everything, help thy servant."

Chu-bu cannot do much, though once I am sure that at a game of bridge he sent me the ace of trumps after I had not held a card worth having for the whole of the evening. And chance alone could have done as much as that for me. But I do not tell this to Chu-bu.

THE WONDERFUL WINDOW

The old man in the Oriental-looking robe was being moved on by the police, and it was this that attracted to him and the parcel under his arm the attention of Mr. Sladden, whose livelihood was earned in the emporium of Messrs. Mergin and Chater, that is to say in their establishment.

Mr. Sladden had the reputation of being the silliest young man in Business; a touch of romance—a mere suggestion of it—would send his eyes gazing away as though the walls of the emporium were of gossamer and London itself a myth, instead of attending to customers.

Merely the fact that the dirty piece of paper that wrapped the old man's parcel was covered with Arabic writing was enough to give Mr. Sladden the idea of romance, and he followed until the little crowd fell off and the stranger stopped by the kerb and unwrapped his parcel and prepared to sell the thing that was inside it. It was a little window in old wood with small panes set in lead; it was not much more than a foot in breadth and was under two feet long. Mr. Sladden had never before seen a window sold in the street, so he asked the price of it.

"Its price is all you possess," said the old man.

"Where did you get it?" said Mr. Sladden, for it was a strange window.

"I gave all that I possessed for it in the streets of Baghdad."

"Did you possess much?" said Mr. Sladden.

"I had all that I wanted," he said, "except this window."

"It must be a good window," said the young man.

"It is a magical window," said the old one.

"I have only ten shillings on me, but I have fifteen-and-six at home."

The old man thought for a while.

"Then twenty-five-and-sixpence is the price of the window," he said.

It was only when the bargain was completed and the ten shillings paid and the strange old man was coming for his fifteen-and-six and to fit the magical window into his only room that it occurred to Mr. Sladden's mind that he did not want a window. And then they were at the door of the house in which he rented a room, and it seemed too late to explain.

The stranger demanded privacy when he fitted up the window, so Mr. Sladden remained outside the door at the top of a little flight of creaky stairs. He heard no sound of hammering.

And presently the strange old man came out with his faded yellow robe and his great beard, and his eyes on far-off places. "It is finished," he said, and he and the young man parted. And whether he remained a spot of colour and an anachronism in London, or whether he ever came again to Baghdad, and what dark hands kept on the circulation of his twenty-five-and-six, Mr. Sladden never knew.

Mr. Sladden entered the bare-boarded room in which he slept and spent all his indoor hours between closing-time and the hour at which Messrs. Mergin and Chater commenced. To the Penates of so dingy a room his neat frock-coat must have been a continual wonder. Mr. Sladden took it off and folded it carefully; and there was the old man's window rather high up in the wall. There had been no window in that wall hitherto, nor any ornament at all but a small cupboard, so when Mr. Sladden had put his frock-coat safely away he glanced through his new window. It was where his cupboard had been in which he kept his tea-things: they were all standing on the table now. When Mr. Sladden glanced through his new window it was late in a summer's evening; the butterflies some while ago would have closed their wings, though the bat would scarcely yet be drifting abroad—but this was in London: the shops were shut and street-lamps not yet lighted.

Mr. Sladden rubbed his eyes, then rubbed the window, and still he saw a sky of blazing blue, and far, far down beneath him, so that no sound came up from it or smoke of chimneys, a mediaeval city set with towers; brown roofs and cobbled streets, and then white walls and buttresses, and beyond them bright green fields and tiny streams. On the towers archers lolled, and along the walls were pikemen, and now and then a wagon went down some old-world street and lumbered through the gateway and out to the country, and now and then a wagon drew up to the city from the mist that was rolling with evening over the fields. Sometimes folks put their heads out of lattice windows, sometimes some idle troubadour seemed to sing, and nobody hurried or troubled about anything. Airy and dizzy though the distance was, for Mr. Sladden seemed higher above the city than any cathedral gargoyle, yet one clear detail he obtained as a clue: the banners floating from every tower over the idle archers had little golden dragons all over a pure white field.

He heard motor-buses roar by his other window, he heard the news-boys howling.

Mr. Sladden grew dreamier than ever after that on the premises, in the establishment of Messrs. Mergin and Chater. But in one matter he was wise and wakeful: he made continuous and careful inquiries about the golden dragons on a white flag, and talked to no one of his wonderful window. He came to know the flags of every king in Europe, he even dabbled in history, he made inquiries at shops that understood heraldry, but nowhere could he learn any trace of little dragons *or* on a field *argent*. And when it seemed that for him alone those golden dragons had fluttered he came to love them as an exile in some desert might love the lilies of his home or as a sick man might love swallows when he cannot easily live to another spring.

As soon as Messrs. Mergin and Chater closed, Mr. Sladden used to go back to his dingy room and gaze though the wonderful window until it grew dark in the city and the guard would go with a lantern round the ramparts and the night came up like velvet, full of strange stars. Another clue he tried to obtain one night by jotting down the shapes of the constellations, but this led him no further, for they were unlike any that shone upon either hemisphere.

Each day as soon as he woke he went first to the wonderful window, and there was the city, diminutive in the distance, all shining in the morning, and the golden dragons dancing in the sun, and the archers stretching themselves or swinging their arms on the tops of the windy towers. The window would not open, so that he never heard the songs that the troubadours sang down there beneath the gilded balconies; he did not even hear the belfries' chimes, though he saw the jack-daws routed every hour from their homes. And the first thing that he always did was to cast his eye round all the little towers that rose up from the ramparts to see that the little golden dragons were flying there on their flags. And when he saw them flaunting themselves on white folds from every tower against the marvelous deep blue of the sky he dressed contentedly, and, taking one last look, went off to his work with a glory in his mind. It would have been difficult for the customers of Messrs. Mergin and Chater to guess the precise ambition of Mr. Sladden as he walked before them in his neat frock-coat: it was that he might be a man-at-arms or an archer in order to fight for the little golden dragons that flew on a white flag for an unknown king in an inaccessible city. At first Mr. Sladden used to walk round and round the mean street that he lived in, but he gained no clue from that; and soon he noticed that quite different winds blew below his wonderful window from those that blew on the other side of the house.

In August the evenings began to grow shorter: this was the very remark that the other employees made to him at the emporium, so that he almost feared that they suspected his secret, and he had much less time for the wonderful window, for lights were few down there and they blinked out early.

One morning late in August, just before he went to Business, Mr. Sladden saw a company of pikemen running down the cobbled road towards the gateway of the mediaeval city—Golden Dragon City he used to call it alone in his own mind, but he never spoke of it to anyone. The next thing that he noticed was that the archers were handling round bundles of arrows in addition to the quivers which they wore. Heads were thrust out of windows more than usual, a woman ran out and called some children indoors, a knight rode down the street, and then more pikemen appeared along the walls, and all the jack-daws were in the air. In the street no troubadour sang. Mr. Sladden took one look along the towers to see that the flags were flying, and all the golden dragons were streaming in the wind. Then he had to go to Business. He took a bus back that evening and ran upstairs. Nothing seemed to be happening in Golden Dragon City except a crowd in the cobbled street that led down to the gateway; the archers seemed to be reclining as usual lazily in their towers, and then a white flag went down with all its golden dragons; he did not see at first that all the archers were dead. The crowd was pouring towards him, towards the precipitous wall from which he looked; men with a white flag covered with golden dragons were moving backwards slowly, men with another flag were pressing them, a flag on which there was one huge red bear. Another banner went down upon a tower. Then he saw it all: the golden dragons were being beaten—his little golden dragons. The men of the bear were coming under the window; what ever he threw from that height would fall with terrific force: fire-irons, coal, his clock, whatever he had—he would fight for his little golden dragons yet. A flame broke out from one of the towers and licked the feet of a reclining archer; he did not stir. And now the alien standard was out of sight directly underneath. Mr. Sladden broke the panes of the wonderful window and wrenched away with a poker the lead that held them. Just as the glass broke he saw a banner covered with golden dragons fluttering still, and then as he drew back to hurl the poker there came to him the scent of mysterious spices, and there was nothing there, not even the daylight, for behind the fragments of the wonderful window was nothing but that small cupboard in which he kept his tea-things.

And though Mr. Sladden is older now and knows more of the world, and even has a Business of his own, he has never been able to buy such another window, and has not ever since, either from books or men, heard any rumour at all of Golden Dragon City.

EPILOGUE

Here the fourteenth Episode of the Book of Wonder endeth and here the relating of the Chronicles of Little Adventures at the Edge of the World. I take farewell of my readers. But it may be we shall even meet again, for it is still to be told how the gnomes robbed the fairies, and of the vengeance that the fairies took, and how even the gods themselves were troubled thereby in their sleep; and how the King of Ool insulted the troubadours, thinking himself safe among his scores of archers and hundreds of halberdiers, and how the troubadours stole to his towers by night, and under his battlements by the light of the moon made that king ridiculous for ever in song. But for this I must first return to the Edge of the World. Behold, the caravans start.

FIFTY-ONE TALES (1915)

THE ASSIGNATION

Fame singing in the highways, and trifling as she sang, with sordid adventurers, passed the poet by.

And still the poet made for her little chaplets of song, to deck her forehead in the courts of Time: and still she wore instead the worthless garlands, that boisterous citizens flung to her in the ways, made out of perishable things.

And after a while whenever these garlands died the poet came to her with his chaplets of song; and still she laughed at him and wore the worthless wreaths, though they always died at evening.

And one day in his bitterness the poet rebuked her, and said to her: "Lovely Fame, even in the highways and the byways you have not foreborne to laugh and shout and jest with worthless men, and I have toiled for you and dreamed of you and you mock me and pass me by."

And Fame turned her back on him and walked away, but in departing she looked over her shoulder and smiled at him as she had not smiled before, and, almost speaking in a whisper, said:

"I will meet you in the graveyard at the back of the Workhouse in a hundred years."

CHARON

Charon leaned forward and rowed. All things were one with his weariness.

It was not with him a matter of years or of centuries, but of wide floods of time, and an old heaviness and a pain in the arms that had become for him part of the scheme that the gods had made and was of a piece with Eternity.

If the gods had even sent him a contrary wind it would have divided all time in his memory into two equal slabs.

So grey were all things always where he was that if any radiance lingered a moment among the dead, on the face of such a queen perhaps as Cleopatra, his eyes could not have perceived it.

It was strange that the dead nowadays were coming in such numbers. They were coming in thousands where they used to come in fifties. It was neither Charon's duty nor his wont to ponder in his grey soul why these things might be. Charon leaned forward and rowed.

Then no one came for a while. It was not usual for the gods to send no one down from Earth for such a space. But the gods knew best.

Then one man came alone. And the little shade sat shivering on a lonely bench and the great boat pushed off. Only one passenger: the gods knew best. And great and weary Charon rowed on and on beside the little, silent, shivering ghost.

And the sound of the river was like a mighty sigh that Grief in the beginning had sighed among her sisters, and that could not die like the echoes of human sorrow failing on earthly hills, but was as old as time and the pain in Charon's arms.

Then the boat from the slow, grey river loomed up to the coast of Dis and the little, silent shade still shivering stepped ashore, and Charon turned the boat to go wearily back to the world. Then the little shadow spoke, that had been a man.

"I am the last," he said.

No one had ever made Charon smile before, no one before had ever made him weep.

THE DEATH OF PAN

When travellers from London entered Arcady they lamented one to another the death of Pan.

And anon they saw him lying stiff and still.

Horned Pan was still and the dew was on his fur; he had not the look of a live animal. And then they said, "It is true that Pan is dead."

And, standing melancholy by that huge prone body, they looked for long at memorable Pan.

And evening came and a small star appeared.

And presently from a hamlet of some Arcadian valley, with a sound of idle song, Arcadian maidens came.

And, when they saw there, suddenly in the twilight, that old recumbent god, they stopped in their running and whispered among themselves. "How silly he looks," they said, and thereat they laughed a little.

And at the sound of their laughter Pan leaped up and the gravel flew from his hooves.

And, for as long as the travellers stood and listened, the crags and the hill-tops of Arcady rang with the sounds of pursuit.

THE SPHINX AT GIZEH

I saw the other day the Sphinx's painted face.

She had painted her face in order to ogle Time.

And he has spared no other painted face in all the world but hers.

Delilah was younger than she, and Delilah is dust. Time hath loved nothing but this worthless painted face.

I do not care that she is ugly, nor that she has painted her face, so that she only lure his secret from Time.

Time dallies like a fool at her feet when he should be smiting cities.

Time never wearies of her silly smile.

There are temples all about her that he has forgotten to spoil.

I saw an old man go by, and Time never touched him.

Time that has carried away the seven gates of Thebes!

She has tried to bind him with ropes of eternal sand, she had hoped to oppress him with the Pyramids.

He lies there in the sand with his foolish hair all spread about her paws.

If she ever finds his secret we will put out his eyes, so that he shall find no more our beautiful things—there are lovely gates in Florence that I fear he will carry away.

We have tried to bind him with song and with old customs, but they only held him for a little while, and he has always smitten us and mocked us.

When he is blind he shall dance to us and make sport.

Great clumsy time shall stumble and dance, who liked to kill little children, and can hurt even the daisies no longer.

Then shall our children laugh at him who slew Babylon's winged bulls, and smote great numbers of the gods and fairies—when he is shorn of his hours and his years.

We will shut him up in the Pyramid of Cheops, in the great chamber where the sarcophagus is. Thence we will lead him out when we give our feasts. He shall ripen our corn for us and do menial work.

We will kiss they painted face, O Sphinx, if thou wilt betray to us Time.

And yet I fear that in his ultimate anguish he may take hold blindly of the world and the moon, and slowly pull down upon him the House of Man.

THE HEN

All along the farmyard gables the swallows sat a-row, twittering uneasily to one another, telling of many things, but thinking only of Summer and the South, for Autumn was afoot and the North wind waiting.

And suddenly one day they were all quite gone. And everyone spoke of the swallows and the South.

"I think I shall go South myself next year," said a hen.

And the year wore on and the swallows came again, and the year wore on and they sat again on the gables, and all the poultry discussed the departure of the hen.

And very early one morning, the wind being from the North, the swallows all soared suddenly and felt the wind in their wings; and a strength came upon them and a strange old knowledge and a more than human faith, and flying high they left the smoke of our cities and small remembered eaves, and saw at last the huge and homeless sea, and steering by grey sea-currents went southward with the wind. And going South they went by glittering fog-banks and saw old islands lifting their heads above them; they saw the slow quests of the wandering ships, and divers seeking pearls, and lands at war, till there came in view the mountains that they sought and the sight of the peaks they knew; and they descended into an austral valley, and saw Summer sometimes sleeping and sometimes singing song.

"I think the wind is about right," said the hen; and she spread her wings and ran out of the poultry-yard. And she ran fluttering out on to the road and some way down it until she came to a garden.

At evening she came back panting.

And in the poultry-yard she told the poultry how she had gone South as far as the high road, and saw the great world's traffic going by, and came to lands where the potato grew, and saw the stubble upon which men live, and at the end of the road had found a garden, and there were roses in it—beautiful roses!—and the gardener himself was there with his braces on.

"How extremely interesting," the poultry said, "and what a really beautiful description!"

And the Winter wore away, and the bitter months went by, and the Spring of the year appeared, and the swallows came again.

"We have been to the South," they said, "and the valleys beyond the sea."

But the poultry would not agree that there was a sea in the South: "You should hear our hen," they said.

WIND AND FOG

"Way for us," said the North Wind as he came down the sea on an errand of old Winter.

And he saw before him the grey silent fog that lay along the tides.

"Way for us," said the North Wind, "O ineffectual fog, for I am Winter's leader in his age-old war with the ships. I overwhelm them suddenly in my strength, or drive upon them the huge seafaring bergs. I cross an ocean while you move a mile. There is mourning in inland places when I have met the ships. I drive them upon the rocks and feed the sea. Wherever I appear they bow to our lord the Winter."

And to his arrogant boasting nothing said the fog. Only he rose up slowly and trailed away from the sea and, crawling up long valleys, took refuge among the hills; and night came down and everything was still, and the fog began to mumble in the stillness. And I hear him telling infamously to himself the tale of his horrible spoils. "A hundred and fifteen galleons of old Spain, a certain argosy that went from Tyre, eight fisher-fleets and ninety ships of the line, twelve warships under sail, with their carronades, three hundred and eighty-seven river-craft, forty-two merchantmen that carried spice, thirty yachts, twenty-one battleships of the modern time, nine thousand admirals...." he mumbled and chuckled on, till I suddenly rose and fled from his fearful contamination.

THE RAFT-BUILDERS

All we who write put me in mind of sailors hastily making rafts upon doomed ships.

When we break up under the heavy years and go down into eternity with all that is ours our thoughts like small lost rafts float on awhile upon Oblivion's sea. They will not carry much over those tides, our names and a phrase or two and little else.

They that write as a trade to please the whim of the day, they are like sailors that work at the rafts only to warm their hands and to distract their thoughts from their certain doom; their rafts go all to pieces before the ship breaks up.

See now Oblivion shimmering all around us, its very tranquility deadlier than tempest. How little all our keels have troubled it. Time in its deeps swims like a monstrous whale; and, like a whale, feeds on the littlest things—small tunes and little unskilled songs of the olden, golden evenings—and anon turneth whale-like to overthrow whole ships.

See now the wreckage of Babylon floating idly, and something there that once was Nineveh; already their kings and queens are in the deeps among the weedy masses of old centuries that hide the sodden bulk of sunken Tyre and make a darkness round Persepolis.

For the rest I dimly see the forms of foundered ships on the sea-floor strewn with crowns.

Our ships were all unseaworthy from the first.

There goes the raft that Homer made for Helen.

THE WORKMAN

I saw a workman fall with his scaffolding right from the summit of some vast hotel. And as he came down I saw him holding a knife and trying to cut his name on the scaffolding. He had time to try and do this for he must have had nearly three hundred feet to fall. And I could think of nothing but his folly in doing this futile thing, for not only would the man be unrecognizably dead in three seconds, but the very pole on which he tried to scratch whatever of his name he had time for was certain to be burnt in a few weeks for firewood.

Then I went home for I had work to do. And all that evening I thought of the man's folly, till the thought hindered me from serious work.

And late that night while I was still at work, the ghost of the workman floated through my wall and stood before me laughing.

I heard no sound until after I spoke to it; but I could see the grey diaphanous form standing before me shuddering with laughter.

I spoke at last and asked what it was laughing at, and then the ghost spoke. It said: "I'm a laughin' at you sittin' and workin' there."

"And why," I asked, "do you laugh at serious work?"

"Why, yer bloomin' life 'ull go by like a wind," he said, "and yer 'ole silly civilization 'ull be tidied up in a few centuries."

Then he fell to laughing again and this time audibly; and, laughing still, faded back through the wall again and into the eternity from which he had come.

THE GUEST

A young man came into an ornate restaurant at eight o'clock in London.

He was alone, but two places had been laid at the table which was reserved for him. He had chosen the dinner very carefully, by letter a week before.

A waiter asked him about the other guest.

"You probably won't see him till the coffee comes," the young man told him; so he was served alone.

Those at adjacent tables might have noticed the young man continually addressing the empty chair and carrying on a monologue with it throughout his elaborate dinner.

"I think you knew my father," he said to it over the soup.

"I sent for you this evening," he continued, "because I want you to do me a good turn; in fact I must insist on it."

There was nothing eccentric about the man except for this habit of addressing an empty chair, certainly he was eating as good a dinner as any sane man could wish for.

After the Burgundy had been served he became more voluble in his monologue, not that he spoiled his wine by drinking excessively.

"We have several acquaintances in common," he said. "I met King Seti a year ago in Thebes. I think he has altered very little since you knew him. I thought his forehead a little low for a king's. Cheops has left the house that he built for your reception, he must have prepared for you for years and years. I suppose you have seldom been entertained like that. I ordered this dinner over a week ago. I thought then that a lady might have come with me, but as she wouldn't I've asked you. She may not after all be as lovely as Helen of Troy. Was Helen very lovely? Not when you knew her, perhaps. You were lucky in Cleopatra, you must have known her when she was in her prime.

"You never knew the mermaids nor the fairies nor the lovely goddesses of long ago, that's where we have the best of you."

He was silent when the waiters came to his table, but rambled merrily on as soon as they left, still turned to the empty chair.

"You know I saw you here in London only the other day. You were on a motor bus going down Ludgate Hill. It was going much too fast. London is a good place. But I shall be glad enough to leave it. It was in London that I met the lady I that was speaking about. If it hadn't been for London I probably shouldn't have met her, and if it hadn't been for London she probably wouldn't have had so much besides me to amuse her. It cuts both ways."

He paused once to order coffee, gazing earnestly at the waiter and putting a sovereign in his hand. "Don't let it be chicory," said he.

The waiter brought the coffee, and the young man dropped a tabloid of some sort into his cup.

"I don't suppose you come here very often," he went on. "Well, you probably want to be going. I haven't taken you much out of your way, there is plenty for you to do in London."

Then having drunk his coffee he fell on the floor by a foot of the empty chair, and a doctor who was dining in the room bent over him and announced to the anxious manager the visible presence of the young man's guest.

DEATH AND ODYSSEUS

In the Olympian courts Love laughed at Death, because he was unsightly, and because She couldn't help it, and because he never did anything worth doing, and because She would.

And Death hated being laughed at, and used to brood apart thinking only of his wrongs and of what he could do to end this intolerable treatment.

But one day Death appeared in the courts with an air and They all noticed it. "What are you up to now?" said Love. And Death with some solemnity said to Her: "I am going to frighten Odysseus"; and drawing about him his grey traveller's cloak went out through the windy door with his jowl turned earthwards.

And he came soon to Ithaca and the hall that Athene knew, and opened the door and saw there famous Odysseus, with his white locks bending close over the fire, trying to warm his hands.

And the wind through the open door blew bitterly on Odysseus.

And Death came up behind him, and suddenly shouted.

And Odysseus went on warming his pale hands.

Then Death came close and began to mouth at him. And after a while Odysseus turned and spoke. And "Well, old servant," he said, "have your masters been kind to you since I made you work for me round Ilion?"

And Death for some while stood mute, for the thought of the laughter of Love.

Then "Come now," said Odysseus, "lend me your shoulder," and he leaning heavily on that bony joint, they went together through the open door.

DEATH AND THE ORANGE

Two dark young men in a foreign southern land sat at a restaurant table with one woman.

And on the woman's plate was a small orange which had an evil laughter in its heart.

And both of the men would be looking at the woman all the time, and they ate little and they drank much.

And the woman was smiling equally at each.

Then the small orange that had the laughter in its heart rolled slowly off the plate on to the floor. And the dark young men both sought for it at once, and they met suddenly beneath the table, and soon they were speaking swift words to one another, and a horror and an impotence came over the Reason of each as she sat helpless at the back of the mind, and the heart of the orange laughed and the woman went on smiling; and Death, who was sitting at another table, tête-à-tête with an old man, rose and came over to listen to the quarrel.

THE PRAYER OF THE FLOWERS

It was the voice of the flowers on the West wind, the lovable, the old, the lazy West wind, blowing ceaselessly, blowing sleepily, going Greece-wards.

"The woods have gone away, they have fallen and left us; men love us no longer, we are lonely by moonlight. Great engines rush over the beautiful fields, their ways lie hard and terrible up and down the land.

"The cancrous cities spread over the grass, they clatter in their lairs continually, they glitter about us blemishing the night.

"The woods are gone, O Pan, the woods, the woods. And thou art far, O Pan, and far away."

I was standing by night between two railway embankments on the edge of a Midland city. On one of them I saw the trains go by, once in every two minutes, and on the other, the trains went by twice in every five.

Quite close were the glaring factories, and the sky above them wore the fearful look that it wears in dreams of fever.

The flowers were right in the stride of that advancing city, and thence I heard them sending up their cry. And then I heard, beating musically up wind, the voice of Pan reproving them from Arcady—

"Be patient a little, these things are not for long."

TIME AND THE TRADESMAN

Once Time as he prowled the world, his hair grey not with weakness but with dust of the ruin of cities, came to a furniture shop and entered the Antique department. And there he saw a man darkening the wood of a chair with dye and beating it with chains and making imitation wormholes in it.

And when Time saw another doing his work he stood by him awhile and looked on critically.

And at last he said: "That is not how I work," and he turned the man's hair white and bent his back and put some furrows in his little cunning face; then turned and strode away, for a mighty city that was weary and sick and too long had troubled the fields was sore in need of him.

THE LITTLE CITY

I was in the pre-destined 11.8 from Goraghwood to Drogheda, when I suddenly saw the city. It was a little city in a valley, and only seemed to have a little smoke, and the sun caught the smoke and turned it golden, so that it looked like an old Italian picture where angels walk in the foreground and the rest is a blaze of gold. And beyond, as one could tell by the lie of land although one could not see through the golden smoke, I knew that there lay the paths of the roving ships.

All round there lay a patchwork of small fields all over the slopes of the hills, and the snow had come upon them tentatively, but already the birds of the waste had moved to the sheltered places for every omen boded more to fall. Far away some little hills blazed like an aureate bulwark broken off by age and fallen from the earthward rampart of Paradise. And aloof and dark the mountains stared unconcernedly seawards.

And when I saw those grey and watchful mountains sitting where they sat while the cities of the civilization of Araby and Asia arose like crocuses, and like crocuses fell, I wondered for how long there would be smoke in the valley and little fields on the hills.

THE UNPASTURABLE FIELDS

Thus spake the mountains: "Behold us, even us; the old ones, the grey ones, that wear the feet of Time. Time on our rocks shall break his staff and stumble: and still we shall sit majestic, even as now, hearing the sound of the sea, our old coeval sister, who nurses the bones of her children and weeps for the things she has done.

"Far, far, we stand above all things; befriending the little cities until they grow old and leave us to go among the myths.

"We are the most imperishable mountains."

And softly the clouds foregathered from far places, and crag on crag and mountain upon mountain in the likeness of Caucasus upon Himalaya came riding past the sunlight upon the backs of storms and looked down idly from their golden heights upon the crests of the mountains.

"Ye pass away," said the mountains.

And the clouds answered, as I dreamed or fancied,

"We pass away, indeed we pass away, but upon our unpasturable fields Pegasus prances. Here Pegasus gallops and browses upon song which the larks bring to him every morning from far terrestrial fields. His hoof-beats ring upon our slopes at sunrise as though our fields were of silver. And breathing the dawn-wind in dilated nostrils, with head tossed upwards and with quivering wings, he stands and stares from our tremendous heights, and snorts and sees far-future wonderful wars rage in the creases and the folds of the togas that cover the knees of the gods."

THE WORM AND THE ANGEL

As he crawled from the tombs of the fallen a worm met with an angel.

And together they looked upon the kings and kingdoms, and youths and maidens and the cities of men. They saw the old men heavy in their chairs and heard the children singing in the fields. They saw far wars and warriors and walled towns, wisdom and wickedness, and the pomp of kings, and the people of all the lands that the sunlight knew.

And the worm spake to the angel saying: "Behold my food."

"Be dakeon para Thina poluphloisboio Thalassaes," murmured the angel, for they walked by the sea, "and can you destroy that too?"

And the worm paled in his anger to a greyness ill to behold, for for three thousand years he had tried to destroy that line and still its melody was ringing in *his head*.

THE SONGLESS COUNTRY

The poet came unto a great country in which there were no songs. And he lamented gently for the nation that had not any little foolish songs to sing to itself at evening.

And at last he said: "I will make for them myself some little foolish songs so that they may be merry in the lanes and happy by the fireside." And for some days he made for them aimless songs such as maidens sing on the hills in the older happier countries.

Then he went to some of that nation as they sat weary with the work of the day and said to them: "I have made you some aimless songs out of the small unreasonable legends, that are somewhat akin to the wind in the vales of my childhood; and you may care to sing them in your disconsolate evenings."

And they said to him:

"If you think we have time for that sort of nonsense nowadays you cannot know much of the progress of modern commerce."

And the poet wept for he said: "Alas! They are damned."

THE LATEST THING

I saw an unclean-feeder by the banks of the river of Time. He crouched by orchards numerous with apples in a happy land of flowers; colossal barns stood near which the ancients had stored with grain, and the sun was golden on serene far hills behind the level lands. But his back was to all these things. He crouched and watched the river. And whatever the river chanced to send him down the unclean-feeder clutched at greedily with his arms, wading out into the water.

Now there were in those days, and indeed still are, certain uncleanly cities upon the river of Time; and from them fearfully nameless things came floating shapelessly by. And whenever the odor of these came down the river before them the unclean-feeder plunged into the dirty water and stood far out, expectant. And if he opened his mouth one saw these things on his lips.

Indeed from the upper reaches there came down sometimes the fallen rhododendron's petal, sometimes a rose; but they were useless to the un-clean-feeder, and when he saw them he growled.

A poet walked beside the river's bank; his head was lifted and his look was afar; I think he saw the sea, and the hills of Fate from which the river ran. I saw the unclean-feeder standing voracious, up to his waist in that evil-smelling river.

"Look," I said to the poet.

"The current will sweep him away," the poet said.

"But those cities that poison the river," I said to him.

He answered: "Whenever the centuries melt on the hills of Fate the river terribly floods."

THE DEMAGOGUE AND THE DEMI-MONDE

A demagogue and a demi-mondaine chanced to arrive together at the gate of Paradise. And the Saint looked sorrowfully at them both.

"Why were you a demagogue?" he said to the first.

"Because," said the demagogue, "I stood for those principles that have made us what we are and have endeared our Party to the great heart of the people. In a word I stood unflinchingly on the plank of popular representation."

"And you?" said the Saint to her of the demi-monde.

"I wanted money," said the demi-mondaine.

And after some moments' thought the Saint said: "Well, come in; though you don't deserve to."

But to the demagogue he said: "We genuinely regret that the limited space at our disposal and our unfortunate lack of interest in those Questions that you have gone so far to inculate and have so ably upheld in the past, prevent us from giving you the support for which you seek."

And he shut the golden door.

THE GIANT POPPY

I dreamt that I went back to the hills I knew, whence on a clear day you can see the walls of Ilion and the plains of Roncesvalles. There used to be woods along the tops of those hills with clearings in them where the moonlight fell, and there when no one watched the fairies danced.

But there were no woods when I went back, no fairies nor distant glimpse of Ilion or plains of Roncesvalles, only one giant poppy waved in the wind, and as it waved it hummed "Remember not." And by its oak-like stem a poet sat, dressed like a shepherd and playing an ancient tune softly upon a pipe. I asked him if the fairies had passed that way or anything olden.

He said: "The poppy has grown apace and is killing gods and fairies. Its fumes are suffocating the world, and its roots drain it of its beautiful strength." And I asked him why he sat on the hills I knew, playing an olden tune.

And he answered: "Because the tune is bad for the poppy, which would otherwise grow more swiftly; and because if the brotherhood of which I am one were to cease to pipe on the hills men would stray over the world and be lost or come to terrible ends. We think we have saved Agamemnon."

Then he fell to piping again that olden tune, while the wind among the poppy's sleepy petals murmured "Remember not. Remember not."

ROSES

I know a roadside where the wild rose blooms with a strange abundance. There is a beauty in the blossoms too of an almost exotic kind, a taint of deeper pink that shocks the Puritan flowers. Two hundred generations ago (generations, I mean, of roses) this was a village street; there was a floral decadence when they left their simple life and the roses came from the wilderness to clamber round houses of men.

Of all the memories of that little village, of all the cottages that stood there, of all the men and women whose homes they were, nothing remains but a more beautiful blush on the faces of the roses.

I hope that when London is clean passed away and the defeated fields come back again, like an exiled people returning after a war, they may find some beautiful thing to remind them of it all; because we have loved a little that swart old city.

THE MAN WITH THE GOLDEN EAR-RINGS

It may be that I dreamed this. So much at least is certain—that I turned one day from the traffic of a city, and came to its docks and saw its slimy wharves going down green and steep into the water, and saw the huge grey river slipping by and the lost things that went with it turning over and over, and I thought of the nations and unpitying Time, and saw and marvelled at the queenly ships come newly from the sea.

It was then, if I mistake not, that I saw leaning against a wall, with his face to the ships, a man with golden ear-rings. His skin had the dark tint of the southern men: the deep black hairs of his moustache were whitened a little with salt; he wore a dark blue jacket such as sailors wear, and the long boots of seafarers, but the look in his eyes was further afield than the ships, he seemed to be beholding the farthest things.

Even when I spoke to him he did not call home that look, but answered me dreamily with that same fixed stare as though his thoughts were heaving on far and lonely seas. I asked him what ship he had come by, for there were many there. The sailing ships were there with their sails all furled and their masts straight and still like a wintry forest; the steamers were there, and great liners, puffing up idle smoke into the twilight. He answered he had come by none of them. I asked him what line he worked on, for he was clearly a sailor; I mentioned well-known lines, but he did not know them. Then I asked him where he worked and what he was. And he said: "I work in the Sargasso Sea, and I am the last of the pirates, the last left alive." And

I shook him by the hand I do not know how many times. I said: "We feared you were dead. We feared you were dead." And he answered sadly: "No. No. I have sinned too deeply on the Spanish seas: I am not allowed to die."

THE DREAM OF KING KARNA-VOOTRA

King Karna-Vootra sitting on his throne commanding all things said: "I very clearly saw last night the queenly Vava-Nyria. Though partly she was hidden by great clouds that swept continually by her, rolling over and over, yet her face was unhidden and shone, being full of moonlight.

"I said to her:

"'Walk with me by the great pools in many-gardened, beautiful Istra-khan where the lilies float that give delectable dreams; or, drawing aside the curtain of hanging orchids, pass with me thence from the pools by a secret path through the else impassable jungle that fills the only way between the mountains that shut in Istrakhan. They shut it in and look on it with joy at morning and at evening when the pools are strange with light, till in their gladness sometimes there melts the deadly snow that kills upon lonely heights the mountaineer. They have valleys among them older than the wrinkles in the moon.

"'Come with me thence or linger with me there and either we shall come to romantic lands which the men of the caravans only speak of in song; or else we shall listlessly walk in a land so lovely that even the but-terflies that float about it when they see their images flash in the sacred pools are terrified by their beauty, and each night we shall hear the myriad nightingales all in one chorus sing the stars to death. Do this and I will send heralds far from here with tidings of thy beauty; and they shall run and come to Séndara and men shall know it there who herd brown sheep; and from Séndara the rumour shall spread on, down either bank of the holy river of Zoth, till the people that make wattles in the plains shall hear of it and sing; but the heralds shall go northward along the hills until they come to Sooma. And in that golden city they shall tell the kings, that sit in theirlofty alabaster house, of thy strange and sudden smiles. And often in distant markets shall thy story be told by merchants out from Sooma as they sit telling careless tales to lure men to their wares.

"'And the heralds passing thence shall come even to Ingra, to Ingra where they dance. And there they shall tell of thee, so that thy name long hence shall be sung in that joyous city. And there they shall borrow camels and pass over the sands and go by desert ways to distant Nirid to tell of thee to the lonely men in the mountain monasteries.

"'Come with me even now for it is Spring.'"

"And as I said this she faintly yet perceptibly shook her head. And it was only then I remembered my youth was gone, and she dead forty years."

THE STORM

They saw a little ship that was far at sea and that went by the name of the *Petite Espérance*. And because of its uncouth rig and its lonely air and the look that it had of coming from strangers' lands they said: "It is neither a ship to greet nor desire, nor yet to succor when in the hands of the sea."

And the sea rose up as is the wont of the sea and the little ship from afar was in his hands, and frailer than ever seemed its feeble masts with their sails of fantastic cut and their alien flags. And the sea made a great and very triumphing voice, as the sea doth. And then there arose a wave that was very strong, even the ninth-born son of the hurricane and the tide, and hid the little ship and hid the whole of the far parts of the sea. Thereat said those who stood on the good dry land:

"'Twas but a little, worthless alien ship and it is sunk at sea, and it is good and right that the storm have spoil." And they turned and watched the course of the merchant-men, laden with silver and appeasing spice; year after year they cheered them into port and praised their goods and their familiar sails. And many years went by.

And at last with decks and bulwarks covered with cloth of gold; with age-old parrots that had known the troubadours, singing illustrious songs and preening their feathers of gold; with a hold full of emeralds and rubies; all silken with Indian loot; furling as it came in its way-worn alien sails, a galleon glided into port, shutting the sunlight from the merchantmen: and lo! it loomed the equal of the cliffs.

"Who are you?" they asked, "far-travelled wonderful ship?"

And they said: "The *Petite Espérance*."

"O," said the people on shore. "We thought you were sunk at sea."

"Sunk at sea?" sang the sailors. "We could not be sunk at sea—we had the gods on board."

A MISTAKEN IDENTITY

Fame as she walked at evening in a city saw the painted face of Notoriety flaunting beneath a gas-lamp, and many kneeled unto her in the dirt of the road.

"Who are you?" Fame said to her.

"I am Fame," said Notoriety.

Then Fame stole softly away so that no one knew she had gone.

And Notoriety presently went forth and all her worshippers rose and followed after, and she led them, as was most meet, to her native Pit.

THE TRUE HISTORY OF THE
HARE AND THE TORTOISE

For a long time there was doubt with acrimony among the beasts as to whether the Hare or the Tortoise could run the swifter. Some said the Hare was the swifter of the two because he had such long ears, and others said the Tortoise was the swifter because anyone whose shell was so hard as that should be able to run hard too. And lo, the forces of estrangement and disorder perpetually postponed a decisive contest.

But when there was nearly war among the beasts, at last an arrangement was come to and it was decided that the Hare and the Tortoise should run a race of five hundred yards so that all should see who was right.

"Ridiculous nonsense!" said the Hare, and it was all his backers could do to get him to run.

"The contest is most welcome to me," said the Tortoise, "I shall not shirk it."

O, how his backers cheered.

Feeling ran high on the day of the race; the goose rushed at the fox and nearly pecked him. Both sides spoke loudly of the approaching victory up to the very moment of the race.

"I am absolutely confident of success," said the Tortoise. But the Hare said nothing, he looked bored and cross. Some of his supporters deserted him then and went to the other side, who were loudly cheering the Tortoise's inspiriting words. But many remained with the Hare. "We shall not be disappointed in him," they said. "A beast with such long ears is bound to win."

"Run hard," said the supporters of the Tortoise.

And "run hard" became a kind of catch-phrase which everybody repeated to one another. "Hard shell and hard living. That's what the country wants. Run hard," they said. And these words were never uttered but multitudes cheered from their hearts.

Then they were off, and suddenly there was a hush.

The Hare dashed off for about a hundred yards, then he looked round to see where his rival was.

"It is rather absurd," he said, "to race with a Tortoise." And he sat down and scratched himself. "Run hard! Run hard!" shouted some.

"Let him rest," shouted others. And "let him rest" became a catch-phrase too.

And after a while his rival drew near to him.

"There comes that damned Tortoise," said the Hare, and he got up and ran as hard as could be so that he should not let the Tortoise beat him.

"Those ears will win," said his friends. "Those ears will win; and establish upon an incontestable footing the truth of what we have said." And some of them turned to the backers of the Tortoise and said: "What about your beast now?"

"Run hard," they replied. "Run hard."

The Hare ran on for nearly three hundred yards, nearly in fact as far as the winning-post, when it suddenly struck him what a fool he looked running races with a Tortoise who was nowhere in sight, and he sat down again and scratched.

"Run hard. Run hard," said the crowd, and "Let him rest."

"Whatever is the use of it?" said the Hare, and this time he stopped for good. Some say he slept.

There was desperate excitement for an hour or two, and then the Tortoise won.

"Run hard. Run hard," shouted his backers. "Hard shell and hard living: that's what has done it." And then they asked the Tortoise what his achievement signified, and he went and asked the Turtle. And the Turtle said, "It is a glorious victory for the forces of swiftness." And then the Tortoise repeated it to his friends. And all the beasts said nothing else for years. And even to this day, "a glorious victory for the forces of swiftness" is a catch-phrase in the house of the snail.

And the reason that this version of the race is not widely known is that very few of those that witnessed it survived the great forest-fire that happened shortly after. It came up over the weald by night with a great wind. The Hare and the Tortoise and a very few of the beasts saw it far off from a high bare hill that was at the edge of the trees, and they hurriedly called a meeting to decide what messenger they should send to warn the beasts in the forest.

They sent the Tortoise.

ALONE THE IMMORTALS

I heard it said that very far away from here, on the wrong side of the deserts of Cathay and in a country dedicate to winter, are all the years that are dead. And there a certain valley shuts them in and hides them, as rumor has it, from the world, but not from the sight of the moon nor from those that dream in his rays.

And I said: I will go from here by ways of dream and I will come to that valley and enter in and mourn there for the good years that are dead. And I said: I will take a wreath, a wreath of mourning, and lay it at their feet in token of my sorrow for their dooms.

And when I sought about among the flowers, among the flowers for my wreath of mourning, the lily looked too large and the laurel looked too solemn and I found nothing frail enough nor slender to serve as an offering to the years that were dead. And at last I made a slender wreath of daisies in the manner that I had seen them made in one of the years that is dead.

"This," said I, "is scarce less fragile or less frail than one of those delicate forgotten years." Then I took my wreath in my hand and went from here. And when I had come by paths of mystery to that romantic land, where the valley that rumour told of lies close to the mountainous moon, I searched among the grass for those poor slight years for whom I bought my sorrow and my wreath. And when I found there nothing in the grass I said: "Time has shattered them and swept them away and left not even any faint remains."

But looking upwards in the blaze of the moon I suddenly saw colossi sitting near, and towering up and blotting out the stars and filling the night with blackness; and at those idols' feet I saw praying and making obeisance kings and the days that are and all times and all cities and all nations and all their gods. Neither the smoke of incense nor of the sacrifice burning reached those colossal heads, they sat there not to be measured, not to be over-thrown, not to be worn away.

I said: "Who are those?"

One answered: "Alone the Immortals."

And I said sadly: "I came not to see dread gods, but I came to shed my tears and to offer flowers at the feet of certain little years that are dead and may not come again."

He answered me: "These *are* the years that are dead, alone the immortals; all years to be are Their children—They fashioned their smiles and their laughter; all earthly kings They have crowned, all gods They have created; all the events to be flow down from their feet like a river, the worlds are flying pebbles that They have already thrown, and Time and all his centuries behind him kneel there with bended crests in token of vassalage at Their potent feet."

And when I heard this I turned away with my wreath, and went back to my own land comforted.

A MORAL LITTLE TALE

There was once an earnest Puritan who held it wrong to dance. And for his principles he labored hard, his was a zealous life. And there loved him all of those who hated the dance; and those that loved the dance respected him too; they said "He is a pure, good man and acts according to his lights."

He did much to discourage dancing and helped to close several Sunday entertainments. Some kinds of poetry, he said, he liked, but not the fanciful kind as that might corrupt the thoughts of the very young. He always dressed in black.

He was quite interested in morality and was quite sincere and there grew to be much respect on Earth for his honest face and his flowing pure-white beard.

One night the Devil appeared unto him in a dream and said "Well done."

"Avaunt," said that earnest man.

"No, no, friend," said the Devil.

"Dare not to call me 'friend,'" he answered bravely.

"Come, come, friend," said the Devil. "Have you not put apart the couples that would dance? Have you not checked their laughter and their accursed mirth? Have you not worn my livery of black? O friend, friend, you do not know what a detestable thing it is to sit in hell and hear people being happy, and singing in theatres and singing in the fields, and whispering after dances under the moon," and he fell to cursing fearfully.

"It is you," said the Puritan, "that put into their hearts the evil desire to dance; and black is God's own livery, not yours."

And the Devil laughed contemptuously and spoke.

"He only made the silly colors," he said, "and useless dawns on hill-slopes facing South, and butterflies flapping along them as soon as the sun rose high, and foolish maidens coming out to dance, and the warm mad West wind, and worst of all that pernicious influence Love."

And when the Devil said that God made Love that earnest man sat up in bed and shouted "Blasphemy! Blasphemy!"

"It's true," said the Devil. "It isn't I that send the village fools muttering and whispering two by two in the woods when the harvest moon is high, it's as much as I can bear even to see them dancing."

"Then," said the man, "I have mistaken right for wrong; but as soon as I wake I will fight you yet."

"O, no you don't," said the Devil. "You don't wake up out of this sleep."

And somewhere far away Hell's black steel doors were opened, and arm in arm those two were drawn within, and the doors shut behind them and still they went arm in arm, trudging further and further into the deeps of Hell, and it was that Puritan's punishment to know that those that he cared for on Earth would do evil as he had done.

THE RETURN OF SONG

"The swans are singing again," said to one another the gods. And looking downwards, for my dreams had taken me to some fair and far Valhalla, I saw below me an iridescent bubble not greatly larger than a star shine beautifully but faintly, and up and up from it looking larger and larger came a flock of white, innumerable swans, singing and singing and singing, till it seemed as though even the gods were wild ships swimming in music.

"What is it?" I said to one that was humble among the gods.

"Only a world has ended," he said to me, "and the swans are coming back to the gods returning the gift of song."

"A whole world dead!" I said.

"Dead," said he that was humble among the gods. "The worlds are not for ever; only song is immortal."

"Look! Look!" he said. "There will be a new one soon."

And I looked and saw the larks, going down from the gods.

SPRING IN TOWN

At a street corner sat, and played with a wind, Winter disconsolate.

Still tingled the fingers of the passers-by and still their breath was visible, and still they huddled their chins into their coats when turning a corner they met with a new wind, still windows lighted sent out into the street the thought of romantic comfort by evening fires; these things still were, yet the throne of Winter tottered, and every breeze brought tidings of further fortresses lost on lakes or boreal hill-slopes. And not any longer as a king did Winter appear in those streets, as when the city was decked with gleaming white to greet him as a conqueror and he rode in with his glittering icicles and haughty retinue of prancing winds, but he sat there with a little wind at the corner of the street like some old blind beggar with his hungry dog. And as to some old blind beggar Death approaches, and the alert ears of the sightless man prophetically hear his far-off footfall, so there came suddenly to Winter's ears the sound, from some neighbouring garden, of Spring approaching as she walked on daisies. And Spring approaching looked at huddled inglorious Winter.

"Begone," said Spring.

"There is nothing for you to do here," said Winter to her. Nevertheless he drew about him his grey and battered cloak and rose and called to his little bitter wind and up a side street that led northward strode away.

Pieces of paper and tall clouds of dust went with him as far as the city's outer gate. He turned then and called to Spring: "You can do nothing in this city," he said; then he marched homeward over plains and sea and heard his old winds howling as he marched. The ice broke up behind him and foundered like navies. To left and to right of him flew the flocks of the sea-birds, and far before him the geese's triumphant cry went like a clarion. Greater and greater grew his stature as he went northwards and ever more kingly his mien. Now he took baronies at a stride and now counties and came again to the snow-white frozen lands where the wolves came out to meet him and, draping himself anew with old grey clouds, strode through the gates of his invincible home, two old ice barriers swinging on pillars of ice that had never known the sun.

So the town was left to Spring. And she peered about to see what she could do with it. Presently she saw a dejected dog coming prowling down the road, so she sang to him and he gambolled. I saw him next day strutting by with something of an air. Where there were trees she went to them and whispered, and they sang the arboreal song that only trees can hear, and the green buds came peeping out as stars while yet it is twilight, secretly one by one. She went to gardens and awaked from dreaming the warm maternal earth. In little patches bare and desolate she called up like a flame the golden crocus, or its purple brother like an emperor's ghost. She gladdened the graceless backs of untidy houses, here with a weed, there with a little grass. She said to the air, "Be joyous."

Children began to know that daisies blew in unfrequented corners. Buttonholes began to appear in the coats of the young men. The work of Spring was accomplished.

HOW THE ENEMY CAME TO THLUNRANA

It had been prophesied of old and foreseen from the ancient days that its enemy would come upon Thlunrana. And the date of its doom was known and the gate by which it would enter, yet none had prophesied of the enemy who he was save that he was of the gods though he dwelt with men. Meanwhile Thlunrana, that secret lamaserai, that chief cathedral of wizardry, was the terror of the valley in which it stood and of all lands round about it. So narrow and high were the windows and so strange when lighted at night that they seemed to regard men with the demoniac leer of something that had a secret in the dark. Who were the magicians and the deputy-magicians and the great arch-wizard of that furtive place nobody knew, for they went veiled and hooded and cloaked completely in black.

Though her doom was close upon her and the enemy of prophecy should come that very night through the open, southward door that was named the Gate of the Doom, yet that rocky edifice Thlunrana remained mysterious still, venerable, terrible, dark, and dreadfully crowned with her doom. It was not often that anyone dared wander near to Thlunrana by night when the moan of the magicians invoking we know not Whom rose faintly from inner chambers, scaring the drifting bats: but on the last night of all the man from the black-thatched cottage by the five pine-trees came, because he would see Thlunrana once again before the enemy that was divine, but that dwelt with men, should come against it and it should be no more. Up the dark valley he went like a bold man, but his fears were thick upon him; his bravery bore their weight but stooped a little beneath them. He went in at the southward gate that is named the Gate of the Doom. He came into a dark hall, and up a marble stairway passed to see the last of Thlunrana. At the top a curtain of black velvet hung and he passed into a chamber heavily hung with curtains, with a gloom in it that was blacker than anything they could account for. In a sombre chamber beyond, seen through a vacant archway, magicians with lighted tapers plied their wizardry and whispered incantations. All the rats in the place were passing away, going whimpering down the stairway. The man from the black-thatched cottage passed through that second chamber: the magicians did not look at him and did not cease to whisper. He passed from them through heavy curtains still of black velvet and came into a chamber of black marble where nothing stirred. Only one taper burned in the third chamber; there were no windows. On the smooth floor and under the smooth wall a silk pavilion stood with its curtains drawn close together: this was the holy of holies of that ominous place, its inner mystery. One on each side of it dark figures crouched, either of men or women or cloaked stone, or of beasts trained to be silent. When the awful stillness of the mystery was more than he could bear the man from the black-thatched cottage by the five pine-trees went up to the silk pavilion, and with a bold and nervous clutch of the hand drew one of the curtains aside, and saw the inner mystery, and laughed. And the prophecy was fulfilled, and Thlunrana was never more a terror to the valley, but the magicians passed away from their terrific halls and fled through the open fields wailing and beating their breasts, for laughter was the enemy that was doomed to come against Thlunrana through her southward gate (that was named the Gate of the Doom), and it is of the gods but dwells with man.

A LOSING GAME

Once in a tavern Man met face to skull with Death. Man entered gaily but Death gave no greeting, he sat with his jowl morosely over an ominous wine.

"Come, come," said Man, "we have been antagonists long, and if I were losing yet I should not be surly."

But Death remained unfriendly watching his bowl of wine and gave no word in answer.

Then Man solicitously moved nearer to him and, speaking cheerily still, "Come, come," he said again, "you must not resent defeat."

And still Death was gloomy and cross and sipped at his infamous wine and would not look up at Man and would not be companionable.

But Man hated gloom either in beast or god, and it made him unhappy to see his adversary's discomfort, all the more because he was the cause, and still he tried to cheer him.

"Have you not slain the Dinatherium?" he said. "Have you not put out the Moon? Why! you will beat me yet."

And with a dry and barking sound Death wept and nothing said; and presently Man arose and went wondering away; for he knew not if Death wept out of pity for his opponent, or because he knew that he should not have such sport again when the old game was over and Man was gone, or whether because perhaps, for some hidden reason, he could never repeat on Earth his triumph over the Moon.

TAKING UP PICADILLY

Going down Picadilly one day and nearing Grosvenor Place I saw, if my memory is not at fault, some workmen with their coats off—or so they seemed. They had pickaxes in their hands and wore corduroy trousers and that little leather band below the knee that goes by the astonishing name of "York-to-London."

They seemed to be working with peculiar vehemence, so that I stopped and asked one what they were doing.

"We are taking up Picadilly," he said to me.

"But at this time of year?" I said. "Is it usual in June?"

"We are not what we seem," said he.

"Oh, I see," I said, "you are doing it for a joke."

"Well, not exactly that," he answered me.

"For a bet?" I said.

"Not precisely," said he.

And then I looked at the bit that they had already picked, and though it was broad daylight over my head it was darkness down there, all full of the southern stars.

"It was noisy and bad and we grew aweary of it," said he that wore corduroy trousers. "We are not what we appear."

They were taking up Picadilly altogether.

AFTER THE FIRE

When that happened which had been so long in happening and the world hit a black, uncharted star, certain tremendous creatures out of some other world came peering among the cinders to see if there were anything there that it were worth while to remember. They spoke of the great things that the world was known to have had; they mentioned the mammoth. And presently they saw man's temples, silent and windowless, staring like empty skulls.

"Some great thing has been here," one said, "in these huge places." "It was the mammoth," said one. "Something greater than he," said another.

And then they found that the greatest thing in the world had been the dreams of man.

THE CITY

In time as well as space my fancy roams far from here. It led me once to the edge of certain cliffs that were low and red and rose up out of a desert: a little way off in the desert there was a city. It was evening, and I sat and watched the city.

Presently I saw men by threes and fours come softly stealing out of that city's gate to the number of about twenty. I heard the hum of men's voices speaking at evening.

"It is well they are gone," they said. "It is well they are gone. We can do business now. It is well they are gone." And the men that had left the city sped away over the sand and so passed into the twilight.

"Who are these men?" I said to my glittering leader.

"The poets," my fancy answered. "The poets and artists."

"Why do they steal away?" I said to him. "And why are the people glad that they have gone?"

He said: "It must be some doom that is going to fall on the city, something has warned them and they have stolen away. Nothing may warn the people."

I heard the wrangling voices, glad with commerce, rise up from the city. And then I also departed, for there was an ominous look on the face of the sky.

And only a thousand years later I passed that way, and there was nothing, even among the weeds, of what had been that city.

THE FOOD OF DEATH

Death was sick. But they brought him bread that the modern bakers make, whitened with alum, and the tinned meats of Chicago, with a pinch of our modern substitute for salt. They carried him into the dining-room of a great hotel (in that close atmosphere Death breathed more freely), and there they gave him their cheap Indian tea. They brought him a bottle of wine that they called champagne. Death drank it up. They brought a newspaper and looked up the patent medicines; they gave him the foods that it recommended for invalids, and a little medicine as prescribed in the paper. They gave him some milk and borax, such as children drink in England.

Death arose ravening, strong, and strode again through the cities.

THE LONELY IDOL

I had from a friend an old outlandish stone, a little swine-faced idol to whom no one prayed.

And when I saw his melancholy case as he sat cross-legged at receipt of prayer, holding a little scourge that the years had broken (and no one heeded the scourge and no one prayed and no one came with squealing sacrifice; and he had been a god), then I took pity on the little forgotten thing and prayed to it as perhaps they prayed long since, before the coming of the strange dark ships, and humbled myself and said:

"O idol, idol of the hard pale stone, invincible to the years, O scourge-holder, give ear for behold I pray.

"O little pale-green image whose wanderings are from far, know thou that here in Europe and in other lands near by, too soon there pass from us the sweets and song and the lion strength of youth: too soon do their cheeks fade, their hair grow grey and our beloved die; too brittle is beauty, too far off is fame and the years are gathered too soon; there are leaves, leaves falling, everywhere falling; there is autumn among men, autumn and reaping; failure there is, struggle, dying and weeping, and all that is beautiful hath not remained but is even as the glory of morning upon the water.

"Even our memories are gathered too with the sound of the ancient voices, the pleasant ancient voices that come to our ears no more; the very gardens of our childhood fade, and there dims with the speed of the years even the mind's own eye.

"O be not any more the friend of Time, for the silent hurry of his malevolent feet have trodden down what's fairest; I almost hear the whimper of the years running behind him hound-like, and it takes few to tear us.

"All that is beautiful he crushes down as a big man tramples daises, all that is fairest. How very fair are the little children of men. It is autumn with all the world, and the stars weep to see it.

"Therefore no longer be the friend of Time, who will not let us be, and be not good to him but pity us, and let lovely things live on for the sake of our tears."

Thus prayed I out of compassion one windy day to the snout-faced idol to whom no one kneeled.

THE SPHINX IN THEBES (MASSACHUSETTS)

There was a woman in a steel-built city who had all that money could buy, she had gold and dividends and trains and houses, and she had pets to play with, but she had no sphinx.

So she besought them to bring her a live sphinx; and therefore they went to the menageries, and then to the forests and the desert places, and yet could find no sphinx.

And she would have been content with a little lion but that one was already owned by a woman she knew; so they had to search the world again for a sphinx.

And still there was none.

But they were not men that it is easy to baffle, and at last they found a sphinx in a desert at evening watching a ruined temple whose gods she had eaten hundreds of years ago when her hunger was on her. And they cast chains on her, who was still with an ominous stillness, and took her westwards with them and brought her home.

And so the sphinx came to the steel-built city.

And the woman was very glad that she owned a sphinx: but the sphinx stared long into her eyes one day, and softly asked a riddle of the woman.

And the woman could not answer, and she died.

And the sphinx is silent again and none knows what she will do.

THE REWARD

One's spirit goes further in dreams than it does by day. Wandering once by night from a factory city I came to the edge of Hell.

The place was foul with cinders and cast-off things, and jagged, half-buried things with shapeless edges, and there was a huge angel with a hammer building in plaster and steel. I wondered what he did in that dreadful place. I hesitated, then asked him what he was building. "We are adding to Hell," he said, "to keep pace with the times." "Don't be too hard on them," I said, for I had just come out of a compromising age and a weakening country. The angel did not answer. "It won't be as bad as the old hell, will it?" I said. "Worse," said the angel.

"How can you reconcile it with your conscience as a Minister of Grace," I said, "to inflict such a punishment?" (They talked like this in the city whence I had come and I could not avoid the habit of it.)

"They have invented a new cheap yeast," said the angel.

I looked at the legend on the walls of the hell that the angel was building, the words were written in flame, every fifteen seconds they changed their color, "Yeasto, the great new yeast, it builds up body and brain, and something more."

"They shall look at it for ever," the angel said.

"But they drove a perfectly legitimate trade," I said, "the law allowed it."

The angel went on hammering into place the huge steel uprights.

"You are very revengeful," I said. "Do you never rest from doing this terrible work?"

"I rested one Christmas Day," the angel said, "and looked and saw little children dying of cancer. I shall go on now until the fires are lit."

"It is very hard to prove," I said, "that the yeast is as bad as you think."

"After all," I said, "they must live."

And the angel made no answer but went on building his hell.

THE TROUBLE IN LEAFY GREEN STREET

She went to the idol-shop in Moleshill Street, where the old man mumbles, and said: "I want a god to worship when it is wet."

The old man reminded her of the heavy penalties that rightly attach to idolatry and, when he had enumerated all, she answered him as was meet: "Give me a god to worship when it is wet."

And he went to the back places of his shop and sought out and brought her a god. The same was carved of grey stone and wore a propitious look and was named, as the old man mumbled, The God of Rainy Cheerfulness.

Now it may be that long confinement to the house affects adversely the liver, or these things may be of the soul, but certain it is that on a rainy day her spirits so far descended that those cheerful creatures came within sight of the Pit, and, having tried cigarettes to no good end, she bethought her of Moleshill Street and the mumbling man.

He brought the grey idol forth and mumbled of guarantees, although he put nothing on paper, and she paid him there and then his preposterous price and took the idol away.

And on the next wet day that there ever was she prayed to the grey-stone idol that she had bought, the God of Rainy Cheerfulness (who knows with what ceremony or what lack of it?), and so brought down on her in Leafy Green Street, in the preposterous house at the corner, that doom of which all men speak.

THE MIST

The mist said unto the mist: "Let us go up into the Downs." And the mist came up weeping.

And the mist went into the high places and the hollows.

And clumps of trees in the distance stood ghostly in the haze.

But I went to a prophet, one who loved the Downs, and I said to him: "Why does the mist come up weeping into the Downs when it goes into the high places and the hollows?"

And he answered: "The mist is the company of a multitude of souls who never saw the Downs, and now are dead. Therefore they come up weeping into the Downs, who are dead and never saw them."

FURROW-MAKER

He was all in black, but his friend was dressed in brown, members of two old families.

"Is there any change in the way you build your houses?" said he in black.

"No change," said the other. "And you?"

"We change not," he said.

A man went by in the distance riding a bicycle.

"He is always changing," said the one in black, "of late almost every century. He is uneasy. Always changing."

"He changes the way he builds his house, does he not?" said the brown one.

"So my family say," said the other. "They say he has changed of late."

"They say he takes much to cities?" the brown one said.

"My cousin who lives in belfries tells me so," said the black one. "He says he is much in cities."

"And there he grows lean?" said the brown one.

"Yes, he grows lean."

"Is it true what they say?" said the brown one.

"Caw," said the black one.

"Is it true that he cannot live many centuries?"

"No, no," said the black one. "Furrow-maker will not die. We must not lose furrow-maker. He has been foolish of late, he has played with smoke and is sick. His engines have wearied him and his cities are evil. Yes, he is very sick. But in a few centuries he will forget his folly and we shall not lose furrow-maker. Time out of mind he has delved and my family have got their food from the raw earth behind him. He will not die."

"But they say, do they not?" said the brown one, "his cities are noisome, and that he grows sick in them and can run no longer, and that it is with him as it is with us when we grow too many, and the grass has the bitter taste in the rainy season, and our young grow bloated and die."

"Who says it?" replied the black one.

"Pigeon," the brown one answered. "He came back all dirty. And Hare went down to the edge of the cities once. He says it too. Man was too sick to chase him. He thinks that Man will die, and his wicked friend Dog with him. Dog, he will die. That nasty fellow Dog. He will die too, the dirty fellow!"

"Pigeon and Hare!" said the black one. "We shall not lose furrow-maker."

"Who told you he will not die?" his brown friend said.

"Who told me!" the black one said. "My family and his have understood each other times out of mind. We know what follies will kill each other and what each may survive, and I say that furrow-maker will not die."

"He will die," said the brown one.

"Caw," said the other.

And Man said in his heart: "Just one invention more. There is something I want to do with petrol yet, and then I will give it all up and go back to the woods."

LOBSTER SALAD

I was climbing round the perilous outside of the Palace of Colquon-hombros. So far below me that in the tranquil twilight and clear air of those lands I could only barely see them lay the craggy tops of the mountains.

It was along no battlements or terrace edge I was climbing, but on the sheer face of the wall itself, getting what foothold I could where the boulders joined.

Had my feet been bare I was done, but though I was in my night-shirt I had on stout leather boots, and their edges somehow held in those narrow cracks. My fingers and wrists were aching.

Had it been possible to stop for a moment I might have been lured to give a second look at the fearful peaks of the mountains down there in the twilight, and this must have been fatal.

That the thing was all a dream is beside the point. We have fallen in dreams before, but it is well known that if in one of those falls you ever hit the ground—you die: I had looked at those menacing mountaintops and knew well that such a fall as the one I feared must have such a termination. Then I went on.

It is strange what different sensations there can be in different boulders—every one gleaming with the same white light and every one chosen to match the rest by minions of ancient kings—when your life depends on the edges of every one you come to. Those edges seemed strangely different. It was of no avail to overcome the terror of one, for the next would give you a hold in quite a different way or hand you over to death in a different manner. Some were too sharp to hold and some too flush with the wall, those whose hold was the best crumbled the soonest; each rock had its different terror: and then there were those things that followed behind me.

And at last I came to a breach made long ago by earthquake, lightning or war: I should have had to go down a thousand feet to get round it and they would come up with me while I was doing that, for certain sable apes that I have not mentioned as yet, things that had tigerish teeth and were born and bred on that wall, had pursued me all the evening. In any case I could have gone no farther, nor did I know what the king would do along whose wall I was climbing. It was time to drop and be done with it or stop and await those apes.

And then it was that I remembered a pin, thrown carelessly down out of an evening-tie in another world to the one where grew that glittering wall, and lying now if no evil chance had removed it on a chest of drawers by my bed. The apes were very close, and hurrying, for they knew my fingers were slipping, and the cruel peaks of those infernal mountains seemed surer of me than the apes. I reached out with a desperate effort of will towards where the pin lay on the chest of drawers. I groped about. I found it! I ran it into my arm. Saved!

THE RETURN OF THE EXILES

The old man with a hammer and the one-eyed man with a spear were seated by the roadside talking as I came up the hill.

"It isn't as though they hadn't asked us," the one with the hammer said.

"There ain't no more than twenty as knows about it," said the other.

"Twenty's twenty," said the first.

"After all these years," said the one-eyed man with the spear. "After all these years. We might go back just once."

"O' course we might," said the other.

Their clothes were old even for laborers, the one with the hammer had a leather apron full of holes and blackened, and their hands looked like leather. But whatever they were they were English, and this was pleasant to see after all the motors that had passed me that day with their burden of mixed and doubtful nationalities.

When they saw me the one with the hammer touched his greasy cap.

"Might we make so bold, sir," he said, "as the ask the way to Stonehenge?"

"We never ought to go," mumbled the other plaintively. "There's not more than twenty as knows, but...."

I was bicycling there myself to see the place so I pointed out the way and rode on at once, for there was something so utterly servile about them both that I did not care for their company. They seemed by their wretched mien to have been persecuted or utterly neglected for many years, I thought that very likely they had done long terms of penal servitude.

When I came to Stonehenge I saw a group of about a score of men standing among the stones. They asked me with some solemnity if I was expecting anyone, and when I said No they spoke to me no more. It was three miles back where I left those strange old men, but I had not been in the stone circle long when they appeared, coming with great strides along the road. When they saw them all the people took off their hats and acted very strangely, and I saw that they had a goat which they led up then to the old altar stone. And the two old men came up with their hammer and spear and began apologizing plaintively for the liberty they had taken in coming back to that place, and all the people knelt on the grass before them. And then still kneeling they killed the goat by the altar, and when the two old men saw this they came up with many excuses and eagerly sniffed the blood. And at first this made them happy. But soon the one with the spear began to whimper. "It used to be men," he lamented. "It used to be men."

And the twenty men began looking uneasily at each other, and the plaint of the one-eyed man went on in that tearful voice, and all of a sudden they all looked at me. I do not know who the two old men were or what any of them were doing, but there are moments when it is clearly time to go, and I left them there and then. And just as I got up on to my bicycle I heard the plaintive voice of the one with the hammer apologizing for the liberty he had taken in coming back to Stonehenge.

"But after all these years," I heard him crying, "After all these years...."

And the one with the spear said: "Yes, after three thousand years...."

NATURE AND TIME

Through the streets of Coventry one winter's night strode a triumphant spirit. Behind him stooping, unkempt, utterly ragged, wearing the clothes and look that outcasts have, whining, weeping, reproaching, an ill-used spirit tried to keep pace with him. Continually she plucked him by the sleeve and cried out to him as she panted after and he strode resolute on.

It was a bitter night, yet it did not seem to be the cold that she feared, ill-clad though she was, but the trams and the ugly shops and the glare of the factories, from which she continually winced as she hobbled on, and the pavement hurt her feet.

He that strode on in front seemed to care for nothing, it might be hot or cold, silent or noisy, pavement or open fields, he merely had the air of striding on.

And she caught up and clutched him by the elbow. I heard her speak in her unhappy voice, you scarcely heard it for the noise of the traffic.

"You have forgotten me," she complained to him. "You have forsaken me here."

She pointed to Coventry with a wide wave of her arm and seemed to indicate other cities beyond. And he gruffly told her to keep pace with him and that he did not forsake her. And she went on with her pitiful lamentation.

"My anemones are dead for miles," she said, "all my woods are fallen and still the cities grow. My child Man is unhappy and my other children are dying, and still the cities grow and you have forgotten me!"

And then he turned angrily on her, almost stopping in that stride of his that began when the stars were made.

"When have I ever forgotten you?" he said, "or when forsaken you ever? Did I not throw down Babylon for you? And is not Nineveh gone? Where is Persepolis that troubled you? Where Tarshish and Tyre? And you have said I forget you."

And at this she seemed to take a little comfort. I heard her speak once more, looking wistfully at her companion. "When will the fields come back and the grass for my children?"

"Soon, soon," he said: then they were silent. And he strode away, she limping along behind him, and all the clocks in the towers chimed as he passed.

THE SONG OF THE BLACKBIRD

As the poet passed the thorn-tree the blackbird sang.

"How ever do you do it?" the poet said, for he knew bird language.

"It was like this," said the blackbird. "It really was the most extraordinary thing. I made that song last Spring, it came to me all of a sudden. There was the most beautiful she-blackbird that the world has ever seen. Her eyes were blacker than lakes are at night, her feathers were blacker than the night itself, and nothing was as yellow as her beak; she could fly much faster than the lightning. She was not an ordinary she-blackbird, there has never been any other like her at all. I did not dare go near her because she was so wonderful. One day last Spring when it got warm again—it had been cold, we ate berries, things were quite different then, but Spring came and it got warm—one day I was thinking how wonderful she was and it seemed so extraordinary to think that I should ever have seen her, the only really wonderful she-blackbird in the world, that I opened my beak to give a shout, and then this song came, and there had never been anything like it before, and luckily I remembered it, the very song that I sang just now. But what is so extraordinary, the most amazing occurence of that marvellous day, was that no sooner had I sung the song than that very bird, the most wonderful she-blackbird in the world, flew right up to me and sat quite close to me on the same tree. I never remember such wonderful times as those.

"Yes, the song came in a moment, and as I was saying…."

And an old wanderer walking with a stick came by and the blackbird flew away, and the poet told the old man the blackbird's wonderful story.

"That song new?" said the wanderer. "Not a bit of it. God made it years ago. All the blackbirds used to sing it when I was young. It was new then."

THE MESSENGERS

One wandering nigh Parnassus chasing hares heard the high Muses.

"Take us a message to the Golden Town."

Thus sang the Muses.

But the man said: "They do not call to me. Not to such as me speak the Muses."

And the Muses called him by name.

"Take us a message," they said, "to the Golden Town."

And the man was downcast for he would have chased hares.

And the Muses called again.

And when whether in valleys or on high crags of the hills he still heard the Muses he went at last to them and heard their message, though he would fain have left it to other men and chased the fleet hares still in happy valleys.

And they gave him a wreath of laurels carved out of emeralds as only the Muses can carve. "By this," they said, "they shall know that you come from the Muses."

And the man went from that place and dressed in scarlet silks as befitted one that came from the high Muses. And through the gateway of the Golden Town he ran and cried his message, and his cloak floated behind him. All silent sat the wise men and the aged, they of the Golden Town; cross-legged they sat before their houses reading from parchments a message of the Muses that they sent long before.

And the young man cried his message from the Muses.

And they rose up and said: "Thou art not from the Muses. Otherwise spake they." And they stoned him and he died.

And afterwards they carved his message upon gold; and read it in their temples on holy days.

When will the Muses rest? When are they weary? They sent another messenger to the Golden Town. And they gave him a wand of ivory to carry in his hand with all the beautiful stories of the world wondrously carved thereon. And only the Muses could have carved it. "By this," they said, "they shall know that you come from the Muses."

And he came through the gateway of the Golden Town with the message he had for its people. And they rose up at once in the Golden street, they rose from reading the message that they had carved upon gold. "The last who came," they said, "came with a wreath of laurels carved out of emeralds, as only the Muses can carve. You are not from the Muses." And even as they had stoned the last so also they stoned him. And afterwards they carved his message on gold and laid it up in their temples.

When will the Muses rest? When are they weary? Even yet once again they sent a messenger under the gateway into the Golden Town. And for all that he wore a garland of gold that the high Muses gave him, a garland of kingcups soft and yellow on his head, yet fashioned of pure gold and by whom but the Muses, yet did they stone him in the Golden Town. But they had the message, and what care the Muses?

And yet they will not rest, for some while since I heard them call to me.

"Go take our message," they said, "unto the Golden Town."

But I would not go. And they spake a second time. "Go take our message," they said.

And still I would not go, and they cried out a third time: "Go take our message."

And though they cried a third time I would not go. But morning and night they cried and through long evenings.

When will the Muses rest? When are they weary? And when they would not cease to call to me I went to them and I said: "The Golden Town is the Golden Town no longer. They have sold their pillars for brass and their temples for money, they have made coins out of their golden doors. It is become a dark town full of trouble, there is no ease in its streets, beauty has left it and the old songs are gone."

"Go take our message," they cried.

And I said to the high Muses: "You do not understand. You have no message for the Golden Town, the holy city no longer."

"Go take our message," they cried.

"What is your message?" I said to the high Muses.

And when I heard their message I made excuses, dreading to speak such things in the Golden Town; and again they bade me go.

And I said: "I will not go. None will believe me."

And still the Muses cry to me all night long.

They do not understand. How should they know?

THE THREE TALL SONS

And at last Man raised on high the final glory of his civilization, the towering edifice of the ultimate city.

Softly beneath him in the deeps of the earth purred his machinery fulfilling all his needs, there was no more toil for man. There he sat at ease discussing the Sex Problem.

And sometimes painfully out of forgotten fields, there came to his outer door, came to the furthest rampart of the final glory of Man, a poor old woman begging. And always they turned her away. This glory of Man's achievement, this city was not for her.

It was Nature that came thus begging in from the fields, whom they always turned away.

And away she went again alone to her fields.

And one day she came again, and again they sent her hence. But her three tall sons came too.

"These shall go in," she said. "Even these my sons to your city."

And the three tall sons went in.

And these are Nature's sons, the forlorn one's terrible children, War, Famine and Plague.

Yea and they went in there and found Man unawares in his city still poring over his Problems, obsessed with his civilization, and never hearing their tread as those three came up behind.

COMPROMISE

They built their gorgeous home, their city of glory, above the lair of the earthquake. They built it of marble and gold in the shining youth of the world. There they feasted and fought and called their city immortal, and danced and sang songs to the gods. None heeded the earthquake in all those joyous streets. And down in the deeps of the earth, on the black feet of the abyss, they that would conquer Man mumbled long in the darkness, mumbled and goaded the earthquake to try his strength with that city, to go forth blithely at night and to gnaw its pillars like bones. And down in those grimy deeps the earthquake answered them, and would not do their pleasure and would not stir from thence, for who knew who they were who danced all day where he rumbled, and what if the lords of that city that had no fear of his anger were haply even the gods!

And the centuries plodded by, on and on round the world, and one day they that had danced, they that had sung in that city, remembered the lair of the earthquake in the deeps down under their feet, and made plans one with another and sought to avert the danger, sought to appease the earthquake and turn his anger away.

They sent down singing girls, and priests with oats and wine, they sent down garlands and propitious berries, down by dark steps to the black depths of the earth, they sent peacocks newly slain, and boys with burning spices, and their thin white sacred cats with collars of pearls all newly drawn from sea, they sent huge diamonds down in coffers of teak, and ointment and strange oriental dyes, arrows and armor and the rings of their queen.

"Oho," said the earthquake in the coolth of the earth, "so they are not the gods."

WHAT WE HAVE COME TO

When the advertiser saw the cathedral spires over the downs in the distance, he looked at them and wept.

"If only," he said, "this were an advertisement of Beefo, so nice, so nutritious, try it in your soup, ladies like it."

THE TOMB OF PAN

"Seeing," they said, "that old-time Pan is dead, let us now make a tomb for him and a monument, that the dreadful worship of long ago may be remembered and avoided by all."

So said the people of the enlightened lands. And they built a white and mighty tomb of marble. Slowly it rose under the hands of the builders and longer every evening after sunset it gleamed with rays of the departed sun.

And many mourned for Pan while the builders built; many reviled him. Some called the builders to cease and to weep for Pan and others called them to leave no memorial at all of so infamous a god. But the builders built on steadily.

And one day all was finished, and the tomb stood there like a steep sea-cliff. And Pan was carved thereon with humbled head and the feet of angels pressed upon his neck. And when the tomb was finished the sun had already set, but the afterglow was rosy on the huge bulk of Pan.

And presently all the enlightened people came, and saw the tomb and remembered Pan who was dead, and all deplored him and his wicked age. But a few wept apart because of the death of Pan.

But at evening as he stole out of the forest, and slipped like a shadow softly along the hills, Pan saw the tomb and laughed.

THE LAST BOOK OF WONDER (1916)

PREFACE

Ebrington Barracks
Aug. 16th, 1916

I do not know where I may be when this preface is read. As I write it in August 1916, I am at Ebrington Barracks, Londonderry, recovering from a slight wound. But it does not greatly matter where I am; my dreams are here before you amongst the following pages; and writing in a day when life is cheap, dreams seem to me all the dearer, the only things that survive.

Just now the civilization of Europe seems almost to have ceased, and nothing seems to grow in her torn fields but death, yet this is only for a while and dreams will come back again and bloom as of old, all the more radiantly for this terrible ploughing, as the flowers will bloom again where the trenches are and the primroses shelter in shell-holes for many seasons, when weeping Liberty has come home to Flanders.

To some of you in America this may seem an unnecessary and wasteful quarrel, as other people's quarrels often are; but it comes to this that though we are all killed there will be songs again, but if we were to submit and so survive there could be neither songs nor dreams, nor any joyous free things any more.

And do not regret the lives that are wasted amongst us, or the work that the dead would have done, for war is no accident that man's care could have averted, but is as natural, though not as regular, as the tides; as well regret the things that the tide has washed away, which destroys and cleanses and crumbles, and spares the minutest shells.

A TALE OF LONDON

"Come," said the Sultan to his hasheesh-eater in the very furthest lands that know Bagdad, "dream to me now of London."

And the hasheesh-eater made a low obeisance and seated himself cross-legged upon a purple cushion broidered with golden poppies, on the floor, beside an ivory bowl where the hasheesh was, and having eaten liberally of the hasheesh blinked seven times and spoke thus:

"O Friend of God, know then that London is the desiderate town even of all Earth's cities. Its houses are of ebony and cedar which they roof with thin copper plates that the hand of Time turns green. They have golden balconies in which amethysts are where they sit and watch the sunset. Musicians in the gloaming steal softly along the ways; unheard their feet fall on the white sea-sand with which those ways are strewn, and in the darkness suddenly they play on dulcimers and instruments with strings. Then are there murmurs in the balconies praising their skill, then are there bracelets cast down to them for reward and golden necklaces and even pearls.

"Indeed but the city is fair; there is by the sandy ways a paving all alabaster, and the lanterns along it are of chrysoprase, all night long they shine green, but of amethyst are the lanterns of the balconies.

"As the musicians go along the ways dancers gather about them and dance upon the alabaster pavings, for joy and not for hire. Sometimes a window opens far up in an ebony palace and a wreath is cast down to a dancer or orchids showered upon them.

"Indeed of many cities have I dreamt but of none fairer, through many marble metropolitan gates hasheesh has led me, but London is its secret, the last gate of all; the ivory bowl has nothing more to show. And indeed even now the imps that crawl behind me and that will not let me be are plucking me by the elbow and bidding my spirit return, for well they know that I have seen too much. 'No, not London,' they say; and therefore I will speak of some other city, a city of some less mysterious land, and anger not the imps with forbidden things. I will speak of Persepolis or famous Thebes."

A shade of annoyance crossed the Sultan's face, a look of thunder that you had scarcely seen, but in those lands they watched his visage well, and though his spirit was wandering far away and his eyes were bleared with hasheesh yet that storyteller there and then perceived the look that was death, and sent his spirit back at once to London as a man runs into his house when the thunder comes.

"And therefore," he continued, "in the desiderate city, in London, all their camels are pure white. Remarkable is the swiftness of their horses, that draw their chariots that are of ivory along those sandy ways and that are of surpassing lightness, they have little bells of silver upon their horses' heads. O Friend of God, if you perceived their merchants! The glory of their dresses in the noonday! They are no less gorgeous than those butterflies that float about their streets. They have overcloaks of green and vestments of azure, huge purple flowers blaze on their overcloaks, the work of cunning needles, the centres of the flowers are of gold and the petals of purple. All their hats are black—" ("No, no," said the Sultan)—"but irises are set about the brims, and green plumes float above the crowns of them.

"They have a river that is named the Thames, on it their ships go up with violet sails bringing incense for the braziers that perfume the streets, new songs exchanged for gold with alien tribes, raw silver for the statues of their heroes, gold to make balconies where the women sit, great sapphires to reward their poets with, the secrets of old cities and strange lands, the earning of the dwellers in far isles, emeralds, diamonds, and the hoards of the sea. And whenever a ship comes into port and furls its violet sails and the news spreads through London that she has come, then all the merchants go down to the river to barter, and all day long the chariots whirl through the streets, and the sound of their going is a mighty roar all day until evening, their roar is even like—"

"Not so," said the Sultan.

"Truth is not hidden from the Friend of God," replied the hasheesh-eater, "I have erred being drunken with the hasheesh, for in the desiderate city, even in London, so thick upon the ways is the white sea-sand with which the city glimmers that no sound comes from the path of the charioteers, but they go softly like a light sea-wind." ("It is well," said the Sultan.) "They go softly down to the port where the vessels are, and the merchandise in from the sea, amongst the wonders that the sailors show, on land by the high ships, and softly they go though swiftly at evening back to their homes.

"O would that the Munificent, the Illustrious, the Friend of God, had even seen these things, had seen the jewellers with their empty baskets, bargaining there by the ships, when the barrels of emeralds came up from the hold. Or would that he had seen the fountains there in silver basins in the midst of the ways. I have seen small spires upon their ebony houses and the spires were all of gold, birds strutted there upon the copper roofs from golden spire to spire that have no equal for splendour in all the woods of the world. And over London the desiderate city the sky is so deep a blue that by this alone the traveller may know where he has come, and may end his fortunate journey. Nor yet for any colour of the sky is there too great heat in London, for along its ways a wind blows always from the South gently and cools the city.

"Such, O Friend of God, is indeed the city of London, lying very far off on the yonder side of Bagdad, without a peer for beauty or excellence of its ways among the towns of the earth or cities of song; and even so, as I have told, its fortunate citizens dwell, with their hearts ever devising beautiful things and from the beauty of their own fair work that is more abundant around them every year, receiving new inspirations to work things more beautiful yet."

"And is their government good?" the Sultan said.

"It is most good," said the hasheesh-eater, and fell backwards upon the floor.

He lay thus and was silent. And when the Sultan perceived he would speak no more that night he smiled and lightly applauded.

And there was envy in that palace, in lands beyond Bagdad, of all that dwell in London.

THIRTEEN AT TABLE

In front of a spacious fireplace of the old kind, when the logs were well alight, and men with pipes and glasses were gathered before it in great easeful chairs, and the wild weather outside and the comfort that was within, and the season of the year—for it was Christmas—and the hour of the night, all called for the weird or uncanny, then out spoke the ex-master of foxhounds and told this tale.

I once had an odd experience too. It was when I had the Bromley and Sydenham, the year I gave them up—as a matter of fact it was the last day of the season. It was no use going on because there were no foxes left in the county, and London was sweeping down on us. You could see it from the kennels all along the skyline like a terrible army in grey, and masses of villas every year came skirmishing down our valleys. Our coverts were mostly on the hills, and as the town came down upon the valleys the foxes used to leave them and go right away out of the county and they never returned. I think they went by night and moved great distances. Well it was early April and we had drawn blank all day, and at the last draw of all, the very last of the season, we found a fox. He left the covert with his back to London and its railways and villas and wire and slipped away towards the chalk country and open Kent. I felt as I once felt as a child on one summer's day when I found a door in a garden where I played left luckily ajar, and I pushed it open and the wide lands were before me and waving fields of corn.

We settled down into a steady gallop and the fields began to drift by under us, and a great wind arose full of fresh breath. We left the clay lands where the bracken grows and came to a valley at the edge of the chalk. As we went down into it we saw the fox go up the other side like a shadow that crosses the evening, and glide into a wood that stood on the top. We saw a flash of primroses in the wood and we were out the other side, hounds hunting perfectly and the fox still going absolutely straight. It began to dawn on me then that we were in for a great hunt, I took a deep breath when I thought of it; the taste of the air of that perfect Spring afternoon as it came to one galloping, and the thought of a great run, were together like some old rare wine. Our faces now were to another valley, large fields led down to it, with easy hedges, at the bottom of it a bright blue stream went singing and a rambling village smoked, the sunlight on the opposite slopes danced like a fairy; and all along the top old woods were frowning, but they dreamed of Spring. The "field" had fallen of and were far behind and my only human companion was James, my old first whip, who had a hound's instinct, and a personal animosity against a fox that even embittered his speech.

Across the valley the fox went as straight as a railway line, and again we went without a check straight through the woods at the top. I remember hearing men sing or shout as they walked home from work, and sometimes children whistled; the sounds came up from the village to the woods at the top of the valley. After that we saw no more villages, but valley after valley arose and fell before us as though we were voyaging some strange and stormy sea, and all the way before us the fox went dead up-wind like the fabulous Flying Dutchman. There was no one in sight now but my first whip and me, we had both of us got on to our second horses as we drew the last covert.

Two or three times we checked in those great lonely valleys beyond the village, but I began to have inspirations, I felt a strange certainty within me that this fox was going on straight up-wind till he died or until night came and we could hunt no longer, so I reversed ordinary methods and only cast straight ahead and always we picked up the scent again at once. I believe that this fox was the last one left in the villa-haunted lands and that he was prepared to leave them for remote uplands far from men, that if we had come the following day he would not have been there, and that we just happened to hit off his journey.

Evening began to descend upon the valleys, still the hounds drifted on, like the lazy but unresting shadows of clouds upon a summer's day, we heard a shepherd calling to his dog, we saw two maidens move towards a hidden farm, one of them singing softly; no other sounds, but ours, disturbed the leisure and the loneliness of haunts that seemed not yet to have known the inventions of steam and gun-powder (even as China, they say, in some of her further mountains does not yet know that she has fought Japan).

And now the day and our horses were wearing out, but that resolute fox held on. I began to work out the run and to wonder where we were. The last landmark I had ever seen before must have been over five miles back and from there to the start was at least ten miles more. If only we could kill! Then the sun set. I wondered what chance we had of killing our fox. I looked at James' face as he rode beside me. He did not seem to have lost any confidence yet his horse was as tired as mine. It was a good clear twilight and the scent was as strong as ever, and the fences were easy enough, but those valleys were terribly trying and they still rolled on and on. It looked as if the light would outlast all possible endurance both of the fox and the horses, if the scent held good and he did not go to ground, otherwise night would end it. For long we had seen no houses and no roads, only chalk slopes with the twilight on them, and here and there some sheep, and scattered copses darkening in the evening. At some moment I seemed to realise all at once that the light was spent and that darkness was hovering, I looked at James, he was solemnly shaking his head. Suddenly in a little wooded valley we saw climb over the oaks the red-brown gables of a queer old house, at that instant I saw the fox scarcely heading by fifty yards. We blundered through a wood into full sight of the house, but no avenue led up to it or even a path nor were there any signs of wheel-marks anywhere. Already lights shone here and there in windows. We were in a park, and a fine park, but unkempt beyond credibility; brambles grew everywhere. It was too dark to see the fox any more but we knew he was dead beat, the hounds were just before us,—and a four-foot railing of oak. I shouldn't have tried it on a fresh horse the beginning of a run, and here was a horse near his last gasp. But what a run! an event standing out in a lifetime, and the hounds close up on their fox, slipping into the darkness as I hesitated. I decided to try it. My horse rose about eight inches and took it fair with his breast, and the oak log flew into handfuls of wet decay—it rotten with years. And then we were on a lawn and at the far end of it the hounds were tumbling over their fox. Fox, hounds and light were all done together at the of a twenty-mile point. We made some noise then, but nobody came out of the queer old house.

I felt pretty stiff as I walked round to the hall door with the mask and the brush while James went with the hounds and the two horses to look for the stables. I rang a bell marvellously encrusted with rust, and after a long while the door opened a little way revealing a hall with much old armour in it and the shabbiest butler that I have ever known.

I asked him who lived there. Sir Richard Arlen. I explained that my horse could go no further that night and that I wished to ask Sir Richard Arlen for a bed for the night.

"O, no one ever comes here, sir," said the butler.

I pointed out that I had come.

"I don't think it would be possible, sir," he said.

This annoyed me and I asked to see Sir Richard, and insisted until he came. Then I apologised and explained the situation. He looked only fifty, but a 'Varsity oar on the wall with the date of the early seventies, made him older than that; his face had something of the shy look of the hermit; he regretted that he had not room to put me up. I was sure that this was untrue, also I had to be put up there, there was nowhere else within miles, so I almost insisted. Then to my astonishment he turned to the butler and they talked it over in an undertone. At last they seemed to think that they could manage it, though clearly with reluctance. It was by now seven o' clock and Sir Richard told me he dined at half past seven. There was no question of clothes for me other than those I stood in, as my host was shorter and broader. He showed me presently to the drawing-room and there he reappeared before half past seven in evening dress and a white waistcoat. The drawing-room was large and contained old furniture but it was rather worn than venerable, an Aubusson carpet flapped about the floor, the wind seemed momently to enter the room, and old draughts haunted corners; the stealthy feet of rats that were never at rest indicated the extent of the ruin that time had wrought in the wainscot; somewhere far off a shutter flapped to and fro, the guttering candles were insufficient to light so large a room. The gloom that these things suggested was quite in keeping with Sir Richard's first remark to me after he entered the room: "I must tell you, sir, that I have led a wicked life. O, a very wicked life."

Such confidences from a man much older than oneself after one has known him for half an hour are so rare that any possible answer merely does not suggest itself. I said rather slowly, "O, really," and chiefly to fore-stall another such remark I said "What a charming house you have."

"Yes," he said, "I have not left it for nearly forty years. Since I left the 'Varsity. One is young there, you know, and one has opportunities; but I make no excuses, no excuses." And the door slipping its rusty latch, came drifting on the draught into the room, and the long carpet flapped and the hangings upon the walls, then the draught fell rustling away and the door slammed to again.

"Ah, Marianne," he said, "we have a guest to-night. Mr. Linton. This is Marianne Gib." And everything became clear to me. "Mad," I said to myself, for no one had entered the room.

The rats ran up the length of the room behind the wainscot ceaselessly, and the wind unlatched the door again and the folds of the carpet fluttered up to our feet and stopped there, for our weight held it down.

"Let me introduce Mr. Linton," said my host—"Lady Mary Errinjer."

The door slammed back again. I bowed politely. Even had I been invit-ed I should have humoured him, but it was the very least that an uninvited guest could do.

This kind of thing happened eleven times, the rustling, and the flut-tering of the carpet and the footsteps of the rats, and the restless door, and then the sad voice of my host introducing me to phantoms. Then for some while we waited while I struggled with the situation; conversation flowed slowly. And again the draught came trailing up the room, while the flaring candles filled it with hurrying shadows. "Ah, late again, Cicely," said my host in his soft, mournful way. "Always late, Cicely." Then I went down to dinner with that man and his mind and the twelve phantoms that haunted it. I found a long table with fine old silver on it and places laid for fourteen. The butler was now in evening dress, there were fewer draughts in the dining-room, the scene was less gloomy there. "Will you sit next to Rosalind at the other end," Richard said to me. "She always takes the head of the table, I wronged her most of all." I said, "I shall be delighted."

I looked at the butler closely, but never did I see by any expression of his face or by anything that he did any suggestion that he waited upon less than fourteen people in the complete possession of all their faculties.

Perhaps a dish appeared to be refused more often than taken but every glass was equally filled with champagne. At first I found little to say, but when Sir Richard speaking from the far end of the table said, "You are tired, Mr. Linton," I was reminded that I owed something to a host upon whom I had forced myself. It was excellent champagne and with the help of a second glass I made the effort to begin a conversation with a Miss Helen Errold for whom the place upon one side of me was laid. It came more easy to me very soon, I frequently paused in my monologue, like Mark Anthony, for a reply, and sometimes I turned and spoke to Miss Rosalind Smith. Sir Richard at the other end talked sorrowfully on, he spoke as a condemned man might speak to his judge, and yet somewhat as a judge might speak to one that he once condemned wrongly. My own mind began to turn to mournful things. I drank another glass of champagne, but I was still thirsty. I felt as if all the moisture in my body had been blown away over the downs of Kent by the wind up which we had galloped. Still I was not talking enough; my host was looking at me. I made another effort, after all I had something to talk about, a twenty-mile point is not often seen in a lifetime, especially south of the Thames. I began to describe the run to Rosalind Smith. I could see then that my host was pleased, the sad look in his face gave a kind of a flicker, like mist upon the mountains on a miserable day when a faint puff comes from the sea and the mist would lift if it could. And the butler refilled my glass very attentively. I asked her first if she hunted, and paused and began my story. I told her where we had found the fox and how fast and straight he had gone, and how I had got through the village by keeping to the road, while the little gardens and wire, and then the river, had stopped the rest of the field. I told her the kind of country that we crossed and how splendid it looked in the Spring, and how mysterious the valleys were as soon as the twilight came, and what a glorious horse I had and how wonderfully he went. I was so fearfully thirsty after the great hunt that I had to stop for a moment now and then, but I went on with my description of that famous run, for I had warmed to the subject, and after all there was nobody to tell of it but me except my old whipper-in, and "the old fellow's probably drunk by now," I thought. I described to her minutely the exact spot in the run at which it had come to me clearly that this was going to be the greatest hunt in the whole history of Kent. Sometimes I forgot incidents that had happened as one well may in a run of twenty miles, and then I had to fill in the gaps by inventing. I was pleased to be able to make the party go off well by means of my conversation, and besides that the lady to whom I was speaking was extremely pretty: I do not mean in a flesh and blood kind of way but there were little shadowy lines about the chair beside me that hinted at an unusually graceful figure when Miss Rosalind Smith was alive; and I began to perceive that what I first mistook for the smoke of guttering candles and a table-cloth waving in the draught was in reality an extremely animated company who listened, and not without interest, to my story of by far the greatest hunt that the world had ever known: indeed I told them that I would confidently go further and predict that never in the history of the world would there be such a run again. Only my throat was terribly dry. And then as it seemed they wanted to hear more about my horse. I had forgotten that I had come there on a horse, but when they reminded me it all came back; they looked so charming leaning over the table intent upon what I said, that I told them everything they wanted to know. Everything was going so pleasantly if only Sir Richard would cheer up. I heard his mournful voice every now and then—these were very pleasant people if only he would take them the right way. I could understand that he regretted his past, but the early seventies seemed centuries away and I felt sure that he misunderstood these ladies, they were not revengeful as he seemed to suppose. I wanted to show him how cheerful they really were, and so I made a joke and they an laughed at it, and then I chaffed them a bit, especially Rosalind, and nobody resented it in the very least. And still Sir Richard sat there with that unhappy look, like one that has ended weeping because it is vain and has not the consolation even of tears.

We had been a long time there and many of the candles had burned out, but there was light enough. I was glad to have an audience for my exploit, and being happy myself I was determined Sir Richard should be. I made more jokes and they still laughed good-naturedly; some of the jokes were a little broad perhaps but no harm was meant. And then—I do not wish to excuse myself—but I had had a harder day than I ever had had before and without knowing it I must have been completely exhausted; in this state the champagne had found me, and what would have been harmless at any other time must somehow have got the better of me when quite tired out—anyhow I went too far, I made some joke—I cannot in the least remember what—that suddenly seemed to offend them. I felt all at once a commotion in the air, I looked up and saw that they had all arisen from the table and were sweeping towards the door: I had not time to open it but it blew open on a wind, I could scarcely see what Sir Richard was doing because only two candles were left, I think the rest blew out when the ladies suddenly rose. I sprang up to apologise, to assure them—and then fatigue overcame me as it had overcome my horse at the last fence, I clutched at the table but the cloth came away and then I fell. The fall, and the darkness on the floor and the pent up fatigue of the day overcame me all three together.

The sun shone over glittering fields and in at a bedroom window and thousands of birds were chanting to the Spring, and there I was in an old four-poster bed in a quaint old panelled bedroom, fully dressed and wearing long muddy boots; someone had taken my spurs and that was all. For a moment I failed to realise and then it all came back, my enormity and the pressing need of an abject apology to Sir Richard. I pulled an embroidered bell rope until the butler came. He came in perfectly cheerful and indescribably shabby. I asked him if Sir Richard was up, and he said he had just gone down, and told me to my amazement that it was twelve o'clock. I asked to be shown in to Sir Richard at once. He was in his smoking-room. "Good morning," he said cheerfully the moment I went in. I went directly to the matter in hand. "I fear that I insulted some ladies in your house—" I began.

"You did indeed," he said, "You did indeed." And then he burst into tears and took me by the hand. "How can I ever thank you?" he said to me then. "We have been thirteen at table for thirty years and I never dared to insult them because I had wronged them all, and now you have done it and I know they will never dine here again." And for a long time he still held my hand, and then he gave it a grip and a kind of a shake which I took to mean "Goodbye" and I drew my hand away then and left the house. And I found James in the stables with the hounds and asked him how he had fared, and James, who is a man of very few words, said he could not rightly remember, and I got my spurs from the butler and climbed on to my horse and slowly we rode away from that queer old house, and slowly we wended home, for the hounds were footsore but happy and the horses were tired still. And when we recalled that the hunting season was ended we turned our faces to Spring and thought of the new things that try to replace the old. And that very year I heard, and have often heard since, of dances and happier dinners at Sir Richard Arlen's house.

THE CITY ON MALLINGTON MOOR

Besides the old shepherd at Lingwold whose habits render him unreliable I am probably the only person that has ever seen the city on Mallington Moor.

I had decided one year to do no London season; partly because of the ugliness of the things in the shops, partly because of the unresisted invasions of German bands, partly perhaps because some pet parrots in the oblong where I lived had learned to imitate cab-whistles; but chiefly because of late there had seized me in London a quite unreasonable longing for large woods and waste spaces, while the very thought of little valleys underneath copses full of bracken and foxgloves was a torment to me and every summer in London the longing grew worse till the thing was becoming intolerable. So I took a stick and a knapsack and began walking northwards, starting at Tetherington and sleeping at inns, where one could get real salt, and the waiter spoke English and where one had a name instead of a number; and though the tablecloth might be dirty the windows opened so that the air was clean, where one had the excellent company of farmers and men of the wold, who could not be thoroughly vulgar, because they had not the money to be so even if they had wished it.

At first the novelty was delightful, and then one day in a queer old inn up Uthering way, beyond Lingwold, I heard for the first time the rumour of the city said to be on Mallington Moor. They spoke of it quite casually over their glasses of beer, two farmers at the inn. "They say the queer folk be at Mallington with their city," one farmer said. "Travelling they seem to be," said the other. And more came in then and the rumour spread. And then, such are the contradictions of our little likes and dislikes and all the whims that drive us, that I, who had come so far to avoid cities, had a great longing all of a sudden for throngs again and the great hives of Man, and then and there determined on that bright Sunday morning to come to Mallington and there search for the city that rumour spoke of so strangely.

Mallington Moor, from all that they said of it, was hardly a likely place to find a thing by searching. It was a huge high moor, very bleak and desolate and altogether trackless. It seemed a lonely place from what they said. The Normans when they came had called it Mal Lieu and afterwards Mallintown and so it changed to Mallington. Though what a town can ever have had to do with a place so utterly desolate I do not know. And before that some say that the Saxons called it Baplas, which I believe to be a corruption of Bad Place.

And beyond the mere rumour of a beautiful city all of white marble and with a foreign look up on Mallington Moor, beyond this I could not get. None of them had seen it himself, "only heard of it like," and my questions, rather than stimulating conversation, would always stop it abruptly. I was no more fortunate on the road to Mallington until the Tuesday, when I was quite near it; I had been walking two days from the inn where I had heard the rumour and could see the great hill steep as a headland on which Mallington lay, standing up on the skyline: the hill was covered with grass, where anything grew at all, but Mallington Moor is all heather; it is just marked Moor on the map; nobody goes there and they do not trouble to name it. It was there where the gaunt hill first came into sight, by the roadside as I enquired for the marble city of some labourers by the way, that I was directed, partly I think in derision, to the old shepherd of Lingwold. It appeared that he, following sometimes sheep that had strayed, and wandering far from Lingwold, came sometimes up to the edge of Mallington Moor, and that he would come back from these excursions and shout through the villages, raving of a city of white marble and gold-tipped minarets. And hearing me asking questions of this city they had laughed and directed me to the shepherd of Lingwold. One well-meant warning they gave me as I went—the old man was not reliable.

And late that evening I saw the thatches of Lingwold sheltering under the edge of that huge hill that Atlas-like held up those miles of moor to the great winds and heaven.

They knew less of the city in Lingwold than elsewhere but they knew the whereabouts of the man I wanted, though they seemed a little ashamed of him. There was an inn in Lingwold that gave me shelter, whence in the morning, equipped with purchases, I set out to find their shepherd. And there he was on the edge of Mallington Moor standing motionless, gazing stupidly at his sheep; his hands trembled continually and his eyes had a blear look, but he was quite sober, wherein all Lingwold had wronged him.

And then and there I asked him of the city and he said he had never heard tell of any such place. And I said, "Come, come, you must pull yourself together." And he looked angrily at me; but when he saw me draw from amongst my purchases a full bottle of whiskey and a big glass he became more friendly. As I poured out the whiskey I asked him again about the marble city on Mallington Moor but he seemed quite honestly to know nothing about it. The amount of whiskey he drank was quite incredible, but I seldom express surprise and once more I asked him the way to the wonderful city. His hand was steadier now and his eyes more intelligent and he said that he had heard something of some such city, but his memory was evidently blurred and he was still unable to give me useful directions. I consequently gave him another tumbler, which he drank off like the first without any water, and almost at once he was a different man. The trembling in his hands stopped altogether, his eye became as quick as a younger man's, he answered my questions readily and frankly, and, what was more important to me still, his old memory became alert and clear for even minutest details. His gratitude to myself I need not mention, for I make no pretence that I bought the bottle of whiskey that the old shepherd enjoyed so much without at least some thought of my own advantage. Yet it was pleasant to reflect that it was due to me that he had pulled himself together and steadied his shaking hand and cleared his mind, recovered his memory and his self-respect. He spoke to me quite clearly, no longer slurring his words; he had seen the city first one moonlight night when he was lost in the mist on the big moor, he had wandered far in the mist, and when it lifted he saw the city by moonlight. He had no food, but luckily had his flask. There never was such a city, not even in books. Travellers talked sometimes of Venice seen from the sea, there might be such a place or there might not, but, whether or no, it was nothing to the city on Mallington Moor. Men who read books had talked to him in his time, hundreds of books, but they never could tell of any city like this. Why, the place was all of marble, roads, walls and palaces, all pure white marble, and the tops of the tall thin spires were entirely of gold. And they were queer folk in the city even for foreigners. And there were camels, but I cut him short for I thought I could judge for myself, if there was such a place, and, if not, I was wasting my time as well as a pint of good whiskey. So I got him to speak of the way, and after more circumlocution than I needed and more talk of the city he pointed to a tiny track on the black earth just beside us, a little twisty way you could hardly see.

I said the moor was trackless; untrodden of man or dog it certainly was and seemed to have less to do with the ways of man than any waste I have seen, but the track the old shepherd showed me, if track it was, was no more than the track of a hare—an elf-path the old man called it, Heaven knows what he meant. And then before I left him he insisted on giving me his flask with the queer strong rum it contained. Whiskey brings out in some men melancholy, in some rejoicing, with him it was clearly generosity and he insisted until I took his rum, though I did not mean to drink it. It was lonely up there, he said, and bitter cold and the city hard to find, being set in a hollow, and I should need the rum, and he had never seen the marble city except on days when he had had his flask: he seemed to regard that rusted iron flask as a sort of mascot, and in the end I took it.

I followed that odd, faint track on the black earth under the heather till I came to the big grey stone beyond the horizon, where the track divides into two, and I took the one to the left as the old man told me. I knew by another stone that I saw far off that I had not lost my way, nor the old man lied.

And just as I hoped to see the city's ramparts before the gloaming fell on that desolate place, I suddenly saw a long high wall of whiteness with pinnacles here and there thrown up above it, floating towards me silent and grim as a secret, and knew it for that evil thing the mist. The sun, though low, was shining on every sprig of heather, the green and scarlet mosses were shining with it too, it seemed incredible that in three minutes' time all those colours would be gone and nothing left all round but a grey darkness. I gave up hope of finding the city that day, a broader path than mine could have been quite easily lost. I hastily chose for my bed a thick patch of heather, wrapped myself in a waterproof cloak, and lay down and made myself comfortable. And then the mist came. It came like the careful pulling of lace curtains, then like the drawing of grey blinds; it shut out the horizon to the north, then to the east and west; it turned the whole sky white and hid the moor; it came down on it like a metropolis, only utterly silent, silent and white as tombstones.

And then I was glad of that strange strong rum, or whatever it was in the flask that the shepherd gave me, for I did not think that the mist would clear till night, and I feared the night would be cold. So I nearly emptied the flask; and, sooner than I expected, I fell asleep, for the first night out as a rule one does not sleep at once but is kept awake some while by the little winds and the unfamiliar sound of the things that wander at night, and that cry to one another far-off with their queer, faint voices; one misses them afterwards when one gets to houses again. But I heard none of these sounds in the mist that evening.

And then I woke and found that the mist was gone and the sun was just disappearing under the moor, and I knew that I had not slept for as long as

I thought. And I decided to go on while I could, for I thought that I was not very far from the city.

I went on and on along the twisty track, bits of the mist came down and filled the hollows but lifted again at once so that I saw my way. The twilight faded as I went, a star appeared, and I was able to see the track no longer. I could go no further that night, yet before I lay down to sleep I decided to go and look over the edge of a wide depression in the moor that I saw a little way off. So I left the track and walked a few hundred yards, and when I got to the edge the hollow was full of mist all white underneath me. Another star appeared and a cold wind arose, and with the wind the mist flapped away like a curtain. And there was the city.

Nothing the shepherd had said was the least untrue or even exaggerated. The poor old man had told the simple truth, there is not a city like it in the world. What he had called thin spires were minarets, but the little domes on the top were clearly pure gold as he said. There were the marble terraces he described and the pure white palaces covered with carving and hundreds of minarets. The city was obviously of the East and yet where there should have been crescents on the domes of the minarets there were golden suns with rays, and wherever one looked one saw things that obscured its origin. I walked down to it, and, passing through a wicket gate of gold in a low wall of white marble, I entered the city. The heather went right up to the city's edge and beat against the marble wall whenever the wind blew it. Lights began to twinkle from high windows of blue glass as I walked up the white street, beautiful copper lanterns were lit up and let down from balconies by silver chains, from doors ajar came the sound of voices singing, and then I saw the men. Their faces were rather grey than black, and they wore beautiful robes of coloured silk with hems embroidered with gold and some with copper, and sometimes pacing down the marble ways with golden baskets hung on each side of them I saw the camels of which the old shepherd spoke.

The people had kindly faces, but, though they were evidently friendly to strangers, I could not speak with them being ignorant of their language, nor were the sounds of the syllables they used like any language I had ever heard: they sounded more like grouse.

When I tried to ask them by signs whence they had come with their city they would only point to the moon, which was bright and full and was shining fiercely on those marble ways till the city danced in light. And now there began appearing one by one, slipping softly out through windows, men with stringed instruments in the balconies. They were strange instruments with huge bulbs of wood, and they played softly on them and very beautifully, and their queer voices softly sang to the music weird dirges of the griefs of their native land wherever that may be. And far off in the heart of the city others were singing too, the sound of it came to me wherever I roamed, not loud enough to disturb my thoughts, but gently turning the mind to pleasant things. Slender carved arches of marble, as delicate almost as lace, crossed and re-crossed the ways wherever I went. There was none of that hurry of which foolish cities boast, nothing ugly or sordid so far as I could see. I saw that it was a city of beauty and song. I wondered how they had travelled with all that marble, how they had laid it down on Mallington Moor, whence they had come and what their resources were, and determined to investigate closely next morning, for the old shepherd had not troubled his head to think how the city came, he had only noted that the city was there (and of course no one believed him, though that is partly his fault for his dissolute ways). But at night one can see little and I had walked all day, so I determined to find a place to rest in. And just as I was wondering whether to ask for shelter of those silk-robed men by signs or whether to sleep outside the walls and enter again in the morning, I came to a great archway in one of the marble houses with two black curtains, embroidered below with gold, hanging across it. Over the archway were carved apparently in many tongues the words: "Here strangers rest." In Greek, Latin and Spanish the sentence was repeated and there was writing also in the language that you see on the walls of the great temples of Egypt, and Arabic and what I took to be early Assyrian and one or two languages I had never seen. I entered through the curtains and found a tesselated marble court with golden braziers burning sleepy incense swinging by chains from the roof, all round the walls were comfortable mattresses lying upon the floor covered with cloths and silks. It must have been ten o'clock and I was tired. Outside the music still softly filled the streets, a man had set a lantern down on the marble way, five or six sat down round him, and he was sonorously telling them a story. Inside there were some already asleep on the beds, in the middle of the wide court under the braziers a woman dressed in blue was singing very gently, she did not move, but sung on and on, I never heard a song that was so soothing. I lay down on one of the mattresses by the wall, which was all inlaid with mosaics, and pulled over me some of the cloths with their beautiful alien work, and almost immediately my thoughts seemed part of the song that the woman was singing in the midst of the court under the golden braziers that hung from the high roof, and the song turned them to dreams, and so I fell asleep.

A small wind having arisen, I was awakened by a sprig of heather that beat continually against my face. It was morning on Mallington Moor, and the city was quite gone.

WHY THE MILKMAN SHUDDERS
WHEN HE PERCEIVES THE DAWN

In the Hall of the Ancient Company of Milkmen round the great fireplace at the end, when the winter logs are burning and all the craft are assembled they tell to-day, as their grandfathers told before them, why the milkman shudders when he perceives the dawn.

When dawn comes creeping over the edges of hills, peers through the tree-trunks making wonderful shadows, touches the tops of tall columns of smoke going up from awakening cottages in the valleys, and breaks all golden over Kentish fields, when going on tip-toe thence it comes to the walls of London and slips all shyly up those gloomy streets the milkman perceives it and shudders.

A man may be a Milkman's Working Apprentice, may know what borax is and how to mix it, yet not for that is the story told to him. There are five men alone that tell that story, five men appointed by the Master of the Company, by whom each place is filled as it falls vacant, and if you do not hear it from one of them you hear the story from no one and so can never know why the milkman shudders when he perceives the dawn.

It is the way of one of these five men, greybeards all and milkmen from infancy, to rub his hands by the fire when the great logs burn, and to settle himself more easily in his chair, perhaps to sip some drink far other than milk, then to look round to see that none are there to whom it would not be fitting the tale should be told and, looking from face to face and seeing none but the men of the Ancient Company, and questioning mutely the rest of the five with his eyes, if some of the five be there, and receiving their permission, to cough and to tell the tale. And a great hush falls in the Hall of the Ancient Company, and something about the shape of the roof and the rafters makes the tale resonant all down the hall so that the youngest hears it far away from the fire and knows, and dreams of the day when perhaps he will tell himself why the milkman shudders when he perceives the dawn.

Not as one tells some casual fact is it told, nor is it commented on from man to man, but it is told by that great fire only and when the occasion and the stillness of the room and the merit of the wine and the profit of all seem to warrant it in the opinion of the five deputed men: then does one of them tell it, as I have said, not heralded by any master of ceremonies but as though it arose out of the warmth of the fire before which his knotted hands would chance to be; not a thing learned by rote, but told differently by each teller, and differently according to his mood, yet never has one of them dared to alter its salient points, there is none so base among the Company of Milkmen. The Company of Powderers for the Face know of this story and have envied it, the Worthy Company of Chin-Barbers, and the Company of Whiskerers; but none have heard it in the Milkmen's Hall, through whose wall no rumour of the secret goes, and though they have invented tales of their own Antiquity mocks them.

This mellow story was ripe with honourable years when milkmen wore beaver hats, its origin was still mysterious when smocks were the vogue, men asked one another when Stuarts were on the throne (and only the Ancient Company knew the answer) why the milkman shudders when he perceives the dawn. It is all for envy of this tale's reputation that the Company of Powderers for the Face have invented the tale that they too tell of an evening, "Why the Dog Barks when he hears the step of the Baker"; and because probably all men know that tale the Company of the Powderers for the Face have dared to consider it famous. Yet it lacks mystery and is not ancient, is not fortified with classical allusion, has no secret lore, is common to all who care for an idle tale, and shares with "The Wars of the Elves," the Calf-butcher's tale, and "The Story of the Unicorn and the Rose," which is the tale of the Company of Horse-drivers, their obvious inferiority.

But unlike all these tales so new to time, and many another that the last two centuries tell, the tale that the milkmen tell ripples wisely on, so full of quotation from the profoundest writers, so full of recondite allusion, so deeply tinged with all the wisdom of man and instructive with the experience of all times that they that hear it in the Milkmen's Hall as they interpret allusion after allusion and trace obscure quotation lose idle curiosity and forget to question why the milkman shudders when he perceives the dawn.

You also, O my reader, give not yourself up to curiosity. Consider of how many it is the bane. Would you to gratify this tear away the mystery from the Milkmen's Hall and wrong the Ancient Company of Milkmen? Would they if all the world knew it and it became a common thing to tell that tale any more that they have told for the last four hundred years? Rather a silence would settle upon their hall and a universal regret for the ancient tale and the ancient winter evenings. And though curiosity were a proper consideration yet even then this is not the proper place nor this the proper occasion for the Tale. For the proper place is only the Milkmen's Hall and the proper occasion only when logs burn well and when wine has been deeply drunken, then when the candles were burning well in long rows down to the dimness, down to the darkness and mystery that lie at the end of the hall, then were you one of the Company, and were I one of the five, would I rise from my seat by the fireside and tell you with all the embellishments that it has gleaned from the ages that story that is the heirloom of the milkmen. And the long candles would burn lower and lower and gutter and gutter away till they liquefied in their sockets, and draughts would blow from the shadowy end of the hall stronger and stronger till the shadows came after them, and still I would hold you with that treasured story, not by any wit of mine but all for the sake of its glamour and the times out of which it came; one by one the candles would flare and die and, when all were gone, by the light of ominous sparks when each milkman's face looks fearful to his fellow, you would know, as now you cannot, why the milkman shudders when he perceives the dawn.

THE BAD OLD WOMAN IN BLACK

The bad old woman in black ran down the street of the ox-butchers.

Windows at once were opened high up in those crazy gables; heads were thrust out: it was she. Then there arose the counsel of anxious voices, calling sideways from window to window or across to opposite houses. Why was she there with her sequins and bugles and old black gown? Why had she left her dreaded house? On what fell errand she hasted?

They watched her lean, lithe figure, and the wind in that old black dress, and soon she was gone from the cobbled street and under the town's high gateway. She turned at once to her right and was hid from the view of the houses. Then they all ran down to their doors, and small groups formed on the pavement; there they took counsel together, the eldest speaking first. Of what they had seen they said nothing, for there was no doubt it was she; it was of the future they spoke, and the future only.

In what notorious thing would her errand end? What gains had tempted her out from her fearful home? What brilliant but sinful scheme had her genius planned? Above all, what future evil did this portend? Thus at first it was only questions. And then the old grey-beards spoke, each one to a little group; they had seen her out before, had known her when she was younger, and had noted the evil things that had followed her goings: the small groups listened well to their low and earnest voices. No one asked questions now or guessed at her infamous errand, but listened only to the wise old men who knew the things that had been, and who told the younger men of the dooms that had come before.

Nobody knew how many times she had left her dreaded house; but the oldest recounted all the times that they knew, and the way she had gone each time, and the doom that had followed her going; and two could remember the earthquake that there was in the street of the shearers.

So were there many tales of the times that were, told on the pavement near the old green doors by the edge of the cobbled street, and the experience that the aged men had bought with their white hairs might be had cheap by the young. But from all their experience only this was clear, that never twice in their lives had she done the same infamous thing, and that the same calamity twice had never followed her goings. Therefore it seemed that means were doubtful and few for finding out what thing was about to befall; and an ominous feeling of gloom came down on the street of the ox-butchers. And in the gloom grew fears of the very worst. This comfort they only had when they put their fear into words—that the doom that followed her goings had never yet been anticipated. One feared that with magic she meant to move the moon; and he would have dammed the high tide on the neighbouring coast, knowing that as the moon attracted the sea the sea must attract the moon, and hoping by his device to humble her spells. Another would have fetched iron bars and clamped them across the street, remembering the earthquake there was in the street of the shearers. Another would have honoured his household gods, the little cat-faced idols seated above his hearth, gods to whom magic was no unusual thing, and, having paid their fees and honoured them well, would have put the whole case before them. His scheme found favour with many, and yet at last was rejected, for others ran indoors and brought out their gods, too, to be honoured, till there was a herd of gods all seated there on the pavement; yet would they have honoured them and put their case before them but that a fat man ran up last of all, carefully holding under a reverent arm his own two hound-faced gods, though he knew well—as, indeed, all men must—that they were notoriously at war with the little cat-faced idols. And although the animosities natural to faith had all been lulled by the crisis, yet a look of anger had come into the cat-like faces that no one dared disregard, and all perceived that if they stayed a moment longer there would be flaming around them the jealousy of the gods; so each man hastily took his idols home, leaving the fat man insisting that his hound-faced gods should be honoured.

Then there were schemes again and voices raised in debate, and many new dangers feared and new plans made.

But in the end they made no defence against danger, for they knew not what it would be, but wrote upon parchment as a warning, and in order that all might know: *"The bad old woman in black ran down the street of the ox-butchers."*

THE BIRD OF THE DIFFICULT EYE

Observant men and women that know their Bond Street well will appreciate my astonishment when in a jewellers' shop I perceived that nobody was furtively watching me. Not only this but when I even picked up a little carved crystal to examine it no shop-assistants crowded round me. I walked the whole length of the shop, still no one politely followed.

Seeing from this that some extraordinary revolution had occurred in the jewelry business I went with my curiosity well aroused to a queer old person half demon and half man who has an idol-shop in a byway of the City and who keeps me informed of affairs at the Edge of the World. And briefly over a pinch of heather incense that he takes by way of snuff he gave me this tremendous information: that Mr. Neepy Thang the son of Thangobrind had returned from the Edge of the World and was even now in London.

The information may not appear tremendous to those unacquainted with the source of jewelry; but when I say that the only thief employed by any West-end jeweller since famous Thangobrind's distressing doom is this same Neepy Thang, and that for lightness of fingers and swiftness of stockinged foot they have none better in Paris, it will be understood why the Bond Street jewellers no longer cared what became of their old stock.

There were big diamonds in London that summer and a few considerable sapphires. In certain astounding kingdoms behind the East strange sovereigns missed from their turbans the heirlooms of ancient wars, and here and there the keepers of crown jewels who had not heard the stockinged feet of Thang, were questioned and died slowly.

And the jewellers gave a little dinner to Thang at the Hotel Great Magnificent; the windows had not been opened for five years and there was wine at a guinea a bottle that you could not tell from champagne and cigars at half a crown with a Havana label. Altogether it was a splendid evening for Thang.

But I have to tell of a far sadder thing than a dinner at a hotel. The public require jewelry and jewelry must be obtained. I have to tell of Neepy Thang's last journey.

That year the fashion was emeralds. A man named Green had recently crossed the Channel on a bicycle and the jewellers said that a green stone would be particularly appropriate to commemorate the event and recommended emeralds.

Now a certain money-lender of Cheapside who had just been made a peer had divided his gains into three equal parts; one for the purchase of the peerage, country house and park, and the twenty thousand pheasants that are absolutely essential, and one for the upkeep of the position, while the third he banked abroad, partly to cheat the native tax-gatherer and partly because it seemed to him that the days of the Peerage were few and that he might at any moment be called upon to start afresh elsewhere. In the upkeep of the position he included jewelry for his wife and so it came about that Lord Castlenorman placed an order with two well-known Bond-street jewellers named Messrs. Grosvenor and Campbell to the extent of £100,000 for a few reliable emeralds.

But the emeralds in stock were mostly small and shop-soiled and Neepy Thang had to set out at once before he had had as much as a week in London. I will briefly sketch his project. Not many knew it, for where the form of business is blackmail the fewer creditors you have the better (which of course in various degrees applies at all times).

On the shores of the risky seas of Shiroora Shan grows one tree only so that upon its branches if anywhere in the world there must build its nest the Bird of the Difficult Eye. Neepy Thang had come by this information, which was indeed the truth, that if the bird migrated to Fairyland before the three eggs hatched out they would undoubtedly all turn into emeralds, while if they hatched out first it would be a bad business.

When he had mentioned these eggs to Messrs. Grosvenor and Campbell they had said, "The very thing": they were men of few words, in English, for it was not their native tongue.

So Neepy Thang set out. He bought the purple ticket at Victoria Station. He went by Herne Hill, Bromley and Bickley and passed St. Mary Cray. At Eynsford he changed and taking a footpath along a winding valley went wandering into the hills. And at the top of a hill in a little wood, where all the anemones long since were over and the perfume of mint and thyme from outside came drifting in with Thang, he found once more the familiar path, age-old and fair as wonder, that leads to the Edge of the World. Little to him were its sacred memories that are one with the secret of earth, for he was on business, and little would they be to me if I ever put them on paper. Let it suffice that he went down that path going further and further from the fields we know, and all the way he muttered to himself, "What if the eggs hatch out and it be a bad business!" The glamour that is at all times upon those lonely lands that lie at the back of the chalky hills of Kent intensified as he went upon his journeys. Queerer and queerer grew the things that he saw by little World-End Path. Many a twilight descended upon that journey with all their mysteries, many a blaze of stars; many a morning came flaming up to a tinkle of silvern horns; till the outpost elves of Fairyland came in sight and the glittering crests of Fairyland's three mountains betokened the journey's end. And so with painful steps (for the shores of the world are covered with huge crystals) he came to the risky seas of Shiroora Shan and saw them pounding to gravel the wreckage of fallen stars, saw them and heard their roar, those shipless seas that between earth and the fairies' homes heave beneath some huge wind that is none of our four. And there in the darkness on the grizzly coast, for darkness was swooping slantwise down the sky as though with some evil purpose, there stood that lonely, gnarled and deciduous tree. It was a bad place to be found in after dark, and night descended with multitudes of stars, beasts prowling in the blackness gluttered [See any dictionary, but in vain.] at Neepy Thang. And there on a lower branch within easy reach he clearly saw the Bird of the Difficult Eye sitting upon the nest for which she is famous. Her face was towards those three inscrutable mountains, far-off on the other side of the risky seas, whose hidden valleys are Fairyland. Though not yet autumn in the fields we know, it was close on midwinter here, the moment as Thang knew when those eggs hatch out. Had he miscalculated and arrived a minute too late? Yet the bird was even now about to migrate, her pinions fluttered and her gaze was toward Fairyland. Thang hoped and muttered a prayer to those pagan gods whose spite and vengeance he had most reason to fear. It seems that it was too late or a prayer too small to placate them, for there and then the stroke of midwinter came and the eggs hatched out in the roar of Shiroora Shan or ever the bird was gone with her difficult eye and it was a bad business indeed for Neepy Thang; I haven't the heart to tell you any more.

"'Ere," said Lord Castlenorman some few weeks later to Messrs. Grosvenor and Campbell, "you aren't 'arf taking your time about those emeralds."

THE LONG PORTER'S TALE

There are things that are known only to the long porter of Tong Tong Tarrup as he sits and mumbles memories to himself in the little bastion gateway.

He remembers the war there was in the halls of the gnomes; and how the fairies came for the opals once, which Tong Tong Tarrup has; and the way that the giants went through the fields below, he watching from his gateway: he remembers quests that are even yet a wonder to the gods. Who dwells in those frozen houses on the high bare brink of the world not even he has told me, and he is held to be garrulous. Among the elves, the only living things ever seen moving at that awful altitude where they quarry turquoise on Earth's highest crag, his name is a byword for loquacity wherewith they mock the talkative.

His favourite story if you offer him bash—the drug of which he is fondest, and for which he will give his service in war to the elves against the goblins, or vice-versa if the goblins bring him more—his favourite story, when bodily soothed by the drug and mentally fiercely excited, tells of a quest undertaken ever so long ago for nothing more marketable than an old woman's song.

Picture him telling it. An old man, lean and bearded, and almost monstrously long, that lolled in a city's gateway on a crag perhaps ten miles high; the houses for the most part facing eastward, lit by the sun and moon and the constellations we know, but one house on the pinnacle looking over the edge of the world and lit by the glimmer of those unearthly spaces where one long evening wears away the stars: my little offering of bash; a long forefinger that nipped it at once on a stained and greedy thumb—all these are in the foreground of the picture. In the background, the mystery of those silent houses and of not knowing who their denizens were, or what service they had at the hands of the long porter and what payment he had in return, and whether he was mortal.

Picture him in the gateway of this incredible town, having swallowed my bash in silence, stretch his great length, lean back, and begin to speak.

It seems that one clear morning a hundred years ago, a visitor to Tong Tong Tarrup was climbing up from the world. He had already passed above the snow and had set his foot on a step of the earthward stairway that goes down from Tong Tong Tarrup on to the rocks, when the long porter saw him. And so painfully did he climb those easy steps that the grizzled man on watch had long to wonder whether or not the stranger brought him bash, the drug that gives a meaning to the stars and seems to explain the twilight. And in the end there was not a scrap of bash, and the stranger had nothing better to offer that grizzled man than his mere story only.

It seems that the stranger's name was Gerald Jones, and he always lived in London; but once as a child he had been on a Northern moor. It was so long ago that he did not remember how, only somehow or other he walked alone on the moor, and all the ling was in flower. There was nothing in sight but ling and heather and bracken, except, far off near the sunset, on indistinct hills, there were little vague patches that looked like the fields of men. With evening a mist crept up and hid the hills, and still he went walking on over the moor. And then he came to the valley, a tiny valley in the midst of the moor, whose sides were incredibly steep. He lay down and looked at it through the roots of the ling. And a long, long way below him, in a garden by a cottage, with hollyhocks all round her that were taller than herself, there sat an old woman on a wooden chair, singing in the evening. And the man had taken a fancy to the song and remembered it after in London, and whenever it came to his mind it made him think of evenings—the kind you don't get in London—and he heard a soft wind going idly over the moor and the bumble-bees in a hurry, and forgot the noise of the traffic. And always, whenever he heard men speak of Time, he grudged to Time most this song. Once afterwards he went to that Northern moor again and found the tiny valley, but there was no old woman in the garden, and no one was singing a song. And either regret for the song that the old woman had sung, on a summer evening twenty years away and daily receding, troubled his mind, or else the wearisome work that he did in London, for he worked for a great firm that was perfectly useless; and he grew old early, as men do in cities. And at last, when melancholy brought only regret and the uselessness of his work gained round him with age, he decided to consult a magician. So to a magician he went and told him his troubles, and particularly he told him how he had heard the song. "And now," he said, "it is nowhere in the world."

"Of course it is not in the world," the magician said, "but over the Edge of the World you may easily find it." And he told the man that he was suffering from flux of time and recommended a day at the Edge of the World. Jones asked what part of the Edge of the World he should go to, and the magician had heard Tong Tong Tarrup well spoken of; so he paid him, as is usual, in opals, and started at once on the journey. The ways to that town are winding; he took the ticket at Victoria Station that they only give if they know you: he went past Bleth: he went along the Hills of Neol-Hungar and came to the Gap of Poy. All these are in that part of the world that pertains to the fields we know; but beyond the Gap of Poy on those ordinary plains, that so closely resemble Sussex, one first meets the unlikely. A line of common grey hills, the Hills of Sneg, may be seen at the edge of the plain from the Gap of Poy; it is there that the incredible begins, infrequently at first, but happening more and more as you go up the hills. For instance, descending once into Poy Plains, the first thing that I saw was an ordinary shepherd watching a flock of ordinary sheep. I looked at them for some time and nothing happened, when, without a word, one of the sheep walked up to the shepherd and borrowed his pipe and smoked it—an incident that struck me as unlikely; but in the Hills of Sneg I met an honest politician. Over these plains went Jones and over the Hills of Sneg, meeting at first unlikely things, and then incredible things, till he came to the long slope beyond the hills that leads up to the Edge of the World, and where, as all guidebooks tell, anything may happen. You might at the foot of this slope see here and there things that could conceivably occur in the fields we know; but soon these disappeared, and the traveller saw nothing but fabulous beasts, browsing on flowers as astounding as themselves, and rocks so distorted that their shapes had clearly a meaning, being too star- tling to be accidental. Even the trees were shockingly unfamiliar, they had so much to say, and they leant over to one another whenever they spoke and struck grotesque attitudes and leered. Jones saw two fir-trees fighting. The effect of these scenes on his nerves was very severe; still he climbed on, and was much cheered at last by the sight of a primrose, the only famil- iar thing he had seen for hours, but it whistled and skipped away. He saw the unicorns in their secret valley. Then night in a sinister way slipped over the sky, and there shone not only the stars, but lesser and greater moons, and he heard dragons rattling in the dark.

With dawn there appeared above him among its amazing crags the town of Tong Tong Tarrup, with the light on its frozen stairs, a tiny cluster of houses far up in the sky. He was on the steep mountain now: great mists were leaving it slowly, and revealing, as they trailed away, more and more astonishing things. Before the mist had all gone he heard quite near him, on what he had thought was bare mountain, the sound of a heavy galloping on turf. He had come to the plateau of the centaurs. And all at once he saw them in the mist: there they were, the children of fable, five enormous cen- taurs. Had he paused on account of any astonishment he had not come so far: he strode on over the plateau, and came quite near to the centaurs. It is never the centaurs' wont to notice men; they pawed the ground and shouted to one another in Greek, but they said no word to him. Nevertheless they turned and stared at him when he left them, and when he had crossed the plateau and still went on, all five of them cantered after to the edge of their green land; for above the high green plateau of the centaurs is nothing but naked mountains, and the last green thing that is seen by the mountaineer as he travels to Tong Tong Tarrup is the grass that the centaurs trample. He came into the snow fields that the mountain wears like a cape, its head being bare above it, and still climbed on. The centaurs watched him with increasing wonder.

Not even fabulous beasts were near him now, nor strange demoniac trees—nothing but snow and the clean bare crag above it on which was Tong Tong Tarrup. All day he climbed and evening found him above the snow-line; and soon he came to the stairway cut in the rock and in sight of that grizzled man, the long porter of Tong Tong Tarrup, sitting mumbling amazing memories to himself and expecting in vain from the stranger a gift of bash.

It seems that as soon as the stranger arrived at the bastion gateway, tired though he was, he demanded lodgings at once that commanded a good view of the Edge of the World. But the long porter, that grizzled man, disappointed of his bash, demanded the stranger's story to add to his memories before he would show him the way. And this is the story, if the long porter has told me the truth and if his memory is still what it was. And when the story was told, the grizzled man arose, and, dangling his musical keys, went up through door after door and by many stairs and led the stranger to the top-most house, the highest roof in the world, and in its parlour showed him the parlour window. There the tired stranger sat down in a chair and gazed out of the window sheer over the Edge of the World. The window was shut, and in its glittering panes the twilight of the World's Edge blazed and danced, partly like glow-worms' lamps and partly like the sea; it went by rippling, full of wonderful moons. But the traveller did not look at the wonderful moons. For from the abyss there grew with their roots in far constellations a row of hollyhocks, and amongst them a small green garden quivered and trembled as scenes tremble in water; higher up, ling in bloom was floating upon the twilight, more and more floated up till all the twilight was purple; the little green garden low down was hung in the midst of it. And the garden down below, and the ling all round it, seemed all to be trembling and drifting on a song. For the twilight was full of a song that sang and rang along the edges of the World, and the green garden and the ling seemed to flicker and ripple with it as the song rose and fell, and an old woman was singing it down in the garden. A bumble-bee sailed across from over the Edge of the World. And the song that was lapping there against the coasts of the World, and to which the stars were dancing, was the same that he had heard the old woman sing long since down in the valley in the midst of the Northern moor.

But that grizzled man, the long porter, would not let the stranger stay, because he brought him no bash, and impatiently he shouldered him away, himself not troubling to glance through the World's outermost window, for the lands that Time afflicts and the spaces that Time knows not are all one to that grizzled man, and the bash that he eats more profoundly astounds his mind than anything man can show him either in the World we know or over the Edge. And, bitterly protesting, the traveller went back and down again to the World.

* * * *

Accustomed as I am to the incredible from knowing the Edge of the World, the story presents difficulties to me. Yet it may be that the devastation wrought by Time is merely local, and that outside the scope of his destruction old songs are still being sung by those that we deem dead. I try to hope so. And yet the more I investigate the story that the long porter told me in the town of Tong Tong Tarrup the more plausible the alternative theory appears—that that grizzled man is a liar.

THE LOOT OF LOMA

Coming back laden with the loot of Loma, the four tall men looked earnestly to the right; to the left they durst not, for the precipice there that had been with them so long went sickly down on to a bank of clouds, and how much further below that only their fears could say.

Loma lay smoking, a city of ruin, behind them, all its defenders dead; there was no one left to pursue them, and yet their Indian instincts told them that all was scarcely well. They had gone three days along that narrow ledge: mountain quite smooth, incredible, above them, and precipice as smooth and as far below. It was chilly there in the mountains; at night a stream or a wind in the gloom of the chasm below them went like a whisper; the stillness of all things else began to wear the nerve—an enemy's howl would have braced them; they began to wish their perilous path were wider, they began to wish that they had not sacked Loma.

Had that path been any wider the sacking of Loma must indeed have been harder for them, for the citizens must have fortified the city but that the awful narrowness of that ten-league pass of the hills had made their crag-surrounded city secure. And at last an Indian had said, "Come, let us sack it." Grimly they laughed in the wigwams. Only the eagles, they said, had ever seen it, its hoard of emeralds and its golden gods; and one had said he would reach it, and they answered, "Only the eagles."

It was Laughing Face who said it, and who gathered thirty braves and led them into Loma with their tomahawks and their bows; there were only four left now, but they had the loot of Loma on a mule. They had four golden gods, a hundred emeralds, fifty-two rubies, a large silver gong, two sticks of malachite with amethyst handles for holding incense at religious feasts, four beakers one foot high, each carved from a rose-quartz crystal; a little coffer carved out of two diamonds, and (had they but known it) the written curse of a priest. It was written on parchment in an unknown tongue, and had been slipped in with the loot by a dying hand.

From either end of that narrow, terrible ledge the third night was closing in; it was dropping down on them from the heights of the mountain and slipping up to them out of the abyss, the third night since Loma blazed and they had left it. Three more days of tramping should bring them in triumph home, and yet their instincts said that all was scarcely well. We who sit at home and draw the blinds and shut the shutters as soon as night appears, who gather round the fire when the wind is wild, who pray at regular seasons and in familiar shrines, know little of the demoniac look of night when it is filled with curses of false, infuriated gods. Such a night was this. Though in the heights the fleecy clouds were idle, yet the wind was stirring mournfully in the abyss and moaning as it stirred, unhappily at first and full of sorrow; but as day turned away from that awful path a very definite menace entered its voice which fast grew louder and louder, and night came on with a long howl. Shadows repeatedly passed over the stars, and then a mist fell swiftly, as though there were something suddenly to be done and utterly to be hidden, as in very truth there was.

And in the chill of that mist the four tall men prayed to their totems, the whimsical wooden figures that stood so far away, watching the pleasant wigwams; the firelight even now would be dancing over their faces, while there would come to their ears delectable tales of war. They halted upon the pass and prayed, and waited for any sign. For a man's totem may be in the likeness perhaps of an otter, and a man may pray, and if his totem be placable and watching over his man a noise may be heard at once like the noise that the otter makes, though it be but a stone that falls on another stone; and the noise is a sign. The four men's totems that stood so far away were in the likeness of the coney, the bear, the heron, and the lizard. They waited, and no sign came. With all the noises of the wind in the abyss, no noise was like the thump that the coney makes, nor the bear's growl, nor the heron's screech, nor the rustle of the lizard in the reeds.

It seemed that the wind was saying something over and over again, and that that thing was evil. They prayed again to their totems, and no sign came. And then they knew that there was some power that night that was prevailing against the pleasant carvings on painted poles of wood with the firelight on their faces so far away. Now it was clear that the wind was saying something, some very, very dreadful thing in a tongue that they did not know. They listened, but they could not tell what it said. Nobody could have said from seeing their faces how much the four tall men desired the wigwams again, desired the camp-fire and the tales of war and the benignant totems that listened and smiled in the dusk: nobody could have seen how well they knew that this was no common night or wholesome mist.

When at last no answer came nor any sign from their totems, they pulled out of the bag those golden gods that Loma gave not up except in flames and when all her men were dead. They had large ruby eyes and emerald tongues. They set them down upon that mountain pass, the cross-legged idols with their emerald tongues; and having placed between them a few decent yards, as it seemed meet there should be between gods and men, they bowed them down and prayed in their desperate straits in that dank, ominous night to the gods they had wronged, for it seemed that there was a vengeance upon the hills and that they would scarce escape, as the wind knew well. And the gods laughed, all four, and wagged their emerald tongues; the Indians saw them, though the night had fallen and though the mist was low. The four tall men leaped up at once from their knees and would have left the gods upon the pass but that they feared some hunter of their tribe might one day find them and say of Laughing Face, "He fled and left behind his golden gods," and sell the gold and come with his wealth to the wigwams and be greater than Laughing Face and his three men. And then they would have cast the gods away, down the abyss, with their eyes and their emerald tongues, but they knew that enough already they had wronged Loma's gods, and feared that vengeance enough was waiting them on the hills. So they packed them back in the bag on the frightened mule, the bag that held the curse they knew nothing of, and so pushed on into the menacing night. Till midnight they plodded on and would not sleep; grimmer and grimmer grew the look of the night, and the wind more full of meaning, and the mule knew and trembled, and it seemed that the wind knew, too, as did the instincts of those four tall men, though they could not reason it out, try how they would.

And though the squaws waited long where the pass winds out of the mountains, near where the wigwams are upon the plains, the wigwams and the totems and the fire, and though they watched by day, and for many nights uttered familiar calls, still did they never see those four tall men emerge out of the mountains any more, even though they prayed to their totems upon their painted poles; but the curse in the mystical writing that they had unknown in their bag worked there on that lonely pass six leagues from the ruins of Loma, and nobody can tell us what it was.

THE SECRET OF THE SEA

In an ill-lit ancient tavern that I know, are many tales of the sea; but not without the wine of Gorgondy, that I had of a private bargain from the gnomes, was the tale laid bare for which I had waited of an evening for the greater part of a year.

I knew my man and listened to his stories, sitting amid the bluster of his oaths; I plied him with rum and whiskey and mixed drinks, but there never came the tale for which I sought, and as a last resort I went to the Huthneth Mountains and bargained there all night with the chiefs of the gnomes.

When I came to the ancient tavern and entered the low-roofed room, bringing the hoard of the gnomes in a bottle of hammered iron, my man had not yet arrived. The sailors laughed at my old iron bottle, but I sat down and waited; had I opened it then they would have wept and sung. I was well content to wait, for I knew my man had the story, and it was such a one as had profoundly stirred the incredulity of the faithless.

He entered and greeted me, and sat down and called for brandy. He was a hard man to turn from his purpose, and, uncorking my iron bottle, I sought to dissuade him from brandy for fear that when the brandy, bit his throat he should refuse to leave it for any other wine. He lifted his head and said deep and dreadful things of any man that should dare to speak against brandy.

I swore that I said nothing against brandy but added that it was often given to children, while Gorgondy was only drunk by men of such depravity that they had abandoned sin because all the usual vices had come to seem genteel. When he asked if Gorgondy was a bad wine to drink I said that it was so bad that if a man sipped it that was the one touch that made damnation certain. Then he asked me what I had in the iron bottle, and I said it was Gorgondy; and then he shouted for the largest tumbler in that ill-lit ancient tavern, and stood up and shook his fist at me when it came, and swore, and told me to fill it with the wine that I got on that bitter night from the treasure house of the gnomes.

As he drank it he told me that he had met men who had spoken against wine, and that they had mentioned Heaven; and therefore he would not go there—no, not he; and that once he had sent one of them to Hell, but when he got there he would turn him out, and he had no use for milksops.

Over the second tumbler he was thoughtful, but still he said no word of the tale he knew, until I feared that it would never be heard. But when the third glass of that terrific wine had burned its way down his gullet, and vindicated the wickedness of the gnomes, his reticence withered like a leaf in the fire, and he bellowed out the secret.

I had long known that there is in ships a will or way of their own, and had even suspected that when sailors die or abandon their ships at sea, a derelict, being left to her own devices, may seek her own ends; but I had never dreamed by night, or fancied during the day, that the ships had a god that they worshipped, or that they secretly slipped away to a temple in the sea.

Over the fourth glass of the wine that the gnomes so sinfully brew but have kept so wisely from man, until the bargain that I had with their elders all through that autumn night, the sailor told me the story. I do not tell it as he told it to me because of the oaths that were in it; nor is it from delicacy that I refrain from writing these oaths verbatim, but merely because the horror they caused in me at the time troubles me still whenever I put them on paper, and I continue to shudder until I have blotted them out. Therefore,

I tell the story in my own words, which, if they possess a certain decency that was not in the mouth of that sailor, unfortunately do not smack, as his did, of rum and blood and the sea.

You would take a ship to be a dead thing like a table, as dead as bits of iron and canvas and wood. That is because you always live on shore, and have never seen the sea, and drink milk. Milk is a more accursed drink than water.

What with the captain and what with the man at the wheel, and what with the crew, a ship has no fair chance of showing a will of her own.

There is only one moment in the history of ships, that carry crews on board, when they act by their own free will. This moment comes when all the crew are drunk. As the last man falls drunk on to the deck, the ship is free of man, and immediately slips away. She slips away at once on a new course and is never one yard out in a hundred miles.

It was like this one night with the Sea-Fancy. Bill Smiles was there himself, and can vouch for it. Bill Smiles has never told this tale before for fear that anyone should call him a liar. Nobody dislikes being hung as much as Bill Smiles would, but he won't be called a liar. I tell the tale as I heard it, relevancies and irrelevancies, though in my more decent words; and as I made no doubts of the truth of it then, I hardly like to now; others can please themselves.

It is not often that the whole of a crew is drunk. The crew of the Sea-Fancy was no drunkener than others. It happened like this.

The captain was always drunk. One day a fancy he had that some spiders were plotting against him, or a sudden bleeding he had from both his ears, made him think that drinking might be bad for his health. Next day he signed the pledge. He was sober all that morning and all the afternoon, but at evening he saw a sailor drinking a a glass of beer, and a fit of madness seized him, and he said things that seemed bad to Bill Smiles. And next morning he made all of them take the pledge.

For two days nobody had a drop to drink, unless you count water, and on the third morning the captain was quite drunk. It stood to reason they all had a glass or two then, except the man at the wheel; and towards evening the man at the wheel could bear it no longer, and seems to have had his glass like all the rest, for the ship's course wobbled a bit and made a circle or two. Then all of a sudden she went off south by east under full canvas till midnight, and never altered her course. And at midnight she came to the wide wet courts of the Temple in the Sea.

People who think that Mr. Smiles is drunk often make a great mistake. And people are not the only ones that have made that mistake. Once a ship made it, and a lot of ships. It's a mistake to think that old Bill Smiles is drunk just because he can't move.

Midnight and moonlight and the Temple in the Sea Bill Smiles clearly remembers, and all the derelicts in the world were there, the old abandoned ships. The figureheads were nodding to themselves and blinking at the image. The image was a woman of white marble on a pedestal in the outer court of the Temple of the Sea: she was clearly the love of all the man-deserted ships, or the goddess to whom they prayed their heathen prayers. And as Bill Smiles was watching them, the lips of the figureheads moved; they all began to pray. But all at once their lips were closed with a snap when they saw that there were men on the Sea-Fancy. They all came crowding up and nodded and nodded and nodded to see if all were drunk, and that's when they made their mistake about old Bill Smiles, although he couldn't move. They would have given up the treasuries of the gulfs sooner than let men hear the prayers they said or guess their love for the goddess. It is the intimate secret of the sea.

The sailor paused. And, in my eagerness to hear what lyrical or blasphemous thing those figureheads prayed by moonlight at midnight in the sea to the woman of marble who was a goddess to ships, I pressed on the sailor more of my Gorgondy wine that the gnomes so wickedly brew.

I should never have done it; but there he was sitting silent while the secret was almost mine. He took it moodily and drank a glass; and with the other glasses that he had had he fell a prey to the villainy of the gnomes who brew this unbridled wine to no good end. His body leaned forward slowly, then fell on to the table, his face being sideways and full of a wicked smile, and, saying very clearly the one word, "Hell," he became silent for ever with the secret he had from the sea.

HOW ALI CAME TO THE BLACK COUNTRY

Shooshan the barber went to Shep the maker of teeth to discuss the state of England. They agreed that it was time to send for Ali.

So Shooshan stepped late that night from the little shop near Fleet Street and made his way back again to his house in the ends of London and sent at once the message that brought Ali.

And Ali came, mostly on foot, from the country of Persia, and it took him a year to come; but when he came he was welcome.

And Shep told Ali what was the matter with England and Shooshan swore that it was so, and Ali looking out of the window of the little shop near Fleet Street beheld the ways of London and audibly blessed King Solomon and his seal.

When Shep and Shooshan heard the names of King Solomon and his seal both asked, as they had scarcely dared before, if Ali had it. Ali patted a little bundle of silks that he drew from his inner raiment. It was there.

Now concerning the movements and courses of the stars and the influence on them of spirits of Earth and devils this age has been rightly named by some The Second Age of Ignorance. But Ali knew. And by watching nightly, for seven nights in Bagdad, the way of certain stars he had found out the dwelling place of Him they Needed.

Guided by Ali all three set forth for the Midlands. And by the reverence that was manifest in the faces of Shep and Shooshan towards the person of Ali, some knew what Ali carried, while others said that it was the tablets of the Law, others the name of God, and others that he must have a lot of money about him. So they passed Slod and Apton.

And at last they came to the town for which Ali sought, that spot over which he had seen the shy stars wheel and swerve away from their orbits, being troubled. Verily when they came there were no stars, though it was midnight. And Ali said that it was the appointed place. In harems in Persia in the evening when the tales go round it is still told how Ali and Shep and Shooshan came to the Black country.

When it was dawn they looked upon the country and saw how it was without doubt the appointed place, even as Ali had said, for the earth had been taken out of pits and burned and left lying in heaps, and there were many factories, and they stood over the town and as it were rejoiced. And with one voice Shep and Shooshan gave praise to Ali.

And Ali said that the great ones of the place must needs be gathered together, and to this end Shep and Shooshan went into the town and there spoke craftily. For they said that Ali had of his wisdom contrived as it were a patent and a novelty which should greatly benefit England. And when they heard how he sought nothing for his novelty save only to benefit mankind they consented to speak with Ali and see his novelty. And they came forth and met Ali.

And Ali spake and said unto them: "O lords of this place; in the book that all men know it is written how that a fisherman casting his net into the sea drew up a bottle of brass, and when he took the stopper from the bottle a dreadful genie of horrible aspect rose from the bottle, as it were like a smoke, even to darkening the sky, whereat the fisherman…" And the great ones of that place said: "We have heard the story." And Ali said: "What became of that genie after he was safely thrown back into the sea is not properly spoken of by any save those that pursue the study of demons and not with certainty by any man, but that the stopper that bore the ineffable seal and bears it to this day became separate from the bottle is among those things that man may know." And when there was doubt among the great ones Ali drew forth his bundle and one by one removed those many silks till the seal stood revealed; and some of them knew it for the seal and others knew it not.

And they looked curiously at it and listened to Ali, and Ali said:

"Having heard how evil is the case of England, how a smoke has darkened the country, and in places (as men say) the grass is black, and how even yet your factories multiply, and haste and noise have become such that men have no time for song, I have therefore come at the bidding of my good friend Shooshan, barber of London, and of Shep, a maker of teeth, to make things well with you."

And they said: "But where is your patent and your novelty?"

And Ali said: "Have I not here the stopper and on it, as good men know, the ineffable seal? Now I have learned in Persia how that your trains that make the haste, and hurry men to and fro, and your factories and the digging of your pits and all the things that are evil are everyone of them caused and brought about by steam."

"Is it not so?" said Shooshan.

"It is even so," said Shep.

"Now it is clear," said Ali, "that the chief devil that vexes England and has done all this harm, who herds men into cities and will not let them rest, is even the devil Steam."

Then the great ones would have rebuked him but one said: "No, let us hear him, perhaps his patent may improve on steam."

And to them hearkening Ali went on thus: "O Lords of this place, let there be made a bottle of strong steel, for I have no bottle with my stopper, and this being done let all the factories, trains, digging of pits, and all evil things soever that may be done by steam be stopped for seven days, and the men that tend them shall go free, but the steel bottle for my stopper I will leave open in a likely place. Now that chief devil, Steam, finding no factories to enter into, nor no trains, sirens nor pits prepared for him, and being curious and accustomed to steel pots, will verily enter one night into the bottle that you shall make for my stopper, and I shall spring forth from my hiding with my stopper and fasten him down with the ineffable seal which is the seal of King Solomon and deliver him up to you that you cast him into the sea."

And the great ones answered Ali and they said: "But what should we gain if we lose our prosperity and be no longer rich?"

And Ali said: "When we have cast this devil into the sea there will come back again the woods and ferns and all the beautiful things that the world hath, the little leaping hares shall be seen at play, there shall be music on the hills again, and at twilight ease and quiet and after the twilight stars."

And "Verily," said Shooshan, "there shall be the dance again."

"Aye," said Shep, "there shall be the country dance."

But the great ones spake and said, denying Ali: "We will make no such bottle for your stopper nor stop our healthy factories or good trains, nor cease from our digging of pits nor do anything that you desire, for an interference with steam would strike at the roots of that prosperity that you see so plentifully all around us."

Thus they dismissed Ali there and then from that place where the earth was torn up and burnt, being taken out of pits, and where factories blazed all night with a demoniac glare; and they dismissed with him both

Shooshan, the barber, and Shep, the maker of teeth: so that a week later Ali started from Calais on his long walk back to Persia.

And all this happened thirty years ago, and Shep is an old man now and Shooshan older, and many mouths have bit with the teeth of Shep (for he has a knack of getting them back whenever his customers die), and they have written again to Ali away in the country of Persia with these words, saying:

"O Ali. The devil has indeed begotten a devil, even that spirit Petrol. And the young devil waxeth, and increaseth in lustihood and is ten years old and becoming like to his father. Come therefore and help us with the ineffable seal. For there is none like Ali."

And Ali turns where his slaves scatter rose-leaves, letting the letter fall, and deeply draws from his hookah a puff of the scented smoke, right down into his lungs, and sighs it forth and smiles, and lolling round on to his other elbow speaks comfortably and says, "And shall a man go twice to the help of a dog?"

And with these words he thinks no more of England but ponders again the inscrutable ways of God.

THE BUREAU D'ECHANGE DE MAUX

I often think of the Bureau d'Echange de Maux and the wondrously evil old man that sate therein. It stood in a little street that there is in Paris, its doorway made of three brown beams of wood, the top one overlapping the others like the Greek letter *pi*, all the rest painted green, a house far lower and narrower than its neighbours and infinitely stranger, a thing to take one's fancy. And over the doorway on the old brown beam in faded yellow letters this legend ran, Bureau Universel d'Echanges de Maux.

I entered at once and accosted the listless man that lolled on a stool by his counter. I demanded the wherefore of his wonderful house, what evil wares he exchanged, with many other things that I wished to know, for curiosity led me; and indeed had it not I had gone at once from that shop, for there was so evil a look in that fattened man, in the hang of his fallen cheeks and his sinful eye, that you would have said he had had dealings with Hell and won the advantage by sheer wickedness.

Such a man was mine host; but above all the evil of him lay in his eyes, which lay so still, so apathetic, that you would have sworn that he was drugged or dead; like lizards motionless on a wall they lay, then suddenly they darted, and all his cunning flamed up and revealed itself in what one moment before seemed no more than a sleepy and ordinary wicked old man. And this was the object and trade of that peculiar shop, the Bureau Universel d'Echange de Maux: you paid twenty francs, which the old man proceeded to take from me, for admission to the bureau and then had the right to exchange any evil or misfortune with anyone on the premises for some evil or misfortune that he "could afford," as the old man put it.

There were four or five men in the dingy ends of that low-ceilinged room who gesticulated and muttered softly in twos as men who make a bargain, and now and then more came in, and the eyes of the flabby owner of the house leaped up at them as they entered, seemed to know their errands at once and each one's peculiar need, and fell back again into somnolence, receiving his twenty francs in an almost lifeless hand and biting the coin as though in pure absence of mind.

"Some of my clients," he told me. So amazing to me was the trade of this extraordinary shop that I engaged the old man in conversation, repulsive though he was, and from his garrulity I gathered these facts. He spoke in perfect English though his utterance was somewhat thick and heavy; no language seemed to come amiss to him. He had been in business a great many years, how many he would not say, and was far older than he looked. All kinds of people did business in his shop. What they exchanged with each other he did not care except that it had to be evils, he was not empowered to carry on any other kind of business.

There was no evil, he told me, that was not negotiable there; no evil the old man knew had ever been taken away in despair from his shop. A man might have to wait and come back again next day, and next day and the day after, paying twenty francs each time, but the old man had the addresses of all his clients and shrewdly knew their needs, and soon the right two met and eagerly exchanged their commodities. "Commodities" was the old man's terrible word, said with a gruesome smack of his heavy lips, for he took a pride in his business and evils to him were goods.

I learned from him in ten minutes very much of human nature, more than I have ever learned from any other man; I learned from him that a man's own evil is to him the worst thing there is or ever could be, and that an evil so unbalances all men's minds that they always seek for extremes in that small grim shop. A woman that had no children had exchanged with an impoverished half-maddened creature with twelve. On one occasion a man had exchanged wisdom for folly.

"Why on earth did he do that?" I said.

"None of my business," the old man answered in his heavy indolent way. He merely took his twenty francs from each and ratified the agreement in the little room at the back opening out of the shop where his clients do business. Apparently the man that had parted with wisdom had left the shop upon the tips of his toes with a happy though foolish expression all over his face, but the other went thoughtfully away wearing a troubled and very puzzled look. Almost always it seemed they did business in opposite evils.

But the thing that puzzled me most in all my talks with that unwieldy man, the thing that puzzles me still, is that none that had once done business in that shop ever returned again; a man might come day after day for many weeks, but once do business and he never returned; so much the old man told me, but when I asked him why, he only muttered that he did not know.

It was to discover the wherefore of this strange thing and for no other reason at all that I determined myself to do business sooner or later in the little room at the back of that mysterious shop. I determined to exchange some very trivial evil for some evil equally slight, to seek for myself an advantage so very small as scarcely to give Fate as it were a grip, for I deeply distrusted these bargains, knowing well that man has never yet benefited by the marvellous and that the more miraculous his advantage appears to be the more securely and tightly do the gods or the witches catch him. In a few days more I was going back to England and I was beginning to fear that I should be sea-sick: this fear of sea-sickness, not the actual malady but only the mere fear of it, I decided to exchange for a suitably little evil. I did not know with whom I should be dealing, who in reality was the head of the firm (one never does when shopping) but I decided that neither Jew nor Devil could make very much on so small a bargain as that.

I told the old man my project, and he scoffed at the smallness of my commodity trying to urge me to some darker bargain, but could not move me from my purpose. And then he told me tales with a somewhat boastful air of the big business, the great bargains that had passed through his hands. A man had once run in there to try and exchange death, he had swallowed poison by accident and had only twelve hours to live. That sinister old man had been able to oblige him. A client was willing to exchange the commodity.

"But what did he give in exchange for death?" I said.

"Life," said that grim old man with a furtive chuckle.

"It must have been a horrible life," I said.

"That was not my affair," the proprietor said, lazily rattling together as he spoke a little pocketful of twenty-franc pieces.

Strange business I watched in that shop for the next few days, the exchange of odd commodities, and heard strange mutterings in corners amongst couples who presently rose and went to the back room, the old man following to ratify.

Twice a day for a week I paid my twenty francs, watching life with its great needs and its little needs morning and afternoon spread out before me in all its wonderful variety.

And one day I met a comfortable man with only a little need, he seemed to have the very evil I wanted. He always feared the lift was going to break. I knew too much of hydraulics to fear things as silly as that, but it was not my business to cure his ridiculous fear. Very few words were needed to convince him that mine was the evil for him, he never crossed the sea, and I on the other hand could always walk upstairs, and I also felt at the time, as many must feel in that shop, that so absurd a fear could never trouble me.

And yet at times it is almost the curse of my life. When we both had signed the parchment in the spidery back room and the old man had signed and ratified (for which we had to pay him fifty francs each) I went back to my hotel, and there I saw the deadly thing in the basement. They asked me if I would go upstairs in the lift, from force of habit I risked it, and I held my breath all the way and clenched my hands. Nothing will induce me to try such a journey again. I would sooner go up to my room in a balloon. And why? Because if a balloon goes wrong you have a chance, it may spread out into a parachute after it has burst, it may catch in a tree, a hundred and one things may happen, but if the lift falls down its shaft you are done. As for sea-sickness I shall never be sick again, I cannot tell you why except that I know that it is so.

And the shop in which I made this remarkable bargain, the shop to which none return when their business is done: I set out for it next day. Blindfold I could have found my way to the unfashionable quarter out of which a mean street runs, where you take the alley at the end, whence runs the cul de sac where the queer shop stood. A shop with pillars, fluted and painted red, stands on its near side, its other neighbour is a low-class jeweller's with little silver brooches in the window. In such incongruous company stood the shop with beams with its walls painted green.

In half an hour I found the cul de sac to which I had gone twice a day for the last week, I found the shop with the ugly painted pillars and the jeweller that sold brooches, but the green house with the three beams was gone.

Pulled down, you will say, although in a single night. That can never be the answer to the mystery, for the house of the fluted pillars painted on plaster and the low-class jeweller's shop with its silver brooches (all of which I could identify one by one) were standing side by side.

A STORY OF LAND AND SEA

It is written in the first Book of Wonder how Captain Shard of the bad ship *Desperate Lark*, having looted the sea-coast city Bombasharna, retired from active life; and resigning piracy to younger men, with the good will of the North and South Atlantic, settled down with a captured queen on his floating island.

Sometimes he sank a ship for the sake of old times but he no longer hovered along the trade-routes; and timid merchants watched for other men.

It was not age that caused him to leave his romantic profession; nor unworthiness of its traditions, nor gun-shot wound, nor drink; but grim necessity and force majeure. Five navies were after him. How he gave them the slip one day in the Mediterranean, how he fought with the Arabs, how a ship's broadside was heard in Lat. 23 N. Long. 4 E. for the first time and the last, with other things unknown to Admiralties, I shall proceed to tell.

He had had his fling, had Shard, captain of pirates, and all his merry men wore pearls in their ear-rings; and now the English fleet was after him under full sail along the coast of Spain with a good North wind behind them. They were not gaining much on Shard's rakish craft, the bad ship *Desperate Lark*, yet they were closer than was to his liking, and they interfered with business.

For a day and a night they had chased him, when off Cape St. Vincent at about six a.m. Shard took that step that decided his retirement from active life, he turned for the Mediterranean. Had he held on Southwards down the African coast it is doubtful whether in face of the interference of England, Russia, France, Denmark and Spain, he could have made piracy pay; but in turning for the Mediterranean he took what we may call the penultimate step of his life which meant for him settling down. There were three great courses of action invented by Shard in his youth, upon which he pondered by day and brooded by night, consolations in all his dangers, secret even from his men, three means of escape as he hoped from any peril that might meet him on the sea. One of these was the floating island that the Book of Wonder tells of, another was so fantastic that we may doubt if even the brilliant audacity of Shard could ever have found it practicable, at least he never tried it so far as is known in that tavern by the sea in which I glean my news, and the third he determined on carrying out as he turned that morning for the Mediterranean. True he might yet have practised piracy in spite of the step that he took, a little later when the seas grew quiet, but that penultimate step was like that small house in the country that the business man has his eye on, like some snug investment put away for old age, there are certain final courses in men's lives which after taking they never go back to business.

He turned then for the Mediterranean with the English fleet behind him, and his men wondered.

What madness was this,—muttered Bill the Boatswain in Old Frank's only ear, with the French fleet waiting in the Gulf of Lyons and the Spaniards all the way between Sardinia and Tunis: for they knew the Spaniards' ways. And they made a deputation and waited upon Captain Shard, all of them sober and wearing their costly clothes, and they said that the Mediterranean was a trap, and all he said was that the North wind should hold. And the crew said they were done.

So they entered the Mediterranean and the English fleet came up and closed the straits. And Shard went tacking along the Moroccan coast with a dozen frigates behind him. And the North wind grew in strength. And not till evening did he speak to his crew, and then he gathered them all together except the man at the helm, and politely asked them to come down to the hold. And there he showed them six immense steel axles and a dozen low iron wheels of enormous width which none had seen before; and he told his crew how all unknown to the world his keel had been specially fitted for these same axles and wheels, and how he meant soon to sail to the wide Atlantic again, though not by the way of the straits. And when they heard the name of the Atlantic all his merry men cheered, for they looked on the Atlantic as a wide safe sea.

And night came down and Captain Shard sent for his diver. With the sea getting up it was hard work for the diver, but by midnight things were done to Shard's satisfaction, and the diver said that of all the jobs he had done—but finding no apt comparison, and being in need of a drink, silence fell on him and soon sleep, and his comrades carried him away to his hammock. All the next day the chase went on with the English well in sight, for Shard had lost time overnight with his wheels and axles, and the danger of meeting the Spaniards increased every hour; and evening came when every minute seemed dangerous, yet they still went tacking on towards the East where they knew the Spaniards must be.

And at last they sighted their topsails right ahead, and still Shard went on. It was a close thing, but night was coming on, and the Union Jack which he hoisted helped Shard with the Spaniards for the last few anxious minutes, though it seemed to anger the English, but as Shard said, "There's no pleasing everyone," and then the twilight shivered into darkness.

"Hard to starboard," said Captain Shard.

The North wind which had risen all day was now blowing a gale. I do not know what part of the coast Shard steered for, but Shard knew, for the coasts of the world were to him what Margate is to some of us.

At a place where the desert rolling up from mystery and from death, yea, from the heart of Africa, emerges upon the sea, no less grand than her, no less terrible, even there they sighted the land quite close, almost in darkness. Shard ordered every man to the hinder part of the ship and all the ballast too; and soon the *Desperate Lark*, her prow a little high out of the water, doing her eighteen knots before the wind, struck a sandy beach and shuddered, she heeled over a little, then righted herself, and slowly headed into the interior of Africa.

The men would have given three cheers, but after the first Shard silenced them and, steering the ship himself, he made them a short speech while the broad wheels pounded slowly over the African sand, doing barely five knots in a gale. The perils of the sea he said had been greatly exaggerated. Ships had been sailing the sea for hundreds of years and at sea you knew what to do, but on land this was different. They were on land now and they were not to forget it. At sea you might make as much noise as you pleased and no harm was done, but on land anything might happen. One of the perils of the land that he instanced was that of hanging. For every hundred men that they hung on land, he said, not more than twenty would be hung at sea. The men were to sleep at their guns. They would not go far that night; for the risk of being wrecked at night was another danger peculiar to the land, while at sea you might sail from set of sun till dawn: yet it was essential to get out of sight of the sea for if anyone knew they were there they'd have cavalry after them. And he had sent back Smerdrak (a young lieutenant of pirates) to cover their tracks where they came up from the sea. And the merry men vigorously nodded their heads though they did not dare to cheer, and presently Smerdrak came running up and they threw him a rope by the stern. And when they had done fifteen knots they anchored, and Captain Shard gathered his men about him and, standing by the land-wheel in the bows, under the large and clear Algerian stars, he explained his system of steering. There was not much to be said for it, he had with considerable ingenuity detached and pivoted the portion of the keel that held the leading axle and could move it by chains which were controlled from the land-wheel, thus the front pair of wheels could be deflected at will, but only very slightly, and they afterwards found that in a hundred yards they could only turn their ship four yards from her course. But let not captains of comfortable battleships, or owners even of yachts, criticise too harshly a man who was not of their time and who knew not modern contrivances; it should be remembered also that Shard was no longer at sea. His steering may have been clumsy but he did what he could.

When the use and limitations of his land-wheel had been made clear to his men, Shard bade them all turn in except those on watch. Long before dawn he woke them and by the very first gleam of light they got their ship under way, so that when those two fleets that had made so sure of Shard closed in like a great crescent on the Algerian coast there was no sign to see of the *Desperate Lark* either on sea or land; and the flags of the Admiral's ship broke out into a hearty English oath.

The gale blew for three days and, Shard using more sail by daylight, they scudded over the sands at little less than ten knots, though on the report of rough water ahead (as the lookout man called rocks, low hills or uneven surface before he adapted himself to his new surroundings) the rate was much decreased. Those were long summer days and Shard who was anxious while the wind held good to outpace the rumour of his own appearance sailed for nineteen hours a day, lying to at ten in the evening and hoisting sail again at three a.m. when it first began to be light.

In those three days he did five hundred miles; then the wind dropped to a breeze though it still blew from the North, and for a week they did no more than two knots an hour. The merry men began to murmur then. Luck had distinctly favoured Shard at first for it sent him at ten knots through the only populous districts well ahead of crowds except those who chose to run, and the cavalry were away on a local raid. As for the runners they soon dropped off when Shard pointed his cannon though he did not dare to fire, up there near the coast; for much as he jeered at the intelligence of the English and Spanish Admirals in not suspecting his manoeuvre, the only one as he said that was possible in the circumstances, yet he knew that cannon had an obvious sound which would give his secret away to the weakest mind. Certainly luck had befriended him, and when it did so no longer he made out of the occasion all that could be made; for instance while the wind held good he had never missed opportunities to revictual, if he passed by a village its pigs and poultry were his, and whenever he passed by water he filled his tanks to the brim, and now that he could only do two knots he sailed all night with a man and a lantern before him: thus in that week he did close on four hundred miles while another man would have anchored at night and have missed five or six hours out of the twenty-four. Yet his men murmured. Did he think the wind would last for ever, they said. And Shard only smoked. It was clear that he was thinking, and thinking hard. "But what is he thinking about?" said Bill to Bad Jack. And Bad Jack answered: "He may think as hard as he likes but thinking won't get us out of the Sahara if this wind were to drop."

And towards the end of that week Shard went to his chart-room and laid a new course for his ship a little to the East and towards cultivation. And one day towards evening they sighted a village, and twilight came and the wind dropped altogether. Then the murmurs of the merry men grew to oaths and nearly to mutiny. "Where were they now?" they asked, and were they being treated like poor honest men?

Shard quieted them by asking what they wished to do themselves and when no one had any better plan than going to the villagers and saying that they had been blown out of their course by a storm, Shard unfolded his scheme to them. Long ago he had heard how they drove carts with oxen in Africa, oxen were very numerous in these parts wherever there was any cultivation, and for this reason when the wind had begun to drop he had laid his course for the village: that night the moment it was dark they were to drive off fifty yoke of oxen; by midnight they must all be yoked to the bows and then away they would go at a good round gallop.

So fine a plan as this astonished the men and they all apologised for their want of faith in Shard, shaking hands with him every one and spitting on their hands before they did so in token of good will.

The raid that night succeeded admirably, but ingenious as Shard was on land, and a past-master at sea, yet it must be admitted that lack of experience in this class of seamanship led him to make a mistake, a slight one it is true, and one that a little practice would have prevented altogether: the oxen could not gallop. Shard swore at them, threatened them with his pistol, said they should have no food, and all to no avail: that night and as long as they pulled the bad ship *Desperate Lark* they did one knot an hour and no more. Shard's failures like everything that came his way were used as stones in the edifice of his future success, he went at once to his chart-room and worked out all his calculations anew.

The matter of the oxen's pace made pursuit impossible to avoid. Shard therefore countermanded his order to his lieutenant to cover the tracks in the sand, and the *Desperate Lark* plodded on into the Sahara on her new course trusting to her guns.

The village was not a large one and the little crowd that was sighted astern next morning disappeared after the first shot from the cannon in the stern. At first Shard made the oxen wear rough iron bits, another of his mistakes, and strong bits too. "For if they run away," he had said, "we might as well be driving before a gale and there's no saying where we'd find ourselves," but after a day or two he found that the bits were no good and, like the practical man he was, immediately corrected his mistake.

And now the crew sang merry songs all day bringing out mandolins and clarionets and cheering Captain Shard. All were jolly except the captain himself whose face was moody and perplexed; he alone expected to hear more of those villagers; and the oxen were drinking up the water every day, he alone feared that there was no more to be had, and a very unpleasant fear that is when your ship is becalmed in a desert. For over a week they went on like this doing ten knots a day and the music and singing got on the captain's nerves, but he dared not tell his men what the trouble was. And then one day the oxen drank up the last of the water. And Lieutenant Smerdrak came and reported the fact.

"Give them rum," said Shard, and he cursed the oxen. "What is good enough for me," he said, "should be good enough for them," and he swore that they should have rum.

"Aye, aye, sir," said the young lieutenant of pirates.

Shard should not be judged by the orders he gave that day, for nearly a fortnight he had watched the doom that was coming slowly towards him, discipline cut him off from anyone that might have shared his fear and discussed it, and all the while he had had to navigate his ship, which even at sea is an arduous responsibility. These things had fretted the calm of that clear judgment that had once baffled five navies. Therefore he cursed the oxen and ordered them rum, and Smerdrak had said "Aye, aye, sir," and gone below.

Towards sunset Shard was standing on the poop, thinking of death; it would not come to him by thirst; mutiny first, he thought. The oxen were refusing rum for the last time, and the men were beginning to eye Captain Shard in a very ominous way, not muttering, but each man looking at him with a sidelong look of the eye as though there were only one thought among them all that had no need of words. A score of geese like a long letter "V" were crossing the evening sky, they slanted their necks and all went twisting downwards somewhere about the horizon. Captain Shard rushed to his chart-room, and presently the men came in at the door with Old Frank in front looking awkward and twisting his cap in his hand.

"What is it?" said Shard as though nothing were wrong.

Then Old Frank said what he had come to say: "We want to know what you be going to do."

And the men nodded grimly.

"Get water for the oxen," said Captain Shard, "as the swine won't have rum, and they'll have to work for it, the lazy beasts. Up anchor!"

And at the word water a look came into their faces like when some wanderer suddenly thinks of home.

"Water!" they said.

"Why not?" said Captain Shard. And none of them ever knew that but for those geese, that slanted their necks and suddenly twisted downwards, they would have found no water that night nor ever after, and the Sahara would have taken them as she has taken so many and shall take so many more. All that night they followed their new course: at dawn they found an oasis and the oxen drank.

And here, on this green acre or so with its palm-trees and its well, beleaguered by thousands of miles of desert and holding out through the ages, here they decided to stay: for those who have been without water for a while in one of Africa's deserts come to have for that simple fluid such a regard as you, O reader, might not easily credit. And here each man chose a site where he would build his hut, and settle down, and marry perhaps, and even forget the sea; when Captain Shard having filled his tanks and barrels peremptorily ordered them to weigh anchor. There was much dissatisfaction, even some grumbling, but when a man has twice saved his fellows from death by the sheer freshness of his mind they come to have a respect for his judgment that is not shaken by trifles. It must be remembered that in the affair of the dropping of the wind and again when they ran out of water these men were at their wits' end: so was Shard on the last occasion, but that they did not know. All this Shard knew, and he chose this occasion to strengthen the reputation that he had in the minds of the men of that bad ship by explaining to them his motives, which usually he kept secret. The oasis he said must be a port of call for all the travellers within hundreds of miles: how many men did you see gathered together in any part of the world where there was a drop of whiskey to be had! And water here was rarer than whiskey in decent countries and, such was the peculiarity of the Arabs, even more precious. Another thing he pointed out to them, the Arabs were a singularly inquisitive people and if they came upon a ship in the desert they would probably talk about it; and the world having a wickedly malicious tongue would never construe in its proper light their difference with the English and Spanish fleets, but would merely side with the strong against the weak.

And the men sighed, and sang the capstan song and hoisted the anchor and yoked the oxen up, and away they went doing their steady knot, which nothing could increase. It may be thought strange that with all sail furled in dead calm and while the oxen rested they should have cast anchor at all. But custom is not easily overcome and long survives its use. Rather enquire how many such useless customs we ourselves preserve: the flaps for instance to pull up the tops of hunting-boots though the tops no longer pull up, the bows on our evening shoes that neither tie nor untie. They said they felt safer that way and there was an end of it.

Shard lay a course of South by West and they did ten knots that day, the next day they did seven or eight and Shard hove to. Here he intended to stop, they had huge supplies of fodder on board for the oxen, for his men he had a pig or so, plenty of poultry, several sacks of biscuits and ninety-eight oxen (for two were already eaten), and they were only twenty miles from water. Here he said they would stay till folks forgot their past, someone would invent something or some new thing would turn up to take folks' minds off them and the ships he had sunk: he forgot that there are men who are well paid to remember.

Half way between him and the oasis he established a little depot where he buried his water-barrels. As soon as a barrel was empty he sent half a dozen men to roll it by turns to the depot. This they would do at night, keeping hid by day, and next night they would push on to the oasis, fill the barrel and roll it back. Thus only ten miles away he soon had a store of water, unknown to the thirstiest native of Africa, from which he could safely replenish his tanks at will. He allowed his men to sing and even within reason to light fires. Those were jolly nights while the rum held out; sometimes they saw gazelles watching them curiously, sometimes a lion went by over the sand, the sound of his roar added to their sense of the security of their ship; all round them level, immense lay the Sahara: "This is better than an English prison," said Captain Shard.

And still the dead calm lasted, not even the sand whispered at night to little winds; and when the rum gave out and it looked like trouble, Shard reminded them what little use it had been to them when it was all they had and the oxen wouldn't look at it.

And the days wore on with singing, and even dancing at times, and at nights round a cautious fire in a hollow of sand with only one man on watch they told tales of the sea. It was all a relief after arduous watches and sleeping by the guns, a rest to strained nerves and eyes; and all agreed, for all that they missed their rum, that the best place for a ship like theirs was the land.

This was in Latitude 23 North, Longitude 4 East, where, as I have said, a ship's broadside was heard for the first time and the last. It happened this way.

They had been there several weeks and had eaten perhaps ten or a dozen oxen and all that while there had been no breath of wind and they had seen no one: when one morning about two bells when the crew were at breakfast the lookout man reported cavalry on the port side. Shard who had already surrounded his ship with sharpened stakes ordered all his men on board, the young trumpeter who prided himself on having picked up the ways of the land, sounded "Prepare to receive cavalry." Shard sent a few men below with pikes to the lower port-holes, two more aloft with muskets, the rest to the guns, he changed the "grape" or "canister" with which the guns were loaded in case of surprise, for shot, cleared the decks, drew in ladders, and before the cavalry came within range everything was ready for them. The oxen were always yoked in order that Shard could manoeuvre his ship at a moment's notice.

When first sighted the cavalry were trotting but they were coming on now at a slow canter. Arabs in white robes on good horses. Shard estimated that there were two or three hundred of them. At sixty yards Shard opened with one gun, he had had the distance measured, but had never practised for fear of being heard at the oasis: the shot went high. The next one fell short and ricochetted over the Arabs' heads. Shard had the range then and by the time the ten remaining guns of his broadside were given the same elevation as that of his second gun the Arabs had come to the spot where the last shot pitched. The broadside hit the horses, mostly low, and ricochetted on amongst them; one cannon-ball striking a rock at the horses' feet shattered it and sent fragments flying amongst the Arabs with the peculiar scream of things set free by projectiles from their motionless harmless state, and the cannon-ball went on with them with a great howl, this shot alone killed three men.

"Very satisfactory," said Shard rubbing his chin. "Load with grape," he added sharply.

The broadside did not stop the Arabs nor even reduce their speed but they crowded in closer together as though for company in their time of danger, which they should not have done. They were four hundred yards off now, three hundred and fifty; and then the muskets began, for the two men in the crow's-nest had thirty loaded muskets besides a few pistols, the muskets all stood round them leaning against the rail; they picked them up and fired them one by one. Every shot told, but still the Arabs came on. They were galloping now. It took some time to load the guns in those days. Three hundred yards, two hundred and fifty, men dropping all the way, two hundred yards; Old Frank for all his one ear had terrible eyes; it was pistols now, they had fired all their muskets; a hundred and fifty; Shard had marked the fifties with little white stones. Old Frank and Bad Jack up aloft felt pretty uneasy when they saw the Arabs had come to that little white stone, they both missed their shots.

"All ready?" said Captain Shard.

"Aye, aye, sir," said Smerdrak.

"Right," said Captain Shard raising a finger.

A hundred and fifty yards is a bad range at which to be caught by grape (or "case" as we call it now), the gunners can hardly miss and the charge has time to spread. Shard estimated afterwards that he got thirty Arabs by that broadside alone and as many horses.

There were close on two hundred of them still on their horses, yet the broadside of grape had unsettled them, they surged round the ship but seemed doubtful what to do. They carried swords and scimitars in their hands, though most had strange long muskets slung behind them, a few unslung them and began firing wildly. They could not reach Shard's merry men with their swords. Had it not been for that broadside that took them when it did they might have climbed up from their horses and carried the bad ship by sheer force of numbers, but they would have had to have been very steady, and the broadside spoiled all that. Their best course was to have concentrated all their efforts in setting fire to the ship but this they did not attempt. Part of them swarmed all round the ship brandishing their swords and looking vainly for an easy entrance; perhaps they expected a door, they were not sea-faring people; but their leaders were evidently set on driving off the oxen not dreaming that the *Desperate Lark* had other means of travelling. And this to some extent they succeeded in doing. Thirty they drove off, cutting the traces, twenty they killed on the spot with their scimitars though the bow gun caught them twice as they did their work, and ten more were unluckily killed by Shard's bow gun. Before they could fire a third time from the bows they all galloped away, firing back at the oxen with their muskets and killing three more, and what troubled Shard more than the loss of his oxen was the way that they manoeuvred, galloping off just when the bow gun was ready and riding off by the port bow where the broadside could not get them, which seemed to him to show more knowledge of guns than they could have learned on that bright morning. What, thought Shard to himself, if they should bring big guns against the *Desperate Lark*! And the mere thought of it made him rail at Fate. But the merry men all cheered when they rode away. Shard had only twenty-two oxen left, and then a score or so of the Arabs dismounted while the rest rode further on leading their horses. And the dismounted men lay down on the port bow behind some rocks two hundred yards away and began to shoot at the oxen. Shard had just enough of them left to manoeuvre his ship with an effort and he turned his ship a few points to the starboard so as to get a broadside at the rocks. But grape was of no use here as the only way he could get an Arab was by hitting one of the rocks with shot behind which an Arab was lying, and the rocks were not easy to hit except by chance, and as often as he manoeuvred his ship the Arabs changed their ground. This went on all day while the mounted Arabs hovered out of range watching what Shard would do; and all the while the oxen were growing fewer, so good a mark were they, until only ten were left, and the ship could manoeuvre no longer. But then they all rode off.

The merry men were delighted, they calculated that one way and another they had unhorsed a hundred Arabs and on board there had been no more than one man wounded: Bad Jack had been hit in the wrist; probably by a bullet meant for the men at the guns, for the Arabs were firing high. They had captured a horse and had found quaint weapons on the bodies of the dead Arabs and an interesting kind of tobacco. It was evening now and they talked over the fight, made jokes about their luckier shots, smoked their new tobacco and sang; altogether it was the jolliest evening they'd had. But Shard alone on the quarter-deck paced to and fro pondering, brooding and wondering. He had chopped off Bad Jack's wounded hand and given him a hook out of store, for captain does doctor upon these occasions and Shard, who was ready for most things, kept half a dozen or so of neat new limbs, and of course a chopper. Bad Jack had gone below swearing a little and said he'd lie down for a bit, the men were smoking and singing on the sand, and Shard was there alone. The thought that troubled Shard was: what would the Arabs do? They did not look like men to go away for nothing. And at back of all his thoughts was one that reiterated guns, guns, guns. He argued with himself that they could not drag them all that way on the sand, that the *Desperate Lark* was not worth it, that they had given it up. Yet he knew in his heart that that was what they would do. He knew there were fortified towns in Africa, and as for its being worth it, he knew that there was no pleasant thing left now to those defeated men except revenge, and if the *Desperate Lark* had come over the sand why not guns? He knew that the ship could never hold out against guns and cavalry, a week perhaps, two weeks, even three: what difference did it make how long it was, and the men sang:

> *Away we go, Oho, Oho, Oho,*
> *A drop of rum for you and me*
> *And the world's as round as the letter O*
> *And round it runs the sea.*

A melancholy settled down on Shard.

About sunset Lieutenant Smerdrak came up for orders. Shard ordered a trench to be dug along the port side of the ship. The men wanted to sing and grumbled at having to dig, especially as Shard never mentioned his fear of guns, but he fingered his pistols and in the end Shard had his way. No one on board could shoot like Captain Shard. That is often the way with captains of pirate ships, it is a difficult position to hold. Discipline is essential to those that have the right to fly the skull-and-cross-bones, and Shard was the man to enforce it. It was starlight by the time the trench was dug to the captain's satisfaction and the men that it was to protect when the worst came to the worst swore all the time as they dug. And when it was finished they clamoured to make a feast on some of the killed oxen, and this Shard let them do. And they lit a huge fire for the first time, burning abundant scrub, they thinking that Arabs daren't return, Shard knowing that concealment was now useless. All that night they feasted and sang, and Shard sat up in his chart-room making his plans.

When morning came they rigged up the cutter as they called the captured horse and told off her crew. As there were only two men that could ride at all these became the crew of the cutter. Spanish Dick and Bill the Boatswain were the two.

Shard's orders were that turn and turn about they should take command of the cutter and cruise about five miles off to the North East all the day but at night they were to come in. And they fitted the horse up with a flagstaff in front of the saddle so that they could signal from her, and carried an anchor behind for fear she should run away.

And as soon as Spanish Dick had ridden off Shard sent some men to roll all the barrels back from the depot where they were buried in the sand, with orders to watch the cutter all the time and, if she signalled, to return as fast as they could.

They buried the Arabs that day, removing their water-bottles and any provisions they had, and that night they got all the water-barrels in, and for days nothing happened. One event of extraordinary importance did indeed occur, the wind got up one day, but it was due South, and as the oasis lay to the North of them and beyond that they might pick up the camel track Shard decided to stay where he was. If it had looked to him like lasting Shard might have hoisted sail but it it dropped at evening as he knew it would, and in any case it was not the wind he wanted. And more days went by, two weeks without a breeze. The dead oxen would not keep and they had had to kill three more, there were only seven left now.

Never before had the men been so long without rum. And Captain Shard had doubled the watch besides making two more men sleep at the guns. They had tired of their simple games, and most of their songs, and their tales that were never true were no longer new. And then one day the monotony of the desert came down upon them.

There is a fascination in the Sahara, a day there is delightful, a week is pleasant, a fortnight is a matter of opinion, but it was running into months. The men were perfectly polite but the boatswain wanted to know when Shard thought of moving on. It was an unreasonable question to ask of the captain of any ship in a dead calm in a desert, but Shard said he would set a course and let him know in a day or two. And a day or two went by over the monotony of the Sahara, who for monotony is unequalled by all the parts of the earth. Great marshes cannot equal it, nor plains of grass nor the sea, the Sahara alone lies unaltered by the seasons, she has no altering surface, no flowers to fade or grow, year in year out she is changeless for hundreds and hundreds of miles. And the boatswain came again and took off his cap and asked Captain Shard to be so kind as to tell them about his new course. Shard said he meant to stay until they had eaten three more of the oxen as they could only take three of them in the hold, there were only six left now.

But what if there was no wind, the boatswain said. And at that moment the faintest breeze from the North ruffled the boatswain's forelock as he stood with his cap in his hand.

"Don't talk about the wind to *me*," said Captain Shard: and Bill was a little frightened for Shard's mother had been a gipsy.

But it was only a breeze astray, a trick of the Sahara. And another week went by and they ate two more oxen.

They obeyed Captain Shard ostentatiously now but they wore ominous looks. Bill came again and Shard answered him in Romany.

Things were like this one hot Sahara morning when the cutter signalled. The lookout man told Shard and Shard read the message, "Cavalry astern" it read, and then a little later she signalled, "With guns."

"Ah," said Captain Shard.

One ray of hope Shard had; the flags on the cutter fluttered. For the first time for five weeks a light breeze blew from the North, very light, you hardly felt it. Spanish Dick rode in and anchored his horse to starboard and the cavalry came on slowly from the port.

Not till the afternoon did they come in sight, and all the while that little breeze was blowing.

"One knot," said Shard at noon. "Two knots," he said at six bells and still it grew and the Arabs trotted nearer. By five o'clock the merry men of the bad ship *Desperate Lark* could make out twelve long old-fashioned guns on low wheeled carts dragged by horses and what looked like lighter guns carried on camels. The wind was blowing a little stronger now. "Shall we hoist sail, sir?" said Bill.

"Not yet," said Shard.

By six o'clock the Arabs were just outside the range of cannon and there they halted. Then followed an anxious hour or so, but the Arabs came no nearer. They evidently meant to wait till dark to bring their guns up. Probably they intended to dig a gun epaulment from which they could safely pound away at the ship.

"We could do three knots," said Shard half to himself as he was walking up and down his quarter-deck with very fast short paces. And then the sun set and they heard the Arabs praying and Shard's merry men cursed at the top of their voices to show that they were as good men as they.

The Arabs had come no nearer, waiting for night. They did not know how Shard was longing for it too, he was gritting his teeth and sighing for it, he even would have prayed, but that he feared that it might remind Heaven of him and his merry men.

Night came and the stars. "Hoist sail," said Shard. The men sprang to their places, they had had enough of that silent lonely spot. They took the oxen on board and let the great sails down, and like a lover coming from over sea, long dreamed of, long expected, like a lost friend seen again after many years, the North wind came into the pirates' sails. And before Shard could stop it a ringing English cheer went away to the wondering Arabs.

They started off at three knots and soon they might have done four but Shard would not risk it at night. All night the wind held good, and doing three knots from ten to four they were far out of sight of the Arabs when daylight came. And then Shard hoisted more sail and they did four knots and by eight bells they were doing four and a half. The spirits of those volatile men rose high, and discipline became perfect. So long as there was wind in the sails and water in the tanks Captain Shard felt safe at least from mutiny. Great men can only be overthrown while their fortunes are at their lowest. Having failed to depose Shard when his plans were open to criticism and he himself scarce knew what to do next it was hardly likely they could do it now; and whatever we think of his past and his way of living we cannot deny that Shard was among the great men of the world.

Of defeat by the Arabs he did not feel so sure. It was useless to try to cover his tracks even if he had had time, the Arab cavalry could have picked them up anywhere. And he was afraid of their camels with those light guns on board, he had heard they could do seven knots and keep it up most of the day and if as much as one shot struck the mainmast...and Shard taking his mind off useless fears worked out on his chart when the Arabs were likely to overtake them. He told his men that the wind would hold good for a week, and, gipsy or no, he certainly knew as much about the wind as is good for a sailor to know.

Alone in his chart-room he worked it out like this, mark two hours to the good for surprise and finding the tracks and delay in starting, say three hours if the guns were mounted in their epaulments, then the Arabs should start at seven. Supposing the camels go twelve hours a day at seven knots they would do eighty-four knots a day, while Shard doing three knots from ten to four, and four knots the rest of the time, was doing ninety and actually gaining. But when it came to it he wouldn't risk more than two knots at night while the enemy were out of sight, for he rightly regarded anything more than that as dangerous when sailing on land at night, so he too did eighty-four knots a day. It was a pretty race. I have not troubled to see if Shard added up his figures wrongly or if he under-rated the pace of camels, but whatever it was the Arabs gained slightly, for on the fourth day Spanish Jack, five knots astern on what they called the cutter, sighted the camels a very long way off and signalled the fact to Shard. They had left their cavalry behind as Shard supposed they would. The wind held good, they had still two oxen left and could always eat their "cutter," and they had a fair, though not ample, supply of water, but the appearance of the Arabs was a blow to Shard for it showed him that there was no getting away from them, and of all things he dreaded guns. He made light of it to the men: said they would sink the lot before they had been in action half an hour: yet he feared that once the guns came up it was only a question of time before his rigging was cut or his steering gear disabled.

One point the *Desperate Lark* scored over the Arabs and a very good one too, darkness fell just before they could have sighted her and now Shard used the lantern ahead as he dared not do on the first night when the Arabs were close, and with the help of it managed to do three knots. The Arabs encamped in the evening and the *Desperate Lark* gained twenty knots. But the next evening they appeared again and this time they saw the sails of the *Desperate Lark*.

On the sixth day they were close. On the seventh they were closer. And then, a line of verdure across their bows, Shard saw the Niger River.

Whether he knew that for a thousand miles it rolled its course through forest, whether he even knew that it was there at all; what his plans were, or whether he lived from day to day like a man whose days are numbered he never told his men. Nor can I get an indication on this point from the talk that I hear from sailors in their cups in a certain tavern I know of. His face was expressionless, his mouth shut, and he held his ship to her course. That evening they were up to the edge of the tree trunks and the Arabs camped and waited ten knots astern and the wind had sunk a little.

There Shard anchored a little before sunset and landed at once. At first he explored the forest a little on foot. Then he sent for Spanish Dick. They had slung the cutter on board some days ago when they found she could not keep up. Shard could not ride but he sent for Spanish Dick and told him he must take him as a passenger. So Spanish Dick slung him in front of the saddle "before the mast" as Shard called it, for they still carried a mast on the front of the saddle, and away they galloped together. "Rough weather," said Shard, but he surveyed the forest as he went and the long and short of it was he found a place where the forest was less than half a mile thick and the *Desperate Lark* might get through: but twenty trees must be cut. Shard marked the trees himself, sent Spanish Dick right back to watch the Arabs and turned the whole of his crew on to those twenty trees. It was a frightful risk, the *Desperate Lark* was empty, with an enemy no more than ten knots astern, but it was a moment for bold measures and Shard took the chance of being left without his ship in the heart of Africa in the hope of being repaid by escaping altogether.

The men worked all night on those twenty trees, those that had no axes bored with bradawls and blasted, and then relieved those that had.

Shard was indefatigable, he went from tree to tree showing exactly what way every one was to fall, and what was to be done with them when they were down. Some had to be cut down because their branches would get in the way of the masts, others because their trunks would be in the way of the wheels; in the case of the last the stumps had to be made smooth and low with saws and perhaps a bit of the trunk sawn off and rolled away. This was the hardest work they had. And they were all large trees, on the other hand had they been small there would have been many more of them and they could not have sailed in and out, sometimes for hundreds of yards, without cutting any at all: and all this Shard calculated on doing if only there was time.

The light before dawn came and it looked as if they would never do it at all. And then dawn came and it was all done but one tree, the hard part of the work had all been done in the night and a sort of final rush cleared everything up except that one huge tree. And then the cutter signalled the Arabs were moving. At dawn they had prayed, and now they had struck their camp. Shard at once ordered all his men to the ship except ten whom he left at the tree, they had some way to go and the Arabs had been moving some ten minutes before they got there. Shard took in the cutter which wasted five minutes, hoisted sail short-handed and that took five minutes more, and slowly got under way.

The wind was dropping still and by the time the *Desperate Lark* had come to the edge of that part of the forest through which Shard had laid his course the Arabs were no more than five knots away. He had sailed East half a mile, which he ought to have done overnight so as to be ready, but he could not spare time or thought or men away from those twenty trees. Then Shard turned into the forest and the Arabs were dead astern. They hurried when they saw the *Desperate Lark* enter the forest.

"Doing ten knots," said Shard as he watched them from the deck. The *Desperate Lark* was doing no more than a knot and a half for the wind was weak under the lee of the trees. Yet all went well for a while. The big tree had just come down some way ahead, and the ten men were sawing bits off the trunk.

And then Shard saw a branch that he had not marked on the chart, it would just catch the top of the mainmast. He anchored at once and sent a hand aloft who sawed it half way through and did the rest with a pistol, and now the Arabs were only three knots astern. For a quarter of a mile Shard steered them through the forest till they came to the ten men and that bad big tree, another foot had yet to come off one corner of the stump for the wheels had to pass over it. Shard turned all hands on to the stump and it was then that the Arabs came within shot. But they had to unpack their gun. And before they had it mounted Shard was away. If they had charged things might have been different. When they saw the *Desperate Lark* under way again the Arabs came on to within three hundred yards and there they mounted two guns. Shard watched them along his stern gun but would not fire. They were six hundred yards away before the Arabs could fire and then they fired too soon and both guns missed. And Shard and his merry men saw clear water only ten fathoms ahead. Then Shard loaded his stern gun with canister instead of shot and at the same moment the Arabs charged on their camels; they came galloping down through the forest waving long lances. Shard left the steering to Smerdrak and stood by the stern gun, the Arabs were within fifty yards and still Shard did not fire; he had most of his men in the stern with muskets beside him. Those lances carried on camels were altogether different from swords in the hands of horsemen, they could reach the men on deck. The men could see the horrible barbs on the lanceheads, they were almost at their faces when Shard fired, and at the same moment the *Desperate Lark* with her dry and suncracked keel in air on the high bank of the Niger fell forward like a diver. The gun went off through the tree-tops, a wave came over the bows and swept the stern, the *Desperate Lark* wriggled and righted herself, she was back in her element.

The merry men looked at the wet decks and at their dripping clothes. "Water," they said almost wonderingly.

The Arabs followed a little way through the forest but when they saw that they had to face a broadside instead of one stern gun and perceived that a ship afloat is less vulnerable to cavalry even than when on shore, they abandoned ideas of revenge, and comforted themselves with a text out of their sacred book which tells how in other days and other places our enemies shall suffer even as we desire.

For a thousand miles with the flow of the Niger and the help of occasional winds, the *Desperate Lark* moved seawards. At first he sweeps East a little and then Southwards, till you come to Akassa and the open sea.

I will not tell you how they caught fish and ducks, raided a village here and there and at last came to Akassa, for I have said much already of Captain Shard. Imagine them drawing nearer and nearer the sea, bad men all, and yet with a feeling for something where we feel for our king, our country or our home, a feeling for something that burned in them not less ardently than our feelings in us, and that something the sea. Imagine them nearing it till sea birds appeared and they fancied they felt sea breezes and all sang songs again that they had not sung for weeks. Imagine them heaving at last on the salt Atlantic again.

I have said much already of Captain Shard and I fear lest I shall weary you, O my reader, if I tell you any more of so bad a man. I too at the top of a tower all alone am weary.

And yet it is right that such a tale should be told. A journey almost due South from near Algiers to Akassa in a ship that we should call no more than a yacht. Let it be a stimulus to younger men.

GUARANTEE TO THE READER

Since writing down for your benefit, O my reader, all this long tale that I heard in the tavern by the sea I have travelled in Algeria and Tunisia as well as in the Desert. Much that I saw in those countries seems to throw doubt on the tale that the sailor told me. To begin with the Desert does not come within hundreds of miles of the coast and there are more mountains to cross than you would suppose, the Atlas mountains in particular. It is just possible Shard might have got through by El Cantara, following the camel road which is many centuries old; or he may have gone by Algiers and Bou Saada and through the mountain pass El Finita Dem, though that is a bad enough way for camels to go (let alone bullocks with a ship) for which reason the Arabs call it Finita Dem—the Path of Blood.

I should not have ventured to give this story the publicity of print had the sailor been sober when he told it, for fear that he I should have deceived you, O my reader; but this was never the case with him as I took good care to ensure: "in vino veritas" is a sound old proverb, and I never had cause to doubt his word unless that proverb lies.

If it should prove that he has deceived me, let it pass; but if he has been the means of deceiving you there are little things about him that I know, the common gossip of that ancient tavern whose leaded bottle-glass windows watch the sea, which I will tell at once to every judge of my acquaintance, and it will be a pretty race to see which of them will hang him.

Meanwhile, O my reader, believe the story, resting assured that if you are taken in the thing shall be a matter for the hangman.

A TALE OF THE EQUATOR

He who is Sultan so remote to the East that his dominions were deemed fabulous in Babylon, whose name is a by-word for distance today in the streets of Bagdad, whose capital bearded travellers invoke by name in the gate at evening to gather hearers to their tales when the smoke of tobacco arises, dice rattle and taverns shine; even he in that very city made mandate, and said: "Let there be brought hither all my learned men that they may come before me and rejoice my heart with learning."

Men ran and clarions sounded, and it was so that there came before the Sultan all of his learned men. And many were found wanting. But of those that were able to say acceptable things, ever after to be named The Fortunate, one said that to the South of the Earth lay a Land—said Land was crowned with lotus—where it was summer in our winter days and where it was winter in summer.

And when the Sultan of those most distant lands knew that the Creator of All had contrived a device so vastly to his delight his merriment knew no bounds. On a sudden he spake and said, and this was the gist of his saying, that upon that line of boundary or limit that divided the North from the South a palace be made, where in the Northern courts should summer be, while in the South was winter; so should he move from court to court according to his mood, and dally with the summer in the morning and spend the noon with snow. So the Sultan's poets were sent for and bade to tell of that city, foreseeing its splendour far away to the South and in the future of time; and some were found fortunate. And of those that were found fortunate and were crowned with flowers none earned more easily the Sultan's smile (on which long days depended) than he that foreseeing the city spake of it thus:

"In seven years and seven days, O Prop of Heaven, shall thy builders build it, thy palace that is neither North nor South, where neither summer nor winter is sole lord of the hours. White I see it, very vast, as a city, very fair, as a woman, Earth's wonder, with many windows, with thy princesses peering out at twilight; yea, I behold the bliss of the gold balconies, and hear a rustling down long galleries and the doves' coo upon its sculptured eaves. O Prop of Heaven, would that so fair a city were built by thine ancient sires, the children of the sun, that so might all men see it even today, and not the poets only, whose vision sees it so far away to the South and in the future of time.

"O King of the Years, it shall stand midmost on that line that divideth equally the North from the South and that parteth the seasons asunder as with a screen. On the Northern side when summer is in the North thy silken guards shall pace by dazzling walls while thy spearsmen clad in furs go round the South. But at the hour of noon in the midmost day of the year thy chamberlain shall go down from his high place and into the midmost court, and men with trumpets shall go down behind him, and he shall utter a great cry at noon, and the men with trumpets shall cause their trumpets to blare, and the spearsmen clad in furs shall march to the North and thy silken guard shall take their place in the South, and summer shall leave the North and go to the South, and all the swallows shall rise and follow after. And alone in thine inner courts shall no change be, for they shall lie narrowly along that line that parteth the seasons in sunder and divideth the North from the South, and thy long gardens shall lie under them.

"And in thy gardens shall spring always be, for spring lies ever at the marge of summer; and autumn also shall always tint thy gardens, for autumn always flares at winter's edge, and those gardens shall lie apart between winter and summer. And there shall be orchards in thy garden, too, with all the burden of autumn on their boughs and all the blossom of spring.

"Yea, I behold this palace, for we see future things; I see its white wall shine in the huge glare of midsummer, and the lizards lying along it motionless in the sun, and men asleep in the noonday, and the butterflies floating by, and birds of radiant plumage chasing marvellous moths; far off the forest and great orchids glorying there, and iridescent insects dancing round in the light. I see the wall upon the other side; the snow has come upon the battlements, the icicles have fringed them like frozen beards, a wild wind blowing out of lonely places and crying to the cold fields as it blows has sent the snowdrifts higher than the buttresses; they that look out through windows on that side of thy palace see the wild geese flying low and all the birds of the winter, going by swift in packs beat low by the bitter wind, and the clouds above them are black, for it is midwinter there; while in thine other courts the fountains tinkle, falling on marble warmed by the fire of the summer sun.

"Such, O King of the Years, shall thy palace be, and its name shall be Erlathdronion, Earth's Wonder; and thy wisdom shall bid thine architects build at once, that all may see what as yet the poets see only, and that prophecy be fulfilled."

And when the poet ceased the Sultan spake, and said, as all men hearkened with bent heads:

"It will be unnecessary for my builders to build this palace, Erlathdronion, Earth's Wonder, for in hearing thee we have drunk already its pleasures."

And the poet went forth from the Presence and dreamed a new thing.

A NARROW ESCAPE

It was underground.

In that dank cavern down below Belgrave Square the walls were dripping. But what was that to the magician? It was secrecy that he needed, not dryness. There he pondered upon the trend of events, shaped destinies and concocted magical brews.

For the last few years the serenity of his ponderings had been disturbed by the noise of the motor-bus; while to his keen ears there came the earthquake-rumble, far off, of the train in the tube, going down Sloane Street; and when he heard of the world above his head was not to its credit.

He decided one evening over his evil pipe, down there in his dank chamber, that London had lived long enough, had abused its opportunities, had gone too far, in fine, with its civilisation. And so he decided to wreck it.

Therefore he beckoned up his acolyte from the weedy end of the cavern, and, "Bring me," he said, "the heart of the toad that dwelleth in Arabia and by the mountains of Bethany." The acolyte slipped away by the hidden door, leaving that grim old man with his frightful pipe, and whither he went who knows but the gipsy people, or by what path he returned; but within a year he stood in the cavern again, slipping secretly in by the trap while the old man smoked, and he brought with him a little fleshy thing that rotted in a casket of pure gold.

"What is it?" the old man croaked.

"It is," said the acolyte, "the heart of the toad that dwelt once in Arabia and by the mountains of Bethany."

The old man's crooked fingers closed on it, and he blessed the acolyte with his rasping voice and claw-like hand uplifted; the motor-bus rumbled above on its endless journey; far off the train shook Sloane Street.

"Come," said the old magician, "it is time." And there and then they left the weedy cavern, the acolyte carrying cauldron, gold poker and all things needful, and went abroad in the light. And very wonderful the old man looked in his silks.

Their goal was the outskirts of London; the old man strode in front and the acolyte ran behind him, and there was something magical in the old man's stride alone, without his wonderful dress, the cauldron and wand, the hurrying acolyte and the small gold poker.

Little boys jeered till they caught the old man's eye. So there went on through London this strange procession of two, too swift for any to follow. Things seemed worse up there than they did in the cavern, and the further they got on their way towards London's outskirts the worse London got. "It is time," said the old man, "surely."

And so they came at last to London's edge and a small hill watching it with a mournful look. It was so mean that the acolyte longed for the cavern, dank though it was and full of terrible sayings that the old man said when he slept.

They climbed the hill and put the cauldron down, and put there in the necessary things, and lit a fire of herbs that no chemist will sell nor decent gardener grow, and stirred the cauldron with the golden poker. The magician retired a little apart and muttered, then he strode back to the cauldron and, all being ready, suddenly opened the casket and let the fleshy thing fall in to boil.

Then he made spells, then he flung up his arms; the fumes from the cauldron entering in at his mind he said raging things that he had not known before and runes that were dreadful (the acolyte screamed); there he cursed London from fog to loam-pit, from zenith to the abyss, motor-bus, factory, shop, parliament, people. "Let them all perish," he said, "and London pass away, tram lines and bricks and pavement, the usurpers too long of the fields, let them all pass away and the wild hares come back, blackberry and briar-rose."

"Let it pass," he said, "pass now, pass utterly."

In the momentary silence the old man coughed, then waited with eager eyes; and the long long hum of London hummed as it always has since first the reed-huts were set up by the river, changing its note at times but always humming, louder now than it was in years gone by, but humming night and day though its voice be cracked with age; so it hummed on.

And the old man turned him round to his trembling acolyte and terribly said as he sank into the earth: "YOU HAVE NOT BROUGHT ME THE HEART OF THE TOAD THAT DWELLETH IN ARABIA NOR BY THE MOUNTAINS OF BETHANY!"

THE WATCH-TOWER

I sat one April in Provence on a small hill above an ancient town that Goth and Vandal as yet have forborne to "bring up to date."

On the hill was an old worn castle with a watch-tower, and a well with narrow steps and water in it still.

The watch-tower, staring South with neglected windows, faced a broad valley full of the pleasant twilight and the hum of evening things: it saw the fires of wanderers blink from the hills, beyond them the long forest black with pines, one star appearing, and darkness settling slowly down on Var.

Sitting there listening to the green frogs croaking, hearing far voices clearly but all transmuted by evening, watching the windows in the little town glimmering one by one, and seeing the gloaming dwindle solemnly into night, a great many things fell from mind that seem important by day, and evening in their place planted strange fancies.

Little winds had arisen and were whispering to and fro, it grew cold, and I was about to descend the hill, when I heard a voice behind me saying, "Beware, beware."

So much the voice appeared a part of the evening that I did not turn round at first; it was like voices that one hears in sleep and thinks to be of one's dream. And the word was monotonously repeated, in French.

When I turned round I saw an old man with a horn. He had a white beard marvellously long, and still went on saying slowly, "Beware, beware." He had clearly just come from the tower by which he stood, though I had heard no footfall. Had a man come stealthily upon me at such an hour and in so lonesome a place I had certainly felt surprised; but I saw almost at once that he was a spirit, and he seemed with his uncouth horn and his long white beard and that noiseless step of his to be so native to that time and place that I spoke to him as one does to some fellow-traveller who asks you if you mind having the window up.

I asked him what there was to beware of.

"Of what should a town beware," he said, "but the Saracens?"

"Saracens?" I said.

"Yes, Saracens, Saracens," he answered and brandished his horn.

"And who are you?" I said.

"I, I am the spirit of the tower," he said.

When I asked him how he came by so human an aspect and was so unlike the material tower beside him he told me that the lives of all the watchers who had ever held the horn in the tower there had gone to make the spirit of the tower. "It takes a hundred lives," he said. "None hold the horn of late and men neglect the tower. When the walls are in ill repair the Saracens come: it was ever so."

"The Saracens don't come nowadays," I said.

But he was gazing past me watching, and did not seem to heed me.

"They will run down those hills," he said, pointing away to the South, "out of the woods about nightfall, and I shall blow my horn. The people will all come up from the town to the tower again; but the loopholes are in very ill repair."

"We never hear of the Saracens now," I said.

"Hear of the Saracens!" the old spirit said. "Hear of the Saracens! They slip one evening out of that forest, in the long white robes that they wear, and I blow my horn. That is the first that anyone ever hears of the Saracens."

"I mean," I said, "that they never come at all. They cannot come and men fear other things." For I thought the old spirit might rest if he knew that the Saracens can never come again. But he said, "There is nothing in the world to fear but the Saracens. Nothing else matters. How can men fear other things?"

Then I explained, so that he might have rest, and told him how all Europe, and in particular France, had terrible engines of war, both on land and sea; and how the Saracens had not these terrible engines either on sea or land, and so could by no means cross the Mediterranean or escape destruction on shore even though they should come there. I alluded to the European railways that could move armies night and day faster than horses could gallop. And when as well as I could I had explained all, he answered, "In time all these things pass away and then there will still be the Saracens."

And then I said, "There has not been a Saracen either in France or Spain for over four hundred years."

And he said, "The Saracens! You do not know their cunning. That was ever the way of the Saracens. They do not come for a while, no not they, for a long while, and then one day they come."

And peering southwards, but not seeing clearly because of the rising mist, he silently moved to his tower and up its broken steps.

HOW PLASH-GOO CAME TO THE LAND OF NONE'S DESIRE

In a thatched cottage of enormous size, so vast that we might consider it a palace, but only a cottage in the style of its building, its timbers and the nature of its interior, there lived Plash-Goo.

Plash-Goo was of the children of the giants, whose sire was Uph. And the lineage of Uph had dwindled in bulk for the last five hundred years, till the giants were now no more than fifteen foot high; but Uph ate elephants which he caught with his hands.

Now on the tops of the mountains above the house of Plash-Goo, for Plash-Goo lived in the plains, there dwelt the dwarf whose name was Lrip-pity-Kang. And the dwarf used to walk at evening on the edge of the tops of the mountains, and would walk up and down along it, and was squat and ugly and hairy, and was plainly seen of Plash-Goo.

And for many weeks the giant had suffered the sight of him, but at length grew irked at the sight (as men are by little things), and could not sleep of a night and lost his taste for pigs. And at last there came the day, as anyone might have known, when Plash-Goo shouldered his club and went up to look for the dwarf.

And the dwarf though briefly squat was broader than may be dreamed, beyond all breadth of man, and stronger than men may know; strength in its very essence dwelt in that little frame, as a spark in the heart of a flint: but to Plash-Goo he was no more than mis-shapen, bearded and squat, a thing that dared to defy all natural laws by being more broad than long.

When Plash-Goo came to the mountain he cast his chimahalk down (for so he named the club of his heart's desire) lest the dwarf should defy him with nimbleness; and stepped towards Lrippity-Kang with gripping hands, who stopped in his mountainous walk without a word, and swung round his hideous breadth to confront Plash-Goo. Already then Plash-Goo in the deeps of his mind had seen himself seize the dwarf in one large hand and hurl him with his beard and his hated breadth sheer down the precipice that dropped away from that very place to the land of None's Desire. Yet it was otherwise that Fate would have it. For the dwarf parried with his little arms the grip of those monstrous hands, and gradually working along the enormous limbs came at length to the giant's body where by dwarfish cunning he obtained a grip; and turning Plash-Goo about, as a spider does some great fly, till his little grip was suitable to his purpose, he suddenly lifted the giant over his head. Slowly at first, by the edge of that precipice whose base sheer distance hid, he swung his giant victim round his head, but soon faster and faster; and at last when Plash-Goo was streaming round the hated breadth of the dwarf and the no less hated beard was flapping in the wind, Lrippity-Kang let go. Plash-Goo shot over the edge and for some way further, out towards Space, like a stone; then he began to fall. It was long before he believed and truly knew that this was really he that fell from this mountain, for we do not associate such dooms with ourselves; but when he had fallen for some while through the evening and saw below him, where there had been nothing to see, or began to see, the glimmer of tiny fields, then his optimism departed; till later on when the fields were greener and larger he saw that this was indeed (and growing now terribly nearer) that very land to which he had destined the dwarf.

At last he saw it unmistakable, close, with its grim houses and its dreadful ways, and its green fields shining in the light of the evening. His cloak was streaming from him in whistling shreds.

So Plash-Goo came to the Land of None's Desire.

THE THREE SAILORS' GAMBIT

Sitting some years ago in the ancient tavern at Over, one afternoon in Spring, I was waiting, as was my custom, for something strange to happen. In this I was not always disappointed for the very curious leaded panes of that tavern, facing the sea, let a light into the low-ceilinged room so mysterious, particularly at evening, that it somehow seemed to affect the events within. Be that as it may, I have seen strange things in that tavern and heard stranger things told.

And as I sat there three sailors entered the tavern, just back, as they said, from sea, and come with sunburned skins from a very long voyage to the South; and one of them had a board and chessmen under his arm, and they were complaining that they could find no one who knew how to play chess. This was the year that the Tournament was in England. And a little dark man at a table in a corner of the room, drinking sugar and water, asked them why they wished to play chess; and they said they would play any man for a pound. They opened their box of chessmen then, a cheap and nasty set, and the man refused to play with such uncouth pieces, and the sailors suggested that perhaps he could find better ones; and in the end he went round to his lodgings near by and brought his own, and then they sat down to play for a pound a side. It was a consultation game on the part of the sailors, they said that all three must play.

Well, the little dark man turned out to be Stavlokratz.

Of course he was fabulously poor, and the sovereign meant more to him than it did to the sailors, but he didn't seem keen to play, it was the sailors that insisted; he had made the badness of the sailors' chessmen an excuse for not playing at all, but the sailors had overruled that, and then he told them straight out who he was, and the sailors had never heard of Stavlokratz.

Well, no more was said after that. Stavlokratz said no more, either because he did not wish to boast or because he was huffed that they did not know who he was. And I saw no reason to enlighten the sailors about him; if he took their pound they had brought it upon themselves, and my boundless admiration for his genius made me feel that he deserved whatever might come his way. He had not asked to play, they had named the stakes, he had warned them, and gave them the first move; there was nothing unfair about Stavlokratz.

I had never seen Stavlokratz before, but I had played over nearly every one of his games in the World Championship for the last three or four years; he was always of course the model chosen by students. Only young chess-players can appreciate my delight at seeing him play first hand.

Well, the sailors used to lower their heads almost as low as the table and mutter together before every move, but they muttered so low that you could not hear what they planned.

They lost three pawns almost straight off, then a knight, and shortly after a bishop; they were playing in fact the famous Three Sailors' Gambit.

Stavlokratz was playing with the easy confidence that they say was usual with him, when suddenly at about the thirteenth move I saw him look surprised; he leaned forward and looked at the board and then at the sailors, but he learned nothing from their vacant faces; he looked back at the board again.

He moved more deliberately after that; the sailors lost two more pawns, Stavlokratz had lost nothing as yet. He looked at me I thought almost irritably, as though something would happen that he wished I was not there to see. I believed at first that he had qualms about taking the sailors' pound, until it dawned on me that he might lose the game; I saw that possibility in his face, not on the board, for the game had become almost incomprehensible to me. I cannot describe my astonishment. And a few moves later Stavlokratz resigned.

The sailors showed no more elation than if they had won some game with greasy cards, playing amongst themselves.

Stavlokratz asked them where they got their opening. "We kind of thought of it," said one. "It just come into our heads like," said another. He asked them questions about the ports they had touched at. He evidently thought as I did myself that they had learned their extraordinary gambit, perhaps in some old dependancy of Spain, from some young master of chess whose fame had not reached Europe. He was very eager to find out who this man could be, for neither of us imagined that those sailors had invented it, nor would anyone who had seen them. But he got no information from the sailors.

Stavlokratz could very ill afford the loss of a pound. He offered to play them again for the same stakes. The sailors began to set up the white pieces. Stavlokratz pointed out that it was his turn for the first move. The sailors agreed but continued to set up the white pieces and sat with the white before them waiting for him to move. It was a trivial incident, but it revealed to Stavlokratz and myself that none of these sailors was aware that white always moves first.

Stavlokratz played them on his own opening, reasoning of course that as they had never heard of Stavlokratz they would not know of his opening; and with probably a very good hope of getting back his pound he played the fifth variation with its tricky seventh move, at least so he intended, but it turned to a variation unknown to the students of Stavlokratz.

Throughout this game I watched the sailors closely, and I became sure, as only an attentive watcher can be, that the one on their left, Jim Bunion, did not even know the moves.

When I had made up my mind about this I watched only the other two, Adam Bailey and Bill Sloggs, trying to make out which was the master mind; and for a long while I could not. And then I heard Adam Bailey mutter six words, the only words I heard throughout the game, of all their consultations, "No, him with the horse's head." And I decided that Adam Bailey did not know what a knight was, though of course he might have been explaining things to Bill Sloggs, but it did not sound like that; so that left Bill Sloggs. I watched Bill Sloggs after that with a certain wonder; he was no more intellectual than the others to look at, though rather more forceful perhaps. Poor old Stavlokratz was beaten again.

Well, in the end I paid for Stavlokratz, and tried to get a game with Bill Sloggs alone, but this he would not agree to, it must be all three or none: and then I went back with Stavlokratz to his lodgings. He very kindly gave me a game: of course it did not last long but I am prouder of having been beaten by Stavlokratz than of any game that I have ever won. And then we talked for an hour about the sailors, and neither of us could make head or tail of them. I told him what I had noticed about Jim Bunion and Adam Bailey, and he agreed with me that Bill Sloggs was the man, though as to how he had come by that gambit or that variation of Stavlokratz's own opening he had no theory.

I had the sailors' address which was that tavern as much as anywhere, and they were to be there all evening. As evening drew in I went back to the tavern, and found there still the three sailors. And I offered Bill Sloggs two pounds for a game with him alone and he refused, but in the end he played me for a drink. And then I found that he had not heard of the "en passant" rule, and believed that the fact of checking the king prevented him from castling, and did not know that a player can have two or more queens on the board at the same time if he queens his pawns, or that a pawn could ever become a knight; and he made as many of the stock mistakes as he had time for in a short game, which I won. I thought that I should have got at the secret then, but his mates who had sat scowling all the while in the corner came up and interfered. It was a breach of their compact apparently for one to play by himself, at any rate they seemed angry. So I left the tavern then and came back again next day, and the next day and the day after, and often saw the sailors, but none were in a communicative mood. I had got Stavlokratz to keep away, and they could get no one to play chess with at a pound a side, and I would not play with them unless they told me the secret.

And then one evening I found Jim Bunion drunk, yet not so drunk as he wished, for the two pounds were spent; and I gave him very nearly a tumbler of whiskey, or what passed for whiskey in that tavern at Over, and he told me the secret at once. I had given the others some whiskey to keep them quiet, and later on in the evening they must have gone out, but Jim Bunion stayed with me by a little table leaning across it and talking low, right into my face, his breath smelling all the while of what passed for whiskey.

The wind was blowing outside as it does on bad nights in November, coming up with moans from the South, towards which the tavern faced with all its leaded panes, so that none but I was able to hear his voice as Jim Bunion gave up his secret. They had sailed for years, he told me, with Bill Snyth; and on their last voyage home Bill Snyth had died. And he was buried at sea. Just the other side of the line they buried him, and his pals divided his kit, and these three got his crystal that only they knew he had, which Bill got one night in Cuba. They played chess with the crystal.

And he was going on to tell me about that night in Cuba when Bill had bought the crystal from the stranger, how some folks might think they had seen thunderstorms, but let them go and listen to that one that thundered in Cuba when Bill was buying his crystal and they'd find that they didn't know what thunder was. But then I interrupted him, unfortunately perhaps, for it broke the thread of his tale and set him rambling a while, and cursing other people and talking of other lands, China, Port Said and Spain: but I brought him back to Cuba again in the end. I asked him how they could play chess with a crystal; and he said that you looked at the board and looked at the crystal, and there was the game in the crystal the same as it was on the board, with all the odd little pieces looking just the same though smaller, horses' heads and whatnots; and as soon as the other man moved the move came out in the crystal, and then your move appeared after it, and all you had to do was to make it on the board. If you didn't make the move that you saw in the crystal things got very bad in it, everything hor-ribly mixed and moving about rapidly, and scowling and making the same move over and over again, and the crystal getting cloudier and cloudier; it was best to take one's eyes away from it then, or one dreamt about it afterwards, and the foul little pieces came and cursed you in your sleep and moved about all night with their crooked moves.

I thought then that, drunk though he was, he was not telling the truth, and I promised to show him to people who played chess all their lives so that he and his mates could get a pound whenever they liked, and I prom-ised not to reveal his secret even to Stavlokratz, if only he would tell me all the truth; and this promise I have kept till long after the three sailors have lost their secret. I told him straight out that I did not believe in the crystal. Well, Jim Bunion leaned forward then, even further across the table, and swore he had seen the man from whom Bill had bought the crystal and that he was one to whom anything was possible. To begin with his hair was vil-lainously dark, and his features were unmistakable even down there in the South, and he could play chess with his eyes shut, and even then he could beat anyone in Cuba. But there was more than this, there was the bargain he made with Bill that told one who he was. He sold that crystal for Bill Snyth's soul.

Jim Bunion leaning over the table with his breath in my face nodded his head several times and was silent.

I began to question him then. Did they play chess as far away as Cuba? He said they all did. Was it conceivable that any man would make such a bargain as Snyth made? Wasn't the trick well known? Wasn't it in hundreds of books? And if he couldn't read books mustn't he have heard from sailors that it is the Devil's commonest dodge to get souls from silly people?

Jim Bunion had leant back in his own chair quietly smiling at my questions but when I mentioned silly people he leaned forward again, and thrust his face close to mine and asked me several times if I called Bill Snyth silly. It seemed that these three sailors thought a great deal of Bill Snyth and it made Jim Bunion angry to hear anything said against him. I hastened to say that the bargain seemed silly though not of course the man who made it; for the sailor was almost threatening, and no wonder for the whiskey in that dim tavern would madden a nun.

When I said that the bargain seemed silly he smiled again, and then he thundered his fist down on the table and said that no one had ever yet got the best of Bill Snyth and that that was the worst bargain for himself that the Devil ever made, and that from all he had read or heard of the Devil he had never been so badly had before as the night when he met Bill Snyth at the inn in the thunderstorm in Cuba, for Bill Snyth already had the damndest soul at sea; Bill was a good fellow, but his soul was damned right enough, so he got the crystal for nothing.

Yes, he was there and saw it all himself, Bill Snyth in the Spanish inn and the candles flaring, and the Devil walking in and out of the rain, and then the bargain between those two old hands, and the Devil going out into the lightning, and the thunderstorm raging on, and Bill Snyth sitting chuckling to himself between the bursts of the thunder.

But I had more questions to ask and interrupted this reminiscence. Why did they all three always play together? And a look of something like fear came over Jim Bunion's face; and at first he would not speak. And then he said to me that it was like this; they had not paid for that crystal, but got it as their share of Bill Snyth's kit. If they had paid for it or given something in exchange to Bill Snyth that would have been all right, but they couldn't do that now because Bill was dead, and they were not sure if the old bargain might not hold good. And Hell must be a large and lonely place, and to go there alone must be bad, and so the three agreed that they would all stick together, and use the crystal all three or not at all, unless one died, and then the two would use it and the one that was gone would wait for them. And the last of the three to go would take the crystal with him, or maybe the crystal would bring him. They didn't think, they said, they were the kind of men for Heaven, and he hoped they knew their place better than that, but they didn't fancy the notion of Hell alone, if Hell it had to be. It was all right for Bill Snyth, he was afraid of nothing. He had known perhaps five men that were not afraid of death, but Bill Snyth was not afraid of Hell. He died with a smile on his face like a child in its sleep; it was drink killed poor Bill Snyth.

This was why I had beaten Bill Sloggs; Sloggs had the crystal on him while we played, but would not use it; these sailors seemed to fear loneliness as some people fear being hurt; he was the only one of the three who could play chess at all, he had learnt it in order to be able to answer questions and keep up their pretence, but he had learnt it badly, as I found. I never saw the crystal, they never showed it to anyone; but Jim Bunion told me that night that it was about the size that the thick end of a hen's egg would be if it were round. And then he fell asleep.

There were many more questions that I would have asked him but I could not wake him up. I even pulled the table away so that he fell to the floor, but he slept on, and all the tavern was dark but for one candle burning; and it was then that I noticed for the first time that the other two sailors had gone, no one remained at all but Jim Bunion and I and the sinister barman of that curious inn, and he too was asleep.

When I saw that it was impossible to wake the sailor I went out into the night. Next day Jim Bunion would talk of it no more; and when I went back to Stavlokratz I found him already putting on paper his theory about the sailors, which became accepted by chess-players, that one of them had been taught their curious gambit and that the other two between them had learnt all the defensive openings as well as general play. Though who taught them no one could say, in spite of enquiries made afterwards all along the Southern Pacific.

I never learnt any more details from any of the three sailors, they were always too drunk to speak or else not drunk enough to be communicative. I seem just to have taken Jim Bunion at the flood. But I kept my promise, it was I that introduced them to the Tournament, and a pretty mess they made of established reputations. And so they kept on for months, never losing a game and always playing for their pound a side. I used to follow them wherever they went merely to watch their play. They were more marvellous than Stavlokratz even in his youth.

But then they took to liberties such as giving their queen when playing first-class players. And in the end one day when all three were drunk they played the best player in England with only a row of pawns. They won the game all right. But the ball broke to pieces. I never smelt such a stench in all my life.

The three sailors took it stoically enough, they signed on to different ships and went back again to the sea, and the world of chess lost sight, for ever I trust, of the most remarkable players it ever knew, who would have altogether spoiled the game.

THE EXILES CLUB

It was an evening party; and something someone had said to me had started me talking about a subject that to me is full of fascination, the subject of old religions, forsaken gods. The truth (for all religions have some of it), the wisdom, the beauty, of the religions of countries to which I travel have not the same appeal for me; for one only notices in them their tyranny and intolerance and the abject servitude that they claim from thought; but when a dynasty has been dethroned in heaven and goes forgotten and outcast even among men, one's eyes no longer dazzled by its power find something very wistful in the faces of fallen gods suppliant to be remembered, something almost tearfully beautiful, like a long warm summer twilight fading gently away after some day memorable in the story of earthly wars. Between what Zeus, for instance, has been once and the half-remembered tale he is today there lies a space so great that there is no change of fortune known to man whereby we may measure the height down which he has fallen. And it is the same with many another god at whom once the ages trembled and the twentieth century treats as an old wives' tale. The fortitude that such a fall demands is surely more than human.

Some such things as these I was saying, and being upon a subject that much attracts me I possibly spoke too loudly, certainly I was not aware that standing close behind me was no less a person than the ex-King of Eritivaria, the thirty islands of the East, or I would have moderated my voice and moved away a little to give him more room. I was not aware of his presence until his satellite, one who had fallen with him into exile but still revolved about him, told me that his master desired to know me; and so to my surprise I was presented though neither of them even knew my name. And that was how I came to be invited by the ex-King to dine at his club.

At the time I could only account for his wishing to know me by supposing that he found in his own exiled condition some likeness to the fallen fortunes of the gods of whom I talked unwitting of his presence; but now I know that it was not of himself he was thinking when he asked me to dine at that club.

The club would have been the most imposing building in any street in London, but in that obscure mean quarter of London in which they had built it it appeared unduly enormous. Lifting right up above those grotesque houses and built in that Greek style that we call Georgian, there was something Olympian about it. To my host an unfashionable street could have meant nothing, through all his youth wherever he had gone had become fashionable the moment he went there; words like the East End could have had no meaning to him.

Whoever built that house had enormous wealth and cared nothing for fashion, perhaps despised it. As I stood gazing at the magnificent upper windows draped with great curtains, indistinct in the evening, on which huge shadows flickered my host attracted my attention from the doorway, and so I went in and met for the second time the ex-King of Eritivaria.

In front of us a stairway of rare marble led upwards, he took me through a side-door and downstairs and we came to a banqueting-hall of great magnificence. A long table ran up the middle of it, laid for quite twenty people, and I noticed the peculiarity that instead of chairs there were thrones for everyone except me, who was the only guest and for whom there was an ordinary chair. My host explained to me when we all sat down that everyone who belonged to that club was by rights a king.

In fact none was permitted, he told me, to belong to the club until his claim to a kingdom made out in writing had been examined and allowed by those whose duty it was. The whim of a populace or the candidate's own misrule were never considered by the investigators, nothing counted with them but heredity and lawful descent from kings, all else was ignored. At that table there were those who had once reigned themselves, others lawfully claimed descent from kings that the world had forgotten, the kingdoms claimed by some had even changed their names. Hatzgurh, the mountain kingdom, is almost regarded as mythical.

I have seldom seen greater splendour than that long hall provided below the level of the street. No doubt by day it was a little sombre, as all basements are, but at night with its great crystal chandeliers, and the glitter of heirlooms that had gone into exile, it surpassed the splendour of palaces that have only one king. They had come to London suddenly most of those kings, or their fathers before them, or forefathers; some had come away from their kingdoms by night, in a light sleigh, flogging the horses, or had galloped clear with morning over the border, some had trudged roads for days from their capital in disguise, yet many had had time just as they left to snatch up some small thing without price in markets, for the sake of old times as they said, but quite as much, I thought, with an eye to the future. And there these treasures glittered on that long table in the banqueting-hall of the basement of that strange club. Merely to see them was much, but to hear their story that their owners told was to go back in fancy to epic times on the romantic border of fable and fact, where the heroes of history fought with the gods of myth. The famous silver horses of Gilgianza were there climbing their sheer mountain, which they did by miraculous means before the time of the Goths. It was not a large piece of silver but its workmanship outrivalled the skill of the bees.

A yellow Emperor had brought out of the East a piece of that incomparable porcelain that had made his dynasty famous though all their deeds are forgotten, it had the exact shade of the right purple.

And there was a little golden statuette of a dragon stealing a diamond from a lady, the dragon had the diamond in his claws, large and of the first water. There had been a kingdom whose whole constitution and history were founded on the legend, from which alone its kings had claimed their right to the scepter, that a dragon stole a diamond from a lady. When its last king left that country, because his favorite general used a peculiar formation under the fire of artillery, he brought with him the little ancient image that no longer proved him a king outside that singular club.

There was the pair of amethyst cups of the turbaned King of Foo, the one that he drank from himself, and the one that he gave to his enemies, eye could not tell which was which.

All these things the ex-King of Eritivaria showed me, telling me a marvelous tale of each; of his own he had brought nothing, except the mascot that used once to sit on the top of the water tube of his favorite motor.

I have not outlined a tenth of the splendour of that table, I had meant to come again and examine each piece of plate and make notes of its history; had I known that this was the last time I should wish to enter that club I should have looked at its treasures more attentively, but now as the wine went round and the exiles began to talk I took my eyes from the table and listened to strange tales of their former state.

He that has seen better times has usually a poor tale to tell, some mean and trivial thing has been his undoing, but they that dined in that basement had mostly fallen like oaks on nights of abnormal tempest, had fallen mightily and shaken a nation. Those who had not been kings themselves, but claimed through an exiled ancestor, had stories to tell of even grander disaster, history seeming to have mellowed their dynasty's fate as moss grows over an oak a great while fallen. There were no jealousies there as so often there are among kings, rivalry must have ceased with the loss of their navies and armies, and they showed no bitterness against those that had turned them out, one speaking of the error of his Prime Minister by which he had lost his throne as "poor old Friedrich's Heaven-sent gift of tactlessness."

They gossiped pleasantly of many things, the tittle-tattle we all had to know when we were learning history, and many a wonderful story I might have heard, many a side light on mysterious wars had I not made use of one unfortunate word. That word was "upstairs."

The ex-King of Eritivaria having pointed out to me those unparalleled heirlooms to which I have alluded, and many more besides, hospitably asked me if there was anything else that I would care to see, he meant the pieces of plate that they had in the cupboards, the curiously graven swords of other princes, historic jewels, legendary seals, but I who had had a glimpse of their marvelous staircase, whose balustrade I believed to be solid gold and wondering why in such a stately house they chose to dine in the basement, mentioned the word "upstairs." A profound hush came down on the whole assembly, the hush that might greet levity in a cathedral.

"Upstairs!" he gasped. "We cannot go upstairs."

I perceived that what I had said was an ill-chosen thing. I tried to excuse myself but knew not how.

"Of course," I muttered, "members may not take guests upstairs."

"Members!" he said to me. "We are not the members!"

There was such reproof in his voice that I said no more, I looked at him questioningly, perhaps my lips moved, I may have said "What are you?" A great surprise had come on me at their attitude.

"We are the waiters," he said.

That I could not have known, here at last was honest ignorance that I had no need to be ashamed of, the very opulence of their table denied it.

"Then who are the members?" I asked.

Such a hush fell at that question, such a hush of genuine awe, that all of a sudden a wild thought entered my head, a thought strange and fantastic and terrible. I gripped my host by the wrist and hushed my voice.

"Are they too exiles?" I asked.

Twice as he looked in my face he gravely nodded his head.

I left that club very swiftly indeed, never to see it again, scarcely pausing to say farewell to those menial kings, and as I left the door a great window opened far up at the top of the house and a flash of lightning streamed from it and killed a dog.

THE THREE INFERNAL JOKES

This is the story that the desolate man told to me on the lonely Highland road one autumn evening with winter coming on and the stags roaring.

The saddening twilight, the mountain already black, the dreadful melancholy of the stags' voices, his friendless mournful face, all seemed to be of some most sorrowful play staged in that valley by an outcast god, a lonely play of which the hills were part and he the only actor.

For long we watched each other drawing out of the solitudes of those forsaken spaces. Then when we met he spoke.

"I will tell you a thing that will make you die of laughter. I will keep it to myself no longer. But first I must tell you how I came by it."

I do not give the story in his words with all his woeful interjections and the misery of his frantic self-reproaches for I would not convey unnecessarily to my readers that atmosphere of sadness that was about all he said and that seemed to go with him where-ever he moved.

It seems that he had been a member of a club, a West-end club he called it, a respectable but quite inferior affair, probably in the City: agents belonged to it, fire insurance mostly, but life insurance and motor-agents too, it was in fact a touts' club. It seems that a few of them one evening, forgetting for a moment their encyclopedias and non-stop tyres, were talking loudly over a card-table when the game had ended about their personal virtues, and a very little man with waxed moustaches who disliked the taste of wine was boasting heartily of his temperance. It was then that he who told this mournful story, drawn on by the boasts of others, leaned forward a little over the green baize into the light of the two guttering candles and revealed, no doubt a little shyly, his own extraordinary virtue. One woman was to him as ugly as another.

And the silenced boasters rose and went home to bed leaving him all alone, as he supposed, with his unequalled virtue. And yet he was not alone, for when the rest had gone there arose a member out of a deep arm-chair at the dark end of the room and walked across to him, a man whose occupation he did not know and only now suspects.

"You have," said the stranger, "a surpassing virtue."

"I have no possible use for it," my poor friend replied.

"Then doubtless you would sell it cheap," said the stranger.

Something in the man's manner or appearance made the desolate teller of this mournful tale feel his own inferiority, which probably made him feel acutely shy, so that his mind abased itself as an Oriental does his body in the presence of a superior, or perhaps he was sleepy, or merely a little drunk. Whatever it was he only mumbled, "O yes," instead of contradict-ing so mad a remark. And the stranger led the way to the room where the telephone was.

"I think you will find my firm will give a good price for it," he said: and without more ado he began with a pair of pincers to cut the wire of the telephone and the receiver. The old waiter who looked after the club they had left shuffling round the other room putting things away for the night.

"Whatever are you doing of?" said my friend.

"This way," said the stranger. Along a passage they went and away to the back of the club and there the stranger leaned out of a window and fastened the severed wires to the lightning conductor. My friend has no doubt of that, a broad ribbon of copper, half an inch wide, perhaps wider, running down from the roof to the earth.

"Hell," said the stranger with his mouth to the telephone; then silence for a while with his ear to the receiver, leaning out of the window. And then my friend heard his poor virtue being several times repeated, and then words like Yes and No.

"They offer you three jokes," said the stranger, "which shall make all who hear them simply die of laughter."

I think my friend was reluctant then to have anything more to do with it, he wanted to go home; he said he didn't want jokes.

"They think very highly of your virtue," I said the stranger. And at that, odd as it seems, my friend wavered, for logically if they thought highly of the goods they should have paid a higher price.

"O all right," he said. The extraordinary document that the agent drew from his pocket ran something like this:

"I...in consideration of three new jokes received from Mr. Montagu-Montague, hereinafter to be called the agent, and warranted to be as by him stated and described, do assign to him, yield, abrogate and give up all recognitions, emoluments, perquisites or rewards due to me Here or Elsewhere on account of the following virtue, to wit and that is to say... that all women are to me equally ugly." The last eight words being filled in in ink by Mr. Montagu-Montague.

My poor friend duly signed it. "These are the jokes," said the agent. They were boldly written on three slips of paper. "They don't seem very funny," said the other when he had read them. "You are immune," said Mr. Montagu-Montague, "but anyone else who hears them will simply die of laughter: that we guarantee."

An American firm had bought at the price of waste paper a hundred thousand copies of The Dictionary of Electricity written when electricity was new,—and it had turned out that even at the time its author had not rightly grasped his subject,—the firm had paid £10,000 to a respectable English paper (no other in fact than the Briton) for the use of its name, and to obtain orders for The Briton Dictionary of Electricity was the occupation of my unfortunate friend. He seems to have had a way with him. Apparently he knew by a glance at a man, or a look round at his garden, whether to recommend the book as "an absolutely up-to-date achievement, the finest thing of its kind in the world of modern science" or as "at once quaint and imperfect, a thing to buy and to keep as a tribute to those dear old times that are gone." So he went on with this quaint though usual business, putting aside the memory of that night as an occasion on which he had "somewhat exceeded" as they say in circles where a spade is called neither a spade nor an agricultural implement but is never mentioned at all, being altogether too vulgar. And then one night he put on his suit of dress clothes and found the three jokes in the pocket. That was perhaps a shock. He seems to have thought it over carefully then, and the end of it was he gave a dinner at the club to twenty of the members. The dinner would do no harm he thought—might even help the business, and if the joke came off he would be a witty fellow, and two jokes still up his sleeve.

Whom he invited or how the dinner went I do not know for he began to speak rapidly and came straight to the point, as a stick that nears a cataract suddenly goes faster and faster. The dinner was duly served, the port went round, the twenty men were smoking, two waiters loitered, when he after carefully reading the best of the jokes told it down the table. They laughed. One man accidentally inhaled his cigar smoke and spluttered, the two waiters overheard and tittered behind their hands, one man, a bit of a raconteur himself, quite clearly wished not to laugh, but his veins swelled dangerously in trying to keep it back, and in the end he laughed too. The joke had succeeded; my friend smiled at the thought; he wished to say little deprecating things to the man on his right; but the laughter did not stop and the waiters would not be silent. He waited, and waited wondering; the laughter went roaring on, distinctly louder now, and the waiters as loud as any. It had gone on for three or four minutes when this frightful thought leaped up all at once in his mind: *it was forced laughter!* However could anything have induced him to tell so foolish a joke? He saw its absurdity as in revelation; and the more he thought of it as these people laughed at him, even the waiters too, the more he felt that he could never lift up his head with his brother touts again. And still the laughter went roaring and choking on. He was very angry. There was not much use in having a friend, he thought, if one silly joke could not be overlooked; he had fed them too. And then he felt that he had no friends at all, and his anger faded away, and a great unhappiness came down on him, and he got quietly up and slunk from the room and slipped away from the club. Poor man, he scarcely had the heart next morning even to glance at the papers, but you did not need to glance at them, big type was bandied about that day as though it were common type, the words of the headlines stared at you; and the headlines said:—Twenty-Two Dead Men at a Club.

Yes, he saw it then: the laughter had not stopped, some had probably burst blood vessels, some must have choked, some succumbed to nausea, heart-failure must have mercifully taken some, and they were his friends after all, and none had escaped, not I even the waiters. It was that infernal joke.

He thought out swiftly, and remembers clear as a nightmare, the drive to Victoria Station, the boat-train to Dover and going disguised to the boat: and on the boat pleasantly smiling, almost obsequious, two constables that wished to speak for a moment with Mr. Watkyn-Jones. That was his name.

In a third-class carriage with handcuffs on his wrists, with forced conversation when any, he returned between his captors to Victoria to be tried for murder at the High Court of Bow.

At the trial he was defended by a young barrister of considerable ability who had gone into the Cabinet in order to enhance his forensic reputation. And he was ably defended. It is no exaggeration to say that the speech for the defence showed it to be usual, even natural and right, to give a dinner to twenty men and to slip away without ever saying a word, leaving all, with the waiters, dead. That was the impression left in the minds of the jury. And Mr. Watkyn-Jones felt himself practically free, with all the advantages of his awful experience, and his two jokes intact. But lawyers are still experimenting with the new act which allows a prisoner to give evidence. They do not like to make no use of it for fear they may be thought not to know of the act, and a lawyer who is not in touch with the very latest laws is soon regarded as not being up to date and he may drop as much as £50,000 a year in fees. And therefore though it always hangs their clients they hardly like to neglect it.

Mr. Watkyn-Jones was put in the witness box. There he told the simple truth, and a very poor affair it seemed after the impassioned and beautiful things that were uttered by the counsel for the defence. Men and women had wept when they heard that. They did not weep when they heard Watkyn-Jones. Some tittered. It no longer seemed a right and natural thing to leave one's guests all dead and to fly the country. Where was Justice, they asked, if anyone could do that? And when his story was told the judge rather happily asked if he could make him die of laughter too. And what was the joke? For in so grave a place as a Court of Justice no fatal effects need be feared. And hesitatingly the prisoner pulled from his pocket the three slips of paper: and perceived for the first time that the one on which the first and best joke had been written had become quite blank. Yet he could remember it, and only too clearly. And he told it from memory to the Court.

"An Irishman once on being asked by his master to buy a morning paper said in his usual witty way, 'Arrah and begorrah and I will be after wishing you the top of the morning.'"

No joke sounds quite so good the second time it is told, it seems to lose something of its essence, but Watkyn-Jones was not prepared for the awful stillness with which this one was received; nobody smiled; and it had killed twenty-two men. The joke was bad, devilish bad; counsel for the defence was frowning, and an usher was looking in a little bag for something the judge wanted. And at this moment, as though from far away, without his wishing it, there entered the prisoner's head, and shone there and would not go, this old bad proverb: "As well be hung for a sheep as for a lamb." The jury seemed to be just about to retire. "I have another joke," said Watkyn-Jones, and then and there he read from the second slip of paper. He watched the paper curiously to see if it would go blank, occupying his mind with so slight a thing as men in dire distress very often do, and the words were almost immediately expunged, swept swiftly as if by a hand, and he saw the paper before him as blank as the first. And they were laughing this time, judge, jury, counsel for the prosecution, audience and all, and the grim men that watched him upon either side. There was no mistake about this joke.

He did not stay to see the end, and walked out with his eyes fixed on the ground, unable to bear a glance to the right or left. And since then he has wandered, avoiding ports and roaming lonely places. Two years have known him on the Highland roads, often hungry, always friendless, always changing his district, wandering lonely on with his deadly joke.

Sometimes for a moment he will enter inns, driven by cold and hunger, and hear men in the evening telling jokes and even challenging him; but he sits desolate and silent, lest his only weapon should escape from him and his last joke spread mourning in a hundred cots. His beard has grown and turned grey and is mixed with moss and weeds, so that no one, I think, not even the police, would recognise him now for that dapper tout that sold The Briton Dictionary of Electricity in such a different land.

He paused, his story told, and then his lip quivered as though he would say more, and I believe he intended then and there to yield up his deadly joke on that Highland road and to go forth then with his three blank slips of paper, perhaps to a felon's cell, with one more murder added to his crimes, but harmless at last to man. I therefore hurried on, and only heard him mumbling sadly behind me, standing bowed and broken, all alone in the twilight, perhaps telling over and over even then the last infernal joke.

TALES OF THREE HEMISPHERES (1920)

THE LAST DREAM OF BWONA KHUBLA

From steaming lowlands down by the equator, where monstrous orchids blow, where beetles big as mice sit on the tent-ropes, and fireflies glide about by night like little moving stars, the travelers went three days through forests of cactus till they came to the open plains where the oryx are.

And glad they were when they came to the water-hole, where only one white man had gone before, which the natives know as the camp of Bwona Khubla, and found the water there.

It lies three days from the nearest other water, and when Bwona Khubla had gone there three years ago, what with malaria with which he was shaking all over, and what with disgust at finding the water-hole dry, he had decided to die there, and in that part of the world such decisions are always fatal. In any case he was overdue to die, but hitherto his amazing resolution, and that terrible strength of character that so astounded his porters, had kept him alive and moved his safari on.

He had had a name no doubt, some common name such as hangs as likely as not over scores of shops in London; but that had gone long ago, and nothing identified his memory now to distinguish it from the memories of all the other dead but "Bwona Khubla," the name the Kikuyus gave him.

There is not doubt that he was a fearful man, a man that was dreaded still for his personal force when his arm was no longer able to lift the kiboko, when all his men knew he was dying, and to this day though he is dead.

Though his temper was embittered by malaria and the equatorial sun, nothing impaired his will, which remained a compulsive force to the very last, impressing itself upon all, and after the last, from what the Kikuyus say. The country must have had powerful laws that drove Bwona Khubla out, whatever country it was.

On the morning of the day that they were to come to the camp of Bwona Khubla all the porters came to the travelers' tents asking for dow.

Dow is the white man's medicine, that cures all evils; the nastier it tastes, the better it is. They wanted down this morning to keep away devils, for they were near the place where Bwona Khubla died.

The travelers gave them quinine.

By sunset the came to Campini Bwona Khubla and found water there. Had they not found water many of them must have died, yet none felt any gratitude to the place, it seemed too ominous, too full of doom, too much harassed almost by unseen, irresistible things.

And all the natives came again for dow as soon as the tents were pitched, to protect them from the last dreams of Bwona Khubla, which they say had stayed behind when the last safari left taking Bwona Khubla's body back to the edge of civilization to show to the white men there that they had not killed him, for the white men might not know that they durst not kill Bwona Khubla.

And the travelers gave them more quinine, so much being bad for the nerves, and that night by the camp-fires there was no pleasant talk; all talking at once of meat they had eaten and cattle that each one owned, but a gloomy silence hung by every fire and the little canvas shelters. They told the white men that Bwona Khubla's city, of which he had thought at the last (and where the natives believed he was once a king), of which he had raved till the loneliness rang with his raving, had settled down all about them; and they were afraid, for it was so strange a city, and wanted more dow. And the two travelers gave them more quinine, for they saw real fear in their faces, and knew they might run away and leave them alone in that place, that they, too, had come to fear with an almost equal dread, though they knew not why. And as the night wore on their feeling of boding deepened, although they had shared three bottles or so of champagne that they meant to keep for days when they killed a lion.

This is the story that each of those two men tell, and which their porters corroborate, but then a Kikuyu will always say whatever he thinks is expected of him.

The travelers were both in bed and trying to sleep but not able to do so because of an ominous feeling. That mournfullest of all the cries of the wild, the hyæna like a damned soul lamenting, strangely enough had ceased. The night wore on to the hour when Bwona Khubla had died three or four years ago, dreaming and raving of "his city"; and in the hush a sound softly arose, like a wind at first, then like the roar of beasts, then unmistakably the sound of motors—motors and motor busses.

And then they saw, clearly and unmistakably they say, in that lonely desolation where the equator comes up out of the forest and climbs over jagged hills,—they say they saw London.

There could have been no moon that night, but they say there was a multitude of stars. Mists had come rolling up at evening about the pinnacles of unexplored red peaks that clustered round the camp. But they say the mist must have cleared later on; at any rate they swear they could see London, see it and hear the roar of it. Both say they saw it not as they knew it at all, not debased by hundreds of thousands of lying advertisements, but transfigured, all its houses magnificent, its chimneys rising grandly into pinnacles, its vast squares full of the most gorgeous trees, transfigured and yet London.

Its windows were warm and happy, shining at night, the lamps in their long rows welcomed you, the public-houses were gracious jovial places; yet it was London.

They could smell the smells of London, hear London songs, and yet it was never the London that they knew; it was as though they had looked on some strange woman's face with the eyes of her lover. For of all the towns of the earth or cities of song; of all the spots there be, unhallowed or hallowed, it seemed to those two men then that the city they saw was of all places the most to be desired by far. They say a barrel organ played quite near them, they say a coster was singing, they admit that he was singing out of tune, they admit a cockney accent, and yet they say that that song had in it something that no earthly song had ever had before, and both men say that they would have wept but that there was a feeling about their heartstrings that was far too deep for tears. They believe that the longing of this masterful man, that was able to rule a safari by raising a hand, had been so strong at the last that it had impressed itself deeply upon nature and had caused a mirage that may not fade wholly away, perhaps for several years.

I tried to establish by questions the truth or reverse of this story, but the two men's tempers had been so spoiled by Africa that they were not up to cross-examination. They would not even say if their camp-fires were still burning. They say that they saw the London lights all round them from eleven o'clock till midnight, they could hear London voices and the sound of the traffic clearly, and over all, a little misty perhaps, but unmistakably London, arose the great metropolis.

After midnight London quivered a little and grew more indistinct, the sound of the traffic began to dwindle away, voices seemed farther off, ceased altogether, and all was quiet once more where the mirage shimmered and faded, and a bull rhinoceros coming down through the stillness snorted, and watered at the Carlton Club.

HOW THE OFFICE OF POSTMAN FELL VACANT IN OTFORD-UNDER-THE-WOLD

The duties of postman at Otford-under-the-Wold carried Amuel Sleggins farther afield than the village, farther afield than the last house in the lane, right up to the big bare wold and the house where no one went, no one that is but the three grim men that dwelt there and the secretive wife of one, and, once a year when the queer green letter came, Amuel Sleggins the postman.

The green letter always came just as the leaves were turning, addressed to the eldest of the three grim men, with a wonderful Chinese stamp and the Otford post-mark, and Amuel Sleggins carried it up to the house.

He was not afraid to go, for he always took the letter, had done so for seven years, yet whenever summer began to draw to a close, Amuel Sleggins was ill at ease, and if there was a touch of autumn about shivered unduly so that all folk wondered.

And then one day a wind would blow from the East, and the wild geese would appear, having left the sea, flying high and crying strangely, and pass till they were no more than a thin black line in the sky like a magical stick flung up by a doer of magic, twisting and twirling away; and the leaves would turn on the trees and the mists be white on the marshes and the sun set large and red and autumn would step down quietly that night from the wold; and the next day the strange green letter would come from China.

His fear of the three grim men and that secretive woman and their lonely, secluded house, or else the cadaverous cold of the dying season, rather braced Amuel when the time was come and he would step out bolder upon the day that he feared than he had perhaps for weeks. He longed on that day for a letter for the last house in the lane, there he would dally and talk awhile and look on church-going faces before his last tramp over the lonely wold to end at the dreaded door of the queer grey house called wold-hut.

When he came to the door of wold-hut he would give the postman's knock as though he came on ordinary rounds to a house of every day, although no path led up to it, although the skins of weasels hung thickly from upper windows.

And scarcely had his postman's knock rung through the dark of the house when the eldest of the three grim men would always run to the door. O, what a face had he. There was more slyness in it than ever his beard could hide. He would put out a gristly hand; and into it Amuel Sleggins would put the letter from China, and rejoice that his duty was done, and would turn and stride away. And the fields lit up before him, but, ominous, eager and low murmuring arose in the wold-hut.

For seven years this was so and no harm had come to Sleggins, seven times he had gone to wold-hut and as often come safely away; and then he needs must marry. Perhaps because she was young, perhaps because she was fair or because she had shapely ankles as she came one day through the marshes among the milkmaid flowers shoeless in spring. Less things than these have brought men to their ends and been the nooses with which Fate snared them running. With marriage curiosity entered his house, and one day as they walked with evening through the meadows, one summer evening, she asked him of wold-hut where he only went, and what the folks were like that no one else had seen. All this he told her; and then she asked him of the green letter from China, that came with autumn, and what the letter contained. He read to her all the rules of the Inland Revenue, he told her he did not know, that it was not right that he should know, he lectured her on the sin of inquisitiveness, he quoted Parson, and in the end she said that she must know. They argued concerning this for many days, days of the ending of summer, of shortening evenings, and as they argued autumn grew nearer and nearer and the green letter from China.

And at last he promised that when the green letter came he would take it as usual to the lonely house and then hide somewhere near and creep to the window at nightfall and hear what the grim folk said; perhaps they might read aloud the letter from China. And before he had time to repent of that promise a cold wind came one night and the woods turned golden, the plover went in bands at evening over the marshes, the year had turned, and there came the letter from China. Never before had Amuel felt such misgivings as he went his postman's rounds, never before had he so much feared the day that took him up to the wold and the lonely house, while snug by the fire his wife looked pleasurably forward to curiosity's gratification and hoped to have news ere nightfall that all the gossips of the village would envy. One consolation only had Amuel as he set out with a shiver, there was a letter that day for the last house in the lane. Long did he tarry there to look at their cheery faces, to hear the sound of their laughter—you did not hear laughter in wold-hut—and when the last topic had been utterly talked out and no excuse for lingering remained he heaved a heavy sigh and plodded grimly away and so came late to wold-hut.

He gave his postman's knock on the shut oak door, heard it reverberate through the silent house, saw the grim elder man and his gristly hand, gave up the green letter from China, and strode away. There is a clump of trees growing all alone in the wold, desolate, mournful, by day, by night full of ill omen, far off from all other trees as wold-hut from other houses. Near it stands wold-hut. Not today did Amuel stride briskly on with all the new winds of autumn blowing cheerily past him till he saw the village before him and broke into song; but as soon as he was out of sight of the house he turned and stooping behind a fold of the ground ran back to the desolate wood. There he waited watching the evil house, just too far to hear voices. The sun was low already. He chose the window at which he meant to eavesdrop, a little barred one at the back, close to the ground. And then the pigeons came in; for a great distance there was no other wood, so numbers shelter there, though the clump is small and of so evil a look (if they notice that); the first one frightened Amuel, he felt that it might be a spirit escaped from torture in some dim parlour of the house that he watched, his nerves were strained and he feared foolish fears. Then he grew used to them and the sun set then and the aspect of everything altered and he felt strange fears again. Behind him was a hollow in the wold, he watched it darkening; and before him he saw the house through the trunks of the trees. He waited for them to light their lamps so that they could not see, when he would steal up softly and crouch by the little back window. But though every bird was home, though the night grew chilly as tombs, though a star was out, still there shone no yellow light from any window. Amuel waited and shuddered. He did not dare to move till they lit their lamps, they might be watching. The damp and the cold so strangely affected him that autumn evening and the remnants of sunset, the stars and the wold and the whole vault of the sky seemed like a hall that they had prepared for Fear. He began to feel a dread of prodigious things, and still no light shone in the evil house. It grew so dark that he decided to move and make his way to the window in spite of the stillness and though the house was dark. He rose and while standing arrested by pains that cramped his limbs, he heard the door swing open on the far side of the house. He had just time to hide behind the trunk of a pine when the three grim men approached him and the woman hobbled behind. Right to the ominous clump of trees they came as though they loved their blackness, passed through within a yard or two of the post-man and squatted down on their haunches in a ring in the hollow behind the trees. They lit a fire in the hollow and laid a kid on the fire and by the light of it Amuel saw brought forth from an untanned pouch the letter that came from China. The elder opened it with his gristly hand and intoning words that Amuel did not know, drew out from it a green powder and sprinkled it on the fire. At once a flame arose and a wonderful savour, the flames rose higher and flickered turning the trees all green; and Amuel saw the gods coming to snuff the savour. While the three grim men prostrated themselves by their fire, and the horrible woman that was the spouse of one, he saw the gods coming gauntly over the wold, beheld the gods of Old England hungrily snuffing the savour, Odin, Balder, and Thor, the gods of the ancient people, beheld them eye to eye clear and close in the twilight, and the office of postman fell vacant in Otford-under-the-Wold.

THE PRAYER OF BOOB AHEERA

In the harbour, between the liner and the palms, as the huge ship's passengers came up from dinner, at moonrise, each in his canoe, Ali Kareeb Ahash and Boob Aheera passed within knife thrust.

So urgent was the purpose of Ali Kareeb Ahash that he did not lean over as his enemy slid by, did not tarry then to settle that long account; but that Boob Aheera made no attempt to reach him was a source of wonder to Ali. He pondered it till the liner's electric lights shone far away behind him with one blaze and the canoe was near to his destination, and pondered it in vain, for all that the eastern subtlety of his mind was able to tell him clearly was that it was not like Boob Aheera to pass him like that.

That Boob Aheera could have dared to lay such a cause as his before the Diamond Idol Ali had not conceived, yet as he drew near to the golden shrine in the palms, that none that come by the great ships ever found, he began to see more clearly in his mind that this was where Boob had gone on that hot night. And when he beached his canoe his fears departed, giving place to the resignation with which he always viewed Destiny; for there on the white sea sand were the tracks of another canoe, the edges all fresh and ragged. Boob Aheera had been before him. Ali did not blame himself for being late, the thing had been planned before the beginning of time, by gods that knew their business; only his hate of Boob Aheera increased, his enemy against whom he had come to pray. And the more his hate increased the more clearly he saw him, until nothing else could be seen by the eye of his mind but the dark lean figure, the little lean legs, the grey beard and neat loin-cloth of Boob Aheera, his enemy.

That the Diamond Idol should have granted the prayers of such a one he did not as yet imagine, he hated him merely for his presumptuousness in approaching the shrine at all, for approaching it before him whose cause was righteous, for many an old past wrong, but most of all for the expression of his face and the general look of the man as he has swept by in his canoe with his double paddle going in the moonlight.

Ali pushed through the steaming vegetation. The place smelt of orchids. There is no track to the shrine though many go. If there were a track the white man would one day find it, and parties would row to see it whenever a liner came in; and photographs would appear in weekly papers with accounts of it underneath by men who had never left London, and all the mystery would be gone away and there would be nothing novel in this story.

Ali had scarcely gone a hundred yards through cactus and creeper underneath the palms when he came to the golden shrine that nothing guards except the deeps of the forest, and found the Diamond Idol. The Diamond Idol is five inches high and its base a good inch square, and it has a greater lustre than those diamonds that Mr. Moses bought last year for his wife, when he offered her an earldom or the diamonds, and Jael his wife had answered, "Buy the diamonds and be just plain Mr. Fortescue."

Purer than those was its luster and carved as they carve not in Europe, and the men thereby are poor and held to be fearless—yet they do not sell that idol. And I may say here that if any one of my readers should ever come by ship to the winding harbour where the forts of the Portuguese crumble in infinite greenery, where the baobab stands like a corpse here and there in the palms, if he goes ashore where no one has any business to go, and where no one so far as I know has gone from a liner before (though it's little more than a mile or so from the pier), and if he finds a golden shrine, which is near enough to the shore, and a five-inch diamond in it carved in the shape of a god, it is better to leave it alone and get back safe to the ship than to sell that diamond idol for any price in the world.

Ali Kareeb Ahash went into the golden shrine, and when he raised his head from the seven obeisances that are the due of the idol, behold! it glowed with such a lustre as only it wears after answering recent prayer. No native of those parts mistakes the tone of the idol, they know its varying shades as a tracker knows blood; the moon was streaming in through the open door and Ali saw it clearly.

No one had been that night but Boob Aheera.

The fury of Ali rose and surged to his heart, he clutched his knife till the hilt of it bruised his hand, yet he did not utter the prayer that he had made ready about Boob Aheera's liver, for he saw that Boob Aheera's prayers were acceptable to the idol and knew that divine protection was over his enemy.

What Boob Aheera's prayer was he did not know, but he went back to the beach as fast as one can go through cacti and creepers that climb to the tops of the palms; and as fast as his canoe could carry him he went down the winding harbour, till the liner shone beside him as he passed, and he heard the sound of its band rise up and die, and he landed and came that night into Boob Aheera's hut. And there he offered himself as his enemy's slave, and Boob Aheera's slave he is to this day, and his master has protection from the idol. And Ali rows to the liners and goes on board to sell rubies made of glass, and thin suits for the tropics and ivory napkin rings, and Manchester kimonos, and little lovely shells; and the passengers abuse him because of his prices; and yet they should not, for all the money cheated by Ali Kareeb Ahash goes to Boob Aheera, his master.

EAST AND WEST

It was dead of night and midwinter. A frightful wind was bringing sleet from the East. The long sere grasses were wailing. Two specks of light appeared on the desolate plain; a man in a hansom cab was driving alone in North China.

Alone with the driver and the dejected horse. The driver wore a good waterproof cape, and of course an oiled silk hat, but the man in the cab wore nothing but evening dress. He did not have the glass door down because the horse fell so frequently, the sleet had put his cigar out and it was too cold to sleep; the two lamps flared in the wind. By the uncertain light of a candle lamp that flickered inside the cab, a Manchu shepherd that saw the vehicle pass, where he watched his sheep on the plain in fear of the wolves, for the first time saw evening dress. And though he saw if dimly, and what he saw was wet, it was like a backward glance of a thousand years, for as his civilization is so much older than ours they have presumably passed through all that kind of thing.

He watched it stoically, not wondering at a new thing, if indeed it be new to China, meditated on it awhile in a manner strange to us, and when he had added to his philosophy what little could be derived from the sight of this hansom cab, returned to his contemplation of that night's chances of wolves and to such occasional thoughts as he drew at times for his comfort out of the legends of China, that have been preserved for such uses. And on such a night their comfort was greatly needed. He thought of the legend of a dragon-lady, more fair than the flowers are, without an equal amongst daughters of men, humanly lovely to look on although her sire was a dragon, yet one who traced his descent from gods of the elder days, and so it was that she went in all her ways divine, like the earliest ones of her race, who were holier than the emperor.

She had come down one day out of her little land, a grassy valley hidden amongst the mountains; by the way of the mountain passes she came down, and the rocks of the rugged pass rang like little bells about her, as her bare feet went by, like silver bells to please her; and the sound was like the sound of the dromedaries of a prince when they come home at evening—their silver bells are ringing and the village-folk are glad. She had come down to pick the enchanted poppy that grew, and grows to this day—if only men might find it—in a field at the feet of the mountains; if one should pick it happiness would come to all yellow men, victory without fighting, good wages, and ceaseless ease. She came down all fair from the mountains; and as the legend pleasantly passed through his mind in the bitterest hour of the night, which comes before dawn, two lights appeared and another hansom went by.

The man in the second cab was dressed the same as the first, he was wetter than the first, for the sleet had fallen all night, but evening dress is evening dress all the world over. The driver wore the same oiled hat, the same waterproof cape as the other. And when the cab had passed the darkness swirled back where the two small lamps had been, and the slush poured into the wheel-tracks and nothing remained but the speculations of the shepherd to tell that a hansom cab had been in that part of China; presently even these ceased, and he was back with the early legends again in contemplation of serener things.

And the storm and the cold and the darkness made one last effort, and shook the bones of that shepherd, and rattled the teeth in the head that mused on the flowery fables, and suddenly it was morning. You saw the outlines of the sheep all of a sudden, the shepherd counted them, no wolf had come, you could see them all quite clearly. And in the pale light of the earliest morning the third hansom appeared, with its lamps still burning, looking ridiculous in the daylight. They came out of the East with the sleet and were all going due westwards, and the occupant of the third cab also wore evening dress.

Calmly that Manchu shepherd, without curiosity, still less with wonder, but as one who would see whatever life has to show him, stood for four hours to see if another would come. The sleet and the East wind continued. And at the end of four hours another came. The driver was urging it on as fast as he could, as though he were making the most of the daylight, his cabby's cape was flapping wildly about him; inside the cab a man in evening dress was being jolted up and down by the unevenness of the plain.

This was of course that famous race from Pittsburg to Piccadilly, going round by the long way, that started one night after dinner from Mr. Flagdrop's house, and was won by Mr. Kagg, driving the Honourable Alfred Fortescue, whose father it will be remembered was Hagar Dermstein, and became (by Letters Patent) Sir Edgar Fortescue, and finally Lord St. George.

The Manchu shepherd stood there till evening, and when he saw that no more cabs would come, turned homeward in search of food.

And the rice prepared for him was hot and good, all the more after the bitter coldness of that sleet. And when he had consumed it her perused his experience, turning over again in his mind each detail of the cabs he had seen; and from that his thoughts slipped calmly to the glorious history of China, going back to the indecorous times before calmness came, and beyond those times to the happy days of the earth when the gods and dragons were here and China was young; and lighting his opium pipe and casting his thoughts easily forward he looked to the time when the dragons shall come again.

And for a long while then his mind reposed itself in such a dignified calm that no thought stirred there at all, from which when he was aroused he cast off his lethargy as a man emerges from the baths, refreshed, cleansed and contented, and put away from his musings the things he had seen on the plain as being evil and of the nature of dreams, or futile illusion, the results of activity which troubleth calm. And then he turned his mind toward the shape of God, the One, the Ineffable, who sits by the lotus lily, whose shape is the shape of peace, and denieth activity, and went out his thanks to him that he had cast all bad customs westward out of China as a woman throws household dirt out of her basket far out into neighbouring gardens.

From thankfulness he turned to calm again, and out of calm to sleep.

A PRETTY QUARREL

On one of those unattained, and unattainable pinnacles that are known as the Bleaks of Eerie, an eagle was looking East with a hopeful presage of blood.

For he knew, and rejoiced in the knowledge, that eastward over the dells the dwarfs were risen in Ulk, and gone to war with the demi-gods.

The demi-gods are they that were born of earthly women, but their sires are the elder gods who walked of old among men. Disguised they would go through the villages sometimes in summer evenings, cloaked and unknown of men; but the younger maidens knew them and always ran to them singing, for all that their elders said: in evenings long ago they had danced to the woods of the oak-trees. Their children dwelt out-of-doors beyond the dells of the bracken, in the cool and heathery lands, and were now at war with the dwarfs.

Dour and grim were the demi-gods and had the faults of both parents, and would not mix with men but claimed the right of their fathers, and would not play human games but forever were prophesying, and yet were more frivolous than their mothers were, whom the fairies had long since buried in wild wood gardens with more than human rites.

And being irked at their lack of rights and ill content with the land, and having no power at all over the wind and snow, and caring little for the powers they had, the demi-gods became idle, greasy, and slow; and the contemptuous dwarfs despised them ever.

The dwarfs were contemptuous of all things savouring of heaven, and of everything that was even partly divine. They were, so it has been said, of the seed of man; but, being squat and hairy like to the beasts; they praised all beastly things, and bestiality was shown reverence among them, so far as reverence was theirs to show. So most of all they despised the discontent of the demi-gods, who dreamed of the courts of heaven and power over wind and snow; for what better, said the dwarfs, could demi-gods do than nose in the earth for roots and cover their faces with mire, and run with the cheerful goats and be even as they?

Now in their idleness caused by their discontent, the seed of the gods and the maidens grew more discontented still, and only spake of or cared for heavenly things; until the contempt of the dwarfs, who heard of all these doings, was bridled no longer and it must needs be war. They burned spice, dipped in blood and dried, before the chief of their witches, sharpening their axes, and made war on the demi-gods.

They passed by night over the Oolnar Mountains, each dwarf with his good axe, the old flint war-axe of his fathers, a night when no moon shone, and they went unshod, and swiftly, to come on the demi-gods in the darkness beyond the dells of Ulk, lying fat and idle and contemptible.

And before it was light they found the heathery lands, and the demi-gods lying lazy all over the side of a hill. The dwarfs stole towards them warily in the darkness.

Now the art that the gods love most is the art of war: and when the seed of the gods and those nimble maidens awoke and found it was war it was almost as much to them as the godlike pursuits of heaven, enjoyed in the marble courts; or power over wind and snow. They all drew out at once their swords of tempered bronze, cast down to them centuries since on stormy nights when their fathers, drew them and faced the dwarfs, and casting their idleness from them, fell on them, sword to axe. And the dwarfs fought hard that night, and bruised the demi-gods sorely, hacking with those huge axes that had not spared the oaks. Yet for all the weight of their blows and the cunning of their adventure, one point they had over-looked: *the demi-gods were immortal.*

As the fight rolled on towards morning the fighters were fewer and fewer, yet for all the blows of the dwarfs men fell upon one side only.

Dawn came and the demi-gods were fighting against no more than six, and the hour that follows dawn, and the last of the dwarfs was gone.

And when the light was clear on that peak of the Bleaks of Eerie the eagle left his crag and flew grimly East, and found it was as he had hoped in the matter of blood.

But the demi-gods lay down in their heathery lands, for once content though so far from the courts of heaven, and even half forgot their heavenly rights, and sighed no more for power over wind and snow.

HOW THE GODS AVENGED MEOUL KI NING

Meoul Ki Ning was on his way with a lily from the lotus ponds of Esh to offer it to the Goddess of Abundance in her temple Aoul Keroon. And on the road from the pond to the little hill and the temple Aoul Keroon, Ap Ariph, his enemy, shot him with an arrow from a bow that he had made out of bamboo, and took his pretty lily up the hill and offered it to the Goddess of Abundance in her temple Aoul Keroon. And the Goddess was pleased with the gift, as all women are, and sent pleasant dreams to Ap Ariph for seven nights straight from the moon.

And on the seventh night the gods held conclave together, on the cloudy peaks they held it, above Narn, Ktoon, and Pti. So high their peak arises that no man heard their voices. They spake on that cloudy mountain (not the highest hamlet heard them). "What doth the Goddess of Abundance," (but naming her Lling, as they name her), "what doth she sending sweet dreams for seven nights to Ap Ariph?"

And the gods sent for their seer who is all eyes and feet, running to and fro on the Earth, observing the ways of men, seeing even their littlest doings, never deeming a doing too little, but knowing the web of the gods is woven of littlest things. He it is that sees the cat in the garden of para-keets, the thief in the upper chamber, the sin of the child with the honey, the women talking indoors and the small hut's innermost things. Standing before the gods he told them the case of Ap Ariph and the wrongs of Meoul Ki Ning and the rape of the lotus lily; he told of the cutting and making of Ap Ariph's bamboo bow, of the shooting of Meoul Ki Ning, and of how the arrow hit him, and the smile on the face of Lling when she came by the lotus bloom.

And the gods were wroth with Ap Ariph and swore to avenge Ki Ning.

And the ancient one of the gods, he that is older than Earth, called up the thunder at once, and raised his arms and cried out on the gods' high windy mountain, and prophesied on those rocks with runes that were older than speech, and sang in his wrath old songs that he had learned in storm from the sea, when only that peak of the gods in the whole of the earth was dry; and he swore that Ap Ariph should die that night, and the thunder raged about him, and the tears of Lling were vain.

The lightning stroke of the gods leaping earthward seeking Ap Ariph passed near to his house but missed him. A certain vagabond was down from the hills, singing songs in the street near by the house of Ap Ariph, songs of a former folk that dwelt once, they say, in those valleys, and begging for rice and curds; it was him the lightning hit.

And the gods were satisfied, and their wrath abated, and their thunder rolled away and the great black clouds dissolved, and the ancient one of the gods went back to his age-old sleep, and morning came, and the birds and the light shone on the mountain, and the peak stood clear to see, the serene home of the gods.

THE GIFT OF THE GODS

There was once a man who sought a boon of the gods. For peace was over the world and all things savoured of sameness, and the man was weary at heart and sighed for the tents and the warfields. Therefore he sought a boon of the ancient gods. And appearing before them he said to them, "Ancient gods; there is peace in the land where I dwell, and indeed to the uttermost parts, and we are full weary of peace. O ancient gods, grant us war!"

And the ancient gods made him a war.

And the man went forth with his sword, and behold it was even war. And the man remembered the little things that he knew, and thought of the quiet days that there used to be, and at night on the hard ground dreamed of the things of peace. And dearer and dearer grew the wonted things, the dull but easeful things of the days of peace, and remembering these he began to regret the war, and sought once more a boon of the ancient gods, and appearing before them he said: "O ancient gods, indeed but a man loves best the days of peace. Therefore take back your war and give us peace, for indeed of all your blessedness peace is best."

And the man returned again to the haunts of peace.

But in a while the man grew weary of peace, of the things that he used to know, and the savour of sameness again; and sighing again for the tents, and appearing once more to the gods, he said to them: "Ancient gods; we do not love your peace, for indeed the days are dull, and a man is best at war."

And the gods made him a war.

And there were drums again, the smoke of campfires again, wind in the waste again, the sound of horses of war, burning cities again, and the things that wanderers know; and the thoughts of that man went home to the ways of peace; moss upon lawns again, light in old spires again, sun upon gardens again, flowers in pleasant woods and sleep and the paths of peace.

And once more the man appeared to the ancient gods and sought from them one more boon, and said to them: "Ancient gods; indeed but the world and we are a-weary of war and long for the ancient ways and the paths of peace."

So the gods took back their war and gave him peace.

But the man took counsel one day and communed long with himself and said to himself: "Behold, the wishes I wish, which the gods grant, are not to be much desired; and if the gods should one day grant a wish and never revoke it, which is a way of the gods, I should be sorely tried because of my wish; my wishes are dangerous wishes and not to be desired."

And therefore he wrote an anonymous letter to the gods, writing: "O ancient gods; this man that hath four times troubled you with his wishes, wishing for peace and war, is a man that hath no reverence for the gods, speaking ill of them on days when they do not hear, and speaking well of them on holy days and at the appointed hours when the gods are hearkening to prayer. Therefore grant no more wishes to this impious man."

And the days of peace wore on and there arose again from the earth, like mist in the autumn from the fields that generations have ploughed, the savour of sameness again. And the man went forth one morning and appeared once more to the gods, and cried: "O ancient gods; give us but one war again, for I would be back to the camps and debateable borders of lands."

And the gods said: "We hear not well of your way of life, yea ill things have come to our hearing, so that we grant no more the wishes you wish."

THE SACK OF EMERALDS

One bad October night in the high wolds beyond Wiltshire, with a north wind chaunting of winter, with the old leaves letting go their hold one by one from branches and dropping down to decay, with a mournful sound of owls, and in fearsome loneliness, there trudged in broken boots and in wet and windy rags an old man, stooping low under a sack of emeralds. It were easy to see had you been travelling late on that inauspicious night, that the burden of the sack was far too great for the poor old man that bore it. And had you flashed a lantern in his face there was a look there of hopelessness and fatigue that would have told you it was no wish of his that kept him tottering on under that bloated sack.

When the menacing look of the night and its cheerless sounds, and the cold, and the weight of the sack, had all but brought him to the door of death, and he had dropped his sack onto the road and was dragging it on behind him, just as he felt that his final hour was come, and come (which was worse) as he held the accursed sack, just then he saw the bulk and the black shape of the Sign of the Lost Shepherd loom up by the ragged way. He opened the door and staggered into the light and sank on a bench with his huge sack beside him.

All this you had seen had you been on that lonely road, so late on those bitter wolds, with their outlines vast and mournful in the dark, and their little clumps of trees sad with October. But neither you nor I were out that night. I did not see the poor old man and his sack until he sank down all of a heap in the lighted inn.

And Yon the blacksmith was there; and the carpenter, Willie Losh; and Jackers, the postman's son. And they gave him a glass of beer. And the old man drank it up, still hugging his emeralds.

And at last they asked him what he had in his sack, the question he clearly dreaded; and he only clasped yet tighter the sodden sack and mumbled he had potatoes.

"Potatoes," said Yon the blacksmith.

"Potatoes," said Willie Losh.

And when he heard the doubt that was in their voices the old man shivered and moaned.

"Potatoes, did you say?" said the postman's son. And they all three rose and tried to peer at the sack that the rain-soaked wayfarer so zealously sheltered.

And from the old man's fierceness I had said that, had it not been for that foul night on the roads and the weight he had carried so far and the fearful winds of October, he had fought with the blacksmith, the carpenter and the postman's son, all three, till he beat them away from his sack. And weary and wet as he was he fought them hard.

I should no doubt have interfered; and yet the three men meant no harm to the wayfarer, but resented the reticence that he displayed to them though they had given him beer; it was to them as though a master key had failed to open a cupboard. And, as for me, curiosity held me down to my chair and forbade me to interfere on behalf of the sack; for the old man's furtive ways, and the night out of which he came, and the hour of his coming, and the look of his sack, all made me long as much to know what he had, as even the blacksmith, the carpenter and the postman's son.

And then they found the emeralds. They were all bigger than hazel nuts, hundreds and hundreds of them: and the old man screamed.

"Come, come, we're not thieves," said the blacksmith.

"We're not thieves," said the carpenter.

"We're not thieves," said the postman's son.

And with awful fear on his face the wayfarer closed his sack, whimpering over his emeralds and furtively glancing round as though the loss of his secret were and utterly deadly thing. And then they asked him to give them just one each, just one huge emerald each, because they had given him a glass of beer. Then to see the wayfarer shrink against his sack and guard it with clutching fingers one would have said that he was a selfish man, were it not for the terror that was freezing his face. I have seen men look sheer at Death with far less fear.

And they took their emerald all three, one enormous emerald each, while the old man hopelessly struggled till he saw his three emeralds go, and fell to the floor and wept, a pitiable, sodden heap.

And about that time I began to hear far off down the windy road, by which that sack had come, faintly at first and slowly louder and louder, the click clack clop of a lame horse coming nearer. Click clack clop and a loose shoe rattling, the sound of a horse too weary to be out upon such a night, too lame to be out at all.

Click clack clop. And all of a sudden the old wayfarer heard it; heard it above the sound of his won sobbing, and at once went white to the lips. Such sudden fear as blanched him in a moment struck right to the hearts of all there. They muttered to him that it was only their play, they hastily whispered excuses, they asked him what was wrong, but seemed scarcely to hope for an answer, nor did he speak, but sat with a frozen stare, all at once dry-eyed, a monument to terror.

Nearer and nearer came the click clack clop.

And when I saw the expression of that man's face and how its horror deepened as the ominous sound drew nearer, then I knew that something was wrong. And looking for the last time upon all four I saw the wayfarer horror-struck by his sack and the other three crowding round to put their huge emeralds back then, even on such a night, I slipped away from the inn.

Outside the bitter wind roared in my ears, and close in the darkness the horse went click clack clop.

And as soon as my eyes could see at all in the night I saw a man in a huge hat looped up in front, wearing a sword in a scabbard shabby and huge, and looking blacker than the darkness, riding on a lean horse slowly up to the inn. Whether his were the emeralds, or who he was, or why he rode a lame horse on such a night, I did not stop to discover, but went at once from the inn as he strode in his great black riding coat up to the door.

And that was the last that was ever seen of the wayfarer; the blacksmith, the carpenter or the postman's son.

THE OLD BROWN COAT

My friend, Mr. Douglas Ainslie, tells me that Sir James Barrie once told him this story. The story, or rather the fragment, was as follows.

A man strolling into an auction somewhere abroad, I think it must have been France, for they bid in francs, found they were selling old clothes. And following some idle whim he soon found himself bidding for an old coat. A man bid against him, he bid against the man. Up and up went the price till the old coat was knocked down to him for twenty pounds. As he went away with the coat he saw the other bidder looking at him with an expression of fury.

That's as far as the story goes. But how, Mr. Ainslie asked me, did the matter develop, and why that furious look? I at once made enquiries at a reliable source and have ascertained that the man's name was Peters, who thus oddly purchased a coat, and that he took it to the Rue de Rivoli, to a hotel where he lodged, from the little low, dark auction room by the Seine in which he concluded the bargain. There he examined it, off and on, all day and much of the next morning, a light brown overcoat with tails, without discovering any excuse, far less a reason, for having spent twenty pounds on so worn a thing. And late next morning to his sitting room looking out on the Gardens of the Tuileries the man with the furious look was ushered in.

Grim he stood, silent and angry, till the guiding waiter went. Not till then did he speak, and his words came clear and brief, welling up from deep emotions.

"How did you dare to bid against me?"

His name was Santiago. And for many moments Peters found no excuse to offer, no apology, nothing in extenuation. Lamely at last, weakly, knowing his argument to be of no avail, he muttered something to the intent that Mr. Santiago could have outbid him.

"No," said the stranger. "We don't want all the town in this. This is a matter between you and me." He paused, then added in his fierce, curt way: "A thousand pounds, no more."

Almost dumbly Peters accepted the offer and, pocketing the thousand pounds that was paid him, and apologizing for the inconvenience he had unwittingly caused, tried to show the stranger out. But Santiago strode swiftly on before him, taking the coat, and was gone.

There followed between Peters and his second thoughts another long afternoon of bitter reproaches. Why ever had he let go so thoughtlessly of a garment that so easily fetched a thousand pounds? And the more he brooded on this the more clearly did he perceive that he had lost an unusual opportunity of a first class investment of a speculative kind. He knew men perhaps better than he knew materials; and, though he could not see in that old brown coat the value of so much as a thousand pounds, he saw far more than that in the man's eager need for it. An afternoon of brooding over lost opportunities led to a night of remorse, and scarcely had day dawned when he ran to his sitting-room to see if he still had safe the card of Santiago. And there was the neat and perfumed *carte de visite* with Santiago's Parisian address in the corner.

That morning he sought him out, and found Santiago seated at a table with chemicals and magnifying glasses beside him examining, as it lay spread wide before him, the old brown coat. And Peters fancied he wore a puzzled air.

They came at once to business. Peters was rich and asked Santiago to name his price, and that small dark man admitted financial straits, and so was willing to sell for thirty thousand pounds. A little bargaining followed, the price came down and the old brown coat changed hands once more, for twenty thousand pounds.

Let any who may be inclined to doubt my story understand that in the City, as any respectable company promoter will tell them, twenty thousand pounds is invested almost daily with less return for it than an old tail coat. And, whatever doubts Mr. Peters felt that day about the wisdom of his investment, there before him lay that tangible return, that something that may be actually fingered and seen, which is so often denied to the investor in gold mines and other Selected Investments. Yet as the days wore on and the old coat grew no younger, nor any more wonderful, nor the least useful, but more and more like an ordinary old coat, Peters began once more to doubt his astuteness. Before the week was out his doubts had grown acute. And then one morning, Santiago returned. A man, he said, had just arrived from Spain, a friend unexpected all of a sudden in Paris, from whom he might borrow money: and would Peters resell the coat for thirty thousand pounds?

It was then that Peters, seeing his opportunity, cast aside the pretence that he had maintained for so long of knowing something about the mysterious coat, and demanded to know its properties. Santiago swore that he knew not, and repeatedly swore the same by many sacred names; but when Peters as often threatened not to sell, Santiago at last drew out a thin cigar and, lighting it and settling himself in a chair, told all he knew of the coat.

He had been on its tracks for weeks with suspicions growing all the time that it was no ordinary coat, and at last he had run it to earth in that auction room but would not bid for it more than twenty pounds for fear of letting every one into the secret. What the secret was he swore he did not know, but this much he knew all along, that the weight of the coat was absolutely nothing; and he had discovered by testing it with acids that the brown stuff of which the coat was made was neither cloth nor silk nor any known material, and would neither burn nor tear. He believed it to be some undiscovered element. And the properties of the coat which he was convinced were marvellous he felt sure of discovering within another week by means of experiments with his chemicals. Again he offered thirty thousand pounds, to be paid within two or three days if all went well. And then they started haggling together as business men will.

And all the morning went by over the gardens of the Tuileries and the afternoons came on, and only by two o'clock they arrived at an understanding, on a basis, as they called it, of thirty thousand guineas. And the old tail coat was brought out and spread on the table, and they examined it together and chatted about its properties, all the more friendly for their strenuous argument. And Santiago was rising up to go, and Peters pleasantly holding out his hand, when a step was heard on the stair. It echoed up to the room, the door opened. And an elderly labouring man came stumping in. He walked with difficulty, almost like a bather who has been swimming and floating all morning and misses the buoyancy of the water when he has come to land. He stumped up to the table without speaking and there at once caught sight of the old brown coat.

"Why," he said, "that be my old coat."

And without another word he put it on. In the fierce glare of his eyes as he fitted on that coat, carefully fastening the buttons, buttoning up the flap of a pocket here, unbuttoning one there, neither Peters nor Santiago found a word to say. They sat there wondering how they had dared to bid for that brown tail coat, how they had dared to buy it, even to touch it, they sat there silent without a single excuse. And with no word more the old labourer stumped across the room, opened wide the double window that looked on the Tuileries gardens and, flashing back over his shoulder one look that was full of scorn, stumped away up through the air at an angle of forty degrees.

Peters and Santiago saw him bear to his left from the window; passing diagonally over the Rue de Rivoli and over a corner of the Tuileries gardens; they saw him clear the Louvre, and thence they dumbly watched him still slanting upwards, stepping out with a firmer and more confident stride as he dwindled and dwindled away with his old brown coat.

Neither spoke till he was no more than a speck in the sky far away over Paris going South Eastwards.

"Well I am blowed," said Peters.

But Santiago sadly shook his head. "I knew it was a good coat," he said. "I *knew* it was a good coat."

AN ARCHIVE OF THE OLDER MYSTERIES

It is told in the Archive of the Older Mysteries of China that one of the house of Tlang was cunning with sharpened iron and went to the green jade mountains and carved a green jade god. And this was in the cycle of the Dragon, the seventy-eighth year.

And for nearly a hundred years men doubted the green jade god, and then they worshipped him for a thousand years; and after that they doubted him again, and the green jade god made a miracle and whelmed the green jade mountains, sinking them down one evening at sunset into the earth so that there is only a marsh where the green jade mountains were. And the marsh is full of the lotus.

By the side of this lotus marsh, just as it glitters at evening, walks Li La Ting, the Chinese girl, to bring the cows home; she goes behind them singing of the river Lo Lang Ho. And thus she sings of the river, even of Lo Lang Ho: she sings that he is indeed of all rivers the greatest, born of more ancient mountains than even the wise men know, swifter than hares, more deep than the sea, the master of other rivers perfumed even as roses and fairer than the sapphires around the neck of a prince. And then she would pray to the river Lo Lang Ho, master of rivers and rival of the heaven at dawn, to bring her down in a boat of light bamboo a lover rowing out of the inner land in a garment of yellow silk with turquoises at his waist, young and merry and idle, with a face as yellow as gold and a ruby in his cap with lanterns shining at dusk.

Thus she would pray of an evening to the river Lo Lang Ho as she went behind the cows at the edge of the lotus marshes and the green jade god under the lotus marshes was jealous of the lover that the maiden Li La Ting would pray for of an evening to the river Lo Lang Ho, and he cursed the river after the manner of gods and turned it into a narrow and evil smelling stream.

And all this happened a thousand years ago, and Lo Lang Ho is but a reproach among travelers and the story of that great river is forgotten, and what became of the maiden no tale saith though all men think she became a goddess of jade to sit and smile at a lotus on a lotus carven of stone by the side of the green jade god far under the marshes upon the peaks of the mountains, but women know that her ghost still haunts the lotus marshes on glittering evenings, singing of Lo Lang Ho.

A CITY OF WONDER

Past the upper corner of a precipice the moon rode into view. Night had for some while now hooded the marvelous city. They had planned it to be symmetrical, its maps were orderly, near; in two dimensions, that is length and breadth, its streets met and crossed each other with regular exactitude, with all the dullness of the science of man. The city had laughed as it were and shaken itself free and in the third dimension had soared away to consort with all the careless, irregular things that know not man for their master.

Yet even there, even at those altitudes, man had still clung to his symmetry, still claimed that these mountains were houses; in orderly rows the thousand windows stood watching each other precisely, all orderly, all alike, lest any should guess by day that there might be mystery here. So they stood in the daylight. The sun set, still they were orderly, as scientific and regular as the labour of only man and the bees. The mists darken at evening. And first the Woolworth Building goes away, sheer home and away from any allegiance to man, to take his place among mountains; for I saw him stand with the lower slopes invisible in the gloaming, while only his pinnacles showed up in the clearer sky. Thus only mountains stand.

Still all the windows of the other buildings stood in their regular rows—all side by side in silence, not yet changed, as though waiting one furtive moment to step from the schemes of man, to slip back to mystery and romance again as cats do when they steal on velvet feet away from familiar hearths in the dark of the moon.

Night fell, and the moment came. Someone lit a window, far up another shone with its orange glow. Window by window, and yet not nearly all. Surely if modern man with his clever schemes held any sway here still he would have turned one switch and lit them all together; but we are back with the older man of whom far songs tell, he whose spirit is kin to strange romances and mountains. One by one the windows shine from the precipices; some twinkle, some are dark; man's orderly schemes have gone, and we are amongst vast heights lit by inscrutable beacons.

I have seen such cities before, and I have told of them in *The Book of Wonder*.

Here in New York a poet met a welcome.

BEYOND THE FIELDS WE KNOW: PUBLISHER'S NOTE

Beyond the fields we know, in the Lands of Dream, lies the Valley of the Yann where the mighty river of that name, rising in the Hills of Hap, idleing its way by massive dream-evoking amethyst cliffs, orchid-laden forests, and ancient mysterious cities, comes to the Gates of Yann and passes to the sea.

Some years since a poet visiting that land voyaged down the Yann on a trading bark named the *Bird of the River* and returning safe to Ireland, set down in a tale that is called *Idle Days on the Yann*, the wonders of that voyage. Now the tale being one of marvellous beauty, found its way into a volume we call *A Dreamer's Tales* where it may be found to this day with other wondrous tales of that same poet.

As the days went by the lure of the river and pleasant memories of his shipmates bore in with a constant urge on the soul of the poet that he might once more journey Beyond the Fields We Know and come to the floor of Yann; and one day it fell out that turning into Go-by Street that leads up from the Embankment toward the Strand and which you and I always do go by and perhaps never see in passing, he found the door which one enters on the way to the Land of Dream.

Twice of late has Lord Dunsany entered that door in Go-by Street and returned to the Valley of the Yann and each time come back with a tale; one, of his search for the *Bird of the River,* the other of the mighty hunter who avenged the destruction of Perdóndaris, where on his earlier voyage the captain tied up his ship and traded within the city. That all may be clear to those who read these new tales and to whom no report has previously come Beyond the Fields We Know the publishers reprint in this volume *Idle Days on the Yann.*

IDLE DAYS ON THE YANN

So I came down through the wood to the bank of Yann and found, as had been prophesied, the ship *Bird of the River* about to loose her cable.

The captain sate cross-legged upon the white deck with his scimitar lying beside him in its jewelled scabbard, and the sailors toiled to spread the nimble sails to bring the ship into the central stream of Yann, and all the while sang ancient soothing songs. And the wind of the evening descending cool from the snowfields of some mountainous abode of distant gods came suddenly, like glad tidings to an anxious city, into the wing-like sails.

And so we came into the central stream, whereat the sailors lowered the greater sails. But I had gone to bow before the captain, and to inquire concerning the miracles, and appearances among men, of the most holy gods of whatever land he had come from. And the captain answered that he came from fair Belzoond, and worshipped gods that were the least and humblest, who seldom sent the famine or the thunder, and were easily appeased with little battles. And I told how I came from Ireland, which is of Europe, whereat the captain and all the sailors laughed, for they said, "There are no such places in all the land of dreams." When they had ceased to mock me, I explained that my fancy mostly dwelt in the desert of Cuppar-Nombo, about a beautiful city called Golthoth the Damned, which was sentinelled all round by wolves and their shadows, and had been utterly desolate for years and years, because of a curse which the gods once spoke in anger and could never since recall. And sometimes my dreams took me as far as Pungar Vees, the red walled city where the fountains are, which trades with the Isles and Thul. When I said this they complimented me upon the abode of my fancy, saying that, though they had never seen these cities, such places might well be imagined. For the rest of that evening I bargained with the captain over the sum that I should pay him for my fare if God and the tide of Yann should bring us safely as far as the cliffs by the sea, which are named Bar-Wul-Yann, the Gate of Yann.

And now the sun had set, and all the colours of the world and heaven had held a festival with him, and slipped one by one away before the imminent approach of night. The parrots had all flown home to the jungle on either bank, the monkeys in rows in safety on high branches of the trees were silent and asleep, the fireflies in the deeps of the forest were going up and down, and the great stars came gleaming out to look on the face of Yann. Then the sailors lighted lanterns and hung them round the ship, and the light flashed out on a sudden and dazzled Yann, and the ducks that fed along his marshy banks all suddenly arose, and made wide circles in the upper air, and saw the distant reaches of the Yann and the white mist that softly cloaked the jungle, before they returned again into their marshes.

And then the sailors knelt on the decks and prayed, not all together, but five or six at a time. Side by side there kneeled down together five or six, for there only prayed at the same time men of different faiths, so that no god should hear two men praying to him at once. As soon as any one had finished his prayer, another of the same faith would take his place. Thus knelt the row of five or six with bended heads under the fluttering sail, while the central stream of the River Yann took them on towards the sea, and their prayers rose up from among the lanterns and went towards the stars. And behind them in the after end of the ship the helmsman prayed aloud the helmsman's prayer, which is prayed by all who follow his trade upon the River Yann, of whatever faith they be. And the captain prayed to his little lesser gods, to the gods that bless Belzoond.

And I too felt that I would pray. Yet I liked not to pray to a jealous God there where the frail affectionate gods whom the heathen love were being humbly invoked; so I bethought me, instead, of Sheol Nugganoth, whom the men of the jungle have long since deserted, who is now unworshipped and alone; and to him I prayed.

And upon us praying the night came suddenly down, as it comes upon all men who pray at evening and upon all men who do not; yet our prayers comforted our own souls when we thought of the Great Night to come.

And so Yann bore us magnificently onwards, for he was elate with molten snow that the Poltiades had brought him from the Hills of Hap, and the Marn and Migris were swollen full with floods; and he bore us in his might past Kyph and Pir, and we saw the lights of Goolunza.

Soon we all slept except the helmsman, who kept the ship in the midstream of Yann.

When the sun rose the helmsman ceased to sing, for by song he cheered himself in the lonely night. When the song ceased we suddenly all awoke, and another took the helm, and the helmsman slept.

We knew that soon we should come to Mandaroon. We made a meal, and Mandaroon appeared. Then the captain commanded, and the sailors loosed again the greater sails, and the ship turned and left the stream of Yann and came into a harbour beneath the ruddy walls of Mandaroon.

Then while the sailors went and gathered fruits I came alone to the gate of Mandaroon. A few huts were outside it, in which lived the guard. A sentinel with a long white beard was standing in the gate, armed with a rusty pike. He wore large spectacles, which were covered with dust. Through the gate I saw the city. A deathly stillness was over all of it. The ways seemed untrodden, and moss was thick on doorsteps; in the market-place huddled figures lay asleep. A scent of incense and burned poppies, and there was a hum of the echoes of distant bells. I said to the sentinel in the tongue of the region of Yann, "Why are they all asleep in this still city?"

He answered: "None may ask questions in this gate for fear they wake the people of the city. For when the people of this city wake the gods will die. And when the gods die men may dream no more." And I began to ask him what gods that city worshipped, but he lifted his pike because none might ask questions there. So I left him and went back to the *Bird of the River*.

Certainly Mandaroon was beautiful with her white pinnacles peering over her ruddy walls and the green of her copper roofs.

When I came back again to the *Bird of the River*, I found the sailors were returned to the ship. Soon we weighed anchor, and sailed out again, and so came once more to the middle of the river. And now the sun was moving towards his heights, and there had reached us on the River Yann the song of those countless myriads of choirs that attend him in his progress round the world. For the little creatures that have many legs had spread their gauze wings easily on the air, as a man rests his elbows on a balcony and gave jubilant, ceremonial praises to the sun, or else they moved together on the air in wavering dances intricate and swift, or turned aside to avoid the onrush of some drop of water that a breeze had shaken from a jungle orchid, chilling the air and driving it before it, as it fell whirring in its rush to the earth; but all the while they sang triumphantly. "For the day is for us," they said, "whether our great and sacred father the Sun shall bring up more life like us from the marshes, or whether all the world shall end to-night." And there sang all those whose notes are known to human ears, as well as those whose far more numerous notes have never been heard by man.

To these a rainy day had been as an era of war that should desolate continents during all the lifetime of a man.

And there came out also from the dark and steaming jungle to behold and rejoice in the Sun the huge and lazy butterflies. And they danced, but danced idly, on the ways of the air, as some haughty queen of distant conquered lands might in her poverty and exile dance, in some encampment of the gipsies, for the mere bread to live by, but beyond that would never abate her pride to dance for a fragment more.

And the butterflies sung of strange and painted things, of purple orchids and of lost pink cities and the monstrous colours of the jungle's decay. And they, too, were among those whose voices are not discernible by human ears. And as they floated above the river, going from forest to forest, their splendour was matched by the inimical beauty of the birds who darted out to pursue them. Or sometimes they settled on the white and wax-like blooms of the plant that creeps and clambers about the trees of the forest; and their purple wings flashed out on the great blossoms as, when the caravans go from Nurl to Thace, the gleaming silks flash out upon the snow, where the crafty merchants spread them one by one to astonish the mountaineers of the Hills of Noor.

But upon men and beasts the sun sent a drowsiness. The river monsters along the river's marge lay dormant in the slime. The sailors pitched a pavilion, with golden tassels, for the captain upon the deck, and then went, all but the helmsman, under a sail that they had hung as an awning between two masts. Then they told tales to one another, each of his own city or of the miracles of his god, until all were fallen asleep. The captain offered me the shade of his pavilion with the gold tassels, and there we talked for a while, he telling me that he was taking merchandise to Perdóndaris, and that he would take back to fair Belzoond things appertaining to the affairs of the sea. Then, as I watched through the pavilion's opening the brilliant birds and butterflies that crossed and recrossed over the river, I fell asleep, and dreamed that I was a monarch entering his capital underneath arches of flags, and all the musicians of the world were there, playing melodiously their instruments; but no one cheered.

In the afternoon, as the day grew cooler again, I awoke and found the captain buckling on his scimitar, which he had taken off him while he rested.

And now we were approaching the wide court of Astahahn, which opens upon the river. Strange boats of antique design were chained there to the steps. As we neared it we saw the open marble court, on three sides of which stood the city fronting on colonnades. And in the court and along the colonnades the people of that city walked with solemnity and care according to the rites of ancient ceremony. All in that city was of ancient device; the carving on the houses, which, when age had broken it remained unrepaired, was of the remotest times, and everywhere were represented in stone beasts that have long since passed away from Earth—the dragon, the griffin, and the hippogriffin, and the different species of gargoyle. Nothing was to be found, whether material or custom, that was new in Astahahn. Now they took no notice at all of us as we went by, but continued their processions and ceremonies in the ancient city, and the sailors, knowing their custom, took no notice of them. But I called, as we came near, to one who stood beside the water's edge, asking him what men did in Astahahn and what their merchandise was, and with whom they traded. He said, "Here we have fettered and manacled Time, who would otherwise slay the gods."

I asked him what gods they worshipped in that city, and he said, "All those gods whom Time has not yet slain." Then he turned from me and would say no more, but busied himself in behaving in accordance with ancient custom. And so, according to the will of Yann, we drifted onwards and left Astahahn, and we found in greater quantities such birds as prey on fishes. And they were very wonderful in their plumage, and they came not out of the jungle, but flew, with their long necks stretched out before them, and their legs lying on the wind behind straight up the river over the mid-stream.

And now the evening began to gather in. A thick white mist had appeared over the river, and was softly rising higher. It clutched at the trees with long impalpable arms, it rose higher and higher, chilling the air; and white shapes moved away into the jungle as though the ghosts of ship-wrecked mariners were searching stealthily in the darkness for the spirits of evil that long ago had wrecked them on the Yann.

As the sun sank behind the field of orchids that grew on the matted summit of the jungle, the river monsters came wallowing out of the slime in which they had reclined during the heat of the day, and the great beasts of the jungle came down to drink. The butterflies a while since were gone to rest. In little narrow tributaries that we passed night seemed already to have fallen, though the sun which had disappeared from us had not yet set.

And now the birds of the jungle came flying home far over us, with the sunlight glistening pink upon their breasts, and lowered their pinions as soon as they saw the Yann, and dropped into the trees. And the widgeon began to go up the river in great companies, all whistling, and then would suddenly wheel and all go down again. And there shot by us the small and arrow-like teal; and we heard the manifold cries of flocks of geese, which the sailors told me had recently come in from crossing over the Lispasian ranges; every year they come by the same way, close by the peak of Mluna, leaving it to the left, and the mountain eagles know the way they come and—men say—the very hour, and every year they expect them by the same way as soon as the snows have fallen upon the Northern Plains. But soon it grew so dark that we saw these birds no more, and only heard the whirring of their wings, and of countless others besides, until they all settled down along the banks of the river, and it was the hour when the birds of the night went forth. Then the sailors lit the lanterns for the night, and huge moths appeared, flapping about the ship, and at moments their gorgeous colours would be revealed by the lanterns, then they would pass into the night again, where all was black. And again the sailors prayed, and thereafter we supped and slept, and the helmsman took our lives into his care.

When I awoke I found that we had indeed come to Perdóndaris, that famous city. For there it stood upon the left of us, a city fair and notable, and all the more pleasant for our eyes to see after the jungle that was so long with us. And we were anchored by the marketplace, and the captain's merchandise was all displayed, and a merchant of Perdóndaris stood looking at it. And the captain had his scimitar in his hand, and was beating with it in anger upon the deck, and the splinters were flying up from the white planks; for the merchant had offered him a price for his merchandise that the captain declared to be an insult to himself and his country's gods, whom he now said to be great and terrible gods, whose curses were to be dreaded. But the merchant waved his hands, which were of great fatness, showing his pink palms, and swore that of himself he thought not at all, but only of the poor folk in the huts beyond the city to whom he wished to sell the merchandise for as low a price as possible, leaving no remuneration for himself. For the merchandise was mostly the thick toomarund carpets that in the winter keep the wind from the floor, and tollub which the people smoke in pipes. Therefore the merchant said if he offered a piffek more the poor folk must go without their toomarunds when the winter came, and without their tollub in the evenings, or else he and his aged father must starve together. Thereat the captain lifted his scimitar to his own throat, saying that he was now a ruined man, and that nothing remained to him but death. And while he was carefully lifting he beard with his left hand, the merchant eyed the merchandise again, and said that rather than see so worthy a captain die, a man for whom he had conceived an especial love when first he saw the manner in which he handled his ship, he and his aged father should starve together and therefore he offered fifteen piffeks more.

When he said this the captain prostrated himself and prayed to his gods that they might yet sweeten this merchant's bitter heart—to his little lesser gods, to the gods that bless Belzoond.

At last the merchant offered yet five piffeks more. Then the captain wept, for he said that he was deserted of his gods; and the merchant also wept, for he said that he was thinking of his aged father, and of how soon he would starve, and he hid his weeping face with both his hands, and eyed the tollub again between his fingers. And so the bargain was concluded, and the merchant took the toomarund and tollub, paying for them out of a great clinking purse. And these were packed up into bales again, and three of the merchant's slaves carried them upon their heads into the city. And all the while the sailors had sat silent, cross-legged in a crescent upon the deck, eagerly watching the bargain, and now a murmur of satisfaction arose among them, and they began to compare it among themselves with other bargains that they had known. And I found out from them that there are seven merchants in Perdóndaris, and that they had all come to the captain one by one before the bargaining began, and each had warned him privately against the others. And to all the merchants the captain had offered the wine of his own country, that they make in fair Belzoond, but could in no wise persuade them to it. But now that the bargain was over, and the sailors were seated at the first meal of the day, the captain appeared among them with a cask of that wine, and we broached it with care and all made merry together. And the captain was glad in his heart because he knew that he had much honour in the eyes of his men because of the bargain that he had made. So the sailors drank the wine of their native land, and soon their thoughts were back in fair Belzoond and the little neighbouring cities of Durl and Duz.

But for me the captain poured into a little glass some heavy yellow wine from a small jar which he kept apart among his sacred things. Thick and sweet it was, even like honey, yet there was in its heart a mighty, ardent fire which had authority over souls of men. It was made, the captain told me, with great subtlety by the secret craft of a family of six who lived in a hut on the mountains of Hian Min. Once in these mountains, he said, he followed the spoor of a bear, and he came suddenly on a man of that family who had hunted the same bear, and he was at the end of a narrow way with precipice all about him, and his spear was sticking in the bear, and the wound not fatal, and he had no other weapon. And the bear was walking towards the man, very slowly because his wound irked him—yet he was now very close. And what the captain did he would not say, but every year as soon as the snows are hard, and travelling is easy on the Hian Min, that man comes down to the market in the plains, and always leaves for the captain in the gate of fair Belzoond a vessel of that priceless secret wine.

And as I sipped the wine and the captain talked, I remembered me of stalwart noble things that I had long since resolutely planned, and my soul seemed to grow mightier within me and to dominate the whole tide of the Yann. It may be that I then slept. Or, if I did not, I do not now minutely recollect every detail of that morning's occupations. Towards evening, I awoke and wishing to see Perdóndaris before we left in the morning, and being unable to wake the captain, I went ashore alone. Certainly Perdóndaris was a powerful city; it was encompassed by a wall of great strength and altitude, having in it hollow ways for troops to walk in, and battlements along it all the way, and fifteen strong towers on it in every mile, and copper plaques low down where men could read them, telling in all the languages of those parts of the Earth—one language on each plaque— the tale of how an army once attacked Perdóndaris and what befell that army. Then I entered Perdóndaris and found all the people dancing, clad in brilliant silks, and playing on the tam-bang as they danced. For a fearful thunderstorm had terrified them while I slept, and the fires of death, they said, had danced over Perdóndaris, and now the thunder had gone leaping away large and black and hideous, they said, over the distant hills, and had turned round snarling at them, showing his gleaming teeth, and had stamped, as he went, upon the hilltops until they rang as though they had been bronze. And often and again they stopped in their merry dances and prayed to the God they knew not, saying, "O, God that we know not, we thank Thee for sending the thunder back to his hills." And I went on and came to the market-place, and lying there upon the marble pavement I saw the merchant fast asleep and breathing heavily, with his face and the palms of his hands towards the sky, and slaves were fanning him to keep away the flies. And from the market-place I came to a silver temple and then to a palace of onyx, and there were many wonders in Perdóndaris, and I would have stayed and seen them all, but as I came to the outer wall of the city I suddenly saw in it a huge ivory gate. For a while I paused and admired it, then I came nearer and perceived the dreadful truth. The gate was carved out of one solid piece!

I fled at once through the gateway and down to the ship, and even as I ran I thought that I heard far off on the hills behind me the tramp of the fearful beast by whom that mass of ivory was shed, who was perhaps even then looking for his other tusk. When I was on the ship again I felt safer, and I said nothing to the sailors of what I had seen.

And now the captain was gradually awakening. Now night was rolling up from the East and North, and only the pinnacles of the towers of Perdóndaris still took the fallen sunlight. Then I went to the captain and told him quietly of the thing I had seen. And he questioned me at once about the gate, in a low voice, that the sailors might not know; and I told him how the weight of the thing was such that it could not have been brought from afar, and the captain knew that it had not been there a year ago. We agreed that such a beast could never have been killed by any assault of man, and that the gate must have been a fallen tusk, and one fallen near and recently. Therefore he decided that it were better to flee at once; so he commanded, and the sailors went to the sails, and others raised the anchor to the deck, and just as the highest pinnacle of marble lost the last rays of the sun we left Perdóndaris, that famous city. And night came down and cloaked Perdóndaris and hid it from our eyes, which as things have happened will never see it again; for I have heard since that something swift and wonderful has suddenly wrecked Perdóndaris in a day—towers, and walls, and people.

And the night deepened over the River Yann, a night all white with stars. And with the night there arose the helmsman's song. As soon as he had prayed he began to sing to cheer himself all through the lonely night. But first he prayed, praying the helmsman's prayer. And this is what I remember of it, rendered into English with a very feeble equivalent of the rhythm that seemed so resonant in those tropic nights

To whatever god may hear.

Wherever there be sailors whether of river or sea: whether their way be dark or whether through storm: whether their perils be of beast or of rock: or from enemy lurking on land or pursuing on sea: wherever the tiller is cold or the helmsman stiff: wherever sailors sleep or helmsman watch: guard, guide, and return us to the old land, that has known us: to the far homes that we know.

To all the gods that are.

To whatever god may hear.

So he prayed, and there was silence. And the sailors laid them down to rest for the night. The silence deepened, and was only broken by the ripples of Yann that lightly touched our prow. Sometimes some monster of the river coughed.

Silence and ripples, ripples and silence again.

And then his loneliness came upon the helmsman, and he began to sing. And he sang the market songs of Durl and Duz, and the old dragon-legends of Belzoond.

Many a song he sang, telling to spacious and exotic Yann the little tales and trifles of his city of Durl. And the songs welled up over the black jungle and came into the clear cold air above, and the great bands of stars that looked on Yann began to know the affairs of Durl and Duz, and of the shepherds that dwelt in the fields between, and the flocks that they had, and the loves that they had loved, and all the little things that they hoped to do. And as I lay wrapped up in skins and blankets listening to those songs, and watching the fantastic shapes of the great trees like to black giants stalking through the night, I suddenly fell asleep.

When I awoke great mists were trailing away from the Yann. And the flow of the river was tumbling now tumultuously, and little waves appeared; for Yann had scented from afar the ancient crags of Glorm, and knew that their ravines lay cool before him wherein he should meet the merry wild Irillion rejoicing from fields of snow. So he shook off from him the torpid sleep that had come upon him in the hot and scented jungle, and forgot its orchids and its butterflies, and swept on turbulent, expectant, strong; and soon the snowy peaks of the Hills of Glorm came glittering into view. And now the sailors were waking up from sleep. Soon we all ate, and then the helmsman laid him down to sleep while a comrade took his place, and they all spread over him their choicest furs.

And in a while we heard the sound that the Irillion made as she came down dancing from the fields of snow.

And then we saw the ravine in the Hills of Glorm lying precipitous and smooth before us, into which we were carried by the leaps of Yann. And now we left the steamy jungle and breathed the mountain air; the sailors stood up and took deep breaths of it, and thought of their own far-off Acroctian hills on which were Durl and Duz—below them in the plains stands fair Belzoond.

A great shadow brooded between the cliffs of Glorm, but the crags were shining above us like gnarled moons, and almost lit the gloom. Louder and louder came the Irillion's song, and the sound of her dancing down from the fields of snow. And soon we saw her white and full of mists, and wreathed with rainbows delicate and small that she had plucked up near the mountain's summit from some celestial garden of the Sun. Then she went away seawards with the huge grey Yann and the ravine widened, and opened upon the world, and our rocking ship came through to the light of day.

And all that morning and all the afternoon we passed through the marshes of Pondoovery; and Yann widened there, and flowed solemnly and slowly, and the captain bade the sailors beat on bells to overcome the dreariness of the marshes.

At last the Irusian Mountains came in sight, nursing the villages of Pen-Kai and Blut, and the wandering streets of Mlo, where priests propitiate the avalanche with wine and maize. Then the night came down over the plains of Tlun, and we saw the lights of Cappadarnia. We heard the Pathnites beating upon drums as we passed Imaut and Golzunda, then all but the helmsman slept. And villages scattered along the banks of the Yann heard all that night in the helmsman's unknown tongue the little songs of cities that they know not.

I awoke before dawn with a feeling that I was unhappy before I remembered why. Then I recalled that by the evening of the approaching day, according to all forseen probabilities, we should come to Bar-Wul-Yann, and I should part from the captain and his sailors. And I had liked the man because he had given me of his yellow wine that was set apart among his sacred things, and many a story he had told me about his fair Belzoond between the Acrotian hills and the Hian Min. And I had liked the ways that his sailors had, and the prayers that they prayed at evening side by side, grudging not one another their alien gods. And I had a liking too for the tender way in which they often spoke of Durl and Duz, for it is good that men should love their native cities and the little hills that hold those cities up.

And I had come to know who would meet them when they returned to their homes, and where they thought the meetings would take place, some in a valley of the Acrotian hills where the road comes up from Yann, others in the gateway of one or another of the three cities, and others by the fireside in the home. And I thought of the danger that had menaced us all alike outside Perdóndaris, a danger that, as things have happened, was very real.

And I thought too of the helmsman's cheery song in the cold and lonely night, and how he had held our lives in his careful hands. And as I thought of this the helmsman ceased to sing, and I looked up and saw a pale light had appeared in the sky, and the lonely night had passed; and the dawn widened, and the sailors awoke.

And soon we saw the tide of the Sea himself advancing resolute between Yann's borders, and Yann sprang lithely at him and they struggled a while; then Yann and all that was his were pushed back northwards, so that the sailors had to hoist the sails, and the wind being favourable, we still held onwards.

And we passed Góndara and Narl and Hoz. And we saw memorable, holy Golnuz, and heard the pilgrims praying.

When we awoke after the midday rest we were coming near to Nen, the last of the cities in the River Yann. And the jungle was all about us once again, and about Nen; but the great Mloon ranges stood up over all things, and watched the city from beyond the jungle.

Here we anchored, and the captain and I went up into the city and found that the Wanderers had come into Nen.

And the Wanderers were a weird, dark, tribe, that once in every seven years came down from the peaks of Mloon, having crossed by a pass that is known to them from some fantastic land that lies beyond. And the people of Nen were all outside their houses, and all stood wondering at their own streets. For the men and women of the Wanderers had crowded all the ways, and every one was doing some strange thing. Some danced astounding dances that they had learned from the desert wind, rapidly curving and swirling till the eye could follow no longer. Others played upon instruments beautiful wailing tunes that were full of horror, which souls had taught them lost by night in the desert, that strange far desert from which the Wanderers came.

None of their instruments were such as were known in Nen nor in any part of the region of the Yann; even the horns out of which some were made were of beasts that none had seen along the river, for they were barbed at the tips. And they sang, in the language of none, songs that seemed to be akin to the mysteries of night and to the unreasoned fear that haunts dark places.

Bitterly all the dogs of Nen distrusted them. And the Wanderers told one another fearful tales, for though no one in Nen knew aught of their language, yet they could see the fear on the listeners' faces, and as the tale wound on, the whites of their eyes showed vividly in terror as the eyes of some little beast whom the hawk has seized. Then the teller of the tale would smile and stop, and another would tell his story, and the teller of the first tale's lips would chatter with fear. And if some deadly snake chanced to appear the Wanderers would greet him like a brother, and the snake would seem to give his greetings to them before he passed on again. Once that most fierce and lethal of tropic snakes, the giant lythra, came out of the jungle and all down the street, the central street of Nen, and none of the Wanderers moved away from him, but they all played sonorously on drums, as though he had been a person of much honour; and the snake moved through the midst of them and smote none.

Even the Wanderers' children could do strange things, for if any one of them met with a child of Nen the two would stare at each other in silence with large grave eyes; then the Wanderers' child would slowly draw from his turban a live fish or snake. And the children of Nen could do nothing of that kind at all.

Much I should have wished to stay and hear the hymn with which they greet the night, that is answered by the wolves on the heights of Mloon, but it was now time to raise the anchor again that the captain might return from Bar-Wul-Yann upon the landward tide. So we went on board and continued down the Yann. And the captain and I spoke little, for we were thinking of our parting, which should be for long, and we watched instead the splendour of the westerning sun. For the sun was a ruddy gold, but a faint mist cloaked the jungle, lying low, and into it poured the smoke of the little jungle cities, and the smoke of them met together in the mist and joined into one haze, which became purple, and was lit by the sun, as the thoughts of men become hallowed by some great and sacred thing. Sometimes one column from a lonely house would rise up higher than the cities' smoke, and gleam by itself in the sun.

And now as the sun's last rays were nearly level, we saw the sight that I had come to see, for from two mountains that stood on either shore two cliffs of pink marble came out into the river, all glowing in the light of the low sun, and they were quite smooth and of mountainous altitude, and they nearly met, and Yann went tumbling between them and found the sea.

And this was Bar-Wul-Yann, the Gate of Yann, and in the distance through that barrier's gap I saw the azure indescribable sea, where little fishing-boats went gleaming by.

And the sunset and the brief twilight came, and the exultation of the glory of Bar-Wul-Yann was gone, yet still the pink cliffs glowed, the fairest marvel that the eye beheld-and this in a land of wonders. And soon the twilight gave place to the coming out of stars, and the colours of Bar-Wul-Yann went dwindling away. And the sight of those cliffs was to me as some chord of music that a master's hand had launched from the violin, and which carries to Heaven of Faëry the tremulous spirits of men.

And now by the shore they anchored and went no farther, for they were sailors of the river and not of the sea, and knew the Yann but not the tides beyond.

And the time was come when the captain and I must part, he to go back again to his fair Belzoond in sight of the distant peaks of the Hian Min, and I to find my way by strange means back to those hazy fields that all poets know, wherein stand small mysterious cottages through whose windows, looking westwards, you may see the fields of men, and looking eastwards see glittering elfin mountains, tipped with snow, going range on range into the region of Myth, and beyond it into the kingdom of Fantasy, which pertain to the Lands of Dream. Long we should meet no more, for my fancy is weakening as the years slip by, and I go ever more seldom into the Lands of Dream. Then we clasped hands, uncouthly on his part, for it is not the method of greeting in his country, and he commended my soul to the care of his own gods, to his little lesser gods, the humble ones, to the gods that bless Belzoond.

A SHOP IN GO-BY STREET

I said I must go back to Yann again and see if *Bird of the River* still plies up and down and whether her bearded captain commands her still or whether he sits in the gate of fair Belzoond drinking at evening the marvellous yellow wine that the mountaineer brings down from the Hian Min. And I wanted to see the sailors again who came from Durl and Duz and to hear from their lips what befell Perdóndaris when its doom came up without warning from the hills and fell on that famous city. And I wanted to hear the sailors pray at night each to his own god, and to feel the wind of the evening coolly arise when the sun went flaming away from that exotic river. For I thought never again to see the tide of Yann, but when I gave up politics not long ago the wings of my fancy strengthened, though they had erstwhile drooped, and I had hopes of coming behind the East once more where Yann like a proud white war-horse goes through the Lands of Dream.

Yet I had forgotten the way to those little cottages on the edge of the fields we know whose upper windows, though dim with antique cobwebs, look out on the fields we know not and are the starting-point of all adventure in all the Lands of Dream.

I therefore made enquiries. And so I came to be directed to the shop of a dreamer who lives not far from the Embankment in the City. Among so many streets as there are in the city it is little wonder that there is one that has never been seen before; it is named Go-by Street and runs out of the Strand if you look very closely. Now when you enter this man's shop you do not go straight to the point but you ask him to sell you something, and if it is anything with which he can supply you he hands it you and wishes you good-morning. It is his way. And many have been deceived by asking for some unlikely thing, such as the oyster-shell from which was taken one of those single pearls that made the gates of Heaven in Revelations, and finding that the old man had it in stock.

He was comatose when I went into the shop, his heavy lids almost covered his little eyes; he sat, and his mouth was open. I said, "I want some of Abama and Pharpah, rivers of Damascus." "How much?" he said. "Two and a half yards of each, to be delivered to my flat." "That is very tiresome," he muttered, "very tiresome. We do not stock it in that quantity." "Then I will take all you have," I said.

He rose laboriously and looked among some bottles. I saw one labelled: Nilos, river of Ægyptos; and others Holy Ganges, Phlegethon, Jordan; I was almost afraid he had it, when I heard him mutter again, "This is very tiresome," and presently he said, "We are out of it." "Then," I said, "I wish you to tell me the way to those little cottages in whose upper chambers poets look out upon the fields we know not, for I wish to go into the Land of Dream and to sail once more upon mighty, sea-like Yann."

At that he moved heavily and slowly in way-worn carpet slippers, panting as he went, to the back part of his shop, and I went with him. This was a dingy lumber-room full of idols: the near end was dingy and dark but at the far end was a blue cærulean glow in which stars seemed to be shining and the heads of the idols glowed. "This," said the fat old man in carpet slippers, "is the heaven of the gods who sleep." I asked him what gods slept and he mentioned names that I had never heard as well as names that I knew. "All those," he said, "that are not worshipped now are asleep."

"Then does Time not kill the gods?" I said to him and he answered, "No. But for three or four thousand years a god is worshipped and for three or four he sleeps. Only Time is wakeful always."

"But they that teach us of new gods"—I said to him, "are they not new?"

"They hear the old ones stirring in their sleep being about to wake, because the dawn is breaking and the priests crow. These are the happy prophets: unhappy are they that hear some old god speak while he sleeps still being deep in slumber, and prophesy and prophesy and no dawn comes, they are those that men stone saying, 'Prophesy where this stone shall hit you, and this.'"

"Then shall Time never slay the gods," I said. And he answered, "They shall die by the bedside of the last man. Then Time shall go mad in his solitude and shall not know his hours from his centuries of years and they shall clamour round him crying for recognition and he shall lay his stricken hands on their heads and stare at them blindly and say, 'My children, I do not know you one from another,' and at these words of Time empty worlds shall reel."

And for some while then I was silent, for my imagination went out into those far years and looked back at me and mocked me because I was the creature of a day.

Suddenly I was aware by the old man's heavy breathing that he had gone to sleep. It was not an ordinary shop: I feared lest one of his gods should wake and call for him: I feared many things, it was so dark, and one or two of those idols were something more than grotesque. I shook the old man hard by one of his arms.

"Tell me the way to the cottages," I said, "on the edge of the fields we know."

"I don't think we can do that," he said.

"Then supply me," I said, "with the goods."

That brought him to his senses. He said, "You go out by the back door and turn to the right"; and he opened a little, old, dark door in the wall through which I went, and he wheezed and shut the door. The back of the shop was of incredible age. I saw in antique characters upon a mouldering board, "Licensed to sell weasels and jade earrings." The sun was setting now and shone on little golden spires that gleamed along the roof which had long ago been thatched and with a wonderful straw. I saw that the whole of Go-by Street had the same strange appearance when looked at from behind. The pavement was the same as the pavement of which I was weary and of which so many thousand miles lay the other side of those houses, but the street was of most pure untrampled grass with such marvellous flowers in it that they lured downward from great heights the flocks of butterflies as they traveled by, going I know not whence. The other side of the street there was pavement again but no houses of any kind, and what there was in place of them I did not stop to see, for I turned to my right and walked along the back of Go-by Street till I came to the open fields and the gardens of the cottages that I sought. Huge flowers went up out of these gardens like slow rockets and burst into purple blooms and stood there huge and radiant on six-foot stalks and softly sang strange songs. Others came up beside them and bloomed and began singing too. A very old witch came out of her cottage by the back door and into the garden in which I stood.

"What are these wonderful flowers?" I said to her.

"Hush! Hush!" she said, "I am putting the poets to bed. These flowers are their dreams."

And in a lower voice I said: "What wonderful songs are they singing?" and she said, "Be still and listen."

And I listened and found they were singing of my own childhood and of things that happened there so far away that I had quite forgotten them till I heard the wonderful song.

"Why is the song so faint?" I said to her.

"Dead voices," she said, "Dead voices," and turned back again to her cottage saying: "Dead voices" still, but softly for fear that she should wake the poets. "They sleep so badly while they live," she said.

I stole on tiptoe upstairs to the little room from whose windows, looking one way, we see the fields we know and, looking another, those hilly lands that I sought—almost I feared not to find them. I looked at once toward the mountains of faëry; the afterglow of the sunset flamed on them, their avalanches flashed on their violet slopes coming down tremendous from emerald peaks of ice; and there was the old gap in the blue-grey hills above the precipice of amethyst whence one sees the Lands of Dream.

All was still in the room where the poets slept when I came quietly down. The old witch sat by a table with a lamp, knitting a splendid cloak of gold and green for a king that had been dead a thousand years.

"Is it any use," I said, "to the king that is dead that you sit and knit him a cloak of gold and green?"

"Who knows?" she said.

"What a silly question to ask," said her old black cat who lay curled by the fluttering fire.

Already the stars were shining on that romantic land when I closed the witch's door; already the glow-worms were mounting guard for the night around those magical cottages. I turned and trudged for the gap in the blue-grey mountains.

Already when I arrived some colour began to show in the amethyst precipice below the gap although it was not yet morning. I heard a rattling and sometimes caught a flash from those golden dragons far away below me that are the triumph of the goldsmiths of Sirdoo and were given life by the ritual incantations of the conjurer Amargrarn. On the edge of the opposite cliff, too near I thought for safety, I saw the ivory palace of Singanee that mighty elephant-hunter; small lights appeared in windows, the slaves were awake, and beginning with heavy eyelids the work of the day.

And now a ray of sunlight topped the world. Others than I must describe how it swept from the amethyst cliff the shadow of the black one that opposed it, how that one shaft of sunlight pierced the amethyst for leagues, and how the rejoicing colour leaped up to welcome the light and shot back a purple glow on the walls of the palace of ivory while down in that incredible ravine the golden dragons still played in the darkness.

At this moment a female slave came out by a door of the palace and tossed a basket-full of sapphires over the edge. And when day was manifest on those marvellous heights and the flare of the amethyst precipice filled the abyss, then the elephant-hunter arose in his ivory palace and took his terrific spear and going out by a landward door went forth to avenge Perdóndaris

I turned then and looked upon the lands of Dream, and the thin white mist that never rolls quite away was shifting in the morning. Rising like isles above it I saw the Hills of Hap and the city of copper, old, deserted Bethmoora, and Utnar Véhi and Kyph and Mandaroon and the wandering leagues of Yann. Rather I guessed than saw the Hian Min whose imperturbable and aged heads scarce recognize for more than clustered mounds the round Acroctian hills, that are heaped about their feet and that shelter, as I remembered, Durl and Duz. But most clearly I discerned that ancient wood through which one going down to the bank of Yann whenever the moon is old may come on *Bird of the River* anchored there, waiting three days for travellers, as has been prophesied of her. And as it was now that season I hurried down from the gap in the blue-grey hills by an elfin path that was coeval with fable, and came by means of it to the edge of the wood. Black though the darkness was in that ancient wood the beasts that moved in it were blacker still. It is very seldom that any dreamer travelling in Lands of Dream is ever seized by these beasts, and yet I ran; for if a man's spirit is seized in the Lands of Dream his body may survive it for many years and well know the beasts that mouthed him far away and the look in their little eyes and the smell of their breath; that is why the recreation field at Hanwell is so dreadfully trodden into restless paths.

And so I came at last to the sea-like flood of proud, tremendous Yann, with whom there tumbled streams from incredible lands—with these he went by singing. Singing he carried drift-wood and whole trees, fallen in far-away, unvisited forests, and swept them mightily by, but no sign was there either out in the river or in the olden anchorage near by of the ship I came to see.

And I built myself a hut and roofed it over with the huge abundant leaves of a marvellous weed and ate the meat that grows on the targar-tree and waited there three days. And all day long the river tumbled by and all night long the tolulu-bird sang on and the huge fireflies had no other care than to pour past in torrents of dancing sparks, and nothing rippled the surface of the Yann by day and nothing disturbed the tolulu-bird by night. I know not what I feared for the ship I sought and its friendly captain who came from fair Belzoond and its cheery sailors out of Durl and Duz; all day long I looked for it on the river and listened for it by night until the dancing fireflies danced me to sleep. Three times only in those three nights the tolulu-bird was scared and stopped his song, and each time I awoke with a start and found no ship and saw that he was only scared by the dawn. Those indescribable dawns upon the Yann came up like flames in some land over the hills where a magician burns by secret means enormous amethysts in a copper pot. I used to watch them in wonder while no bird sang—till all of a sudden the sun came over a hill and every bird but one began to sing, and the tolulu-bird slept fast, till out of an opening eye he saw the stars.

I would have waited three more days, but on the third day I had gone in my loneliness to see the very spot where first I met *Bird of the River* at her anchorage with her bearded captain sitting on the deck. And as I looked at the black mud of the harbour and pictured in my mind that band of sailors whom I had not seen for two years, I saw an old hulk peeping from the mud. The lapse of centuries seemed partly to have rotted and partly to have buried in the mud all but the prow of the boat and on the prow I faintly saw a name. I read it slowly—it was *Bird of the River.* And then I knew that, while in Ireland and London two years had barely passed over my head, ages had gone over the region of Yann and wrecked and rotted that once familiar ship, and buried years ago the bones of the youngest of my friends, who so often sang to me of Durl and Duz or told the dragon-legends of Belzoond.For beyond the world we know there roars a hurricane of centuries whose echo only troubles—though sorely—our fields; while elsewhere there is calm. I stayed a moment by that battered hulk and said a prayer for whatever may be immortal of those who were wont to sail it down the Yann, and I prayed for them to the gods to whom they loved to pray, to the little lesser gods that bless Belzoond. Then leaving the hut that I built to those ravenous years I turned my back to the Yann and entering the forest at evening just as its orchids were opening their petals to perfume the night came out of it in the morning, and passed that day along the amethyst gulf by the gap in the blue-grey mountains. I wondered if Singanee, that mighty elephant-hunter, had returned again with his spear to his lofty ivory palace or if his doom had been one with that of Perdóndaris. I saw a merchant at a small back door selling new sapphires as I passed the palace, then I went on and came as twilight fell to those small cottages where the elfin mountains are in sight of the fields we know. And I went to the old witch that I had seen before and she sat in her parlour with a red shawl round her shoulders still knitting the golden cloak, and faintly through one of her windows the elfin mountains shone and I saw again through another the fields we know.

"Tell me something," I said, "of this strange land!"

"How much do you know?" she said. "Do you know that dreams are illusion?"

"Of course I do," I said. "Every one knows that."

"Oh no they don't," she said, "the mad don't know it."

"That is true," I said.

"And do you know," she said, "that Life is illusion?"

"Of course it is not," I said. "Life is real, Life is earnest———."

At that the witch and her cat (who had not moved from her old place by the hearth) burst into laughter. I stayed some time, for there was much that I wished to ask, but when I saw that the laughter would not stop I turned and went away.

THE AVENGER OF PERDÓNDARIS

I was rowing on the Thames not many days after my return from the Yann and drifting eastwards with the fall of the tide away from Westminster Bridge, near which I had hired my boat. All kinds of things were on the water with me—sticks drifting, and huge boats—and I was watching, so absorbed the traffic of that great river that I did not notice I had come to the City until I looked up and saw that part of the Embankment that is nearest to Go-by Street. And then I suddenly wondered what befell Singanee, for there was a stillness about his ivory palace when I passed it by, which made me think that he had not then returned. And though I had seen him go forth with his terrific spear, and mighty elephant-hunter though he was, yet his was a fearful quest for I knew that it was none other than to avenge Perdóndaris by slaying that monster with the single tusk who had overthrown it suddenly in a day. So I tied up my boat as soon as I came to some steps, and landed and left the Embankment, and about the third street I came to I began to look for the opening of Go-by Street; it is very narrow, you hardly notice it at first, but there it was, and soon I was in the old man's shop. But a young man leaned over the counter. He had no information to give me about the old man—he was sufficient in himself. As to the little old door in the back of the shop, "We know nothing about that, sir." So

I had to talk to him and humour him. He had for sale on the counter an instrument for picking up a lump of sugar in a new way. He was pleased when I looked at it and he began to praise it. I asked him what was the use of it, and he said that it was of no use but that it had only been invented a week ago and was quite new and was made of real silver and was being very much bought. But all the while I was straying towards the back of the shop. When I enquired about the idols there he said that they were some of the season's novelties and were a choice selection of mascots; and while I made a pretence of selecting one I suddenly saw the wonderful old door. I was through it at once and the young shop-keeper after me. No one was more surprised than he when he saw the street of grass and the purple flowers on it; he ran across in his frock-coat on to the opposite pavement and only just stopped in time, for the world ended there. Looking downward over the pavement's edge he saw, instead of accustomed kitchen-windows, white clouds and a wide, blue sky. I led him to the old back door of the shop, looking pale and in need of air, and pushed him lightly and he went limply through, for I thought the air was better for him on the side of the street that he knew. As soon as the door was shut on that astonished man I turned to the right and went along the street till I saw the gardens and the cottages, and a little red patch moving in a garden, which I knew to be the old witch wearing her shawl.

"Come for a change of illusion again?" she said.

"I have come from London," I said. "And I want to see Singanee. I want to go to his ivory palace over the elfin mountains where the amethyst precipice is."

"Nothing like changing your illusions," she said, "or you grow tired. London's a fine place but one wants to see the elfin mountains sometimes."

"Then you know London?" I said.

"Of course I do," she said. "I can dream as well as you. You are not the only person that can imagine London." Men were toiling dreadfully in her garden; it was in the heat of the day and they were digging with spades; she suddenly turned from me to beat one of them over the back with a long black stick that she carried. "Even my poets go to London sometimes," she said to me.

"Why did you beat that man?" I said.

"To make him work," she answered.

"But he is tired," I said.

"Of course he is," said she.

And I looked and saw that the earth was difficult and dry and that every spadeful that the tired men lifted was full of pearls; but some men sat quite still and watched the butterflies that flitted about the garden and the old witch did not beat them with her stick. And when I asked her who the diggers were she said, "These are my poets, they are digging for pearls."

And when I asked her what so many pearls were for she said to me: "To feed the pigs of course."

"But do the pigs like pearls?" I said to her.

"Of course they don't," she said. And I would have pressed the matter further but the old black cat had come out of the cottage and was looking at me whimsically and saying nothing so that I knew I was asking silly questions. And I asked instead why some of the poets were idle and were watching butterflies without being beaten. And she said: "The butterflies know where the pearls are hidden and they are waiting for one to alight above the buried treasure. They cannot dig until they know where to dig." And all of a sudden a faun came out of a rhododendron forest and began to dance upon a disk of bronze in which a fountain was set; and the sound of his two hooves dancing on the bronze was beautiful as bells.

"Tea-bell," said the witch; and all the poets threw down their spades and followed her into the house, and I followed them; but the witch and all of us followed the black cat, who arched his back and lifted his tail and walked along the garden-path of blue enamelled tiles and through the black-thatched porch and the open, oaken door and into a little room where tea was ready. And in the garden the flowers began to sing and the fountain tinkled on the disk of bronze. And I learned that the fountain came from an otherwise unknown sea, and sometimes it threw gilded fragments up from the wrecks of unheard-of galleons, foundered in storms of some sea that was nowhere in the world; or battered to bits in wars waged with we know not whom. Some said that it was salt because of the sea and others that it was salt with mariners' tears. And some of the poets took large flowers out of vases and threw their petals all about the room, and others talked two at a time and other sang. "Why they are only children after all," I said.

"Only children!" repeated the old witch who was pouring out cowslip wine.

"*Only* children," said the old black cat. And every one laughed at me.

"I sincerely apologize," I said. "I did not mean to say it. I did not intend to insult any one."

"Why he knows nothing at all," said the old black cat. And everybody laughed till the poets were put to bed.

And then I took one look at the fields we know, and turned to the other window that looks on the elfin mountains. And the evening looked like a sapphire. And I saw my way though the fields were growing dim, and when I found it I went downstairs and through the witch's parlour, and out of doors and came that night to the palace of Singanee.

Lights glittered through every crystal slab—and all were uncurtained—in the palace of ivory. The sounds were those of a triumphant dance. Very haunting indeed was the booming of a bassoon, and like the dangerous advance of some galloping beast were the blows wielded by a powerful man on the huge, sonourous drum. It seemed to me as I listened that the contest of Singanee with the more than elephantine destroyer of Perdóndaris had already been set to music. And as I walked in the dark along the amethyst precipice I suddenly saw across it a curved white bridge. It was one ivory tusk. And I knew it for the triumph of Singanee. I knew at once that this curved mass of ivory that had been dragged by ropes to bridge the abyss was the twin of the ivory gate that once Perdóndaris had, and had itself been the destruction of that once famous city—towers and walls and people. Already men had begun to hollow it and to carve human figures life-size along its sides. I walked across it; and half way across, at the bottom of the curve, I met a few of the carvers fast asleep. On the opposite cliff by the palace lay the thickest end of the tusk and I came down a ladder which leaned against the tusk for they had not yet carved steps.

Outside the ivory palace it was as I had supposed and the sentry at the gate slept heavily; and though I asked of him permission to enter the palace he only muttered a blessing on Singanee and fell asleep again. It was evident that he had been drinking bak. Inside the ivory hall I met with servitors who told me that any stranger was welcome there that night, because they extolled the triumph of Singanee. And they offered me bak to drink to commemorate the splendour but I did not know its power nor whether a little or much prevailed over a man so I said that I was under an oath to a god to drink nothing beautiful; and they asked me if he could not be appeased by a prayer, and I said, "In nowise," and went towards the dance; and they commiserated me and abused that god bitterly, thinking to please me thereby, and then they fell to drinking bak to the glory of Singanee. Outside the curtains that hung before the dance there stood a chamberlain and when I told him that though a stranger there, yet I was well known to Mung and Sish and Kib, the gods of Pegana, whose signs I made, he bade me ample welcome. Therefore I questioned him about my clothes asking if they were not unsuitable to so august an occasion and he swore by the spear that had slain the destroyer of Perdóndaris that Singanee would think it a shameful thing that any stranger not unknown to the gods should enter the dancing hall unsuitably clad; and therefore he led me to another room and took silken robes out of an old sea-chest of black and seamy oak with green copper hasps that were set with a few pale sapphires, and requested me to choose a suitable robe. And I chose a bright green robe, with an under-robe of light blue which was seen here and there, and a light blue sword-belt. I also wore a cloak that was dark purple with two thin strips of dark-blue along the border and a row of large dark sapphires sewn along the purple between them; it hung down from my shoulders behind me. Nor would the chamberlain of Singanee let me take any less than this, for he said that not even a stranger, on that night, could be allowed to stand in the way of his master's munificence which he was pleased to exercise in honour of his victory. As soon as I was attired we went to the dancing hall and the first thing that I saw in that tall, scintillant chamber was the huge form of Singanee standing among the dancers and the heads of the men no higher than his waist. Bare were the huge arms that had held the spear that had avenged Perdóndaris. The chamberlain led me to him and I bowed, and said that I gave thanks to the gods to whom he looked for protection; and he said that he had heard my gods well spoken of by those accustomed to pray but this he said only of courtesy, for he knew not whom they were.

Singanee was simply dressed and only wore on his head a plain gold band to keep his hair from falling over his forehead, the ends of the gold were tied in the back with a bow of purple silk. But all his queens wore crowns of great magnificence, though whether they were crowned as the queens of Singanee or whether queens were attracted there from the thrones of distant lands by the wonder of him and the splendour I did not know.

All there wore silken robes of brilliant colours and the feet of all were bare and very shapely for the custom of boots was unknown in those regions. And when they saw that my big toes were deformed in the manner of Europeans, turning inwards towards the others instead of being straight, one or two asked sympathetically if an accident had befallen me. And rather than tell them truly that deforming out big toes was our custom and our pleasure I told them that I was under the curse of a malignant god at whose feet I had neglected to offer berries in infancy. And to some extent I justified myself, for Convention is a god though his ways are evil; and had I told them the truth I would not have been understood. They gave me a lady to dance with who was of marvellous beauty, she gold me that her name was Saranoora, a princess from the North, who had been sent as tribute to the palace of Singanee. And partly she danced as Europeans dance and partly as the fairies of the waste who lure, as legend has it, lost travellers to their doom. And if I could get thirty heathen men out of fantastic lands, with their long black hair and little elfin eyes and instruments of music even unknown to Nebuchadnezzar the King; and if I could make them play those tunes that I heard in the ivory palace on some lawn, gentle reader, at evening near your house then you would understand the beauty of Saranoora and the blaze of light and colour in that stupendous hall and the lithesome movement of those mysterious queens that danced round Singanee. Then gentle reader you would be gentle no more but the thoughts that run like leopards over the far free lands would come leaping into your head even were it London, yes, even in London: you would rise up then and beat your hands on the wall with its pretty pattern of flowers, in the hope that the bricks might break and reveal the way to that palace of ivory by the amethyst gulf where the golden dragons are. For there have been men who have burned prisons down that the prisoners might escape, and even such incendiaries those dark musicians are who dangerously burn down custom that the pining thoughts may go free. Let your elders have no fear, have no fear. I will not play those tunes in any streets we know. I will not bring those strange musicians here, I will only whisper the way to the Lands of Dream, and only a few frail feet shall find the way, and I shall dream alone of the beauty of Saranoora and sometimes sigh. We danced on and on at the will of the thirty musicians, but when the stars were paling and the wind that knew the dawn was ruffling up the edge of the skirts of night, then Saranoora the princess of the North led me out into a garden. Dark groves of trees were there which filled the night with perfume and guarded night's mysteries from the arising dawn. There floated over us, wandering in that garden, the triumphant melody of those dark musicians, whose origin was unguessed even by those that dwelt there and knew the Lands of Dream. For only a moment once sang the tolulu-bird, for the festival of that night had scared him and he was silent. For only a moment once we heard him singing in some far grove because the musicians rested and our bare feet made no sound; for a moment we heard that bird of which once our nightingale dreamed and handed on the tradition to his children. And Saranoora told me that they have named the bird the Sister of Song; but for the musicians, who presently played again, she said they had no name, for no one knew who they were or from what country. Then some one sang quite near us in the darkness to an instrument of strings telling of Singanee and his battle against the monster. And soon we saw him sitting on the ground and singing to the night of that spear-thrust that had found the thumping heart of the destroyer of Perdóndaris; and we stopped awhile and asked him who had seen so memorable a struggle and he answered none but Singanee and he whose tusk had scattered Perdóndaris, and now the last was dead. And when we asked him if Singanee had told him of the struggle he said that that proud hunter would say no word about it and that therefore his mighty deed was given to the poets and become their trust forever, and he struck again his instrument of strings and sang on.

When the strings of pearls that hung down from her neck began to gleam all over Saranoora I knew that dawn was near and that that memorable night was all but gone. And at last we left the garden and came to the abyss to see the sunrise shine on the amethyst cliff. And at first it lit up the beauty of Saranoora and then it topped the world and blazed upon those cliffs of amethyst until it dazzled our eyes, and we turned from it and saw the workman going out along the tusk to hollow it and to carve a balustrade of fair professional figures. And those who had drunken bak began to awake and to open their dazzled eyes at the amethyst precipice and to rub them and turn them away. And now those wonderful kingdoms of song that the dark musicians established all night by magical chords dropped back again to the sway of that ancient silence who ruled before the gods, and the musicians wrapped their cloaks about them and covered up their marvellous instrumentsand stole away to the plains; and no one dared ask them whither they went or why they dwelt there, or what god they served. And the dance stopped and all the queens departed. And then the female slave came out again by a door and emptied her basket of sapphires down the abyss as I saw her do before. Beautiful Saranoora said that those great queens would never wear their sapphires more than once and that every day at noon a merchant from the mountains sold new ones for that evening. Yet I suspected that something more than extravagance lay at the back of that seemingly wasteful act of tossing sapphires into an abyss, for thee were in the depths of it those two dragons of gold of whom nothing seemed to be known. And I thought, and I think so still, that Singanee, terrific though he was in war with the elephants, from whose tusks he had built his palace, well knew and even feared those dragons in the abyss, and perhaps valued those priceless jewels less than he valued his queens, and that he to whom so many lands paid beautiful tribute out of their dread of his spear, himself paid tribute to the golden dragons. Whether those dragons had wings I could not see; nor, if they had, could I tell if they could bear that weight of solid gold from the abyss; nor by what paths they could crawl from it did I know. And I know not what use to a golden dragon should sapphires be or a queen. Only it seemed strange to me that so much wealth of jewels should be thrown by command of a man who had nothing to fear—to fall flashing and changing their colours at dawn into an abyss.

I do not know how long we lingered there watching the sunrise on those miles of amethyst. And it is strange that that great and famous wonder did not move me more than it did, but my mind was dazzled by the fame of it and my eyes were actually dazzled by the blaze, and as often happens I thought more of little things and remember watching the day-light in the solitary sapphire that Saranoora had and that she wore upon her finger in a ring. Then, the dawn wind being all about her, she said that she was cold and turned back into the ivory palace. And I feared that we might never meet again, for time moves differently over the Lands of Dream than over the fields we know; like ocean-currents going different ways and bearing drifting ships. And at the doorway of the ivory palace I turned to say farewell and yet I found no words that were suitable to say. And often now when I stand in other lands I stop and think of many things to have said; yet all I said was "Perhaps we shall meet again." And she said that it was likely that we should often meet for that this was a little thing for the gods to permit not knowing that the gods of the Lands of Dream have little power upon the fields we know. Then she went in through the doorway. And having exchanged for my own clothes again the raiment that the chamberlain had given me I turned from the hospitality of mighty Singanee and set my face towards the fields we know. I crossed that enormous tusk that had been the end of Perdóndaris and met the artists carving it as I went; and some by way of greeting as I passed extolled Singanee, and in answer I gave honour to his name. Daylight had not yet penetrated wholly to the bottom of the abyss but the darkness was giving place to a purple haze and I could faintly see one golden dragon there. Then looking once towards the ivory palace, and seeing no one at the windows, I turned sorrowfully away, and going by the way that I knew passed through the gap in the mountains and down their slopes till I came again in sight of the witch's cottage. And as I went to the upper window to look for the fields we know, the witch spoke to me; but I was cross, as one newly waked from sleep, and I would not answer her. Then the cat questioned me as to whom I had met, and I answered him that in the fields we know cats kept their place and did not speak to man. And then I came downstairs and walked straight out of the door, heading for Go-by Street. "You are going the wrong way," the witch called through the window; and indeed I had sooner gone back to the ivory palace again, but I had no right to trespass any further on the hospitality of Singanee and one cannot stay always in the Lands of Dream, and what knowledge had that old witch of the call of the fields we know or the little though many snares that bind our feet therein? So I paid no heed to her, but kept on, and came to Go-by Street. I saw the house with the green door some way up the street but thinking that the near end of the street was closer to the Embankment where I had left my boat I tried the first door I came to, a cottage thatched like the rest, with little golden spires along the roof-ridge, and strange birds sitting there and preening marvellous feathers. The door opened, and to my surprise I found myself in what seemed like a shepherd's cottage; a man who was sitting on a log of wood in a little low dark room said something to me in an alien language. I muttered something and hurried through to the street. The house was thatched in front as well as behind. There were not golden spires in front, no marvellous birds; but there was no pavement. There was a row of houses, byres, and barns but no other sign of a town. Far off I saw one or two little villages. Yet there was the river—and no doubt the Thames, for it was the width of the Thames and had the curves of it, if you can imagine the Thames in that particular spot without a city around it, without any bridges, and the Embankment fallen in. I saw that there had happened to me permanently and in the light of day some such thing as happens to a man, but to a child more often, when he awakes before morning in some strange room and sees a high, grey window where the door ought to be and unfamiliar objects in wrong places and though knowing where he is yet knows not how it can be that the place should look like that.

A flock of sheep came by me presently looking the same as ever, but the man who led them had a wild, strange look. I spoke to him and he did not understand me. Then I went down to the river to see if my boat was there and at the very spot where I had left it, in the mud (for the tide was low) I saw a half-buried piece of blackened wood that might have been part of a boat, but I could not tell. I began to feel that I had missed the world. It would be a strange thing to travel from far away to see London and not be able to find it among all the roads that lead there, but I seemed to have travelled in Time and to have missed it among the centuries. And when as I wandered over the grassy hills I came on a wattled shrine that was thatched with straw and saw a lion in it more worn with time than even the Sphinx at Gizeh and when I knew it for one of the four in Trafalgar Square then I saw that I was stranded far away in the future with many centuries of treacherous years between me and anything that I had known. And then I sat on the grass by the worn paws of the lion to think out what to do. And I decided to go back through Go-by Street and, since there was nothing left to keep me any more to the fields we know, to offer myself as a servant in the palace of Singanee, and to see again the face of Saranoora and those famous, wonderful, amethystine dawns upon the abyss where the golden dragons play. And I stayed no longer to look for remains of the ruins of London; for there is little pleasure in seeing wonderful things if there is no one at all to hear of them and to wonder. So I returned at once to Go-by Street, the little row of huts, and saw no other record that London had been except that one stone lion. I went to the right house this time. It was very much altered and more like one of those huts that one sees on Salisbury plain than a shop in the city of London, but I found it by counting the houses in the street for it was still a row of houses though pavement and city were gone. And it was still a shop. A very different shop to the one I knew, but things were for sale there—shepherd's crooks, food, and rude axes. And a man with long hair was there who was clad in skins. I did not speak to him for I did not know his language. He said to me something that sounded like "Everkike." It conveyed no meaning to me; but when he looked towards one of his buns, light suddenly dawned in my mind, and I knew that England was even England still and that still she was not conquered, and that though they had tired of London they still held to their land; for the words that the man had said were, "Av er kike," and then I knew that that very language that was carried to distant lands by the old, triumphant cockney was spoken still in his birthplace and that neither his politics nor his enemies had destroyed him after all these thousand years. I had always disliked the Cockney dialect—and with the arrogance of the Irishman who hears from rich and poor the English of the splendour of Elizabeth; and yet when I heard those words my eyes felt sore as with impending tears—it should be remembered how far away I was. I think I was silent for a little while. Suddenly I saw that the man who kept the shop was asleep. That habit was strangely like the ways of a man who if he were then alive would be (if I could judge from the time-worn look of the lion) over a thousand years old. But then how old was I? It is perfectly clear that Time moves over the Lands of Dream swifter or slower than over the fields we know. For the dead, and the long dead, live again in our dreams; and a dreamer passes through the events of days in a single moment of the Town-Hall's clock. Yet logic did not aid me and my mind was puzzled. While the old man slept—and strangely like in face he was to the old man who had shown me first the little, old backdoor—I went to the far end of his wattled shop. There was a door of a sort on leather hinges. I pushed it open and there I was again under the notice-board at the back of the shop, at least the back of Go-by Street had not changed. Fantastic and remote though this grass street was with its purple flowers and the golden spires, and the world ending at its opposite pavement, yet I breathed more happily to see something again that I had seen before. I thought I had lost forever the world I knew, and now that I was at the back of Go-by Street again I felt the loss less than when I was standing where familiar things ought to be; and I turned my mind to what was left me in the vast Lands of Dream and thought of Saranoora. And when I saw the cottages again I felt less lonely even at the thought of the cat though he generally laughed at the things I said. And the first thing that I saw when I saw the witch was that I had lost the world and was going back for the rest of my days to the palace of Singanee. And the first thing that she said was: "Why! You've been through the wrong door," quite kindly for she saw how unhappy I looked. And I said, "Yes, but it's all the same street. The whole street's altered and London's gone and the people I used to know and the houses I used to rest in, and everything; and I'm tired."

"What did you want to go through the wrong door for?" she said.

"O, that made no difference," I said.

"O, didn't it?" she said in a contradictory way.

"Well I wanted to get to the near end of the street so as to find my boat quickly by the Embankment. And now my boat, and the Embankment and—and——."

"Some people are always in such a hurry," said the old black cat. And I felt too unhappy to be angry and I said nothing more.

And the old witch said, "Now which way do you want to go?" and she was talking rather like a nurse to a small child. And I said, "I have nowhere to go."

And she said, "Would you rather go home or go to the ivory palace of Singanee." And I said, "I've got a headache, and I don't want to go anywhere, and I'm tired of the Lands of Dream."

"Then suppose you try going in through the right door," she said.

"That's no good," I said. "Everyone's dead and gone, and they're selling buns there."

"What do you know about Time?" she said.

"Nothing," answered the old, black cat, though nobody spoke to him.

"Run along," said the old witch.

So I turned and trudged away to Go-by Street again. I was very tired. "What does he know about anything?" said the old black cat behind me. I knew what he was going to say next. He waited a moment and then said, "Nothing." When I looked over my shoulder he was strutting back to the cottage. And when I got to Go-by Street I listlessly opened the door through which I had just now come. I saw no use in doing it, I just did wearily as I was told. And the moment I got inside I saw it was just the same as of old, and the sleepy old man was there who sold idols. And I bought a vulgar thing that I did not want, for the sheer joy of seeing accustomed things. And when I turned from Go-by Street which was just the same as ever, the first thing that I saw was a taximeter running into a hansom cab. And I took off my hat and cheered. And I went to the Embankment and there was my boat, and the stately river full of dirty, accustomed things. And I rowed back and bought a penny paper, (I had been away it seemed for one day) and I read it from cover to cover—patent remedies for incurable illnesses and all—and I determined to walk, as soon as I was rested, in all the streets that I knew and to call on all the people that I had ever met, and to be content for long with the fields we know.

UNHAPPY FAR-OFF THINGS (1916)

PREFACE

I have chosen a title that shall show that I make no claim for this book to be "up-to-date." As the first title indicates, I hoped to show, to as many as might to read my words, something of the extent of the wrongs that the people of France had suffered. There is no such need any longer. The tales, so far as they went, I gather together here for the few that seem to read my books in England.

—Dunsany

A DIRGE OF VICTORY (SONNET)

Lift not thy trumpet, Victory, to the sky,
*   Nor through battalions nor by batteries blow,*
*   But over hollows full of old wire go,*
Where among dregs of war the long-dead lie
With wasted iron that the guns passed by.
*   When they went eastwards like a tide at flow;*
*   There blow thy trumpet that the dead may know,*
Who waited for thy coming, Victory.
It is not we that have deserved thy wreath,
*   They waited there among the towering weeds.*
The deep mud burned under the thermite's breath,
*   And winter cracked the bones that no man heeds:*
Hundreds of nights flamed by: the seasons passed.
And thou last come to them at last, at last!

THE CATHEDRAL OF ARRAS

On the great steps of Arras Cathedral I saw a procession, in silence, standing still.

They were in orderly and perfect lines, stirring or swaying slightly: sometimes they bent their heads, sometimes two leaned together, but for the most part they were motionless. It was the time when the fashion is just changing and some were newly all in shining yellow, while others still wore green.

I went up the steps amongst them, the only human thing, for men and women worship no more in Arras Cathedral, and the trees have come instead; little humble things, all less than four years old, in great numbers thronging the steps processionally, and growing in perfect rows just where step meets step. They have come to Arras with the wind and the rain; which enter the aisles together whenever they will, and go wherever man went; they have such a reverent air, the young limes on the three flights of steps, that you would say they did not know that Arras Cathedral was fallen on evil days, that they did not know they looked on ruin and vast disaster, but thought that these great walls open to stars and sun were the natural and fitting place for the worship of little weeds.

Behind them the shattered houses of Arras seemed to cluster about the cathedral as, one might fancy easily, hurt and frightened children, so wistful are their gaping windows and old, grey empty gables, so melancholy and puzzled. They are more like a little old people come upon trouble, gazing at their great elder companion and not knowing what to do.

But the facts of Arras are sadder than a poet's most tragic fancies. In the western front of Arras Cathedral stand eight pillars rising from the ground; above them stood four more. Of the four upper pillars the two on the left are gone, swept away by shells from the north: and a shell has passed through the neck of one of the two that is left, just as a bullet might go through a daffodil's stem.

The left-hand corner of that western wall has been caught from the north, by some tremendous shell which has torn the whole corner down in a mound of stone: and still the walls have stood.

I went in through the western doorway. All along the nave lay a long heap of white stones, with grass and weeds on the top, and a little trodden path over the grass and weeds. This is all that remained of the roof of Arras Cathedral and of any chairs or pews there may have been in the nave, or anything that may have hung above them. It was all down but one slender arch that crossed the nave just at the transept; it stood out against the sky, and all who saw it wondered how it stood.

In the southern aisle panes of green glass, in twisted frame of lead, here and there lingered, like lonely leaves on an apple-tree-after a hailstorm in spring. The aisles still had their roofs over them which those stout old walls held up in spite of all.

Where the nave joins the transept the ruin is most enormous. Perhaps there was more to bring down there, so the Germans brought it down: there may have been a tower there, for all I know, or a spire.

I stood on the heap and looked towards the altar. To my left all was ruin. To my right two old saints in stone stood by the southern door. The door had been forced open long ago, and stood as it was opened, partly broken. A great round hole gaped in the ground outside; it was this that had opened the door.

Just beyond the big heap, on the left of the chancel, stood something made of wood, which almost certainly had been the organ.

As I looked at these things there passed through the desolate sanctuaries, and down an aisle past pillars pitted with shrapnel, a sad old woman, sad even for a woman of North-East France. She seemed to be looking after the mounds and stones that had once been the cathedral; perhaps she had once been the Bishop's servant, or the wife of one of the vergers; she only remained of all who had been there in other days, she and the pigeons and jackdaws. I spoke to her. All Arras, she said, was ruined. The great cathedral was ruined, her own family were ruined utterly, and she pointed to where the sad houses gazed from forlorn dead windows. Absolute ruin, she said; but there must be no armistice. No armistice. No. It was necessary that there should be no armistice at all. No armistice with Germans.

She passed on, resolute and sad, and the guns boomed on beyond Arras.

A French interpreter, with the Sphinxes' heads on his collar, showed me a picture postcard with a photograph of the chancel as it was five years ago. It was the very chancel before which I was standing. To see that photograph astonished me, and to know that the camera that took it must have stood where I was standing, only a little lower down, under the great heap. Though one knew there had been an altar there, and candles and roof and carpet, and all the solemnity of a cathedral's interior, yet to see that photograph and to stand on that weedy heap, in the wind, under the jackdaws, was a contrast with which the mind fumbled.

I walked a little with the French interpreter. We came to a little shrine in the southern aisle. It had been all paved with marble, and the marble was broken into hundreds of pieces, and someone had carefully picked up all the bits, and laid them together on the altar.

And this pathetic heap that was gathered of broken bits had drawn many to stop and gaze at it; and idly, as soldiers will, they had written their names on them: every bit had a name on it, with but a touch of irony the Frenchman said, "All that is necessary to bring your name to posterity is to write it on one of these stones.," "No," I said, "I will do it by describing all this." And we both laughed.

I have not done it yet: there is more to say of Arras. As I begin the tale of ruin and wrong, the man who did it totters. His gaudy power begins to stream away like the leaves of autumn. Soon his throne will be bare, and I shall have but begun to say what I have to say of calamity in cathedral and little gardens of Arras.

The winter of the Hohenzollerns will come; sceptre, uniforms, stars and courtiers all gone; still the world will not know half of the bitter wrongs of Arras. And spring will bring a new time and cover the trenches with green, and the pigeons will preen themselves on the shattered towers, and the lime-trees along the steps will grow taller and brighter, and happier men will sing in the streets untroubled by any War Lord; by then, perhaps, I may have told, to such as care to read, what such a war did in an ancient town, already romantic when romance was young, when war came suddenly without mercy, without pity, out of the north and east, on little houses, carved galleries, and gardens; churches, cathedrals and the jackdaws' nests.

A GOOD WAR

Nietsche said, "You have heard that a good cause justifies any war, but I say unto you that a good war justifies any cause."

A man was walking alone over a plain so desolate that, if you have never seen it, the mere word desolation could never convey to you the melancholy surroundings that mourned about this man on his lonely walk. Far off a vista of trees followed a cheerless road all dead as mourners suddenly stricken dead in some funereal procession. By this road he had come; but when he had reached a certain point he turned from the road at once, branching away to the left, led by a line of bushes that may once have been a lane. For some while his feet had rustled through long neglected grass; sometimes he lifted them up to step over a telephone wire that lolled over old entanglements and bushes; often he came to rusty strands of barbed wire and walked through them where they had been cut, perhaps years ago, by huge shells; then his feet hissed on through the grass again, dead grass that had hissed about his boots all through the afternoon.

Once he sat down to rest on the edge of a crater, weary with such walking as he had never seen before; and after he had stayed there a little while a cat that seemed to have its home in that wild place started suddenly up and leaped away over the weeds. It seemed an animal totally wild, and utterly afraid of man.

Grey bare hills surrounded the waste: a partridge called far off: evening was drawing in. He rose wearily, and yet with a certain fervour, as one that pursues With devotion a lamentable quest. Looking round him as he left his resting-place he saw a cabbage or two that after some while had come back to what was a field and had sprouted on the edge of a shell-hole. A yellowing convolvulus climbed up a dead weed. Weeds, grass and tumbled earth were all about him. It would be no better when he went on. Still he went on. A flower or two peeped up among the weeds. He stood up and looked at the landscape and drew no hope from that, the shattered trunk of a stricken tree leered near him, white trenches scarred the hillside. He followed an old trench through a hedge of elder, passed under more wire, by a great rusty shell that had not burst, passed by a dug-out where something grey seemed to lie down at the bottom of many steps. Black fungi grew near the entrance. He went on and on over shell-holes, passing round them where they were deep, stepping into or over the small ones. Little burrs clutched at him; he went rustling on, the only sound in the waste but the clicking of shattered iron. Now he was among nettles. He came by many small unnatural valleys. He passed more trenches only guarded by fungi. While it was light he followed little paths, marvelling who made them. Once he got into a trench. Dandelions leaned across it as though to bar his way, believing man to have gone and to have no right to return. Weeds thronged, in thousands here. It was the day of the weeds. It was only they that seemed to triumph in those fields deserted of man. He passed on down the trench and never knew whose trench it once had been. Frightful shells had smashed it here and there, and had twisted iron as though round gigantic fingers that had twiddled it idly a moment and let it drop to lie in the rain for ever. He passed more dug-outs and black fungi, watching them; and then he left the trench, going straight on over the open: again dead grasses hissed about his feet, sometimes small wire sang faintly He passed through a belt of nettles and thence to dead grass again. And now the light of the afternoon was beginning to dwindle away. He had intended to reach his journey's end by daylight, for he was past the time of life when one wanders after dark, but he had not contemplated the difficulty of walking over that road, or dreamed that lanes he knew could be so foundered and merged, in that mournful desolate moor.

Evening was filling fast, still he kept on. It was the time when the cornstacks would once have begun to grow indistinct, and slowly turn grey in the greyness, and homesteads one by one would have lit their innumerable lights. But evening now came down on a dreary desolation: and a cold wind arose; and the traveller heard the mournful sound of iron flapping on broken things, and knew that this was the sound that would haunt the waste for ever.

And evening settled down, a huge grey canvas waiting for sombre pictures; a setting for all the dark tales of the world, haunted forever a grizzly place was haunted ever, in any century, in any land; but not by mere ghosts from all those thousands of graves and half-buried bodies and sepulchral shell-holes; haunted by things huger and more disastrous than that; haunted by wailing ambitions, under the stars or moon, drifting across the rubbish that once was villages, which strews the lonely plain; the lost ambitions of two Emperors and a Sultan wailing from wind to wind and whimpering for dominion of the world.

The cold wind blew over the blasted heath and bits of broken iron flapped on and on.

And now the traveller hurried, for night was falling, and such a night as three witches might have brewed in a cauldron. He went on eagerly but with infinite sadness. Over the sky-line strange rockets went up from the war, peered oddly over the earth and went down again. Very far off a few soldiers lit a little fire of their own. The night grew colder; tap, tap, went broken iron.

And at last the traveller stopped in the lonely night and looked round him attentively, and appeared to be satisfied that he had come within sight of his journey's end, although to ordinary eyes the spot to which he had come differed in no way from the rest of the waste.

He went no further, but turned round and round, peering piece by piece at that weedy and cratered earth.

He was looking for the village where he was born.

THE HOUSE WITH TWO STOREYS

I came again to Croisilles.

I looked for the sunken road that we used to hold in support, with its row of little shelters in the bank and the carved oak saints above them here and there that had survived the church in Croisilles. I could have found it with my eyes shut. With my eyes open I could not find it. I did not recognize the lonely metalled road down which lorries were rushing for the little lane so full of life, whose wheel-ruts were three years old.

As I gazed about me looking for our line, I passed an old French civilian looking down at a slight mound of white stone that rose a little higher than the road. He was walking about uncertainly, when first I noticed him, as though he was not sure where he was. But now he stood quite still looking down at the mound.

"Voilà ma maison," he said.

He said no more than that: this astounding remark, this gesture that indicated such calamity, were quite simply made. There was nothing whatever of theatrical pose that we wrongly associate with the French, because they conceal their emotions less secretly than we; there were no tragic tones in his voice: only a trace of deep affection showed in one of the words he used. He spoke as a woman might say of her only child, "Look at *my* baby."

"Voilà ma maison," he said.

I tried to say in his language what I felt; and after my attempt he spoke of his house.

It was very old. Down underneath, he said, it dated from feudal times; though I did not quite make out whether all that lay under that mound had been so old or whether he only meant the cellars of his house. It was a fine high house, he said, as much as two storeys high. No one that is familiar with houses of fifty storeys, none even that has known palaces, will smile at this old man's efforts to tell of his high house, and to make me believe that it rose to two storeys high, as we stood together by that sad white mound. He told me that his son was killed. And that disaster strangely did not move me so much as the white mound that had been a house and had had two storeys, for it seems to be common to every French family with whose fathers I have chanced to speak in ruined cities or on busy roads of France.

He pointed to a huge white mound beyond on the top of which someone had stuck a small cross of wood. "The church," he said. And that I knew already.

In very inadequate French I tried to comfort him. I told him that surely France would build his house again. Perhaps even the allies; for I could not believe that we shall have done enough if we merely drive the Germans out of France and leave this poor old man still wandering homeless. I told him that surely in the future Croisilles would stand again.

He took no interest in anything that I said. His house of two storeys was down, his son was dead, the little village of Croisilles had gone away; he had only one hope from the future. When I had finished speaking of the future, he raised a knobbed stick that he carried, up to the level of his throat, surely his son's old trench stick, and there he let it dangle from a piece of string in the handle, which he held against his neck. He watched me shrewdly and attentively meanwhile, for I was a stranger and was to be taught something I might not know—a thing that it was necessary for all men to learn. "Le Kaiser," he said. "Yes;" I said, "the Kaiser." But I pronounced the word Kaiser differently from him, and he repeated again "Le Kaiser," and watched me closely to be sure that I understood. And then he said "Pendu," and made the stick quiver a little as it dangled from its string. "Oui," I said, "Pendu."

Did I understand? He was not yet quite sure. It was important that this thing should be quite decided between us as we stood on this road through what had been Croisilles, where he had lived through many sunny years and I had dwelt for a season amongst rats. "Pendu" he said. Yes, I agreed.

It was all right. The old man almost smiled.

I offered him a cigarette and we lit two from an apparatus of flint and steel and petrol that the old man had in his pocket.

He showed me a photograph of himself and a passport to prove, I suppose, that he was not a spy. One could not recognize the likeness, for it must have been taken on some happier day, before he had seen his house of two storeys lying there by the road. But he was no spy, for there were tears in his eyes; and Prussians I think have no tears for what we saw across the village of Croisilles.

I spoke of the rebuilding of his house no more, I spoke no more of the new Croisilles shining through future years; for these were not the things that he saw in the future, and these were not the hopes of the poor old man. He had one dark hope of the future, and no others. He hoped to see the Kaiser hung for the wrong he had done to Croisilles. It was for this hope he lived.

Madame or señor of whatever far country, who may chance to see these words, blame not this old man for the fierce hope he cherished. It was the only hope he had. You, Madame, with your garden, your house, your church, the village where all know you, you may hope as a Christian should, there is wide room for hope in your future. You shall see the seasons move over your garden, you shall busy yourself with your home, and speak and share with your neighbours innumerable small joys, and find consolation and beauty, and at last rest, in and around the church whose spire you see from your home. You, señor, with your son perhaps growing up, perhaps wearing already some sword that you wore once, you can turn back to your memories or look with hope to the future with equal ease.

The man that I met in Croisilles had none of these things at all. He had that one hope only.

Do not, I pray you, by your voice or vote, or by any power or influence that you have, do anything to take away from this poor old Frenchman the only little hope he has left. The more trivial his odd hope appears to you compared with your own high hopes that come so easily to you amongst all your fields and houses, the more cruel a thing must it be to take it from him.

I learned many things in Croisilles, and the last of them is this strange one the old man taught me. I turned and shook hands with him and said good-bye, for I wished to see again our old front line that we used to hold over the hill, now empty, silent at last. "The Boche is defeated," I said.

"Vaincu, vaincu," he repeated. And I left him with something almost like happiness looking out of his tearful eyes.

BERMONDSEY VERSUS WURTEMBURG

The trees grew thinner and thinner along the road, then ceased altogether, and suddenly we saw Albert in the wood of the ghosts of murdered trees, all grey and deserted.

Descending into Albert past trees in their agony we came all at once on the houses. You did not see them far off as in other cities; we came on them all at once as you come on a corpse in the grass.

We stopped and stood by a house that was covered with plaster marked off to look like great stones, its pitiful pretence laid bare, the slates gone and the rooms gone, the plaster all pitted with shrapnel. Near it lay an iron railing, a hand-rail blown there from the railway bridge; a shrapnel bullet had passed through its twisted stem as though it had gone through butter. And beside the hand-rail lay one of the great steel supports of the bridge that had floated there upon some flaming draught; the end of it bent and splayed as though it had been a slender cane that someone had shoved too hard into the earth.

There had been a force abroad in Albert that could do these things, an iron force that had no mercy for iron, a mighty mechanical contrivance that could take machinery and pull it all to pieces in a moment as a child takes a flower to pieces petal by petal.

When such a force was abroad what chance had man? It had come down upon Albert suddenly, and railway lines and bridges had drooped and withered and the houses had stooped down in the blasting heat, and in that attitude I found them still, worn-out, melancholy heaps overcome by disaster.

Pieces of paper rustled about like footsteps, dirt covered the ruins, fragments of rusty shells lay as unsightly and dirty as that which they had destroyed. Cleaned up and polished, and priced at half a crown apiece, these fragments may look romantic some day in a London shop, but to-day in Albert they look unclean and untidy, like a cheap knife sticking up from a murdered woman's ribs, whose dress is long out of fashion.

The stale smell of war arose from the desolation.

A British helmet dinted in like an old bowler, but tragic not absurd, lay near a barrel and a teapot.

On a wall that rose above a heap of dirty and smashed rafters was written in red paint KOMPe I.M.B.K. 184. The red paint had dripped down the wall from every letter. Verily we stood upon the scene of the murder.

Opposite those red letters across the road was a house with traces of a pleasant ornament below the sills of the windows, a design of grapes and vine. Someone had stuck up a wooden boot on a peg outside the door.

Perhaps the cheery design on the wall attracted me. I entered the house and looked round.

A chunk of shell lay on the floor, and a little decanter, only chipped at the lip, and part of a haversack of horse-skin. There were pretty tiles on the floor, but dry mud buried them deep: it was like the age-old dirt that gathers in temples in Africa. A man's waistcoat lay on the mud and part of a woman's stays: the waistcoat was black and was probably kept for Sundays. That was all that there was to see on the ground floor, no more flotsam than that had come down to these days from peace.

A forlorn stairway tried still to wind upstairs. It went up out of a corner of the room. It seemed still to believe that there was an upper storey, still to feel that this was a house, there seemed a hope in the twists of that battered staircase that men would yet come again and seek sleep at evening by way of those broken steps; the hand-rail and the banisters streamed down from the top, a woman's dress lolled down from the upper room above those aimless steps, the laths of the ceiling gaped, the plaster was gone; of all the hopes men hope that can never be fulfilled, of all desires that ever come too late, most futile was the hope expressed by that stairway's posture that ever a family would come home there again or tread those steps once more. And, if in some far country one should hope, who has not seen Albert, out of compassion for these poor people of France, that where a staircase still remains there may be enough of a house to shelter those who called it home again, I will tell one thing more: there blew inside that house the same wind that blew outside, the wind that wandered free over miles of plains wandered unchecked through that house; there was no indoors or outdoors any more.

And on the wall of the room in which I stood, someone had proudly written his regiment's name, The 156th Wurtemburgers. It was written in chalk; and another man had come and had written two words before it and had recorded the name of his own regiment too. And the writing remains after these two men are gone, and the lonely house is silent but for the wind and the things that creak as it blows, the only message of this deserted house, is this mighty record, this rare line of history, ill-written: "Lost by the 156th Wurtemburgers, retaken by the Bermondsey Butterflies."

Two men wrote that sentence between them. And, as with Homer, no one knows who they were. And; like Homer, their words were epic.

ON AN OLD BATTLE-FIELD

I entered an old battle-field through a garden gate, a pale green gate by the. Bapaume-Arras road. The cheerful green attracted me in the deeps of the desolation as an emerald might in a dust-bin. I entered through that homely garden gate, it had no hinges, no pillars, it lolled on a heap of stone: I came to it from the road; this alone was not battle-field; the road alone was made and tended and kept; all the rest was battle-field, as far as the eye could see. Over a large whitish heap lay a Virginia creeper, turning a dull crimson. And the presence of this creeper mourning there in the waste showed unmistakably that the heap had been a house. All the living things were gone that had called this white heap Home: the father would be fighting, somewhere; the children would have fled, if there had been time; the dog would have gone with them, or perhaps, if there was not time, he served other masters; the cat would have made a lair for herself and stalked mice at night through the trenches. All the live things that we ever consider were gone; the creeper alone remained, the only mourner, clinging to fallen stones that had supported it once.

And I knew by its presence here there had been a house. And by the texture or composition of the ruin all round I saw that a village had stood there. There are calamities one does not contemplate, when one thinks of time and change. Death, passing away, even ruin, are all the human lot; but one contemplates ruin as brought by kindly ages, coming slowly at last, with lichen and ivy and moss, its harsher aspects all hidden with green, coming with dignity and in due season. Thus our works should pass away; our worst fears contemplated no more than this.

But here in a single day, perhaps in a moment with one discharge from a battery, all the little things that one family cared for, their house, their garden; and the garden paths, and then the village and the road through the village, and the old landmarks that the old people remembered, and count-less treasured things, were all turned into rubbish.

And these things that one did not contemplate, have happened for hun-dreds of miles, with such disaster vast plains and hills are covered, because of the German war.

Deep wells, old cellars, battered trenches and dug-outs, lie in the rub-bish and weeds under the intricate wreckage of peace and war. It will be a bad place years hence for wanderers lost at night.

When the village went, trenches came; and, in the same storm that had crumbled the village, the trenches withered too; shells still thump on to the north, but peace and war alike have deserted the village. Grass has begun to return over torn earth on edges of trenches. Abundant wire rusts away by its twisted stakes of steel. Not a path of old, not a lane nor a doorway there, but is barred and cut off by wire; and the wire in its turn has been cut by shells and lies in ungathered swathes. A pair of wheels moulders amongst weeds, and may be of peace or of war, it is too broken down for anyone to say. A great bar of iron lies cracked across as though one of the elder giants had handled it carelessly. Another mound near by, with an old green beam sticking out of it, was also once a house. A trench runs by it. A Ger-man bomb with its wooden handle, some bottles, a bucket, a petrol tin and some bricks and stones, lie in the trench. A young elder tree grows amongst them. And over all the ruin and rubbish Nature, with all her wealth and luxury, comes back to her old inheritance, holding again the land that she held so long, before the houses came.

A garden gate of iron has been flung across a wall. Then a deep cellar into which a whole house seems to have slanted down. In the midst of all this is an orchard. A huge shell has uprooted, but not killed, an apple-tree; another apple-tree stands stone dead on the edge of a crater: most of the trees are dead. British aeroplanes drone over continually. A great gun goes by towards Bapaume, dragged by a slow engine with caterpillar wheels. The gun is all blotched green and yellow. Four or five men are seated on the huge barrel alone.

Dark old steps near the orchard run down into a dug-out, with a car-tridge-case tied to a piece of wood beside it to beat when the gas came. A telephone wire lies listlessly by the opening. A patch of Michaelmas dai-sies, deep mauve and pale mauve, and a bright yellow flower beside them, show where a garden used to stand near by. Above the dug-out a patch of jagged earth shows in three clear layers under the weeds: four inches of grey road metal, imported, for all this country is chalk and clay; two inches of flint below it, and under that an inch of a bright red stone. We are look-ing then at a road—a road through a village trodden by men and women, and the hooves of horses and familiar modern things, a road so buried, so shattered, so overgrown, showing by chance an edge in the midst of the wilderness, that I could seem rather to have discovered the track of the

Dinosaur in prehistoric clays than the highway, of a little village that only five years ago was full of human faults and joys and songs and tiny tears. Down that road before the plans, of the Kaiser began to fumble with the earth, down that road—but it is useless to look back, we are too far away from five years ago, too far away from thousands of ordinary things, that never seemed as though they would ever peer at us over chasms of time, out of another age, utterly far off, irrevocably removed from our ways and days. They are gone, those times, gone like the Dinosaur; gone with bows and arrows and the old knightlier days. No splendour marks their sunset where I sit, no dignity of houses, or derelict engines of war, mined all equally are scattered dirtily in the mud, and common weeds overpower them; it is not ruin but rubbish that covers the ground here and spreads its untidy flood for hundreds and hundreds of miles.

A band plays in Arras, to the north and east the shells go thumping on.

The very origins of things are in doubt, so much is jumbled together. It is as hard to make out just where the trenches ran, and which was No-Man's-Land, as it is to tell the houses from garden and orchard and road: the rubbish covers all. It is as though the ancient forces of Chaos had come back from the abyss to fight against order and man, and Chaos had won. So lies this village of France.

As I left it a rat, with something in its mouth, holding its head high, ran right across the village.

THE REAL THING

Once at manoeuvres as the Prussian Crown Prince charged at the head of his regiment, as sabres gleamed, plumes streamed, and hooves thundered behind him, he is reported to have said to one that galloped near him: "Ah, if only this were the real thing!"

One need not doubt that the report is true. So a young man might feel as he led his regiment of cavalry, for the scene would fire the blood; all those young men and fine uniforms and good horses, all coming on behind, everything streaming that could float on the air, everything jingling then which could ever make a sound, a bright sky no doubt over the uniforms, a good fresh wind for men and horses to gulp; and behind, the clinking and jingling, the long roll of hooves thundering. Such a scene might well stir emotions to sigh for the splendours of battle.

This is one side of war. Mutilation and death are another; misery, cold and dirt; pain, and the intense loneliness of men left behind by armies, with much to think of; no hope, and a day or two to live. But we understand that glory covers that.

There is yet a third side.

I came to Albert when the fight was far from it: only at night you saw any signs of war, when clouds flashed now and then and curious rockets peered. Albert robbed of peace was deserted even by war.

I will not say that Albert was devastated or desolate, for these long words have different interpretations and may easily be exaggerated. A German agent might say to you, "Devastated is rather a strong word, and desolate is a matter of opinion." And so you might never know what Albert is like.

I will tell you what I saw.

Albert was a large town. I will not write of all of it.

I sat down near a railway bridge at the edge of the town; I think I was near the station; and small houses had stood there with little gardens; such as porters and other railway folk would have lived in. I sat down on the railway and looked at one of these houses, for it had clearly been a house. It was at the back of it that most remained, in what must have been a garden. A girder torn up like a pack of cards lay on the leg of a table amongst a brick wall by an apple-tree.

Lower down in the heap was the frame-work of a large four-poster bed; through it all a vine came up quite green and still alive; and at the edge of the heap lay a doll's green pram. Small though the house had been there was evidence in that heap of some prosperity in more than one generation. For the four-poster bed had been a fine one, good work in sound old timber, before the bits in the girder had driven it into the wall; and the green pram must have been the dowry of no ordinary, doll, but one with the best yellow curls whose blue eyes could move. One blue columbine close by mourned alone for the garden.

The wall and the vine and the bed and the girder lay in an orchard, and some of the apple-trees were standing yet, though the orchard had been terribly wrecked by shell fire. All that still stood were dead. Some stood upon the very edge of craters; their leaves and twigs and bark had been stripped by one blast in a moment; and they had tottered, with stunted, black, gesticulating branches; and so they stood today.

The curls of a mattress lay on the ground, clipped once from a horse's mane.

After looking for some while across the orchard one suddenly noticed that the cathedral had stood on the other side. It was draped, when we saw it closer, as with a huge grey cloak, the lead of its roof having come down and covered it.

Near the house of that petted doll (as I came to think of it) a road ran by on the other side of the railway. Great shells had dropped along it with terrible regularity. You could imagine Death striding down it with exact five-yard paces, on his own day, claiming his own. As I stood on the road something whispered behind me; and I saw, stirring round with the wind, in one of those footsteps of Death, a double page of a book open at Chapter

II: and Chapter II was headed with the proverb, "Un Malheur Ne Vient Jamais Seul;" Misfortunes never come singly! And on that dreadful road, with shell-holes every five yards as far as the eye could see, and flat beyond it the whole city in ruin. What harmless girl or old man had been reading that dreadful prophecy when the Germans came down upon Albert and involved it, and themselves, and that book, all except those two pages, in such multiplication of ruin?

Surely, indeed, there is a third side to war: for what had the doll done, that used to have a green pram, to deserve to share thus in the fall and punishment of an Emperor?

A GARDEN OF ARRAS

As I walked through Arras from the Spanish gate, gardens flashed as I went, one by one, through the houses.

I stepped in over the window-sill of one of the houses, attracted by the gleam of a garden dimly beyond: and went through the empty house, empty of people, empty of furniture, empty of plaster, and entered the garden through an empty doorway.

When I came near it seemed less like a garden. At first it had almost seemed to beckon to passers-by in the street, so rare are gardens now in this part of France, that it seemed to have more than a garden's share of mystery, all in the silence there at the back of the silent house; but when one entered it some of the mystery went, and seemed to hide in a further part of the garden amongst wild shrubs and innumerable weeds.

British aeroplanes frequently roared over, disturbing the congregation of Arras Cathedral a few hundred yards away, who rose cawing and wheeled over the garden; for only jackdaws come to Arras Cathedral now, besides a few pigeons.

Unkempt beside me a bamboo flourished wildly, having no need of man. On the other side of the small wild track that had been the garden path the skeletons of hothouses stood, surrounded by nettles; their pipes lay all about, shattered and riddled through.

Branches of rose break up through the myriad nettles, but only to be seized and choked by columbine. A late moth looks for flowers not quite in vain. It hovers on wing-beats that are invisibly swift by its lonely autumn flower, then darts away over the desolation which is no desolation to a moth: man has destroyed man; nature comes back; it is well: that must be the brief philosophy of myriads of tiny things whose way of life one seldom considered before; now that man's cities are down, now that ruin and misery confront us whichever way we turn, one notices more the small things that are left.

One of the greenhouses is almost all gone, a tumbled mass that might be a piece of Babylon, if archæologists should come to study it. But it is too sad to study, too untidy to have any interest, and, alas, too common: there are hundreds of miles of this.

The other greenhouse, a sad, ungainly skeleton, is possessed by grass and weeds. On the raised centre many flower-pots were neatly arranged once: they stand in orderly lines, but each separate one is broken: none contain flowers any more, but only grass. And the glass of the greenhouse lies there in showers, all grey. No one has tidied anything up there for years.

A meadow-sweet had come into that greenhouse and dwelt there in that abode of fine tropical flowers, and one night an elder tree had entered and is now as high as the house, and at the end of the greenhouse grass has come in like a wave; for change and disaster are far-reaching and are only mirrored here. This desolate garden and its mined house are a part of hundreds of thousands such, or millions. Mathematics will give you no picture of what France has suffered. If I tell you what one garden is like, one village, one house, one cathedral, after the German war has swept by, and if you read my words, I may help you perhaps to imagine more easily what France has suffered than if I spoke of millions. I speak of one garden in Arras; and you might walk from there, south by east for weeks, and find no garden that has suffered less.

It is all weeds and elders. An apple-tree rises out of a mass of nettles, but it is quite dead. Wild rose-trees show here and there, or roses that have ran wild like the cats of No-Man's-Land: And once I saw a rose-bush that had been planted in a pot and still grew there, as though it still remembered man, but the flower-pot was shattered, like all the pots in that garden, and the rose grew wild as any in any hedge.

The ivy alone grows on over a mighty wall, and seems to care not. The ivy alone seems not to mourn, but to have added the last four years to its growth as though they were ordinary years. That corner of the wall alone whispers not of disaster, it only seems to tell of the passing of years, which makes the ivy strong, and for which in peace as in war there is no cure. All the rest speaks of war, of war that comes to gardens, without banners or trumpets or splendour, and roots up everything, and turns round and smashes the house, and leaves it all desolate, and forgets and goes away. And when the histories of the war are written, attacks and counter-attacks and the doom of Emperors, who will remember that garden?

Saddest of all, as it seemed to me watching the garden paths, were spiders' webs that had been spun across them, so grey and stout and strong, fastened from weed to weed, with the spiders in their midst sitting in obvious ownership. You knew then as you looked at those webs across all the paths in the garden that any that you might fancy walking the small paths still, were but grey ghosts gone from thence, no more than dreams, hopes and imaginings, something altogether weaker than spiders webs.

And the old wall of the garden that divides it from its neighbour, of solid stone and brick, over fifteen feet high, it is that mighty old wall that held the romance of the garden. I do not tell the tale of that garden of Arras, for that is conjecture, and I only tell what I saw, in order that someone perhaps in some far country may know what happened in thousands and thousands of gardens because an Emperor sighed, and longed for the splendour of war. The tale is but conjecture, yet all the romance is there; for picture a wall over fifteen feet high built as they built long ago, standing for all those ages between two gardens. For would not the temptation arise to peer over the wall if a young man heard, perhaps songs, one evening the other side? And at first he would have some pretext and afterwards none at all, and the pretext would vary wonderfully little with the generations, while the ivy went on growing thicker and thicker. The thought might come of climbing the wall altogether and down the other side, and it might seem too daring and be utterly put away. And then one day, some wonderful summer evening, the west all red and a new moon in the sky, far voices heard clearly and white mists rising, one wonderful summer day, back would come that thought to climb the great old wall and go down the other side. Why not go in next door from the street, you might say. That would be different, that would be calling; that would mean ceremony, black hats, and awkward new gloves, constrained talk and little scope for romance. It would all be the fault of the wall.

With what diffidence, as the generations passed, would each first peep over the wall be undertaken. In some years it would be scaled from one side, in some ages from the other. What a barrier that old red wall would have seemed! How new the adventure would have seemed in each age to those that dared it, and how old to the wall! And in all those years the elders never made a door, but kept that huge and haughty separation. And the ivy quietly grew greener. And then one day a shell came from the east, and, in a moment, without plan or diffidence or pretext, tumbled away some yards of the proud old wall, and the two gardens were divided no longer: but there was no one to walk in them any more.

Wistfully round the edge of the huge breach in the wall, a Michaelmas daisy peered into the garden, in whose mined paths I stood.

AFTER HELL

He heard an English voice shouting, "Paiper! Paiper!" No mere spelling of the word will give the intonation. It was the voice of English towns he heard again. The very voice of London in the morning. It seemed like magic, or like some wonderfully vivid dream.

He was only a hundred miles or so from England; it was not very long since he had been there; yet what he heard seemed like an enchanted dream, because only the day before he had been in the trenches.

They had been twelve days in the trenches and had marched out at evening. They had marched five miles and were among tin huts in quite a different world. Through the doorways of the huts green grass could be seen and the sun was shining on it. It was morning. Everything was strangely different. You saw more faces smiling. Men were not so calm as they had been during the last twelve days, the last six especially: someone was kicking a football at somebody else's hut and there was excitement about it.

Guns were still firing: but they thought of death now as one who walked on the other side of the hills, no longer as a neighbour, as one who might drop in at any moment, and sometime did, while they were taking tea. It was not that they had been afraid of him, but the strain of expectancy was over; and that strain being suddenly gone in a single night, they all had a need, whether they knew it or not, of something to take its place, so the football loomed very large.

It was morning and he had slept long. The guns that grew active at dawn had not woke him; in those twelve days they had grown too familiar, but he woke wide when he heard the young English soldier with a bundle of three-days-old papers under his arm calling "Paiper, paiper!"—bringing to that strange camp the voice of the English towns. He woke wide at that wonder; and saw the sun shining cheerily, on desolation with a tinge of green in it, which even by itself rejoiced him on that morning after those twelve days amongst mud, looking at mud, surrounded by mud, protected by mud, sharing with mud the liability to be suddenly blown high and to come down in a shower on other men's helmets and coats.

He wondered if Dante when he came up from Hell heard anyone calling amongst the Verdure, in sunlight, any familiar call such as merchants use, some trivial song or cry of his native city.

A HAPPY VALLEY

"The enemy attacked the Happy Valley." I read these words in a paper at the time of the taking of Albert, for the second time, by our troops. And the words brought back Albert to me like a spell, Albert at the end of the mighty Bapaume-Albert road, that pathway Of Mars down which he had stalked so tremendously through his garden, the wide waste battlefields of the Somme. The words brought back Albert at the end of that road in the sunset and the cathedral seen against the west, and the gilded Virgin half cast down, but incapable of losing dignity, and evening coming down over the marshes. They brought it back like a spell. Like two spells rather, that some magician had mixed. Picture some magician of old in his sombre wonderful, chamber wishing dreams to transport him far off to delectable valleys. He sits him down and writes out a spell on parchment, slowly and with effort of aged memory, though he remembered it easily once. The shadows of crocodiles and antique gods flicker on walls and ceiling from a gusty flame as he writes; and in the end he writes the spell out wrongly and mixes up with the valleys where he would rest dark bits of the regions of Hell. So one sees Albert again and its Happy Valley.

I do not know which the Happy Valley is, for so many little valleys run in and out about Albert; and with a little effort of imagination, having only seen them full of the ruin of war, one can fancy any of them being once named happy. Yet one there is away to the east of Albert, which even up to last autumn seemed able to bear this name, so secluded it was in that awful garden of Mars; a tiny valley running into the wood of Bécourt. A few yards, higher up and all was desolation, a little further along a lonely road and you saw Albert mourning over irreparable vistas of ruin and wasted fields; but the little valley ran into the wood of Bécourt and sheltered there, and there you saw scarcely any signs of war. It might almost have been an English valley, by the side of an English wood. The soil was the same brown clay that you see in the south Of England above the downs and the chalk; the wood was a hazel wood, such as grow in England, thinned a good deal, as English hazels are, but with several tall trees still growing; and plants were there and late flowers, such as grow in Surrey and Kent. And at the end of the valley, just in the shadow of that familiar homely wood, a hundred British officers rest for ever.

As the world is today perhaps that obscure spot, as fittingly as any, might be named the Happy Valley.

IN BETHUNE

Under all ruins is history, as every tourist knows. Indeed, the dust that gathers above the ruin of cities may be said to be the cover of the most wonderful of the picture-books of Time, those secret books into which we sometimes peep. We turn no more, perhaps, than the corner of a single page in our prying, but we catch a glimpse there of things so gorgeous, in the book that we are not meant to see, that it is worth while to travel to far countries, whoever can, to see one of those books, and where the edges are turned up a little to catch sight of those strange winged bulls and mysterious kings and lion-headed gods that were not meant for us. And out of the glimpses, one catches from odd comers of those volumes of Time, where old centuries hide, one builds up part by guesses, part by fancy mixed with but little knowledge, a tale or theory of how men and women lived in unknown ages in the faith of forgotten gods.

Such a people lived in Timgad and left it probably about the time that waning Rome began to call home her outposts. Long after the citizens left the city stood on that high plateau in Africa, teaching shepherd Arabs what Rome had been: even to-day its great arches and parts of its temples stand: its paved streets are still grooved clearly with the wheel-ruts of chariots, and beaten down on each side of the centre by the pairs of horses that drew them two thousand years ago. When all the clatter had died away Timgad stood there in silence.

At Pompeii, city and citizens ended together. Pompeii did not mourn among strangers, a city without a people: but was buried at once, closed like an ancient book.

I doubt if anyone knows why its gods deserted Luxor, or Luxor lost faith in its gods, or in itself; conquest from over the desert or down the Nile, I suppose, or corruption within. Who knows? But one day I saw a woman come out from the back of her house and empty a basket full of dust and rubbish right into the temple at Luxor, where a dark green god is seated, three times the size of a man, buried as high as his waist. I suppose that what I saw had been happening off and on pretty well every morning for the last four thousand years. Safe under the dust that that woman threw, and the women that lived before her, Time hid his secrets.

And then I have seen the edges of stones in deserts that might or might not have been cities: they had fallen so long that you could hardly say.

At all these cities, whether disaster met them, and ruin came suddenly on to crowded streets; or whether they passed slowly out of fashion, and grew quieter year by year while the jackals drew nearer and nearer; at all these cities one can look with interest and not be saddened by the faintest sorrow—for anything that happened to such a different people so very long ago. Ram-headed gods, although their horns be broken and all their worshippers gone; armies whose elephants have turned against them; kings whose ancestors have eclipsed their faces in heaven and left them helpless against the onslaught of the stars; not a tear is given for one of these to-day.

But when in ruins as complete as Pompeii, as desolate as Timgad amongst its African hills, you see the remnant of a pack of cards lying with what remains of the stock of a draper's shop; and the front part of the shop and the snug room at the back gape side by side together in equal, misery, as though there had never been a barrier between the counter with its wares and the good mahogany table with its decanters; then in the rustling of papers that blow with dust along long-desolate floors one hears the whisper of Disaster, saying, "See; I have come." For under plaster shaken down by calamity, and red dust that once was bricks, it is our own age that is lying; and the little things that lie about the floors are relics of the twentieth century. Therefore in the streets of Bethune the wistful appeal that is in all things lost far off and utterly passed away cries out with an insistence that is never felt in the older fallen cities. No doubt to future times the age that lies under plaster in Bethune, with thin, bare laths standing over it, will appear an age of glory; and yet to thousands that went one day from its streets, leaving all manner of small things behind, it may well have been an age full of far other promises, no less golden to them, no less magical even, though too little to stir the pen of History, busy with batteries and imperial dooms. So that to these, whatever others may write, the twentieth-century

will not be the age of strategy, but will only seem to have been those fourteen lost quiet summers whose fruits lie under the plaster.

That layer of plaster and brick-dust lies on the age that has gone, as final, as fatal, as the layer of flints that covers the top of the chalk and marks
the end of an epoch and some unknown geologic catastrophe.

It is only by the little things in Bethune, lying where they were left,
that one can trace at all what kind of house each was, or guess at the people
who dwelt in it. It is only by a potato growing where Pavement was, and
flowering vigorously under a vacant window, that one can guess that the
battered, house beside it was once a fruiterer's shop, whence the potato
rolled away when man fell on evil days, and found the street, no longer
harsh and unfriendly; but soft and fertile like the primal waste, and took
root and throve there as its forbears throve before it in another continent
before the coming of man.

Across the street, in the dust of a stricken house, the implements of
his trade show where a carpenter lived when disaster came so suddenly,
quite good tools, some still upon shelves, some amongst broken things
that lie all over the floor. And further along the street in which these things
are someone has put up a great iron shutter that was to protect his shop. It
has a graceful border of painted, irises all the way up each side. It might
have been a jeweller that would have had such a shutter. The shutter alone
remains standing straight upright, and the whole shop is gone.

And just here the shaken street ends and all the streets end together.
The rest is a mound of white stones and pieces of bricks with low, leaning
walls surrounding it, and the halves of hollow houses; and eyeing it round
a comer, one old tower of the cathedral, as though still gazing over its
congregation of houses, a mined, melancholy watcher. Over the bricks lie
tracks, but no more streets. It is about the middle of the town, a hawk goes
over, calling as though he flew over the waste, and as though the waste
were his. The breeze that carries him opens old shutters and flaps them
to again. Old, useless hinges moan; wall-paper whispers. Three French
soldiers trying to find their homes walk over the bricks and groundsel.

It is the Abomination of Desolation, not seen by prophecy far off in
some fabulous future, nor remembered from terrible ages by the aid of
papyrus and stone, but fallen on our own century, on the homes of folk like
ourselves: common things that we knew are become the relics of bygone
days. It is our own time that has ended in blood and broken bricks.

IN AN OLD DRAWING-ROOM

There was one house with a roof on it in Peronne. And there an officer came by moonlight on his way back from leave. He was looking for
his battalion which had moved and was now somewhere in the desolation out in front of Peronne, or else was marching there—no one quite

knew. Someone said he had seen it marching through Tincourt; the R.T.O. said Brie. Those who did not know were always ready to help, they made suggestions and even pulled out maps. Why should they not? They were giving away no secret, because they did not know, and so they followed a soldier's natural inclination to give all the help they could to another soldier. Therefore they offered their suggestions like old friends. They had never met before, might never meet again; but La France introduces you, and five minute acquaintance in a place like Peronne, where things may change so profoundly in one night, and where all is so tense by the strange background of ruin that little portions of time seem very valuable, five minutes there seem quite a long time. And so they are, for what may not happen in five minutes any day now in France. Five minutes may be a page of history, a chapter even, perhaps a volume. Little children with inky fingers years hence may sit for a whole hour trying to learn up and remember just what happened during five minutes in France some time about now. These are just reflections such as pass through the mind in the moonlight among vast ruins and are at once forgotten.

Those that knew where the battalion was that the wandering officer looked for were not many; these were reserved and spoke like one that has a murder on his conscience, not freely and openly: for of one thing no one speaks in France, and that is the exact position of a unit. One may wave one's hand vaguely eastwards and say "Over there,," but to name a village and the people that occupy it is to offend against the silence that in these days broods over France, the solemn hush befitting so vast a tragedy.

And in the end it seemed better to that officer to obey the R.T.O. and to go by his train to Brie that left in the morning, and that question settled, there remained only food and sleep.

Down in the basement of the big house with a roof there was a kitchen, in fact there was everything that a house should have; and the more that one saw of simple household things, tables, chairs, the fire in the kitchen, pieces of carpet, floors, ceilings, and even windows, the more one wondered; it did not seem natural in Peronne.

Picture to yourself a fine drawing-room with high ornamental walls and all the air about it of dignity, peace and ease, that were so recently gone; only just, as it might have been, stepped through the double doorway; skirts, as it were, of ladies only just trailed out of sight; and then turn in fancy to that great town streaming with moonlight, full of the mystery that moonlight always brings, but without the light of it; all black, dark as caverns of earth where no light ever came, blacker for the moonlight than if no moon were there; sombre, mourning and accursed, each house in the great streets sheltering darkness amongst its windowless walls; as though it nursed disaster, having no other children left, and would not let the moon peer in on its grief or see the monstrous orphan that it fondled.

In the old drawing-room with twenty others, the wandering officer lay down to sleep on the floor, and thought of old wars that came to the cities of France a long while ago. To just such houses as this, he thought, men must have come before and gone on next day to fight in other centuries; it seemed to him that it must have been more romantic then. Who knows?

He had a bit of carpet to lie on. A few more officers came in in the early part of the night, and talked a little and lay down. A few candles were stuck on tables here and there. Midnight would have struck from the towers had any clock been left to strike in Peronne. Still talk went on in low voices here and there. The candles burned low and were fewer. Big shadows float-ed along those old high walls. Then the talk ceased and everyone was still: nothing stirred but the shadows. An officer muttered in sleep of things far thence, and was silent. Far away shells thumped faintly. The shadows, left to themselves, went round and round the room, searching in every corner for something that was lost. Over walls and ceiling they went and could not find it. The last candle was failing. It flared and guttered. The shadows raced over the room from comer to corner. Lost, and they could not find it. They hurried desperately in those last few moments. Great shadows searching for some little thing. In the smallest nook they sought for it. Then the last candle died. As the flame went up with the smoke from the fallen wick all the great shadows turned and mournfully trailed away.

THE HOMES OF ARRAS

As you come to Arras by the western road, by the red ramparts and the Spanish gate, Arras looks like a king. With such a dignity as clings to the ancient gateway so might a king be crowned; with such a sweep of dull red as the old ramparts show, so might he be robed; but a dead king with crowned skull. For the ways of Arras are empty but for brown soldiers, and her houses are bare as bones.

Arras sleeps profoundly, roofless, windowless, carpetless; Arras sleeps as a skeleton sleeps, with all the dignity of former days about it, but the life that stirs in its streets is not the old city's life, the old city is murdered. I came to Arras and went down a street, and saw back gardens glinting through the bare ribs of the houses. Garden after garden shone, so far as it could, though it was in October and after four years of war; but what was left of those gardens shining there in the sun was like sad faces trying to smile after many disasters.

I came to a great wall that no shell had breached. A cascade of scarlet creeper poured over it, as though on the other side some serene garden grew, where no disaster came, tended by girls who had never heard of war, walking untrodden paths. It was not so. But one's fancy, weary of ruin, readily turns to such scenes wherever facts are hidden, though but by a tottering wall, led by a few bright leaves or the glimpse of a flower.

But not for any fancy of mine must you picture ruin any more as something graced with splendour, or as it were an argosy reaching the shores of our day laden with grandeur and dignity out of antiquity. Ruin to-day is not covered with ivy, and has no curious architecture or strange secrets of history, and is not beautiful or romantic at all. It has no tale to tell of old civilizations, not otherwise known, told of by few grey stones. Ruin to-day is destruction and sorrow and debt and loss, come down untidily upon modern homes and cutting off ordinary generations, smashing the implements of familiar trades and making common avocations obsolete. It is no longer the guardian and the chronicle of ages that we should otherwise forget: ruin to-day is an age heaped up in rubble around us before it has ceased to be still green in our memory. Quite ordinary wardrobes in unseemly attitudes gape out from bedrooms whose front walls are gone, in houses whose most inner design shows unconcealed to the cold gaze of the street. The rooms have neither mystery nor adornment. Burst mattresses loll down from bedraggled beds. No one has come to tidy them up for years. And roofs have slanted down as low as the first floor.

I saw a green door ajar in an upper room: the whole of the front wall of the house was gone: the door partly opened oddly on to a little staircase, whose steps one could just see, that one wondered whither it went. The door seemed to beckon and beckon to some lost room, but if one could ever have got there, up through that shattered house, and if the steps of that little staircase would bear, so that one came to, the room that is hidden away at the top, yet there could only be silence and spiders there, and broken plaster and the dust of calamity; it is only to memories that the green door beckons; nothing remains.

And some day they may come to Arras to see the romance of war, to see where the shells struck and to pick up pieces of iron. It is not this that is romantic, not Mars, but poor, limping Peace. It is what is left that appeals to you, with pathos and infinite charm; little desolate gardens that no one has tended for years, wall-paper left in forlorn rooms when all else is Scattered, old toys buried in rubbish, old steps untrodden on inaccessible landings: it is what is left that appeals to you, what remains of old peaceful things. The great guns throb on, all round is the panoply of war, if panoply be the right word for this vast disaster that is known to Arras as innumerable separate sorrows; but it is not to this great event that-the sympathy turns in Arras, nor to its thunder and show, nor the trappings of it, guns lorries, and fragments of shells: it is to the voiceless, deserted inanimate things, so greatly wronged, that all the heart goes out: floors fallen in festoons, windows that seem to be wailing, roofs as though crazed with grief and then petrified in their craziness; railings, lamp-posts, sticks, all hit, nothing spared by that frenzied iron: the very earth clawed and-torn: it is what is left that appeals to you.

As I went from Arras I passed by a grey, gaunt shape, the ghost of a railway station standing in the wilderness haunting a waste of weeds, and mourning, as it seemed, over rusted railway lines lying idle and purposeless as though leading nowhere, as though all roads had ceased, and all lands were deserted, and all travellers dead: sorrowful and lonely that ghostly shape stood dumb in the desolation among houses whose doors were shut and their windows broken. And in all that stricken assembly no voice spoke but the sound of iron tapping on broken things, which was dumb awhile when the wind dropped. The wind rose and it tapped again.

TALES OF WAR (1918)

INTRODUCTION BY DARRELL SCHWEITZER

This is a melancholy, atypical, and occasionally surprising book by the author of The Gods of Pegana and The King of Elfland's Daughter. It was written for a political rather than artistic purpose, but because it was painfully inspired from life (and death) and because it is written by a great writer, it is far more than just a curio.

The stories in this book were written for the British War Office in 1918. They were intended as propaganda, to be published in newspapers and magazines to bolster public morale, to demonstrate the rightness of the Allied cause and the personal wickedness of the Kaiser, and so forth. That being so, the quietly mournful tone seems, at first, out of place, but it is precisely that tone which keeps the book honest and raises it above jingoism.

Consider the context. It is hard for readers today (particular American readers) to appreciate precisely how appalling the First World War (or the Great War as it was known then) was for the long-term combatants. It doesn't matter if you've seen Saving Private Ryan, or any amount of war footage. Remember that the Allied casualties at D-Day were only about 9000. About 3000 Americans were killed at Iwo Jima. But on the first day of the Battle of the Somme in 1916 the British lost 40,000 in an afternoon, a rate the horrendously incompetent commander, Field Marshall Douglas Haig, did not "consider severe." Sure enough, he wasted that number again, and again, and again, racking up 1,200,000 dead on both sides by the end of the year without an inch of ground gained. And there were more battles like that. It would be impossible to believe, without the old war footage, that men really did make wave after wave of useless bayonet charges into machine-gun fire, the first wave taking 100% casualties, followed by another, which also loses 100%, and a third, mowed down like wheat.

One can only begin to faintly grasp the magnitude of the horror when traveling in England today. It isn't that military graveyards are everywhere, but World War I memorials certainly are. Most of the ones I've seen are elaborate works in bronze, with long lists of the names of the dead. They're much more common than World War II memorials.

For all the war may have begun in a blaze of patriotic fervor, it soon settled into relentlessly growing lists of the fallen. Everyone knew someone killed. Dunsany lost many friends. This was a war in which all classes fought, all professions. The list of eminent writers killed is a long one: Joyce Kilmer, Wilfred Owen, Saki, and William Hope Hodgson come immediately to mind. Dunsany himself was, in an odd way, lucky. He'd seen the war coming. A couple months before the outbreak he was calling the Kaiser a "homicidal maniac," a judgment since borne out by history (unless you accept the revisionist theory that he was an ineffectual mama's boy who just let the carnage happen).

In August, 1914, for a member of Dunsany's class (he was, after all, a Peer of the Realm) there was no question of his duty to crown and country. He first joined the Irish Volunteers, a unit which the British military managed to ignore for some months, which left him inactive. (Later the Volunteers were taken over by anti-British radicals, and participated in the Easter Rebellion of 1916, about which, more below.) Dunsany finally managed to get into the regular army, but an officer who disliked him got him transferred to the reserves before the unit was sent to Gallipoli in 1915.

Dunsany was bitterly disappointed. As the troops marched away, someone shouted, "But you're the one we would have followed anywhere!" and the soldiers cheered. Dunsany was moved, but didn't, perhaps, realize that the unfriendly officer had saved his life. The Gallipoli campaign was a bloody fiasco even by the standards of the First World War, and very likely, if he had gone, we would still have *The Sword of Welleran* and *A Dreamer's Tales*, enough to insure Dunsany's reputation as a great and seminal fantasy writer, but there would have been no Jorkens, no *The King of Elfland's Daughter*, or *The Curse of the Wise Woman*.

After much time "lamentably bored" behind the lines, Dunsany's first real brush with death (at least his first since his service in the Boer War) came, not in France, but at home in Ireland, when the Easter Rebellion broke out in 1916. Firing was audible from Dunsany castle. There was a tense moment when a mob was reported to be on the way to loot the castle. Had it not turned back, there would have been no one to stop the looters. But, worst of all for the family, Lord Dunsany seemed to have disappeared a bit earlier.

Once more, his duty had seemed clear. He may have thought of himself as half-Irish, but he never wavered in his loyalty to the British Empire. As soon as the rebellion broke out, he and another officer, along with Dunsany's chauffeur, motored into Dublin to offer services to the British. At one point the car turned down a street and found itself facing a barricade manned by Republican riflemen, who opened fire.

The other officer was not hurt. The chauffeur lost a finger.

Dunsany was hit in the face, below the left eye. (A half an inch higher, and the bullet would have gone into his brain through the eye, and, again, no *The King of Elfland's Daughter*.) This is the "slight wound" he says he is recovering from in the introduction to *The Last Book of Wonder*, written the following August. Having wounded him, the Irish rebels promptly apologized and took him to a hospital, where he waited out the rest of the uprising with bullets occasionally chipping away at the windowsill ("Nasty little things," an attendant nun is reported to have described them).

He didn't see any actual action in the main war, the World War, until later in 1917, when he was indeed sent to France and spent time in the trenches. At one point he procured a piano for the regiment and concerts were given. (Another officer remarked that when the Big Advance came, that piano would prove a liability.)

At this point Dunsany experienced the same misery and danger common to the Western front. One of his letters remarks how one of the orderlies, "inoculated me in the chest with anti-tetanus serum which I enjoyed so much last time." Of course he is being ironic about enjoyment. He got the serum because he cut his hand on old barbed wire while "crawling about" in the mud, very likely under fire, to string up new.

Meanwhile, the death toll of friends and acquaintances mounted. Since late 1914, he had written virtually nothing. This was not a time to dream of ethereal beauty in the lands Beyond the Fields We Know. It was a problem Dunsany later described in an essay called "The Fantastic Dreams." He couldn't imagine wild and fantastic things when reality around him was so extreme.

In January 1918 he was offered a job in the War Office, and he began to write the sketches found in the present volume, and in its companion, *Unhappy Far-Off Things* (1919). Some of the items in *Tales of War* are not really stories at all, just descriptive sketches, but the descriptions are vivid and sometimes there is a very apt, quietly sinister phrase, as in "A Walk to the Trenches," which begins with the beauty of nature and ends, "we go on for another mile over the hills where the black fountains are rising." The black fountains are of course of mud, rising where shells crash into the ground.

There are even a few fantasies here, two dealing with the posthumous punishment of the Kaiser. "The Road" is a ghost story, and a tribute to Francis Ledwidge, a friend and a poet whose work Dunsany had discovered and sponsored. (Dunsany wrote the introductions to all three of Ledgwidge's collections, including the posthumous *Last Songs*, 1919). Ledwidge was killed by a shell while working on a road.

Certainly *Tales of War* is a minor addition to the Dunsanian canon, not something which, alone, would have made his name remembered at the beginning of the twenty-first century, but the book does have obvious merits in the gracefulness of its prose, and more subtle ones in what it chooses to dwell upon: loss, the devastation of the land, and the actual universality of the experience of soldiers (and grieving families) on all sides. The Kaiser may be to blame, but Dunsany does not ask us to hate the Germans. This moral point may be what moves the book from propaganda into literature. *Tales of War* is hardly of the stature of *All Quiet on the Western Front*; but it is, in its own way, authentic and sincere.

—Darrell Schweitzer
Philadelphia PA, June 2002

THE PRAYER OF THE MEN OF DALESWOOD

He said: "There were only twenty houses in Daleswood. A place you would scarcely have heard of. A village up top of the hills.

"When the war came there was no more than thirty men there between sixteen and forty-five. They all went.

"They all kept together; same battalion, same platoon. They was like that in Daleswood. Used to call the hop pickers foreigners, the ones that come from London. They used to go past Daleswood, some of them, every year, on their way down to the hop fields. Foreigners they used to call them. Kept very much to themselves, did the Daleswood people. Big woods all round them.

"Very lucky they was, the Daleswood men. They'd lost no more than five killed and a good sprinkling of wounded. But all the wounded was back again with the platoon. This was up to March when the big offensive started.

"It came very sudden. No bombardment to speak of. Just a burst of Tok Emmas going off all together and lifting the front trench clean out of it; then a barrage behind, and the Boche pouring over in thousands. 'Our luck is holding good,' the Daleswood men said, for their trench wasn't getting it at all. But the platoon on their right got it. And it sounded bad too a long way beyond that. No one could be quite sure. But the platoon on their right was getting it: that was sure enough.

"And then the Boche got through them altogether. A message came to say so. 'How are things on the right?' they said to the runner. 'Bad,' said the runner, and he went back, though Lord knows what he went back to. The Boche was through right enough. 'We'll have to make a defensive flank,' said the platoon commander. He was a Daleswood man too. Came from the big farm. He slipped down a communication trench with a few men, mostly bombers. And they reckoned they wouldn't see any of them any more, for the Boche was on the right, thick as starlings.

"The bullets were snapping over thick to keep them down while the Boche went on, on the right: machine guns, of course. The barrage was screaming well over and dropping far back, and their wire was still all right just in front of them, when they put up a head to look. There was the left platoon of the battalion. One doesn't bother, somehow, so much about another battalion as one's own. One's own gets sort of homely. And there they were wondering how their own officer was getting on, and the few fellows with them, on his defensive flank. The bombs were going off thick. All the Daleswood men were firing half right. It sounded from the noise as if it couldn't last long, as if it would soon be decisive, and the battle be won, or lost, just there on the right, and perhaps the war ended. They didn't notice the left. Nothing to speak of.

"Then a runner came from the left. 'Hullo!' they said, 'How are things over there?'

"'The Boche is through,' he said. 'Where's the officer?' 'Through!' they said. It didn't seem possible. However did he do that? they thought. And the runner went on to the right to look for the officer.

"And then the barrage shifted further back. The shells still screamed over them, but the bursts were further away. That is always a relief. Probably they felt it. But it was bad for all that. Very bad. It meant the Boche was well past them. They realized it after a while.

"They and their bit of wire were somehow just between two waves of attack. Like a bit of stone on the beach with the sea coming in. A platoon was nothing to the Boche; nothing much perhaps just then to anybody. But it was the whole of Daleswood for one long generation.

"The youngest full-grown man they had left behind was fifty, and some one had heard that he had died since the war. There was no one else in Daleswood but women and children, and boys up to seventeen.

"The bombing had stopped on their right; everything was quieter, and the barrage further away. When they began to realize what that meant they began to talk of Daleswood. And then they thought that when all of them were gone there would be nobody who would remember Daleswood just as it used to be. For places alter a little, woods grow, and changes come, trees get cut down, old people die; new houses are built now and then in place of a yew tree, or any old thing, that used to be there before; and one way or another the old things go; and all the time you have people thinking that the old times were best, and the old ways when they were young. And the Daleswood men were beginning to say, 'Who would there be to remember it just as it was?'

"There was no gas, the wind being wrong for it, so they were able to talk, that is if they shouted, for the bullets alone made as much noise as breaking up an old shed, crisper like, more like new timber breaking; and the shells of course was howling all the time, that is the barrage that was bursting far back. The trench still stank of them.

"They said that one of them must go over and put his hands up, or run away if he could, whichever he liked, and when the war was over he would go to some writing fellow, one of those what makes a living by it, and tell him all about Daleswood, just as it used to be, and he would write it out proper and there it would be for always. They all agreed to that. And then they talked a bit, as well as they could above that awful screeching, to try and decide who it should be. The eldest, they said, would know Daleswood best. But he said, and they came to agree with him, that it would be a sort of waste to save the life of a man what had had his good time, and they ought to send the youngest, and they would tell him all they knew of Daleswood before his time, and everything would be written down just the same and the old time remembered.

"They had the idea somehow that the women thought more of their own man and their children and the washing and what-not; and that the deep woods and the great hills beyond, and the plowing and the harvest and snaring rabbits in winter and the sports in the village in summer, and the hundred things that pass the time of one generation in an old, old place like Daleswood, meant less to them than the men. Anyhow they did not quite seem to trust them with the past.

"The youngest of them was only just eighteen. That was Dick. They told him to get out and put his hands up and be quick getting across, as soon as they had told him one or two things about the old time in Daleswood that a youngster like him wouldn't know.

"Well, Dick said he wasn't going, and was making trouble about it, so they told Fred to go. Back, they told him, was best, and come up behind the Boche with his hands up; they would be less likely to shoot when it was back towards their own supports.

"Fred wouldn't go, and so on with the rest. Well, they didn't waste time quarrelling, time being scarce, and they said what was to be done? There was chalk where they were, low down in the trench, a little brown clay on the top of it. There was a great block of it loose near a shelter. They said they would carve with their knives on the big bowlder of chalk all that they knew about Daleswood. They would write where it was and just what it was like, and they would write something of all those little things that pass with a generation. They reckoned on having the time for it. It would take a direct hit with something large, what they call big stuff, to do any harm to that bowlder. They had no confidence in paper, it got so messed up when you were hit; besides, the Boche had been using thermite. Burns, that does.

"They'd one or two men that were handy at carving chalk; used to do the regimental crest and pictures of Hindenburg, and all that. They decided they'd do it in reliefs.

"They started smoothing the chalk. They had nothing more to do but just to think what to write. It was a great big bowlder with plenty of room on it. The Boche seemed not to know that they hadn't killed the Daleswood men, just as the sea mightn't know that one stone stayed dry at the coming in of the tide. A gap between two divisions probably.

"Harry wanted to tell of the woods more than anything. He was afraid they might cut them down because of the war, and no one would know of the larks they had had there as boys. Wonderful old woods they were, with a lot of Spanish chestnut growing low, and tall old oaks over it. Harry wanted them to write down what the foxgloves were like in the wood at the end of summer, standing there in the evening, 'Great solemn rows,' he said, 'all odd in the dusk. All odd in the evening, going there after work; and makes you think of fairies.' There was lots of things about those woods, he said, that ought to be put down if people were to remember Daleswood as it used to be when they knew it. What were the good old days without those woods? he said.

"But another wanted to tell of the time when they cut the hay with scythes, working all those long days at the end of June; there would be no more of that, he said, with machines come in and all.

"There was room to tell of all that and he woods too, said the others, so long as they put it short like.

"And another wanted to tell of the valleys beyond the wood, far afield where the men went working; the women would remember the hay. The great valleys he'd tell of. It was they that made Daleswood. The valleys beyond the wood and the twilight on them in summer. Slopes covered with mint and thyme, all solemn at evening. A hare on them perhaps, sitting as though they were his, then lolloping slowly away. It didn't seem from the way he told of those old valleys that he thought they could ever be to other folk what they were to the Daleswood men in the days he remembered. He spoke of them as though there were something in them, besides the mint and the thyme and the twilight and hares, that would not stay after these men were gone, though he did not say what it was. Scarcely hinted it even.

"And still the Boche did nothing to the Daleswood men. The bullets had ceased altogether. That made it much quieter. The shells still snarled over, bursting far, far away.

"And Bob said tell of Daleswood itself, the old village, with queer chimneys, of red brick, in the wood. There weren't houses like that nowadays. They'd be building new ones and spoiling it, likely, after the war. And that was all he had to say.

"And nobody was for not putting down anything any one said. It was all to go in on the chalk, as much as would go in the time. For they all sort of understood that the Daleswood of what they called the good old time was just the memories that those few men had of the days they had spent there together. And that was the Daleswood they loved, and wanted folks to remember. They were all agreed as to that. And then they said how was they to write it down. And when it came to writing there was so much to be said, not spread over a lot of paper I don't mean, but going down so deep like, that it seemed to them how their own talk wouldn't be good enough to say it. And they knew no other, and didn't know what to do. I reckon they'd been reading magazines and thought that writing had to be like that muck. Anyway, they didn't know what to do. I reckon their talk would be good enough for Daleswood when they loved Daleswood like that. But they didn't, and they were puzzled.

"The Boche was miles away behind them now, and his barrage with him. Still in front he did nothing.

"They talked it all over and over, did the Daleswood men. They tried everything. But somehow or other they couldn't get near what they wanted to say about old summer evenings. Time wore on. The bowlder was smooth and ready, and that whole generation of Daleswood men could find no words to say what was in their hearts about Daleswood. There wasn't time to waste. And the only thing they thought of in the end was 'Please, God, remember Daleswood just like it used to be.' And Bill and Harry carved that on the chalk between them.

"What happened to the Daleswood men? Why, nothing. There come one of them counter-attacks, a regular bastard for Jerry. The French made it and did the Boche in proper. I got the story from a man with a hell of a great big hammer, long afterwards when that trench was well behind our line. He was smashing up a huge great chunk of chalk because he said they all felt it was so damn silly."

THE ROAD

The Battery Sergeant-Major was practically asleep. He was all worn out by the continuous roar of bombardments that had been shaking the dugouts and dazing his brains for weeks. He was pretty well fed up.

The officer commanding the battery, a young man in a very neat uniform and of particularly high birth, came up and spat in his face. The Sergeant-Major sprang to attention, received an order, and took a stick at once and beat up the tired men. For a message had come to the battery that some English (God punish them!) were making a road at X.

The gun was fired. It was one of those unlucky shots that come on days when or luck is out. The shell, a 5.9, lit in the midst of the British working party. It did the Germans little good. It did not stop the deluge of shells that was breaking up their guns and was driving misery down like a wedge into their spirits. It did not improve the temper of the officer commanding the battery, so that the men suffered as acutely as ever under the Sergeant-Major. But it stopped the road for that day.

I seemed to see that road going on in a dream.

Another working party came along next day, with clay pipes and got to work; and next day and the day after. Shells came, but went short or over; the shell holes were neatly patched up; the road went on. Here and there a tree had to be cut, but not often, not many of them were left; it was mostly digging and grubbing up roots, and pushing wheelbarrows along planks and duck-boards, and filling up with stones. Sometimes the engineers would come: that was when streams were crossed. The engineers made their bridges, and the infantry working party went on with the digging and laying down stones. It was monotonous work. Contours altered, soil altered, even the rock beneath it, but the desolation never; they always worked in desolation and thunder. And so the road went on.

They came to a wide river. They went through a great forest. They passed the ruins of what must have been quite fine towns, big prosperous towns with universities in them. I saw the infantry working party with their stumpy clay pipes, in my dream, a long way on from where that shell had lit, which stopped the road for a day. And behind them curious changes came over the road at X. You saw the infantry going up to the trenches, and going back along it into reserve. They marched at first, but in a few days they were going up in motors, grey busses with shuttered windows. And then the guns came along it, miles and miles of guns, following after the thunder which was further off over the hills. And then one day the cavalry came by. Then stores in wagons, the thunder muttering further and further away. I saw farm-carts going down the road at X. And then one day all manner of horses and traps and laughing people, farmers and women and boys all going by to X. There was going to be a fair.

And far away the road was growing longer and longer amidst, as always, desolation and thunder. And one day far away from X the road grew very fine indeed. It was going proudly through a mighty city, sweeping in like a river; you would not think that it ever remembered duck-boards. There were great palaces there, with huge armorial eagles blazoned in stone, and all along each side of the road was a row of statues of kings. And going down the road towards the palace, past the statues of the kings, a tired procession was riding, full of the flags of the Allies. And I looked at the flags in my dream, out of national pride to see whether we led, or whether France or America. America went before us, but I could not see the Union Jack in the van nor the Tricolour either, nor the Stars and Stripes: Belgium led and then Serbia, they that had suffered most.

And before the flags, and before the generals, I saw marching along on foot the ghosts of the working party that were killed at X, gazing about them in admiration as they went, at the great city and at the palaces. And one man, wondering at the Sièges Allée, turned round to the Lance Corporal in charge of the party: "That is a fine road that we made, Frank," he said.

AN IMPERIAL MONUMENT

It is an early summer's morning: the dew is all over France: the train is going eastwards. They are quite slow, those troop trains, and there are few embankments or cuttings in those flat plains, so that you seem to be meandering along through the very life of the people. The roads come right down to the railways, and the sun is shining brightly over the farms and the people going to work along the roads, so that you can see their faces clearly as the slow train passes them by.

They are all women and boys that work on the farms; sometimes perhaps you see a very old man, but nearly always women and boys; they are out working early. They straighten up from their work as we go by and lift their hands to bless us.

We pass by long rows of the tall French poplars, their branches cut away all up the trunk, leaving only an odd round tuft at the top of the tree; but little branches are growing all up the trunk now, and the poplars are looking unkempt. It would be the young men who would cut the branches of the poplars. They would cut them for some useful thrifty purpose that I do not know; and then they would cut them because they were always cut that way, as long ago as the times of the old men's tales about France; but chiefly, I expect, because youth likes to climb difficult trees; that is why they are clipped so very high. And the trunks are all unkempt now.

We go on by many farms with their shapely red-roofed houses; they stand there, having the air of the homes of an ancient people; they would not be out of keeping with any romance that might come, or any romance that has come in the long story of France, and the girls of those red-roofed houses work all alone in the fields.

We pass by many willows and come to a great marsh. In a punt on some open water an old man is angling. We come to fields again, and then to a deep wood. France smiles about us in the open sunlight.

But towards evening we pass over the border of this pleasant country into a tragical land of destruction and gloom. It is not only that murder has walked here to and fro for years, until all the fields are ominous with it, but the very fields themselves have been mutilated until they are unlike fields, the woods have been shattered right down to the anemones, and the houses have been piled in heaps of rubbish, and the heaps of rubbish have been scattered by shells. We see no more trees, no more houses, no more women, no cattle even now. We have come to the abomination of desolation. And over it broods, and will probably brood for ever, accursed by men and accursed by the very fields, the hyena-like memory of the Kaiser, who has whitened so many bones.

It may be some satisfaction to his selfishness to know that the monument to it cannot pass away, to know that the shell holes go too deep to be washed away by the healing rains of years, to know that the wasted German generations will not in centuries gather up what has been spilt on the Somme, or France recover in the sunshine of many summers from all the misery that his devilish folly has caused. It is likely to be to such as him a source of satisfaction, for the truly vain care only to be talked of in many mouths; they hysterically love to be thought of, and the notice of mankind is to them a mirror which reflects their futile postures. The admiration of fools they love, and the praise of a slavelike people, but they would sooner be hated by mankind than be ignored and forgotten as is their due. And the truly selfish care only for their imperial selves.

Let us leave him to pass in thought from ruin to ruin, from wasted field to field, from crater to crater; let us leave his fancy haunting cemeteries in the stricken lands of the world, to find what glee he can in this huge manifestation of his imperial will.

We neither know to what punishment he moves nor can even guess what fitting one is decreed. But the time is surely appointed and the place. Poor trifler with Destiny, who ever had so much to dread?

A WALK TO THE TRENCHES

To stand at the beginning of a road is always wonderful; for on all roads before they end experience lies, sometimes adventure. And a trench, even as a road, has its beginnings somewhere. In the heart of a very strange country you find them suddenly. A trench may begin in the ruins of a house, may run up out of a ditch; may be cut into a rise of ground sheltered under a hill, and is built in many ways by many men. As to who is the best builder of trenches there can be little doubt, and any British soldier would probably admit that for painstaking work and excellence of construction there are few to rival Von Hindenburg. His Hindenburg line is a model of neatness and comfort, and it would be only a very ungrateful British soldier who would deny it.

You come to the trenches out of strangely wasted lands, you come perhaps to a wood in an agony of contortions, black, branchless, sepulchral trees, and then no more trees at all. The country after that is still called Picardy or Belgium, still has its old name on the map as though it smiled there yet, sheltering cities and hamlet and radiant with orchards and gardens, but the country named Belgium — or whatever it be — is all gone away, and there stretches for miles instead one of the world's great deserts, a thing to take its place no longer with smiling lands, but with Sahara, Gobi, Kalahari, and the Karoo; not to be thought of as Picardy, but more suitably to be named the Desert of Wilhelm. Through these sad lands one goes to come to the trenches. Overhead floats until it is chased away an aëroplane with little black crosses, that you can scarcely see at his respectful height, peering to see what more harm may be done in the desolation and ruin. Little flashes sparkle near him, white puffs spread out round the flashes: and he goes, and our airmen go away after him; black puffs break out round our airmen. Up in the sky you hear a faint tap-tapping. They have got their machine guns working.

You see many things there that are unusual in deserts: a good road, a railway, perhaps a motor bus; you see what was obviously once a village, and hear English songs, but no one who has not seen it can imagine the country in which the trenches lie, unless he bear a desert clearly in mind, a desert that has moved from its place on the map by some enchantment of wizardry, and come down on a smiling country. Would it not be glorious to be a Kaiser and be able to do things like that?

Past all manner of men, past no trees, no hedges, no fields, but only one field from skyline to skyline that has been harrowed by war, one goes with companions that this event in our history has drawn from all parts of the earth. On that road you may hear all in one walk where is the best place to get lunch in the City; you may hear how they laid a drag for some Irish pack, and what the Master said; you may hear a farmer lamenting over the harm that rhinoceroses do to his coffee crop; you may hear Shakespeare quoted and *La vie Parisienne*.

In the village you see a lot of German orders, with their silly notes of exclamation after them, written up on notice boards among the ruins. Ruins and German orders. That turning movement of Von Kluck's near Paris in 1914 was a mistake. Had he not done it we might have had ruins and German orders everywhere. And yet Von Kluck may comfort himself with the thought that it is not by his mistakes that Destiny shapes the world: such a nightmare as a world-wide German domination can have had no place amongst the scheme of things.

Beyond the village the batteries are thick. A great howitzer near the road lifts its huge muzzle slowly, fires and goes down again, and lifts again and fires. It is as though Polyphemus had lifted his huge shape slowly, leisurely, from the hillside where he was sitting, and hurled the mountain top, and sat down again. If he is firing pretty regularly you are sure to get the blast of one of them as you go by, and it can be a very strong wind indeed. One's horse, if one is riding, does not very much like it, but I have seen horses far more frightened by a puddle on the road when coming home from hunting in the evening: one 12-inch howitzer more or less in France calls for no great attention from man or beast.

And so we come in sight of the support trenches where we are to dwell for a week before we go on for another mile over the hills, where the black fountains are rising.

A WALK IN PICARDY

Picture any village you know. In such a village as that the trench begins. That is to say, there are duck-boards along a ditch, and the ditch runs into a trench. Only the village is no longer there. It was like some village you know, though perhaps a little merrier, because it was further south and nearer the sun; but it is all gone now. And the trench runs out of the ruins, and is called Windmill Avenue. There must have been a windmill standing there once.

When you come from the ditch to the trench you leave the weeds and soil and trunks of willows and see the bare chalk. At the top of those two white walls is a foot or so of brown clay. The brown clay grows deeper as you come to the hills, until the chalk has disappeared altogether. Our alliance with France is new in the history of man, but it is an old, old union in the history of the hills. White chalk with brown clay on top has dipped and gone under the sea; and the hills of Sussex and Kent are one with the hills of Picardy.

And so you may pass through the chalk that lies in that desolate lane with memories of more silent and happier hills; it all depends on what the chalk means to you: you may be unfamiliar with it and in that case you will not notice it; or you may have been born among those thyme-scented hills and yet have no errant fancies, so that you will not think of the hills that watched you as a child, but only keep your mind on the business in hand; that is probably best.

You come after a while to other trenches: notice boards guide you, and you keep to Windmill Avenue. You go by Pear Lane, Cherry Lane, and Plum Lane. Pear trees, cherry trees and plum trees must have grown there. You are passing through either wild lanes banked with briar, over which these various trees peered one by one and showered their blossoms down at the end of spring, and girls would have gathered the fruit when it ripened, with the help of tall young men; or else you are passing through an old walled garden, and the pear and the cherry and plum were growing against the wall, looking southwards all through the summer. There is no way whatever of telling which it was; it is all one in war; whatever was there is gone; there remain to-day, and survive, the names of those three trees only. We come next to Apple Lane. You must not think that an apple tree ever grew there, for we trace here the hand of the wit, who by naming Plum Lane's neighbour "Apple Lane" merely commemorates the inseparable connection that plum has with apple forever in the minds of all who go to modern war. For by mixing apple with plum the manufacturer sees the opportunity of concealing more turnip in the jam, as it were, at the junction of the two forces, than he might be able to do without this unholy alliance.

We come presently to the dens of those who trouble us (but only for our own good), the dugouts of the trench mortar batteries. It is noisy when they push up close to the front line and play for half an hour or so with their rivals: the enemy sends stuff back, our artillery join in; it is as though, while you were playing a game of croquet, giants hundreds of feet high, some of them friendly, some unfriendly, carnivorous and hungry, came and played football on your croquet lawn.

We go on past Battalion Headquarters, and past the dugouts and shelters of various people having business with History, past stores of bombs and the many other ingredients with which history is made, past men coming down who are very hard to pass, for the width of two men and two packs is the width of a communication trench and sometimes an inch over; past two men carrying a flying pig slung on a pole between them; by many turnings; and Windmill Avenue brings you at last to Company Headquarters in a dugout that Hindenburg made with his German thoroughness.

And there, after a while, descends the Tok Emma man, the officer commanding a trench mortar battery, and is given perchance a whiskey and water, and sits on the best empty box that we have to offer, and lights one of our cigarettes.

"There's going to be a bit of a strafe at 5.30," he says.

WHAT HAPPENED ON THE NIGHT OF THE TWENTY-SEVENTH

The night of the twenty-seventh was Dick Cheeser's first night on sentry. The night was far gone when he went on duty; in another hour they would stand to. Dick Cheeser had camouflaged his age when he enlisted: he was barely eighteen. A wonderfully short time ago he was quite a little boy; now he was in a frontline trench. It hadn't seemed that things were going to alter like that. Dick Cheeser was a plowboy: long brown furrows over haughty, magnificent downs seemed to stretch away into the future as far as his mind could see. No narrow outlook either, for the life of nations depends upon those brown furrows. But there are the bigger furrows that Mars makes, the long brown trenches of war; the life of nations depends on these too; Dick Cheeser had never pictured these. He had heard talk about a big navy and a lot of Dreadnoughts; silly nonsense he called it. What did one want a big navy for? To keep the Germans out, some people said. But the Germans weren't coming. If they wanted to come, why didn't they come? Anybody could see that they never did come. Some of Dick Cheeser's pals had votes.

And so he had never pictured any change from plowing the great downs; and here was war at last, and here was he. The Corporal showed him where to stand, told him to keep a good lookout and left him.

And there was Dick Cheeser alone in the dark with an army in front of him, eighty yards away: and, if all tales were true, a pretty horrible army.

The night was awfully still. I use the adverb not as Dick Cheeser would have used it. The stillness awed him. There had not been a shell all night. He put his head up over the parapet and waited. Nobody fired at him. He felt that the night was waiting for him. He heard voices going along the trench: some one said it was a black night: the voices died away. A mere phrase; the night wasn't black at all, it was grey. Dick Cheeser was staring at it, and the night was staring back at him, and seemed to be threatening him; it was grey, grey as an old cat that they used to have at home, and as artful. Yes, thought Dick Cheeser, it was an artful night; that was what was wrong with it. If shells had come or the Germans, or anything at all, you would know how to take it; but that quiet mist over huge valleys, and stillness! Anything might happen. Dick waited and waited, and the night waited too. He felt they were watching each other, the night and he. He felt that each was crouching. His mind slipped back to the woods on hills he knew. He was watching with eyes and ears and imagination to see what would happen in No Man's Land under that ominous mist: but his mind took a peep for all that at the old woods that he knew. He pictured himself, he and a band of boys, chasing squirrels again in the summer. They used to chase a squirrel from tree to tree, throwing stones, till they tired it: and then they might hit it with a stone: usually not. Sometimes the squirrel would hide, and a boy would have to climb after it. It was great sport, thought Dick Cheeser. What a pity he hadn't had a catapult in those days, he thought. Somehow the years when he had not had a catapult seemed all to be wasted years. With a catapult one might get the squirrel almost at once, with luck: and what a great thing that would be. All the other boys would come round to look at the squirrel, and to look at the catapult, and ask him how he did it. He wouldn't have to say much, there would be the squirrel; no boasting would be necessary with the squirrel lying dead. It might spread to other things, even rabbits; almost anything, in fact. He would certainly get a catapult first thing when he got home. A little wind blew in the night, too cold for summer. It blew away, as it were, the summer of Dick's memories; blew away hills and woods and squirrel. It made for a moment a lane in the mist over No Man's Land. Dick Cheeser peered down it, but it closed again. "No," Night seemed to say, "you don't guess my secret." And the awful hush intensified. "What would they do?" thought the sentry. "What were they planning in all those miles of silence?" Even the Verys were few. When one went up, far hills seemed to sit and brood over the valley: their black shapes seemed to know what would happen in the mist and seemed sworn not to say. The rocket faded, and the hills went back into mystery again, and Dick Cheeser peered level again over the ominous valley.

All the dangers and sinister shapes and evil destinies, lurking between the armies in that mist, that the sentry faced that night cannot be told until the history of the war is written by a historian who can see the mind of the soldier. Not a shell fell all night, no German stirred; Dick Cheeser was relieved at "Stand to" and his comrades stood to beside him, and soon it was wide, golden, welcome dawn.

And for all the threats of night the thing that happened was one that the lonely sentry had never foreseen: in the hour of his watching Dick Cheeser, though scarcely eighteen, became a full-grown man.

STANDING TO

One cannot say that one time in the trenches is any more tense than another. One cannot take any one particular hour and call it, in modern nonsensical talk, "typical hour in the trenches." The routine of the trenches has gone on too long for that. The tensest hour ought to be half an hour before dawn, the hour when attacks are expected and men stand to. It is an old convention of war that that is the dangerous hour, the hour when defenders are weakest and attack most to be feared. For darkness favours the attackers then as night favours the lion, and then dawn comes and they can hold their gains in the light. Therefore in every trench in every war the garrison is prepared in that menacing hour, watching in greater numbers than they do the whole night through. As the first lark lifts from meadows they stand there in the dark. Whenever there is any war in any part of the world you may be sure that at that hour men crowd to their parapets: when sleep is deepest in cities they are watching there.

When the dawn shimmers a little, and a grey light comes, and widens, and all of a sudden figures become distinct, and the hour of the attack that is always expected is gone, then perhaps some faint feeling of gladness stirs the newest of the recruits; but chiefly the hour passes like all the other hours there, an unnoticed fragment of the long, long routine that is taken with resignation mingled with jokes.

Dawn comes shy with a wind scarce felt, dawn faint and strangely perceptible, feeble and faint in the east while men still watch the darkness. When did the darkness go? When did the dawn grow golden? It happened as in a moment, a moment you did not see. Guns flash no longer: the sky is gold and serene; dawn stands there like Victory that will shine, on one of these years when the Kaiser goes the way of the older curses of earth. Dawn, and the men unfix bayonets as they step down from the fire-step and clean their rifles with pull-throughs. Not all together, but section by section, for it would not do for a whole company to be caught cleaning their rifles at dawn, or at any other time.

They rub off the mud or the rain that has come at night on their rifles, they detach the magazine and see that its spring is working, they take out the breechblock and oil it, and put back everything clean: and another night is gone; it is one day nearer victory.

THE SPLENDID TRAVELLER

A traveller threw his cloak over his shoulder and came down slopes of gold in El Dorado. From incredible heights he came. He came from where the peaks of the pure gold mountain shone a little red with the sunset; from crag to crag of gold he stepped down slowly. Sheer out of romance he came through the golden evening.

It was only an incident of every day; the sun had set or was setting, the air turned chill, and a battalion's bugles were playing "Retreat" when this knightly stranger, a British aëroplane, dipped, and went homeward over the infantry. That beautiful evening call, and the golden cloud bank towering, and that adventurer coming home in the cold, happening all together, revealed in a flash the fact (which hours of thinking sometimes will not bring) that we live in such a period of romance as the troubadours would have envied.

He came, that British airman, over the border, sheer over No Man's Land and the heads of the enemy and the mysterious land behind, snatching the secrets that the enemy would conceal. Either he had defeated the German airmen who would have stopped his going, or they had not dared to try. Who knows what he had done? He had been abroad and was coming home in the evening, as he did every day.

Even when all its romance has been sifted from an age (as the centuries sift) and set apart from the trivial, and when all has been stored by the poets; even then what has any of them more romantic than these adventurers in the evening air, coming home in the twilight with the black shells bursting below?

The infantry look up with the same vague wonder with which children look at dragon flies; sometimes they do not look at all, for all that comes in France has its part with the wonder of a terrible story as well as with the incidents of the day, incidents that reoccur year in and year out, too often for us to notice them. If a part of the moon were to fall off in the sky and come tumbling to earth, the comment on the lips of the imperturbable British watchers that have seen so much would be, "Hullo, what is Jerry up to now?"

And so the British aëroplane glides home in the evening, and the light fades from the air, and what is left of the poplars grows dark against the sky, and what is left of the houses grows more mournful in the gloaming, and night comes, and with it the sounds of thunder, for the airman has given his message to the artillery. It is as though Hermes had gone abroad sailing upon his sandals, and had found some bad land below those winged feet wherein men did evil and kept not the laws of gods or men; and he had brought this message back and the gods were angry.

For the wars we fight to-day are not like other wars, and the wonders of them are unlike other wonders. If we do not see in them the saga and epic, how shall we tell of them?

ENGLAND

"And then we used to have sausages," said the Sergeant.

"And mashed?" said the Private.

"Yes," said the Sergeant, "and beer. And then we used to go home. It was grand in the evenings. We used to go along a lane that was full of them wild roses. And then we come to the road where the houses were. They all had their bit of a garden, every house."

"Nice, I calls it, a garden," the Private said.

"Yes," said the Sergeant, "they all had their garden. It came right down to the road. Wooden palings: none of that there wire."

"I hates wire," said the Private.

"They didn't have none of it," the N. C. O. went on. "The gardens came right down to the road, looking lovely. Old Billy Weeks he had them tall pale-blue flowers in his garden nearly as high as a man."

"Hollyhocks?" said the Private.

"No, they wasn't hollyhocks. Lovely they were. We used to stop and look at them, going by every evening. He had a path up the middle of his garden paved with red tiles, Billy Weeks had; and these tall blue flowers growing the whole way along it, both sides like. They was a wonder. Twenty gardens there must have been, counting them all; but none to touch Billy Weeks with his pale-blue flowers. There was an old windmill away to the left. Then there were the swifts sailing by overhead and screeching: just about as high again as the houses. Lord, how them birds did fly. And there was the other young fellows, what were not out walking, standing about by the roadside, just doing nothing at all. One of them had a flute: Jim Booker, he was. Those were great days. The bats used to come out, flutter, flutter, flutter; and then there'd be a star or two; and the smoke from the chimneys going all grey; and a little cold wind going up and down like the bats; and all the colour going out of things; and the woods looking all strange, and a wonderful quiet in them, and a mist coming up from the stream. It's a queer time that. It's always about that time, the way I see it: the end of the evening in the long days, and a star or two, and me and my girl going home."

"Wouldn't you like to talk about things for a bit the way you remember them?"

"Oh, no, Sergeant," said the other, "you go on. You do bring it all back so."

"I used to bring her home," the Sergeant said, "to her father's house. Her father was keeper there, and they had a house in the wood. A fine house with queer old tiles on it, and a lot of large friendly dogs. I knew them all by name, same as they knew me. I used to walk home then along the side of the wood. The owls would be about; you could hear them yelling. They'd float out of the wood like, sometimes: all large and white."

"I knows them," said the Private.

"I saw a fox once so close I could nearly touch him, walking like he was on velvet. He just slipped out of the wood."

"Cunning old brute," said the Private.

"That's the time to be out," said the Sergeant. "Ten o'clock on a summer's night, and the night full of noises, not many of them, but what there is, strange, and coming from a great way off, through the quiet, with nothing to stop them. Dogs barking, owls hooting, an old cart; and then just once a sound that you couldn't account for at all, not anyhow. I've heard sounds on nights like that that nobody 'ud think you'd heard, nothing like the flute that young Booker had, nothing like anything on earth."

"I know," said the Private.

"I never told any one before, because they wouldn't believe you. But it doesn't matter now. There'd be a light in the window to guide me when I got home. I'd walk up through the flowers of our garden. We had a lovely garden. Wonderful white and strange the flowers looked of a nighttime."

"You bring it all back wonderful," said the Private.

"It's a great thing to have lived," said the Sergeant.

"Yes, Sergeant," said the other, "I wouldn't have missed it, not for anything."

For five days the barrage had rained down behind them: they were utterly cut off and had no hope of rescue: their food was done, and they did not know where they were.

SHELLS

When the aëroplanes are home and the sunset has flared away, and it is cold, and night comes down over France, you notice the guns more than you do by day, or else they are actually more active then, I do not know which it is.

It is then as though a herd of giants, things of enormous height, came out from lairs in the earth and began to play with the hills. It is as though they picked up the tops of the hills in their hands and then let them drop rather slowly. It is exactly like hills falling. You see the flashes all along the sky, and then that lumping thump as though the top of the hill had been let drop, not all in one piece, but crumbled a little as it would drop from your hands if you were three hundred feet high and were fooling about in the night, spoiling what it had taken so long to make. That is heavy stuff bursting, a little way off.

If you are anywhere near a shell that is bursting, you can hear in it a curious metallic ring. That applies to the shells of either side, provided that you are near enough, though usually of course it is the hostile shell and not your own that you are nearest to, and so one distinguishes them. It is curious, after such a colossal event as this explosion must be in the life of a bar of steel, that anything should remain at all of the old bell-like voice of the metal, but it appears to, if you listen attentively; it is perhaps its last remonstrance before leaving its shape and going back to rust in the earth again for ages.

Another of the voices of the night is the whine the shell makes in coming; it is not unlike the cry the hyena utters as soon as it's dark in Africa: "How nice traveller would taste," the hyena seems to say, and "I want dead White Man." It is the rising note of the shell as it comes nearer, and its dying away when it has gone over, that make it reminiscent of the hyena's method of diction. If it is not going over then it has something quite different to say. It begins the same as the other, it comes up, talking of the back areas with the same long whine as the other. I have heard old hands say "That one is going well over." "Whee-oo," says the shell; but just where the "oo" should be long drawn out and turn into the hyena's final syllable, it says something quite different. "Zarp," it says. That is bad. Those are the shells that are looking for you.

And then of course there is the whizz-bang coming from close, along his flat trajectory: he has little to say, but comes like a sudden wind, and all that he has to do is done and over at once.

And then there is the gas shell, who goes over gurgling gluttonously, probably in big herds, putting down a barrage. It is the liquid inside that gurgles before it is turned to gas by the mild explosion; that is the explanation of it; yet that does not prevent one picturing a tribe of cannibals who have winded some nice juicy men and are smacking their chops and dribbling in anticipation.

And a wonderful thing to see, even in those wonderful nights, is our thermite bursting over the heads of the Germans. The shell breaks into a shower of golden rain; one cannot judge easily at night how high from the ground it breaks, but about as high as the tops of trees seen at a hundred yards. It spreads out evenly all round and rains down slowly; it is a bad shower to be out in, and for a long time after it has fallen, the sodden grass of winter, and the mud and old bones beneath it, burn quietly in a circle. On such a night as this, and in such showers, the flying pigs will go over, which take two men to carry each of them; they go over and root right down to the German dugout, where the German has come in out of the golden rain, and they fling it all up in the air.

These are such nights as Scheherazade with all her versatility never dreamed of; or if such nightmares came she certainly never told of them, or her august master, the Sultan, light of the age, would have had her at once beheaded; and his people would have deemed that he did well. It has been reserved for a modern autocrat to dream such a nightmare, driven to it perhaps by the tales of a white-whiskered Scheherazade, the Lord of the Kiel Canal; and being an autocrat he has made the nightmare a reality for the world. But the nightmare is stronger than its master, and grows mightier every night; and the All-Highest War Lord learns that there are powers in Hell that are easily summoned by the rulers of earth, but that go not easily home.

TWO DEGREES OF ENVY

It was night in the front line and no moon, or the moon was hidden. There was a strafe going on. The Tok Emmas were angry. And the artillery on both sides were looking for the Tok Emmas.

Tok Emma, I may explain for the blessed dwellers in whatever far happy island there be that has not heard of these things, is the crude language of Mars. He has not time to speak of a trunk mortar battery, for he is always in a hurry, and so he calls them T. M.'s. But Bellona might not hear him saying T. M., for all the din that she makes: might think that he said D. N; and so he calls it Tok Emma. Ak, Beer, C, Don: this is the alphabet of Mars.

And the huge minnies were throwing old limbs out of No Man's Land into the frontline trench, and shells were rasping down through the air that seemed to resist them until it was torn to pieces: they burst and showers of mud came down from heaven. Aimlessly, as it seemed, shells were bursting now and then in the air, with a flash intensely red: the smell of them was drifting down the trenches.

In the middle of all this Bert Butterworth was hit. "Only in the foot," his pals said. "Only!" said Bert. They put him on a stretcher and carried him down the trench. They passed Bill Britterling, standing in the mud, an old friend of Bert's. Bert's face, twisted with pain, looked up to Bill for some sympathy.

"Lucky devil," said Bill.

Across the way on the other side of No Man's Land there was mud the same as on Bill's side: only the mud over there stank; it didn't seem to have been kept clean somehow. And the parapet was sliding away in places, for working parties had not had much of a chance. They had three Tok Emmas working in that battalion front line, and the British batteries did not quite know where they were, and there were eight of them looking.

Fritz Groedenschasser, standing in that unseemly mud, greatly yearned for them to find soon what they were looking for. Eight batteries searching for something they can't find, along a trench in which you have to be, leaves the elephant hunter's most desperate tale a little dull and insipid. Not that Fritz Groedenschasser knew anything about elephant hunting: he hated all things sporting, and cordially approved of the execution of Nurse Cavell. And there was thermite too. Flammenwerfer was all very well, a good German weapon: it could burn a man alive at twenty yards. But this accursed flaming English thermite could catch you at four miles. It wasn't fair.

The three German trench mortars were all still firing. When would the English batteries find what they were looking for, and this awful thing stop? The night was cold and smelly.

Fritz shifted his feet in the foul mud, but no warmth came to him that way.

A gust of shells was coming along the trench. Still they had not found the minnewerfer! Fritz moved from his place altogether to see if he could find some place where the parapet was not broken. And as he moved along the sewerlike trench he came on a wooden cross that marked the grave of a man he once had known, now buried some days in the parapet, old Ritz Handelscheiner.

"Lucky devil," said Fritz.

THE MASTER OF NO MAN'S LAND

When the last dynasty has fallen and the last empire passed away, when man himself has gone, there will probably still remain the swede[1]. There grew a swede in No Man's Land by Croisille near the Somme, and it had grown there for a long while free from man.

It grew as you never saw a swede grow before. It grew tall and strong and weedy. It lifted its green head and gazed round over No Man's Land. Yes, man was gone, and it was the day of the swede.

The storms were tremendous. Sometimes pieces of iron sang through its leaves. But man was gone and it was the day of the swede.

A man used to come there once, a great French farmer, an oppressor of swedes. Legends were told of him and his herd of cattle, dark traditions that passed down vegetable generations. It was somehow known in those fields that the man ate swedes.

And now his house was gone and he would come no more.

The storms were terrible, but they were better than man. The swede nodded to his companions: the years of freedom had come.

They had always known among them that these years would come. Man had not been there always, but there had always been swedes. He would go some day, suddenly, as he came. That was the faith of the swedes. And when the trees went the swede believed that the day was come. When hundreds of little weeds arrived that were never allowed before, and grew unchecked, he knew it.

After that he grew without any care, in sunlight, moonlight and rain; grew abundantly and luxuriantly in the freedom, and increased in arrogance till he felt himself greater than man. And indeed in those leaden storms that sang often over his foliage all living things seemed equal.

There was little that the Germans left when they retreated from the Somme that was higher than this swede. He grew the tallest thing for miles and miles. He dominated the waste. Two cats slunk by him from a shattered farm: he towered above them contemptuously.

A partridge ran by him once, far, far below his lofty leaves. The night winds mourning in No Man's Land seemed to sing for him alone.

It was surely the hour of the swede. For him, it seemed, was No Man's Land. And there I met him one night by the light of a German rocket and brought him back to our company to cook.

---

1   The rutabaga or Swedish turnip

WEEDS AND WIRE

Things had been happening. Divisions were moving. There had been, there was going to be, a stunt. A battalion marched over the hill and sat down by the road. They had left the trenches three days march to the north and had come to a new country. The officers pulled their maps out; a mild breeze fluttered them; yesterday had been winter and to-day was spring; but spring in a desolation so complete and far-reaching that you only knew of it by that little wind. It was early March by the calendar, but the wind was blowing out of the gates of April. A platoon commander, feeling that mild wind blowing, forgot his map and began to whistle a tune that suddenly came to him out of the past with the wind. Out of the past it blew and out of the South, a merry vernal tune of a Southern people. Perhaps only one of those that noticed the tune had ever heard it before. An officer sitting near had heard it sung; it reminded him of a holiday long ago in the South.

"Where did you hear that tune?" he asked the platoon commander.

"Oh, the hell of a long way from here," the platoon commander said.

He did not remember quite where it was he had heard it, but he remembered a sunny day in France and a hill all dark with pine woods, and a man coming down at evening out of the woods, and down the slope to the village, singing this song. Between the village and the slope there were orchards in blossom. So that he came with his song for hundreds of yards through orchards. "The hell of a way from here," he said.

For a long while then they sat silent.

"It mightn't have been so very far from here," said the platoon commander. "It was in France, now I come to think of it. But it was a lovely part of France, all woods and orchards. Nothing like this, thank God." And he glanced with a tired look at the unutterable desolation.

"Where was it?" said the other.

"In Picardy," he said.

"Aren't we in Picardy now?" said his friend.

"Are we?" he said.

"I don't know. The maps don't call it Picardy."

"It was a fine place, anyway," the platoon commander said. "There seemed always to be a wonderful light on the hills. A kind of short grass grew on them, and it shone in the sun at evening. There were black woods above them. A man used to come out of them singing at evening."

He looked wearily round at the brown desolation of weeds. As far as the two officers could see there was nothing but brown weeds and bits of brown barbed wire. He turned from the desolate scene back to his reminiscences.

"He came singing through the orchards into the village," he said. "A quaint old place with queer gables, called Ville-en-Bois."

"Do you know where we are?" said the other.

"No, said the platoon commander."

"I thought not," he said. "Hadn't you better take a look at the map?"

"I suppose so," said the platoon commander, and he smoothed out his map and wearily got to the business of finding out where he was.

"Good Lord!" he said. "Ville-en-Bois!"

SPRING IN ENGLAND AND FLANDERS

Very soon the earliest primroses will be coming out in woods wherever they have been sheltered from the north. They will grow bolder as the days go by, and spread and come all down the slopes of sunny hills. Then the anemones will come, like a shy pale people, one of the tribes of the elves, who dare not leave the innermost deeps of the wood: in those days all the trees will be in leaf, the bluebells will follow, and certain fortunate woods will shelter such myriads of them that the bright fresh green of the beech trees will flash between two blues, the blue of the sky and the deeper blue of the bluebells. Later the violets come, and such a time as this is the perfect time to see England: when the cuckoo is heard and he surprises his hearers; when evenings are lengthening out and the bat is abroad again; and all the flowers are out and all the birds sing. At such a time not only Nature smiles but our quiet villages and grave old spires wake up from winter in the mellow air and wear their centuries lightly. At such a time you might come just at evening on one of those old villages in a valley and find it in the mood to tell you the secret of the ages that it hid and treasured there before the Normans came. Who knows? For they are very old, very wise, very friendly; they might speak to you one warm evening. If you went to them after great suffering they might speak to you; after nights and nights of shelling over in France, they might speak to you and you might hear them clearly.

It would be a long, long story that they would tell, all about the ages; and it would vary wonderfully little, much less perhaps than we think; and the repetitions rambling on and on in the evening, as the old belfry spoke and the cottages gathered below it, might sound so soothing after the boom of shells that perhaps you would nearly sleep. And then with one's memory tired out by the war one might never remember the long story they told, when the belfry and the brown-roofed houses all murmured at evening, might never remember even that they had spoken all through that warm spring and evening. We may have heard them speak and forgotten that they have spoken. Who knows? We are at war, and see so many strange things: some we must forget, some we must remember; and we cannot choose which.

To turn from Kent to Flanders is to turn to a time of mourning through all seasons alike. Spring there brings out no leaf on myriad oaks, nor the haze of green that floats like a halo above the heads of the birch trees, that stand with their fairylike trunks haunting the deeps of the woods. For miles and miles and miles summer ripens no crops, leads out no maidens laughing in the moonlight, and brings no harvest home. When Autumn looks on orchards in all that region of mourning he looks upon barren trees that will never blossom again. Winter drives in no sturdy farmers at evening to sit before cheery fires, families meet not at Christmas, and the bells are dumb in belfries; for all by which a man might remember his home has been utterly swept away: has been swept away to make a maniacal dancing ground on which a murderous people dance to their death led by a shallow, clever, callous, imperial clown.

There they dance to their doom till their feet shall find the precipice that was prepared for them on the day that they planned the evil things they have done.

THE NIGHTMARE COUNTRIES

There are certain lands in the darker dreams of poetry that stand out in the memory of generations. There is for instance Poe's "Dark tarn of Auber, the ghoul-haunted region of Weir"; there are some queer twists in the river Alph as imagined by Coleridge; two lines of Swinburne:

By the tideless dolorous inland sea
In a land of sand and ruin and gold

are as haunting as any. There are in literature certain regions of gloom, so splendid that whenever you come on them they leave in the mind a sort of nightmare country which one's thoughts revisit on hearing the lines quoted.

It is pleasant to picture such countries sometimes when sitting before the fire. It is pleasant because you can banish them by the closing of a book; a puff of smoke from a pipe will hide them altogether, and back come the pleasant, wholesome, familiar things. But in France they are there always. In France the nightmare countries stand all night in the starlight; dawn comes and they still are there. The dead are buried out of sight and others take their places among men; but the lost lands lie unburied gazing up at the winds; and the lost woods stand like skeletons all grotesque in the solitude; the very seasons have fled from them. The very seasons have fled; so that if you look up to see whether summer has turned to autumn, or if autumn has turned to winter yet, nothing remains to show you. It is like the eccentric dream of some strange man, very arresting and mysterious, but lacking certain things that should be there before you can recognize it as earthly. It is a mad, mad landscape. There are miles and miles and miles of it. It is the biggest thing man has done. It looks as though man in his pride, with all his clever inventions, had made for himself a sorry attempt at creation.

Indeed when we trace it all back to its origin we find at the beginning of this unhappy story a man who was only an emperor and wished to be something more. He would have ruled the world but has only meddled with it; and his folly has brought misery to millions, and there lies his broken dream on the broken earth. He will never take Paris now. He will never be crowned at Versailles as Emperor of Europe; and after that, most secret dream of all, did not the Cæsars proclaim themselves divine? Was it not whispered among Macedonian courtiers that Alexander was the child of God? And was the Hohenzollern less than these?

What might not force accomplish? All gone now, that dream and the Hohenzollern line broken. A maniacal dream and broken farms all mixed up together: they make a pretty nightmare and the clouds still gleam at night with the flashes of shells, and the sky is still troubled by day with uncouth balloons and the black bursts of the German shells and the white of our anti-aircraft.

And below there lies this wonderful waste land where no girls sing, and where no birds come but starlings; where no hedgerows stand, and no lanes with wild roses, and where no pathways run through fields of wheat, and there are no fields at all and no farms and no farmers; and two haystacks stand on a hill I know, undestroyed in the desolation, and nobody touches them for they know the Germans too well; and the tops have been blown off hills down to the chalk. And men say of this place that it is Pozières and of that place that it is Ginchy; nothing remains to show that hamlets stood there at all, and a brown, brown weed grows over it all for ever; and a mighty spirit has arisen in man, and no one bows to the War Lord though many die. And Liberty is she who sang her songs of old, and is fair as she ever was, when men see her in visions, at night in No Man's Land when they have the strength to crawl in: still she walks of a night in Pozières and in Ginchy.

A fanciful man once called himself the Emperor of the Sahara: the German Kaiser has stolen into a fair land and holds with weakening hands a land of craters and weed, and wire and wild cabbages and old German bones.

SPRING AND THE KAISER

While all the world is waiting for Spring there lie great spaces in one of the pleasantest lands to which Spring cannot come.

Pear trees and cherry and orchards flash over other lands, blossoming as abundantly as though their wonder were new, with a beauty as fresh and surprising as though nothing like it before had ever adorned countless centuries. Now with the larch and soon with the beech trees and hazel, a bright green blazes forth to illumine the year. The slopes are covered with violets. Those who have gardens are beginning to be proud of them and to point them out to their neighbours. Almond and peach in blossom peep over old brick walls. The land dreams of summer all in the youth of the year.

But better than all this the Germans have found war. The simple content of a people at peace in pleasant countries counted for nothing with them. Their Kaiser prepared for war, made speeches about war, and, when he was ready, made war. And now the hills that should be covered with violets are full of murderous holes, and the holes are half full of empty meat tins, and the garden walls have gone and the gardens with them, and there are no woods left to shelter anemones. Boundless masses of brown barbed wire straggle over the landscape. All the orchards there are cut down out of ruthless spite to hurt France whom they cannot conquer. All the little trees that grow near gardens are gone, aspen, laburnum and lilac. It is like this for hundreds of miles. Hundreds of ruined towns gaze at it with vacant windows and see a land from which even Spring is banished. And not a ruined house in all the hundred towns but mourns for some one, man, woman or child; for the Germans make war equally on all in the land where Spring comes no more.

Some day Spring will come back; some day she will shine all April in Picardy again, for Nature is never driven utterly forth, but comes back with her seasons to cover up even the vilest things.

She shall hide the raw earth of the shell holes till the violets come again; she shall bring back even the orchards for Spring to walk in once more; the woods will grow tall again above the southern anemones; and the great abandoned guns of the Germans will rust by the rivers of France. Forgotten like them, the memory of the War Lord will pass with his evil deeds.

TWO SONGS

Over slopes of English hills looking south in the time of violets, evening was falling.

Shadows at edges of woods moved, and then merged in the gloaming.

The bat, like a shadow himself, finding that spring was come, slipped from the dark of the wood as far as a clump of beech trees and fluttered back again on his wonderful quiet wings.

Pairing pigeons were home.

Very young rabbits stole out to gaze at the calm still world. They came out as the stars come. At one time they were not there, and then you saw them, but you did not see them come.

Towering clouds to the west built palaces, cities and mountains; bastions of rose and precipices of gold; giants went home over them draped in mauve by steep rose-pink ravines into emerald-green empires. Turbulences of colour broke out above the departed sun; giants merged into mountains, and cities became seas, and new processions of other fantastic things sailed by. But the chalk slopes facing south smiled on with the same calm light, as though every blade of grass gathered a ray from the gloaming. All the hills faced the evening with that same quiet glow, which faded softly as the air grew colder; and the first star appeared.

Voices came up in the hush, clear from the valley, and ceased. A light was lit, like a spark, in a distant window: more stars appeared and the woods were all dark now, and shapes even on the hill slopes began to grow indistinct.

Home by a laneway in the dim, still evening a girl was going, singing the Marseillaise.

In France where the downs in the north roll away without hedges, as though they were great free giants that man had never confined, as though they were stretching their vast free limbs in the evening, the same light was smiling and glimmering softly away.

A road wound over the downs and away round one of their shoulders. A hush lay over them as though the giants slept, or as though they guarded in silence their ancient, wonderful history.

The stillness deepened and the dimness of twilight; and just before colours fade, while shapes can still be distinguished, there came by the road a farmer leading his Norman horse. High over the horse's withers his collar pointed with brass made him fantastic and huge and strange to see in the evening.

They moved together through that mellow light towards where unseen among the clustered downs the old French farmer's house was sheltered away.

He was going home at evening humming "God Save the King."

THE PUNISHMENT

An exhalation arose, drawn up by the moon, from an old battlefield after the passing of years. It came out of very old craters and gathered from trenches, smoked up from No Man's Land, and the ruins of farms; it rose from the rottenness of dead brigades, and lay for half the night over two armies; but at midnight the moon drew it up all into one phantom and it rose and trailed away eastwards.

It passed over men in grey that were weary of war; it passed over a land once prosperous, happy and mighty, in which were a people that were gradually starving; it passed by ancient belfries in which there were no bells now; it passed over fear and misery and weeping, and so came to the palace at Potsdam. It was the dead of the night between midnight and dawn, and the palace was very still that the Emperor might sleep, and sentries guarded it who made no noise and relieved others in silence. Yet it was not so easy to sleep. Picture to yourself a murderer who had killed a man. Would you sleep? Picture yourself the man that planned this war! Yes, you sleep, but nightmares come.

The phantom entered the chamber. "Come," it said.

The Kaiser leaped up at once as obediently as when he came to attention on parade, years ago, as a subaltern in the Prussian Guard, a man whom no woman or child as yet had ever cursed; he leaped up and followed. They passed the silent sentries; none challenged and none saluted; they were moving swiftly over the town as the felon Gothas go; they came to a cottage in the country. They drifted over a little garden gate, and there in a neat little garden the phantom halted like a wind that has suddenly ceased. "Look," it said.

Should he look? Yet he must look. The Kaiser looked; and saw a window shining and a neat room in the cottage: there was nothing dreadful there; thank the good German God for that; it was all right, after all. The Kaiser had had a fright, but it was all right; there was only a woman with a baby sitting before the fire, and two small children and a man. And it was quite a jolly room. And the man was a young soldier; and, why, he was a Prussian Guardsman, — there was his helmet hanging on the wall, — so everything was all right. They were jolly German children; that was well. How nice and homely the room was. There shone before him, and showed far off in the night, the visible reward of German thrift and industry. It was all so tidy and neat, and yet they were quite poor people. The man had done his work for the Fatherland, and yet beyond all that had been able to afford all those little knickknacks that make a home so pleasant and that in their humble little way were luxury. And while the Kaiser looked the two young children laughed as they played on the floor, not seeing that face at the window.

Why! Look at the helmet. That was lucky. A bullet hole right through the front of it. That must have gone very close to the man's head. How ever did it get through? It must have glanced upwards as bullets sometimes do. The hole was quite low in the helmet. It would be dreadful to have bullets coming by close like that. The firelight flickered, and the lamp shone on, and the children played on the floor, and the man was smoking out of a china pipe; he was strong and able and young, one of the wealth-winners of Germany.

"Have you seen?" said the phantom.

"Yes," said the Kaiser. It was well, he thought, that a Kaiser should see how his people lived.

At once the fire went out and the lamp faded away, the room fell sombrely into neglect and squalor, and the soldier and the children faded away with the room; all disappeared phantasmally, and nothing remained but the helmet in a kind of glow on the wall, and the woman sitting all by herself in the darkness.

"It has all gone," said the Kaiser.

"It has never been," said the phantom.

The Kaiser looked again. Yes, there was nothing there, it was just a vision. There were the grey walls all damp and uncared for, and that helmet standing out solid and round, like the only real thing among fancies. No, it had never been. It was just a vision.

"It might have been," said the phantom.

Might have been? How might it have been?

"Come," said the phantom.

They drifted away down a little lane that in summer would have had roses, and came to an Uhlan's house; in times of peace a small farmer. Farm buildings in good repair showed even in the night, and the black shapes of haystacks; again a well-kept garden lay by the house. The phantom and the Kaiser stood in the garden; before them a window glowed in a lamplit room.

"Look," said the phantom.

The Kaiser looked again and saw a young couple; the woman played with a baby, and all was prosperous in the merry room. Again the hard-won wealth of Germany shone out for all to see, the cosy comfortable furniture spoke of acres well cared for, spoke of victory in the struggle with the seasons on which wealth of nations depends.

"It might have been," said the phantom. Again the fire died out and the merry scene faded away, leaving a melancholy, ill-kept room, with poverty and mourning haunting dusty corners and the woman sitting alone.

"Why do you show me this?" said the Kaiser. "Why do you show me these visions?"

"Come," said the phantom.

"What is it?" said the Kaiser. "Where are you bringing me?"

"Come," said the phantom.

They went from window to window, from land to land. You had seen, had you been out that night in Germany, and able to see visions, an imperious figure passing from place to place, looking on many scenes. He looked on them, and families withered away, and happy scenes faded, and the phantom said to him "Come." He expostulated but obeyed; and so they went from window to window of hundreds of farms in Prussia, till they came to the Prussian border and went on into Saxony; and always you would have heard, could you hear spirits speak, "It might have been," "It might have been," repeated from window to window.

They went down through Saxony, heading for Austria. And for long the Kaiser kept that callous, imperious look. But at last he, even he, at last he nearly wept. And the phantom turned then and swept him back over Saxony, and into Prussia again and over the sentries' heads, back to his comfortable bed where it was so hard to sleep.

And though they had seen thousands of merry homes, homes that can never be merry now, shrines of perpetual mourning; though they had seen thousands of smiling German children, who will never be born now, but were only the visions of hopes blasted by him; for all the leagues over which he had been so ruthlessly hurried, dawn was yet barely breaking.

He had looked on the first few thousand homes of which he had robbed all time, and which he must see with his eyes before he may go hence. The first night of the Kaiser's punishment was accomplished.

THE ENGLISH SPIRIT

By the end of the South African war Sergeant Cane had got one thing very well fixed in his mind, and that was that war was an overrated amusement. He said he "was fed up with it," partly because that misused metaphor was then new, partly because every one was saying it: he felt it right down in his bones, and he had a long memory. So when wonderful rumours came to the East Anglian village where he lived, on August 1, 1914, Sergeant Cane said: "That means war," and decided then and there to have nothing to do with it: it was somebody else's turn; he felt he had done enough. Then came August 4th, and England true to her destiny, and then Lord Kitchener's appeal for men. Sergeant Cane had a family to look after and a nice little house: he had left the army ten years.

In the next week all the men went who had been in the army before, all that were young enough, and a good sprinkling of the young men too who had never been in the army. Men asked Cane if he was going, and he said straight out "No."

By the middle of August Cane was affecting the situation. He was a little rallying point for men who did not want to go. "He knows what it's like," they said.

In the smoking room of the Big House sat the Squire an his son, Arthur Smith; and Sir Munion Boomer-Platt, the Member for the division. The Squire's son had been in the last war as a boy, and like Sergeant Cane had left the army since. All the morning he had been cursing an imaginary general, seated in the War Office at an imaginary desk with Smith's own letter before him, in full view but unopened. Why on earth didn't he answer it, Smith thought. But he was calmer now, and the Squire and Sir Munion were talking of Sergeant Cane.

"Leave him to me," said Sir Munion.

"Very well," said the Squire. So Sir Munion Boomer-Platt went off and called on Sergeant Cane.

Mrs Cane knew what he had come for.

"Don't let him talk you over," Bill, she said.

"Not he," said Sergeant Cane.

Sir Munion came on Sergeant Cane in his garden.

"A fine day," said Sir Munion. And from that he went on to the war. "If you enlist," he said, "they will make you a sergeant again at once. You will get a sergeant's pay, and your wife will get the new separation allowance."

"Sooner have Cane," said Mrs Cane.

"Yes, yes, of course," said Sir Munion. "But then there is the medal, probably two or three medals, and the glory of it, and it is such a splendid life."

Sir Munion did warm to a thing whenever he began to hear his own words. He painted war as it has always been painted, one of the most beautiful things you could imagine. And then it mustn't be supposed that it was like those wars that there used to be, a long way off. There would be houses where you would be billeted, and good food, and shady trees and villages wherever you went. And it was such an opportunity of seeing the Continent ("the Continent as it really is," Sir Munion called it) as would never come again, and he only wished he were younger. Sir Munion really did wish it, as he spoke, for his own words stirred him profoundly; but somehow or other they did not stir Sergeant Cane. No, he had done his share, and he had a family to look after.

Sir Munion could not understand him: he went back to the Big House and said so. He had told him all the advantages he could think of that were there to be had for the asking, and Sergeant Cane merely neglected them.

"Let me have a try," said Arthur Smith. "He soldiered with me before."

Sir Munion shrugged his shoulders. He had all the advantages at his fingers' ends, from pay to billeting: there was nothing more to be said. Nevertheless young Smith went.

"Hullo, Sergeant Cane," said Smith.

"Hello, sir," said the sergeant.

"Do you remember that night at Reit River?"

"Don't I, sir," said Cane.

"One blanket each and no ground sheet?"

"I remember, sir," said Cane.

"Didn't it rain," said Smith.

"It rained that night, proper."

"Drowned a few of the lice, I suppose."

"Not many," said Cane.

"No, not many," Smith reflected. "The Boers had the range all right that time."

"Gave it us proper," said Cane.

"We were hungry that night," said Smith. "I could have eaten biltong."

"I did eat some of it," said Cane. "Not bad stuff, what there was of it, only not enough."

"I don't think," said Smith, "that I've ever slept on the bare earth since."

"No, sir?" said Cane. "It's hard. You get used to it. But it will always be hard."

"Yes, it will always be hard," said Smith. "Do you remember the time we were thirsty?"

"Oh, yes, sir," said Cane, "I remember that. One doesn't forget that."

"No. I still dream of it sometimes," said Smith. "It makes a nasty dream. I wake with my mouth all dry too, when I dream that."

"Yes," said Cane, "one doesn't forget being thirsty."

"Well," said Smith, "I suppose we're for it all over again?"

"I suppose so, sir," said Cane.

AN INVESTIGATION INTO THE CAUSES AND ORIGIN OF THE WAR

The German imperial barber has been called up. He must have been called up quite early in the war. I have seen photographs in papers that leave no doubt of that. Who he is I do not know: I once read his name in an article but have forgotten it; few even know if he still lives. And yet what harm he has done! What vast evils he has unwittingly originated! Many years ago he invented a frivolity, a *jeu d'esprit* easily forgivable to an artist in the heyday of his youth, to whom his art was new and even perhaps wonderful. A craft, of course, rather than an art, and a humble craft at that; but then, the man was young, and what will not seem wonderful to youth?

He must have taken the craft very seriously, but as youth takes things seriously, fantastically and with laughter. He must have determined to out-shine rivals: he must have gone away and thought, burning candles late perhaps, when all the palace was still. But how can youth think seriously? And there had come to him this absurd, this fantastical conceit. What else would have come? The more seriously he took the tonsorial art, the more he studied its tricks and phrases and heard old barbers lecture, the more sure were the imps of youth to prompt him to laughter and urge him to something outrageous and ridiculous. The background of the dull pomp of Potsdam must have made all this more certain. It was bound to come.

And so one day, or, as I have suggested, suddenly late one night, there came to the young artist bending over tonsorial books that quaint, mad, odd, preposterous inspiration. Ah, what pleasure there is in the madness of youth; it is not like the madness of age, clinging to outworn formulæ; it is the madness of breaking away, of galloping among precipices, of dallying with the impossible, of courting the absurd. And this inspiration, it was in none of the books; the lecturer barbers had not lectured on it, could not dream of it and did not dare to; there was no tradition for it, no precedent; it was mad; and to introduce it into the pomp of Potsdam, that was the daring of madness. And this preposterous inspiration of the absurd young barber-madman was nothing less than a moustache that without any curve at all, or any suggestion of sanity, should go suddenly up at the ends very nearly as high as the eyes!

He must have told his young fellow craftsmen first, for youth goes first to youth with its hallucinations. And they, what could they have said? You cannot say of madness that it is mad, you cannot call absurdity absurd. To have criticized would have revealed jealousy; and as for praise you could not praise a thing like that. They probably shrugged, made gestures; and perhaps one friend warned him. But you cannot warn a man against a madness; if the madness is in possession it will not be warned away: why should it? And then perhaps he went to the old barbers of the Court. You can picture their anger. Age does not learn from youth in any case. But there was the insult to their ancient craft, bad enough if only imagined, but here openly spoken of. And what would come of it? They must have feared, on the one hand, dishonour to their craft if this young barber were treated as his levity deserved; and, on the other hand, could they have feared his success? I think they could not have guessed it.

And then the young idiot with his preposterous inspiration must have looked about to see where he could practise his new absurdity. It should have been enough to have talked about it among his fellow barbers; they would have gone with new zest to their work next day for this delirious interlude, and no harm would have been done. "Fritz," (or Hans) they would have said, "was a bit on last night, a bit full up," or whatever phrase they use to touch on drunkenness; and the thing would have been forgotten. We all have our fancies. But this young fool wanted to get his fancy mixed up with practice: that's where he was mad. And in Potsdam, of all places.

He probably tried his friends first, young barbers at the Court and others of his own standing. None of them were fools enough to be seen going about like that. They had jobs to lose. A Court barber is one thing, a man who cuts ordinary hair is quite another. Why should they become outcasts because their friend chose to be mad?

He probably tried his inferiors then, but they would have been timid folk; they must have seen the thing was absurd, and of course daren't risk it. Again, why should they?

Did he try to get some noble then to patronize his invention? Probably the first refusals he had soon inflamed his madness more, and he threw caution insanely to the winds, and went straight to the Emperor.

It was probably about the time that the Emperor dismissed Bismarck; certainly the drawings of that time show him still with a sane moustache.

The young barber probably chanced on him in this period, finding him bereft of an adviser, and ready to be swayed by whatever whim should come. Perhaps he was attracted by the barber's hardihood, perhaps the absurdity of his inspiration had some fascination for him, perhaps he merely saw that the thing was new and, feeling jaded, let the barber have his way.

And so the frivolity became a fact, the absurdity became visible, and honour and riches came the way of the barber.

A small thing, you might say, however fantastical. And yet I believe the absurdity of that barber to be among the great evils that have brought death nearer to man; whimsical and farcical as it was, yet a thing deadlier than Helen's beauty or Tamerlane's love of skulls. For just as character is outwardly shown so outward things react upon the character; and who, with that daring barber's ludicrous fancy visible always on his face, could quite go the sober way of beneficent monarchs? The fantasy must be mitigated here, set off there; had you such a figure to dress, say for amateur theatricals, you would realize the difficulty. The heavy silver eagle to balance it; the glittering cuirass lower down, preventing the eye from dwelling too long on the barber's absurdity. And then the pose to go with the cuirass and to carry off the wild conceit of that mad, mad barber. He has much to answer for, that eccentric man whose name so few remember. For pose led to actions; and just when Europe most needed a man of wise counsels, restraining the passions of great empires, just then she had ruling over Germany and, unhappily, dominating Austria, a man who every year grew more akin to the folly of that silly barber's youthful inspiration.

Let us forgive the barber. For long I have known from pictures that I have seen of the Kaiser that he has gone to the trenches. Probably he is dead. Let us forgive the barber. But let us bear in mind that the futile fancies of youth may be deadly things, and that one of them falling on a fickle mind may so stir its shallows as to urge it to disturb and set in motion the avalanches of illimitable grief.

LOST

Describing a visit, say the papers of March 28th, which the Kaiser paid incognito to Cologne Cathedral on March 18th before the great battle, the Cologne correspondent of the *Tyd* says:

> There were only a few persons in the building. Under high arches and in spacious solitude the Kaiser sat, as if in deep thought, before the priests' choir. Behind him his military staff stood respectfully at a distance. Still musing as he rose, the monarch resting both hands on his walking-stick remains standing immovable for some minutes . . . I shall never forget this picture of the musing monarch praying in Cologne Cathedral on the eve of the great battle.

Probably he won't forget it. The German casualty lists will help to remind him. But what is more to the point is that this expert propagandist has presumably received orders that we are not to forget it, and that the sinister originator of the then impending holocaust should be toned down a little in the eyes at least of the *Tyd* to something a little more amiable.

And no doubt the little piece of propaganda gave every satisfaction to those who ordered it, or they would not have passed it out to the *Tyd*, and the touching little scene would never have reached our eyes. At the same time the little tale would have been better suited to the psychology of other countries if he had made the War Lord kneel when he prayed in Cologne Cathedral, and if he had represented the Military Staff as standing out of respect to One who, outside Germany, is held in greater respect than the All Highest.

And had the War Lord really knelt is it not possible that he might have found pity, humility, or even contrition? Things easily overlooked in so large a cathedral when sitting erect, as a War Lord, before the priests' choir, but to be noticed perhaps with one's eyes turned to the ground.

Perhaps he nearly found one of those things. Perhaps he felt (who knows?) just for a moment, that in the dimness of those enormous aisles was something he had lost a long, long while ago.

One is not mistaken to credit the very bad with feeling far, faint appeals from things of glory like Cologne Cathedral; it is that the appeals come to them too far and faint on their headlong descent to ruin.

For what was the War Lord seeking? Did he know that pity for his poor slaughtered people, huddled by him on to our ceaseless machine guns, might be found by seeking there? Or was it only that the lost thing, whatever it was, made that faint appeal to him, passing the door by chance, and drew him in, as the scent of some herb or flower in a moment draws us back years to look for something lost in our youth; we gaze back, wondering, and do not find it.

And to think that perhaps he lost it by very little! That, but for that proud attitude and the respectful staff, he might have seen what was lost, and have come out bringing pity for his people. Might have said to the crowd that gave him that ovation, as we read, outside the door: "My pride has driven you to this needless war, my ambition has made a sacrifice of millions, but it is over, and it shall be no more; I will make no more conquests."

They would have killed him. But for that renunciation, perhaps, however late, the curses of the widows of his people might have kept away from his grave.

But he did not find it. He sat at prayer. Then he stood. Then he marched out: and his staff marched out behind him. And in the gloom of the floor of the vast Cologne Cathedral lie the things that the Kaiser did not find and never will find now. Unnoticed thus, and in some silent moment, passes a man's last chance.

THE LAST MIRAGE

The desolation that the German offensive has added to the dominions of the Kaiser cannot easily be imagined by any one who has never seen a desert. Look at it on the map and it is full of the names of towns and villages; it is in Europe, where there are no deserts; it is a fertile province among places of famous names. Surely it is a proud addition to an ambitious monarch's possessions. Surely there is something there that it is worth while to have conquered at the cost of army corps. No, nothing. They are mirage towns. The farms grow Dead Sea fruit. France recedes before the imperial clutch. France smiles, but not for him. His new towns seem to be his because their names have not yet been removed from any map, but they crumble at his approach because France is not for him. His deadly ambition makes a waste before it as it goes, clutching for cities. It comes to them and the cities are not there.

I have seen mirages and have heard others told of, but the best mirages of all we never hear described; the mirage that waterless travellers see at the last. Those fountains rising out of onyx basins, blue and straight into incredible heights, and falling and flooding cool white marble; the haze of spray above their feathery heads through which the pale green domes of weathered copper shimmer and shake a little; mysterious temples, the tombs of unknown kings; the cataracts coming down from rose-quartz cliffs, far off but seen quite clearly, growing to rivers bearing curious barges to the golden courts of Sahara. These things we never see; they are seen at the last by men who die of thirst.

Even so has the Kaiser looked at the smiling plains of France. Even so has he looked on her famous ancient cities and the farms and the fertile fields and the woods and orchards of Picardy. With effort and trouble he has moved towards them. As he comes near to them the cities crumble, the woods shrivel and fall, the farms fade out of Picardy, even the hedgerows go; it is bare, bare desert. He had been sure of Paris, he had dreamed of Versailles and some monstrous coronation, he had thought his insatiable avarice would be sated. For he had plotted for conquest of the world, that boundless greed of his goading him on as a man in the grip of thirst broods upon lakes.

He sees victory near him now. That also will fade in the desert of old barbed wire and weeds. When will he see that a doom is over all his ambitions? For his dreams of victory are like those last dreams that come in deceptive deserts to dying men.

There is nothing good for him in the desert of the Somme. Bapaume is not really there, though it be marked on his maps; it is only a wilderness of slates and brick. Peronne looks like a city a long way off, but when you come near it is only the shells of houses. Pozière, Le Sars, Sapigny, are gone altogether.

And all is Dead Sea fruit in a visible desert. The reports of German victories there are mirage like all the rest; they too will fade into weeds and old barbed wire.

And the advances that look like victories, and the ruins that look like cities, and the shell-beaten broken fields that look like farms, — they and the dreams of conquest and all the plots and ambitions, they are all the mirage of a dying dynasty in a desert it made for its doom.

Bones lead up to the desert, bones are scattered about it, it is the most menacing and calamitous waste of all the deadly places that have been inclement to man. It flatters the Hohenzollerns with visions of victory now because they are doomed by it and are about to die. When their race has died the earth shall smile again, for their deadly mirage shall oppress us no more. The cities shall rise again and the farms come back; hedgerows and orchards shall be seen again; the woods shall slowly lift their heads from the dust; and gardens shall come again where the desert was, to bloom in happier ages that forget the Hohenzollerns.

A FAMOUS MAN

Last winter a famous figure walked in Behagnies. Soldiers came to see him from their billets all down the Arras road, from Ervillers and from Sapigny, and from the ghosts of villages back from the road, places that once were villages but are only names now. They would walk three or four miles, those who could not get lorries, for his was one of those names that *all* men know, not such a name as a soldier or poet may win, but a name that all men know. They used to go there at evening.

Four miles away on the left as you went from Ervillers, the guns mumbled over the hills, low hills over which the Verys from the trenches put up their heads and peered around, — greeny, yellowy heads that turned the sky sickly, and the clouds lit up and went grey again all the night long. As you got near to Behagnies you lost sight of the Verys, but the guns mumbled on. A silly little train used to run on one's left, which used to whistle loudly, as though it asked to be shelled, but I never saw a shell coming its way; perhaps it knew that the German gunners could not calculate how slow it went. It crossed the road as you got down to Behagnies.

You passed the graves of two or three German soldiers with their names on white wooden crosses, — men killed in 1914; and then a little cemetery of a French cavalry regiment, where a big cross stood in the middle with a wreath and a tricolor badge, and the names of the men. And then one saw trees. That was always a wonder, whether one saw their dark shapes in the evening, or whether one saw them by day, and knew from the look of their leaves whether autumn had come yet, or gone. In winter at evening one just saw the black bulk of them, but that was no less marvellous than seeing them green in summer; trees by the side of the Arras-Bapaume road, trees in mid-desert in the awful region of Somme. There were not many of them, just a cluster, fewer than the date palms in an oasis in Sahara, but an oasis is an oasis wherever you find it, and a few trees make it. There are little places here and there, few enough as the Arabs know, that the Sahara's deadly sand has never been able to devastate; and there are places even in the Somme that German malice, obeying the Kaiser as the sand of Sahara obeys the accursed sirocco, has not been able to destroy quite to the uttermost. That little cluster of trees at Behagnies is one of these; Divisional Headquarters used to shelter beneath them; and near them was a statue on a lawn which probably stood by the windows of some fine house, though there is no trace of the house but the lawn and that statue now.

And over the way on the left a little further on, just past the officers' club, a large hall stood where one saw that famous figure, whom officers and men alike would come so far to see.

The hall would hold perhaps four or five hundred seats in front of a stage fitted up very simply with red, white and blue cloths, but fitted up by some one that understood the job; and at the back of that stage on those winter evenings walked on his flat and world-renowned feet the figure of Charlie Chaplin.

When aëroplanes came over bombing, the dynamos used to stop for they supplied light to other places besides the cinema, and the shade of Charlie Chaplin would fade away. But the men would wait till the aëroplanes had gone and that famous figure came waddling back to the screen. There he amused tired men newly come from the trenches, there he brought laughter to most of the twelve days that they had out of the line.

He is gone from Behagnies now. He did not march in the retreat a little apart from the troops, with head bent forward and hand thrust in jacket, a flat-footed Napoleon: yet he is gone; for no one would have left behind for the enemy so precious a thing as a Charlie Chaplin film. He is gone but he will return. He will come with his cane one day along that Arras road to the old hut in Behagnies; and men dressed in brown will welcome him there again.

He will pass beyond it through those desolate plains, and over the hills beyond them, beyond Bapaume. Far hamlets to the east will know his antics.

And one day surely, in old familiar garb, without court dress, without removing his hat, armed with that flexible cane, he will walk over the faces of the Prussian Guard and, picking up the Kaiser by the collar, with infinite nonchalance in finger and thumb, will place him neatly in a prone position and solemnly sit on his chest.

THE OASES OF DEATH

While the German guns were pounding Amiens and the battle of dull Prussianism against Liberty raged on, they buried Richthofen in the British lines.

They had laid him in a large tent with his broken machine outside it. Thence British airmen carried him to the quiet cemetery, and he was buried among the cypresses in this old resting place of French generations just as though he had come there bringing no harm to France.

Five wreaths were on his coffin, placed there by those who had fought against him up in the air. And under the wreaths on the coffin was spread the German flag.

When the funeral service was over three volleys were fired by the escort, and a hundred aviators paid their last respects to the grave of their greatest enemy; for the chivalry that the Prussians have driven from earth and sea lives on in the blue spaces of the air.

They buried Richthofen at evening, and the planes came droning home as they buried him, and the German guns roared on and guns answered, defending Amiens. And in spite of all, the cemetery had the air of quiet, remaining calm and aloof, as all French graveyards are. For they seem to have no part in the cataclysm that shakes all the world but them; they seem to withdraw amongst memories and to be aloof from time, and, above all, to be quite untroubled by the war that rages to-day, upon which they appear to look out listlessly from among their cypress and yew, and dimly, down a vista of centuries. They are very strange, these little oases of death that remain unmoved and green with their trees still growing, in the midst of a desolation as far as the eye can see, in which cities and villages and trees and hedges and farms and fields and churches are all gone, and where hugely broods a desert. It is as though Death, stalking up and down through France for four years, sparing nothing, had recognized for his own his little gardens, and had spared only them.

ANGLO-SAXON TYRANNY

"We need a sea," says Big-Admiral von Tirpitz, "freed of Anglo-Saxon tyranny." Unfortunately neither the British Admiralty nor the American Navy permit us to know how much of the Anglo-Saxon tyranny is done by American destroyers and how much by British ships and even trawler. It would interest both countries to know, if it could be known. But the Big-Admiral is unjust to France, for the French navy exerts a tyranny at sea that can by no means be overlooked, although naturally from her position in front of the mouth of the Elbe England practises the culminating insupportable tyranny of keeping the High Seas Fleet in the Kiel Canal.

It is not I, but the Big-Admiral, who chose the word tyranny as descriptive of the activities of the Anglo-Saxon navies. He was making a speech at Dusseldorf on May 25th and was reported in the Dusseldorfer *Nachrichten* on May 27th.

Naturally it does not seem like tyranny to us, even the contrary; but for an admiral, *ein Grosse-Admiral*, lately commanding a High Seas Fleet, it must have been more galling than we perhaps can credit to be confined in a canal. There was he, who should have been breasting the blue, or at any rate doing something salty and nautical, far out in the storms of that sea that the Germans call an Ocean, with the hurricane raging angrily in his whiskers and now and then wafting tufts of them aloft to white the halyards; there was he constrained to a command the duties of which however nobly he did them could be equally well carried out by any respectable bargee. He hoped for a piracy of which the *Lusitania* was merely a beginning; he looked for the bombardment of innumerable towns; he pictured slaughter in many a hamlet of fishermen; he planned more than all those things of which U-boat commanders are guilty; he saw himself a murderous old man, terrible to seafarers, and a scourge of the coasts, and fancied himself chronicled in after years by such as told dark tales of Captain Kidd or the awful buccaneers; but he followed in the end no more desperate courses than to sit and watch his ships on a wharf near Kiel like one of Jacob's night watchmen.

No wonder that what appears to us no more than the necessary protection of women and children in seacoast towns from murder should be to him an intolerable tyranny. No wonder that the guarding of travellers of the allied countries at sea, and even those of the neutrals, should be a most galling thing to the Big-Admiral's thwarted ambition, looking at it from the point of view of one who to white-whiskered age has retained the schoolboy's natural love of the black and yellow flag. A pirate, he would say, has as much right to live as wasps or tigers. The Anglo-Saxon navies, he might argue, have a certain code of rules for use at sea; they let women get first into the boats, for instance, when ships are sinking, and they rescue drowning mariners when they can: no actual harm in all this, he would feel, though it would weaken you, as Hindenburg said of poetry; but if all these little rules are tyrannously enforced on those who may think them silly, what is to become of the pirate? Where, if people like Beattie and Sims had always had their way, would be those rollicking tales of the jolly Spanish Main, and men walking the plank into the big blue sea, and long, low, rakish craft putting in to Indian harbours with a cargo of men and women all hung from the yard-arm? A melancholy has come over the spirit of Big-Admiral von Tirpitz in the years he has spent in the marshes between the Elbe and Kiel, and in that melancholy he sees romance crushed; he sees no more pearl earrings and little gold rings in the hold, he sees British battleships spoiling the Spanish Main, and hateful American cruisers in the old Sargasso Sea; he sees himself, alas, the last of all the pirates.

Let him take comfort. There were always pirates. And in spite of the tyranny of England and America, and of France, which the poor old man perplexed with his troubles forgot, there will be pirates still. Not many perhaps, but enough U-boats will always be able to slip through that tyrannous blockade to spread indiscriminate slaughter amongst the travellers of any nation, enough to hand on the old traditions of murder at sea. And one day Captain Kidd, with such a bow as they used to make in ports of the Spanish Main, will take off his ancient hat, sweeping it low in Hell, and be proud to clasp the hand of the Lord of the Kiel Canal.

MEMORIES

... far-off things
And battles long ago.

Those who live in an old house are necessarily more concerned with paying the plumber, should his art be required, or choosing wall paper that does not clash with the chintzes, than with the traditions that may haunt its corridors. In Ireland, — and no one knows how old that is, for the gods that lived there before the Red Branch came wrote few chronicles on the old grey Irish stones and wrote in their own language, — in Ireland we are more concerned with working it so that Tim Flanagan gets the job he does be looking for.

But in America those who remember Ireland remember her, very often, from old generations; maybe their grandfather migrated, perhaps his grandfather, and Ireland is remembered by old tales treasured among them. Now Tim Flanagan will not be remembered in a year's time when he has the job for which he has got us to agitate, and the jobberies that stir us move not the pen of History.

But the tales that Irish generations hand down beyond the Atlantic have to be tales that are worth remembering. They are tales that have to stand the supreme test, tales that a child will listen to by the fireside of an evening, so that they go down with those early remembered evenings that are last of all to go of the memories of a lifetime. A tale at a child will listen to must have much grandeur. Any cheap stuff will do for us, bad journalism, and novels by girls that could get no other jobs; but a child looks for those things in a tale that are simple and noble and epic, the things that Earth remembers. And so they tell, over there, tales of Sarsfield and of the old Irish Brigade; they tell, of an evening, of Owen Roe O'Neill. And into those tales come the plains of Flanders again and the ancient towns of France, towns famous long ago and famous yet: let us rather think of them as famous names and not as the sad ruins we have seen, melancholy by day and monstrous in the moonlight.

Many an Irishman who sails from America for those historic lands knows that the old trees that stand there have their roots far down in soil once richened by Irish blood. When the Boyne was lost and won, and Ireland had lost her King, many an Irishman with all his wealth in a scabbard looked upon exile as his sovereign's court. And so they came to the lands of foreign kings, with nothing to offer for the hospitality that was given them but a sword; and it usually was a sword with which kings were well content. Louis XV had many of them, and was glad to have them at Fontenoy; the Spanish King admitted them to the Golden Fleece; they defended Maria Theresa. Landen in Flanders and Cremona knew them. A volume were needed to tell of all those swords; more than one Muse has remembered them. It was not disloyalty that drove them forth; their King was gone, they followed, the oak was smitten and brown were the leaves of the tree.

But no such mournful metaphor applies to the men who march to-day towards the plains where the "Wild Geese" were driven. They go with no country mourning them, but their whole land cheers them on; they go to the inherited battlefields. And there is this difference in their attitude to kings, that those knightly Irishmen of old, driven homeless over-sea, appeared as exiles suppliant for shelter before the face of the Grand Monarch, and he, no doubt with exquisite French grace, gave back to them all they had lost except what was lost forever, salving so far as he could the injustice suffered by each. But to-day when might, for its turn, is in the hands of democracies, the men whose fathers built the Statue of Liberty have left their country to bring back an exiled king to his home, and to right what can be righted of the ghastly wrongs of Flanders.

And if men's prayers are heard, as many say, old saints will hear old supplications going up by starlight with a certain wistful, musical intonation that has linked the towns of Limerick and Cork with the fields of Flanders before.

THE MOVEMENT

For many years Eliphaz Griggs was comparatively silent. Not that he did not talk on all occasions whenever he could find hearers, he did that at great length; but for many years he addressed no public meeting, and was no part of the normal life of the northeast end of Hyde Park or Trafalgar Square. And then one day he was talking in a public house where he had gone to talk on the only subject that was dear to him. He waited, as was his custom, until five or six men were present, and then he began. "Ye're all damned, I'm saying, damned from the day you were born. Your portion is Tophet."

And on that day there happened what had never happened in his experience before. Men used to listen in a tolerant way, and say little over their beer, for that is the English custom; and that would be all. But to-day a man rose up with flashing eyes and went over to Eliphaz and gripped him by the hand: "They're *all* damned," said the stranger.

That was the turning point in the life of Eliphaz. Up to that moment he had been a lonely crank, and men thought he was queer; but now there were two of them and he became a Movement. A Movement in England may do what it likes: there was a Movement, before the War, for spoiling tulips in Kew Gardens and breaking church windows; it had its run like the rest.

The name of Eliphaz's new friend was Ezekiel Pim: and they drew up rules for their Movement almost at once; and very soon country inns knew Eliphaz no more. And for some while they missed him where he used to drop in of an evening to tell them they were all damned: and then a man proved one day that the earth was flat, and they all forgot Eliphaz.

But Eliphaz went to Hyde Park and Ezekiel Pim went with him, and there you would see them close to the Marble Arch on any fine Sunday afternoon, preaching their Movement to the people of London. "You are all damned," said Eliphaz. "Your portion shall be damnation for everlasting."

"*All* damned," added Ezekiel.

Eliphaz was the orator. He would picture Hell to you as it really is. He made you see pretty much what it will be like to wriggle and turn and squirm, and never escape from burning. But Ezekiel Pim, though he seldom said more than three words, uttered those words with such alarming sincerity and had such a sure conviction shining in his eyes that searched right in your face as he said them, and his long hair waved so weirdly as his head shot forward when he said "You're *all* damned," that Ezekiel Pim brought home to you that the vivid descriptions of Eliphaz really applied to *you*.

People who lead bad lives get their sensibilities hardened. These did not care very much what Eliphaz said. But girls at school, and several governesses, and even some young clergy, were very much affected. Eliphaz Griggs and Ezekiel Pim seemed to bring Hell so near to you. You could almost feel it baking the Marble Arch from two to four on Sundays. And at four o'clock the Surbiton Branch of the International Anarchists used to come along, and Eliphaz Griggs and Ezekiel Pim would pack up their flag and go, for the pitch belonged to the Surbiton people till six; and the crank Movements punctiliously recognize each other's rights. If they fought among themselves, which is quite unthinkable, the police would run them in; it is the one thing that an anarchist in England may never do.

When the War came the two speakers doubled their efforts. The way they looked at it was that here was a counter-attraction taking people's minds off the subject of their own damnation just as they had got them to think about it. Eliphaz worked as he had never worked before; he spared nobody; but it was still Ezekiel Pim who somehow brought it most home to them.

One fine spring afternoon Eliphaz Griggs was speaking at his usual place and time; he had wound himself up wonderfully. "You are damned," he was saying, "for ever and ever and ever. Your sins have found you out. Your filthy lives will be as fuel round you and shall burn for ever and ever."

"Look here," said a Canadian soldier in the crowd, "we shouldn't allow that in Ottawa."

"What?" asked an English girl.

"Why, telling us we're all damned like that," he said.

"Oh, this is England," she said. "They may all say what they like here."

"You are all damned," said Ezekiel, jerking forward his head and shoulders till his hair flapped out behind. "*All, all, all* damned."

"I'm damned if I am," said the Canadian soldier.

"Ah," said Ezekiel, and a sly look came into his face.

Eliphaz flamed on. "Your sins are remembered. Satan shall grin at you. He shall heap cinders on you for ever and ever. Woe to you, filthy livers. Woe to you, sinners. Hell is your portion. There shall be none to grieve for you. You shall dwell in torment for ages. None shall be spared, not one. Woe everlasting . . . Oh, I beg pardon, gentlemen, I'm sure." For the Pacifists' League had been kept waiting three minutes. It was their turn to-day at four.

NATURE'S CAD

The claim of Professor Grotius Jan Beek to have discovered, or learned, the language of the greater apes has been demonstrated clearly enough. He is not the original discoverer of the fact that they have what may be said to correspond with a language; nor is he the first man to have lived for some while in the jungle protected by wooden bars, with a view to acquiring some knowledge of the meaning of the various syllables that gorillas appear to utter. If so crude a collection of sounds, amounting to less than a hundred words, if words they are, may be called a language, it may be admitted that the Professor has learned it, as his recent experiments show. What he has not proved is his assertion that he has actually conversed with a gorilla, or by signs, or grunts, or any means whatever obtained an insight, as he put it, into its mentality, or, as we should put it, its point of view. This Professor Beek claims to have done; and though he gives us a certain plausible corroboration of a kind which makes his story appear likely, it should be borne in mind that it is not of the nature of proof.

The Professor's story is briefly that having acquired this language, which nobody that has witnessed his experiments will call in question, he went back to the jungle for a week, living all the time in the ordinary explorer's cage of the Blik pattern. Towards the very end of the week a big male gorilla came by, and the Professor attracted it by the one word "Food." It came, he says, close to the cage, and seemed prepared to talk but became very angry on seeing a man there, and beat the cage and would say nothing. The Professor says that he asked it why it was angry. He admits that he had learned no more than forty words of this language, but believes that there are perhaps thirty more. Much however is expressed, as he says, by mere intonation. Anger, for instance; and scores of allied words, such as terrible, frightful, kill, whether noun, verb or adjective, are expressed, he says, by a mere growl. Nor is there any word for "Why," but queries are signified by the inflexion of the voice.

When he asked it why it was angry the gorilla said that men killed him, and added a noise that the professor said was evidently meant to allude to guns. The only word used, he says, in this remark of the gorilla's was the word that signified "man." The sentence as understood by the professor amounted to "Man kill me. Guns." But the word "kill" was represented simply by a snarl, "me" by slapping its chest, and "guns" as I have explained was only represented by a noise. The Professor believes that ultimately a word for guns may be evolved out of that noise, but thinks that it will take many centuries, and that if during that time guns should cease to be in use, this stimulus being withdrawn, the word will never be evolved at all, nor of course will it be needed.

The Professor tried, by evincing interest, ignorance, and incredulity, and even indignation, to encourage the gorilla to say more; but to his disappointment, all the more intense after having exchanged that one word of conversation with one of the beasts, the gorilla only repeated what it had said, and beat on the cage again. For half an hour this went on, the Professor showing every sign of sympathy, the gorilla raging and beating upon the cage.

It was half an hour of the most intense excitement to the Professor, during which time he saw the realization of dreams that many considered crazy, glittering as it were within his grasp, and all the while this ridiculous gorilla would do nothing but repeat the mere shred of a sentence and beat the cage with its great hands; and the heat of course was intense. And by the end of the half hour the excitement and the heat seem to have got the better of the Professor's temper, and he waved the disgusting brute angrily away with a gesture that probably was not much less impatient than the gorilla's own. And at that the animal suddenly became voluble. He beat more furiously than ever upon the cage and slipped his great fingers through the bars, trying to reach the Professor, and poured out volumes of ape-chatter.

Why, why did men shoot at him, he asked. He made himself terrible, therefore men ought to love him. That was the whole burden of what the Professor calls its argument."Me, me terrible," two slaps on the chest and then a growl. "Man love me." And then the emphatic negative word, and the sound that meant guns, and sudden furious rushes at the cage to try to get at the Professor.

The gorilla, Professor Beek explains, evidently admired only strength; whenever he said "I make myself terrible to Man," a sentence he often repeated, he drew himself up and thrust out his huge chest and bared his frightful teeth; and certainly, the Professor says, there was something terribly grand about the menacing brute. "Me terrible," he repeated again and again, "Me terrible. Sky, sun, stars with me. Man love me. Man love me. No?" It meant that all the great forces of nature assisted him and his terrible teeth, which he gnashed repeatedly, and that therefore man should love him, and he opened his great jaws wide as he said this, showing all the brutal force of them.

There was to my mind a genuine ring in Professor Beek's story, because he was obviously so much more concerned, and really troubled, by the dreadful depravity of this animal's point of view, or mentality as he called it, than he was concerned with whether or not we believed what he had said.

And I mentioned that there was a circumstance in his story of a plausible and even corroborative nature. It is this. Professor Beek, who noticed at the time a bullet wound in the tip of the gorilla's left ear, by means of which it was luckily identified, put his analysis of its mentality in writing and showed it to several others, before he had any way of accounting for the beast having such a mind.

Long afterwards it was definitely ascertained that this animal had been caught when young on the slopes of Kilimanjaro and trained and even educated, so far as such things are possible, by an eminent German Professor, a *persona grata* at the Court of Berlin.

THE HOME OF HERR SCHNITZELHAASER

The guns in the town of Greinstein were faintly audible. The family of Schnitzelhaaser lived alone there in mourning, an old man and old woman. They never went out or saw any one, for they knew they could not speak as though they did not mourn. They feared that their secret would escape them. They had never cared for the war that the War Lord made. They no longer cared what he did with it. They never read his speeches; they never hung out flags when he ordered flags: they hadn't the heart to.

They had had four sons.

The lonely old couple would go as far as the shop for food. Hunger stalked behind them. They just beat hunger every day, and so saw evening: but there was nothing to spare. Otherwise they did not go out at all. Hunger had been coming slowly nearer of late. They had nothing but the ration, and the ration was growing smaller. They had one pig of their own, but the law said you might not kill it. So the pig was no good to them.

They used to go and look at that pig sometimes when hunger pinched. But more than that they did not dare to contemplate.

Hunger came nearer and nearer. The war was going to end by the first of July. The War Lord was going to take Paris on this day and that would end the war at once. But then the war was always going to end. It was going to end in 1914, and their four sons were to have come home when the leaves fell. The War Lord had promised that. And even if it did end, that would not bring their four sons home now. So what did it matter what the War Lord said.

It was thoughts like these that they knew they had to conceal. It was because of thoughts like these that they did not trust themselves to go out and see other people, for they feared that by their looks if by nothing else, or by their silence or perhaps their tears, they might imply a blasphemy against the All Highest. And hunger made one so hasty. What might one not say? And so they stayed indoors.

But now. What would happen now? The War Lord was coming to Greinstein in order to hear the guns. One officer of the staff was to be billeted in their house. And what would happen now?

They talked the whole thing over. They must struggle and make an effort. The officer would be there for one evening. He would leave in the morning quite early in order to make things ready for the return to Potsdam: he had charge of the imperial car. So for one evening they must be merry. They would suppose, it was Herr Schnitzelhaaser's suggestion, they would think all the evening that Belgium and France and Luxemburg all attacked the Fatherland, and that the Kaiser, utterly unprepared, quite unprepared, called on the Germans to defend their land against Belgium.

Yes, the old woman could imagine that; she could think it all the evening.

And then, — it was no use not being cheerful altogether, — then one must imagine a little more, just for the evening: it would come quite easy; one must think that the four boys were alive.

Hans too? (Hans was the youngest).

Yes, all four. Just for the evening.

But if the officer asks?

He will not ask. What are four soldiers?

So it was all arranged; and at evening the officer came. He brought his own rations, so hunger came no nearer. Hunger just lay down outside the door and did not notice the officer.

A this supper the officer began to talk. The Kaiser himself, he said, was at the Schartzhaus.

"So," said Herr Schnitzelhaaser; "just over the way." So close. Such an honour.

And indeed the shadow of the Schartzhaus darkened their garden in the morning.

It was such an honour, said Frau Schnitzelhaaser too. And they began to praise the Kaiser. So great a War Lord, she said; the most glorious war there had ever been.

Of course, said the officer, it would end on the first of July.

Of course, said Frau Schnitzelhaaser. And so great an admiral, too. One must remember that also. And how fortunate we were to have him: one must not forget that. Had it not been for him the crafty Belgians would have attacked the Fatherland, but they were struck down before they could do it. So much better to prevent a bad deed like that than merely to punish after. So wise. And had it not been for him, if it had not been for him . . .

The old man saw that she was breaking down and hastily he took up that feverish praise. Feverish it was, for their hunger and bitter loss affected their minds no less than illness does, and the things they did they did hastily and intemperately. His praise of the War Lord raced on as the officer ate. He spoke of him as of those that benefit man, as of monarchs who bring happiness to their people. And now, he said, he is here in the Schartzhaus beside us, listening to the guns just like a common soldier.

Finally the guns, as he spoke, coughed beyond ominous hills. Contentedly the officer went on eating. He suspected nothing of the thoughts his host and hostess were hiding. At last he went upstairs to bed.

As fierce exertion is easy to the fevered, so they had spoken; and it wears them, so they were worn. The old woman wept when the officer went out of hearing. But old Herr Schnitzelhaaser picked up a big butcher's knife. "I will bear it no more," he said.

His wife watched him in silence as he went away with his knife. Out of the house he went and into the night. Through the open door she saw nothing; all was dark; even the Schartzhaus, where all was gay to-night, stood dark for fear of aëroplanes. The old woman waited in silence.

When Herr Schnitzelhaaser returned there was blood on his knife.

"What have you done?" the old woman asked him quite calmly. "I have killed our pig," he said.

She broke out then, all the more recklessly for the long restraint of the evening; the officer must have heard her.

"We are lost! We are lost!" she cried. "We may not kill our pig. Hunger has made you mad. You have ruined us."

"I will bear it no longer," he said. "I have killed our pig."

"But they will never let us eat it," she cried. "Oh, you have ruined us!"

"If you did not dare to kill our pig," he said, "why did you not stop me when you saw me go? You saw me go with the knife?"

"I thought," she said, "you were going to kill the Kaiser."

A DEED OF MERCY

As hindenburg and the Kaiser came down, as we read, from Mont d'Hiver, during the recent offensive, they saw on the edge of a crater two wounded British soldiers. The Kaiser ordered that they should be cared for: their wounds were bound up and they were given brandy, and brought round from unconsciousness. That is the German account of it, and it may well be true. It was a kindly act.

Probably had it not been for this the two men would have died among those desolate craters; no one would have known, and no one could have been blamed for it.

The contrast of this spark of imperial kindness against the gloom of the background of the war that the Kaiser made is a pleasant thing to see, even though it illuminates for only a moment the savage darkness in which our days are plunged. It was a kindness that probably will long be remembered to him. Even we, his enemies, will remember it. And who knows but that when most he needs it his reward for the act will be given him.

For Judas, they say, once in his youth, gave his cloak, out of compassion, to a shivering beggar, who sat shaken with ague, in rags, in bitter need. And the years went by and Judas forgot his deed. And long after, in Hell, Judas they say was given one day's respite at the end of every year because of this one kindness he had done so long since in his youth. And every year he goes, they say, for a day and cools himself among the Arctic bergs; once every year for century after century.

Perhaps some sailor on watch on a misty evening blown far out of his course away to the north saw something ghostly once on an iceberg floating by, or heard some voice in the dimness that seemed like the voice of man, and came home with this weird story. And perhaps, as the story passed from lip to lip, men found enough justice in it to believe it true. So it came down the centuries.

Will seafarers ages hence on dim October evenings, or on nights when the moon is ominous through mist, red and huge and uncanny, see a lonely figure sometimes on the loneliest part of the sea, far north of where the *Lusitania* sank, gathering all the cold it can? Will they see it hugging a crag of iceberg wan as itself, helmet, cuirass and ice pale-blue in the mist together? Will it look towards them with ice-blue eyes through the mist, and will they question it, meeting on those bleak seas? Will it answer — or will the North wind howl like voices? Will the cry of seals be heard, and ice floes grinding, and strange birds lost upon the wind that night, or will it speak to them in those distant years and tell them how it sinned, betraying man?

It will be a grim, dark story in that lonely part of the sea, when he confesses to sailors, blown too far north, the dreadful thing he plotted against man. The date on which he is seen will be told from sailor to sailor. Queer taverns of distant harbours will know it well. Not many will care to be at sea that day, and few will risk being driven by stress of weather on the Kaiser's night to the bergs of the haunted part of sea.

And yet for all the grimness of the pale-blue phantom, with cuirass and helmet and eyes shimmering on deadly icebergs, and yet for all the sorrow of the wrong he did against man, the women drowned and the children, and all the good ships gone, yet will the horrified mariners meeting him in the mist grudge him no moment of the day he has earned, or the coolness he gains from the bergs, because of the kindness he did to the wounded men. For the mariners in their hearts are kindly men, and what a soul gains from kindness will seem to them well deserved.

LAST SCENE OF ALL

After John Calleron was hit he carried on in a kind of twilight of the mind. Things grew dimmer and calmer; harsh outlines of events became blurred; memories came to him; there was a singing in his ears like far-off bells. Things seemed more beautiful than they had a while ago; to him it was for all the world like evening after some quiet sunset, when lawns and shrubs and woods and some old spire look lovely in the late light, and one reflects on past days. Thus he carried on, seeing things dimly. And what is sometimes called "the roar of battle," those aërial voices that snarl and moan and whine and rage at soldiers, had grown dimmer too. It all seemed further away, and littler, as far things are. He still heard the bullets: there is something so violently and intensely sharp in the snap of passing bullets at short ranges that you hear them in deepest thought, and even in dreams. He heard them, tearing by, above all things else. The rest seemed fainter and dimmer, and smaller and further away.

He did not think he was very badly hit, but nothing seemed to matter as it did a while ago. Yet he carried on.

And then he opened his eyes very wide and found he was back in London again in an underground train. He knew it at once by the look of it. He had made hundreds of journeys, long ago, by those trains. He knew by the dark, outside, that it had not yet left London; but what was odder than that, if one stopped to think of it, was that he knew exactly where it was going. It was the train that went away out into the country where he used to live as a boy. He was sure of that without thinking.

When he began to think how he came to be there he remembered the war as a very far-off thing. He supposed he had been unconscious a very long time. He was all right now.

Other people were sitting beside him on the same seat. They all seemed like people he remembered a very long time ago. In the darkness opposite, beyond the windows of the train, he could see their reflections clearly. He looked at the reflections but could not quite remember.

A woman was sitting on his left. She was quite young. She was more like some one that he most deeply remembered than all the others were. He gazed at her, and tried to clear his mind.

He did not turn and stare at her, but he quietly watched her reflection before him in the dark. Every detail of her dress, her young face, her hat, the little ornaments she wore, were minutely clear before him, looking out of the dark. So contented she looked you would say she was untouched by war.

As he gazed at the clear calm face and the dress that seemed neat though old and, like all things, so faraway, his mind grew clearer and clearer. It seemed to him certain it was the face of his mother, but from thirty years ago, out of old memories and one picture. He felt sure it was his mother as she had been when he was very small. And yet after thirty years how could he know? He puzzled to try and be quite sure. But how she came to be there, looking like that, out of those oldest memories, he did not think of at all.

He seemed to be hugely tired by many things and did not want to think. Yet he was very happy, more happy even than tired men just come home all new to comfort.

He gazed and gazed at the face in the dark. And then he felt quite sure.

He was about to speak. Was she looking at him? Was she watching him, he wondered. He glanced for the first time to his own reflection in that clear row of faces.

His own reflection was not there, but blank dark showed between his two neighbours. And then he knew he was dead.

OLD ENGLAND

Towards winter's end on a high, big, bare down, in the south of England, John Plowman was plowing. He was plowing the brown field at the top of the hill, good soil of the clay; a few yards lower down was nothing but chalk, with shallow flinty soil and steep to plow; so they let briars grow there. For generations his forbears had plowed on the top of that hill. John did not know how many. The hills were very old; it might have been always.

He scarcely looked to see if his furrow was going straight. The work he was doing was so much in his blood that he could almost feel if furrows were straight or not. Year after year they moved on the same old landmarks; thorn trees and briars mostly guided the plow, where they stood on the untamed land beyond; the thorn trees grew old at their guiding, and still the furrows varied not by the breadth of a hoof-mark.

John, as he plowed, had leisure to meditate on much besides the crops; he knew so much of the crops that his thoughts could easily run free from them; he used to meditate on who they were that lived in briar and thorn tree, and danced as folk said all through midsummer night, and sometimes blessed and sometimes harmed the crops; for he knew that in Old England were wonderful ancient things, odder and older things than many folks knew. And his eyes had leisure to see much beside the furrows, for he could almost feel the furrows going straight.

One day at his plowing, as he watched the thorn ahead, he saw the whole big hill besides, looking south, and the lands below it; one day he saw in the bright sun of late winter a horseman riding the road through the wide lands below. The horseman shone as he rode, and wore white linen over what was shining, and on the linen was a big red cross. "One of them knights," John Plowman said to himself or his horse, "going to them crusades." And he went on with his plowing all that day satisfied, and remembered what he had seen for years, and told his son.

For there is in England, and there always was, mixed with the needful things that feed or shelter the race, the wanderer-feeling for romantic causes that runs deep and strange through the other thoughts, as the Gulf Stream runs through the sea. Sometimes generations of John Plowman's family would go by and no high romantic cause would come to sate that feeling. They would work on just the same though a little sombrely, as though some good thing had been grudged them. And then the Crusades had come, and John Plowman had seen the Red Cross knight go by, riding towards the sea in the morning, and Jon Plowman was satisfied.

Some generations later a man of the same name was plowing the same hill. They still plowed the brown clay at the top and left the slope wild, though there were many changes. And the furrows were wonderfully straight still. And half he watched a thorn tree ahead as he plowed and half he took in the whole hill sloping south and the wide lands below it, far beyond which was the sea. They had a railway now down in the valley. The sunlight glittering near the end of winter shone on a train that was marked with great white squares and red crosses on them.

John Plowman stopped his horses and looked at the train. "An ambulance train," he said, "coming up from the coast." He thought of the lads he knew and wondered if any were there. He pitied the men in that train and envied them. And then there came to him the thought of England's cause and of how those men had upheld it, at sea and in crumbling cities. He thought of the battle whose echoes reached sometimes to that field, whispering to furrows and thorn trees that had never heard them before. He thought of the accursed tyrant's cruel might, and of the lads that had faced it. He saw the romantic splendour of England's cause. He was old but had seen the glamour for which each generation looked. Satisfied in his heart and cheered with a new content he went on with his age-old task in the business of man with the hills.

9 UNCOLLECTED AND RARE STORIES

*The first 8 stories in this section were never collected in Lord Dun-
sany's lifetime; the 9th only appeared in England. Dunsany scholars S.T.
Joshi provided the text for "One More Tale," and Martin Andersson the
text for "The Poet Speaks with Earth." The remaining stories come from
the original publications, via online resources at archive.org.*

—Editor

ONE MORE TALE

On a long, straight, dusty road between the Moon and the World,
where I wandered once while dreaming, I met a poor old woman coming
towards the World. Never before had I seen one so shabby, never before an
old woman in dress, in face and in manner, so utterly downcast, or fallen so
far as she from the world's esteem. She had the appearance of being outcast
for ever from the genteel. Her pace was as sorry as her poor jaded eyes, and
yet she seemed to run. Her feet made the motion of running as she hurried
along. Yet never before had I seen one go so slow.

And the road to the World was hard, and long, and white, and dusty.

She seemed no more like to a traveller than to a lady of good repute,
yet there she was with her shawl and her abject look and her poor old feet
that padded on that great road. She carried in her hand a dirty and shrivelled palm, such a thing as might stay on in a bankrupt lodging-house, in
some unfashionable square by the sea, with no one to dust it, when all the
other furniture was carried away for debt. She clasped it still.

"I'm sure there's a lot as needs me," she mumbled as she went; and
sighed; and said over and over again, "O dearie, dearie me."

Far over her poor bowed head and dejected face flew and turned and
gambolled, going no faster than she, so that they ever soared exactly above
her head, a flock of doves that shone so purely white in the twilight, which
gleams between Earth and Moon, that I knew her by this to be Peace.

She was hobbling, all unwitting, straight for the World,

"You can't come here," I said as soon as I saw what she wanted. "You
can't come here, you know."

The words were on my lips as réveillé woke me.

THE GERMAN SPY

Originally published in *The Saturday Review*, 10 August 1912.

*From a page specially stolen from the secret
annals of the Chancelleries of Europe.*

Friedrich Holtschz was marching along with a perfectly straight knee, a step that he particularly enjoyed, when an orderly rode up with a Warofficecommunicationlike envelope in his hand, which he opened and at once proceeded to read aloud to Holtschz. Holtschz halted, presented arms and listened in silence. The order was in a few terse words, but the words were very long; when at last he had finished the orderly rode away, and Holtschz was left alone on the parade-ground where twenty minutes ago he had been marching up and down so happily with a straight knee. Now he sighed heavily and almost wept, almost his knees bent under him as he marched. Holtschz was to be a spy. That was the order in the Warofficecommunicationlike envelope. Holtschz was to go into the very citadel of the hypothetical enemy. He was to go disguised and alone and count the lions in Trafalgar Square, and if he came back, ah! *if* he came back, he was to report in cypher. He thought of his bairns along the banks of the Rhine; the Swiss, the Dutch and German Rhine; he thought of his frau, never was such a frau, in all the years that he had wedded her never for an hour night or day had she once ceased to cook.

He disguised himself as a desirable alien and entered England, and took by Royal license and letters patent the name of Montague.

He made his plans with the swiftness of desperation; he would approach Trafalgar Square by the way of Piccadilly, as less suspicion attaches to travellers from the West than those that come from the East, especially through the City; he would go down S. James' Street right past the sentries and along Pall Mall, the very daring of this being likely to screen his purpose; and he would go by night; yet he scarcely hoped ever again to sit in a lust-garden drinking gallons of beer.

The night of his arrival he dined in a great hotel not far from Piccadilly. The soup and fish he enjoyed, but then an incident occurred that robbed him of his appetite for the rest of that fateful evening. The vegetables were splashed on to his plate from between a spoon and fork held in one hand by the commander-in-chief of the army of occupation. Poor Holtschz leaped to attention, and suddenly realised that he had betrayed himself, and that he would be hung by the English, or discharged at Bow Street without a caution, or created a peer: it was the uncertainty of what to fear that made the suspense so deadly. When he sat down again he found his plate piled high with vegetables which the commander-in-chief had continued to splash down upon it from fork and spoon with that sangfroid that had already won for him on manoeuvres the cordon of Saint Minerva. And in the end there were no English present, only Americans, Swiss and the army of occupation. But it was a fearful escape.

And after dinner Holtschz stepped out and slipped down Piccadilly; then began the difficult time. He had to answer five questions:

Firstly: Had the crowd torn down any of the lions on the grounds that they were not peace-loving animals and constituted a menace to Germany? If so, how many?

Secondly: Did the crowd consist of politicians or persons of better standing?

Thirdly: Had the number of lions been recently added to in vainglorious allusion to military power and as a taunt to Germany? If so, by how many?

Fourthly: How many field-guns could be cast from metal contained in lions?

Fifthly: Are the lions alive?

These were the questions that Holtschz had to answer alone and at dead of night with no friendly hand to guide him. He had got unperceived to the end of S. James' Street, commiserating himself on his difficulties as he went, when suddenly he saw on a placard "A Speech upon Revolution by a Member of Parliament," announced for Trafalgar Square that very night; he glanced up swiftly and saw that Pall Mall was crowded, and, turning on his heel, was about to slip away to await a better occasion when an Englishman suddenly accosted him with the words: "Ah! You are an enemy."

Holtschz desperately explained that he was English, but the other would have none of it, and, joyfully shouting, "No, you're an enemy, I see it in your eye," he shook him warmly by the hand. "For I used to be a pro-Boer," he said, "and I am a pro-spy now."

When Holtschz perceived that the man's intentions were friendly, he decided suddenly and not unwisely that here was the very man to obtain for him the dangerous information. Drawing him aside into Chandos Street, which is less frequented, Holtschz told the man the five questions, and explained that if he could obtain the information a hundred pfennigs were his; and partly from national pride and partly from motives of cunning he somewhat exaggerated the value of the pfennig. But the Englishman said that all men were brothers, and that he would do it though the reward were less, and his name transpired to be Bykes.

So Holtschz arranged a meeting place for midnight within easy reach of the great hotel where he lodged, and, elated at his release from anxiety and peril of the short but desperate journey up Pall Mall, slipped quietly away, and unsuspected gained that hotel, so near to Piccadilly, in which he almost felt himself at home.

Two or three Englishmen that knew no better had dined there and were sitting in the hall but soon these left, and Holtschz heard unbroken around him the long and succulent words of his native land.

Towards midnight he crept out and safely reached the corner of a mews which he had appointed as the meeting-place for Bykes, and there he saw Bykes leaning against the wall in the careless, weary attitude of one whose work is accomplished.

For a long while he was unable to recognise Holtschz, and just when Holtschz began to fear that his friend had forgotten him that earnest man shook hands with him and wept. He said that it had been a glorious meeting and a credit to the brotherhood of man, and that a new era had dawned, and Holtschz was his brother and the day of the tyrant was over. When Holtschz put in a word about the lions he said that they were prowling all round the Square, and there were forty of them, and they went in couples and often growled at Bykes, but that he did not mind them because Holtschz was his brother and because it was a glorious day for the brotherhood of man. The War department of a mighty empire does not choose those for its spies that do not know men, and Holtschz perceived at once from the man's rambling statement, and especially from the fact that all the lions he saw had appeared to him in pairs, that Bykes was very drunk.

Yet did not Holtschz make the mistake that might be so easily fatal of offending one that knew his guilty secret in the country of a hypothetical enemy; but he promised Bykes his vote for the Parliament of Man and listened to him until he fell asleep, when Holtschz slipped back to the large hotel with the grim work still to do. I do not think that our country's reputation in the eyes of Friedrich Holtschz would have been lost merely through the festivities of Bykes, but that Holtschz had unluckily once read in a book that all the English were faithless, and his little experience with Bykes clinched the idea in his mind, so that even now, as he sits beside the Rhine with his fair-haired bairns around him, he holds—but I anticipate my story's happy ending.

The work was still to do, and Holtschz decided on that anxious day that followed the lapse of Bykes to trust his original plan, and to seek no aid from a perfidious people; and when night fell he stepped away alone, and came again to the terrible end of Pall Mall.

Almost more than poor Holtschz could bear, so far away from his home, were the unsympathetic faces of the sentries. He wished as he saw them that he had come from the other side through Henrietta Street from the City, in spite of all the things that go on in the City and the suspicion that must attach to all that come that way. But now he was committed to his route, Pall Mall and Pall Mall East, and then the dreaded Square and the work that he had to do: he knew the way well enough, for there had been before him a pioneer, one who had once subscribed to the Party Funds and been elected to a club that stood in that very street, from one of whose bow-windows he had secretly mapped the approach to Trafalgar Square.

That map was now in the heel of Holtschz's boot.

He saw, as he went cautiously up Pall Mall, those implacable hall-porters that stood on the steps of the clubs that were not for Holtschz because he was an alien and unknown. And suddenly the thought came to him that he would claim sanctuary in one of these clubs, whence he might steal away when the street grew empty; perhaps, like Bykes, the hall-porter had abnormally loved the Boers. Holtschz decided to appeal to him. And then as he reached the steps he saw that it was the wrong kind of club for the members that he saw through a lighted window looked ignorant of the Brotherhood of Man, and the hall-porter wore medals on his coat that looked as though he was once unkind to the Boers, and Holtschz turned away in despair and continued his lonely journey so far from his native land. And so he came sorrowfully but safely to Pall Mall East, where he saw at once a bank of which he made a note for military purposes, and, finding nothing further of importance, came undetected to Trafalgar Square. Then all was haste with Holtschz; one rapid glance betrayed a lion in front of him, another showed one to his left, another, one on his right—three lions; he saw no more.

It was not a moment to dally; hastily noting in cypher his precious information he secretly slipped away, and, adroitly joining that very night a party of English spies that with justifiable curiosity were going to visit the Elbe, he safely came to the Vaterland once more. There he reported that there were only three lions now in Trafalgar Square, about eight field-guns could be cast from the metal contained in them, and as it was night at the time he could not tell if the lions were alive.

And Holtschz after all his dangers saw his bairns again playing along the banks of the Swiss-Dutch-German Rhine, and sat once more in a lust-garden at evening, singing "hoch hoch hoch" over gallons of beer, and marched again on his parade-ground with a perfectly straight knee.

And some weeks afterwards proceedings were instituted at the High Court of Bow against a person or persons for trespassing in pursuit of information in that part of England, Scotland and the town of Berwick-on-Tweed known as Trafalgar Square, not moved thereto by due respect for this Realm, and neither By nor With the Consent of Parliament.

THE HEART OF EARTH

Originally published in *The Saturday Review*, 16 October 1909.

As the poet walked through the moist, grey town thinking of Faëry and imperious Death, he saw the unthought-of pavement, monotonous, wet, clad with dirt, desolate. And, thinking of the long time that they had lain there under unheeding feet, unprotected by soil or grass against the will of the rain, he, being at peace because it was now evening, pitied the old grey stones. And the pavement felt his pity. Every stone felt it; stone told it unto stone for quite a mile. It had been trodden on for two hundred years by dogs as well as men, it had been spat upon and covered with filth, but had not before been pitied.

Deep in its core it felt the poet's pity; it had felt an earthquake less.

The pavement said nought in answer, but the echoes of the poet's footsteps felt its anger as they fled, and from stone to stone these thoughts whirled up and down through the pavement's fiery soul that was welded of old in the volcanic Prime or ever the hills were dumb. (The poet knew not what the pavement thought, for his dreams were now in Arcady.)

"What is this that dares to pity the heart of Earth? A thing of a few years and the toy of Time!

"Is not Earth's heart of the lineage of the stars? What should it do with a man's pity when Earth has none for man?

"Is not Earth true unto her old love Seismos? Or hath man lured her from Him?

"Man dallies awhile with Earth, but soon Seismos sees him. Man could not protect Earth against her old fierce lover even if she had willed it.

"Am I not the heart of wandering Earth, child of the sun?

"Who? Who has pitied me?

"Brethren of mine stand watch by companies over trivial human dead. And the dead moulder, but not my brethren.

"Twin am I to the granite who used to frolic with me when the old earthquake rocked our native hills.

"The wind greets me and passes by, and then comes back again. He brings me foundered armies as a cloak and old uprooted cities. Still goeth about with the wind Tyre; and still he carrieth Sidon. Hannibal hath rested awhile with me and rested lightly; no heavier are all his elephants. All rest for a while with me. Then to drifting cities and armies the wind saith 'Come Unto me cometh also the soft far-travelled rain, the child of Heaven and Sea, coming from hovering uncertain over forests and fields. And in the name of the stars, whose herald she is, the soft rain giveth me greeting. For the stars come to me whenever the rain is here. They glide down between her chariots and shine with me; thou shalt find them even here, whosoever passeth at night when the rain has come and her chariots rolled away.

"One has dared to pity the intimate of the stars, the wind's confidant and whom the rain loveth. And this pity hath come from his detested heart.

"Dear to me indeed are the boots of men, but their hearts I hate. What love should Earth's heart have for the hearts of men, who have chosen cities as their foster-mothers, rejecting Earth? But their boots I love, for I have an enemy that lurks and waits, mine enemy the moss, and against him they guard me. If the boots came not forth, the rumour would spread at once through all the wild things; the moss would know it first and then the grass, the dandelion would launch his airy armies on the first townward breeze, and the great brambles would come creeping in, and they would all hide me away where the great stars could not find me or the soft rain come.

"Vile indeed was this man's despised heart. Earth taught it not pity, but it learnt it from some unearthly evil thing.

"Behold now coming down to me the lamps and stars because the rain is here.

"I love the red lamps that watch, because they flame like the heads of the olden hills or ever they were dumb.

"Am I not beautiful among my lamps and stars? See now the mud upon me: here rests Persepolis and here Troy: the East wind brought them and the rain eased their wandering.

"I am older than gods.

"Here comes a man forgetful of me, scorning me; here comes one spitting at me, cursing me when he slips. They do not pity me.

"That is well, very well. Even so Earth feels towards them, who is one with her old love Seismos whose child the avalanche is."

Thus thought the pavement, and awaited with hopeful joy the coming again of the old grey earthquake, Seismos.

The poet had long since passed into the distance; the echoes of his footsteps had fled away through the air from the pavement's sudden anger like bats disturbed in some terrific temple: and anger still burned like the primeval fires in the core of that heart of Earth.

EXCHANGE NO ROBBERY

Originally published in *The Saturday Review*, 19 October 1912.

The poet travelled so far from his native land that he came at last to the country where poets have honour.

And there he met with a ruffian.

And the faces of the ruffian and the poet were so much alike that they might have been brothers. Therefore they talked together. And the ruffian asked the poet what he was. And the poet answered him: "I am only a poet, and I make verses, but none cares for them."

And the ruffian said: "In this country poets have honour."

And the poet said to the ruffian: "What are you?"

And the ruffian said: "I am a common ruffian. I go into houses and set the husband against the wife or stir up strife amongst the children. Or I go out into the fields to put hatred into the labourer's heart and make the servant rise against his master. And sometimes I make men to curse their lot and bring discontent among them. It is my amusement."

And the poet said to him: "Why do you do these things?"

And the ruffian said again: "It is my amusement. Men are made in all manner of ways."

And suddenly the poet seized him by the wrist: "Quick," he said, "let us change, for we are like in face so that we might be brothers, and in this country you say that poets have honour! And in my country such men as you are in high places and get great wealth and verily they have much honour."

And the eyes of the ruffian twinkled for he was a greedy man; and he and the poet changed places there and then; and in that far country the poet at last had honour, and the other has dwelt in our midst for many years. Reader, I dare not tell you his honoured name.

THE WAY OF THE WORLD

Originally published in *The Saturday Review*, 23 November 1912.

As the women came by carrying the world they met the man with the vote, and stopped when they met him.

"What do you want?" said he.

"We want the vote," said the women.

"What vote?" said the man.

"The vote for Parliament," the women said.

"Well, well," he said in his slow, stupid way.

"Give us the vote," they repeated.

"But what will you do with the world if I do?" said he.

"A few of our sisters can carry the world," they said, "while we are in London."

And the man scratched his head very slowly, then led the way to the ballot, and the women followed to vote, with the sounds of a great rejoicing.

But a few remained with the world and would tarry no longer, but went on their old way singing, to carry it round the sun.

THE LITTLE DOINGS OF DEMOS

Originally published in *The Saturday Review*, 23 November 1912.

Now Demos and those that he loved arose in their cities and said to the Kings of the World: "Behold our meanness and our littleness. Begone from our sight that there may be nought any longer whereby to gauge our littleness."

And the Kings of the World made answer unto Demos: "Are we not even as you?"

And they did the little things that Demos loved, and Demos rejoiced in his heart and said: "Lo, they are even as us."

But others of the Kings of the World said: "Yet we are Kings," and they hardened their hearts and hearkened not unto Demos. Then Demos spake unto them, and Demos said: "We will put a resolution against you and vote with our votes and see if it be carried."

And Demos put the resolution even as he had said, and lo! it was carried unanimously. Then Demos and those that he loved said: "Behold, we were right and just."

But Mars arose as of old again from his sleep, with never a rumour of his going forth, nor runners to go before him, and strode through the nations and appeared suddenly before Demos and those that Demos loved, and said to them: "How have you dared to speak to my children?"

And Demos excused himself and spoke of his conscience.

"Cease, cease," said Mars. "Go you and plough my fields, you and your wives and daughters."

And Demos was slave unto Mars for many years, even till Mars slept again and Demos thought him dead and once more made resolutions and put them to the vote.

THE RETURN OF IBRAHIM

Originally published in *The Saturday Review*, 27 December 1913.

Ibrahim Ben Suleiman, whom evil chance, and not the will of God, had sent to London, had returned again to his tent. Two jackals came out to yelp at it that evening down the face of the cliff, and his two white fox-like dogs and the one that he thought was a bull-dog went out to bark at the jackals. They soon returned to the camp; but seeing that Ibrahim was home again, and the jackals had come so close, and there was a moon that night, and one thing and another, they considered it better that they should bark all night. A violent wind arose and repeatedly beat the side of his tent against Ibrahim's head; his camel stank; his hobbled mules limped noisily, for they were close to the tent for fear of robbers; a cock or two crowed at midnight; but Ibrahim, long before that, had dreamily rubbed his chin and mumbled with infinite luxury, "At last one can sleep."

HOW CARE WOULD HAVE DEALT WITH THE NOMADS

Originally published in *The Saturday Review*, 27 December 1913.

At a street corner I saw Hurry and Care.

"Let us come away," said Care, "to the tents of the Arabs."

"Quick, quick!" said Hurry, "there's not a moment to lose. The Nomads change their camps, and we shall miss them."

And Hurry rushed away towards the mountains. But he came back soon to Care.

"It's not that way," he said. "This way. Quick, quick!"

But Care went to say farewell to the folk of the city. "I will come back soon," she said, "for some terrible thing is soon about to befall you, and I wish to be with you before it happens to see what we can do."

She spoke to many that day, saying mostly the same thing, but to each she spoke as though she spoke but to him alone. Then she went through the town after Hurry towards the desert, greeting all that she met in the hard ways as she went. And everyone bowed to her, for they all knew Care. To some she said as she passed: "Have you not left unlocked the door of your house? I fear that thieves will enter."

In the desert, so men say, they wandered long and did not find the Nomads. One day, with prying eyes and restless fingers, one day, with a rush of dust and wind and noises, Care and Hurry came back. And at a little civic dinner, that Money gave that night in honour of Death, one of the city's principal diseases asked them if they had seen the Nomads.

"Well, no," said Hurry. "No, we hadn't time. Besides, they're a lazy lot and not worth seeing." And Care said, "No, they are a dirty people and, I fear, dreadfully rustic. No, we didn't see them."

THE POET SPEAKS WITH EARTH

**Published in the British edition of *Fifty-One Tales* but
replaced with another story in the U.S. edition. The version
of *Fifty-One Tales* in this volume follows the U.S. text.**

Returning late one night from roaming amongst the stars I came on Mother Earth sitting all dark in Space, murmuring tales of her children.

"Dreams and battles," she said. "Dreams and battles." I heard her say nothing more.

I said to her: "O Mother, your sons have done marvellous things." I told her of all our machinery, politics, science; the famous inventions of Man.

Of all these things she had remembered nothing.

"But Steam!" I said. "And Electricity."

No, she remembered nothing, but muttered of poets and heroes. Not even mention of our Parliament moved her.

"Dreams and battles," she said. "Dreams and battles," and fell to muttering poems and crooning of ancient wars.

Mother, mother, you shall remember us.

www.ingramcontent.com/pod-product-compliance
Lightning Source LLC
Chambersburg PA
CBHW020244030726
47499CB00001B/52